CURTAIN CALLS: THREE GREAT MYSTERIES

Ngaio Marsh

NELSON DOUBLEDAY, INC.
Garden City, New York

CURTAIN CALLS:
THREE
GREAT MYSTERIES

Contents

ENTER
A MURDERER

Contents

Foreword

When I showed this manuscript to my friend, Chief Detective-Inspector Alleyn, of the Criminal Investigation Department, he said:

"It's a perfectly good account of the Unicorn case, but isn't it usual in detective stories to conceal the identity of the criminal?"

I looked at him coldly.

"Hopelessly *vieux jeu,* my dear Alleyn. Nowadays the identity of the criminal is always revealed in the early chapters."

"In that case," he said, "I congratulate you."

I was not altogether delighted.

Chapter I

Prologue to a Play

On May 25th Arthur Surbonadier, whose real name was Arthur Simes, went to visit his uncle, Jacob Saint, whose real name was Jacob Simes. Jacob was an actor before he went into management and had chosen Saint as his stage name, and stuck to it for the rest of his life. He made bad jokes about it—"I'm no Saint"—and wouldn't allow his nephew to adopt it when he in turn took to the boards. "Only one Saint in the profession," he roared out. "Call yourself what you like, Arthur, but keep off my grass. I'll start you off at the Unicorn and I'll leave you the cash —or most of it. If you're a bad actor you won't get the parts—that's business."

As Arthur Surbonadier ("Surbonadier" had been suggested by Stephanie Vaughan) walked after the footman towards his uncle's library, he remembered this conversation. He was not a bad actor. He was an adequate actor. He was, he told himself, a damn' good actor. He tried to stiffen himself for the encounter. A damn' good actor with personality. He would dominate Jacob Saint. He would, if necessary, use that final weapon—the weapon that Saint knew nothing about. The footman opened the library door.

"Mr. Surbonadier, sir."

Arthur Surbonadier walked in.

Jacob Saint was sitting at his ultra-modern desk in his ultra-modern chair. A cubistic lamp lit up the tight rolls of fat at the back of his neck. His grey and white check jacket revealed the muscles of his back. His face was turned away from Surbonadier. Wreaths of cigar smoke rose above his pink head. The room smelt of cigar smoke and the scent he used—it was specially made for him, that scent, and none of his ladies— not even Janet Emerald—had ever been given a flask of it.

"Sit down, Arthur," he rumbled. "Have a cigar; I'll talk to you in a moment."

Arthur Surbonadier sat down, refused the cigar, lit a cigarette, and fidgeted. Jacob Saint wrote, grunted, thumped a blotter and swung round in his steel chair.

He was like a cartoon of a theatre magnate. He was as if he played his own character, with his enormous red dewlaps, his coarse voice, his light blue eyes and his thick lips.

"What d'yer want, Arthur?" he said and waited.

"How are you, Uncle Jacob? Rheumatism better?"

"It isn't rheumatism, it's gout, and it's bloody. What d'yer want?"

"It's about the new show at the Unicorn." Surbonadier hesitated, and again Saint waited. "I—I don't know if you've seen the change in the casting."

"I have."

"Oh!"

"Well?"

"Well," said Surbonadier, with a desperate attempt at lightness, "do you approve of it, uncle?"

"I do."

"I don't."

"What the hell does that matter?" asked Jacob Saint. Surbonadier's heavy face whitened. He tried to act the part of himself dominant, himself in control of the stage. Mentally he fingered his weapon.

"Originally," he said, "I was cast for Carruthers. I can play the part and play it well. Now it's been given to Gardener—to Master Felix, whom everybody loves so much."

"Whom Stephanie Vaughan loves so much."

"That doesn't arise," said Surbonadier. His lips trembled. With a kind of miserable exultation he felt his anger welling up.

"Don't be childish, Arthur," rumbled Saint, "and don't come whining to me. Felix Gardener plays Carruthers because he is a better actor than you are. He probably gets Stephanie Vaughan for the same reason. He's got more sex appeal. You're cast for the Beaver. It's a very showy part and they've taken it away from old Barclay Crammer, who would have done it well enough."

"I tell you I'm not satisfied. I want you to make the alteration. I want 'Carruthers.'"

"You won't get it. I told you before you'd ever faced the foots that our relationship was not going to be used to jack you up into star parts. I gave you your chance, and you wouldn't have got that if I wasn't your uncle. Now it's up to you." He stared dully at his nephew and then swung his chair towards the desk. "I'm busy," he added. Surbonadier wetted his lips and crossed to him.

"You've bullied me," he said, "all my life. You paid for my education because it suited your vanity to do it, and because you like power."

"Spoken deliberately—comes down-stage slowly! Quite the little actor, aren't you?"

"You've got to get rid of Felix Gardener!"

Jacob Saint for the first time gave his nephew his whole attention. His eyes protruded slightly. He thrust his head forward—it was a trick that was strangely disconcerting and it had served him well when dealing with harder men than Surbonadier.

"Try that line of talk again," he said very quietly, "and you're finished. Now get out."

"Not yet." Surbonadier gripped the top of the desk and cleared his throat. "I know too much about you," he said at last. "More than you realize. I know why you—why you paid Mortlake two thousand." They stared at each other. A dribble of cigar smoke escaped through Saint's half-open lips. When he spoke it was with venomous restraint.

"So we thought we'd try an odd spot of blackmail, did we?" His voice had thickened. "What have you been doing, you——?"

"Did you never miss a letter you had from him last February—when—when I was——"

"When you were my guest. By God, my money's been well spent on you, Arthur!"

"Here's a copy." Surbonadier's shaking hand went to his pocket. He could not take his eyes off Saint. There was something automaton-like about him. Saint glanced at the paper and dropped it.

"If there's any more of this"—his voice rose to a shocking, raucous yell—"I'll have you up for blackmail. I'll ruin you. You'll never get another shop in London. You hear that?"

"I'll do it." Surbonadier backed away, actually as though he feared he would be attacked. "I'll do it." His hand was on the door. Jacob Saint stood up. He was six feet tall and enormous. He should have dominated the room—he was much the better animal of the two. Yet Surbonadier, unhealthy, too soft, and shaking visibly, had about him an air of sneaking mastery.

"I'm off," he said.

"No," said Saint. "No. Sit down again. I'll talk."

Surbonadier went back to his chair.

On the night of June 7th, after the first performance of *The Rat and the Beaver*, Felix Gardener gave a party in his flat in Sloane Street. He had invited all the other members of the cast, even old Susan Max, who got buccaneerish over the champagne, and talked about the parts she had played with Julius Knight in Australia. Janet Emerald, the "heavy" of the play, listened to her with an air of gloomy profundity. Stephanie Vaughan was very much the leading lady, very tranquil, very gracious, carelessly kind to everyone and obviously pliant to Felix Gardener himself. Nigel Bathgate, the only journalist at the party and an old Cambridge friend of Felix, wondered if he and Miss Vaughan were about to announce their engagement. Surely their mutual attentiveness meant something more than mere theatrical effusion. Arthur Surbonadier was there, rather too friendly with everybody, thought Nigel, who disliked him; and J. Barclay Crammer, who disliked him even more, glared at Surbonadier across the table. Dulcie Deamer, the *jeune fille* of the play, was also the *jeune fille* of the party. And Howard Melville ran her a good second in registering youthful charm, youthful bashfulness and something else that was genuinely youthful and rather pleasing. Jacob Saint was there, loudly jovial and jovially loud. "My company, my actors, my show," he seemed to shout continually, and indeed did. To the playwright, who was present and submissive, Saint actually referred as "my author." The playwright remained submissive. Even George Simpson, the stage manager, was present, and it was he who began the conversation that Nigel was to recall a few weeks later, and relate to his friend, Detective-Inspector Alleyn.

"That business with the gun went off all right, Felix," Simpson said, "though I must say I was nervous about it. I hate a fake."

"Was it all right from the front?" asked Surbonadier, turning to Nigel Bathgate.

"What do you mean?" asked Nigel. "What business with the gun?"

"My God, he doesn't even remember it!" sighed Felix Gardener. "In the third act, my dear chap, I shoot the Beaver—Arthur—Mr. Surbonadier at close range and he falls down dead."

"Of course I remember that," said Nigel, rather nettled. "It was perfectly all right. Most convincing. The gun went off."

"The gun went off!" screamed Miss Dulcie Deamer hilariously. "Did you hear him, Felix?"

"The gun didn't go off," said the stage manager. "That's just the point. I fired another off in the prompt corner and Felix jerks his hand. You see, he shoots the Beaver at close range—actually presses the barrel of the revolver into his waistcoat, so we can't use a blank—it would scorch his clothes. The cartridges that the Beaver loads his gun with are all duds—empty shells."

"I'm damned glad you don't," said Arthur Surbonadier. "I loathe guns and I sweat blood in that scene. The price one pays," he added heavily, "for being an actor." He glanced at his uncle, Jacob Saint.

"Oh, for Heaven's sake!" muttered J. Barclay Crammer in a bitterly scornful aside to Gardener.

"It's your own gun, isn't it, Felix?" he said aloud.

"Yes," said Felix Gardener. "It was my brother's—went all through Flanders with him." His voice deepened. "I'm not leaving it in the theatre. Too precious. Here it is." A little silence fell upon the company as he produced a service revolver and laid it on the table.

"It makes the play seem rather paltry," said the author of the play.

They spoke no more of the gun.

On the morning of June 14th, when *The Rat and the Beaver* had run a week to full houses, Felix Gardener sent Nigel Bathgate two complimentary tickets for the stalls. Angela North, who does not come into this story, was away from London, so Nigel rang up Scotland Yard and asked for his friend, Chief Detective-Inspector Alleyn.

"Are you doing anything to-night?" he said.

"What do you want me to do?" said the voice in the receiver.

"How cautious you are!" said Nigel. "I've got a couple of seats for the show at the Unicorn. Felix Gardener gave them to me."

"You do know a lot of exciting people!" remarked the inspector. "I'll come with pleasure. Dine with me first, won't you?"

"You dine with me. It's my party."

"Really? This promises well."

"That's splendid!" said Nigel. "I'll pick you up at a quarter to seven."

"Right you are. I'm due for a night off," said the voice. "Thank you, Bathgate. Good-bye."

"Hope you enjoy it," said Nigel, but the receiver had gone dead.

At cocktail-time on that same day, June 14th, Arthur Surbonadier called on Miss Stephanie Vaughan at her flat in Shepheard's Market and asked her to marry him. It was not the first time he had done so. Miss Vaughan felt herself called upon to use all her professional and personal *savoir-faire*. The scene needed some handling and she gave it her full attention.

"Darling," she said, taking her time over lighting a cigarette and quite unconsciously adopting the best of her six by-the-mantelpiece poses. "Darling, I'm so terribly, terribly upset by all this. I feel I'm to blame. I *am* to blame."

Surbonadier was silent. Miss Vaughan changed her pose. He knew quite well, through long experience, what her next pose would be, and equally well that it would charm him as though he were watching her for the first time. Her voice would drop. She would purr. She did purr.

"Arthur darling, I'm all nervy. This piece has exhausted my vitality. I don't know where I am. You must be patient with me. I feel I'm incapable of loving anybody." She let her arms fall limply to her sides and then laid one hand delicately on her *décolletage* for him to look at. "Quite incapable," she added on a drifting sigh.

"Even of loving Felix Gardener?" said Surbonadier.

"Ah—Felix!" Miss Vaughan gave her famous three-cornered smile, lifted her shoulders a little, looked meditative and resigned. She managed to convey a world of something or another, quite beyond her control.

"It comes to this," said Surbonadier. "Has Gardener"—he paused and looked away from her—"has Gardener cut me out?"

"My sweet, *what* an Edwardianism. Felix talks one of my languages. You talk another."

"I wish to God," said Surbonadier, "that you would confine yourself to plain English. I can talk that as well as he. I love you. I want you. Does that come into any of your languages?"

Miss Vaughan sank into a chair and clasped her hands.

"Arthur," she said, "I must have my freedom. I can't be closed in emotionally. Felix *gives* me something."

"The hell he does," said Surbonadier. He too sat down, and such was the habit of the stage, he sat down rather stagily. His hands shook with genuine emotion, though, and Stephanie Vaughan eyed him and knew it.

"Arthur," she said, "you must forgive me, darling. I'm very attached to you and I hate hurting you, but—if you can—leave off wanting me. Don't ask me to marry you—I might say 'Yes' and make you even more unhappy than you are now."

Even while she spoke she knew she had made a false step. He had moved quickly to her side and taken her in his arms.

"I'd risk the unhappiness," he muttered. "I want you so much." He pressed his face into her neck. She shivered a little. Unseen by him her face expressed a kind of exultant disgust. Her hands were on his hair. Suddenly she thrust him away.

"No, no, no," she said. "Don't! Leave me alone. Can't you see I'm sick of it all? Leave me alone."

In all the "bad men" parts he had played Surbonadier had never looked quite so evil as he did at that moment.

"I'm damned if I'll leave you alone," he said. "I'm not going to be kicked out. I don't care if you hate me. I want you, and by God I'll have you."

He took her by the wrists. She did not attempt to resist him. They stared, full of antagonism, into each other's faces.

Distantly an electric bell sounded and at once her moment of surrender, if it had been a moment of surrender, was past.

"That's the front door," she said. "Let me go, Arthur." She had to struggle before she could break away from him, and he was still beside her, in a state of rather blatant agitation, when Felix Gardener walked into the room.

Chapter II

"Overture and Beginners, Please"

The stage door-keeper of the Unicorn glanced up at the grimy face of the clock—7.10. All the artists were snug in their dressing rooms now. All, that was, except old Susan Max, who played an insignificant part in the last act and was given a bit of licence by the stage manager. Susan usually came in about eight.

Footsteps sounded in the alley outside. Old Blair uttered a kind of groaning sigh peculiar to himself, got creakily off his stool, and peered out into the warmish air. In a moment two men in evening dress stepped into the pool of uncertain light cast by the stage door lamp. Blair moved into the doorway and looked at them in silence.

"Good evening," said the shorter of the two men.

"'Evening, sir," said Blair, and waited.

"Can we see Mr. Gardener, do you think? He's expecting us. Mr. Bathgate." He opened a cigarette-case and produced a card. Old Blair took it and shifted his gaze to the taller of the two visitors. "Mr. Alleyn is with me," said Nigel Bathgate.

"Will you wait a moment, please?" said Blair, and holding the card in the palm of his hand as if he were rather ashamed of it, he walked off down the passage.

"That old gentleman had a good look at you," said Nigel Bathgate. He offered his cigarette-case.

"Perhaps he knew me," said Chief Detective-Inspector Alleyn. "I'm as famous as anything, you know."

"Are you, now? Too famous, perhaps, to be amused at this sort of thing?" Nigel waved his cigarette in the direction of the passage.

"Not a bit. I'm as simple as I am clever—a lovable trait in my character. An actor in his dressing-room will thrill me to mincemeat. I shall sit and goggle at him, I promise you."

"Felix is more likely to goggle at you. When he gave me a couple of stalls for to-night I told him Angela couldn't come and—I mean," said Nigel hurriedly, "I said I'd ask you, and he was quite startled by the importance of me."

"So he ought to be—all took aback. When your best girl's away ask a policeman. Sensible man, Felix Gardener, as well as a damn' good actor. And I do love a crook play, I do."

"Oh," said Nigel, "I never thought of that. Rather a busman's holiday for you, I'm afraid."

"Not it. Is it the sort where you have to guess the murderer?"

"It is. And you'll look a bit silly if you can't, won't you, inspector?"

"Shut up. I shall bribe this old gentleman to tell me. Here he comes."

Old Blair appeared at the end of the passage.

"Will you come this way, please?" he said, without returning to the door.

Nigel and Alleyn stepped inside the stage door of the Unicorn, and at that precise moment Chief Detective-Inspector Alleyn, all unknowingly, walked into one of the toughest jobs of his career.

They at once sensed the indescribable flavour of the working half of a theatre when the nightly show is coming on. The stage door opens into a little realm, strange or familiar, but always apart and shut in. The passage led directly on to the stage, which was dimly lit and smelt of dead scene paint, of fresh grease paint, of glue-size, and of dusty darkness, time out of mind the incense of the playhouse. A pack of scene flats leaned against the wall and a fireman leaned against the outer flat, which was painted to represent a section of a bookcase. A man in shirt sleeves and rubber-soled shoes ran distractedly round the back of the set. A boy carrying a bouquet of sweet peas disappeared into a brightly-lit entry on the right. The flats of the "set" vanished up into an opalescent haze. Beyond them, lit by shaded lamps, the furniture of a library mutely faced the reverse side of the curtain. From behind the curtain came the disturbing and profoundly exciting murmur of the audience, and the immemorial squall of tuning fiddle-strings. Through the prompt entrance another man in shirt sleeves stared into the flies.

"What are you doing with those bloody blues?" he inquired. His voice was deadened by carpets and furniture. Someone far above answered. A switch clicked and the set was suddenly illuminated. A pair of feet appeared above Nigel's face; he looked up and saw dimly the electricians' platform, on which one man stood with his hand on the switch-board and another sat dangling his legs. Blair led them into the bright entry, which turned out to be another passage. Along this passage on the left were the dressing-room doors, the first marked with a tarnished star. From behind all the doors came the sound of muffled voices—cosy, busy, at home. It was very warm. A man with a worried expression hurried round an elbow in the passage. As he passed he looked at them inquisitively.

"That's George Simpson, the stage manager," whispered Nigel importantly. Old Blair knocked on the second door.

There was a pause and then a pleasant baritone voice called:

"Hullo, who is it?"

Blair opened the door two inches and said: "Your visitors, Mr. Gardener."

"What? Oh, yes. Half a second," called the voice. And then to someone inside: "I quite agree with you, old boy, but what can you do? No, don't go." A chair scraped and in a moment the door was opened. "Come in, come in," said Felix Gardener.

They crossed the threshold and Inspector Alleyn found himself, for the first time in his life, in an actor's dressing-room and shaking hands with the actor.

Felix Gardener was not a preposterously good-looking man; not, that is to say, so handsome that the male section of his audience longed at times to give him a kick in the pants. He had, however, the elusive quality of distinction. His straw-coloured hair was thick and lay sleekly on his neatly shaped head. His eyes, scarcely the width of an eye apart, were surprisingly blue, his nose straight and narrow; his mouth, generously large and curiously folded in at the corners, was a joy to newspaper cartoonists. His jaw-line was sharply marked, giving emphasis to a face otherwise rather fine-drawn. He was tall, carried himself beautifully, but not too much like a showman, and he had a really delightful speaking voice, light but resonant. He was said by women to have "It"; by men to be a very decent fellow; and by critics to be an actor of outstanding ability.

"I'm so glad you've come round," he said to Alleyn. "Do sit down. Oh—may I introduce Mr. Barclay Crammer? Mr. Alleyn. Bathgate you've met."

J. Barclay Crammer was a character actor. He was just sufficiently well known for people to say "Who *is* that man?" when he walked on to the stage, and not quite distinctive enough for them to bother to look him up in the programme. He was dark, full-faced, and a good character actor. He looked bad-tempered, thought Nigel, who had met him once before at Gardener's first-night supper-party.

"Can you all find somewhere to sit?" asked Gardener. He seated himself in front of his dressing-table. Alleyn and Nigel found a couple of arm-chairs.

The room was a blaze of lights and extremely warm. A gas jet protected by an open cage bubbled above the dressing-table, on which stood a mirror and all the paraphernalia of make-up. The room smelt of grease paint. Near the mirror lay a revolver and a pipe. A full-length glass hung on the right-hand wall by a wash-basin. On the left-hand wall a looped-up sheet half covered a collection of suits. Through the wall came the sound of women's voices in the star room.

"So glad you've both come, Nigel," said Gardener. "I never see you nowadays. You journalists are devilish hard to get hold of."

"Not more elusive than you actors," rejoined Nigel, "and not half as slippery as the police. I may tell you it's rather a feather in my cap producing Alleyn to-night."

"I know," agreed Gardener, turning to his mirror and dabbing his face with brown powder. "It makes me quite nervous. Do you realise, J.B., that Mr. Alleyn is a kingpin in the C.I.D.?"

"Really?" intoned Mr. Barclay Crammer deeply. He hesitated a moment and then added with rather ponderous gaiety: "Makes me even more nervous as I'm one of the villains of the piece. A very, very minor villain," he added with unmistakable bitterness.

"Now, don't tell me you're the murderer," said Alleyn. "It would ruin my evening."

"Nothing so important," said Barclay Crammer. "A little 'cameo part,' the management tells me. And that's throwing roses at it."

He uttered a short, scornful noise which Nigel recognized as part of his stock-in-trade.

A voice outside in the passage called:

"Half-hour, please. Half-hour, please."

"I must be off," said Mr. Crammer, sighing heavily. "I'm not made up yet and I begin this revolting piece. Pah!" He rose majestically and made a not unimpressive exit.

"Poor old J.B.'s very disgruntled," said Gardener in an undertone. "He was to play the Beaver and then it was given to Arthur Surbonadier. Great heart-burning, I assure you." He smiled charmingly. "It's a rum life, Nigel," he said.

"You mean they are rum people?" said Nigel.

"Yes—partly. Like children and terribly, terribly like actors. They run too true to type."

"You were not so critical in our Trinity days."

"Don't remind me of my callow youth."

"Youth!" said Alleyn. "You children amuse me. Twenty years ago next month I came down from Oxford. Ah me! Fie, fie! Out upon it!"

"All the same," persisted Nigel, "you can't persuade me, Felix, that you are out of conceit with your job."

"That's another matter," said Felix Gardener.

There was a light tap on the door, which opened far enough to disclose a rather fat face, topped by a check cap and garnished with a red spotted handkerchief. It was accompanied by an unmistakable gust of alcohol, only partially disguised by violet cachous.

"Hullo—hullo, Arthur, come in," said Gardener pleasantly, but without any great enthusiasm.

"So sorry," said the face unctuously. "Thought you were alone, old man. Wouldn't intrude for the world."

"Rot!" said Gardener. "Do come in and shut the door. There's a hellish draught in this room."

"No, no, it's not important. Just that little matter of—I'll see you later." The face withdrew and the door was shut, very gently.

"That's Arthur Surbonadier," Gardener explained to Alleyn. "He's pinched J.B.'s part and thinks I've pinched his. Result, J.B. hates him and he hates me. That's what I mean about actors."

"Oh!" said Nigel, with youthful profundity. "Jealousy."

"And whom do you hate?" asked Alleyn lightly.

"I?" Gardener said. "I'm at the top of this particular tree and can afford to be generous. I dare say I'll get like it sooner or later."

"Do you think Surbonadier a good actor?" asked Nigel.

Gardener lifted one shoulder.

"He's Jacob Saint's nephew."

"I see. Or do I?"

"Jacob Saint owns six theatres, of which this is one. He gives good parts to Surbonadier. He never engages poor artists. Therefore Surbonadier must be a good actor. I refuse to be more catty than that. Do you know this play?" he said, turning to Alleyn.

"No," said the inspector. "Not a word of it. I have been trying to discover from your make-up whether you are a hero, a racketeer, one of us police, or all three. The pipe on your dressing table suggests a hero, the revolver a racketeer, and the excellent taste of the coat you are about to put on, a member of my own profession. I deduced, my dear Bathgate, that Mr. Gardener is a hero disguised as a gun-man, and a member of the C.I.D."

"There!" said Nigel triumphantly. He turned proudly to Gardener. For once Alleyn was behaving nicely as a detective.

"Marvellous!" said Gardener.

"You don't mean to tell me I'm right?" said Alleyn.

"Not far out. But I use the revolver as a policeman, the pipe as a gun-man, and don't wear that suit in this piece at all."

"Which only goes to show," said Alleyn, grinning, "that intuition is as good as induction any day." They lit cigarettes and Nigel and Gardener began a long reminiscent yarn about their Cambridge days.

The door opened again and a little dried-up man in an alpaca jacket came in.

"Ready, Mr. Gardener?" he asked, scarcely glancing at the others.

Gardener took off his wrap, and the dresser got a coat from under the sheet and helped him into it. "You need a touch more powder, sir, if I may say so," he remarked. "It's a warm night."

"That gun business all right?" asked Gardener, turning back to the mirror.

"Props says so. Let me give you a brush, if you please, Mr. Gardener."

"Oh, get along with you, Nannie," rejoined Gardener. He submitted good-humouredly to the clothes brush.

"Handkerchief," murmured the dresser, flicking one into the jacket. "Pouch in side pocket. Pipe, Are you right, sir?"

"Right as rain—run along."

"Thank you, sir. Shall I take the weapon to Mr. Surbonadier, sir?"

"Yes. Go along to Mr. Surbonadier's room. My compliments, and will he join these gentlemen as my guests for supper?" He took up the revolver.

"Certainly, sir," said the dresser, and went out.

"Bit of a character, that," said Gardener. "You will sup with me, won't you? I've asked Surbonadier because he dislikes me. It will add piquancy to the dressed crab."

"Quarter hour, please. Quarter hour, please," said the voice outside.

"We'd better go round to the front," said Nigel.

"Plenty of time. I want you to meet Stephanie Vaughan, Alleyn. She's madly keen on criminology and would never forgive me if I hid you." (Alleyn looked politely resigned.) "Stephanie!" Gardener shouted loudly. A muffled voice from beyond the wall sang:

"Hullo—oh?"

"Can I bring visitors in to see you?"

"Of *course,* dar-ling," trilled the voice, histrionically cordial.

"Marvellous woman!" said Gardener. "Let's go."

Behind the tarnished star they found Miss Stephanie Vaughan in a rather bigger room, with thicker carpets, larger chairs, a mass of flowers and an aproned dresser. She received them with much gaiety, gave them cigarettes and dealt out her charm lavishly, with perhaps an extra liba- tion for Gardener and a hint, thought Nigel, of something more subtly challenging in her manner towards Inspector Alleyn. Even with blue grease on her eyelids and scarlet grease on her nostrils, she was a very lovely woman, with beautifully groomed hair, enormous eyes, and a heart-shaped face. Her three-cornered smile was famous. She began to talk shop—Alleyn's shop—to the inspector, and asked him if he had read H. B. Irving's book on famous criminals. He said he had, and thought it jolly good. She asked him if he had read other books on criminals and psychology; if he had read Freud, if he had read Ernest Jones. Mr. Alleyn said he thought them all jolly good. Nigel felt nervous.

"I've saturated myself in the literature of crime," said Miss Vaughan. "I've tried to understand, deep down, the psychology of the criminal. I'm greedy for more. Tell me of more books to read, Mr. Alleyn."

"Have you read Edgar Wallace?" asked Alleyn. "He's jolly good."

There was a nasty silence, and then Miss Vaughan decided to let loose her lovely laugh. It rang out—a glorious, bubbling cascade of joyousness. Gardener and Nigel joined in, the latter unconvincingly. Gardener flung his head back and shouted. He put his hand lightly on Stephanie Vaughan's shoulder.

Then quite suddenly they were aware that the door had been flung open and that Arthur Surbonadier was standing in the room. With one hand he held on to the door—with the other he fumbled at the spotted neckerchief below his scrubby beard. His mouth was half open and he seemed to be short of breath. At last he spoke.

"Quite a jolly little party," he said. His voice was thick and they saw how his lips trembled. They stopped short in their laughter, Gardener still with his hand on that lovely shoulder, Stephanie Vaughan open- mouthed and frozen into immobility—rather as though they were posing for a theatrical photograph. There was a quite appalling little silence.

"Charming picture," said Surbonadier. "All loving and bright. Mayn't I know the joke?"

"The joke," said Alleyn quickly, "was a bad one—of mine."

"The cream of the jest," said Surbonadier, "is on me. Stephanie will explain it to you. You're the detective, aren't you?"

Gardener and Nigel both started talking. Nigel heard himself intro- duce Alleyn. Gardener was saying something about his supper-party. Alleyn had got to his feet and was offering Miss Vaughan a cigarette.

She took it without moving her gaze off Surbonadier, and Alleyn lit it for her.

"I'm sure we ought to go round to the front," he said. "Don't let's miss the first scene, Nigel—I can't bear to be late."

He took Nigel by the arm, said something courteous to Miss Vaughan, shook Gardener's hand, and propelled Nigel towards the door.

"Don't let me drive you away," said Surbonadier, without moving from the doorway. "I've come to see the fun. Came to see Gardener really, and found him—having his fun."

"Arthur!" Stephanie Vaughan spoke for the first time.

"Well," said Surbonadier loudly, "I've made up m' mind to stop the fun—see? No reason why you shouldn't hear"—he turned slightly towards Nigel. "You're a journalist. Literary man. Here's a surprise—Gardener's a literary man, too."

"Arthur, you're tight," said Gardener. He moved towards Surbonadier, who took a step towards him. Alleyn seized his chance and shoved Nigel through the door.

"Good-bye for the moment," he called. "See you after the show"—and in a second or two they were back on the stage staring at one another.

"That was pretty beastly," said Nigel.

"Yes," said Alleyn. "Come on."

"The brute's drunk," said Nigel.

"Yes," said Alleyn. "This way."

They crossed the stage and made for the exit door, standing aside to let an elderly woman come in; they heard old Blair say: "'Evening, Miss Max." As they went out a voice in the passage behind them called:

"Overture and beginners, please. Overture and beginners, please."

Chapter III

Death of the Beaver

"It's amazing to me," said Nigel, in the second interval, "how that fellow Surbonadier can play a part in the state he's in. You'd never guess he was tight now, would you?"

"I *think* I would have known," said Alleyn. "From where we are you can see his eyes—they don't quite focus."

"I call it a damn' good performance," said Nigel.

"Yes," murmured Alleyn. "Yes. You've seen the piece before, haven't you?"

"Reviewed it," said Nigel, rather grandly.

"Has Surbonadier's reading of the part altered at all?"

Nigel turned and stared at his friend. "Well," he said slowly, "now I come to think of it I believe it has. It's—it's sort of more intense. I mean in that last scene with Felix, when they were alone on the stage. What is it he says to Felix? Something about getting him?"

"'I'll get you, Carruthers,'" quoted Alleyn, with an uncannily just rendering of Surbonadier's thick voice. "'I'll get you, and just when you least expect it!'"

"Good Lord, Alleyn, what a memory you've got!" said Nigel, very startled.

"I've never before seen anything on the stage that impressed me so deeply."

"All carried away like," jibed Nigel, but Alleyn refused to laugh.

"It was uncanny," he said. "The atmosphere of the dressing-room intensified on the stage. Intensified and bigger than life, like emotion in a nightmare. And then he said: 'You think I'm bluffing, playing a part, don't you?' And 'Carruthers'—Gardener, you know—said: 'I think you're bluffing, Beaver—yes. But if you're not—look out!'"

"You're a damn' good mimic, inspector."

"Clap-trap stuff it is really," said Alleyn uneasily.

"What's the matter with you?"

"I don't know. Got the ooble-boobles. Let's have a drink."

They went to the bar. The inspector was very silent and read his programme. Nigel looked at his curiously. He felt apologetic about the horribly uncomfortable scene in the dressing-room and wondered very much what was brewing between Gardener, Surbonadier and Miss Vaughan.

"I suppose old Felix has cut that bounder out?" he ventured.

"Yes," said Alleyn. "Oh, yes—that, of course." The warning bell set up its intolerable racket. "Come on," said Alleyn. "Don't let's miss any of it." He fidgeted while Nigel finished his drink, and led the way back to their stalls.

"The supper-party won't be much fun, I'm afraid," said Nigel.

"Oh—the supper-party. Perhaps it'll be off."

"Perhaps. What'll we do if it's on? Apologize and get out?"

"Wait and see."

"Helpful suggestion!"

"I don't think the supper-party will happen."

"Here she goes," remarked Nigel, as the lights slowly died away, leaving the auditorium in thick-populated darkness.

At the bottom of the blackness in front of them a line of light appeared. It widened, and in a silence so complete that the sound of the pulleys could be heard, the curtain rose on the last act of *The Rat and the Beaver*.

It opened with a scene between the Beaver (Surbonadier), his castoff mistress (Janet Emerald), and her mother (Susan Max). They were all involved in the opium trade. One of their number had been murdered. They had suspected him of being a stool-pigeon in the employ of Carruthers, *alias* the Rat (Felix Gardener). Miss Emerald threatened, Miss Max snivelled, Surbonadier snarled. He took a revolver from his pocket and loaded it while they watched him significantly.

"What are you going to do?" whispered Janet Emerald.

"Pay a little visit to Mister Carruthers."

The stage was blacked out for a quick change.

Carruthers (Felix Gardener) was discovered in his library among the leather chairs that Nigel and Alleyn had seen from the wings. It was still uncertain, to all but the wariest playgoer, whether he was the infamous Rat, organizer of illicit drug traffic, agent of the Nazis, enemy of the people, or the heroic servant of the British Secret Service. He sat at his desk and rapped out a letter on the typewriter, the keyboard of which was not visible.

"He pounds away at the letter Q," whispered Nigel, full of inside knowledge.

To Gardener came Jennifer (Stephanie Vaughan), passionately in love with him, believing him false, fascinated in spite of her nobler self, by the famous Felix charm. Miss Vaughan did this sort of thing remarkably well, the audience was enchanted, especially as at any moment the bookcase might slide back revealing the Butler (J. Barclay Crammer), whom they knew to be a gun-man of gun-men. It was, as Nigel had remarked in reviewing the play, a generous helping out of the old stock-pot, but Felix Gardener and Stephanie Vaughan played it with subtlety and restraint. The lines were sophisticated if the matter was melodramatic, and "it went." Even when the sliding bookcase slid and the gun-man did seize Miss Vaughan by her lovely elbows and pinion her, he did it, as it were, on the turn of an epigram, since as well as being a butler and a gun-man he was also an Etonian.

Miss Vaughan was borne off registering a multitude of conflicting emotions and Felix Gardener remained wrapped in the closest inscrutability. He took out his pipe, filled and lit it, gave a little audible sigh and sank into one of the leather chairs. "Isn't he marvellous!" breathed a woman's voice from behind Nigel. Nigel smiled a superior but tolerant smile and glanced at Alleyn. The inspector's dark eyes were fixed on the stage.

"Positively," thought Nigel, more tolerant than ever, "positively old Alleyn's all het up." Then he saw Alleyn's eyebrow jerk up and his lips tighten and he himself turned to the stage and experienced an emotional shock.

Surbonadier, in his character of the Beaver, was standing in the up-stage entrance facing the audience. With one hand he held on to the door and with the other he fumbled with his spotted neckerchief below his scrubby beard. His mouth was half open and he seemed to be short of breath.

At last he spoke. So complete was the duplication of the scene in the dressing-room that Nigel expected to hear him repeat: "Quite a jolly little party," and got another shock when he said very softly:

"So the Rat's in his hole at last!"

"Beaver!" whispered Felix Gardener. It was a line that most actors would have played for a laugh. Few actors could have played it otherwise, but Felix Gardener did. He made it sound horrible.

The Beaver came downstage. His right hand now held a revolver. *"You're not a killer, Rat,"* he said. *"I am. Put 'em up."*

Gardener's hands went slowly above his head. Surbonadier patted him all over, still covering him with the gun. Then he backed away. He began to arraign Gardener. The intensity of his fury, repressed and controlled apparently by the most stringent effort, touched the audience like venom. The emotional contact between the players and the house was tightened to an almost unendurable tension. Nigel felt profoundly uncomfortable. It seemed to him that this was no fustian scene between the Rat and the Beaver, but a development of the antagonism of two men, indecently played out in public. "Carruthers, the Rat" was his friend Felix Gardener, and the "Beaver" was Arthur Surbonadier, who hated him. The whole business was beastly and he would have liked to look away from it, but for the life of him he couldn't do so.

"*Round every corner, Rat, you've waited for me,*" Surbonadier was saying now. "*Every job I've done this last year you've bitched for me, Rat—Rat. You've mucked round my girl.*" His voice rose hysterically. "*I've had enough. I'm through—I've come to finish it and, by God, I've come to finish you!*"

"*Not this evening, Beaver. It's a lovely little plan and I hate to spoil your party, but you see we're not alone.*"

"*What are you saying?*"

"*We're not alone.*" Gardener spoke with the exasperating facetiousness of the popular hero. "*There's a good angel watching over you, Beaver. You're covered, my Beaver.*"

"*Do I look easy?*"

"*You look lovely, my Beaver, but if you don't believe me take a step to your right and glance in the mirror behind me, and I think you'll see the image of the angel that's watching you.*"

Surbonadier moved upstage. His right hand still held the revolver levelled at Gardener, but for a second he shifted his gaze to the mirror above Gardener's head. Then slowly he turned and stared at the upstage entrance. A moment, and Stephanie Vaughan stood in the doorway. She too held a revolver, pointed at Surbonadier.

"*Jenny!*" whispered Surbonadier. He dropped his hand and the barrel of the gun shone blue. It hung limply from his fingers and as though in a dream he let Gardener take it from him.

"*Thank you, Jennifer,*" said Gardener. Miss Vaughan, with a little laugh, lowered her gun.

"*You don't have any luck, do you, Beaver?*" she said.

Surbonadier uttered a curious little whinnying sound, turned, and clawed at Gardener's neck, forcing up his chin. Gardener's hand jerked up. The report of the revolver, anticipated by every nerve in the audience, was deafeningly loud. Surbonadier crumpled up and, turning a face that was blank of every expression but that of profound astonishment, fell in a heap at Gardener's feet. So far the acting honours in the scene had been even, but now Felix Gardener surpassed anything that had gone before. His face reflected, horribly, the surprise on Surbonadier's. He stood looking foolishly at the gun in his hand and then let it fall to the floor. He turned, bewildered, and peering at the audience as though asking a question. He looked at the stage exits as if he meditated an escape. Then he gazed at Stephanie Vaughan, who, in her turn, was looking with horror from him to what he had done. When at last he spoke—and his lips moved once or twice before any words were heard—it was with the voice of an automaton. Miss Vaughan replied like an echo. They spoke as though they were talking machines. Gardener kept his gaze fixed on the revolver. Once he made as if he would pick it up, but drew his hand back as though it were untouchable.

"God, that man can act!" said a voice behind Nigel. He woke up to feel Alleyn's hand on his knee.

"Is this the end?" the inspector whispered.

"Yes," said Nigel. "The curtain comes down in a moment."

"Then let's get out."

"What!"

"Let's get out," repeated Alleyn; and then, with a change of voice: "Are you looking for me?"

Their seats were on the aisle. Glancing up, Nigel saw that an usher was bending over his friend.

"Are you Inspector Alleyn, sir?"

"Yes. You want me. I'll come. Get up, Bathgate."

Completely at a loss, Nigel rose and followed Alleyn and the usher up the aisle, into the foyer, and out by a sort of office to the stage door alley. No one spoke until then, when the usher said:

"It's terrible, sir—it's terrible."

"Quite," said Alleyn coldly. "I know."

"Did you guess, sir? Have they all guessed?"

"I don't think so. Is someone going to ask for a doctor? Not that there's any hurry for that."

"My Gawd, sir, is he dead?"

"Of course he's dead."

As they approached the stage door old Blair came running out, wringing his hands.

Alleyn walked past him, followed by Nigel. A man in a dinner jacket, his face very white, came down the passage.

"Inspector Alleyn?" he said.

"Here," said Alleyn. "Is the curtain down?"

"I don't think so. Shall I go out in front and ask for a doctor? We didn't realize. I didn't stop the show. Nobody realized—they don't know in front—I don't think they know in front. He said we ought to send for you," the man gabbled on madly. They reached the wings just as the curtain came down; Stephanie Vaughan and Gardener were still on the stage. The applause from the auditorium broke like a storm of hail. Simpson, the stage manager, darted out of the prompt corner. As soon as the fringe of the curtain touched the stage Miss Vaughan screamed and hurled her arms round Gardener's neck. Simpson held back the curtain, looking with horror at Surbonadier, who lay close to his feet. The man in evening dress, who was the business manager, stopped through. The orchestra blared out the first note of the National Anthem, but the man must have held up his hand or spoken to them, because the noise of the one note petered out foolishly. On the stage they heard the business manager speaking to the audience.

"If there is a doctor in front, will he kindly come round to the stage door? Thank you."

The orchestra again struck up the National Anthem. Behind the curtain Alleyn spoke to Simpson.

"Go to the street door and stop anyone from leaving. No one is to go out. You understand? Bathgate, find a telephone and get the Yard. Tell them from me what has happened and ask them to send the usual people. Say I'll want constables." He turned to the business manager, who had come through the curtain. "Show Mr. Bathgate the way to the nearest telephone and then come back here." He knelt down by Surbonadier.

The business manager glanced at Nigel.

"Where's a telephone?" asked Nigel.

"Yes, of course," said the business manager. "I'll show you."

They went together through a door in the proscenium that led to the auditorium, almost colliding with a tall man in a tail coat.

"I'm the doctor," he said. "What's it all about?"

"On the stage," said Nigel, "if you'll go through." The doctor glanced at him and went on to the stage.

In the auditorium the last stragglers were still finding their way out. Some women with their heads together stood with bundles of dust sheets in their arms.

"Get on with your work," said the business manager savagely. "My name's Stavely, Mr.—Mr.——"

"Bathgate," said Nigel.

"Yes, of course. This is a terrible business, Mr. Bathgate."

"No one," thought Nigel, "seems to be able to say anything but this."

They crossed the foyer into an office. People were still standing about the entrance and a woman said:

"You're not very clever about taxis, are you, darling?"

Nigel, at the telephone, remembered the Yard number. A man's voice answered him very quickly.

"I'm speaking for Chief Detective-Inspector Alleyn," said Nigel. "There's been an accident at the Unicorn—a—a fatal accident. He wants you to send the usual people and constables at once."

"Very good," said the voice. "Did you say fatal accident?"

"Yes," said Nigel, "I think so, and I think——" He stopped, gulped, and then his voice seemed to add of its own accord: "I think it looks like murder."

Chapter IV

Alleyn Takes Over

When Nigel got back to the stage he was surprised to find little alteration in the scene he had left. He did not realize how short a time he had been away. The doctor had finished his examination of Surbonadier's body and stood looking down at him.

Miss Vaughan was still on the stage. She was sobbing in the arms of old Susan Max. Felix Gardener was near her, but he seemed unaware of anyone but Alleyn and the doctor. He looked from one to the other, distractedly moving his head like someone in pain. When he saw Nigel he walked over to him swiftly and stood beside him. Nigel took hold of his arm and squeezed it. In the wings, masked in shadows, were groups of people.

"I haven't moved him," said the doctor. "It's a very superficial examination, but quite enough for your purpose. He was shot through the heart and died instantly."

"I shot him," said Gardener suddenly. "I've killed him. I've killed Arthur."

The doctor glanced at him uneasily.

"Shut up, Felix," Nigel murmured. He looked at Alleyn. The inspector was standing talking to George Simpson. They walked to the prompt box. Simpson was showing Alleyn something. It was the gun he used for the faked report.

"I never knew," he kept saying. "They went off at the same time. I never knew. This was a blank. I never even pointed it. It couldn't have done anything, could it?"

Alleyn came back on to the stage. He spoke to all the people in the wings and on the set. "Will you all go to the wardrobe-room, please? I shall take statements later. You will, of course, want to change and take off your war paint. I am afraid I must forbid any access to the dressing-rooms until I have been through them, but I understand there is a wash-basin and a mirror in the wardrobe-room and I shall have your things sent in to you there. Just a moment, please. Don't go yet."

Six men were making their way through the crowd in the wings. Three of the newcomers were uniformed constables. The others were plain clothes men. They were given place and walked on to the stage.

"Well, Bailey," said Alleyn.

"Well, sir," said one of the plain clothes men. "What's the trouble?"

"As you see." Alleyn turned towards the body. The men pulled off their hats. One of them put a handbag down by Alleyn, who nodded. Detective-Sergeant Bailey, a fingerprint official, bent down and looked at the body.

"You men," said Alleyn to the constables, "take everyone to the wardrobe-room. One of you stay outside and one at the stage door. Nobody to come out or go in. Mr. Simpson will show you. He goes in too. Please, Mr. Simpson."

The stage manager started forward and looked wanly round the stage.

"Everybody in the wardrobe-room, please," he said, as though he was calling a rehearsal. He turned to the constables. "This way, please," he added.

He walked off the stage, a policeman following him. A second man waited a moment and then said:

"Just move along, please, ladies and gentlemen." Old Susan Max, roundabout, sensible, said: "Come along, dear," to Miss Vaughan. Miss Vaughan stretched out her hands dumbly to Gardener, who did not look at her. She turned towards Alleyn, who watched her curiously, and then, with a very touching dignity, she let herself be led off by Susan Max. At the doorway she turned and looked again at the dead man, shuddered, and disappeared into the wings.

"Lovely exit, wasn't it?" said the inspector.

"Alleyn!" exclaimed Nigel, really shocked.

Miss Janet Emerald, the "heavy" woman, said: "Bounder!" from behind a piece of scenery.

"Let us go," replied the voice of J. Barclay Crammer. "We are in these people's hands." He appeared on the stage, crossed it, and gripped Gardener's hand. "Come, old man," he said. "With me. Together."

"Oh, get along, the whole lot of you," exclaimed Alleyn with the utmost impatience. Mr. Crammer looked at him, more in sorrow than in anger, and did as he suggested. Gardener straightened his back and managed the veriest ghost of a smile. "You agree with me about actors, I see," he said.

Alleyn responded instantly: "They are a bit thick, aren't they?"

"I want to say," said Gardener, "that I know I've killed him; but, before God, Mr. Alleyn, I didn't load that revolver."

"Don't talk," said Nigel. "They'll find out everything—they'll clear you. Don't worry more than you can help, you know."

Gardener waited a moment. He looked like a man coming round from concussion to realize gradually his abominable surroundings.

"Look here," he said suddenly. "Somebody must have——" He stopped short. A terrified look came into his eyes. Nigel took him by the elbow again and gently urged him forward. "You're a decent old sausage, Nigel," he said uncertainly. "Oh, well——"

"Now!" said Alleyn with relief.

They all turned to him.

"Can we have the whole story?" asked the older of the two C.I.D. men.

"You can. Here it is——"

Alleyn was interrupted by a shrill scream that seemed to come from the dressing-room passage. A woman's voice raised in hideous falsetto was mingled with an exasperated baritone. "Let me alone, let me alone, let me alone!"

"Oh, Lord, more highstrikes!" said Chief Detective-Inspector Alleyn. "Go and see what it's about, Bailey."

Detective-Sergeant Bailey did as he was told. His voice, a deep bass, soon mingled reasonably in the uproar: "Now, then, now then, this won't do"; and then the constable:

"Only obeying orders, miss."

The noise grew fainter. A door slammed. Bailey reappeared, looking scandalized. "One of the ladies, sir," he said. "Trying to get into her room."

"Did she get in?" asked Alleyn sharply.

"Well, yes, she did for a minute. Kind of slipped away from the rest of the mob before the P.C. could stop her. He yanked her out of it, quick time."

"Who was it?"

"I think the name was Emerald," said Bailey disgustedly. "Surname, I mean," he added quickly.

"What did she do it for?"

"Something about getting something for her face, she said, sir."

"Well, she's stowed away with the others now," commented Alleyn grimly. "Sit down, all of you. Bathgate, stay if you like, and you too, Dr. Milner."

"Shall I wait?" asked the business manager.

"Yes, if you will, Mr. Stavely. I may want you." They all sat in the heavy leather chairs, and Nigel thought they looked as if they were arranging themselves for the curtain to go up.

"The situation, briefly, is this," Alleyn began. "The body is that of Mr. Arthur Surbonadier. During the course of the last act he played a scene with Mr. Gardener and Miss Vaughan. He threatened Gardener with that revolver lying there. Miss Vaughan covered him from the doorway. Gardener took the revolver from him. He made as if he would strangle Gardener, who raised the gun and shot him at close quarters. The gun business has always been faked. The report comes from the wings. A blank was never used on the stage, as it would have scorched Surbonadier's clothes. There's no doubt where the shot came from. To-night the revolver was loaded, and not with 'dummies.' Let's have a photo of the body, and one of the stage."

One of the plain clothes men went into the stage door passage and returned with a camera. Several photos were taken. The camera-man, a completely silent individual, then removed himself and his paraphernalia.

"This is our divisional surgeon, Dr. Milner."

"Good evening," said the two medicos simultaneously. The divisional surgeon made a brief examination of the body and stood apart talking to Dr. Milner.

"Run a chalk round the body, Bailey, and turn it over," said Alleyn.

Bailey knelt down and did this. Surbonadier was lying half on his face. When he was turned over Nigel forced himself to look at him. He had the same astonished expression as they had seen from their place in the stalls. The grease paint shone dully on the dead face. The eyes were wide open.

"You notice the scorched clothes. He was killed instantly."

"Shot through the heart," said the doctor.

"God, it's awful!" said the manager suddenly.

"I think that will do." Alleyn turned to the divisional surgeon, who knelt beside Surbonadier and closed the painted eyelids. Bailey, who had just gone off the stage for a moment, reappeared with a length of brocade, with which he covered the body. It was a flamboyant thing, flame-coloured and gold.

"The revolver will, of course, show Mr. Gardener's prints," Alleyn said. "But you will test it for others, please, Bailey. It was in his dressing-room at seven-twenty, when I saw it." Bailey glanced at him in surprise. "The dresser took it to Mr. Surbonadier some time between seven-thirty and seven-forty-five. It was then unloaded and Surbonadier himself loaded it on the stage. We must remember that everyone in the cast knew exactly what would happen. Mr. Gardener was certain to do precisely what he did do—press the barrel of the revolver into Surbonadier above the heart and pull the trigger. There may be a remote possibility that Surbonadier was accidentally supplied with genuine ammunition. It seems scarcely likely. If he was deliberately supplied with live cartridges, the person responsible would be tolerably certain of results. Surbonadier was scarcely off the stage after he loaded the gun, and while on the stage would not fire, since even an unloaded revolver makes a loud click if this is done. Gardener would be certain to pull the trigger. His hand was in full view of the audience and the illusion had to be complete. Am I right, Mr. Stavely?"

"Yes. Yes, I think so, but, you know, the production is not my province, inspector. I belong to the front of the house. The producer is in Manchester, but Mr. Simpson, the general manager, would be your best authority—or Gardener himself."

"Of course, yes. Will you be kind enough to get Mr. Simpson for me? Oh—and, Mr. Stavely, take Detective-Sergeant Bailey with you and show him the dressing-rooms. Bailey, don't disturb any room but Miss Max's. From that you may take a towel and soap and a pot of grease. They take their paint off with grease, don't they? Take the stuff to the wardrobe-room, then lock the dressing-room doors and let 'em wash. And, Fox"—he turned to the second plain clothes man—"be a saint and ring for the mortuary van. Mr. Stavely will take you to the telephone. Sorry to be a bit Hitlerish, but it'll save time." He smiled charmingly at Stavely and the doctor. "Thank you very much, Dr. Milner. I shan't bother you any more tonight, but I've got your address. I'm sure you're longing to get away."

The doctor looked very much as though he was longing to stay. However, he departed meekly, escorted by the divisional surgeon. The others went on their errands and Nigel was left alone with Alleyn.

The theatre had become very silent. Far away in the front of the house a door slammed and immediately afterwards they heard a clock strike. Eleven. Twenty minutes ago the dead man under the length of brocade had been vigorous and alert; the echo of his voice had scarcely died away. To Nigel it seemed more like two hours.

"Alleyn," he said suddenly, "you don't think it was Felix, do you?"

"Bless the boy, I'm not a medium. I haven't the foggiest idea who it was, but he's no likelier than any of the others. He didn't load the revolver. The fact of his pulling the trigger doesn't appear to be particularly relevant. I say it doesn't *appear* to be. He may have to answer a technical charge of manslaughter. I don't know. Don't understand law."

"Bosh."

"Don't say bosh to me, child. Can you write shorthand?"

"Yes."

"Then take this notebook, sit on the other side of the scenery, and write down the ensuing conversations. Do it quietly. Your finger on your lips and all that."

"I don't want your notebook. Got one of my own."

"As you please. Here comes Simpson. Skedaddle." Nigel slipped out of the upstage entrance, leaving the door ajar. In the half-light offstage he saw a large round footstool of the type known as a "pouf." He pulled it quietly towards the entrance, sat down, and took out his scribbling pad and stylo. He heard someone come down the dressing-room passage and walk on to the stage at the prompt corner. From behind the scene flat, and quite close to him, Alleyn spoke.

"Oh, here you are, Mr. Simpson. Frightfully sorry to keep you all hanging about like this, but I want to do as much as I can before the scent, if there is a scent, grows cold. Do sit down."

There was a gentle sound of a soft impact, and the rustle of a silk cushion. Then Simpson spoke. "Of course—anything I can do to help."

"I want you to tell me 'in your own words,' as leading counsel loves to say, the exact procedure that took place every evening, and particularly this evening, in regard to the ammunition used in the revolver. As I remember, Mr. Surbonadier loaded the revolver with cartridges that he took from a drawer in a writing-desk during the first scene in the last act. Who put those cartridges there?"

"The murderer."

"I see," said Alleyn good-humouredly, "that you take my point. I should have said: Who put the dummy cartridges there?"

"I did," said George Simpson.

Chapter V

Statement of the Stage Manager

Nigel experienced a slight thrill in taking down Simpson's last statement—a thrill that was at once tempered by the reflection that the
placing of the dummy cartridges was of little importance in tracing the
deadly ones. Alleyn went on easily:

"You did. Splendid. Now, when exactly did you put the dummies in
that drawer?"

"During the second act wait, just before the curtain went up."

"The desk was then on the stage, or should I say on the set?"

"Only if you're a talkie actor. The scene was set and the desk was in
position."

"I wish there had been no further change of scene. Where exactly
was the desk? As I remember, it was about here."

Nigel heard Alleyn walk across the stage. By dint of squinting
through the crack in the doorway he saw that the inspector was standing
in the prompt first entrance, that is to say, in the doorway on the audience's right of the stage.

"It was just upstage of there," said Simpson.

"And the face of the desk towards the door, wasn't it?" asked Alleyn.

"That is so."

"Now, when you put the dummies in the drawer who was on the
stage?"

"The beginners for the third act. Miss Max, Miss Emerald, and—Mr.
Surbonadier."

"Did they see you put them there?"

"Oh, yes. Janet said: 'I'm always terrified you'll forget those things,
George. You leave it so late!'"

"The drawer was empty when you pulled it out?"

"I think so. I don't know that I'd swear it was—I may not have
looked at the back of it."

"Do you remember if any of the others afterwards came near the desk? Perhaps sat down at it while waiting for the curtain to go up?"

"I don't remember," said Simpson in a great hurry.

"Mr. Simpson—try to remember." There was a pause.

"I can't remember," said Simpson querulously.

"Let me try and help. Did you speak to any of them, now?"

"Yes. Yes, I did. I spoke to Miss Max, who was over on the O.P. She said the rug on that side was in the way of the door opening, and I moved it for her. Then she sat down in the chair over there and took out her knitting. The knitting is 'business' in the part."

"Yes. She had it in a red bag."

"That's right." Simpson began to speak very rapidly. "And she didn't move again before the curtain went up. I remember that because she laughed about her knitting and said she was trying to get it finished before we had run three weeks. It's a scarf. She put it round my neck to measure it."

"Now, didn't she sit in that chair for some time after the curtain went up? Wasn't she still sitting there when Surbonadier loaded the revolver?"

Through the crack in the door Nigel saw Simpson's surprised glance at the inspector.

"You've got a good memory," he said. "That's perfectly true."

"I've got a rotten memory really," said Alleyn, "but the scene impressed me, you know. If you think back it's a great help. Now, what did you do after you had straightened the mat and had your merry jape with the knitting?"

"I think I had a look round the stage to see everything was in place."

"And then——?"

"Then I went to the prompt box. I remember now that Surbonadier and Miss Emerald were standing upstage by the window and——" He stopped short.

"Yes?"

"That's all."

"I don't think so, Mr. Simpson. What were you going to say?"

"Nothing."

"I can't force you to speak, but do—do let me urge you to consider the seriousness of your position. It's no good my pretending or trying to bluff. I'm no actor, Mr. Simpson. You put the cartridges in the drawer. It's of first importance from your point of view to prove that they were dummy cartridges."

"It's not for myself——" began Simpson hotly.

"Then don't for the love of Mike start some fool game of shielding another person. That sort of thing is either damn' dangerous or just plain silly. However, it's as you please."

Simpson moved away from the range of Nigel's vision and when he did speak his voice sounded remote.

"You're quite right, I suppose," he said. "As for myself, I think I can clear up the cartridge business."

"All to the good. Now what were you going to say about Miss Janet Emerald?"

"Honestly, it's nothing really. Arthur Surbonadier seemed a bit upset. He—well, it's my job as stage manager to look after that sort of thing—he was not himself."

"You mean he was drunk—I know he was."

"Oh—well—yes, that and something else. Sort of dangerous drunk. Well, when I went back to the prompt box Janet Emerald came after me and she said: 'Arthur's tight, George, and I'm nervous,' and I said: 'He's giving a damn' good show, anyway.' (He was, you know.) Then she said: 'That may be right, but he's a beast, a filthy beast.' And I heard her whisper——Oh, lord, it meant nothing——"

"Well?"

"She whispered to herself: 'I could kill him'; and then she turned her back to me and stood with her hands on the desk. She talks that way. It meant nothing. I didn't look at her again. I glanced at the book and said: 'All clear, please,' and they took up positions."

"And then?"

"Then I said: 'House lights' to the switchboard man and flicked on the orchestra warning and the black-out warning. That scene opens on a black-out."

"Yes."

"Well, then I said: 'Stand by please,' and we blacked out and the scene went up."

"How long did the black-out last?"

"For the first few speeches of the dialogue. About four minutes altogether, because we black out for a little before the curtain goes up. Then Surbonadier switched on the stage lamp."

"Who was on the stage, behind the scenes, all that time?"

"Oh, the staff were up at the back. The property master and others. Props was standing beside me in the prompt box, I remember. He stayed there after he had given me the dummies and was there all the time until after the black-out. I know that because he kept whispering something about one of the dummies being loose. He seemed scared it might come to bits when Surbonadier loaded the gun."

"I see. And the others?"

"I think young Howard Melville was somewhere round—he's assistant S.M. I was on the book. It's a short scene, but the beginners in the next bit aren't called until half-way through."

"One more point and then I'm done. Where did you get the dummies?"

"Props made them. He's a positive genius at anything like that. Takes a pride in it. He got empty shells and filled them with sand, and then shoved the bullets in."

"Rather unnecessarily thorough, one would think."

"Lord, yes!" Simpson sounded much more at ease now. "But that's Props all over. He was shell-shocked during the war, poor devil, and he's—not exactly queer—but kind of intensely concentrated. He was as proud as Punch when he showed them to me, and said no one could tell they weren't the goods."

"Where were they kept?"

"Props always picked up the revolver at the end of the show and took them out. Then he used to take the gun to Felix Gardener. It was his brother's gun and Felix sets great store by it and always takes it home. Props used to put the dummies into the property-room and bring them to me before that scene. I made him do that because I wanted to be quite certain they were in the right drawer."

"And that's what happened to-night?"

"Yes."

"Did you examine them before you put them in the drawer?"

"I don't think so—I—I don't know."

"Would you have known if they were genuine ammunition?"

"I don't know—yes, I'm sure I would."

"In spite of the property master's art?"

"I don't know, I tell you."

"All right, all right, keep your hair on. If the property man was worried about the loose cartridge——"

"Yes. Yes, of course. They must have been dummies."

"Q.E.D. Now, Mr. Simpson, that's all for the moment. I see Inspector Fox is waiting out there. Just give him your address, will you, and get him to take you to your dressing-room? Show him which clothes you want to change into—no, wait a second; you're in a dinner jacket, and I imagine won't need to change. Fox!"

"Hullo!"

"Has the van come?"

"Outside now."

"Oh. Well, see if Mr. Simpson wants anything from his dressing-room. And, Mr. Simpson, will you let Inspector Fox just have a look at you? Pure formality and whatnot. You needn't if you don't want to. Don't get all het up over it."

Simpson's reply to this speech was indistinguishable.

Nigel, by dint of widening his peephole, could see Fox going rapidly and thoroughly through the stage manager's pockets.

"Cigarette-case, two pounds in notes and cash, pocketbook, handkerchief, matches, no written matter at all. Want to see anything, sir?" he asked cheerfully.

"Not a thing. One last question. Would Gardener be certain to pull the trigger when he pretended to fire the shot into the Beaver?"

"Definitely certain. It was rehearsed most carefully. He always closed his left hand a fraction of a second before he pulled the trigger. That gave me the cue for the blank shot."

"I see, yes. Thank you so much. Good night, Mr. Simpson."

Fox and the stage manager walked away. Nigel was wondering if he might speak when Alleyn's face suddenly appeared close to the door. The inspector laid his finger on his nose and made a face at Nigel, who was rather shocked at this display. Alleyn opened the door and came out. Nigel saw men with a stretcher on the stage and suddenly shut the door to. Alleyn looked curiously, but not unsympathetically, at him.

"Exit an actor, eh?" he said.

"You're a callous old pig," said Nigel.

"Did you get all that down?"

"I did."

"Good boy. Hullo, who's this? Stay where you are and stand by."

Voices, noisy in argument, could be heard from somewhere near the stage door.

"What the hell d'yer mean?" someone inquired loudly. "It's my theatre. Get out of my light."

Nigel returned to his peephole. The body of Surbonadier had gone. Inspector Fox appeared in hot pursuit of a monster of a man in tails, with a gardenia in his coat. He advanced truculently upon Alleyn, uttering a sort of roaring noise.

"Mr. Jacob Saint, I believe," said the inspector politely.

"And who the devil are you?"

"From the Yard, Mr. Saint, and in charge of this unhappy business. I am sorry you should have to meet such shocking news—I see you have heard of the tragedy. Mr. Surbonadier was your nephew, wasn't he? May I offer my sympathy?"

"Who's the swine that did him in?"

"At present we don't know."

"Was he drunk?"

"Since you ask me—yes."

Jacob Saint eyed the inspector and suddenly threw his bulk into an arm-chair. Nigel was seized with an idea and began taking notes again.

"I was in front to-night," said Saint.

"I saw you," said Alleyn brightly.

"I didn't know he was dead, but I knew he was drunk. He did it himself."

"You think so?" Alleyn seemed quite unmoved by this announcement.

"Stavely rang me up at the Savoy. I was behind, earlier in the evening, and saw Arthur. He was tight then. I told him he'd have to get out at the end of the week. Couldn't face the music and killed himself."

"It would take extraordinary fortitude to load a revolver, play a part, and wait for another man to shoot you, I should have thought," remarked Alleyn mildly.

"He was drunk."

"So we agreed. He had provided himself with live cartridges before he was drunk perhaps."

"What d'yer mean? Oh. Wouldn't put it past him. Where's Janet?"

"Who?"

"Miss Emerald."

"The artists are all in the wardrobe-room."

"I'll go and see her."

"Please don't move, Mr. Saint. I'll let her know. Miss Emerald, please, Fox."

Inspector Fox went. Saint glared after him, appeared to hesitate and then produced a cigar-case. "Smoke?" he said.

"No, thank you so much," said Alleyn. "I'm for a pipe."

Saint lit a cigar.

"Understand this," he said. "I'm no hypocrite and I don't spill any sob stuff over Arthur. He was a rotten failure. When one of my shows crashes I forget about it—a dud speculation. So was Arthur. Rotten all through, and a coward, but enough of an actor to see himself in a star part at last—and play it. He was crazy to play a big part, and when I wouldn't give him 'Carruthers' he—he actually threatened me—me!"

"Where did you see him to-night?"

"In his dressing-room. I had business in the office here and went behind."

"Would you care to tell me what happened?"

"Told you already. He was drunk and I fired him."

"What did he say?"

"Didn't wait to listen. I had an appointment in the office for seven-fifteen. Janet!" Saint's voice changed. He got to his feet. Nigel moved a little and saw that Janet Emerald had appeared in the prompt doorway. She gave a loud cry, rushed across the stage and threw herself into Saint's arms.

"Jacco! Jacco!" she sobbed.

"Poor baby—poor baby," Saint murmured, and Nigel marvelled at the kindness in his voice as he soothed the somewhat large and over-whelming Miss Emerald.

"It wasn't you," she said suddenly. "They can't say it was you!" She threw her head back distractedly and her face, cleaned now of its make-up, looked ghastly. Saint had his back to Nigel, but it was sufficiently eloquent of the shock her words had given him. Still holding her, he was frozen into immobility. When he spoke his voice was controlled but no longer tender.

"Poor kid," he said, in the best theatre-magnate manner. "You're all hysterical. Me! Do I seem like a murderer, baby?"

"No, no—I'm mad. It was so awful, Jacco. Jacco, it was so awful."

"M-m—m-m—m-m," growled Mr. Saint soothingly.

"Quite," Alleyn's voice cut in. "Most unpleasant. I am sure you must be longing to get away from it all, Miss Emerald."

"I'll drive you home," offered Jacob Saint. He and Miss Emerald stood side by side now and Nigel could see how pale they both were.

"An excellent idea." Alleyn's voice sounded close to the door. "But first of all may I just put a few questions to Miss Emerald?"

"You may not," said Saint. "If you want anything you can come and see her to-morrow. Get that?"

"Oh, yes, rather. Full in the teeth. Afraid, however, it makes no difference. There's a murder charge hovering round waiting for somebody, Mr. Saint, and shall we say a drama is being produced which you do not control and in which you play a part that may or may not be significant? To carry my flight of fancy a bit farther, I may add that the flat-footed old Law is stage manager, producer, and critic. And I, Mr. Saint, in the words of an old box-office success, 'I, my Lords, embody the law.' Sit down if you want to and please keep quiet. Now then, Miss Emerald."

Chapter VI

Into the Small Hours

Nigel took down every word of Alleyn's little speech with the liveliest enthusiasm. At the conclusion he wrote in brackets: "Noise of theatre magnate sitting down." In a moment he was busy again. Alleyn had concentrated on Miss Janet Emerald.

"Do you mind if I light my pipe, Miss Emerald? Thank you. Oh—cigarette? Those are Turks and those are—but I expect you know that one."

"No, thank you."

A match scraped, and Alleyn spoke between sucks at his pipe.

"Well, now. Will you tell me, as far as you know, how the business of loading the revolver was managed?" ("But he knows all that," thought Nigel impatiently.)

"I—I know nothing about it—I had nothing to do with it," said Janet Emerald.

"Of course not. But perhaps you noticed who put the blank cartridges in the drawer, and when."

"I didn't notice at all—anything about the cartridges."

"Did you never see them put in the drawer?"

"I didn't notice."

"Really? You didn't concern yourself about whether they were there, or say to Mr. Simpson that you were terrified he would forget them?"

"I couldn't have done so. What makes you think I said anything of the sort? Jacco! I don't know what I'm saying. Please—please, can't I go?"

"Don't move, Mr. Saint, I shall soon be done. Now, Miss Emerald, please answer my questions as best you can and as simply as you can. Believe me, an innocent person has nothing to fear and everything to gain in telling the truth. You are not the silly, bewildered little thing you pretend to be. You are a large and, I should say, very intelligent woman."

"Jacco!"

"And I suggest that you behave like one. Now, please—did you or did you not notice Mr. Simpson placing the cartridges to-night, and did you, or did you not, remark that you were afraid he'd forget to do so?"

"No, no, no—it's all a lie."

"And did you afterwards go and stand with your hands on the desk?"

"Never—I was talking to Arthur—I didn't notice what George Simpson was doing—he's telling lies. If that's what he says, he's lying."

"What were you saying to Mr. Surbonadier? It must have been of some interest to absorb all your attention."

"I don't remember."

"Really?"

"I don't remember. I don't remember."

"Thank you. Fox, ask Miss Susan Max if she'll be good enough to come here."

"That mean we can go?" Saint's voice made Nigel jump—he had forgotten the proprietor of the Unicorn.

"In a minute. The night is young. How impatient you are, to be sure."

"What sort of a breed are you?" asked Saint suddenly. "Gentleman 'tec, or the comedian of the Yard, or what?"

"My dear Mr. Saint, you make me feel quite shy."

"Ow yow—yow—yow," Saint echoed the inspector's pleasant voice with the exasperated facetiousness of a street urchin. "All Oxford and Cambridge and hot air," he added savagely.

"Only Oxford, and that's nothing nowadays," said Alleyn apologetically. "Oh, here you are, Miss Max." His voice was cordial, "I can't tell you how bad I feel about giving you all this trouble." Miss Max had waddled into Nigel's line of sight.

"Never you mind," she said comfortably. "You're only doing your job, I suppose."

"Miss Max, if only everyone felt like that a policeman's lot would be a happier one."

"I played Ruth in *Pirates* on the Australian circuit," said Miss Max, letting herself down into the chair the inspector had pushed forward.

"Did you really? Do you remember the trio about the paradox? Frederick, Ruth, and Pirate King?"

"Indeed I do.

> "'A paradox,
> A paradox,
> A most ingenious paradox,'"

sang Miss Max in a jolly wheeze.

"Susan!" wailed Miss Emerald. "How can you?"

"Why not, dear? It's a lovely number."

"There's something of a paradox here," said Alleyn, "that you can solve for us."

"And you're the policeman."

"Yes—would you call me 'Frederick' and may I call you 'Ruth'?"

"Get along with you!" said old Susan Max.

"Well, here it is. Perhaps I won't tell you the paradox but ask you a question and hope that your answer will explain it. Can you tell me just what happened on the stage before the curtain went up on the last act?"

"Susan," began Janet Emerald. "You remember——"

"Please!" (Alleyn made Nigel jump.) "Now, Miss Max."

"Well, let me think. I was sitting on the O.P. knitting my scarf and scolding George Simpson about that mat. 'George,' I said, 'do you want me to break my neck?' So he fixed it. Little things like that look so bad from the front, and it quite spoilt my eggzit at the end of that scene."

"I enjoyed your reading of the part enormously."

"Well, dear, I made it a type, you know."

"Is this a cosy chat or a statement?" inquired Saint.

"It's a dialogue between two people only," answered Alleyn. "It's a great thing to be able to study types, Miss Max—I have to do a bit of that myself."

"It's all observation," said Miss Max in a gratified tone.

"Of course it is. You've learnt to observe. You can be of the greatest help to me. Now, can you tell me, Miss Max, exactly what happened after Mr. Simpson put the mat straight?"

"Now, let me think," said Susan Max. There was a dead silence. Miss Emerald gave a sob.

"Yes," said Susan suddenly. "Janet was upset and talking to poor Arthur, who was a little pizzicato."

"Pizzicato?"

"A little too much wine taken. Pity. Well, they whispered together and then he said to her——No. I'm telling stories. *She* said to *him:* 'Are you all right?'; and *he* said to *her:* 'No, I'm all blanky wrong,' using language as he did so. I didn't hear the next bit, but presently he said in an extremely disagreeable manner: 'You can't talk about influence, Janet. You wouldn't be where you are without it.' More whispers. I didn't listen. I measured my scarf round George Simpson's neck. Then when he went off to the prompt corner——No, I've left out a bit. Wait. *Before* that, when George put the cartridges in the drawer, Janet said she was always afraid he'd forget them—do you remember, dear? And then *after* all the other bit about poor Arthur being drunk and influence and so forth, you followed over to the prompt corner and I recollect that you had another whisper with him—with George Simpson, I mean, of course. There you are!" Miss Max ended with a sort of triumphant gaiety.

"Bravo!" cried Alleyn. "Top marks. We shall have to get you into the force."

"Oh, yes, I dare say. Well, now. Is that all? Can I go?"

"I shall be sorry to lose you."

Nigel had waited for an outburst from Miss Emerald—a denial, an explanation, another bout of hysteria. Instead there was dead silence. He wished he could see Janet Emerald and Jacob Saint.

"It's a shocking thing," said Susan Max abruptly. "It's a very shocking thing for a young man to die as Arthur Surbonadier died. Not himself. Angry. For he *was* angry, you know."

"What about?"

"All sorts of things. Not satisfied with the casting. Unhappy over other matters too, I believe. I suppose it's murder?"

"It looks like it."

"And poor Felix. You're not running away with the idea Felix had anything to do with it, I hope? Except pulling the trigger, poor fellow. Um?"

"Why not?" Janet Emerald demanded. "Why not Felix Gardener? He shot him. It was his revolver. Why is everybody so sure he knew nothing about it? Stephanie doing brave heroine stuff all over him. Everybody treating him like an invalid. While I I am treated like a criminal. It's infamous."

"There's only one thing more," said Alleyn, exactly as if she had not spoken. "It's unavoidable or I wouldn't press it. I should like everyone behind the scenes to-night to be searched before they leave. I can't insist, but it will save a lot of bother if you consent. Miss Max, I expect you know what we are looking for?"

"I don't, then."

"For the dummy cartridges."

"Oh."

"They will be fairly bulky. Miss Emerald, will you take off your wrap?"

"Here!" said Jacob Saint. "Whaddeyer going to do?"

"Oh, hold your tongue, Jacco!"

A slithery noise. Nigel craned his neck and saw Janet Emerald move forward. She was clad in a sequinned sheath that fitted her like a skin.

"Miss Emerald, will you let me make a very superficial examination or would you prefer to go to a police station, where there will be a wardress?"

"Don't let him touch you, Janet."

"Oh, Jacco, don't be a fool." There was no touch of hysteria here, only a harsh and wearied contempt. "Do whatever you like," said Janet Emerald. She held up her magnificent arms and closed her eyes. Alleyn passed his delicate hands lightly over the surface of her dress. He too had closed his eyes. He looked as though his brain was in his fingertips. There was something uncannily remote about him. Lightly the hands swept down the sides and front of the sequinned dress, down the flanks, pausing at the knees and then dropping disinterestedly away. He picked up the fallen wrap, felt it all over, shook it and held it out politely by the collar. "You would like to put it on again," he said.

Janet Emerald breathed unevenly and a curious, distorted smile visited her lips. She slid into the wrap.

"And what about you, Miss Max?" said Alleyn.

"I'm more bulky—you'll have to prod," said Susan Max cheerfully. She took off her overcoat and stood, a round, and somehow pathetic, figure in blouse and skirt.

"You are very courteous," said Alleyn gravely. "And very wise."

He searched her and then Jacob Saint, who stood up for it without protest or comment. Alleyn looked carefully at the papers in his pocketbook, but appeared to find nothing that interested him.

"That is all," he said at last. "I'll keep you no longer. How will you get home, Miss Max?"

"I live in South Kensington—I suppose I've missed the last bus."

"Fox. Be a good fellow and tell the constable at the door to get a taxi. My party, Miss Max."

"You *are* kind," said Susan Max.

"Good night—'Ruth.' Good night, Miss Emerald. Mr. Saint. Inspector Fox will take your addresses."

"Here!" said Saint suddenly. "Maybe I've been short with you, inspector. This thing's upset me. You're doing your duty and I respect that. I'd like to see you to-morrow."

"I shall be at the Yard at eleven, should you wish to make a statement, Mr. Saint."

"Statement be damned."

"By all means. Good night."

Footsteps and then silence.

"Still awake, Bathgate?" asked Alleyn.

"Just," said Nigel. "Let me come out there for a minute. I'm all pins and needles."

"Come out, come out, my dearest dear. What did you think of little Janet? And Uncle Jacob?"

"Not much." Nigel emerged and stood blinking. "By Jove, she told some stinking big whoppers."

"She did rather."

"I say—do you think——"

"Only very confusedly. It's all so muddly."

"I distrust you intensely," said Nigel, "when you go on like that."

"Get back to your corner. Who shall we have next?"

"Don't ask me. It's beastly cold on this stage."

"Shall we adjourn to a dressing-room?"

"Good idea—whose?"

"Bailey has been searching them while you were in your cosy corner. I rather fancy Arthur Surbonadier's."

"You old ghoul. May I ask if you intend to search all the ladies?"

"Don't you think it quate nayce?"

"No, I don't."

"P'r'aps you're right. Hullo, Bailey."

The fingerprint expert reappeared.

"I've been through the rooms," he said in a bored voice. "No sign of the blanks. Got all their prints."

"Really—how?"

"Oh, asked for them." Bailey grinned sardonically. "You weren't there, sir."

"That's all right." Alleyn disliked asking directly for fingerprints and preferred to pick them up without the owners' knowledge. "Well," he said, "we'd better get on with the good work."

"We could do with those dummies," Bailey remarked. "Inspector Fox is searching the other men now, sir. Thought it would save you the trouble."

"Intelligent as well as kind. But he won't find them."

"The dummies?" Bailey eyed his surprise.

"The dummies. Unless our murderer is particularly vindictive."

"What's this," demanded Nigel suspiciously. "Isn't a murderer usually rather vindictive?"

"You don't understand, I'm afraid," said Alleyn kindly. "I think—" he added, turning to Bailey—"I think the cartridges will be in the obvious place."

"Obvious!" repeated Bailey. "You've got me beat, sir. Is there an obvious place?"

"You'll never make a murderer, Bailey. Before we move away let us have a look at that desk. It's in the wings, there. Give me a hand."

Nigel stood near the centre of the stage. He had moved forward towards the wings, when a voice, raucous and detached, yelled above their heads.

"Look out!"

An instant later, Inspector Alleyn hurled himself full at Nigel, driving him backwards. He fell, sprawling across a chair, and at the same moment was aware of something else that fell from above, and crashed down deafeningly on to the stage. Something that raised a cloud of dust.

He got to his feet shaken and bewildered. Lying on the stage was a shattered heap of broken glass. Alleyn stood near it, looking up into the flies.

"Come down out of that," he shouted.

"Yessir. Coming, sir."

"Who the devil are you?" bawled Bailey suddenly.

"Only the props, sir. I'm coming."

They stumbled into the wings, where they were all met by Inspector Fox who had run agitatedly from the wardrobe-room. They all peered up the wall of the stage. An iron ladder ran aloft into the shadows. Soft footsteps padded up there in the dark, and presently among the shadows a darker shape could be seen. The iron ladder vibrated very faintly. Somebody was coming down.

Chapter VII

Props

The shadowy figure came very deliberately down the ladder. Nigel, Alleyn and Bailey did not speak, but fell back a little. Nigel was still shaken by his escape from the chandelier. He felt bewildered, and watched, without thinking, the rubber soles of a pair of dilapidated tennis shoes come down, rung by rung. The man did not turn his face away from the wall until he had completed his descent. Then he swung round slowly.

Bailey moved forward and seized his arm.

"Now then—you," he said.

"Don't you act old-fashioned at me," snarled the man.

"Just a minute, Bailey," said Alleyn. Bailey stared indignantly round.

"You're the property master," said Alleyn. The man stood with his heels together and his hands held tidily at the seams of his trousers. His face was long, thin, and white; with eyebrows that grew together. He looked fixedly at a spot on the scenery above the inspector's head.

"Yessir," he said.

"Been at this job long?"

"Ever since I was demobbed."

"In the Brigade of Guards, weren't you?"

"Yessir. Grenadiers, sir. King's Company."

"You made the dummy cartridges for this show?"

"Yessir."

"Where are they?"

"I gave them to Mr. Simpson."

"The dummy cartridges. Are you sure of that?"

"Yessir."

"How are you so sure? They might have been the real thing."

"No, sir." The man swallowed. "I was looking at them. I dropped a cartridge, and the bullet was loose, sir."

"Where are they now?"

"I dunno, sir."

"How did you come to drop that chandelier?"

Silence.

"How is it fixed up there?"

"On a pulley."

"And the rope turned round a piece of wood or something, to make it fast?"

"Yessir."

"Did the rope break or did you unwind it?"

"I can't say, sir."

"Very well. Sergeant Bailey, go up and have a look at the rope there, will you? Now, Props, you go up to the switchboard and give us some light behind the scenes."

Props turned smartly and did as he was told. In a moment, light flooded the back-stage harshly while, with the facial expression popularly attributed to a boot, Bailey climbed the ladder.

"Now come back." Props returned.

Alleyn had moved over to the desk which stood a little way out from the wings. Nigel, Fox, and the property master followed him. He drew out a pocket-knife and slipped the front of the blade under the top left-hand drawer and pulled it out.

"That's where Surbonadier got the cartridges," he said. "It's empty. Bailey had better get to work on it, but he'll only find stage hands' prints and Surbonadier's, I expect. Now then."

Using the very greatest care to avoid touching the surface, Alleyn next drew out the second drawer with the point of his blade.

"And here we are," he said brightly.

The others bent forward. Lying in the drawer were six cartridges.

"By gum," said Fox, "you've got 'em."

With one accord he and Nigel turned to look at the property master. He was standing in his ridiculous posture of attention, staring, as usual, above their heads. Alleyn, still bent over the drawer, addressed him mildly.

"Look into that drawer. Don't touch anything. Are those the dummies you made?"

Props craned his long neck and bent forward stiffly.

"Well?"

"Yessir."

"Yes. And there—look—is the loose one. There is a grain or two of sand fallen out. You made a job of them. Why didn't you want me to find them?"

Props gave another exhibition of masterly silence.

"You bore me," said Alleyn. "And you behave oddly, and rather like an ass. You knew those dummies were in the drawer; you heard me say I was going to look for them. You were listening up there in the dark. So you cheerfully dropped half a ton of candelabrum on the stage, first warning us of its arrival, as apparently you weren't keen on staging another murder to-night. I suppose you hoped for a scene of general confusion, during which you would shin down the ladder and remove the dummies. It was a ridiculous manoeuvre. The obvious inference is that you dumped the darn' things there yourself, and took to the rigging when the murder came off."

"That's right, sir," said Props surprisingly. "It looks that way, but I never."

"You are, as I have said, an ass; and I'm not sure I oughtn't to arrest you as a something-or-other after the fact."

"My Gawd, I never done it, sir!"

"I'm delighted to hear you say so. Why, then, should you wish to shield the murderer? Oh, well, if you won't answer me, you won't; and I refuse to go on giving an imitation of a gentleman talking to himself. I shall have to detain you in a police station, Props."

A kind of tremor seemed to shake the man. His arms twitched convulsively and his eyes widened. Nigel, who was not familiar with the after-effects of shell-shock, watched him with reluctant curiosity. Alleyn looked at him attentively.

"Well?" he said.

"I never done it," said Props in a breathless whisper. "I never done it. You don't want to lock me up. I was standing in the prompt box and if I thought I seen a bloke or it might have been a woman, moving round in the dark——" He stopped short.

"You'd much better say so," said Alleyn.

"I don't want to get nobody in for the job. He was a swine. Whoever done it, done no 'arm, to my way of thinking."

"You didn't care for Mr. Surbonadier?"

Props uttered a few well-chosen and highly illuminating words. "He was" were the only two of them that were printable.

"Why do you say that?" asked Alleyn. "Has he ever done you any harm?"

The man made as if to speak, hesitated, and then, to Nigel's horror and embarrassment, began to cry.

"Fox," said Alleyn, "will you and Mr. Bathgate muster the rest of the stage staff, one by one, in a dressing-room or somewhere, and see if you can get any information from them? You know what we want. Unless anything crops up, you can let them go home. I'll sing out when I've finished."

Nigel thankfully followed Inspector Fox down the dressing-room passage and, Fox having unlocked the door, into Felix Gardener's room. It seemed an age since they had sat there, listening to his friend's views on the characteristics of actors.

"Well, sir," said Inspector Fox, "I reckon that's our man."

"Do you really think so? Poor devil!"

"He's just the type. Neurotic, highly-strung sort of bloke."

"But," objected Nigel, "his alibi is supported by the stage manager."

"Yes—but suppose the cartridges he gave to the stage manager were the real Mackay?"

"What about the loose shell and the sand? That was true enough."

"Might have been loose when he put them in that drawer earlier in the evening—long before the black-out. Looks pretty queer, you must admit, sir. He scuttles up there into the grid when we are rounding up everyone else, and then, when Chief Inspector Alleyn says he'll take a look in the desk, Master Props lets loose that glass affair, hoping to get down in the confusion and slip out the dummies."

"Yes, but that chandelier business was so darn' silly," protested Nigel, "and if he did the murder, he's by no means silly. And why plant the dummies there, and then take such a clumsy and suspicious way of trying to divert your attention?"

"We'll have to get you in the force, sir," said Inspector Fox good-humouredly. "But all the same I think he's our man. The chief will be getting something now, I don't doubt. Well, sir, I'll just get the rest of the staff along."

The observations made by the rest of the staff of the Unicorn were singularly uninteresting. They were all in the property-room at the time of the black-out, preparing to enjoy a game of poker. In the words of their head, one Mr. Bert Willings: "They didn't know nuffing abaht it." Questioned about Props, Mr. Willings said: "Props was a funny bloke, very jumpy-like, and kep' hisself to hisself."

"Married?" asked Inspector Fox.

No, Props was not married, but he kep' company with Trixie Beadle, Miss Vaughan's dresser, wot was ole Bill Beadle's daughter. Ole Bill Beadle was Mr. Gardener's dresser.

"Who dressed Mr. Surbonadier?"

Old Bill also, it appeared. At this juncture one of the underlings remarked, unexpectedly and dramatically:

" 'E 'ated 'im."

"Who hated who?"

"Ole Bill 'e 'ated Mr. Sirbonbadier. For why? Because Mr. Sirbonbadier 'e was a-mucking arahnd Trixie."

"Er—" said Mr. Willings uneasily.

Fox pricked up his ears. "And how did Props like—er—the deceased—paying attention to his girl?"

" 'E 'ated 'im, too."

"Did he now," said Fox.

There was a short silence. Mr. Willings looked at his boots, stood uncertainly on one leg, grinned, and ran out of information. He and his myrmidons were told they might go home, having first left their names and addresses. They departed. Fox almost rubbed his hands together. "There you are!" he exclaimed. "Deceased was interfering with his girl. He's just the type to go off the deep end. I think before we go any further I'd better let the big noise know about this."

They returned to the wings. Neither Alleyn nor Props were to be seen.

"Well now," remarked Inspector Fox. "Where's he gone popping off to, I wonder?"

"Here I am," said Alleyn's voice. Nigel and Fox started slightly and walked round the prompt wing.

Alleyn and Bailey were on their knees by the prompt box. Bailey was busy with an insufflator and the chief inspector seemed to be peering at the floor through a magnifying glass. Beside him, opened, was the bag they had brought him from the Yard. Nigel looked into it and saw a neat collection of objects, among which he distinguished magnifying glasses, tape, scissors, soap, a towel, an electric torch, rubber gloves, sealing wax, and a pair of handcuffs.

"What are you doing?" asked Nigel.

"Being a detective. Can't you see?"

"What are you looking for?"

"Little signs of footprints, little grains of sand. Fox, my valued old one, my little brush is not in my case. Wing your way to Miss Vaughan's dressing-room and get the foot of my grandmother's hare which you will find on the dressing-table. Fetch me that foot and be thou here again 'ere the Leviathan can swim a league'."

Inspector Fox cast his eyes towards heaven and did as he was bid, returning with a roughed hare's foot.

"Thank you. Any luck with the hirelings?"

"Quite a bit," said Fox. "Surbonadier had been fooling round with the property man's girl, and she's Miss Vaughan's dresser, and her old man's Mr. Gardener's dresser."

"Oh, that."

"What do you mean, 'Oh that'?" asked Fox.

"I knew all that."

"How?"

"Props told me. Carry on with the rest of 'em except Miss Vaughan, and Mr. Gardener. See them one by one. Find out where they all were during the black-out."

"Very good, sir," said Fox formally.

"And don't be cross with me, my Foxkin. You're doing well—excellent well, i'faith."

"Is that Shakespeare?"

"What if it is? Away you go."

"May I stay?" asked Nigel, as Fox went off.

"Do!" Alleyn took a small bottle and a rag from his bag and thoroughly cleaned the hare's foot. He then began to use it as a tiny broom, sweeping up what appeared to be dust from the floor, into a little phial out of the bag. "What have you found, Bailey?" he asked.

"Prints from Prop's rubber shoes, and Simpson's evening ones. Nobody else has stood right inside the prompt box."

"Well, I've got enough sand to be conclusive, if it tallies with what's in the blanks, and I think it will. Gosh, it's getting late!"

"Why the sand?" asked Nigel.

"Think. Think. Think."

"Oh, I see. If it's sand out of the cartridge case, it means Props did bring the dummies to Simpson and they must have been changed during the black-out."

"Stop laughing," said Alleyn to an imaginary audience. "The child's quite right. Now Bailey, will you get what you can in the way of prints from the revolver and the desk. Oh, lummie, what a muddle it all is! Let's have a look at the cartridges in the revolver."

The revolver, held delicately by the extreme end of the barrel, was laid on a table. Bailey, using the insufflator, tested it for fingerprints and, referring to those he had already got, disclosed sufficiently clear evidence of Gardener, Surbonadier, and the dresser having handled it. They broke it open and Bailey turned his attention to the butt ends of the shells. The revolver was a Smith and Wesson and the cartridges ordinary .455. The ends yielded no prints, except Surbonadier's, neither did any other part of the cartridges nor the empty shell.

"Blast!" said Bailey.

"Couldn't expect anything else," said Alleyn philosophically. "Hullo—what's this?"

He picked up one cartridge and held it under a stage lamp. Nigel followed him hopefully. He took out his magnifying glass and looked through it at the shell. He did this with all the other cartridges.

"What is it?" asked Nigel.

Alleyn handed him the glass and he in turn examined the cartridges. Alleyn waited.

"There's—there's a kind of whitish look," ventured Nigel, "on all of them. It's very faint on most, but here's one where it looks clearer. It looks almost like paint."

"Smell it."

"I can smell nothing but brass."

"Put your cigarette out. Blow your nose. Now smell."

"There *is* something else. It reminds me of something. What is it?"

"It looks like one person. It smells like another."

"What on earth do you mean?"

"It looks like cosmetic and it smells like Jacob Saint."

Chapter VIII

Felix Gardener

"What's the time?" said Alleyn, yawning.

"Nearly two o'clock and a dirty night."

"Oh, horror! I loathe late hours."

"Two's not late."

"Not for a journalist, perhaps. Hullo, here come the mummers."

Voices and footsteps sounded in the passage and presently a little procession appeared. Miss Dulcie Deamer, Mr. Howard Melville, Mr. J. Barclay Crammer, Inspector Fox. Miss Dulcie Deamer had her street make-up on—that is to say she had aimed a blow at her cheeks with the rouge puff, and had painted a pair of lips somewhere underneath her nose. She still contrived to be *jeune fille*. J. Barclay Crammer's face showed signs of No. 5 grease paint lingering round the eyebrows and a hint of rather pathetic grey stubble on the chin. He wore a plaid muffler, with one end tossed over his shoulder, and he looked profoundly disgusted. Mr. Melville was pale and anxious.

"Dulcie, how are you going home?" he asked querulously.

"Oh, my God, in a taxi!" she answered drearily.

"I live at Hampstead," Mr. Crammer intoned.

"We are very sorry about all this," said Alleyn, "and will, of course, make ourselves responsible for getting all of you home. The constable at the door will fix it up. Fox, just look after them, will you? Good night."

"*Good* night, everybody, *good* night," mimicked Mr. Crammer bitterly. Miss Deamer glanced timidly and confidingly at Alleyn, who bowed formally. Mr. Melville said: "Oh—ah—good night." Alleyn glanced at him and seemed to get an idea.

"Half a minute, Mr. Melville," he said.

Mr. Melville instantly became green in the face.

"I'll only keep you a few moments," explained the inspector, "but we'll let the others go on, I think. Just wait for me in the wardrobe-room, will you?"

The others turned alarmed glances on Mr. Melville, who looked rather piteously after them and then returned to the wardrobe-room. They filed out towards the stage door.

"Fox," said Alleyn, "have they been searched?"

"The men have thoroughly. I—I kind of patted the lady. She's wearing hardly anything."

"Is there room for a glove there, do you think?"

"Oh—a glove. That's different."

"I know it is, and I've let two of 'em out without a complete search, benighted dolt that I am. Still, old Miss Max is really out of the picture, and there was nothing under those sequins except the Emerald. She doesn't wear stays."

"Nor does Dulcie," said Inspector Fox gloomily.

"Fox, we forget ourselves. If you're not sure, persuade her to go to the station and be searched there. If not, send 'em home in taxis and pay for them."

"Right-oh, sir."

"Where's Mr. Gardener?"

"Waiting for you in his dressing-room."

"Thank you. Are you coming, Bathgate, or do you yearn for your bed?"

"I'll come," said Nigel.

Felix Gardener stood in the middle of the doorway with his hands in his pockets. He started nervously when they came in and then gave a little laugh at himself.

"Is it an arrest?" he said jerkily.

"Not unless you are going to surprise me with a confession," said Alleyn cheerfully. "Let's sit down."

"A confession. My God, it's clear enough without that! I shot him. No matter who planned this ghastly business, I shot him. I'll never get rid of that."

"If you are innocent, Mr. Gardener, you are entirely innocent. You are no more to blame than Mr. Simpson, who put the dummies, or it might have been the cartridges"—Nigel glanced at him in surprise—"in the drawer of the desk. You are as much an instrument as the revolver— as Surbonadier was himself, in loading it."

"I've been repeating that to myself over and over again, but it doesn't make much difference. Nigel, if you could have seen the way he looked at me—as if he knew—as if, in that tiniest fraction of time, he knew what had happened, and thought I'd done it. He looked so surprised. I didn't know myself at first. I got such a shock—you can't think—with the revolver going off. I just went on with the lines. It's Bill's revolver, you know. He said he never shot at a Hun with it. Good job he's dead and can't see all this. He fell just like he always did. Limp. Arthur played the part well. Didn't you think so? And you know I didn't like him. I said so, didn't I—this evening? Oh, God!"

"Mr. Gardener, you can do no good by this," said Alleyn quietly. "Perhaps the truest of all our tiresome clichés is the one that says time cures all things. As a policeman, I should like to say 'time solves all things,' but that unfortunately is not always the case. As a policeman I must ask you certain questions."

"You mean you want to find out if I did it on purpose?"

"I want to prove that you didn't. Where were you at the beginning of the first scene in the last act?"

"The first scene in the last act? You mean the scene when Arthur took the revolver and loaded it."

"That scene—yes. Where were you?"

"I was—where was I?—in my dressing-room."

"When did you come out?"

Gardener buried his face in his hands and then looked up helplessly.

"I don't know. I suppose soon after I was called. Let me think—I can't think collectedly at all. I was called, and I came out into the passage."

"When was this?"

"During the front scene, I think."

"Before or after the black-out, during which the first part of that scene is played?"

"I can't remember. I've really no recollection of anything that happened just before——"

"Some little thing may bring it back. Did you, for instance, walk out of the passage on to a pitch-black stage?"

"Somebody trod on my foot," said Gardener suddenly.

"Somebody trod on your foot—in the dark?"

"Yes. A man."

"Where was this?"

"In the wings—I don't quite know where—it was pitch dark."

"Any idea who it was?"

Gardener looked with quick apprehension at Nigel. "Shall I implicate anyone by this?"

"For Heaven's sake," said Nigel, "tell the truth."

Gardener was silent for a moment. "No," he said at last. "If I had an idea, it was altogether too slight to be of use, and it would carry undue weight; you couldn't help yourself—you'd be influenced. I can see that. I've done enough harm for one night, haven't I?" He stared fiercely at Alleyn.

Alleyn smiled.

"I'm not terribly easily influenced," he said, "and I promise it won't carry one ounce overweight."

"No," said Gardener obstinately. "I'm not even sure myself. The more I think the less sure I get."

"Was it something to do with your sense of smell?"

"My God!" whispered Gardener.

"Thank you," said Alleyn.

Gardener and Nigel stared at him. Gardener began to laugh hysterically.

"Proper detective stuff. 'This man is clever.' Actor-proof part."

"Be quiet," said Alleyn. "I don't want any more histrionics. I'm sick of scenes, Mr. Gardener."

"Sorry."

"So I should hope. Now this revolver. I understand it belonged to your brother. How long have you had it, please?"

"Ever since he died."

"Had you any ammunition?"

"I gave Props the cartridges he turned into dummies."

"Any more at home?"

"No, couldn't find any more. Just the six that were in it. Oh, I supplied everything."

"What did you do after you ran into the man in the dark offstage?"

"Swore and rubbed my foot. It was still hurting when the lights went up."

"Did you go anywhere near the desk that was standing on the stage—almost in the wings?"

"I've no idea. I suppose I must have done so. You mean the desk that—the cartridges were in. It must have been close by."

"About that scene we all witnessed in Miss Vaughan's dressing-room. Why did Surbonadier make that very unpleasant to-do?"

"He was tight."

"Nothing else behind it?"

"He disliked me. I told you that."

"So you did," agreed Alleyn. "But it seemed to me that he disliked you for more reason than that of professional jealousy."

"Yes. You must have seen how it was."

"Miss Vaughan?"

"At least, let us keep Stephanie out of this."

"She is in it. She must take her place in the jig-saw puzzle. I'm sorry. The nicer delicacies do not enter into murder cases. I take it you are engaged to Miss Vaughan and that Surbonadier was the unsuccessful suitor."

"We are not publicly engaged. *We're* not. I've no doubt killed my chances along with my only serious rival. The engagement was to be announced at our supper-party."

"Yes, I see. Mr. Gardener, have you a pair of gloves here in your dressing-room?"

Gardener turned very white.

"Yes," he said, "I have."

"Where?"

"I don't know. Probably in my overcoat pocket. I don't wear any in the piece."

Alleyn felt in the pockets of an overcoat that hung under the sheet. He found a pair of white wash-leather gloves which he examined very carefully. He smelt them, held them under the light, looked at each finger, and then threw them to Gardener.

"A perfectly innocent pair of gloves," he said. "Thank you, Mr. Gardener, I appreciate your frankness. Now, if you agree, I'm going to search you, as I have searched all the others."

Nigel watched this proceeding with the liveliest anxiety. He did not know what Alleyn expected to find, or, indeed, if he expected to find anything. He found nothing.

"That's all, Mr. Gardener," he said. "I'll keep you no longer."

"I'll wait if I may," said Gardener, "for Stephanie. She wanted me to see you first."

"Certainly. Wait on the stage, will you?"

"Shall I come?" asked Nigel diffidently.

"No thanks, old thing. If you don't mind I'd rather be alone."

He went out.

"Well?" asked Nigel anxiously.

"Well, Bathgate, we don't progress very fast. What's happened to your shorthand notes?"

"I—I couldn't report old Felix for you."

"I'm not quite a machine," said Alleyn gently. He raised his voice. "Got everything, Fox?"

"Everything O.K.," answered Inspector Fox from the next room. In a moment he appeared.

"He's been taking it down outside the door," said Alleyn. "I really can't trust my filthy memory."

"Oh, Lord."

"Like to go home?" asked Alleyn.

"Not unless you want to get rid of me," said Nigel.

"Stay put then. Fox, you saw the dressers, Mr. and Miss Beadle?"

"Yes. The girl howled, and said she never done no harm to anybody, and that Mr. Surbonadier was always trying on his funny business, and that Props was her boy. Old Beadle said much the same. He'd warned the girl to look out for Mr. Surbonadier. They were both in the wardrobe-room during the black-out. Alone there together, they said. They met in the elbow of the passage, and went along together. She's a flighty bit of goods, I should say. Deceased was evidently"—Inspector Fox stopped and grimaced—"a nasty kind of chap. You might like to see the girl yourself, some time. The old father's a decent old bird and seems very fond of her."

"All right, I'll remember them. And now I'll have to see Miss Vaughan. I should have done so earlier and let her go home."

"She wanted the others to go first," said Fox. "I—took her clothes into the wardrobe-room and she said she'd change. She's not quite ready."

It was obvious from Inspector Fox's manner that he put Miss Vaughan in a superior catalogue to the rest of the cast. Alleyn looked at him and grinned.

"What's the joke?" inquired Fox suspiciously.

"No offence in the world. Have you carried on with routine work?"

"Mr. Melville helped Bailey re-set the scene in which the revolver was loaded. Haven't found the gloves."

"I'll just take a look at it while she's changing." They returned to the stage. Felix Gardener was walking up and down the passage to the outside exit, and paid little attention to them. Nigel went and spoke to Gardener, but he answered at random and looked at him as though they were strangers.

"It'll be all right, Felix," ventured Nigel lamely.

"What'll be all right?"

"Alleyn will find out who did it. Innocent people are never accused nowadays."

"Do you think I'm worrying about that?" asked Gardener, and fell to walking up and down again. Nigel left him alone.

On the stage Alleyn looked critically at the reconstruction of the penultimate scene. The desk was in position. Miss Max's arm-chair was on the O.P. side, and the window-seat in position, near which Janet Emerald had had her last conversation with Arthur Surbonadier.

"We've had all the chair-seats out, and so on," said Bailey, who was in shirt sleeves. The two constables, who had been helping him, stared solemnly at the furniture. Melville had gone.

"There's something missing," said Alleyn.

"Mr. Melville said not, sir," said Bailey.

"Yes, there is. A spot of colour. What is it?" He turned to Nigel. "There was a spot of colour somewhere in that scene. Something red."

"I know," said Nigel suddenly. "Miss Max's bag for her knitting. It hung on that chair arm."

"Good man," exclaimed Alleyn. "Let's find it." They hunted about. One of the constables disappeared in the direction of the property room.

"Damn the thing, where is it?" murmured Alleyn. "It hung on the chair throughout the scene, and at the end she stuffed her knitting into it and left it there." He hunted round offstage and muttered to himself.

"Does it matter much?" Nigel asked wearily.

"What?"

"Does it matter much?"

"No. I just want to make the stage look pretty."

Nigel was silent.

"Is this the affair, sir?" said the constable, reappearing. In his paw he held a large red bag. Alleyn strode over and took it.

"That's it."

He drew out a long and loud strip of knitting, and then thrust his hand deeper into the bag. A singularly blank look stole over his face, and the others, who knew him, pricked up their ears.

"Has any gentleman in the audience missed an article of clothing?" asked Alleyn. He made a face at Nigel, and looked round, most provokingly. Then so suddenly that they all jumped, he whisked out his hand and held it high above his head.

In it was a pair of grey suede gloves. "Eureka!" said Chief Detective-Inspector Alleyn.

Chapter IX

Stephanie Vaughan's Shoulder

"Yes, but look here," Nigel began indignantly.

"Old Miss Max—I mean to say, that's a bit too thick. She's a nice old thing."

Alleyn gave one of his rare laughs. "All right, all right," he said. "Don't bite my head off. I didn't plant the things."

"Well, somebody else did, then."

"Quite possible. During the black-out. Oh, it's a very nasty bit of goods, this is. And so clever, so filthily clever. Everything nice and simple. No fancy touches. I tell you one thing, all of you, for what it's worth. I've been telling it to myself ever since this started. We're up against good acting."

"Yes," said Nigel thoughtfully, "the very best."

"As you say. It's a West End production, bad luck to it."

"Anything on the thumb of the right-hand glove?" asked Fox abruptly.

"Oh, Mr. Fox, aren't you wonderful?" he said. "Such a lovely quality, moddom, or, rather, sir. Yes, definitely, 'sir.' Have a sniff." He held them out.

"I've got it," said Fox. "They smell of cigars, and scent, and—damn it—where did I smell that scent?"

"On Mr. Jacob Saint."

"By gum, you're right, sir."

"It's a very good scent. Something rather special. But how careless of Mr. Saint to lose his gloves, how rather surprisingly careless." He handed the glove over to his colleague.

"When were they lost? He was wearing none when he came round," Fox declared. "I know that because he shoved me aside at the door, and his ring dug into my hand."

"His altogether too big signet ring," murmured Alleyn. "It does dig in. Look!"

He held up the little finger of the left-hand glove. The base showed a distinct bulge.

"He was behind the scenes earlier in the evening, you know. Before the curtain went up. Then he was in front."

"Could he have come round again, later?" asked Nigel.

"We must find out. By George, Fox, what happened to the old gentleman?"

"Who's he?"

"The stage door keeper."

"I never saw one. He must have gone home during the first few moments."

"He was there when we came round. Not very good. He'll have to be traced. Oh well, let's have Miss Vaughan. I think I'll see her alone, if you please, Fox. There's nothing much else to be done here that I can think of. Have you looked closely at the thumb?"

"Yes," said Fox carefully. "There's a bit of whitish stain on it."

"There is, indeed. We may want an analysis of that to compare with the cartridges."

"What do you make it out to be?"

"Oh, cosmetic, Fox, cosmetic. While I'm talking to Miss Vaughan, see if you two can match it in any of the dressing-rooms. Take samples of any make-up that looks like it and note where from, and all that. And now would you take my compliments to Miss Vaughan and ask her if she would be kind enough to come out here?"

Fox and Bailey went off. Presently the constable who had been stationed outside the wardrobe-room came back and with a glance at Alleyn disappeared in the direction of the stage door. Alleyn followed him, said something that Nigel did not catch and returned.

"Any objection to noting this down for me?" asked Alleyn.

"No," said Nigel. "If I had any, they are overruled by curiosity. I'll go back to my cache-cache."

"Thank you. Here she comes."

Nigel slipped through the doorway in the set. He discovered that, by moving his seat, he could leave the door half open and get a fuller view of the stage without being visible. In this way he was able to see Stephanie Vaughan when she came on to the scene. She had changed her dress and was wearing a dark fur wrap. The stage make-up was gone, and she looked pale and rather tired. There was no hint of histrionics in her manner now. She was grave and dignified, and a little remote. "Why, it's not the same woman," thought Nigel.

"You sent for me," she said quietly.

"I'm sorry if my message sounded peremptory," answered Alleyn.

"Why not? You're in charge."

"Will you sit down?"

She sank into an arm-chair, and there was a little silence.

"What do you want to ask me?" she said at last.

"Several questions. The first—where were you during the black-out at the beginning of the last act?"

"In my dressing-room, changing. Then I went in to see Felix."

"Was anyone with you? In your own room, I mean?"

"My dresser."

"All the time?"

"I've no idea. From my dressing-room I couldn't see when the stage lights went on."

"I should have thought you could hear the dialogue."

"Possibly. I didn't listen."

"Was Mr. Gardener still in his room when you left it?"

"No. He went out first. He came on before I did."

"When did you go out on to the stage?"

"When the scene was over."

"Yes. Thank you. What happened after Bathgate and I left your dressing-room?"

The question must have taken her by surprise. Nigel heard her draw in her breath. When she spoke, however, her voice was quite even.

"After you left," she said, "there was a scene."

"There was the making of one while we were there. What happened?"

She leant back wearily, her wrap slipped down. She winced, as if something had hurt her, and sat forward again, pulling the fur collar over her shoulders.

"You are hurt?" said Alleyn. "Your shoulder. You put your hand up to it."

"Arthur hit me."

"What!"

"Oh, yes."

"Let me see it."

She let her wrap fall, and pulled aside her dress, hunching up her shoulder. Nigel could see the bruise. Alleyn bent over her without touching her.

"What did Gardener do?"

"He wasn't there. I'm beginning half-way, I suppose. The moment you had gone I made Felix leave me. He didn't want to, of course, but I had to deal with Arthur alone, and I insisted. He didn't like going, but he went."

"And then?"

"And then there was a scene—a scene in a whisper. We had had them before. I was used to it. He was quite beside himself with jealousy, and threatened me with all sorts of things. Then he became maudlin and shed tears. I'd never seen him like that before."

"With what did he threaten you?"

"He told me," said Miss Vaughan gently, "that he would drag my name in the mud. He said he would stop Felix marrying me. Really, if Felix had been shot, I should not have wondered. Arthur looked murderous. I think he did it himself."

"Do you? Had he that sort of rogue's courage?"

"I think so. He hoped Felix would be accused."

"Where was he?" asked Alleyn, "when he struck you?"

"How do you mean? I was sitting where you left me—on the small chair in my room. He was standing, I think, about as far off as you are now."

"With his left hand, then?"

"No. I don't know. I can't remember, I'm afraid. Perhaps if you were to do it—but gently, please—I might remember."

Alleyn moved his right arm and Nigel saw his hand against the left side of her throat.

"It would be there, on your face," he said, "I think it must have been with his left hand, and even then it would be a strange sort of blow."

"He was drunk."

"So everyone keeps telling me. Could he not have been behind you? Like this."

Alleyn stood behind her and laid his right hand on her right shoulder. Nigel was suddenly and vividly reminded of the scene in the dressing-room, when Gardener had stood, touching her in the same way, and laughing at Alleyn's remark about Edgar Wallace.

"My hand falls exactly over the bruise," said Alleyn. "Am I hurting you?"

"No."

"Let me draw up your wrap. You are cold."

"Thank you."

"Do you think that could have been the way of it?"

"Perhaps. He was lurching about the room. I really don't remember."

"You must have been terrified."

"No. He was not a terrifying man, but I was glad Felix had gone. I managed to get rid of Arthur and then I went to Felix's room."

"Next door?"

"Yes. I said nothing about the blow on my shoulder. Beadle was there but left as soon as I went in. Then I told Felix it had all petered out."

"What did he say?"

"He said that Arthur was a drunken pig, but that in a way he was sorry for him. He said I must let him speak to Master Surbonadier and tell him to behave himself, and that he wouldn't have me worried like that."

"Quite temperate about it?"

"Yes. He knew that sort of thing didn't really count and we both had a horror of more scenes. We only spoke a few words, and then Felix went out on to the stage. The lights were still out, I remember. Have you got a cigarette, Mr. Alleyn? I should like one."

"I'm very sorry. I didn't think."

She took one from his case and he lit it for her. She touched her fingers against the back of his hand, and they seemed to look full in each other's face. Then she leant back again in her chair. They smoked in silence for a little time—Alleyn very composedly, Miss Vaughan not so composedly.

"Please tell me this," she said at last, very earnestly, "do you suspect anyone?"

"You cannot expect me to answer that," said Alleyn.

"Why not?"

"Everyone is under suspicion. Everyone is lying and acting."

"Even me? Have I lied or played a part?"

"I don't know," said Alleyn sombrely. "How should I?"

"How you dislike me, Inspector Alleyn!"

"You think so?" said Alleyn swiftly, and then, after a pause: "Do you ever do jig-saw puzzles?"

"Sometimes."

"And do you ever conceive an ardent distaste for a bit that won't fit in?"

"Yes."

"That is the only kind of personal prejudice a policeman can allow himself. I have that feeling for the pieces that don't fit. For the ones that do, I develop a queer sort of affection."

"And you can't fit me into your puzzle?"

"On the contrary, I think I have you—just where you belong."

"My cigarette is finished. Have you anything more to ask me? No, I don't want another."

"Only one more point. May I have your hand?"

She held out both her hands. Nigel was astonished to see him take them very lightly in his, and raise them to his face. He turned them over in his palms, and stood with his eyes closed, his lips almost touching them. She made no attempt to withdraw them, but she was less pale, and Nigel thought her hands trembled very slightly. Then he let them drop.

"Chanel No. 5," he said. "Thank you very much, Miss Vaughan."

She hid her hands swiftly in the fur sleeves of her coat. "I thought you were going to kiss them," she said lightly.

"I trust I know my place," said Alleyn. "Good night. Mr. Gardener is waiting for you."

"Good night. Do you want my address?"

"Please."

"Flat 10, The Nun's House, Shepheard's Market. Will you write it down?"

"There is no need. Good night."

She looked at him an instant and then went down the passage to the stage door. Nigel heard her calling:

"There you are, Felix"—and in a moment her footsteps had died away.

"Have you got that address down, Bathgate?" asked Alleyn anxiously.

"You old devil," said Nigel.

"Why?"

"Well, I don't know. I thought you didn't like her before, in the dressing-room."

"So did she."

"Now I'm not so sure."

"Nor is she."

"Are you being a cad, Mr. Alleyn?"

"Yes, Mr. Bathgate."

"What were you driving at about that bruise?"

"Didn't you guess? Can't you see?"

"No, I can't. Unless you wanted an excuse to dally with the lady."

"Have it that way, if you like," said Alleyn.

"I think you're very silly," said Nigel, grandly, "and I'm going home."

"So am I. Thank you for giving me such a lovely evening."

"Not a bit. So glad you were able to come. I must do a job of work before I go to bed."

"What's this—what's this?"

"Story for my paper. It's a scoop."

"You'll bring whatever gup you write to me in the morning, young fella."

"Oh, I say, Alleyn!" Nigel protested.

"Yes, indeed. I'd forgotten your horrible evening shocker. The officer outside has turned away a collection of your boy friends already."

"Well, let me do a bit. It's a scoop—really it is."

"Bring it to my study to-morrow morning, sir."

"Oh, all right."

Alleyn assembled his men and they filed out of the stage door. The lights were turned off.

"A final black-out," said Alleyn's voice in the dark.

The stage of the Unicorn was completely silent and quite given over to the memory of dead plays. Nigel was oppressed by the sense of uneasy expectation that visits all interlopers in deserted buildings. Now, he thought, was the time for ghosts of old mummers to step out from behind the waiting doorways and mouth their way silently through forgotten scenes. Somewhere above their heads a rope creaked, and a little draught of air soughed among the hanging canvas.

"Let's go," said Nigel.

Alleyn switched on an electric torch and they found their way down the passage to the stage door. Nigel stepped out into the cool air. The others were talking to a night-watchman, and to two young men, whom Nigel recognized as journalists.

"Just a moment," said Alleyn's voice in the passage. "Look here!"

The others turned back. The light from the torch had penetrated a kind of dark cubby-hole on the left of the doorway. It shone on old Blair's closed eyes.

"Good God!" exclaimed Nigel. "Is he dead?"

"No—only asleep," said Alleyn. "What's his name?"

"Blair," said the night-watchman.

"Wake up, Blair," said Alleyn. "It's long past the final curtain, and they've all gone home to bed."

Chapter X

The Day After

By nine o'clock on the following morning Nigel had got his story ready to go to press. He warned his sub-editors of his activities and they agreed, with a certain display of irritated enthusiasm, to hold back the front page while he submitted his copy to Alleyn. The morning papers were blazing with effective headlines, supported by exceedingly meagre information. Nigel sought out his friend at Scotland Yard and found him more amenable to persuasion than he had anticipated. The article laid great emphasis on the view that Gardener's part in the tragedy, painful though it had been for himself, did not point in any way to his complicity in the murder. Alleyn did not dispute this, or censor a word of it. Nigel had made little of the personal relationships of Surbonadier, Gardener and Miss Vaughan, beyond using the romantic appeal of the engagement between the last two. He made a lot of his first-hand impression of the tragedy, and of the subsequent scenes behind the curtain.

"Less culpable than I anticipated," said Chief Detective-Inspector Alleyn. "With the few deletions I've pencilled it can go through. Are you returning to your office?"

"Not if you'll have me here," said Nigel promptly. "I've got a boy to take back the copy."

"Aren't you a one? All right—come back. I've come to the stage when I can do with a Boswell."

"Throwing bouquets at yourself, I see," said Nigel. "I'll be back in a jiffy."

Having sent the boy off to Fleet Street, he returned to find Alleyn at the telephone.

"Very well," he said into the instrument as he glanced round at Nigel, "I'll see you in twenty minutes"—and hung up the receiver.

"A very unpleasant gentleman," he grunted.

"How—unpleasant?"

"An informer, or hopes to be."

"Who is it?"

"Mr. Saint's footman. Wait and see."

"I will," said Nigel enthusiastically. "How are you getting on, inspector?"

"Oh, it's a devil of a job," Alleyn complained.

"I've been trying to get it straight in my mind," ventured Nigel, "as far as I know it. I made a sort of amateur dossier."

"I don't suppose you know what a dossier is," said Alleyn. "However, let's see your effort."

Nigel produced several sheets of typewritten paper.

"Here are the notes I took for you."

"Thank you so much, Bathgate. Now do show me your summary. It may be very useful. I'm bad at summarizing."

Nigel glanced suspiciously at him, but Alleyn seemed to be quite serious. He lit his pipe and applied himself to the sheet of foolscap, at the top of which Nigel had typed in capital letters:

"MURDER AT THE UNICORN.

"Circumstances.

"Surbonadier was shot by Gardener with the revolver used in the piece. According to the evidence of the stage manager and the property man, dummy cartridges, of which one was faulty, were placed in the drawer of the desk, immediately before the scene in which Surbonadier loaded the gun. Traces of sand, found in the prompt box, seem to support this theory."

"There was also sand in the top drawer," said Alleyn, glancing up. "Was there? That's pretty conclusive, then."

Alleyn read on:

"Props says the faulty cartridge only went wrong that night, when he dropped it. Unless he is lying, and he and the stage manager are in collusion, that means the dummies were in the top drawer just before the scene opened. Therefore the murderer substituted the lethal cartridges either immediately prior to, or during, the black-out, which lasted four minutes. He used gloves, took the dummies from the top drawer, substituted the real ones, put the dummies in the lower drawer, and got rid of the gloves. A pair of men's grey suede gloves was found in the bag that hung on an armchair on the stage. Surbonadier took the cartridges from the top drawer and loaded the revolver. During the scene that followed Gardener took the gun from him and fired point-blank in the usual way. The cartridges afterwards found in the gun were all live ones.

"Opportunity.

"Everyone behind the scenes had the chance of changing the cartridges. The people on the stage, perhaps, the greatest opportunity. These were Miss Max, Miss Emerald, Surbonadier himself, and the stage manager. On the other hand, anyone may have come out on to the darkened stage and done it. Miss Vaughan, Barclay Crammer, Howard Melville, Miss Deamer, the dressers and the staff, all come under the heading.

"Motive.

"The characters involved may now be taken in turn.

"Miss Emerald. She was on the stage. She had an altercation with Surbonadier. She was seen by the S.M. and Miss Max to cross to the desk and lean over it. Told lies. Motive.—Unknown, but she had quarrelled with S. *N.B.*—She seems to be on *very* friendly terms with Jacob Saint, uncle of S.

"Miss Max. On the stage. Handled bag where gloves were found. Did not go near desk while lights were up. Motive.—None known.

"Stage Manager. On the stage. Handled dummy cartridges. Would be able to go to desk unnoticed or during black-out. Peculiar witness. Motive.—None known.

"Property Master. Handed dummies to S.M. Easy access to desk after black-out. Behaved suspiciously after murder. Dropped candelabrum from above. Hid in gallery. Concealed locality of dummies in second drawer. Motive.—Engaged to Trixie Beadle. Surbonadier had interfered with her. Shellshock case.

"Stephanie Vaughan. In dressing-room. Says Trixie Beadle, her dresser, was there with her, but can't remember how long. Says she went to Gardener's room and remained there until after the black-out. Motive.—Had been threatened by Surbonadier, who was madly in love with her. Possibly afraid of something he might reveal to Gardener. Engaged to Gardener.

"Felix Gardener. Fired the revolver. His own weapon. Admits he came on to stage during the black-out. Says someone trod on

his foot. Supplied cartridges that Props converted into dummies.
Motive.—Possibly Surbonadier's threats to Miss Vaughan."

"J.B. Crammer.
"Dulcie Deamer. ⎫ See Fox's report."
"Howard Melville. ⎭

Alleyn looked up.
"Didn't you hear? Melville and Crammer were together in Crammer's
room during the black-out. Before that Melville had been on the stage.
Miss Deamer was next door and heard their voices. I'll write it in for
you."
He went on with the summary.

"See Fox's report. Motive.—None, except professional jealousy
in Barclay Crammer's case.
"Trixie Beadle. Was helping Miss Vaughan, but told Fox she
was with her father in wardrobe-room during black-out. May have
gone there from dressing-room. Motive.—Had possibly been seduced by deceased, and was afraid of him telling Props. Engaged
to Props.
"Beadle. Father of above. Told Fox he was in wardrobe-room
with his daughter. Met daughter in passage first. Motive.—Surbonadier meddling with the girl.
"Old Blair. Stage door-keeper. Most unlikely.
"Jacob Saint. Owns the show. Was behind earlier in the evening. Deceased's uncle. Had a row with him. Hypothetical owner
of the gloves found in bag. Gardener seemed to remember noticing
a scent on the person who trod on his foot. Saint uses a very noticeable scent. Motive.—Unknown, except for the row about
casting.
"Stage Staff. All in the property-room.
"Notes. Points of interest. Janet Emerald exclaimed: 'It wasn't
you. They can't say it was you,' when Saint appeared. She lied
about herself. Props behaved very strangely and suspiciously. Was
Miss Vaughan telling the truth? Had Saint come back on to the
stage? At first-night party Barclay Crammer seemed to dislike Surbonadier intensely. I noticed coolness between Saint and Surbonadier at studio party."

Here Nigel's document ended abruptly. Alleyn laid it down on his
desk.

"It's all quite correct," he approved. "It's even rather suggestive. If you were a policeman, what would you do next?"

"I haven't any idea."

"Really? Well, I'll tell you what we have done. We've been delving in the murky past of Mr. Jacob Saint."

"Jimini!"

"Yes. Rather a chequered career. You can help me."

"I say—can I really?"

"How long have you been a Pressman?"

"Ever since I came down from Cambridge."

"Almost the G.O.M. of Fleet Street. It's a matter of a year, isn't it?"

"And three months."

"Then you don't remember the illicit drug scandal of some six years ago, and an article in the *Morning Express* that resulted in a libel action in which Jacob Saint featured as plaintiff, and triumphed to the tune of five thousand pounds?"

Nigel whistled shrilly and then became thoughtful. "I do remember vaguely," he said.

"The case was spectacular. The article hinted pretty broadly that Saint's fortune had been amassed through the rather wholesale supply of proscribed drugs. Ladies and gentlemen with unattractive portmanteaux under their yellow eyeballs were, said the writer, constantly being obliged with opium and cocaine by some agency controlled by a 'well-known theatre magnate whose recent successes in a playhouse not a thousand yards from Piccadilly . . .' and so on. As I have said, Saint took it to court, won hands down, and emerged a little tarnished but triumphant. One very curious fact came out. The identity of the author was unknown. A leading reporter on the *Morning Express* was away on holiday. The article arrived at the office purporting to have come from him. A typewritten note was signed with a clever forgery of his name. He denied any knowledge of the business and made his case good. For once in its cocksure career, the *Morning Express* had been had. The address on the notepaper was 'Mossburn,' a village near Cambridge, and the postmark, noticed by the secretary, bore this out. A half-hearted attempt was made to trace the authorship, but in any case the 'Mex,' as I believe your journalists call it, was responsible. Mr. Saint was dreadfully annoyed, and, oh, so virtuous."

"What's all this leading to?"

"The postmark was of a village near Cambridge."

"Are you thinking of Felix?" said Nigel hotly.

"Of Gardener? Where was he this time six years ago?"

Nigel paused. He eyed Alleyn uncomfortably. "Well, since you must know," he said at last, "he had just gone up to Cambridge. He was two years ahead of me."

"I see."

"Look here—what are you thinking?"

"I'm only wondering. That article reads like undergraduate stuff. There's an unmistakable flavour."

"Suppose there is? What are you driving at?"

"Literally only this. Gardener may possibly be able to throw some light on the matter."

"Oh, if that's all——" Nigel looked relieved. "I thought you meant he might have written it."

Alleyn looked curiously at him.

"That particular year," he said, "Surbonadier was sent down from Cambridge."

"*Surbonadier?*" said Nigel slowly.

"Yes," said Alleyn. "Now do you see?"

"You mean—you mean Surbonadier may have written the article and, therefore, knew too much about his uncle."

"That is possible."

"Yes."

"The catch in it is that all this happened six years ago."

"Surbonadier may have blackmailed Saint for six years."

"He may."

The telephone rang. Alleyn took off the receiver. "Yes. Who? Oh, send him up, will you?" He turned to Nigel. "This may help," he said.

"Who is it?"

"Mr. Jacob Saint's footman."

"The informer."

"Yes. I hate this sort of thing. He's going to make me feel ashamed."

"Really? You don't want me to go?"

"Stay where you are. Have a cigarette, and look as if you belonged. Have you seen Gardener this morning?"

"No, I'm going to ring him up. I'm afraid he's not going to forget this business in a hurry."

"I don't suppose so. Would you, in his place?"

"Never. But I think I'd worry a bit more about whether the police thought me guilty. It's the shock of having fired the revolver that seems to have got him down."

"Isn't that what you'd expect in an innocent man?"

"I'm glad to hear you call him that," said Nigel warmly.

"I talk a great deal too much," declared Alleyn. "Come in!"

The door opened to admit a tall, thin, and rather objectionably good-looking man. His face was a little too pale, his eyes were a little too large, and his mouth a little too soft. He closed the door tenderly, and stood quietly inside it.

"Good morning," said Alleyn.

"Good morning, sir."

"You wanted to see me in reference to the murder of Mr. Arthur Surbonadier."

"I thought you might wish to see me, sir."

"Why?"

The footman glanced at Nigel. Alleyn paid no attention to this indication of caution.

"Well?" he said.

"If I might inquire, sir, whether a little inside information about the late Mr. Surbonadier's relationships with my employer——"

"Oh," Alleyn cut him short, "you want to make a statement."

"Oh, no, sir. I only wanted to inquire. I don't want to mix myself up in anything unpleasant, sir. On the other hand, there was an incident that might be worth the police's while."

"If you are withholding any evidence that may be of value to the police, you will get into quite serious trouble. If you are expecting a bribe, however——"

"Oh, please, sir."

"You won't get one. Should your information be relevant you'll be called as a witness, and you'll be paid for that."

"Well, sir," said the man, with an angry smirk, "I must say you're very outspoken."

"I should advise you to follow my example."

The footman thought for a moment, and shot a rather apprehensive glance at the inspector.

"It's merely an incident," he said at last.

"Let's have it," said Alleyn. "Will you take it down for me, Bathgate?"

Nigel moved up to the desk.

"I understand you are a footman in the employ of Mr. Jacob Saint."

"Yes, sir. Or rather I was."

"Name?"

"Joseph Mincing. Age twenty-three. Address 299A, Hanover Square," volunteered Mr. Mincing, with a little burst of frankness.

"Tell me, in your own words, what this incident was."

"It took place a month ago before this play come on. The twenty-fifth of May to be exact. I took special notice. It was in the afternoon. Mr. Surbonadier came to see Mr. Saint. I showed him into the library and waited outside in the 'all. Angry words passed, of which I heard many." Mr. Mincing paused and looked self-conscious.

"Yes?" said Alleyn.

"My attention was first aroused by hearing Mr. Surbonadier say very loud that he knew why Mr. Saint had paid Mr. Mortlake two thousand pounds. This seemed to make Mr. Saint very wild, sir. He didn't speak so loud at first, but his tones are penetrating at the best of times. Mr. Surbonadier says: 'I'll do it,' very defiant, and over and over again. I rather gathered, sir, that he was using pressure to force Mr. Saint to give him another part in the play. At first Mr. Saint took on something dreadful and ordered Mr. Surbonadier out, but presently they settled down a bit and spoke quieter and more reasonable."

"You still heard them, however?"

"Not everything. Mr. Saint seemed to promise Mr. Surbonadier a leading part in the next production, saying he couldn't alter this one. They argued a bit, and then it was settled. I heard Mr. Saint say he'd left his money to Mr. Surbonadier, sir. 'Not all of it,' he says. 'Janet gets some, and if you go first she gets the lot.' They looked at the will, sir."

"How do you know?"

"Mr. Saint came out with Mr. Surbonadier later on, and I saw it on the desk."

"And read it?"

"Just glanced, as you might say, sir. I was familiar with it, in a manner of speaking. The butler and me had witnessed it the week before. It was quite short and on those lines—two thousand pounds a year to Miss Emerald, and the rest to Mr. Surbonadier, and a few legacies. The fortune was to go to Miss Emerald if Mr. Surbonadier was no more."

"Anything else?"

"They seemed to get quieter after that. Mr. Surbonadier said something about sending back a letter when the next piece was cast. Soon after that he left."

"Were you with Mr. Saint six years ago?"

"Yes, sir. As knife boy."

"Used Mr. Mortlake to call on him then?"

The man looked surprised. "Yes, sir."

"But not recently?"

"Very occasionally."

"Why did you get the sack?"

"I—I beg pardon, sir?"

"I think you heard what I said."

"Through no fault of my own," said Mincing sullenly.

"I see. Then you bear him a grudge?"

"No wonder if I do."

"Who is Mr. Jacob Saint's doctor?"

"His doctor, sir?"

"Yes."

"Er—it's Sir Everard Sim, sir."

"Has he been called in lately?"

"He comes in, quite regular."

"I see. No other information or incidents? Then you may go. Wait outside for half an hour. There will be a statement for you to sign."

"Thank you, sir."

The man opened the door quietly. He hesitated a moment and then said softly:

"Mr. Saint—he fair hated Mr. Surbonadier."

He went out, closing the door very gently after him.

Chapter XI

Nigel Turns Sleuth

"That's a pretty little pet," said Alleyn. "There's a typewriter over there. Do you mind putting those squiggles into language?"

"Of course I will. Who's Mortlake?"

"He's a most elusive gentleman whom we have been brooding over for some years. At the time of the libel case his name wasn't even mentioned, but it fairly hummed between the lines. He's a Yank, and his pet names are 'Snow' and 'Dopey.'"

"Golly! It looks rum for Saint, doesn't it?"

"Yes, doesn't it? Get on with your typing."

"If he did it," announced Nigel, above the rattle of the machine, "he must have come round a second time, behind the scenes."

"And old Blair swears he didn't. I spoke to him last night while you were hunting up the taxi."

"May have been asleep."

"Says he wasn't. Says he retired to his cubby-hole, after we had gone through, and waited there. The bluebottle at the door thought he was with the others on the stage."

"Funny. Blair didn't speak to the bluebottle."

"I thought so too. He said he believed in keeping himself to himself, and such a thing had never happened before at the Unicorn."

"Why did you ask about Saint's doctor?"

"I wanted to know if the dear old gentleman was enjoying bonny health."

"Oh, rats!"

"I did. He looks like a heart subject. Such rosy cheeks."

Nigel returned, in exasperation, to his typing.

"There," he said presently. "That's done."

Alleyn touched a bell and brought forth a constable. "Is Mincing out there? The man I saw just now?"

"He is, sir."

"Read this through to him and get him to sign it. Then let him go. He's a horrid man."

"Very good, sir." The constable grinned and withdrew.

"Now, Bathgate," began Alleyn. "If you really want to be a help, there's something you can do for me. You can find out who the journalist was whose name was taken in vain over that article. Seek him out and do a bit of ferreting. Discover, if you can, any connection between him and the characters in our cast. See if he knew Surbonadier or Gardener—wait a moment; don't be so touchy—and if either of them is likely to have introduced him to the other. Got that?"

"Yes. I suppose I'll find his name in the files."

"The report of the case will give it. Hullo! Come in!"

Detective-Sergeant Bailey put his head round the door.

"Busy, inspector?" he inquired.

"Not if it's the Unicorn case."

"It is," announced Bailey. He came in and, at Alleyn's invitation, sat down. Nigel kept quiet and hoped to hear something.

"It's the report on the cartridges," began Bailey. "The white stain was stuff used by Miss Vaughan. It's in a bottle labelled 'Stage-White'! It has been upset, but there was plenty left, and quite enough for the analyst on the glove. All the ladies used some sort of stuff, but hers was different. Specially made up for her. I've seen the chemist."

"And the same on the thumb of the glove?"

"Yes. It beats me, sir. What would she want to dong him off for? I reckoned it was the other lady."

"Your exquisite reason, Bailey?"

"Well, look how she carried on," said Bailey disgustedly. "Making a break for her dressing-room and lying away like a good 'un. Now I've seen the statements it looks still more like it."

"And she's one step nearer Mr. Saint's fortune by this—she was his heir after the deceased. And Mr. Saint consults a heart specialist regularly and, no doubt, does not obey his orders. That makes your eyes bulge, doesn't it?"

"I must say it does, sir. Now look at it this way. Suppose my lady Emerald takes Mr. Saint's glove when he's round behind. She's sure to meet him, seeing how things are between them. She plants the gloves and the cartridges somewhere—likely enough in one of the unused drawers of the desk. She's on the stage. She's by the desk. She waits for the lights to be blacked out and then puts on the glove, changes over the cartridges, and drops the gloves in Miss Max's bag. It would look too obvious to leave them near the desk. She knows all this stuff about bad blood between Saint and his nephew will come out. Saint gets rigged out with the hug-me-tight necktie, and she romps home with the dibs."

"Could anything be better put? And I suppose she dips the thumb of the glove into Miss Vaughan's wet-white just to make it more difficult."

"That's the catch in it," admitted Bailey gloomily.

"Look here," said Nigel loudly. "Listen!"

"Ssh!" whispered Alleyn excitedly.

"Don't be silly, now. Listen to me. Miss Vaughan showed you how Surbonadier struck her on the shoulder. Suppose he got the stuff on his hand and—oh no. Sorry."

"As we were, Bailey," said Alleyn.

"We all of us make mistakes, sir," said Detective Bailey kindly.

Nigel looked foolish.

"Well, anyway," he said, "I bet Surbonadier upset the stuff."

"More than likely," agreed Alleyn.

At this juncture Inspector Fox walked in.

"Here's the Props fancier," said Alleyn.

"Good morning, Mr. Bathgate. Yes, that's me. I don't see how you can get past that funny business with the chandelier. And he *knew* the dummies were in the second drawer. There's motive, behaviour and everything else."

"And the gloves?" Alleyn asked.

"Left on the stage by Mr. Saint, and used by Props for the job."

"And the stage-white of Miss Vaughan, on the glove of Mr. Saint, used by Props for the job?"

"Oh, it was hers, was it?" grumbled Inspector Fox. "Well, Saint must have gone into her room."

"It's ingenious, Fox," said Alleyn, "but I don't think it's quite right. I take it, this stage-white dries like a particularly clinging powder. Now if Saint had got it on his glove, earlier in the evening, it would be dry when the glove was used for the cartridges, and if any came off, it would be powdery and not likely to stick to the brass. Through the lens those marks looked as if the stuff had been smeared on, wet."

"The same thing applies to Felix," ventured Nigel. "According to Miss Vaughan, he left her room soon after we did, and after that they only met in his room."

Alleyn swung round slowly.

"That's quite true," he said; "leaving her room vacant, during the black-out."

"I get you," said Fox heavily.

"I don't," confessed Nigel.

"Don't you? Well I'm jolly well going to be inscrutable. The next thing to do is to see Mr. Jacob Saint again. He *said* he might call in. Do you know, I believe I'll ask the old darling. Run and do your job, Bathgate."

"Oh, I say," Nigel protested. "Can't I wait and hear Uncle Jacob?"

"Away you go!"

Nigel attempted persuasion and was cheerfully invited to get out before he was thrown out. He departed, conscious of smiles on the faces of Inspector Fox and Detective-Sergeant Bailey. A hunt through the file in his own office rewarded him with a complete account of the Jacob Saint libel action, and the discovery of the reporter's name. He was one Edward Wakeford, whom Nigel knew slightly and who was now literary editor on the staff of a weekly paper. Nigel rang him up and arranged a meeting in the bar of a Fleet Street tavern much patronized by Pressmen. They forgathered at eleven o'clock, and over enormous tankards of lager the subject of the trial was broached.

"You doing this Unicorn murder?" asked Wakeford.

"Yes, I am. I know Alleyn, of the Yard, and was with him at the show. It was a marvellous chance, but, of course, I have to play fair. He vets everything."

"By George, he's a marvel, that man," said Wakeford; "I could tell you of a case"—and did.

"It was Alleyn who asked me to look you up," Nigel told him. "He wants to know if you've any idea who wrote the article in the 'Mex' in the Saint libel action. The story that was supposed to be yours."

Wakeford's reply was startling. "I've always thought it was Arthur Surbonadier," he said.

"Gosh, Wakeford—this—this is simply terrific, honestly it is! Why did you think so?"

"Oh, I've nothing much to go on, but I knew the blighter and I'd written to him, so he could have forged my signature. He was Saint's nephew and likely enough to have inside information."

"But why would he do it? Old Saint paid for his education, and gave him everything he had."

"They never got on though. And Surbonadier was always in debt. By the way, he wasn't 'Surbonadier' in those days. He was Arthur Simes. Saint's name is Simes, you know. Arthur crashed heavily soon after that, and was sent down. It was a very unsavoury business. Then Uncle Jacob gave him a chance on the boards and he hurriedly changed to 'Surbonadier.' "

"And he wasn't paid for the article?"

"No, of course not."

"Then I don't see why——"

"Nor can I, except that he was an extraordinarily vindictive sort of chap, and was drinking heavily, even then."

"Didn't Saint suspect him?"

"Saint always swore that forgery was a ramp and that the story was written by me. Legally it didn't arise. The 'Mex' was responsible, whoever wrote the stuff, and, thank the Lord, they believed me. It wasn't quite my style, but it wasn't a bad imitation."

"Have you ever met Felix Gardener?"

"No. Why?"

"He's a friend of mine. It's a ghastly situation for him."

"Awful. But the police don't suspect him, surely?"

"No, I'm sure they don't. But, you see, he did actually shoot Surbonadier. It's an unpleasant thought for him."

"Oh, terrible, I quite agree. Well, that's all I can do to help you. What do I get? It's not my line or I'd pinch your story."

Nigel gave him a friendly but rather absentminded punch.

"Felix must have been a freshman when it happened. I wonder if he could let any light in on it himself. He may have known Surbonadier."

"Try him. I must push off."

"I'm terribly obliged to you, Wakeford."

"Not a bit. Bung-oh," said Wakeford genially, and went his ways.

Nigel was in two minds whether to rush off to Alleyn with his booty, or to seek out Gardener with what, he could not help feeling, was a piece of heartening news. In the end he plumped for Gardener and, in the fury of his zest, took a taxi to the studio-flat in Sloane Street.

Gardener was in. Nigel found him looking wretchedly lost and miserable. He had apparently been staring out of his window, and turned from there with a terribly startled face as Nigel walked in.

"Nigel!" he said breathlessly. "It's—it's you!"

"Hullo, old thing," said Nigel.

"Hullo. I've been thinking. Look here, I believe they'll get me for this. Last night I couldn't think of anything, except how he looked when he fell, and then later—when it was getting light, you know—I began to see what would happen. I'll be arrested for murder. And I won't be able to prove anything. It'll mean—being hanged."

"Oh, shut your silly face up," implored Nigel. "Why the devil should they think you did it? Don't be fatuous."

"I know why he asked me all that stuff. He thinks I planted the cartridges."

"He damn' well doesn't. He's on an entirely different tack, and it's about that I've come to see you."

"I'm sorry." Gardener dropped into a chair and pressed his hand over his eyes. "I'm making an ass of myself. Fire away."

"Do you remember the Jacob Saint libel case?"

Gardener stared.

"It's funny you should ask that. I suddenly thought of it a little while ago."

"That's good. Think again. Did you know Surbonadier then?"

"He was sent down soon after I went to Cambridge, and we were at different colleges. His real name was Simes. Yes, I'd met him."

"Did you ever think he wrote the article in the *Morning Express* that Saint brought the case about?"

"I'm afraid I'm rather vague about it now, but I remember hearing third-year men talk about it at the time."

"Well, the article was sent in by an unknown writer purporting to be one of the 'Mex' staff. It came from Mossburn, near Cambridge."

"I remember, now." Gardener paused for a moment. "I should think it most unlikely Surbonadier wrote it. He'd hardly want to kill the goose that laid the golden eggs."

"He was supposed to be on bad terms with his uncle."

"Yes, that's true. I remember hearing it. He was a most unaccountable chap, and subject to fits of the vilest sort of temper."

"Why was he sent down?"

"On several accounts. A woman. And then he was mixed up with a drug-taking set. Fearful scandal."

"Drugs, eh?"

"Yes. When Saint found out, he threatened to cut him off altogether. He survived that, and went down for good over some affair with a farmer's daughter, I imagine. Oh, Lord, what's the good of all this?"

"Can't you see? If he wrote that article it's quite possible he's been blackmailing Saint for years."

"You mean Saint—oh no."

"Somebody did it."

"I'm half inclined to think he did it himself. He'd have loved to send me to the gallows." Gardener looked as though he forced himself to say this for the sheer horror of hearing the words. He reminded Nigel of a child opening the pages of a book that he knew would terrify him.

"Do get that idea out of your head, Felix. You're the last man they're thinking of," he declared, and hoped he spoke the truth. "Can you remember the names of any men who were friendly with Surbonadier then?"

"There was a fearful swine called—what was his name?—oh, Gaynor. I can't think of anyone else. He was killed in an aeroplane accident, I believe."

"Not much good. If you remember anything more let me know. I'll go now, and do, for the love of Mike, pull yourself together, old thing."

"I'll try. Good-bye, Nigel."

"Good-bye. Don't ring, I'll let myself out."

Gardener walked to the door and opened it. Nigel paused to collect his cigarette-case, which had slipped into a crevice of his chair. That was why Stephanie Vaughan didn't see him as she came to the door.

"Felix," she said, "I had to see you. You must help me. If they ask you about——"

"Do you remember Nigel Bathgate?" said Gardener.

She saw Nigel then, and couldn't speak. He walked past her and downstairs without uttering another word.

Chapter XII

Surbonadier's Flat

Big Ben struck twelve noon as Nigel made his way back to Scotland Yard. Chief Detective-Inspector Alleyn was engaged, but Nigel was invited to take a seat in the passage outside his room. Presently the door opened and a roaring noise informed him of the presence of Mr. Jacob Saint.

"That's all I know. You can ferret round till you're blue in the face, but you won't find anything else. I'm a plain man, inspector——"

"Oh, I don't think so at all, Mr. Saint," Alleyn said politely.

"And your comedy stuff makes me tired. It's a suicide case. When's the inquest?"

"To-morrow at eleven."

Mr. Saint uttered a rumbling sound and walked out into the passage. He stared at Nigel, failed to recognize him, and made off in the direction of the stairs.

"Hullo, Bathgate," said Alleyn from the doorway. "Come in."

Nigel, by dint of terrific self-suppression, managed to report Wakeford with a certain air of nonchalance. Alleyn listened attentively.

"Wakeford's theory is possible," he said. "Surbonadier was a peculiar individual. He may have written the article, fathered it on to Wakeford, and hugged himself with the thought that he was dealing a sly blow at Uncle Jacob. We know he tried to blackmail him a week or so ago. It's not as inconsistent as it seems."

"Saint himself swore he didn't do it—at the time of the trial, I mean."

"Of course he did. If his nephew had proved to be the author, he would have seemed a better authority than a reporter eager for sensational copy. No—in a way it's a reasonable theory."

"You sound doubtful."

"I am."

"So's Gardener. He doesn't think Surbonadier did it."

"What? You've seen him?"

"Yes. He's got the wind up now and thinks you're going to pull him in."

"He doesn't think Surbonadier wrote the article?"

"He said so, quite honestly, though I'm sure he understood how the theory would point to Saint rather than to himself. All the same, I got the feeling he really believed there might be something in it."

"Tell me exactly what was said."

Nigel repeated, as closely as he could, his conversation with Gardener. Rather reluctantly he described Miss Vaughan's appearance and her unfinished sentence.

"What was she going to warn him about?" he wondered.

"Can't you guess?" Alleyn asked.

"No, I can *not*."

"Think. Think. Think."

"Oh, shut up," said Nigel crossly. "You talk like a Thorndyke."

"Why not? I wish I could sleuth like one. I'll have to have a stab at it, too. Dig up some old dirt at Cambridge."

"Do you think there's anything in the suicide theory?"

"No. He hadn't the guts. I suppose you realize the significance of Gardener's information about the drug coterie at Cambridge?"

"It suggests that Surbonadier might be 'in the know,' that way as well as any other, about his uncle's goings on," said Nigel confusedly.

"I must go," said Alleyn, looking at his watch.

"Where to?"

"The deceased's flat."

"May I come, too?"

"You? I don't know. You're rather a prejudiced party in this case."

"You mean about Felix?"

"Yes. If you come you'll have to give me your word you'll keep quiet about it."

"I will, I swear."

"Not a word to anyone. Nor with arms encumbered thus or this head-shake, or by pronouncing of some doubtful phrase——"

"No—no—no."

"Swear!"

"I swear."

"All right. Let's have lunch and go."

They lunched together at Alleyn's flat, and, after a liqueur and a cigarette, made their way to Surbonadier's rooms in Gerald's Row. A police constable was on guard there and produced the keys. At the door Alleyn turned to Nigel.

"I've little idea," he said, "what we shall find in here. It's an ugly case. Are you sure you wouldn't rather keep out of it?"

"How you do go on," said Nigel. "I'm in on the deal."

"So be it. Here we go." He unlocked the door and they walked in.

The flat comprised four rooms and a bathroom and kitchenette, all opening on the right from a passage that ran their length. The first was Surbonadier's bedroom and the second a sitting-room with folding doors leading to a small dining-room. The kitchenette and bathroom came next and another bedroom at the end. This seemed to be unused, and was filled with trunks, boxes, and odds and ends of furniture. The flats were served by a married couple and their son, who all lived in the basement. Alleyn, after a glance at the small bedroom, sighed and rang up the Yard, suggesting that Inspector Fox or Detective Bailey should come and help. The sitting-room was luxuriously and rather floridly furnished. A framed supplement from *La Vie Parisienne* was a striking note above the sideboard. The cushions, of which there were many, were orange and purple. Alleyn sniffed distastefully.

"May as well begin in here," he said. "He *would* have a satinwood desk, wouldn't he? Disgusting object."

He produced a bunch of keys, selected one, and fitted it in the lock.

"Are those his keys?" asked Nigel.

"They are, indeed."

The lock clicked and Alleyn let down the front of the desk. A conglomerate welter of paper fell forward and spilled on to the floor.

"Oh, Lord! Come on, Bathgate. Bills in one pile, receipts in another. Circulars here. Letters there. Read everything and tell me if you strike anything interesting. Wait a moment. You'd better hand over all private letters to me. Here we go. Try and get the bills into chronological order, will you?"

There were a great many bills, and the separate accounts had been sent in a great many times, with added reminders that began obsequiously and worked their way through the humble, the plaintive, the reproachful, and the exasperated tenor, until they reached the final and threatening note that indicates "Immediate proceedings." These, however, never appeared to eventuate, and after half an hour's work Nigel made a discovery.

"I say, Alleyn," he said. "He paid all his bills about a year ago, when the shops threatened to dun him, and, as far as I can see, he hasn't paid one since, and they're all threatening to dun him again! I suppose old Saint must have made him a yearly allowance!"

"Old Saint says he made Surbonadier no allowance. He cleared up his debts at Cambridge, gave him a start on the stage, and intimated it was up to little Arthur."

"Really? Well, he was evidently expecting something to come in as far as one can judge by the letters from the shops."

"What did the total of his last pay-out amount to?"

"Wait a bit."

Nigel did some feverish sums, swore under his breath, began again, and finally said, triumphantly:

"Two thousand pounds. That's what he paid out last May and he owes about the same amount again now."

"What's that you've got?" asked Alleyn.

"It's his pass-book. He's overdrawn. Let me see now. May, last year. There's no note of any large sum to his credit. It must have been cash. No, by Jove—here it is. Two thousand paid in on the twenty-fifth of May last year."

"I see," said Alleyn thoughtfully. "I see."

"Doesn't that look like blackmail money?"

"It does."

"From Saint. I bet it was from Saint."

"Maybe."

"You sound dubious."

"I am. Here's old Fox."

Inspector Fox heard the news without enthusiasm.

"He's still wedded to Props," said Alleyn. "Let's get on with the horrid job."

"Deceased seems to have kept every letter that was ever sent to him," said Fox. "Here's a little pile from somebody called Steff."

"Steff?" echoed Alleyn sharply. "Let me see."

He took the letters and walked to the window with them. He stood very still, glancing swiftly at page after page, and placing each face downwards on the sill as he finished it.

"A pig of a man," he said suddenly.

"That's what Felix called him," remarked Nigel.

"So she told me."

"She?"

"Stephanie—Vaughan."

"Steff—oh, I see," said Nigel eagerly. "The letters are from her."

"Oh, Lord," said Alleyn, looking at him wearily, "you're there, are you?"

"Is there anything useful, sir?" asked Fox.

"There's a good deal that's painful. They start off in her best leading-lady manner—all ecstasy and style, and fashionable dalliance. Then he must have shown up in his true colours. She is horrified by something, but still rather mannered and flowery. She keeps it up until about a week—no—two days ago. Then there are two little notes. 'Please let's stop, Arthur. I'm sorry. I can't help it if I've changed,' and the signature. That was written two days ago. The last, which is in a different key, was actually sent yesterday morning."

"Carrying on with him and Mr. Gardener together, seemingly," said Fox; "but I don't see that it helps."

"I'm afraid it does help a little," Alleyn rejoined. "Ah well—on with the hunt."

At last the contents of the desk were exhausted, and Alleyn led them to the spare bedroom, where the search began again and went on wearily. The Yard men were terribly thorough. Finally they unearthed an old trunk that had been put away in the wardrobe. Nigel switched the lights on and drew the curtains. It was already beginning to get dark in the room. Alleyn opened the trunk. Here they found letters from a great many women, but beyond throwing a little extra light on Mr. Surbonadier's unsavoury character, they were of no value.

At the bottom were two old newspapers, carefully folded. Alleyn pounced on one, shook it open, and folded it back. Fox and Nigel looked over his shoulder and read in flaring capitals the single word "Cocaine!" and underneath: "Amazing revelation of the illicit drug trade. Fool's Paradise—and after."

The paper was the *Morning Express* of March, 1929.

"The story itself!" shouted Nigel. "Look, Alleyn, look! And there's Wakeford's signature, reproduced across the top."

"Was that done with all his articles?"

"I think so. All the middle-page, special articles. The 'Mex' always did it."

"It's quite a clear-cut reproduction," said Alleyn. "Good enough to forge from, any day. And an easy one to copy, too."

"Of course," said Fox slowly, "the deceased would be interested even if he had no hand in the matter."

"Quite so," agreed Alleyn absently. He read some of the letterpress. "It certainly points very directly at Saint," he said. "There's another paper left. That will be the account of the libel action."

"You're quite right, sir—it is."

"Yes. Well, now we turn to little Arthur's bedroom. We are looking for a small strong box. Perhaps a cash box. What are you staring at, Bathgate?"

"You," said Nigel simply.

The bedroom was extremely ornate, and smelt of stale incense. *"Quite* disgusting," muttered Alleyn, and opened a window. They set to work again, leaving Fox to deal with the bathroom. He made the first discovery—a hypodermic syringe in the cupboard above the basin. Nigel found another in the bedside-table drawer, and with it a little oblong packet.

"Dope," said Alleyn. "I thought he was still at it. Let me see." He examined the packet closely. "It's the same as the lot we got from Sniffy Quarles," he said. " 'Oh, what a tangled web we weave when first we practise to deceive.' "

"That's right," said Inspector Fox, and returned to the bathroom.

"I adore Fox," said Alleyn. "He's the perfect embodiment, the last loveliest expression, of horse sense. There is nothing in this chest of drawers, nor in any of the pockets of Mr. Surbonadier's suits, except— hullo, what's this?"

It was another letter, this time a very humble affair, written on common paper. Alleyn handed it to Nigel, who read:

"Dear Mr. Surbonadier, please don't take no more notice of me because I'm sorry about what I done and Dad's that angry he found out and Bert is a decent fellow so I told him, and he's forgiven me but if you ever look at me agen he says he will do for you so please do not look at me and oblige yours sincerly Trixie. p.s. I said nothink about getting them little parcels but will not get any more T."

"Who's Bert?" asked Nigel.

"Albert Hickson is the property master's name," said Alleyn.

"One up to Fox," said Nigel.

"He'll think so—yes. So Trixie got it for him. I must see Trixie again."

He got a chair, put it by the wardrobe and stood on it. Then he reached up and groped at the back of the top shelf.

"Stand by!" he said suddenly.

Nigel hurried to his side. From behind a leather hat box Alleyn drew out a small tin, very sturdily made, and bound with iron.

"That's what we're looking for," he said.

Chapter XIII

Contents of an
Iron-Bound Box

"How the devil did you know he had this?" asked Nigel.

Alleyn climbed down from his perch, put his hand in his pocket and produced a small key hanging on a long, very fine, steel chain.

"We found this round his neck. It suggested something of the sort to me. These boxes are made by one particular firm and the keys are rather individual. Now let us open it."

He inserted the little key and turned it twice. The lock gave a sharp click and opened. Alleyn lifted the lid.

"More paper," said Nigel.

"Yes. Wait a moment."

Alleyn put the box down on the glass top of the dressing-table. From his pocket he took two pairs of tweezers and, using them delicately, lifted out a sheet of blue notepaper. It was folded. He opened it up carefully, and bent over it. Nigel heard him draw in his breath.

"Don't touch it," he said, "but look."

And Nigel looked. On the paper two words were written over and over again:

"Edward Wakeford. Edward Wakeford. Edward Wakeford."

Without a word Alleyn went out of the room, returning, followed by Fox, with the newspaper they had found in the trunk. He folded down the heading of the special article and laid it beside the paper on the dressing-table. The writing of the signature was identical.

"Why, in Heaven's name, did he keep it?" whispered Nigel.

"You may well ask," said Fox. "Human nature's very rum, sir, very rum indeed. Vanity, as like as not."

"*Vanitas vanitatum,*" Alleyn murmured. "But not this time, Fox."

The second paper proved to be another letter. It was signed H.J.M., and began: "Dear Mr. Saint."

"Hullo!" said Alleyn. "Here's the ex-footman coming out in a blaze of dubious glory. He mentioned this. It's from Mortlake. 'Please find enclosed my cheque for five hundred pounds in settlement of our little debt. The goods have all been disposed of, as per arrangement. The trade in Shantung silk is particularly satisfactory, but I have great hopes of Celanese next June when our Mr. Charles comes over. Yours faithfully——' Oh, joy, oh rapture, my Foxkin, this is Mortlake himself! It's a relic of our last little catch. Do you remember? Please to remember, my Fox."

"I remember all right. Shantung was heroin and Celanese was cocaine. We rounded 'em all up except Mortlake."

"And 'our Mr. Charles' was none other than Sniffy Quarles, who got five of the best, bless his little soul. This will just about settle Mr. Mortlake. So *that's* what Surbonadier had had up his sleeve for Jacob Saint."

"Well, sir, I must say it begins to look more as if Saint's our man. Although you've got to admit Trixie's letter still points my way."

"Aren't you both excited?" Nigel observed perkily.

"You must allow us our drab thrills. There's nothing more in the box."

Alleyn refolded the papers, using the utmost care not to touch the surfaces. He put them in a black japanned case that Fox produced. Then he shut the iron-bound box, returned it to the wardrobe shelf, and lit a cigarette.

"Bailey had better get to work on the papers," he said. "There's nothing else here. I'm going to call on Miss Vaughan. No. Wait a moment. I think I'll ring her up."

He sat on the bed, nursing his foot and rocking backwards and forwards. An expression of extreme distaste crossed his face. He took up the telephone directory, consulted it, and with a fastidious lift of his shoulders, dialled a number on the bedside telephone. The others waited.

"Is that Miss Stephanie Vaughan's flat? May I speak to her? Will you say it's Mr. Roderick Alleyn? Thank you."

A pause. Alleyn traced his finger slowly round the base of the telephone.

"Is that Miss Vaughan? Please forgive me for bothering you. I am ringing up from Surbonadier's flat. We intended to go through his papers this afternoon, but I find it's going to be a very big job. There are some letters." He paused. "Yes. I realise it is very disagreeable and I think it would be easiest for you if you could meet me here, and should there be any questions I can ask them straight away. That is extremely kind of you. I am locking the place up now and leaving it, but I thought of returning about nine this evening? Could you come then? May I pick you up? Oh, I see. At nine o'clock, then. Goodbye." He hung up the receiver. "What's the time?" he asked.

"Five o'clock," said Nigel.

"Fox—will you take the papers back to the Yard and let Bailey have them? And tell the constable outside he can go."

"Go!" echoed Fox dazedly.

"Yes, and don't send anyone to relieve him. I'm staying on here myself."

"Until nine?" asked Nigel.

"Until nine—or earlier."

"Anything I can do?"

"Yes," said Alleyn. "You can get hold of Felix Gardener again. You can tell him the police believe Surbonadier to have written the article in the *Morning Express*. Ask him if he can give us more information about Surbonadier's Cambridge days. Anything at all that he can remember. There may be something he's holding back. He's feeling jumpy, you tell me. If he's got the idea we're suspecting him his natural reaction will be to disclaim any previous relationship with Surbonadier."

Nigel looked uncomfortable.

"I don't like the idea of pumping him."

"Then you are useless. I'll see him myself."

"Sorry if I'm tiresome."

"All amateurs are tiresome. You want to be in on this, but you shy off anything that is at all unpleasant. We had this out before in the Wilde case. You'd much better keep out of it, Bathgate. I should have said so at the beginning."

"If you can assure me Felix is safe——"

"I can give you no assurances about anybody who was behind the scenes. I have my own theory, but it may be all wrong. It's by no means cast-iron and a new development might set us off on a completely new track after any one of them, from Gardener himself down to old Blair. You want me to assure you with my hand on my heart that I am not interested in Gardener. I can't do it. Of course I'm interested in him. He fired the revolver. I might have arrested him there and then. He's one of the mob, and I've got to prove to myself he didn't plant the cartridges. Like everyone else in the case, he isn't volunteering information. As an innocent man he's a fool if he tries to blind the police. He may have a specific reason for doing so. He's in love. Think that out. If you choose, you may tell him the theory as regards Saint, and if he knows anything about Surbonadier's past that may throw light on that theory, and cares to tell you, and you are still on the side of justice—well and good. Otherwise I shall have to ask you to regard me as you would any other detective on his job, and to expect to get no information but the sort of stuff you can publish in your paper. Have I made myself intelligible?"

"Abundantly. I can take a snub with as good a grace as anyone else, I hope," said Nigel miserably.

"I'm sorry you look at it like that. What line do you mean to take?"

"May I think it over? If I decide to pull out, you may be quite sure I shall treat this afternoon's discoveries as entirely confidential. I promised that, anyway. And I'll let you see my copy, of course."

"That's a very fair answer. Let me know at my flat this evening, will you? Now I must ask you both to go."

Nigel followed Fox into the passage. At the door he turned and looked back.

"Well—good-bye for the present," he muttered.

"Good-bye, you old sausage," said Inspector Alleyn.

Fox told the constable at the entrance to the flat to go off. Then he turned to the still discomfited Nigel.

"I dare say you think the Chief's been a bit hard, sir," he ventured, "but you don't want to look at it that way. It's a matter of what you might call professional etiquette. The Chief likes you, you see, and he's so—so blasted honest, if you'll excuse me. His job has to come before anything. Don't you worry about Mr. Gardener. He's been the cat's-paw, and nothing else, and if he starts holding back information he's very foolish."

"I don't think he has done anything of the sort," complained Nigel.

"Well, all the better. If you decide to help us, Mr. Bathgate, I'm sure you won't regret it and I'm sure Chief Inspector Alleyn will be very pleased."

Nigel looked at his large, comfortable face and suddenly liked him very much.

"It's nice of you to bother, inspector," he said. "I was a bit disgruntled. He made me feel such an ass and—and I do admire him so very much."

"You're not alone in that, sir. Well, I must be off. Going my way, sir?"

"I'm for Chester Terrace."

"And I'm for the Yard. No rest for the wicked. Good night, sir."

"Good night, inspector."

Nigel's flat in Chester Terrace was a short walk from Gerald's

Row. He strode along quickly, still rather miserable over his lecture from Alleyn. He had only gone a couple of hundred yards when a taxi passed him, moving slowly along the kerb as though cruising for a passenger. Nigel automatically shook his head, and then saw that the man had a fare—a woman. As the cab passed him a streamer of light from the street lamp caught her face. It was Stephanie Vaughan. She gave no hint of recognition, and in a moment had passed him. He turned and stared after the taxi. She must have misunderstood, he thought, and is going now to the flat. However, the man drove slowly down the little street, past Surbonadier's windows, and then turned off to the left and disappeared.

"Rum!" thought Nigel and walked on thoughtfully. "Very rum!" he said aloud.

Back in his own flat he turned on the light and, after further cogitation, decided to try and put himself in a better mood by writing to Angela North, who does not come into this story. She was an ardent admirer of Chief Detective-Inspector Alleyn and would know just how raw Nigel felt. Would she suggest he kept in the game? Would she tell him his scruples about "pumping" Gardener were ridiculous? He couldn't ask her without breaking confidence. Damn it all, what *was* he going to do? Perhaps he'd better go to the Queen's in Cliveden Place and have an evening meal. He wasn't hungry. Alleyn was fed up with him and had made him feel young, and a prig. He knew, Good Lord, that Felix hadn't murdered Arthur Surbonadier. Why shouldn't he ask him if——

The telephone pealed shrilly. Nigel muttered and grumbled and took off the receiver.

Gardener's voice came urgently.

"Is that you, Nigel? Look here, I want to see you. There's something I didn't tell you, about Cambridge, this morning. I was a fool. Could I see you now?"

"Yes," said Nigel. "Yes."

"Will you come here or would you rather I came to you? How about dining here with me? Will you?"

"Yes," said Nigel. "Thank you, Felix."

"Well, don't change—come along now."

"Yes," said Nigel. "Thank you, Felix."

They rang off. He could have shouted with joy. His problem was solved. He rushed to the bathroom and washed, lavishly. He changed his shirt and brushed his hair. Seized with a desire to acquire a little merit in Alleyn's eyes, he rang up Surbonadier's flat. He could hear the telephone ringing there and waited for some time, but nobody answered it. Alleyn had gone, after all. He would ring up again later. He seized his hat and ran downstairs. He hailed a taxi, gave Gardener's address, and flung himself back. Only then did it occur to him that it was very clever of Chief Detective-Inspector Alleyn to have guessed that Gardener would be able to tell them something more about the peculiar behaviour of Arthur Surbonadier, during the days when he was an undergraduate. Gradually he was conscious of an idea that edged in at the back of his mind, an idea that was still only half sensed. He examined it now more closely, letting it come up to the front of his consciousness. For a moment he shied round it nervously, but it was insistent, and presently he fell to reasoning it out with logical persistence. Then a great light dawned on Nigel.

"That's it," he whispered. "That's it. Gosh, what a blind fool I've been." And then with complete understanding he thought: "Poor old Felix!"

Meanwhile in Surbonadier's flat it had grown very dark.

Chapter XIV

Gardener Looks Backwards

"If you don't mind, Nigel," said Gardener, "I'm going to get this off my chest, right away. It'll clear the air. There's a drink. Sit down." He looked less jumpy and nightmare ridden, thought Nigel, and had the air of a man who has come to a decision and is glad of it.

"It's this," he began. "When you came this morning, I was properly under the weather. Hadn't slept a wink and the—the awfulness of having killed Arthur Surbonadier had given place to the terror of being suspected by your friend, Alleyn. You simply can't imagine what that sort of fear is like. Perhaps, if a man's guilty, he is less panic-stricken than I was. It seemed to me I couldn't prove I was *not* guilty, and that, in spite of everything you said, I was the man they really suspected."

"You were quite wrong."

"I hope so. Then, I was sure I was right. Well, I couldn't think of anything coherently, but when you started asking me about the libel case and if I knew Surbonadier at Cambridge I thought: 'He's been sent to ask that. Alleyn thinks I'll be off my guard with Nigel.' I can't tell you how awful I felt. No—let me go on. So I half lied. I said I didn't know Arthur well in those days. It wasn't true—I did know him pretty well for a short time—before I realized quite how unpleasant he was. I was younger than he, and perhaps even more of an ass than most youths. I thought it thrillingly daring and sort of 'draining life to the dregs' kind of thing, when he asked me to a heroin party."

"Good Lord!" apostrophized Nigel.

"Yes. I only went once and it was quite beastly. I didn't take nearly as much as the others, and it didn't have a great effect. I probably offered more resistance. Next morning I felt I'd made a fool of myself, and I thought I'd make a clean break. So I called on Surbonadier to tell him so. I wanted to put it straight. He was still pretty dopey, and inclined to be maudlin. He began to confide in me. He told me things about his uncle and—and he talked about Stephanie Vaughan." Gardener stopped speaking, hesitated, and then said:

"I'd seen her. She'd come up for a production of *Othello*. If I said I loved her from then onwards, I suppose you'd think it very highfalutin. It's true, though. And when Surbonadier began to tell me how friendly they were, I hated him. Then he said his uncle was going to give her leading parts and he began to tell me how he hated his uncle, and what a lot he knew about him. He told me how Saint was mixed up in the drug trade. He told me about his mistresses. Stephanie seemed so innocent, and when I thought of her in that *galère* it had a terrible effect on me. I was dreadfully young. Saint seemed like the embodiment of all evil. It was nightmarish. I don't understand psychology, and I expect the heroin had something to do with it. We were neither of us normal. Anyway, when Surbonadier told me, in a dopey sort of way, that he could, if he chose, deal his uncle a pretty shrewd blow, I encouraged him feverishly. He said that Saint was refusing to pay his bills, but that he knew too much and could make him. He then suggested writing that article, and I urged him to do it and egged him on. Then I suddenly remembered what I'd come for, and tried to tell him I wouldn't go to any more of his parties. He didn't seem to pay much attention. He was engrossed with the idea of the article. I left him and, from that time on, I had nothing to do with him. When the article came out I guessed who had done it, and once, when we met, he tried to pump me. I told him, shortly enough, that he'd nothing to fear from me and, until tonight, I've never spoken of it."

"What made you decide to tell me?" Nigel asked.

Gardener did not answer immediately. Then he said slowly: "I thought the police would start ferreting round in Surbonadier's past, and would find out I had known him."

"That's not it," said Nigel compassionately. "You thought they were —on another trail altogether. I'm right, aren't I? You realised that unless they knew Surbonadier had been blackmailing Saint, they might suspect someone else altogether. Isn't that it?"

"Then they *are*——?"

"I don't think so. Anyhow, this will clinch it. Surely *she* doesn't think *you* are guilty?"

"Each of us was afraid——And then this morning when she came in— —My God, they couldn't suspect her."

"You needn't worry about that now, and as for you——"

"Yes—as for me?" Gardener looked at him. "Nigel," he said. "Do you mind telling me this? Do you in your heart of hearts hide a sort of doubt about me? Do you?"

"No. On my word of honour."

"Then, on my word of honour, I'm not guilty of Surbonadier's death and neither is she. There's something I can't tell you, but—we're not guilty."

"I believe you, old thing."

"I feel better," said Felix Gardener. "Let's dine."

The dinner was an excellent one, and the wine extremely good. They talked about many things, sometimes harking back to the case, but now with less sense of restraint. Once Gardener said suddenly:

"It's pretty gruesome to think of the immediate future of—of the Simes family."

"Then don't think of it. What's happening at the Unicorn?"

"You mean about production? Would you believe it, he actually thought of going on with *The Rat and the Beaver*."

"What!"

"Yes, he did. As soon as the police were out of it. Of course I refused to carry on, and so did Stephanie. The others didn't like it, but didn't actually refuse. Then he began to wonder if after all it *would* be a big attraction—with other people playing the leads. The papers might comment unfavourably. So a new piece goes into rehearsal next week."

"What'll you do?"

"Oh, I'll wait. There are other managements." He grimaced wryly. "They tell me I'm a sort of popular figure, and it's helped my publicity. Maudlin sympathy coupled with morbid curiosity, I suppose. Come into the studio room."

They sat down in front of the fire. The front door bell of the flat rang, and Gardener's servant came through with a letter.

"This has just come by special messenger, sir," he said. "There's no answer."

Gardener slit the envelope and drew out a sheet of paper. Nigel lit a cigarette and wandered round the room. He had paused in front of a photograph of Gardener's brother when he was recalled by an exclamation from his host.

"For Heaven's sake," murmured Gardener, "what's all this in aid of?"

He held out the sheet of paper.

It contained a solitary typewritten paragraph, which Nigel read with bewilderment:

"If your job and your life are any use to you, mind your business or you'll lose both. Forget what's past, or you will get worse than a sore foot."

Nigel and Gardener stared at one another in utter bewilderment.

"Coo lumme!" said Nigel at last.

"Not 'alf," agreed Gardener with emphasis.

"Have you got a sore foot?" Nigel inquired.

"Yes, I have. I told you somebody trod on it."

"Somebody who smelt like Jacob Saint?"

"I only thought so. I wasn't sure."

"Look here," said Nigel, "this is no joke. Alleyn ought to know about it."

"Oh, help."

"Well, he ought to, anyway. I'll ring him up, if I may."

"Where will you find him?"

Nigel paused and considered. Possibly Alleyn might not want him to disclose his whereabouts. Nigel did not even know if he would still be at Surbonadier's flat. He looked up the number in the directory and dialled it.

"He may not be at home," he said deceitfully. Again, he could hear the bell pealing in the flat in Gerald's Row. Again there was no answer. He felt vaguely uneasy.

"Nobody there?" said Gardener.

"I could try the Yard," mumbled Nigel. "But I'll leave it for the moment. Let's have another squint at that paper."

He and Gardener spent the next hour in speculation on the authorship of the letter. Gardener said he didn't think Saint would do it. Nigel said if he was rattled, there was no knowing what he would do.

"If he's a murderer——" he began.

"I'm not sure that he is. Another view is that he's scared I may know something of what Surbonadier found out about him, and thinks I may do exactly what I have done—come clean."

"Did he know you were friendly with Surbonadier?"

"Yes, Arthur introduced us in those days. Afterwards, when I took to the boards, he saw me in the first decent part I played, and remembered me. That's partly how I got my first shop under his management. Not nice to think of now. Arthur resented it very much. He used to tell people I'd got in on his family ticket. God, what a dirty game it is! Do you remember what I said about actors?"

"I do."

"Look at the way they behaved last night, with Surbonadier lying dead on the stage. All of them acting their socks off—except Stephanie."

Nigel looked at him curiously. He seemed to hear Alleyn's sardonic "Lovely exit, wasn't it?" after Miss Vaughan had left the stage. He remembered the curiously seductive note she struck afterwards, in her interview with the inspector. Even he, Alleyn, had stood longer than was necessary with his hand on her bruised shoulder. Nigel thought virtuously of his Angela and felt a little superior.

"I wonder what she's doing?" Gardener said presently. "I wanted to go and see her to-night, but she said she'd ring up."

"What's she so frightened about?" Nigel blurted out. Gardener's face whitened. The look that had been there that morning returned.

"Of course she's frightened," he said at last. "She thinks Alleyn realised Surbonadier was pestering her and threatening her. It wasn't hard last night to see how the land lay. She always made nothing of it to me. Until this morning I didn't realise myself what he was up to. This morning she showed me her shoulder, and told me that after I left her he struck her—the swine! My God, if I'd known that!"

"It's damn' lucky for you that you didn't," said Nigel. "And he's dead now, Felix."

"She told me Alleyn had seen the bruise. She thought Alleyn suspected her. She's terribly highly strung and the shock has been almost overwhelming."

"And you were afraid for her, too?"

"Yes—after this morning. Until then, selfish imbecile that I was, I thought only of myself. That they should even think of her! It's monstrous."

"Well, don't worry. I haven't heard one of them ever hint it. I tell you they are off on different tacks. I'd be breaking confidence if I said more than that. And now, if you don't mind, Felix, I'll be off. It was a devilish late night last night and you look as if you wanted sleep too. Take a couple of aspirins and a peg and leave off worrying. Good night."

"Good night, Nigel. We've never known each other particularly well, but I hope we may from now on. I'm rather grateful to you."

"Bosh. Good night."

It was half-past ten when Nigel got back to Chester Terrace, and he was, he discovered, dead tired. He had, however, a story to write for to-morrow, and he didn't want to leave it till the morning.

Very wearily he sat down to his typewriter and ran in a sheet of paper. He thought for a moment and then began to tap at the keys:

"THE UNICORN MURDER.

"Fresh Developments
Saint Libel Case Recalled."

As he worked his thoughts kept turning to Alleyn. The inspector ought to know about Felix. At last he reached out his hand and took up the telephone. Surely by this time Alleyn would be home. He dialled the number of his flat, rested his head on his hand and waited.

Chapter XV

Achilles' Heel

After Nigel and Inspector Fox had gone out of the room, and the door was shut, Inspector Alleyn stood very still and listened to their footsteps dying away down the passage. He heard Fox speak to the constable at the entrance door, and a little later their voices floated up from the footpath beneath.

If an onlooker had been there, he might perhaps have supposed Alleyn's thoughts were unpleasant ones. The inspector had the type of face that is sometimes described as "winged." The corners of his mouth made two deep depressions such as a painter will render with a crisp upward stroke of the brush. His nostrils, too, slanted up, and so did the outside corners of his very dark eyebrows. It was an attractive and fastidious face and, when nobody watched him, a very expressive one. At the moment it suggested extreme distaste. One might have guessed that he had just done something that was repugnant to him, or that he was about to undertake a task which displeased him.

Alleyn looked at his watch, sighed, turned out the lights, and went to the window, where he was careful to stand behind the curtains. From here he could watch, unseen, the desultory traffic of Gerald's Row. Perhaps only two minutes had passed since Nigel and Fox had gone. A solitary taxi came very slowly down the little street. It loitered past the flat. He had an aeroplane view of it, but he fancied that the occupant's face was in an unusual and uncomfortable position, below the window, for all the world as though its owner were kneeling on the floor, enjoying a worm's-eye view of the flat, and taking rather particular care not to be seen. At this Inspector Alleyn smiled sideways. He was trying to remember the exact location of the nearest telephone booth. The taxi disappeared and he moved away from the window, took out his cigarette-case, thought better of it, and pocketed it again. Three or four minutes passed. His meditations were uncannily checked by the bedside telephone, which came to life abruptly with a piercing double ring.

Alleyn smiled rather more broadly, and sat on the bed with his hands in his pockets. The telephone rang twenty times and then inconsequently went dead. He returned to the window. It was now very quiet in the street, so that when someone came briskly on foot from Elizabeth Street, he heard the steps a long way off. Suddenly he drew back from the window, and with a very desolate groan, crawled under the bed, which was a low one. He was obliged to lie flat on his front. He rearranged the valance, which he had noted disgustedly was of rose-coloured taffeta. Then he lay perfectly still.

Presently a key turned in the entrance door to the flat, and whoever it was who came in must have taken off their shoes, because only the faintest sound, a kind of sensation of movement, told him someone was coming, step by stealthy step, along the passage. Then he heard the handle of the door turn and from under the edge of the valance, in the dim light reflected from the street lamps, he saw the door itself swing forward. The faintest rustle told him that someone had come into the room. Another rustle and the scaly sound of curtain rings. The light from the street was blotted out. When the silence had become intolerable, the telephone above him rang out again shrilly. The bell pealed on and on. The bed above him sank down and touched his shoulders stealthily. The noise of the telephone changed into a stupidly coarse clatter. Something had been pressed down over it. Alleyn counted twenty more double rings before it stopped.

Nigel over in Chester Terrace had hung up his receiver and gone to dine with Gardener.

A faint sigh of relief sounded above Alleyn's head. He could have echoed it with heartfelt enthusiasm when the bed rustled again and the weight on his shoulders was lifted. Next came the sound of chair legs, dragging a little on the carpet, and coming down finally across the room. The wardrobe door creaked. A pause, followed by furtive scrabblings. Then a metallic click. Alleyn cleared his throat.

"You'll simply have to turn up the light, Miss Vaughan," he said.

She didn't scream, but he knew how near she came to it by the desperate little gasp she gave. Then she whispered bravely:

"Who is it?"

"The Law," said Alleyn grandly.

"You!"

"Yes. Do turn the light on. There's no reason at all why you shouldn't. The switch is just inside the door." He sneezed violently. "Bless you, Mr. Alleyn," he said piously.

The room was flooded with pink light. Alleyn had thrust his head and shoulders out from the end of the bed.

She stood with one hand still on the switch. In the other she carried the little iron-bound box. Her eyes were dilated like those of a terrified child. She looked fantastically beautiful.

Alleyn wriggled out and stood up.

"I think bed dust is quite the beastliest kind of dust there is," he complained.

Her fingers slid away from the switch. Her figure slackened. As she pitched forward he caught her. The box fell with a clatter to the floor.

"No, no," he said. "This won't do. You're not a woman who faints when she meets a reverse. You, with your iron nerve. You haven't fainted. Your heart beats steadily."

"Yours, on the contrary," she whispered, "is hammering violently."

He put her on her feet and held her elbows.

"Sit down," he said curtly.

She pulled herself away, and sat in the arm-chair he lugged forward.

"All the same," said Miss Vaughan, "you did give me a fright." She looked at him very steadily. "What a fool I've been. Such an obvious trap."

"I was surprised that it caught you. When I saw you in the taxi, I knew I had succeeded, and then a little later, when you rang—I *thought* Surbonadier would have given you a latch-key."

"I had meant to return it."

"Really? I must say, I can't think where the attraction lay. Evidently you are a bad selector."

"Not always."

"Perhaps not always."

"After all, you have nothing against me. Why shouldn't I come here? You yourself suggested it."

"At nine, with me. What were you looking for in that box?"

"My letters," she said quickly. "I wanted to destroy them."

"They are not there."

"Then like Ophelia I was the more deceived."

"You weren't deceived," he said bitterly.

"Mr. Alleyn—give me my letters. If I give you my word, my solemn word, that they had nothing whatever to do with his death——"

"I've read them."

She turned very white.

"All of them?"

"Yes. Even yesterday's note."

"What are you going to do—arrest me? You are alone here."

"I do not think you would struggle and make a scene. I can't picture myself dragging you, dishevelled and breathless, into the street, and blowing a fanfare on my police whistle while you lacerated my face with your nails."

"No, that would be too undignified."

She began to weep, not noisily or with ugly distortions of her face, but beautifully. Her eyes flooded and then overflowed. She held her handkerchief over them for a moment.

"I'm cold," she said.

He took the eiderdown cover off the bed and gave it to her. It slipped out of her hands and she looked at him helplessly. He put it round her, tucking it into the chair. Suddenly she seized the collar of his coat.

"Look at me!" said Stephanie Vaughan. "Look at me. Do I look like a murderess?"

He took her wrists and tried to pull them down, but she clung to his coat.

"I promise you I didn't mean what I said in that letter. I wanted to frighten him. He threatened me. I only wanted to frighten him."

He wrenched her hands away, and straightened himself.

"You've hurt me," she said.

"You obliged me to. We'd better not prolong this business."

"At least let me explain myself. If, after you've heard me, you still think I'm guilty, I'll go with you without another word."

"I must warn you——"

"I know. But I must speak. Sit down for five minutes and listen to me. I won't bolt. Lock the door, if you like."

"Very well."

He locked the door and pocketed the key. Then he sat on the end of the bed, and waited.

"I've known Arthur Surbonadier for six years," she said at last. "I went to Cambridge to take part in a charity show that was being got up by some of the undergraduates. They engaged me to play Desdemona. I was a novice, then, and very young. Arthur was good-looking in those days and he always had a charm for women. I don't expect you to understand that. He introduced me to Felix, but I hardly remembered Felix when we met again. He had never forgotten me, he says. Arthur was attracted to me. He introduced me to Jacob Saint, and through that I got a real start in my profession. We were both given parts in a Saint show that was produced at the end of the year. He was passionately in love with me. That doesn't begin to express it. He was completely and utterly absorbed as though, apart from me, he had no reality. I was fascinated and—and so it happened. He asked me over and over again to marry him, but I didn't want to get married, and I soon knew he was a rotter. He told me about all sorts of things he had done. He had a fantastic hatred of his uncle, and once, at Cambridge, he wrote an article that attributed all sorts of things to Saint. There was a case about it—I expect you remember—but Saint never thought Arthur had done it, because Arthur was so dependent on him. He told me all about that and his own vices. He still attracted me. Then I met Felix and——" She made a little gesture with her hands, a gesture that he might have recognized as one of her stage tricks.

"From that time onwards, I wanted to break off my relationship with Arthur. He terrified me, and he threatened to tell Felix about—all sorts of things." She paused, and a different note came into her voice. "Felix," she said, "was a different type. He belongs to another caste. In a funny sort of way he's intolerant. But—he's dreadfully honourable. If Arthur had told him! I was terrified. I began to write those letters, at the time I went to New York, but when I got back Arthur still dominated me. Yesterday—it seems years ago—he came to see me, and there was a scene. I thought I would try to frighten him and, after he left, I wrote that note."

"In which you said: 'If you don't promise to-night to let me go I'll put you out of it altogether.'"

"My God, I meant I'd tell Saint what he'd done—how he'd written that article!"

"He's been blackmailing Saint for years. Surely you knew that?"

She looked as if she were thunderstruck.

"Did you know?" asked Alleyn.

"No. He never told me that."

"I see," said Alleyn.

She looked piteously at him. She was rubbing her wrists where he had gripped them. As if on an impulse, she held out her hand.

"Can't you believe me—and pity me?" she whispered.

A silence fell between them. For some seconds neither moved or spoke, and then he was beside her, her hand held close between both of his. He raised it, her fingers threaded through his own. He had bent his head and stood in what seemed to be a posture of profound meditation.

"You've won," he said at last.

She leant forward and touched her face against his fingers, and then, with her free hand, she pulled aside the eiderdown quilt and let it slide to the floor.

"Last night I thought you were going to kiss my hand," she said.

"To-night——" He kissed it deliberately. In the silence that followed they heard someone come at a brisk walk down the narrow street. The sound of footsteps seemed to bring her back to earth. She drew her hand away and stood up.

"I congratulate you," she said.

"On what?"

"On your intelligence. You would have made a bad gaffe if you had arrested me. Will you let me go away now?"

"If you must."

"Indeed I must. Tell me—what made you first suspect me?"

"Your cosmetic was on the cartridges."

She turned away to the window and looked into the street.

"But how extraordinary," she said quietly. "That bottle was overturned on my table. Arthur himself knocked it over." She seemed to ponder this for a moment and then she said quickly: "That means whoever did it was in my room?"

"Yes. Your room was empty just before it happened. You were talking to Gardener next door."

"No, no. That's all wrong. At least he *may* have gone in there. No, he didn't. He was on the stage by that time. Arthur knocked the bottle over. He was splashed with the stuff. When he put the cartridges in the drawer, there was some on his hands. Probably there was still some more of it on his thumb when he loaded the revolver. He realised it was all up with him, and he wanted Felix accused of murder. Or me. He may have deliberately used my wet-white. It would have been like him."

"Would it? You poor child!"

"Yes. Oh, I *know* that's it."

"I wonder if you can be right," said Alleyn.

"I'm sure I am."

"I'll approach it again from that angle," he said, but he scarcely seemed aware of what he said. He looked at her hungrily, as though he would never be satisfied with looking.

"I must go now. May I take—the letters—or must they come out?"

"You may have them."

He went into the next room and got the letters. When he came back with them she looked them through carefully.

"But there's one missing," she said.

"I don't think so."

"Indeed, there is. Are you sure you didn't drop it?"

"Those are all we found."

She looked distractedly round the room.

"I must find it," she insisted. "It must be somewhere here. He threatened to show that one, in particular, to Felix."

"We sifted everything. He must have burnt it."

"No, no. I'm sure he didn't. Please let me look. I know where he kept all his things." She hunted frantically through all the rooms. Once she stopped and looked at him.

"You wouldn't——?"

"I have held back none of your letters, on my word of honour."

"Forgive me," she said, and fell to hunting again. At last she confessed herself defeated.

"If it's found you shall have it," Alleyn assured her. She thanked him, but was clearly not satisfied. At last he persuaded her to stop hunting.

"I'll telephone for a taxi," he said.

"No, don't do that. I'll walk to the corner and get one. I'd rather."

"I'll come with you. I've just got to lock up."

"No. We'll say good night now," she laughed. "I can't be seen out with you—you're too compromising."

"*Nous avons changé tout cela.*"

"You think so, do you, inspector? Good night."

"Good night, Stephanie. If I weren't a policeman——"

"Yes?"

"Give me that key, madam."

"Oh! The key of the flat. Where did I put it? Now that's lost."

"Is it on the chain?"

He pulled at the chain round her neck, found the key, which had been hidden under her dress, and slipped it off. This brought them closer together, and he saw she was trembling.

"You are quite done up," he said. "Shan't I come with you? Give me that pleasure."

"No, please. Good night again."

He touched her hand.

"Good night."

She took a step towards him, looked into his eyes, and smiled. In a moment he had her close-held in his arms.

"What's this?" he said roughly. "I know you're everything I most deplore—and yet—look at this. Shall I kiss you?"

"Why not?"

"Every reason why not."

"How strangely you look at me. As if you were examining my face inch by inch."

He released her suddenly.

"Please go," he said.

In a moment she had gone. He leaned from the window and watched her come out on the pavement below. She turned towards South Eaton Place. A few seconds later, a man came out of an alley-way by the flat, paused to light a cigarette, and then strolled off in the same direction.

Alleyn closed the window carefully and put out the light. In walking to the door he stubbed his toe on the little iron-bound box which was still lying where she had dropped it. He stooped down and opened it. A look of intense relief lightened his face. He picked it up and went out of the flat.

Left to itself the telephone rang again, insistently.

Chapter XVI

The Inquest

About ten minutes after Alleyn got back to his own flat that night, Nigel's call came through.

"Got you at last," he said.

"Did you ring up at Surbonadier's flat about twenty minutes after you left it?" asked Alleyn.

"Yes. How did you know?"

"I heard you."

"Well, why the deuce didn't you answer?"

"I was under the bed."

"What? This telephone's very bad."

"Never mind. What's the matter?"

"I've been to see Felix. He asked me to. You were right."

"Well, not over the telephone. Come to the Yard at nine to-morrow."

"All right," said Nigel. "Good night."

"Flights of angels sing thee to thy rest," said Alleyn wearily, and went to bed.

Next morning Nigel arrived at Scotland Yard with his copy and his messenger boy.

"This is becoming a habit," said Alleyn. He censored the story and the remains were dispatched to Fleet Street.

"Now," said Nigel, "listen!"

He told his story of Gardener's confession, and of the anonymous letter, which he produced. Alleyn listened attentively and examined the paper very carefully.

"I'm glad he decided to tell you this," he said. "Do you think he would repeat it and sign a statement to the same effect?"

"I think so. As far as I could gather, after he had got over the first shock of having killed Surbonadier, he began to think you'd suspect him of malice aforethought. Later on, after I'd heard Miss Vaughan ask him not to repeat whatever it was, he felt it was she who was in danger and

that he must tell you everything he knew that would be likely to draw
your suspicions away from her. He realizes that what he has said definitely implicates Saint, and may implicate himself. He's not at all sure
Saint did it. He's inclined to think it's suicide."

"So is our Mr. Saint—very much inclined," said Alleyn grimly. He
pressed the bell on his desk.

"Ask Inspector Fox to come in," he said to the constable who answered it.

He examined the paper again in silence, until the inspector arrived.

"Glad tidings, Fox," said Alleyn. "Our little murderer has come all
over literary. He's writing letters. One begins to see a glim."

"Does one?" asked Nigel.

"But certainly. Fox, this letter arrived at Mr. Gardener's flat, by district messenger, at about eight-thirty last night. There's the envelope.
The district messenger offices will have to be combed out. Have it tested
for prints. You'll find Gardener and an 'unknown.' I've a pretty good
idea who the unknown is."

"May I ask who?" Fox ventured eagerly.

"A man who, in all honesty, I think I may say we have never, in the
course of our speculation, suspected of this crime; a man who, by his
apparent eagerness to help the police, by his frequent suggestions, as
well as by his singular charm of manner, has succeeded so far in escap-
ing even our casual attention. And that man's name is —"

"You can search me, sir."

"Nigel Bathgate."

"You fatuous old bag of tripe!" shouted Nigel furiously. And then
when he saw Fox's scandalised face: "I beg your pardon, inspector.
Like Mr. Saint, I don't always appreciate your comedy. It is true, Inspector Fox," he added with quiet dignity, "that my fingerprints will be
on that paper; but *not* all over it. Only at one edge, and then I remembered not to."

"You'll escape us this time, I'm afraid, sir," said Fox solemnly. He
began to heave with subterranean chuckles. "Your face was a fair treat,
Mr. Bathgate," he added.

"Well," said Alleyn, "having worked off my professional facetiousness, let's get down to it. In your list of properties offstage is there
a typewriter?"

"There is. A Remington used in the first and last act."

"Where's it kept?"

"In the property-room, between whiles. I think they re-set the first
act after the show, as a rule, so it would be on the stage when they all

got down to the theatre, and in the property-room after the last act. We tested it for prints first just in case it might be in the picture. It showed Mr. Gardener's on the keys, and Props's prints at the sides, where he had carried it on."

"The fingerprint system's too well advertised nowadays for the poorest criminal to fall directly foul of it. Who used the typewriter in the last act? Oh, I remember—Gardener. Just let me get a copy of the letter and then give it to Bailey, will you, Fox? And get him to test the typewriter again. No, I'm not dotty. And now I must get things in order for the inquest. Thank the Lord it's a presentable coroner."

"Ah," agreed Fox heavily. "You may say that."

"How do you mean?" Nigel asked.

"Some of them," said Alleyn, "I positively believe, keep black caps in their hip pockets. Tiresome old creatures. However, this one is a sensible fellow, and we'll be through in no time."

"I'll get back to Fleet Street," said Nigel. "I'm meeting Felix and going to the inquest with him. His lawyer is going to be there."

"I expect there'll be a covey of 'em. My spies tell me St. Jacob has employed Phillip Phillips to watch the wheels go round. He's a brother of Phillips, K.C., who did St. Jacob so proud in the libel action. Very big game afoot."

"Well," said Nigel at the door, "we meet——"

"At Phillipi, in fact. *Au revoir,* Bathgate."

Nigel spent a couple of hours in his office, writing up cameo portraits of the leading characters in the case. His chief expressed himself as being not displeased with the stories, and Nigel, at twenty to eleven, went underground to Sloane Square, and thence to Gardener's flat. The lawyer, a young and preternaturally solemn one, was already there. They discussed a glass of sherry and Nigel attempted to enliven the occasion with a few *facetiæ,* which did not go down particularly well. The lawyer, whose unsuitably Congrevian name was Mr. Reckless, eyed him owlishly, and Gardener was too nervous and upset to be amused. They finished their sherry, and sought a taxi.

The inquest proved, on the whole, a disappointment to the crowds of people who attended it. Very little information as regards police activity came out. Alleyn gave a concise account of the actual scene in the theatre, and was treated with marked respect by the coroner. Nigel watched his friend, and experienced something of the sensation that visited him as a small boy, when the chief god of Pop walked on to a dais and grasped the hand of Royalty. Alleyn described the revolver, and the cartridges—.455.

"Did you notice anything remarkable about either the weapon or the cartridges?" asked the coroner.

"They were the regulation .455, used in that type of Smith and Wesson. There were no fingerprints."

"A glove had been used?"

"Probably."

"What about the dummy cartridges?"

Alleyn described them, and said he had found traces of sand from the faulty cartridge in the prompt corner, and in both drawers.

"What do you deduce from that?"

"That the property master gave the dummies to the stage manager, who put them as usual in the top drawer."

"You suggest that someone afterwards moved them to the second drawer, replacing them with genuine cartridges?"

"Yes, sir."

"Is there anything else you noted as regards the cartridges?"

"I saw whitish stains on them."

"Have you any explanation for this?"

"I believe them to be caused by a certain cosmetic used as a hand make-up by actresses."

"Not by actors?"

"I imagine not. There was none in the actors' dressing-rooms."

"You found bottles of this cosmetic in the actresses' dressing-rooms?"

"I did."

"Are the contents of these bottles all alike?"

"Not precisely."

"Could you distinguish from which, if any, of these bottles, the stains on the revolver had come?"

"An analysis shows that it came from the star dressing-room. A bottle of cosmetic had been spilt there, earlier in the evening."

"The star dressing-room is used—by whom?"

"By Miss Stephanie Vaughan and her dresser. Miss Vaughan received visits from other members of the company during the evening. I myself called on Miss Vaughan, before the first act. The cosmetic was not spilt then. I met, in this room, the deceased, who appeared to be under the influence of alcohol."

"Will you describe to the jury your investigations, immediately after the tragedy?"

Alleyn did so, at some length.

"You searched the stage. Did you find anything that threw any light on the matter?"

"I found a pair of gloves in a bag that had been used on the stage, and I found the dummy cartridges in a lower drawer of the desk."

"What did you remark about the gloves?"

"One had a white stain which, on analysis, proved to be similar to that on the cartridges."

This statement caused a stir among the onlookers. Alleyn's evidence went on for some time. He described his interviews with the performers, and said they had all since signed the notes taken at the time of their statements. This was news to Nigel, who wondered how they had reacted to the evidence of his activities. Alleyn said little about the subsequent investigations by the police, and was not pressed to do so by the coroner, who left him a very free hand.

Felix Gardener was called. He was very pale, but gave his evidence clearly. He admitted ownership of the revolver, said it was his brother's, and that he gave the six cartridges to the property man, who converted them into dummies.

"Did you visit Miss Vaughan's dressing-room before the fatality?"

"Yes. I was there with Chief Detective-Inspector Alleyn, who visited me with a friend, before the first act. I did not return after the first act."

"Did you notice a bottle of white cosmetic upset on the dressing-table?"

"No, sir."

"Mr. Gardener, will you describe the actual scene when you fired the revolver?"

Gardener did so. His voice shook over this, and he was very pale.

"Did you realize at once what had happened?"

"Not at once, I think," Gardener answered. "I was dazed with the report of the revolver. I think it flashed through my mind that one of the blanks, fired in the wings, had got into the chamber of the gun."

"You continued in the character of your part?"

"Yes," said Gardener in a low voice. "Quite automatically. Then I began to realize. But we went on."

"We?"

Gardener hesitated.

"Miss Vaughan was also on, in that scene."

A pair of grey suede gloves was produced, to the infinite satisfaction of the onlookers.

"Are those your property?"

"No." Gardener looked both surprised and relieved.

"Have you seen them before?"

"No. Not to my knowledge."

The anonymous letter was produced, and identified by Gardener, who described how it arrived and explained the reference to his "sore foot."

"Did you get any impression of the identity of the person who trod on your foot?"

Gardener hesitated, and glanced at Alleyn.

"I received a vague impression, but afterwards decided it was not definite enough to count for anything."

"Whom did this impression suggest?"

"Must I answer that?"

He looked again towards Alleyn.

"You told Chief Detective-Inspector Alleyn of this impression?"

"Yes. But I added that it really was not reliable."

"What name did you mention?"

"None. Inspector Alleyn asked if I noticed a particular scent. I thought I had done so."

"You meant a perfume of sorts?"

"Yes."

"With whom did you associate it?"

"With Mr. Jacob Saint."

Mr. Phillip Phillips was on his feet, in righteous indignation. The coroner dealt with him, and turned to Gardener.

"Thank you, Mr. Gardener."

Stephanie Vaughan appeared next. She was very composed and dignified, and gave her evidence lucidly. She confirmed everything that Alleyn had said as regards the stage-white and said that Surbonadier himself upset it after the others had gone. She believed it to be a case of suicide. The jury looked sympathetic and doubtful.

The rest of the cast followed in turn. Barclay Crammer gave a good all-round performance of a heart-broken gentleman of the old school. Janet Emerald achieved the feat known to leading ladies as "running through the gamut of the emotions." Asked to account for the striking discrepancies between her statement and those of Miss Max and the stage manager, she wept unfeignedly and said her heart was broken. The coroner stared at her coldly, and told her she was an unsatisfactory witness. Miss Deamer was youthfully sincere, and used a voice with an effective little broken gasp. Her evidence was supremely irrelevant. The stage manager and Miss Max were sensible and direct. Props looked and behaved so precisely like a murderer, that he left the box in a perfect gale of suspicion. Trixie Beadle struck the "I was an innocent girl" note, but was obviously frightened and was treated gently.

"You say you knew deceased well. You mean you were on terms of great intimacy?"

"I suppose you'd call it that," said poor Trixie.

Her father was sparse, respectful and rather pathetic. Howard Melville was earnest, sincere, and unhelpful. Old Blair gave his evidence rather mulishly. He was asked to give the names of the people who went in at the stage door, and did so, including those of Inspector Alleyn, Mr. Bathgate, and Mr. Jacob Saint. Had he noticed anybody wearing these gloves come in at the stage door?

"Yes," said old Blair, in a bored voice.

"Who was this person?"

"Mr. Saint."

"Mr. Jacob Saint? (If there is a repetition of this noise, I shall have the court cleared.) Are you certain of this?"

"Yes," said old Blair and withdrew.

Mr. Jacob Saint stated that he was the proprietor of the theatre, that deceased was his nephew, and that he had seen him before the show. He identified the gloves as his, and said he had left them behind the scenes. He did not know where. He had visited Miss Emerald's room, but did not think he was wearing them then. Probably he had put them down somewhere on the stage. To Nigel's surprise no mention was made of the tension between Saint and Surbonadier. Mincing, the footman, was not called. Mr. Saint had not returned to the stage until after the tragedy.

The coroner summed up at some length. He touched on the possibility of suicide, and rather belittled it. He directed the jury discreetly towards the verdict which, after an absence of twenty minutes, they ultimately returned—a verdict of murder against some person or persons unknown. As he left the court Nigel found himself walking behind Alleyn, and immediately in front of Janet Emerald and Saint. He was about to join the inspector when Miss Emerald pushed past him, and seized Alleyn by the arm.

"Inspector Alleyn," she said.

Alleyn stopped and looked at her.

"*You* were behind that." She spoke quietly enough, but with a kind of suppressed violence. "*You* told that man to treat me as he did. Why was I singled out to be insulted and suspected? Why was Felix Gardener let off so lightly? Why isn't he arrested? He shot Arthur. It's infamous." Her voice rose hysterically. Several people who had passed them stopped and looked back.

"Janet," said Saint hurriedly, "are you mad? Come away."

She turned and stared at him, burst into a passion of the most hair-raising sobs, and allowed herself to be led off.

Alleyn looked after her thoughtfully.

"Not mad, Mr. Saint," he murmured. "No. I don't think the Emerald is mad. Shall we say venomous to the point of foolhardiness?"

He followed them out into the street, without noticing Nigel.

Chapter XVII

Sloane Street to the Yard

Nigel spent the afternoon in writing up his report of the inquest. He was greatly intrigued by the vast amount of information that had *not* come out. The coroner had skated nimbly over the Jacob Saint libel action, had made no comment at all on Surbonadier's state of intoxication, and had walked like Aga in and out of Stephanie Vaughan's dressing-room. The jury, an unusually docile one, had apparently felt no urge to ask independent questions. Their foreman, like the Elephant's Child, had the air of saying "this is too buch for be." Nigel imagined that, in their brief retirement, they had discussed the possibility of suicide, decided it wouldn't wash, and agreed that the whole thing was too complex for any decision but the usual one, which they had given. He had sensed Alleyn's extreme satisfaction; and now, once more, revised his own view of the case.

He found that he had made up his mind that Saint was responsible for the murder. Yet Saint's was the best of all the alibis. He had been alone in the audience, but Blair had sworn positively that he had not seen the proprietor of the Unicorn return to the stage between the acts. Saint had been in a box, and it was just possible that he could have slipped out during the black-out. At this point Nigel got his brain-wave. Suppose Jacob Saint had left his box under cover of the black-out and had gone through the door in the proscenium, on to the stage. This door had been locked when Stavely and Nigel went through, but Saint might easily have got hold of a key. There he would be, before the lights went out, in his box facing the audience, as large as life. Then complete darkness. Saint had left the box, slipped through the door, which he had perhaps previously unlocked, gone straight to the desk, colliding with Gardener on the way, pulled out the drawers and replaced the dummies with the cartridges. When the lights went up again—there was Mr. Saint sitting in his box at the Unicorn. Nigel was thrilled with himself and rang up Scotland Yard. Alleyn was out, but had made an appointment for four o'clock. Nigel said he would be there at 4.30.

He felt fidgety and unable to settle down to anything. He was big with his theory. Presently he thought of Felix Gardener, and decided to walk round to Sloane Street and talk it over with him. He didn't ring up. If Felix was out he would walk on down to Knightsbridge and take a bus to the Yard. He wanted exercise.

Sloane Square, that full stop between Eatonia and Chelsea, had a look of sunny friendliness. Nigel bought a carnation for his coat, sent a silly telegram to his Angela, and walked lightly onwards. Sloane Street, with its air of quality and hint of boredom, was busier than usual. Nigel felt a sudden inclination to run, to whistle, to twirl his stick round. He glanced jauntily at a shabby-genteel man, who stood looking into the furniture shop next the flat. Gardener's windows on the first floor were open. He spoke blithely to the commissionaire, refused the lift, and ran two steps at a time up the thickly-carpeted stairs to Gardener's door.

It was open and Nigel, without ringing, went into the little entrance hall that opened into the studio sitting-room. He was about to call out, cheerfully, and had actually drawn in his breath to do so, when he was brought up short by a woman's voice coming from the studio room.

"If I did it," it cried urgently, "it was for you—for you, Felix. He was your worst enemy."

Nigel heard Gardener say slowly: "I can't believe it. I can't believe it."

The woman began to laugh.

"All for nothing!" she said, between paroxysms of choking. "Never mind—I don't regret it. Do you hear that? But I don't think you were worth it."

Scarcely aware of what he did, and conscious only of cataclysmic panic, Nigel banged the front door, and heard himself shout:

"Hullo, Felix, are you at home?"

Dead silence and then a sound of footsteps, and the studio door was thrown open.

"Oh—it's you, Nigel," said Felix Gardener.

Nigel didn't look at him, but beyond, into the studio, where he saw Stephanie Vaughan, very attractive, in an arm-chair by the window. She held a handkerchief to her lips.

"Why, it's Nigel Bathgate," she cried, with exactly the same inflexion as the one she used when she said: "Hullo, all you people," in her first entrance in the play.

"You've—you've met before," said Gardener.

Nigel managed to say something, even to take the hand she held out cordially towards him.

"I only came in for a second," he told Gardener.

"I'm sure you didn't," said Miss Vaughan gaily. "You've come to have a boy friend chat—the sort that consists of drinks, cigarettes, long silences and a few *risqué* stories. I'm off, anyway, so you needn't bother about me."

She rose to her feet in one lithe movement. She looked Nigel full in the face, and gave him the three-cornered smile.

"Make Felix bring you to see me," she commanded. "I rather like you, Nigel Bathgate. Felix—you hear? You're to bring him to see me."

"Is this your purse?" asked Gardener. Nigel saw him put it on a table near her, and knew he didn't want to touch her hand. He opened the door to her and she floated out, still talking. Gardener followed her, shut the door, and Nigel heard her voice, very low, outside. In another second the outer door slammed, and Gardener came back into the room.

"It was decent of you to come, Nigel," he said. "I'm all in."

He looked it. He sat down in front of the fire and held his hands to it. Nigel saw he was shaking:

"I think you ought to see a doctor, Felix," he ventured.

"No, no. It's only the after-effects of shock, I imagine. I'll be all right. Think I'll turn in presently and try for a little sleep. I haven't been able to sleep much."

"Jolly sound idea. Why don't you carry it out now? I'll give you some aspirin and a stiff whisky, and leave you in peace."

"Oh, in a minute. Any news?"

They had both managed to avoid speaking of Miss Vaughan. Nigel's theory about Saint came into his mind. He smiled rather wryly to himself at the remembrance of his so recent enthusiasm. Did Gardener wonder if he had overheard anything? Nigel believed that idea had not entered his friend's head. As Felix himself said, he was suffering from shock. Nigel forced himself to speak at random. It was hard to find anything to talk about. He who, hitherto, had barely impinged upon the edge of the theatrical world now found himself drawn into it. He felt, suddenly, as though he were surrounded by these people, as though, against his will, he was obliged to witness a play they had staged and as though he had been compelled to leave his seat in the auditorium and mingle confusedly with the action of the piece. The two men must have been silent for some time, for Nigel was startled to hear Gardener say suddenly:

"She gave her evidence well, didn't she?"

"Who?"

"Stephanie."

"Very well."

Some inflexion in Nigel's voice arrested Gardener's attention. He looked at his friend with a kind of agony in his eyes.

"Nigel—you remember what I said. Neither of us is guilty. I gave you my word and you said you believed me."

"I know I did," said Nigel miserably.

"*Are you beginning—to wonder?*"

"Are you *sure* you're right, Felix? She——Oh, Lord!"

Gardener laughed.

"You *are* beginning to wonder. My God, if you only knew what a heroine she is!"

"Can't you come clean, Felix?"

"I can't—I can't. Not about Stephanie. Oh, well, I suppose I can't blame you. It looks pretty damning, for both of us. What does Alleyn say about the suicide theory?"

"He tells me very little," said Nigel.

"The verdict of the inquest was wrong," Gardener said urgently. "It was suicide. I'll see Alleyn myself and try and make him——" He broke off short. "He must be made to accept that it was suicide."

"I must go. Do try and get some sleep, Felix."

"Sleep! 'Sleep that knits up the ravelled sleeve of care.' Ugh! There goes the actor! Good-bye, Nigel."

"I'll let myself out. Good-bye."

Nigel walked sombrely downstairs and out again into Sloane Street.

He realized now that he had a terrible decision to make. Was he to tell Alleyn of the conversation he had overheard? A woman! He shied off the logical consequence of his statement, and then, despising himself, came back to it again. If he held his tongue what would happen? Would Felix, who loved her, let Saint be accused of the murder? He thought of Alleyn's attitude towards his scruples, and suddenly realized that it was his own peace of mind that he was trying to salvage. He was in Knightsbridge, and walking down to Hyde Park Corner, when he made his decision. He had no right to withhold his knowledge. He would tell Alleyn. With a heavy heart he stopped a taxi.

"Scotland Yard," he said.

It was not yet four o'clock when he got there, but the chief inspector was in and could see him. He went up at once.

"Hullo, Bathgate," Alleyn said. "What's the matter with you? Found the murderer again?"

"Please don't rag me," Nigel begged him. "It's not a theory I've come to give you. It's a statement."

"Sit down. Now then, what is it?"

"I suppose you won't understand how awful this feels, Alleyn. To you, it's all got to be completely impersonal. I can't feel like that. It's been rather an effort to come to you with this information. That sounds theatrical, I know, but you see—it's a woman."

"What do you mean?" said Alleyn harshly. "What's this information? You say you've got a statement to make—well, make it. I beg your pardon, Bathgate—I'm unbearable these days, aren't I?"

Nigel gulped.

"I've overheard a confession," he said.

Alleyn waited a second, and then took up a pencil.

"When?"

"This afternoon about an hour ago."

"Where?"

"At Felix's flat."

"All right. Go ahead."

"It's soon told. I went up into his little lobby, without knocking and I heard voices in the 'studio' as he calls it. A woman said: 'If I did, it was for you, Felix. He was your worst enemy.' Felix said: 'I can't believe it. I can't believe it,' and she began to laugh, horribly, and said: 'It was all for nothing. Never mind, I don't regret it. Do you hear that? But I don't think you were worth it.' Then I shut the front door noisily and called out. Felix came and let me in. She was there."

"It was—?"

"Stephanie Vaughan."

"Impossible," said Alleyn fiercely.

"You don't think I could make a mistake over a thing like that, do you? I tell you I'll never forget their voices for as long as I live."

Alleyn was silent for so long that Nigel stared at him in some discomfort. He looked as though he had made a shutter of his face. At last he said:

"After all, Bathgate, this is not conclusive. 'If I did, it was for you. He was your worst enemy.' Suppose she had told Gardener that she had used some threat to Surbonadier, to choke him off, and that she believed she had driven him to suicide? Suppose they were not speaking of Surbonadier?"

"If you had seen Felix you wouldn't suggest that."

"Why—what do you mean?"

"He's a broken man," said Nigel simply.

"A broken man! A broken man! You're getting as stagy as any of them. Barclay Crammer was a 'broken man' in the witness-box this morning, silly old ass."

Nigel got up.

"Well, that's all," he said. "If you don't think it's conclusive, I'm damn' thankful."

Alleyn leant over the desk and looked at him as though he were a museum piece.

"If Diogenes had rolled up against you," he observed, "he'd have got out of his barrel, filled it with booze and made whoopee."

"I suppose you mean to be nice," said Nigel in a relieved voice.

"I suppose I do. What happened afterwards?"

"We made perfectly dreadful conversation. I must say she gave a marvellous performance."

"I believe you."

"She asked me to go and see her." Nigel shuddered.

"You're not to go."

"Am I likely to?"

"Listen to me. You're to pay no more visits to these people. Understand?"

"Yes—but what's biting you?"

"Unless I'm with you. Write your little articles, and mind your little business."

"This is what I get for doing the beastliest job of my life."

"My dear Bathgate, I do honestly appreciate your difficulty and am genuinely grateful," said Inspector Alleyn, with one of his rather charming turns of formality. "But I do ask you to behave as I suggest. I can reward you with a very choice bit of copy."

"What's that?"

"You may inform your public that Mr. Jacob Saint has been arrested, but that the nature of the charge is not known."

Chapter XVIII

Arrest

"As a matter of hard fact," Alleyn continued, when he had noted, with satisfaction, Nigel's dropped jaw, "Mr. Saint is still at large. I am just off now to do my stuff. Care to come?"

"You bet I would. May I just ring up the office? I'll catch the stop press for the last edition."

"Very well. Say no more than what I've told you. You'd better warn them to hold it back for another twenty minutes. If he's not arrested, you can ring up. Aren't I good to you?"

"Very," said Nigel fervently. He rang up and was well received. "That's that," he said.

"Well, we must hustle along as soon as I get the word from my myrmidon. Don't let me forget my handcuffs. Dear me, I'm quite excited!"

"Five minutes ago," observed Nigel, "you looked as though I'd punched you between the eyes. What's come over you?"

"I've taken thought, or rose leaves, or something, and am 'no longer a Golden Ass.'"

"Are you arresting Saint for the murder?"

"*Wouldn't* you like to know?"

A single knock on the door heralded the entrance of Inspector Fox.

"Our man's just rung up," he said. "The gentleman is in the office of the Unicorn. Evening, Mr. Bathgate."

"Away we go then," cried Alleyn.

"Handcuffs," said Nigel.

"What would I do without you! Handcuffs, Fox?"

"Have got. You'd better put your top coat on, Chief. It's a cold evening."

"Here's the warrant," murmured Alleyn. He struggled into his overcoat and pulled on his felt hat at a jaunty angle.

"Am I tidy?" he asked. "It looks so bad not to be tidy for an arrest."

Nigel thought dispassionately, that he looked remarkably handsome, and wondered if the chief inspector had "It." "I must ask Angela," thought Nigel.

Alleyn led the way into the passage. Inspector Fox took the opportunity to say, in a hoarse whisper:

"He's very worried over this case, Mr. Bathgate. You always know. All this funny business." He had the air of a Nannie, discussing her charge.

A policeman and two plain clothes men awaited them. "Unicorn Theatre," said Alleyn.

"There's a couple of those blasted Pressmen outside," said Fox as they started. "Begging your pardon, Mr. Bathgate."

"Oh," said Alleyn, "we'll go in at the little street behind the theatre. It connects with one of the exits. We can go through the stalls, into the office. Bathgate, you can walk round to the front and swap a bit of agony column with your brother-pests, and then come down the stage door alley-way, all casual. Show this card to the officer on duty there, and he'll let you in. You'll get there as soon as we do. Spin them a yarn."

"Watch me!" said Nigel enthusiastically.

Alleyn gave Fox an account of Nigel's experience in the Sloane Street flat. Fox stared at Nigel as though he was an adventurous child.

The car threaded its way through a maze of narrow streets. Presently Fox tapped on the window, and they stopped.

"This is the back of the Unicorn," said Alleyn. "Out you get, Bathgate. Up there, and round to the left, will bring you out in front. I'll give you a start."

Nigel was conscious that his heart beat thickly as he ran up the side street. He dropped into a walk as he turned towards the impressive modern front of the theatre, with its bas-relief, in black glass and steel, of a star-spotted unicorn. There, sure enough, were two brother-journalists, both of whom he knew slightly.

"Nosing round?" asked Nigel cheerfully.

"And you?" answered one politely.

"I've got a date with the comedienne. If you watch this alley-way, you may see something to your advantage."

"What are you up to?" they asked him suspiciously. "You with your pals in the force."

"Watch me, and see."

He walked airily down the stage door alley-way, till he came to a side door into the front of the house. A uniformed constable was on duty here. He assumed a patiently reproachful air as Nigel drew near him, but when he read Alleyn's card he grinned and opened the door.

"Straight up those stairs, sir," he said.

Nigel cocked a snook at his friends and walked in.

The stairs, which were heavily carpeted, ran up to the dress circle foyer. Here Nigel found Alleyn, Fox, and the two plain clothes detectives, talking to a fifth man whom he had not seen before.

"He came along about a quarter of an hour ago," this man said quietly. "I was up here, but I told the P.C. downstairs to let him in. He looked sideways at me, and asked me when the police were going to clear out and let him have the run of his own property. He said there were letters waiting for him which he must attend to. I made difficulties and held him here. My man downstairs was instructed to ring the Yard as soon as Saint walked into the trap. He's just gone along now, sir, into the office at the end of that passage."

"Well done," said Alleyn. "Come along."

"You got a gun, sir?" asked Fox.

"No. I knew you'd have one, you old blood-thirster. Bathgate, you follow last, will you?"

They walked in silence down the long passage. Nigel was acutely aware of the odour of officialdom. Suddenly, these men whom he knew and liked had become simply policemen. "They are walking in step, I do believe," thought Nigel.

They stopped outside a steel-framed door. He could hear somebody moving about on the other side.

Alleyn knocked once, turned the handle, and walked in. The others followed, Fox with his hand in his jacket pocket.

Between their shoulders Nigel saw Jacob Saint. He had his bowler hat on, and a cigar in his mouth. He seemed to have swung round from a heap of papers on an opened desk.

"What's this?" he said.

The other officers moved apart. Alleyn walked up to him.

"Mr. Saint," he said quietly, "I have a warrant for your arrest——"

Saint made some sort of incoherent sound. Alleyn paused.

"You're mad," said Saint thickly. "I didn't do it. I wasn't there. I was in front."

"Before you go any further, you had better hear the charge."

Saint dropped into the swivel chair. He looked quickly from one man to another. His hand fumbled at the side of the desk.

"You're covered, Mr. Saint," Fox remarked suddenly. With something like a sneer, the proprietor of the Unicorn let his hands drop on to the arms of his chair.

"What's the charge?" he asked.

"You are charged with being concerned with traffic in illicit drugs. Read it out, please Fox. I get the language wrong."

Thus urged, Inspector Fox broke instantly into a monotonous sing-song to which Saint listened closely, feasting unattractively the while on his little fingernail.

"It's infamous," he said, when Fox had stopped as abruptly as he began. "It's infamous. You—Alleyn. You'll make a laughing-stock of yourself over this. You'll lose your job."

"And that'll learn me," said Alleyn. "Come along, Mr. Saint."

Saint took his hand from his lips and let it fall to the lapel of his coat. He rose ponderously, and half turned aside.

The next second Alleyn had him by the wrist. The thick fingers held a piece of paper.

"Please, Mr. Saint," said Alleyn. "We can't have you eating paper, you know."

The next second they were struggling bitterly. Saint seemed to have gone mad. In a moment the chair was overturned. The two men had crashed across the desk. An inkpot fell to the floor, splashing Saint's light check trousers. The other men had got hold of him. Alleyn still held his wrist. It was now strained across his back, making the rolls of fat and muscle on his arm and shoulder bulge. He stopped struggling abruptly.

"Pick up that chair," Alleyn ordered sharply. Nigel, who had hovered impotently on the outskirts of the battle, set the heavy swivel chair on its feet.

"Let him down gently. You'll be all right, Mr. Saint. Open those windows, one of you."

Saint lay back in the chair. His face was purple and his breathing terribly distressed. Alleyn took off his tie, and unfastened his collar. The pulse in his neck throbbed laboriously. Alleyn loosened his clothes and stood looking at him. Then he turned to the desk telephone and dialled a number.

"Yard? Chief Inspector Alleyn. Get the divisional surgeon to come round to the Unicorn Theatre at once. Heart attack, tell him. Got that? Upstairs. The constable at the door will show him. At once. Thank you." He put the receiver down.

"You'd better go outside, I think," said Alleyn. "He wants to be quiet. Fox, will you wait here?"

The three detectives filed out quietly. Fox stood still. Nigel walked over to the darkest corner and sat down, hoping to remain unnoticed.

"Heart attack?" asked Fox quietly.

"Evidently. He'll do though, I fancy." They looked in silence at the empurpled face. Alleyn switched on an electric fan and moved it across the desk. Saint's thin hair was blown sideways. He opened his eyes. They were terribly bloodshot.

"Don't try to talk," said Alleyn. "A doctor will be here in a moment."

He pulled forward another chair, put Saint's feet on it, and then moved him a little, until he was almost lying flat. He did all this very quickly and efficiently, lifting the huge bulk without apparent effort. Then he moved across to the window. Nigel saw that he held the piece of paper. Alleyn leant out of the window, looked at it, and then put it in his pocket.

The room was very silent. Saint was breathing more easily. Presently he gave a deep sigh and closed his eyes again. Fox walked over to Alleyn, who spoke to him in a low voice. The electric fan made a high, thrumming noise and blandly turned from side to side. Saint's hair blew out in fine strands, fell, and blew out again, regularly. Nigel stared at Saint's heavy face, and wondered if it was the face of a murderer.

Before long they heard voices in the passage outside. The door opened and the divisional surgeon came in. He walked over to Saint and bent down to make an examination. He took the pulse, holding up the fat, white wrist and looking placidly at his watch. Then he injected something. Saint's lips parted and came together again clumsily.

"Better," he whispered breathlessly.

"I think so," said the doctor. "We'll keep you quiet a little longer and then take you away, where you'll be more comfortable."

He looked at Alleyn and the others.

"We'll leave him for a moment, I think," he said. They went out of the room. Nigel followed, leaving Fox, who shut the door. They walked along the passage a little way.

"Yes, it's his heart," said the doctor. "It's pretty nasty. He's a sick man. Who's his doctor?"

"Sir Everard Sim," said Alleyn.

"Oh, yes. Well, he'd better see him. Is he under arrest?"

"He is."

"H'm. Nuisance. I'll get an ambulance and wait for him. Leave me a couple of men. I'll ring up Sir Everard. Saint's pretty dickey, but he'll pull round."

"Right," said Alleyn. "You'll fix up here then, will you? I'll leave Fox to see to it."

"Oh," said the doctor, "while I think of it. There's a message for you at the Yard. They asked me to tell you. Someone called Albert Hickson is very anxious to see you. It's about this case. He wouldn't talk to anyone else."

"Albert Hickson," Nigel exclaimed. "Why, that's Props!"

"Hullo," said Alleyn, "you've come to life, have you? You've no business here at all. I must get back to the Yard."

Nigel retreated, but he managed to slip innocently back into the car with Alleyn, who raised no objection. The chief inspector was rather silent. As they drew near Scotland Yard he turned to Nigel.

"Bathgate," he said, "is your news of the arrest out by now?"

"Yes," Nigel assured him. "I didn't ring up to stop it—it will be all over London already. Wonderful, isn't it?" he added modestly.

"All over London already. Yes. That'll be it," murmured Alleyn.

Nigel followed him, dog-like, into the Yard. The man who had seen Props was produced.

"Was he carrying a newspaper?"

"Yes, sir."

"Notice which one?"

The constable had noticed and was eager to say so. Props had carried Nigel's paper.

"You're rather wasted at this job," said Alleyn curtly. "You use your eyes."

The constable flushed with pleasure, and produced a sheet of paper.

"He left this message, sir, and said that he'd call again."

"Thank you."

Nigel, still hopeful, followed Alleyn to his room. At the door Alleyn paused politely.

"May I come in?" he asked. "Or do you wish to be alone?"

Nigel assumed the frank and manly deportment of an eager young American in a crook film. He gazed raptly at Alleyn, wagged his head sideways, and said with emotion:

"Gee, Chief, you're—you're a regular guy."

"Aw, hell, buddy," snarled Alleyn. "C'm on in."

Once in his room he took out a file, opened it, and laid beside it the paper he had taken from Saint, and the one Props had left at the Yard.

"What's that?" asked Nigel.

"With your passion for the word I think you would call it a dossier. It's the file of the Unicorn murder."

"And you're going to add those fresh documents?" Nigel strolled up to the desk.

"Can you read from there?" asked Alleyn anxiously. "Or shall I put them closer?"

Nigel was silent.

"The Saint exhibit is a second letter from Mortlake that lands St. Jacob with a crash at the bottom of his ladder. The note from Props——" Alleyn paused.

"Well?"

"Oh, there you are."

Nigel read the following message, written in rather babyish characters:

"I know who done it and you got the wrong man. J. Saint never done it you did not ought to of arested an innocent man yrs respectfully A. Hickson."

"What's it mean?" asked Nigel.

"It means Props will shortly pay a call on the murderer," said Alleyn.

Chapter XIX

Nigel Warned Off

"Now, don't start badgering me with questions," begged Alleyn. "If you must stay, stay quiet. I've got work to do." He pressed his bell, hung up his hat, and lit a cigarette. Then he took off the receiver of his telephone.

"Give me Inspector Boys. Hullo, is that you, Boys? Who's shadowing that fellow Hickson? Oh, Thompson, is it? When is he relieved? That's in about a quarter of an hour. Has he rung up? He has! Where is he? I see. Thank you very much."

To the constable who answered the bell he said: "Ask the man who saw Hickson to come and speak to me."

The man in question appeared in remarkably short time. He stood to attention like a private soldier. Nigel was reminded of Props.

"What's your name?" Alleyn asked.

"Naseby, sir."

"Well, Naseby, I've got a job for you. You know Thompson?"

"Yes, sir."

"He's shadowing Hickson—the man you saw this afternoon. At the moment they are both in an eating-house at the corner of Westbourne Street and the Pimlico Road. Go there in a taxi. Wait till Hickson comes out, and then run across him casually in the street. Recognize him and say you're going off duty. Get into conversation, if you can, but don't let him suspect you. Tell him you gave me his note and you don't think it's much use his coming back here. Say you overheard me remark to Mr. Bathgate here that I thought he was a bit touched and that we've got the right man. Say I told you to tell him I couldn't see him if he came back. I want him to think I'm quite uninterested in him and his information. He's only just gone in there—you may be in time to sit down by him and stand him a drink. Say, in your opinion, Saint will hang. Don't try and pump him—treat the matter as settled. Then let him go. The detective who relieves Thompson must carry on, and tell him from me if he loses his man I'll murder him. He's not to come away until he's certain Hickson is bedded down for the night. Then he can ring up, and we'll relieve him. He is to note down most particularly the number of every house Props—I mean Hickson—goes to. The more information he can get the better I'll be pleased. Now, do you understand?"

"Yes, sir. I'll just go over it if I may, sir."

"Right."

Naseby repeated his instructions, quickly and accurately.

"That's it," said Alleyn. "Now, away you go. Come here when you return. He's a smart fellow, that," he added when Naseby had gone.

He next asked for a report from the district messenger offices that had been combed through that afternoon.

The anonymous letter to Gardener was traced to an office in Piccadilly. They had been particularly busy when the gentleman called and hadn't much noticed him. He had worn an overcoat, a muffler, a soft hat, and gloves. He had put the letter on the counter and said: "See that's delivered at once. The boy can keep the change. I'm in a hurry," and had gone out. Height? Medium. Voice? Couldn't really say. Clean-shaven? They thought so. Figure? Perhaps on the stout side. "Ugh?" said Alleyn. "Our old pal, the man in the street. Might be anybody."

He sent for Detective-Sergeant Bailey, who came in looking puzzled.

"About that typewriter," he said at once. "It's a rum thing. There's no doubt about it; the anonymous letter was written on the machine in the theatre. We tested that machine on the night of the affair, and found only Mr. Gardener's and Props's prints. Mr. Gardener used it in the play, so that was all right. Well, according to your instructions, sir, we've tested it again, and it's got no prints on the keyboard at all now, except on the letter Q, which still has Mr. Gardener's. I couldn't make it out at all, at first, but I reckon I've got an idea now."

"Yes? What is it, Bailey?"

"Well, sir—after we'd tested the machine it was put into the property-room. All the actors, as you know, were in the wardrobe-room. But Jacob Saint wasn't. He came in afterwards. Now, suppose he went into the property-room and rattled that off? The doors were shut. We wouldn't hear him on the stage, and it would only take a second or two. The paper was in the machine. He could put it in his pocket—you'd already searched him—and go off comfortably. The letter Q is out at the side, and he'd miss it when he wiped his prints off the keys."

"Where is the property-room?" asked Nigel.

"All down that passage to the stage door. It's a dock really. Big double doors open on to the stage, and, beyond old Blair's perch, there are other doors opening into the yard. See what I mean, sir? When Saint goes off with Miss Emerald he passes our man at the stage door, goes out into the yard, and slips into the dock by the pilot door that's cut in the big ones. The double doors on to the stage are shut. He turns on one light, types his letter, wipes over the keys, and slips out. And that dame knows what he's doing and keeps a lookout."

"Still after the Emerald, I see," said Alleyn.

Nigel remembered his theory about Saint and the proscenium door. He advanced it modestly and was listened to by Detective Bailey with a kind of grudging respect peculiar to that official.

"Well," said Alleyn, "it's possible, Bailey. But any of the others could have done the typewriter business—or, at any rate, some of them could. Simpson could, for instance. Think a moment. Who was nearest to the stage door and most able to slip out unnoticed?"

Bailey stared at him.

"Gosh!" he said at last.

"*You mean—old Blair?*" Nigel said slowly.

"Who was asleep," added Alleyn placidly. The other two gaped at him.

"Well," said Alleyn, "nothing's conclusive, but everything is healthier. It all begins to come together very nicely."

"Glad you're pleased, sir," said Bailey with unexpected sarcasm.

"What about prints on the letter?"

"Only Mr. Gardener and Mr. Bathgate."

"And the paper from Surbonadier's flat? The one with the forged signature?"

"Plenty of Mr. Surbonadier's, sir, and something else that's very indistinct and old. I'm having an enlarged photograph taken and can't give an opinion till I've got it. It may turn out to be the deceased, too."

"Let me know at once if it is, Bailey. I'd like to see the photograph."

"Very good, sir."

Bailey was at the door when Alleyn stopped him.

"By the way, Bailey," he said, "I suppose you've heard that we couldn't get any forrader with the cartridges. Inspector Fox tells me every gunsmith's and sports shop in the country has been probed."

"That's right, sir. Very unsatisfactory," said Bailey, and withdrew.

"Alleyn," said Nigel, after a pause, "can't you *force* Props to say whom he saw moving round in the dark?"

"I could try, but he can so easily say he doesn't know who it was. His words were: 'If I thought I saw a bloke, or it might have been a woman, moving round in the dark . . .' Not very conclusive."

"But surely he now thinks you've got the wrong man, and will tell you who it was, to save Saint."

"He's very anxious," said Alleyn, "to save—the murderer."

"Who is probably Saint," said Nigel. "I see. But what about Stephanie Vaughan? Alleyn, if you'd heard her as I did——Oh, my God, I believe she did it! I believe she did."

"Look here, Bathgate. Could you take a day off tomorrow and go into the country on a job for me?"

"Not possible," said the astonished Nigel. "What sort of job? I've got my own job, you might remember."

"I want you to go to High Wycombe and see if you can trace a man called Septimus Carewe."

"You want to get rid of me," said Nigel indignantly. "Septimus Carewe, my foot!" he added with conviction.

"I mean it."

"What on earth for!"

"I'm uneasy about you."

"Bosh!"

"Have it your own way."

"What are *you* doing to-morrow, may I ask?"

"I," said Alleyn, "am putting on a show at the Unicorn."

"What the devil do you mean?"

"The company is under notice to report at various police stations every day. They have all been asked to report at the Unicorn at eleven to-morrow. I intend to hold a reconstruction of the murder."

"As you did in the Frantock case?"

"The conditions are very different. In this instance I am simply using the characters to prove my theory. In the Arthur Wilde case I forced his confession. This, unless these unspeakable mummers insist on dramatising themselves, will be less theatrical."

"I shall be there, however."

"I don't want you there."

"Why ever not?"

"It's a very unpleasant business. I loathe homicide cases and the result of this investigation will be perfectly beastly."

"If I could stand the Frantock case, when my own cousin was murdered, I can stand this."

"You'd much better keep away."

"I do think you're bloody," said Nigel fretfully.

Fox came in.

"Hullo," said Alleyn. "Everything fixed up?"

"Yes. Saint's tucked up in bed and the specialist's been sent for."

"I've just been telling Mr. Bathgate," said Alleyn, "that I don't want him at the theatre to-morrow, and he's got the huff in consequence."

"Inspector Alleyn's quite right, sir," said Fox. "You'd better keep clear of this business. After what you overheard this morning."

"Do you suppose Miss Vaughan is going to ram an arsenic chocolate down my maw?"

The two detectives exchanged a look.

"Oh, well, I'm off," said Nigel angrily.

"Good evening," said Alleyn cheerfully.

Nigel allowed himself the doubtful luxury of slamming the door.

Once out in the street he began to feel rather foolish, and angrier than ever with Chief Detective-Inspector Alleyn for causing this uncomfortable sensation. It was now seven o'clock and Nigel was hungry. He walked rapidly to Regent Street and went into the downstairs restaurant at the Hungaria, where he had a morose and extravagant dinner. He ordered himself brandy, and a cigar which he did not want and did not enjoy. When these were exhausted Nigel called for his bill, tipped his waiter, and marched out of the restaurant.

"Damn it," he said to Lower Regent Street. "I'm going there to-morrow whether he likes it or not."

He took a taxi to his flat in Chester Terrace.

Chief Detective-Inspector Alleyn also dined alone, at a restaurant near the Yard. He returned to his room soon after eight, opened the file of the Unicorn case and went over it very carefully with Inspector Fox. They were two hours at this business. Naseby came in and reported. He had seen Props and had brought off his conversation nicely. Props had seemed very much upset and when last seen was walking in the direction of the King's Road. Naseby had seen him go into a telephone-box, and had then left him to Detective Thompson, who preferred to carry on without being relieved.

Alleyn and Fox returned to the file. Bit by bit they strung together the events of the last three days, and Alleyn talked and Fox listened. At one stage he cast himself back in his chair and stared for fully ten seconds at his superior.

"Do you agree?" asked Alleyn.

"Oh, yes," said Fox heavily, "I agree."

He thought for a moment and then he said:

"I've been thinking that in difficult homicide cases you either get no motive or too many motives. In this instance there are too many. Jacob Saint had been blackmailed by the deceased; Stephanie Vaughan was pestered and threatened. Trixie Beadle was probably ruined by him; Props was what lawyers called 'deeply wronged.' So was the girl's father. That Emerald woman gets Saint's money by it. Well, I don't mind owning I've had my eye on all of 'em in turn. There you are."

"I know," said Alleyn, "I've been through the same process myself. Now look here, Fox. It seems to me there are one or two key pieces in this puzzle. One is the, to me, inexplicable fact that Surbonadier kept that sheet of paper with the experimental signatures: Edward Wakeford, Edward Wakeford, Edward Wakeford. I say inexplicable, in the light of any theory that has been advanced. Another is the evidence of the prints on the typewriter. A third in the behaviour of Stephanie Vaughan last night in Surbonadier's flat. Why did she pretend one of her letters was missing and get me hunting for it? I may tell you I left a folded piece of plain paper in the iron-bound box. While I was out of the room she took that paper. Why? Because she thought it was the document she was after."

"The Mortlake letter or the signatures?"

"Not the Mortlake letter. Why should she risk all that to save Saint?"

"The signatures then?"

"I think so. Now put that together with the fragment of conversation Mr. Bathgate overheard this morning, and what do you get?"

"The *fragment* of conversation," said Fox slowly.

"Exactly."

"I believe you're right, sir. But have you got enough to put before a jury?"

"I've got a man down at Cambridge now, ferreting about in past history. If he fails I'm still going for it. The reconstruction to-morrow morning will help."

"But he won't be there—Saint, I mean."

"*You* are going to climb Jacob's ladder for me tomorrow, my Foxkin."

The telephone rang. Alleyn answered it.

"Hullo. Yes. Where? But what about our men at the doors? Simon's Alley. I see. Well, get back to it and if he comes out detain him. I'll be there. No, don't go in alone. How long have you left the place? I see. Get back there quickly."

Alleyn clapped the receiver down.

"Fox," he said, "we're going to the Unicorn."

"Now?"

"Yes, and damn' quick. I'll tell you on the way."

Chapter XX

Exit Props

"After Naseby left the King's Road," said Alleyn, when they were in
the car, "Thompson watched Props in the telephone-box. He put two
calls through. As soon as he had gone Thompson went in and asked for
the numbers. The operator had lost them. Thompson darted out and
managed to pick Props up again. He spent the time wandering about the
streets, but always drawing nearer this part of the world. Just before
Thompson rang up, Props had led him into the jumble of streets round
the back of the Unicorn. He kept him in sight until he turned up a cul-
de-sac called Simon's Alley. Thompson followed and came to a gate
leading into a yard. He looked round and decided that he was somewhere at the back of the theatre. He climbed the gate and found an
open window that he believes gives into some part of the Unicorn. It
was pitch-dark inside. Thompson was in a quandary. He decided to call
me. First of all he managed to find one of our men and told him what
he'd seen. That took some time. The man hailed a constable and left
him in his place while he himself came round to the gate. That took
longer. Thompson, whom Allah preserve, for I won't, prowled round on
a Cooks' tour in search of a telephone and finally rang me up. Lord
knows how long the gate was left unguarded. Quite five minutes, I
should say, if not longer."

"Well, sir, whatever Props was up to it would probably take longer
than that."

"Yes. Of course it was difficult for Thompson. He didn't want to
start blowing his whistle and the gaff at the same time. Now here's
where we get out and grope for Simon's Alley. I'll just see the others
first."

They left the car and went back a little way to where a second police
car was drawn up. Alleyn gave instructions to the six constables who
were in it. They were to split up singly, go to the several doors of the
theatre, and enter it, leaving the men already on guard in their places.

"I don't know what we'll find," said Alleyn, "but I expect it'll be in the stage half of the theatre. You four come quietly through the stalls, from the several doors, and wait by the orchestra well. Don't use your torches unless you've got to. You come in at the back entrance, and at the stage door. Don't make a move until you get the word from Inspector Fox or myself. If you meet anything, grab it. Right?"

"Right, sir."

"Away you go then. Come on, Fox."

They had pulled up some little way from the back of the Unicorn. Alleyn led the way through a confused jumble of bystreets into the dingy thoroughfare behind the theatre. At last they came into a very narrow, blind street. Alleyn pointed up at the corner building and Fox read the notice: "Simon's Alley."

They walked quietly along the left-hand pavement. The roof of the Unicorn, looking gigantic, cut across the night-blue sky. No one was abroad in Simon's Alley and the traffic of Piccadilly and Trafalgar Square sounded remote. They heard Big Ben strike eleven. In a little while they saw the figure of a man standing very still in the shadows. Alleyn waited until he had come up with him.

"Is that you, Thompson?" he said very quietly.

"Yes, sir. I'm sorry if I've gone wrong over this."

"Not altogether your fault, but it would have been better if you'd kept your relief with you. Sure Hickson went in here?"

"Yes, sir. I had to leave this gate unwatched while I got the constable to come round. It's a long way round, too, but it wasn't more than eight minutes. I hope Hickson's still inside."

"Stay here. Don't move unless you hear my whistle. Come on, Fox."

He put his foot on the gate handle and climbed up. For a moment his silhouette showed dark against the sky. Then he disappeared. Fox followed him. The yard was strewn with indistinguishable rubbish. They picked their way cautiously towards the wall in front of them, and turned a corner, where the yard narrowed into an alley-way behind a low building. Here they found the open window. Alleyn noticed the old and broken shutter and the hole in the pane that would allow access to the catch. With a mental shrug at the watchman's idea of a burglar-proof theatre, Alleyn put his hands on the sill, wriggled through, and waited for Fox, who soon stood beside him. They took off their shoes and stayed there in the dark, listening.

Alleyn's eyes became accustomed to the murk; he saw that they were in a small lumber-room of sorts, that its only door stood open, and that there was a wall beyond. The place smelt disused and dank. He switched on his torch for a moment. From the room they went into a narrow stone passage, up half a dozen steps, and through another door. They took a right-angled turn and passed a row of doors, all of them locked. The passage turned again and grew lighter. Alleyn touched Fox on the hand and pointed to the side and then forward. Fox nodded. They were in country they knew. These were the dressing-rooms. They moved now with the utmost caution and came to the elbow in the passage where Alleyn and Nigel had met Simpson on the night of the murder. There was Gardener's dressing-room and there on the door beyond it hung the tarnished star. A thin flood of light met them. Props had turned on a lamp, somewhere beyond, where the stage was. Alleyn crept forward hugging the wall. He held up his hand. From somewhere out on the stage came a curious sound. It was a kind of faint sibilation as of two surfaces that brushed together, parted, brushed together again. They stayed very still, listening to this whisper, and presently thought it was accompanied by the echo of a creak.

"Scenery," breathed Fox. "Hanging."

"Perhaps."

Alleyn edged down the passage until he could see part of the stage. Nothing stirred. It was very ill-lit out there. He thought what light there was must come from the pilot-lamp above the book in the prompt corner. They waited again for some minutes. Alleyn could see through one of the stage entrances that the curtain was up. Beyond, in the darkness, two of his men must be waiting. Round on his left in the stage door passage, yet another man stood and listened, and a fourth had come in at the back door and was motionless, somewhere in the shadows across the stage. He knew they must all be there, as silent as himself and as silent as Props.

At last he went out on to the stage. He went to the stage door passage and stood there, knowing his man must see him against the light. Presently a hand touched his arm.

"Nobody here or in the dock, sir."

Fox was out on the stage and had crossed through the wings. Alleyn gave him a few minutes longer, and then made his way to the prompt corner. He went out by the footlights, where he knew the men in the stalls would see him. He pointed his torch out into the house and switched it on. A face leapt out of the dark and blinked. One of his own men. He hunted round the stage which was set as he had left it. His stocking foot trod on a piece of glass that must have been left there from the broken chandelier. All this time the faint, sibilant noise and the intermittent creak persisted. He now realised that they came from above his head.

Perhaps Props was back in his perch up there in the grid. Perhaps he waited with a rope in his hands ready to loose another bulk of dead weight. But why should Props let that noise go on up there? There was no draught of air.

From the centre of the stage Alleyn spoke aloud. He was conscious of a dread to hear his own voice. When it came it sounded strange.

"Fox!" he said. "Where are you?"

"Here, sir." Fox was over near the prompt corner.

"Get up that little iron ladder to the switchboard. If he's here he's lying low. Give us all the light in the house. I refuse to play sardines with Mr. Hickson."

Fox climbed the ladder slowly. From down in front one of the constables gave a deprecatory cough.

Click. Click.

The circle came into view, then the stalls. The constables were standing in the two aisles.

Click.

The footlights sprang up in a white glare. Then the proscenium was cinctured with warmth. The lamp on the stage suddenly came alive. The passages glowed. A blaze of light sprang up above the stage. The theatre was awake.

In the centre of the stage Alleyn stood with his eyes screwed up, blinded by light. The two constables came through the wings, their hands arched over their faces. From the switchboard Fox said:

"That's light enough to see an invisible man."

Alleyn, still peering, bent over the footlights. "You two in front," he said, "search the place thoroughly—offices upstairs—cloak-rooms—everything. We'll deal with this department."

He turned to the men on the stage.

"We'll go about this in pairs. He's a shell-shocked man and he's a bit desperate. Somewhere or another in this rabbit warren he's hidden. I think he'll be in his own department behind the scenes. We'll wait till these fellows in the front of the house come back."

They lit cigarettes and stayed uneasily on the stage. The sound of doors shutting announced the activities of the men in front.

"Rum sort of place this, when there's nothing doing," said Fox.

"Yes," Alleyn agreed. "It feels expectant."

"Any idea why he came here, sir?"

"Unfortunately I have. A particularly nasty idea."

The others waited hopefully.

Alleyn stubbed his cigarette on the floor.

"I think he had a rendezvous," he said. "With a murderer."

Fox looked scandalised and perturbed.

"Or murderess as the case may be," added Alleyn.

"Cuh!" said one of the plain clothes men under his breath.

"But," said Fox, "they're all under surveillance."

"I know. Thompson's man gave him the slip. There may be another of our wonderful police who's lost his sheep and doesn't know where to find it. Not a comfortable thought, but it arises. What's the time?"

"Eleven-twenty, sir."

"What the devil is that whispering noise?" asked Alleyn restively. He peered up into the flies; a ceiling-cloth was stretched across under the lowest gallery and the grids were hidden.

"I noticed something of the sort the night of the murder," said Fox. "There must be a draught up there making the canvas swing a bit."

Apparently Alleyn did not hear him. He walked across to the ladder by which Props had descended. He stood there, very still, for a moment. When he spoke his voice sounded odd.

"I think," he said, "we will begin with the grid."

The two men returned from the front of the house. Alleyn walked over to the proscenium door, which was locked. The key hung on a nail beside it. He opened the door. It emitted a loud shriek.

"So much for Bathgate's theory," murmured Alleyn.

The men came through.

"Wait here," said Alleyn. "I'm going into the grid."

"Not on your own, sir," chided Fox. "That chap may be sitting there ready to dong you one."

"I think not. Follow me up if you like."

He climbed the iron ladder that ran flat up the wall. Slowly the shadow of the ceiling-cloth enfolded him. Fox followed.

The other four men stood with their faces tipped back, watching. Alleyn's stockinged feet disappeared above the ceiling-cloth. The ladder vibrated slightly.

"Wait a moment, Fox."

Alleyn's voice sounded eerily above their heads. Fox paused.

Alleyn's dulled footsteps thumped on the gallery overhead. The cloth quivered and sagged. He had unloosed the ropes that fastened it. Presently, with a sort of swishing sigh, the border fell away and the whole thing collapsed in a cloud of dust on to the tops of the wings.

When the dust had settled, the men who looked upwards saw the soles of a pair of rubber shoes. The shoes turned slowly to the right, stopped, turned slowly to the left. The canvas having been taken away they no longer fretted it with a sibilant whisper, but every time they swung, the rope round Props's neck creaked on the wooden cleat above.

Chapter XXI

This Ineffable Effrontery

Inspector Fox was accustomed to what he termed unpleasantness, but for a moment he nearly lost his grip on the iron ladder.

"Props," he said slowly. "So Props was the man, after all."

"Come up here," said Alleyn.

They stood together on the first gallery. Their faces were on a level with the shoulders of the swinging body. The rope that had hanged him was a slack end of the pulley that had suspended the chandelier. It was made fast to a cleat on the top gallery. Fox leant out and touched the hand.

"He's still warm."

"It happened," said Alleyn, "just before Thompson rang up the Yard."

He stood with his hands clenched to the rail of the gallery, gazing, as if against his will, at the body.

"I should have prevented this," he said. "I should have made the arrest this afternoon."

"I don't see that," said Fox in his ponderous way. "How could you have foretold——"

"This ineffable effrontery," finished Alleyn. "Poor Props."

"That sort's very liable to suicide."

"Suicide?" Alleyn turned to him. "This is not suicide."

"Not——?"

"It's murder. Come up to the gallery here."

They climbed the upper length of the ladder. Alleyn paused when his head and shoulders were above the top gallery and switched on his torch.

"Swept!" he said, with a kind of triumph. "Now, my beauty—I've got you!"

"What's that, sir?" asked Fox from below.

"The gallery's been swept. Do suicides tidy up the ground when they set about it? Thick dust farther along. The typewriter was too tidy and so's this gallows. There'll be no prints, but the mark of the criminal is all over it. We can take the body down now, Fox. I'll stay here a moment. You go back."

They had to draw the body in to the first gallery and then get it down the ladder—no easy job. At last Props lay on the stage in his accustomed surroundings. In answer to Fox's whistle the others had come in from the doors. Thompson was white about the gills and couldn't speak. Alleyn turned to him.

"We've had ill luck to-day, Thompson," he said. "I should have made more sure of him."

"It's my fault, sir."

"No," said Alleyn; "the poor devil was too quick for you."

"I still don't see how it was worked."

"Suppose I said I'd meet you here. Suppose I'd killed a man and you knew it. I get here first. I go up there to the platform, put a noose in that rope, and make the other end fast. Then I climb down again. You come in, very nervous. You've been followed, you say, but you've shaken them off. We start to talk. Then I say I can hear someone coming along that passage. 'By God, they're after us,' I say. 'Come on up this ladder. Quick.' I go up first, past the lower landing. He follows. I get to the top landing and wait with the noose in my hands. As his head comes up, I drop it over. One fierce tug. He loosens his hands and claws his neck. Then a heavy thrust and——That's how it worked."

"My oath!" said Fox.

"Yes, but I've left a broom up there because I know my stockinged feet will leave prints in the dust—the thick dust. So while Props is jerking in the air I sweep away the dust. He's hidden by the ceiling-cloth. He won't be missed until to-morrow. It's an old building—some more dust will have fallen then. They may not find him at once, and if they do it looks like suicide. So I take the broom down with me and leave it on the stage in its usual place. Then I run down those nightmare passages into the little store-room. Thompson is in the yard outside. I wait. Presently I hear him go off to get his man from the front of the theatre. That's my chance. When he comes back—I'm not there."

"I see," said Fox heavily. "Yes. I see."

"Now, look here." Alleyn bent over the body. "The head and shoulders are covered in dust. It was there while he was still hanging. It was swept off the top gallery. Analysis will prove it. We've got to come all over scientific, Fox."

"It can't be Saint and it wasn't Props. That's two people cleared away in favour of your theory, sir."

"It is."

"What do we do now, then?"

"Get hold of the men who were watching the rest of the party."

"I'll ring up the Yard. Reports should have come through by now."

"Yes," said Alleyn. "Do that, Fox. I'm especially anxious for the report from Cambridge."

"Yes."

"And from—who's that fellow? Oh, Detective-Sergeant Watkins. Find out if he's been relieved, and if he has tell them to get hold of him and send him round here."

"Very good, sir."

"And ring up Bailey. He'll be in bed now, poor creature, but we'll have to beat him up. And the divisional surgeon. Oh, Lord—here we go again."

Fox disappeared through the proscenium door. Alleyn went back along the stone passages. He turned up the lights and examined the floor and walls carefully. He walked, hugging the wall, all the way to the room with the broken window. Here he examined the floor, the walls, the window sill and the yard outside. He turned his torch on the gate, climbed it, and scrutinized the top meticulously. Here he found a tiny scrap of black cloth which he preserved.

Then he returned to the stage.

He shook some of the dust from Props's hair into an envelope, sealed it up, and, taking a fresh envelope, turned his attention to the shoulders of the coat. He climbed the ladder to the top gallery, where he took a further sample of dust. Using his pocket-lens and his torch he examined the rope carefully, paying particular attention to the noose and the three or four feet above it. He also scrutinized the rail and floor of the gallery for some distance beyond the place where the ladder came up. He then measured the length of the drop. Returning to the stage he found a broom under the electrician's gallery, and from this also he obtained a specimen of dust. He examined the body, paying particular attention to the hands. Bailey and the divisional surgeon arrived while he was still about this business.

"You'll find no prints except his," said Alleyn.

The surgeon made his examination.

"I hear the verdict is murder," he said. "I don't know your reading of it, inspector, but he died from strangulation and a broken neck. I can see no signs of anything else, except a slight bruise at the back of the neck."

"Could that have been caused by a downward kick from a stockinged foot?" Alleyn asked.

"Yes," said the surgeon. He looked up to where the iron ladder ran into the galleries. "I see," he said.

"What about Watkins?"

Fox, who had returned to the stage, answered:

"He'd gone home but they are turning him out."

"Any news from Cambridge?"

"A long statement from a servant at Peterhouse. They're sending it round with the officer who went down there. The mortuary van's here."

"Right. They can come in now."

Fox went to the stage door and returned followed by two men with a stretcher.

Props was carried out of the Unicorn at exactly midnight.

"I feel like Hamlet when he killed Polonius," said Alleyn.

"Shakespeare," said Fox. "I don't read that sort of thing myself."

But the surgeon stood on the stage and said quietly: " 'Thou wretched, rash, intruding fool, farewell.' I suppose the words have been spoken here before," he reflected.

"Under somewhat different circumstances," said Alleyn harshly.

"Here's Watkins," said Fox.

Detective-Sergeant Watkins was a stocky, sandy-haired man. He looked worried.

"You want to see me, sir?" he said to Alleyn.

"I want an account of your day, Watkins."

"Very monotonous it was really. The party I was looking after stayed indoors from the time I relieved until the time I came off."

"Are you sure of that?"

Watkins flushed.

"I sat on a bench in the gardens opposite and I stood by the lamp-post. I never took my eyes off the door, sir."

"Who passed in and out?"

"Other people in the building. I saw my party several times—looked out of the window."

"When was the last time you noted that?"

"At fifteen minutes to ten, sir," said Watkins triumphantly.

"Who came out of the building after that?"

"Quite a number of people, sir. Going out for supper-parties and so on. I recognized most of them as residents."

"Any that you did not recognize?"

"There was a woman. Looked like a working woman, I thought, and a couple of housemaids, and before them an old gentleman in a soft hat and a dinner suit and a sort of opera cloak. He was a bit lame. The commissionaire got him a taxi. I heard him say 'The Platza Theatre' to the driver. I asked the commissionaire about them just to be on the safe side. He's a dense sort of bloke. He thought the woman must have been doing odd work in one of the flats. The old gent he didn't know, but said he came from the top floor, and had probably been dining there. The housemaids came from the street-level flat."

"That's all?"

"No, sir. One other. A young fellow wearing a shepherd's plaid double-breasted suit, a bowler hat, and a dark blue tie with pale blue stripes, came along. I crossed the street and heard him name our party's floor to the liftman."

"Had he a fair moustache and a carnation in his coat?"

"Yes, sir."

"Did he reappear?" Alleyn asked sharply.

"He came out again after about five minutes and walked off towards the square. That's all, sir. I was relieved at ten-fifteen by Detective-Sergeant Allison. He's still on duty."

"Thank you. That's all, Watkins."

"Have I gone wrong anywhere, sir?"

"Yes. You've mistaken a murderer for an innocent person. I don't know that I blame you. Get one of these men to relieve Allison and ask him to report here immediately."

Watkins said nothing, but looked miserable. He and Thompson conferred sympathetically. After a few moments Watkins said diffidently:

"If I may, sir, I'd like to relieve Allison myself."

"Very well, Watkins. If anybody comes away from the building, man or woman, stop them, speak to them, get their names and addresses and make sure they are what they seem. Thompson, you can go too if you like. Don't look so injured, both of you. We've all gone wrong over this."

A pause, and then Thompson addressed the lining of his hat with some feeling.

"We'd both go back on P.C. night-duty before we'd let you down, if you know what I mean, sir."

"That's right," said Watkins fervently.

"Well, push off, you couple of boobies," said Alleyn. He turned to Fox. "I'm going to the telephone. The statement from Peterhouse ought to be here any moment. If Allison comes before I'm back, get a report on those lines from him."

"Are you going for a warrant-to-arrest tonight?" asked Fox.

"I don't think so. I'll still stage my performance tomorrow morning."

Alleyn went through the front of the house and sought out the telephone in the box-office. Enlargements of actresses smiled or stared soulfully at him from the walls. "All the best," "To dear Robert," "Ever yours," he read. In the centre was a magnificent picture of a woman standing in an open window. Written firmly across the mount were two words only: "Stephanie Vaughan." When he had dialled his number Alleyn turned and gazed steadfastly at this picture.

"Hullo!" said a sleepy voice in the receiver.

"Hullo. I thought I said there were to be no more little visits."

"Oh—it's you."

"It is," said Alleyn grimly.

"I had an idea. You needn't get all hot and bothered, I didn't see anybody. I rang for five minutes and then came away. Even the servant was out."

"You rang for five minutes, did you?"

"Yes. I say, is everything all right?"

"Perfectly splendid. There's been another murder at the Unicorn."

"What!!"

"Go to bed and stay there," advised Alleyn and hung up the receiver.

He crossed over and looked more closely at the photograph on the opposite wall.

"Oh, hell!" he said and went back to the stage of the Unicorn.

Chapter XXII

Final Curtain

On the morning of June 17th, at a quarter to eleven, old Blair hung his dilapidated bowler above the tall stool in his cubbyhole behind the stage door. He glanced at the grimy clock and clicked disapproval when he saw that it had been allowed to run down. He inspected the letter rack which was garnished with a solitary postcard, addressed to Miss Susan Max. Blair advanced his nose to within four inches of its surface and read it:

> "Susan darling, how terrible this all is dear my heart goes out to you in this terrible time it must be quite dreadful for you dear, our show goes big in this place and we are doing wonderful business dear. All the best, Daisy."

Blair sucked his teeth, but whether in scorn or appreciation it would be impossible to say.

Footsteps sounded in the alley outside. Old Blair groaned slightly and returned to the stage door. The constable at the stalls entrance saluted. Chief Detective Inspector Alleyn and Inspector Fox followed by Detective-Sergeant Bailey and three plain clothes men walked up to the entrance.

"Good morning, Blair," said Alleyn.

" 'Morning, sir."

The party went in at the stage door and down the long passage past the wall of the dock. On the stage they were met by two more plain clothes men—Thompson and Watkins.

"Everything fixed up?" asked Alleyn.

"Yes, sir."

Alleyn looked up towards the flies. A ceiling-cloth had been stretched across and tied back to the first of the grid galleries.

"If you'll just listen, sir," said Thompson.

They all stood still. A sibilant whisper came from above the canvas cloth. It alternated with a faint creak. At a place near its border, the cloth bulged slightly as if some small object was touching it on the upper surface. The impress made by this object appeared and disappeared regularly, synchronising with the sibilant whisper.

"That will do very well," said Alleyn. "Have you unlocked the dressing-room doors?"

Apparently this had been done. Alleyn went on to the stage and glanced round. It was still set for the scene when Surbonadier loaded the revolver. The curtain was up and the shrouded seats looked very faint in the dark. A lance of sunlight slanted through a crevice in a blind above the gallery. Footsteps sounded in the passage and Mr. George Simpson appeared. He looked nervously round the wings, saw Alleyn, and uttered a little apologetic noise.

"Oh, there you are, Mr. Simpson," said Alleyn. "I've been trying to pretend I'm a stage manager. Any fault to find with the scene?"

Simpson walked down to the float and surveyed the stage. Something of his professional manner seemed to return to the little man.

"It's quite in order, I think," he said.

"Perhaps I'd better wait until the company appears before I explain my motive in calling you all this morning."

"Some of them are outside now."

"Right. Will you treat Detective-Sergeant Wilkins as your call-boy? As soon as everybody's here we'll have them on the stage and I'll speak to them."

Sergeant Wilkins was produced. He and Simpson eyed each other doubtfully.

"What's that you've got in your hand, Wilkins?" asked Alleyn suddenly.

"It's one of your cards, sir. The young gentleman I saw yesterday, if you remember, sir, came along. He just wanted to sit in the stalls."

"Let me see it."

Alleyn surveyed, rather grimly, his own visiting-card with: "Admit bearer to theatre. R.A." scribbled across it in his own writing. It was the one he had given Nigel before they arrested Saint. With remarkable forethought Mr. Bathgate had clung to the bit of pasteboard and had produced it again when occasion arose.

With a slightly accentuated jaw-line, Inspector Alleyn advanced to the footlights and gazed into the swimming darkness of the stalls.

"Mr. Bathgate," he said.

Silence.

"Mr. Bathgate," lied Alleyn, "I can see you."

"You're not looking in my direction at all," declared an indignant voice.

"Come here," Alleyn said.

"I won't."

"If you please."

There was a mulish silence and then Alleyn said mildly:

"House lights, Mr. Simpson, if you please."

Simpson scuttled up the iron ladder and in a moment the stalls were revealed in all their shrouded grimness.

In the centre of Row F, a lonely little figure among the dust sheets, sat Nigel. Alleyn beckoned. Nigel rose sheepishly and processed down the centre aisle.

"Now," said Alleyn, when the culprit reached the curtain of the well. "Now, my enterprising Pressman."

Nigel smirked but did not reply.

"I've a good mind to have you turfed out at the end of a boot," continued Alleyn. He looked seriously at Nigel. "However, I won't do that. I will merely return my card with an additional memorandum. If you still want to stay here you may."

He wrote something on the back of the card and flipped it across the orchestra well.

Nigel caught it and held it to the light. Inspector Alleyn wrote in tiny but exceedingly clear characters, yet, though there were only seven words on the card, Nigel appeared to take an unconscionable time deciphering them. At last he raised his head and he and Alleyn looked at each other.

"It's a mistake," said Nigel.

"No."

"But——" He stopped short and wetted his lips. "No motive," said Nigel at last.

"Every motive."

"I'll stay," said Nigel.

"Very well. House lights, please, Mr. Simpson."

Once again the front of the house was dark.

"I think they are all here now, Inspector Alleyn," said Simpson nervously.

"Ask them to come here, will you, Wilkins?" said Alleyn.

The company of *The Rat and the Beaver* reassembled for the last time on the stage of the Unicorn. They came down the passage in single file. Susan Max and Stephanie Vaughan appeared first. Then came Janet Emerald walking with the gait she used in the provinces for the last act of *Madam X*. Dulcie Deamer followed, expressing tragic bewilderment. Next came Felix Gardener, very white-faced and alone. Howard Melville and J. Barclay Crammer delayed their entrance and made it arm-in-arm with heads held high, like French aristocrats approaching the tumbrels.

"Everybody on the stage, please," said George Simpson.

The players walked through the wings and stood quietly in a semi-circle. They looked attentive and businesslike. It was almost as though they had needed the stage and the lights to give them full solidity. They no longer seemed preposterous or even artificial. They were in their right environment and had become real.

Alleyn stood down by the float, facing the stage. From the auditorium, with the full stage lighting behind him, it was he who now looked a strange shadow, but for the actors there was no suggestion of this; to them he was in the accustomed place of the producer, and they watched him attentively.

"Ladies and gentlemen," said Alleyn, "I have asked you to come here this morning in order that we may stage a reconstruction of the first scene in the last act of *The Rat and the Beaver*. In that scene, as you know, the deceased man, Mr. Arthur Surbonadier, loaded the revolver by which he was subsequently shot. You are all aware that Mr. Jacob Saint is under arrest. He will not be present. Otherwise, with the exception of the deceased, whose part will be read by Mr. Simpson, we are all here."

He paused for a moment. The stage manager looked as though he wanted to say something.

"Yes, Mr. Simpson?"

"Er—I don't know if it matters. The property master has not turned up. As he gave me the dummies I thought perhaps——?"

"We shall have to do without him," said Alleyn. "Are the dressers here?"

Simpson glanced offstage. Beadle and Trixie Beadle came through the wings and stood awkwardly at the end of the semi-circle.

"First I must tell you, all of you, that the police have formed a definite theory as regards this crime. It is in order to substantiate this theory that the reconstruction is necessary. I want to impress upon you that, apart from its distressing associations, there is nothing to worry about in the business. I merely ask the innocent members of the company to rehearse a particular scene in order to verify my theory as regards the movements of the guilty individual. I most earnestly beg of you to behave exactly as you did, so far as you can remember, during the last performance of this scene. I give you this opportunity to vindicate yourselves and at the same time establish the case which we shall bring before the court. I appeal to you to play fair. As innocent individuals you have nothing to fear. Is it agreed?"

He waited for a moment and then Barclay Crammer cleared his throat portentously. He advanced two paces and gazed into the auditorium.

"I do not know if Miss Vaughan or Mr. Gardener have anything to say——" he began.

"Nothing," said Stephanie Vaughan quickly. "I'm quite ready to do it."

"I too," said Gardener.

"In that case," continued Mr. Crammer deeply, "I may say at once that I am prepared to play out this horrible farce—to the end." He let his voice break slightly. "God grant we may be the instruments to avenge poor Arthur." He made a slight gesture expressive of noble resignation and very nearly bowed to the empty auditorium. The hidden Nigel refrained, with something of an effort, from giving him a heartfelt clap. Alleyn caught Gardener's eye. Gardener looked as though he wanted to wink.

"That's all settled, then," said Alleyn. "Now the only difference between this and the real show is that I am not going to black-out the lights. I will ask those of you who were in your dressing rooms at the end of the interval to go to them now. Any movement that you made from one room to another you will repeat. You will see that I have stationed officers along the passages. Please behave exactly as if they were not there. The conversation on the stage between Miss Max, Mr. Surbonadier, Miss Emerald, and Mr. Simpson before the curtain went up, we will reproduce as closely as possible. I will blow this whistle at the point when you are to imagine the black-out takes place, and again when the lights would go on. Now will you all go to your dressing-rooms?"

They filed off quietly. Simpson went to the prompt box and Sergeant Wilkins joined him there.

Alleyn had a word with both of them. Fox and Bailey stood offstage by the first and third left entrances. Two other men went to the O.P. Thompson and a third man disappeared down the dressing-room passage.

"Right," said Alleyn, and walked down to the float.

"Call the last act, please," said Simpson to Sergeant Wilkins.

Wilkins went off down the dressing-room passage. His voice could be heard on the stage.

"Last act, please, last act, please!"

Miss Max, who dressed in a room round the elbow of the passage, came out first, walked on to the stage, sat in the chair on the O.P. side, and took out her knitting. She was followed by Janet Emerald who went straight to the upstage window.

"Stay there as if you were speaking to Surbonadier," said Alleyn quietly. "Now, Mr. Simpson."

Simpson came out of the prompt box and went to the desk. He mimed the business of putting something in the top drawer.

"Now, Miss Emerald," said Alleyn.

"I don't remember—what I said."

"About the cartridges, dear," said Miss Max quietly.

"I—I'm always afraid you'll forget those cartridges," said Janet Emerald.

"Trust little Georgie," said Simpson.

"George, come over here. I want to show you something. This mat is bad where it is, dear."

"What's wrong with the mat, Susan?"

"It jams the door and spoils my eggzit."

"Is that better?"

"That's where it should be. Come here and let me measure my scarf."

"Now, Miss Emerald, you spoke to Surbonadier."

"I—I can't. It's too horrible."

"Go across to the left and meet Mr. Simpson. You say: 'Arthur's tight, George, and I'm nervous.' "

"Arthur's tight, George, and I'm nervous."

"He's giving a damn' good show, anyway."

"Now you whisper: 'I'd like to kill him,' and stand with your hands on the desk."

"I'd—like—to kill——"

"All clear, please."

Janet Emerald stood up and faced upstage.

"House lights. Stand by, please. Black-out."

Alleyn blew a long blast on his whistle. Simpson with the book in his hand went on to the stage. Alleyn stood in the wings, where he could see the stage and dressing-room passage. Melville, who had stood near the prompt box, went tiptoe down the passage and round the elbow. Miss Vaughan came out of her room, leaving the door open; she knocked on Gardener's door. He called: "Come in," and she entered, closing the door behind her. It reopened to let out old Beadle. He stood outside, produced a cigarette and held it, unlit, in his mouth. Trixie Beadle came out of the star-room and joined him. They moved into the elbow of the passage.

Felix Gardener came out of his room and walked softly on to the stage. Here he paused, started, bent down and rubbed his foot, whispered: "What the hell!" and limped on a few paces. The Beadles walked away down the passage towards the wardrobe-room. All this took a very short space of time. On the stage Simpson called: "Curtain up." The actors began to speak the dialogue, muttering their lines and raising their voices loudly at the end of each speech. This dialogue continued for perhaps half a minute and then the stage manager said:

"Lights."

Alleyn blew his whistle and called out:

"Everyone on the stage, please."

Once more the company assembled.

"Thank you very much," said Alleyn. "You have helped me. I am sure it has been difficult and unpleasant for all of you. I can now explain myself a little further. I think you are entitled to an explanation. This reconstruction has proved that no one, who was beyond the elbow in the passage, could have come out on to the stage without running into the two dressers, who did not go to the wardrobe-room until late in the black-out period. Mr. Gardener has stated that when he went on to the stage someone trod on his foot. There are only three men who could have been offstage at that time—Mr. Simpson, the property master—and Mr. Jacob Saint."

Janet Emerald began some sort of demonstration. Alleyn glanced coldly at her and she subsided.

"Mr. Saint was in his box on the prompt side. One theory was that he came through the proscenium door, substituted the cartridges, and returned by the same route. Wilkins, will you go to that door, open it and walk to the desk?"

Sergeant Wilkins marched to the proscenium exit and opened the door. It gave tongue to an ear-splitting shriek.

"That disposes of that," said Alleyn. "Mr. Simpson and Props are left. The theory as regards Props is this. Props was on the stage during the black-out. He substituted the cartridges, and then made himself scarce. No one remembered seeing him offstage when the lights went up. Where did he go? The theory suggests that he went up that ladder and disappeared above the ceiling-cloth. If you'll be good enough to help me I'll demonstrate that. Mr. Simpson is in the prompt box; Miss Max, Miss Emerald, and the deceased are on the stage. Mr. Gardener comes out of the passage and runs into Props, who has just planted the cartridges. He shies off Mr. Gardener and goes up that ladder. He is wearing rubber shoes and is not heard. He wears Mr. Saint's gloves that were left on the stage. Now, Mr. Simpson, will you be good enough to play his part?"

Simpson wetted his lips.

"I—I—can't stand going up those ladders. I've no head for heights. It would—make——I can't."

Alleyn looked doubtfully at the bulk of Crammer and the greenish face of Mr. Melville. He turned resignedly to Gardener.

"Be a good fellow," he said.

"Certainly," said Gardener quietly.

"If your nerves will allow you, Mr. Simpson, perhaps you will impersonate Mr. Gardener."

Simpson did not speak.

"Surely you can do that?"

"I'll do it," said Melville.

"Thank you—I should prefer Mr. Simpson to play this little scene. Now, Mr. Simpson."

Simpson turned and went into Gardener's room.

"Away you go," said Alleyn to Gardener, who nodded and went to the desk. He drew out the top drawer, mimed the business of taking something out, putting something else in. He opened the lower drawer and shut it again, hesitated, glanced interrogatively at Alleyn, and came back to the wings.

"Come out, Mr. Simpson," called Alleyn.

The dressing-room door opened and Simpson came out. He walked down the passage and on to the stage. Gardener bumped into him, stepped aside and began to climb the ladder.

"Right up?" he asked.

"Yes, please."

Gardener went on up the ladder. They watched him. Suddenly they were all aware of the sibilant whisper and of the moving indentation in the cloth. His steps rang on the iron rungs. His head disappeared above the cloth. Then a terrible cry rang out.

"My God, what's that!" screamed Simpson.

Gardener's body swung out from the ladder. It seemed as if he would fall. His feet slipped and for a moment he hung by his hands. Then he righted himself.

"Alleyn!" he cried in a terrible voice, "Alleyn!"

"What's the matter?" shouted Alleyn.

"He's here—he's hanged himself—he's here."

"Who?"

"Props—it's Props."

His horrified face looked down at them.

"It's Props!" he repeated.

Fox, Bailey, Wilkins and Thompson came and stood by the foot of the ladder.

"Come down," said Alleyn.

Gardener came down. Within six rungs of the stage he turned and saw the men that awaited him. With an incoherent cry he stopped short. His lips were drawn back, showing his gums. A streak of saliva trickled down his chin. He squinted.

"And how do you know it is Props?" asked Alleyn.

Gardener kicked down savagely at his face.

"Not again," said Alleyn. "The other time was once too often."

Fox had to drag Gardener down by his ankles. This time Alleyn had remembered his handcuffs.

Chapter XXIII

Epilogue to a Play

If Chief Detective-Inspector Alleyn was interested in the dramatic unities it may have given him some sort of satisfaction to note that the epilogue to the Unicorn murder was spoken on the stage of the theatre.

Gardener had been taken away. Miss Emerald had indulged in a fit of genuine hysterics and had departed. Barclay Crammer, George Simpson, Howard Melville and Dulcie Deamer, all strangely unreal in the harsh light of actual tragedy, had walked down the stage door alley-way and disappeared. The Beadles had gone with old Blair.

Only Alleyn, Stephanie Vaughan, and a very shaken Nigel remained. The ceiling-cloth had been removed and the weighted sack that had hung from the top gallery lay in a rubbishy heap on the floor. Alleyn picked it up, and threw it into the dock, and shut the doors. Nigel stood in the stage door passage. Alleyn looked at him.

"Well, Bathgate," he said. "Never make friends with a policeman."

"I don't think I feel that way about it," decided Nigel slowly.

"You are generous," said Alleyn.

"Why didn't you tell me?"

"If I had told you what would you have done?"

Nigel couldn't answer that.

"I don't know," he said.

"Neither did I know."

"I see."

"Did the thought of it never enter your head?" Alleyn asked him compassionately.

"At first I thought it was Saint and then——" He looked through the wings on to the stage.

Stephanie Vaughan sat there in the arm-chair she had occupied on the night of the murder when Alleyn had first questioned her. She seemed lost in a profound meditation.

"Wait for me," said Alleyn, "somewhere else."

Nigel walked out into the yard. Alleyn went on to the stage.

"Come back from wherever you are," he said softly.

She raised her head and looked at him.

"I can't feel anything at all," she murmured.

He put his hand over hers for a second.

"Cold," he said. "That's the shock. Whenever I have touched your hands they have been cold. Small wonder. Shall I get you a taxi?"

"Not yet. I want to get my bearings."

She looked frowningly at her fingers as though she tried to remember something.

"I suppose you knew what I was up to all along?" she said at last.

"Not quite. I began to wonder, when you said the bruise on your shoulder was made by Surbonadier. I remember how Gardener had stood with his hand on your shoulder when Surbonadier insulted you. I noticed how he gripped you."

She shivered.

"I was afraid then that he would do something dreadful," she said.

"If it's any comfort to you he would have done just what he did if you hadn't existed."

"I know. I was only an accessory after the fact, isn't it? At any rate, not a motive."

"In Surbonadier's flat," Alleyn told her, "I knew how much you were prepared to risk for him. I let you play your part. I let you think you had succeeded."

"Why do you rub it in?"

"Why, to put it rather floridly, because I thought it would help you to hate me and so provide a counter-irritant."

"Oh," she said thoughtfully, "I don't hate you."

"That's strange."

"You were far too clever for me."

"And yet," said Alleyn, "half the victory is yours. From my heart I am sorry that it had to happen as it did. If I thought it would make any difference I would say I hated myself when I held you in my arms. It would only be half true. My thoughts were a mixture of grovel and glory."

"What will happen to him?" she said suddenly. Her eyes dilated.

"I don't know. He will be tried. He's guilty and he's a bad hat. You don't love him. Don't act. Don't pretend. It's going to be ghastly for you, but you left off loving him when you knew he'd done it."

"Yes, that's quite true."

She began to weep, not at all beautifully, but with her face screwed up and with harsh sobs. He looked gravely at her and when she put out her hand, put his handkerchief into it. He went to Surbonadier's dressing-room and found a nickel flask with whisky in it. With a grimace he washed a glass out and poured out a stiff nip. He took it back to her.

"Drink this. It'll put you together."

She swallowed it, gasped, and shuddered.

"Now I'll get you a taxi," said Alleyn.

Nigel turned into the dock when he saw them come out. She got into the taxi.

"Good-bye," she said. "You know where to find me if—I'm wanted."

"Yes, you poor thing."

She held out her hand and, after a moment's hesitation, he kissed it.

"You'll recover," he told her. "Good-bye."

He gave the address to the driver and stood for some time in the empty yard. Then he went back to Nigel.

"Well?" he said. "What do you want to know?"

"Everything," said Nigel.

"All right. Lay back your ears. Here goes."

He pulled forward a couple of dingy arm-chairs and rolled back the doors of the dock, letting in a thin flood of sunshine.

"Here goes," he repeated and, lighting a cigarette, began his discourse.

"In homicide cases the police generally go for the obvious man. In spite of everything the psychologists say, and mind you they know what they're talking about, the obvious man is generally the 'he' in the game. In this case the obvious man was the one who pulled the trigger—Gardener. So from the first I considered him carefully. Would anyone else have risked planting the cartridges? Suppose Gardener had not pulled the trigger or had pulled it too soon? Would anyone else be likely to chance this? Well, they might. But if Gardener himself was the murderer he stood to risk nothing. The next thing I reminded myself of was the fact that I was up against good acting. Gardener was a consummately good actor. So I discounted all his remorseful bewilderment. How cleverly he talked about the insincerity of actors, quietly building up a picture of himself as the only genuine one amongst them. I deliberately refused to accept all this. When we took the statements from the others I noted at once that he and Stephanie Vaughan were nearest to the stage.

"At this time I was, of course, still watching everybody. But he was in his room with her and her room next door was unoccupied and close to the stage. How easy for him to dart in there when he left her, pull on Saint's gloves that he'd found on the stage (a stroke of luck that—he'd meant to use his own), make sure no one was in the passage, and then slip out, go on to the stage and in the dark change the cartridges. I wondered if his story of the sore foot was a fabrication, and deliberately I suggested the scent and he fell into the trap. That made me consider him seriously. Then he allowed you to get all that business about the libel case out of him, but only when he knew we'd find it out for ourselves. He told you Surbonadier had written the article. I wondered if he'd written it himself. When I found the forged signatures in Surbonadier's flat I felt sure Gardener had been the author. Suppose Surbonadier had blackmailed him, threatening to expose him to Saint? Saint would have ruined his career. Suppose Surbonadier threatened to tell Stephanie Vaughan what I suspected was the truth about their Cambridge days? All supposition—but suggestive. I sent a man to Cambridge, who found the old servant who had looked after Gardener and who had overheard a conversation between him and Surbonadier in which Surbonadier accused him of writing the article. Gardener was much deeper in the drug-party stunts than he gave you to understand. No doubt his description of the passion he had for Stephanie Vaughan and the hatred he felt for Saint was true. This passion was drug-fed and inspired the article. I only got the Cambridge statement last night. It clinched matters.

"Then the wet-white. It was spilled after we left the dressing-room. Miss Vaughan said no one but herself and Trixie had been in the room after Surbonadier left it. Gardener was the only person who could have gone there. Anyone else would have run into the Beadles, who stood in the elbow of the passage before they went to the wardrobe-room. Gardener left her in his room to go to the stage. If Props had done the job he would not have gone near the star-room. Nor would Simpson, who was on the stage. Nor would Saint, if he'd come through the proscenium door, which squeaks like sour hell, anyway. But Gardener would."

"You mean," said Nigel, "he left her in his room, went into hers and put on the gloves, made sure there was no one in the passage and darted on to the stage. That was when he got the wet-white on the gloves?"

"Yes."

"What about the threatening letter?"

"Aha! His first bad break. He typed that letter on the stage during the last act for future use in case he wanted to substantiate that little romance of the sore toe. Then he must suddenly have remembered that after the murder he would probably be searched. He had prepared no plan to circumvent that; the whole business of the note was an impromptu effort suggested by his chance encounter in the dark. One imagines him regretting his cleverness then, for he couldn't possibly destroy the paper completely while on the stage. On the spur of the moment he must have slipped it out of sight somewhere about the desk, perhaps simply in the pile of unused typepaper. After I'd searched him he had the opportunity to retrieve it while he waited on the stage for Miss Vaughan. You told me he always hammered away at the letter Q in that scene. He must have remembered telling you that, and when he recovered the paper he wiped away the prints on the machine from every letter except Q. *Most* artistic, but fortunately Bailey had already tested the machine, careful creature that he is, and found Gardener's prints all over it. When we tested it again—no prints on any letter but Q. All would have been well if Bailey had been a little less industrious."

"But Stephanie Vaughan's confession——" began Nigel.

"Her confession! Her confession that she'd gone to Surbonadier's flat and tried to get back the forged paper that she knew he kept in his box. Her confession that I'd found her and she hoped she'd bamboozled me into thinking she was after her letters. Her confession that I'd held her in my arms and that I was his worst enemy——" Alleyn stopped short.

There was a long pause, during which Nigel gazed speculatively at his friend.

"And Props?" he said at last.

"Props I never suspected. A guilty man would never have blackguarded Surbonadier as he did and he was too silly, poor chap, to have done it. He had recognized Gardener somehow in the dark. He may have brushed against him and given him the idea of the toe tarradiddle. Quite possible. Anyway, Props was all for shielding the murderer of his girl's betrayer. Until he saw the news of Saint's arrest. Then he wrote that note to me. He rang up Gardener and I suppose told him he knew something. Gardener suggested the theatre as a rendezvous, probably Props mentioned the window in Simon's Alley. Gardener dressed up as the old boy in an opera cloak and completely diddled our Mr. Wilkins. Disguise is usually a figment of detective fictionists' imagination, but again—Gardener was a consummate actor. He could risk it. You called while he was away murdering Props."

Alleyn described his views as regards the second murder. Nigel listened appalled.

"Wilkins's successor saw the old gentleman in the opera cloak return and failed to recognize him. The flat had been searched this morning. We hope to find evidence of the disguise. I think the overwhelming conceit of most murderers proved a little too much for Felix Gardener. The killing of Props was a bad mistake and yet—what could he do? Props, poor silly oaf that he was, evidently told him he wouldn't stand for an innocent man's trial and possible conviction. Props had to be got rid of. The method was not without points. If you hadn't called and found him out, if the old servant had not overheard that years-old conversation between himself and Surbonadier, if he hadn't got wet-white on his gloves —ah, well, there it is. We haven't been very clever. I'm handing no bouquets to myself over this case."

"Why did you want to get me out of the way?"

"My dear creature, because you were his friend, because he wondered how much you'd overheard in the flat, because—in short, because he's a murderer."

"I'm not convinced, Alleyn."

"You mean you don't want to be. It's perfectly beastly for you, I know. Were you greatly attached to him? Come now—were you?"

"I—well, perhaps not greatly attached, but we are by way of being friends."

"Where were you when I arrested him?"

"I had come round to the back. I stood under the electrician's platform."

"Then you saw him come down the ladder. You saw him kick down at me as he had kicked down at Props. You saw——"

"Yes—yes, I saw his face."

"His behaviour was more damning than I dared hope it would be. When I sent him up the ladder I knew he was planning how he would play the part of the horrified discoverer of the suicide. I thought he would very likely recognize the dummy—it was simply a weighted sack—and I wanted to see how he would react. I hardly dared hope he would do what he did."

"What do you mean?"

"He didn't even look at it. He saw something that scraped the upper surface of the cloth and he thought it was the feet of the body. In his mind was the vivid picture of the swinging corpse and in the violent turbulence of his emotion he did not pause to look—did not want to look— —He gave his magnificent performance of horror-struck discovery and —recognized Props! An innocent man would have looked and seen at once that a weighted sack hung from a rope."

"I wonder he consented to go up the ladder."

"He couldn't refuse. I treated the unfortunate Simpson to a display of official suspicion. The little man was scared out of his life, and Gardener was reassured. To refuse would have been impossible."

"There seems," said Nigel, "so little motive for so big a risk."

"Not when you go into the case. If Surbonadier had blown the gaff, Gardener would have been scrapped by Saint. If his authorship of the article in the *Morning Express* had come out, Saint could and would have done him incalculable harm. You may depend upon it that Surbonadier had been bleeding him for pretty hefty sums. A drug addict gets through lots of money. And Surbonadier could have given Stephanie Vaughan some very nasty information about Felix Gardener. I wonder how much Gardener himself had told her. Enough to make her risk that visit to the flat. She's a courageous creature."

Nigel looked curiously at him.

"She attracts you very much, doesn't she?" he ventured.

Alleyn got up and stood looking out into the yard.

"When she's not being a leading lady, she does," he said coolly.

"You're a rum old fish."

"Think so? Come and have some lunch. I must get back to the Yard."

"I don't feel like eating," said Nigel.

"You'd better try."

They walked down the alley-way to the front of the theatre. The gigantic unicorn in steel and black glass glittered against its starry background. Alleyn and Nigel looked up at it for a moment.

"There's one unique feature in this case," said Alleyn.

"What's that?"

"Thanks to you I was able to watch the murder in comfort from a fifteen-and-sixpenny stall provided by the murderer."

He held up his stick to a taxi and they drove away in silence.

NIGHT
AT THE
VULCAN

Contents

Cast of Characters

Martyn Tarne
Bob Grantley, *business manager*
Fred Badger, *night-watchman*
Clem Smith, *stage-manager*
Bob Cringle, *dresser to* Adam Poole
Adam Poole, *actor-manager*   of the
Helena Hamilton, *leading lady*   Vulcan
Clark Bennington, *her husband*   Theatre
Gay Gainsford, *his niece*
J. G. Darcey, *character actor*
Parry Percival, *juvenile*
Jacques Doré, *designer and assistant to* Adam Poole
Dr. John James Rutherford, *playwright*

Chief Detective-Inspector Alleyn
Detective-Inspector Fox
Detective-Sergeant Gibson   of the
Detective-Sergeant Bailey,   Criminal
finger-print expert   Investigation
Detective-Sergeant Thompson,   Department,
photographer   New Scotland
P. C. Lord Michael Lamprey   Yard
Dr. Curtis

Chapter I

The Vulcan

As she turned into Carpet Street the girl wondered at her own obstinacy. To what a pass it had brought her, she thought. She lifted first one foot and then the other, determined not to drag them. They felt now as if their texture had changed: their bones, it seemed, were covered by sponge and burning wires.

A clock in a jeweller's window gave the time as twenty-three minutes to five. She knew by the consequential scurry of its second-hand that it was alive. It was surrounded by other clocks that made mad dead statements of divergent times as if, she thought, to set before her the stages of that day's fruitless pilgrimage. Nine o'clock, the first agent. Nine thirty-six, the beginning of the wait for auditions at the Unicorn; five minutes past twelve, the first dismissal. "Thank you, Miss—ah— Thank you, dear. Leave your name and address. Next, please." No record of her flight from the smell of restaurants, but it must have been about ten to two, a time registered by a gilt carriage-clock in the corner, that she had climbed the stairs to Garnet Marks's Agency on the third floor. Three o'clock exactly at the Achilles where the auditions had already closed, and the next hour in and out of film agencies. "Leave your picture if you like, dear. Let you know if there's anything." Always the same. As punctual as time itself. The clocks receded, wobbled, enlarged themselves and at the same time spread before their dials a tenuous veil. Beneath the arm of a bronze nude that brandished an active swinging dial, she caught sight of a face: her own. She groped in her bag, and presently in front of the mirrored face a hand appeared and made a gesture at its own mouth with the stub of a lipstick. There was a coolness on her forehead, something pressed heavily against it. She discovered that this was the shop-window.

Behind the looking-glass was a man who peered at her from the shop's interior. She steadied herself with her hand against the window, lifted her suitcase and turned away.

The Vulcan Theatre was near the bottom of the street. Although she did not at first see its name above the entry, she had, during the past fortnight, discovered a sensitivity to theatres. She was aware of them at a distance. The way was downhill: her knees trembled and she resisted with difficulty an impulse to break into a shamble. Among the stream of faces that approached and sailed past there were now some that, on seeing hers, sharpened into awareness and speculation. She attracted notice.

The stage-door was at the end of an alleyway. Puddles of water obstructed her passage and she did not altogether avoid them. The surface of the wall was crenellated and damp.

"She knows," a rather shrill uncertain voice announced inside the theatre, "but she *mustn't* be told." A second voice spoke unintelligibly. The first voice repeated its statement with a change of emphasis: "She *knows* but she mustn't be *told,*" and after a further interruption added dismally: "Thank you very much."

Five young women came out of the stage-door and it was shut behind them. She leant against the wall as they passed her. The first two muttered together and moved their shoulders petulantly, the third stared at her and at once she bent her head. The fourth passed by quickly with compressed lips. She kept her head averted and heard, but did not see, the last girl halt beside her.

"Well, for God's sake!" She looked up and saw, for the second time that day, a too-large face, over-painted, with lips that twisted downwards, tinted lids, and thickly mascaraed lashes.

She said: "I'm late, aren't I?"

"You've had it, dear. I gave you the wrong tip at Marks's. The show here, with the part I told you about, goes on this week. They were auditioning for a tour—'That'll be all for to-day, ladies, thank you. What's the hurry, here's your hat!' For what it's worth, it's all over."

"I lost my way," she said faintly.

"Too bad." The large face swam nearer. "Are you all right?" it demanded. She made a slight movement of her head. "A bit tired. All right, really."

"You look shocking. Here: wait a sec. Try this."

"No, no. Really. Thank you so much but—"

"It's O.K. A chap who travels for a French firm gave it to me. It's marvellous stuff: cognac. Go *on.*"

A hand steadied her head. The cold mouth of the flask opened her lips and pressed against her teeth. She tried to say: "I've had nothing to eat," and at once was forced to gulp down a burning stream. The voice encouraged her: "Do you a power of good. Have the other half."

She shuddered, gasped and pushed the flask away. "No, please!"

"Is it doing the trick?"

"This is wonderfully kind of you. I am so grateful. Yes, I think it must be doing the trick."

"Gra-a-a-nd. Well, if you're sure you'll be O.K. . . ."

"Yes, indeed. I don't even know your name."

"Trixie O'Sullivan."

"I'm Martyn Tarne."

"Look nice in the programme, wouldn't it? If there's nothing else I can do . . ."

"Honestly. I'll be fine."

"You look better," Miss O'Sullivan said doubtfully. "We may run into each other again. The bloody round, the common task." She began to move away. "I've got a date, actually, and I'm running late."

"Yes, of course. Good-bye, and thank you."

"It's open in front. There's a seat in the foyer. Nobody'll say anything. Why not sit there for a bit?" She was half-way down the alley. "Hope you get fixed up," she said. "God, it's going to rain. What a life!"

"What a life," Martyn Tarne echoed, and tried to sound gay and ironic.

"I hope you'll be all right. 'Bye."

"Good-bye and thank you."

The alley was quiet now. Without moving she took stock of herself. Something thrummed inside her head and the tips of her fingers tingled but she no longer felt as if she were going to faint. The brandy glowed at the core of her being, sending out ripples of comfort. She tried to think what she should do. There was a church, back in the Strand: she ought to know its name. One could sleep there, she had been told, and perhaps there would be soup. That would leave two and fourpence for to-morrow: all she had. She lifted her suitcase—it was heavier than she had remembered—and walked to the end of the alleyway. Half a dozen raindrops plopped into a puddle. People hurried along the footpath with upward glances and opened their umbrellas. As she hesitated, the rain came down suddenly and decisively. She turned towards the front of the theatre and at first thought it was shut. Then she noticed that one of the plate-glass doors was ajar.

She pushed it open and went in.

The Vulcan was a new theatre, fashioned from the shell of an old one. Its foyer was an affair of geranium-red leather, chromium steel and double glass walls housing cacti. The central box-office, marked RE-

SERVED TICKETS ONLY, was flanked by doors and beyond them, in the corners, were tubular steel and rubber-foam seats. She crossed the heavily carpeted floor and sat in one of these. Her feet and legs, released from the torment of supporting and moving her body, throbbed ardently.

Facing Martyn, on a huge easel, was a frame of photographs under a printed legend:

Opening at this theatre

on

THURSDAY, MAY 11TH

THUS TO REVISIT

—*A New Play*—

by

JOHN JAMES RUTHERFORD

She stared at two large familiar faces and four strange smaller ones. Adam Poole and Helena Hamilton: those were famous faces. Monstrously enlarged, they had looked out at the New Zealand and Australian public from hoardings and from above cinema entrances. She had stood in queues many times to see them, separately and together. They were in the centre, and surrounding them were Clark Bennington with a pipe and stick and a look of faded romanticism in his eyes, J. G. Darcey with pince-nez and hair *en brosse*, Gay Gainsford, young and intense, and Parry Percival, youngish and dashing. The faces swam together and grew dim.

It was very quiet in the foyer and beginning to get dark. On the other side of the entrance doors the rain drove down slantways, half-blinding her vision of homeward-bound pedestrians and the traffic of the street beyond them. She saw the lights go on in the top of a bus, illuminating the passive and remote faces of its passengers. The glare of headlamps shone pale across the rain. A wave of loneliness, excruciating in its intensity, engulfed Martyn and she closed her eyes. For the first time since her ordeal began, panic rose in her throat and sickened her. Phrases drifted with an aimless rhythm on the tide of her desolation: "You're sunk, you're sunk, you're utterly sunk, you asked for it, and you've got it. What'll happen to you now?"

She was drowning at night in a very lonely sea. She saw lights shine on some unattainable shore. Pieces of flotsam bobbed indifferently against her hands. At the climax of despair, metallic noises, stupid and commonplace, set up a clatter in her head.

Martyn jerked galvanically and opened her eyes. The whirr and click of her fantasy had been repeated behind an obscured-glass wall on her left. Light glowed beyond the wall and she was confronted by the image of a god, sand-blasted across the surface of the glass and beating at a forge under the surprising supervision, it appeared, of Melpomene and Thalia. Further along, a notice in red light, dress circle and stalls, jutted out from an opening. Beyond the hammer-blows of her heart a muffled voice spoke peevishly.

". . . not much use to *me*. What? Yes, I know, old boy, but that's not the point."

The voice seemed to listen. Martyn thought: "This is it. In a minute I'll be turned out."

". . . something pretty bad," the voice said irritably. "She's gone to hospital. . . . They *said* so but nobody's turned up. . . . Well, you know what she's like, old boy, don't you? We've been snowed under all day and *I* haven't been able to do anything about it . . . auditions for the northern tour of the old piece . . . yes, yes, that's all fixed but . . . Look, another thing: the *Onlooker* wants a story and pictures for this week . . . yes, on stage. In costume. Nine-thirty in the morning and everything still in the boxes. . . . Well, can't you think of *anyone?* . . . Who? . . . Oh, God, I'll give it a pop. All right, old boy, thanks."

To Martyn, dazed with brandy and sleep, it was a distortion of a day-dream. Very often had she dreamt herself into a theatre where all was confusion because the leading actress had laryngitis and the understudy was useless. She would present herself modestly: "I happen to know the lines. I could perhaps . . ." The sudden attentiveness, when she began to speak the lines . . . the opening night . . . the grateful tears streaming down the boiled shirts of the management . . . the critics . . . no image had been too gross for her.

"Eileen?" said the voice. "Thank God! Listen, darling, it's Bob Grantley here. Listen, Eileen, I want you to do something terribly kind. I know it's asking a hell of a lot but I'm in trouble and you're my last hope. Helena's dresser's ill. Yes, indeed, poor old Tansley. Yes, I'm afraid so. Just this afternoon, and we haven't been able to raise anybody. First dress rehearsal to-morrow night and a photograph call in the morning and nothing unpacked or anything. I know what a good soul you are and I wondered . . . Oh, God! I see. Yes, I see. No, of course. Oh, well, never mind. I know you would. Yes. 'Bye."

Silence. Precariously alone in the foyer, she meditated an advance upon the man beyond the glass wall and suppressed a dreadful impulse in herself towards hysteria. This was her day-dream in terms of reality.

She must have slept longer than she had thought. Her feet were sleeping still. She began to test them, tingling and pricking, against the floor. She could see her reflection in the front doors, a dingy figure with a pallid face and cavernous shadows for eyes.

The light behind the glass wall went out. There was, however, still a yellow glow coming through the box-office door. As she got to her feet and steadied herself, the door opened.

"I believe," she said, "you are looking for a dresser."

ii

As he had stopped dead in the lighted doorway she couldn't see the man clearly but his silhouette was stocky and trim.

He said with what seemed to be a mixture of irritation and relief: "Good Lord, how long have you been here?"

"Not long. You were on the telephone. I didn't like to interrupt."

"Interrupt!" he ejaculated as if she talked nonsense. He looked at his watch, groaned, and said rapidly: "You've come about this job? From Mrs. Greenacres, aren't you?"

She wondered who Mrs. Greenacres could be? An employment agent? She hunted desperately for the right phrase, the authentic language.

"I understood you required a dresser and I would be pleased to apply." Should she have added "sir"?

"It's for Miss Helena Hamilton," he said rapidly. "Her own dresser who's been with her for years—for a long time—has been taken ill. I explained to Mrs. Greenacres. Photograph call for nine in the morning and first dress rehearsal to-morrow night. We open on Thursday. The dressing's heavy. Two quick changes and so on. I suppose you've got references?"

Her mouth was dry. She said: "I haven't brought—" and was saved by the telephone bell. He plunged back into the office and she heard him shout "Vulcan!" as he picked up the receiver. "Grantley, here," he said. "Oh, hullo, darling. Look, I'm desperately sorry, but I've been held up or I'd have rung you before. For God's sake apologize for me. Try and keep them going till I get there. I know, I know. Not a smell of one until—" The voice became suddenly muffled: she caught isolated words. "I think so . . . yes, I'll ask . . . yes . . . Right. 'Bye, darling."

He darted out, now wearing a hat and struggling into a raincoat. "Look," he said, "Miss—"

"Tarne."

"Miss Tarne. Can you start right away? Miss Hamilton's things are in her dressing-room. They need to be unpacked and hung out to-night. There'll be a lot of pressing. The cleaners have been in but the room's not ready. You can finish in the morning but she wants the things that can't be ironed—I wouldn't know—hung out. Here are the keys. We'll see how you get on and fix up something definite to-morrow if you suit. The night-watchman's there. He'll open the room for you. Say I sent you. Here!"

He fished out a wallet, found a card and scribbled on it. "He's a bit of a stickler: you'd better take this."

She took the card and the keys. "To-night?" she said. "Now?"

"Well, can you?"

"I—yes. But—"

"Not worrying about after-hours are you?"

"No."

For the first time he seemed, in the darkish foyer, to be looking closely at her. "I suppose," he muttered, "it's a bit—" and stopped short.

Martyn said in a voice that to herself sounded half-choked. "I'm perfectly trustworthy. You spoke of references. I have—"

"Oh, yes, yes," he said. "Good. That'll be O.K. then. I'm late. Will you be all right? You can go through the house. It's raining outside. Through there, will you? Thank you. Good night."

Taking up her suitcase, she went through the door he swung open and found herself in the theatre.

She was at the back of the stalls, standing on thick carpet at the top of the ramp and facing the centre aisle. It was not absolutely dark. The curtain was half-raised and a bluish light filtered in from off-stage through some opening—a faintly discerned window—in the scenery. This light was dimly reflected on the shrouded boxes. The dome was invisible, lost in shadow, and so far above that the rain, hammering on the roof beyond it, sounded much as a rumour of drums to Martyn. The deadened air smelt of naphthalene and plush.

She started off cautiously down the aisle. "I forgot," said Mr. Grantley's voice behind her. She managed to choke back a yelp. "You'd better get some flowers for the dressing-room. She likes roses. Here's another card."

"I don't think I've—"

"Florian's at the corner," he shouted. "Show them the card."

The door swung to behind him and a moment later she heard a more remote slam. She waited for a little while longer, to accustom herself to the dark. The shadows melted and the shape of the auditorium filtered through them like an image on a film in the darkroom. She thought it beautiful: the curve of the circle, the fanlike shell that enclosed it, the elegance of the proscenium and modesty of the ornament—all these seemed good to Martyn, and her growing sight of them refreshed her. Though this encouragement had an unreal, rather dream-like character, yet it did actually dispel something of her physical exhaustion so that it was with renewed heart that she climbed a little curved flight of steps on the Prompt side of the proscenium, pushed open the pass-door at the top and arrived backstage.

She was on her own ground. A single blue working-light, thick with dust, revealed a baize letter-rack and hinted at the batten-and-canvas backs of scenery fading upwards into yawning blackness. At her feet a litter of flex ran down into holes in the stage. There were vague, scarcely discernible shapes that she recognized as stacked flats, light bunches, the underside of perches, a wind machine and rain box. She smelt paint and glue size. As she received the assurance of these familiar signs she heard a faint scuffling noise—a rattle of paper, she thought. She moved forward.

In the darkness ahead of her a door opened on an oblong of light which widened to admit the figure of a man in an overcoat. He stood with bent head, fumbled in his pocket and produced a torch. The beam shot out, hunted briefly about the set and walls and found her. She blinked into a dazzling white disk and said: "Mr. Grantley sent me round. I'm the dresser."

"Dresser?" the man said hoarsely. He kept his torchlight on her face and moved towards her. "I wasn't told about no dresser," he said.

She held Mr. Grantley's card out. He came closer and flashed his light on it without touching it. "Ah," he said with a sort of grudging cheerfulness, "that's different. Now I know where I am, don't I?"

"I hope so," she said, trying to make her voice friendly. "I'm sorry to bother you. Miss Hamilton's dresser has been taken ill and I've got the job."

"Aren't you lucky," he said with obvious relish and added, "not but what she isn't a lady when she takes the fit for it."

He was eating something. The movement of his jaws, the succulent noises he made and the faint odour of food were an outrage. She could have screamed her hunger at him. Her mouth filled with saliva.

" 'E says to open the star room," he said. "Come on froo while I get the keys. I was 'avin' me bit er supper."

She followed him into a tiny room choked with junk. A kettle stuttered on a gas ring by a sink clotted with dregs of calcimine and tea leaves. His supper was laid out on a newspaper—bread and an open tin of jam. He explained that he was about to make a cup of tea and suggested she should wait while he did so. She leant against the door and watched him. The fragrance of freshly brewed tea rose above the reek of stale size and dust. She thought, "If he drinks it now I'll have to go out."

"Like a drop of char?" he said. His back was turned to her.

"Very much."

He rinsed out a stained cup under the tap.

Martyn said loudly: "I've got a tin of meat in my suitcase. I was saving it. If you'd like to share it and could spare some of your bread . . ."

He swung round and for the first time she saw his face. He was dark and thin and his eyes were brightly impertinent. Their expression changed as he stared at her.

" 'Ullo, 'ullo!" he said. "Who give *you* a tanner and borrowed 'alf-a-crahn? What's up?"

"I'm all right."

"*Are* you? Your looks don't flatter you, then."

"I'm a bit tired and—" Her voice broke and she thought in terror that she was going to cry. "It's nothing," she said.

" 'Ere!" He dragged a box out from under the sink and not ungently pushed her down on it. "Where's this remarkable tin of very pertikler meat? Give us a shine at it."

He shoved her suitcase over and while she fumbled at the lock busied himself with pouring out tea. "Nothin' to touch a drop of the old char when you're browned off," he said. He put the reeking cup of dark fluid beside her and turned away.

"With any luck," Martyn thought, folding back the garments in her case, "I won't have to sell these now."

She found the tin and gave it to him. "Coo!" he said. "Looks lovely, don't it? Tongue and veal and a pitcher of sheep to show there's no deception. Very tempting."

"Can you open it?"

"Can I open it? Oh, dear."

She drank her scalding tea and watched him open the tin and turn its contents out on a more dubious plate. Using his clasp knife he perched chunks of meat on a slab of bread and held it out to her. "You're in luck," he said. "Eat it slow."

She urged him to join her but he said he would set his share aside for later. They could both, he suggested, take another cut at it to-morrow. He examined the tin with interest while Martyn consumed her portion. She had never before given such intense concentration to a physical act. She would never have believed that eating could bring so fierce a satisfaction.

"Comes from Australia, don't it?" her companion said, still contemplating the tin.

"New Zealand."

"Same thing."

Martyn said: "Not really. There's quite a big sea in between."

"Do you come from there?"

"Where?"

"Australia."

"No. I'm a New Zealander."

"Same thing."

She looked up and found him grinning at her. He made the gesture of wiping the smile off his face. "Oh, dear," he said.

Martyn finished her tea and stood up. "I must start my job," she said.

"Feel better?"

"Much, much better."

"Would it be quite a spell since you ate anything?"

"Yesterday."

"I never fancy drinkin' on an empty stomach, myself."

Her face burnt against the palms of her hands. "But I don't . . . I mean, I know. I mean I was a bit faint and somebody . . . a girl . . . she was terribly kind . . ."

"Does yer mother know yer aht?" he asked ironically, and took a key from a collection hung on nails behind the door. "If you *must* work," he said.

"Please."

"Personally escorted tour abaht to commence. Follow in single file and don't talk to the guide. I thank you."

She followed him to the stage and round the back of the set. He warned her of obstructions by bobbing his torchlight on them and, when she stumbled against a muffled table, took her hand. She was disquieted by the grip of his fingers, calloused and wooden, and by the warmth of his palm, which was unexpectedly soft. She was oppressed with renewed loneliness and fear.

"End of the penny section," he said, releasing her. He unlocked a door, reached inside and switched on a light.

"They call this the Greenroom," he said. "That's what it was in the old days. It's been done up. Guv'nor's idea."

It was a room without a window, newly painted in green. There were a number of armchairs in brown leather, a round table littered with magazines, a set of well-stocked bookshelves and a gas fire. Groups of framed Pollock's prints decorated the walls: "Mr. Dale as Claude Amboine," "Mr. T. Hicks as Richard I," "Mr. S. French as Harlequin." This last enchanted Martyn because the diamonds of Mr. French's costume had been filled in with actual red and green sequins and he glittered in his frame.

Above the fireplace hung a largish sketch—it was little more than that —of a man of about thirty-five in mediaeval dress, with a hood that he was in the act of pushing away from his face. The face was arresting. It had great purity of form, being wide across the eyes and heart-shaped. The mouth, in particular, was of a most subtle character, perfectly masculine but drawn with extreme delicacy. It was well done: it had both strength and refinement. Yet it was not these qualities that disturbed Martyn. Reflected in the glass that covered the picture she saw her own face lying ghost-wise across the other, their forms intermingled like those in a twice-exposed photograph. It seemed to Martyn that her companion must be looking over her shoulder at this double image and she moved away from him and nearer to the picture. The reflection disappeared. Something was written faintly in one corner of the sketch. She drew closer and saw that it was a single word: *Everyman*.

"Spittin' image of 'im, ain't it?" said the night-watchman behind her.

"I don't know," she said quickly. "Is it?"

"*Is* it! Don't you know the Guv'nor when you see 'im?"

"The Governor?"

"'Strewth you're a caution and no error. Don't you know who owns this show? That's the great Mr. Adam Poole, that is."

"Oh," she murmured after a pause, and added uneasily: "I've seen him in the pictures, of course."

"Go on!" he jeered. "Where would that be? Australia? Fancy!"

He had been very kind to her, but she found his remorseless vein of irony exasperating. It would have been easier and less tedious to have let it go but she found herself embarked on an explanation. Of course she knew all about Mr. Adam Poole, she said. She'd seen his photograph in the foyer. All his pictures had been shown in New Zealand. She knew he was the most distinguished of the younger contemporary actor-managers. She was merely startled by the painting because . . . But it was impossible to explain why the face in the painting disturbed her and the unfinished phrase trailed away into an embarrassed silence.

Her companion listened to this rigmarole with an equivocal grin and when she gave it up merely remarked: "Don't apologize. It's the same with all the ladies. 'E fair rocks 'em. Talk about 'aving what it takes."

"I don't mean that at all," she shouted angrily.

"You should see 'em clawing at each other to get at 'im rahnd the stage-door, first nights. Something savage! Females of the speeches? Disgrace to their sexes more like. There's an ironing board etceterer in the wardrobe-room further along. You can plug in when you're ready. 'Er royal 'ighness is over the way."

He went out, opened a further door, switched on a light and called to her to join him.

iii

As soon as she crossed the threshold of the star dressing-room she smelt greasepaint. The dressing-shelf was bare, the room untenanted, but the smell of cosmetics mingled with the faint reek of gas. There were isolated dabs of colour on the shelves and the looking-glass; the lamp-bulbs were smeared with cream and red where sticks of greasepaint had been warmed at them; and on a shelf above the wash-basin somebody had left a miniature frying-pan of congealed mascara in which a hair-pin was embedded.

It was a largish room, windowless and dank, with an air of submerged grandeur about it. The full-length cheval-glass swung from a gilt frame. There was an Empire couch, an armchair and an ornate stool before the dressing-shelf. The floor was carpeted in red with a florid pattern that use had in part obliterated. A number of dress-boxes bearing the legend *Costumes by Pieroot et Cie* were stacked in the middle of the room, and there were two suitcases on the shelf. A gas heater stood against one wall and there was a caged jet above the wash-basin.

"Here we are," said the night-watchman. "All yer own."

She turned to thank him and encountered a speculative stare. "Cosy," he said, "ain't it?" and moved nearer. "Nice little hidey hole, ain't it?"

"You've been very kind," Martyn said. "I'll manage splendidly, now. Thank you very much indeed."

"Don't mention it. Any time." His hand reached out clumsily to her arm. "Been aht in the rain," he said thickly. "Naughty girl."

"It'll soon dry off. I'm quite all right."

She moved behind the pile of dress-boxes and fumbled with the string on the top one. There was a hissing noise. She heard him strike a match and a moment later was horribly jolted by an explosion from the gas heater. It forced an involuntary cry from her.

"'Ullo, *'ullo!*" her companion said. "Ain't superstitious, are we?"

"Superstitious?"

He made an inexplicable gesture towards the gas fire. "*You* know," he said, grinning horridly at her.

"I'm afraid I don't understand?"

"Don't tell me you never 'eard abaht the great Jupiter case! Don't they learn you nothing in them antypodes?"

The heater reddened and purred.

"Come to think of it," he said, "it'd be before your time. I wasn't 'ere myself when it occurred, a-course, but them that was don't give you a chance to forget it. Not that they mention it direct-like, but it don't get forgotten."

"What was it?" Martyn asked against her will.

"Sure yer not superstitious?"

"No, I'm not."

"You ain't been long in this business, then. Nor more am I. Shake 'ands." He extended his hand so pointedly that she was obliged to put her own in it and had some difficulty in releasing herself.

"It must be five years ago," he said, "all of that. A bloke in Number Four dressing-room did another bloke in, very cunning, by blowing dahn the tube of 'is own gas fire. Like if I went nex' door and blew dahn the tube, this fire'd go aht. And if you was dead drunk, like you might of been if this girl-friend of yours'd been very generous with 'er brandy, you'd be commy-tose and before you knew where you was you'd be dead. Which is what occurred. It made a very nasty impression and the theatre was shut dahn for a long while until they 'ad it all altered and pansied up. The Guv'nor won't 'ave it mentioned. 'E changed the name of the 'ouse when 'e took it on. But call it what you like, the memory, as they say, lingers on. Silly, though, ain't it? You and me don't care. That's right, ain't it? We'd rather be cosy. Wouldn't we?" He gave a kind of significance to the word "cosy." Martyn unlocked the suitcases. Her fingers were unsteady and she turned her back in order to hide them from him. He stood in front of the gas fire and began to give out a smell of hot dirty cloth. She took sheets from a suitcase, hung them under the clothes pegs round the walls, and began to unpack the boxes. Her feet throbbed cruelly and she surreptitiously shuffled them out of her wet shoes.

"That's the ticket," he said. "Dry 'em orf, shall we?"

He advanced upon her and squatted to gather up the shoes. His hand, large and prehensile, with a life of its own, darted out and closed over her foot. " 'Ow abaht yer stockings?"

Martyn felt not only frightened but humiliated and ridiculous—wobbling, dead tired, on one foot. It was as if she were half-caught in some particularly degrading kind of stocks.

She said: "Look here, you're a good chap. You've been terribly kind. Let me get on with the job."

His grip slackened. He looked up at her without embarrassment, his thin London face sharp with curiosity. "O.K.," he said. "No offence meant. Call it a day, eh?"

"Call it a day."

"You're the boss," he said, and got to his feet. He put her shoes down in front of the gas fire and went to the door. "Live far from 'ere?" he asked. A feeling of intense desolation swept through her and left her without the heart to prevaricate.

"I don't know," she said. "I've got to find somewhere. There's a women's hostel near Paddington, I think."

"Broke?"

"I'll be all right, now I've got this job."

His hand was in his pocket. " 'Ere," he said.

"No, no. Please."

"Come orf it. We're pals, ain't we?"

"No, really. I'm terribly grateful but I'd rather not. I'm all right."

"You're the boss," he said again, and after a pause: "I can't get the idea, honest I can't. The way you speak and be'ave and all. What's the story? 'Ard luck or what?"

"There's no story, really."

"Just what you say yourself. No questions asked." He opened the door and moved into the passage. "Mind," he said over his shoulder, "it's against the rules but I won't be rahnd again. My mate relieves me at eight ack emma but I'll tip 'im the wink if it suits you. Them chairs in the Greenroom's not bad for a bit of kip and there's the fire. I'll turn it on. Please yerself, a-course."

"Oh," she said, "could I? *Could* I?"

"Never know what you can do till you try. Keep it under your titfer, though, or I'll be in trouble. So long. Don't get down'earted. It'll be all the same in a fahsand years."

He had gone. Martyn ran into the passage and saw his torchlight bobbing out on the stage. She called after him: "Thank you—thank you so much! I don't know your name, but thank you and good night."

"Badger's the name," he said, and his voice sounded hollow in the empty darkness. "Call me Fred."

The light bobbed out of sight. She heard him whistling for a moment and then a door slammed and she was alone.

With renewed heart she turned back to her job.

iv

At ten o'clock she had finished. She had traversed with diligence all the hazards of fatigue: the mounting threat of sleep, the clumsiness that makes the simplest action an ordeal, the horror of inertia and the temptation to let go the tortured muscles and give up, finally and indifferently, the awful struggle.

Five carefully ironed dresses hung sheeted against the walls, the make-up was laid out on the covered dressing-shelf. The boxes were stacked away, the framed photographs set out. It only remained to buy roses in the morning for Miss Helena Hamilton. Even the vase was ready and filled with water.

Martyn leant heavily on the back of a chair and stared at two photographs of the same face in a double leather case. They were not theatre photographs but studio portraits, and the face looked younger than the face in the Greenroom: younger and more formidable, with the mouth set truculently and the gaze withdrawn. But it had the same effect on Martyn. Written at the bottom of each of these photographs, in a small incisive hand, was: *Helena from Adam, 1950.* "Perhaps," she thought, "he's married to her."

Hag-ridden by the fear that she had forgotten some important detail, she paused in the doorway and looked round the room. No, she thought, there was nothing more to be done. But as she turned to go she saw herself, cruelly reflected in the long cheval-glass. It was not, of course, the first time she had seen herself that night; she had passed before the looking-glasses a dozen times and had actually polished them, but her attention had been ruthlessly fixed on the job in hand and she had not once focussed her eyes on her own image. Now she did so. She saw a girl in a yellow sweater and dark skirt with black hair that hung in streaks over her forehead. She saw a white, heart-shaped face with smudges under the eyes and a mouth that was normally firm and delicate but now drooped with fatigue. She raised her hand, pushed the hair back from her face and stared for a moment or two longer. Then she switched off the light and blundered across the passage into the Greenroom. Here, collapsed in an armchair with her overcoat across her, she slept heavily until morning.

Chapter II

In a Glass Darkly

Martyn slept for ten hours. A wind got up in the night and found its way into the top of the stagehouse at the Vulcan. Up in the grid old back-cloths moved a little and, since the Vulcan was a hemp-house, there was a soughing among the forest of ropes. Flakes of paper, relics of some Victorian snowstorm, were dislodged from the top of a batten and fluttered down to the stage. Rain, driven fitfully against the theatre, ran in cascades down pipes and dripped noisily from ledges into the stage-door entry. The theatre mice came out, explored the contents of paste-pots in the sink-room and scuttled unsuccessfully about a covered plate of tongue and veal. Out in the auditorium there arose at intervals a vague whisper, and in his cubby-hole off the dock Fred Badger dozed and woke uneasily. At one o'clock he went on his rounds. He padded down corridors, flicking his torchlight on framed sketches for décor and costumes, explored the foyer and examined the locked doors of the offices. He climbed the heavily carpeted stairs and, lost in meditation, stood for a long time in the dress circle among shrouded rows of seats and curtained doorways. Sighing dolorously he returned backstage and made a stealthy entrance onto the set. Finally he creaked to the Greenroom door and, impelled by who knows what impulse, furtively opened it.

Martyn lay across the chair, her knees supported by one of its arms and her head by the other. The glow from the gas fire was reflected in her face. Fred Badger stood for quite a long time eyeing her and scraping his chin with calloused fingers. At last he backed out, softly closed the door and tiptoed to his cubby-hole, where he telephoned the fire-station to make his routine report.

At dawn the rain stopped and cleaning-vans swept the water down Carpet Street with their great brushes. Milk-carts clinked past the Vulcan and the first bus roared by. Martyn heard none of them. She woke to the murmur of the gas fire, and the confused memory of a dream in which someone tapped gently at a door. The windowless room was still dark but she looked at her watch in the fire-glow and found it was eight o'clock. She got up stiffly, crossed the room and opened the door on grey diffused daylight. A cup of tea with a large sandwich balanced on it had been left on the floor of the passage. Underneath it was a torn scrap of paper on which was scrawled: *Keep your pecker up matey see you some more.*

With a feeling of gratitude and timid security she breakfasted in the Greenroom, and afterwards explored the empty passage, finding at the far end an unlocked and unused dressing-room. To this room she brought her own suitcase and here, with a chair propped under the door-handle, she stripped and washed in icy water. In clean clothes, with her toilet complete, and with a feeling of detachment, as if she herself looked on from a distance at these proceedings, she crossed the stage and went out through the side door and up the alleyway into Carpet Street.

It was a clean sunny morning. The air struck sharply at her lips and nostrils and the light dazzled her. A van had drawn up outside the Vulcan and men were lifting furniture from it. There were cleaners at work in the foyer and a telegraph boy came out whistling. Carpet Street was noisy with traffic. Martyn turned left and walked quickly downhill until she came to a corner shop called Florian. In the window a girl in a blue coverall was setting out a large gilt basket of roses. The door was still locked but Martyn, emboldened by fresh air and a sense of freedom and adventure, tapped on the window and when the girl looked up pointed to the roses and held up Mr. Grantley's card. The girl smiled and, leaving the window, came to let her in.

Martyn said. "I'm sorry to bother you, but Mr. Grantley at the Vulcan told me to get some roses for Miss Helena Hamilton. He didn't give me any money and I'm afraid I haven't got any. Is all this very irregular and tiresome?"

"That will be quayte O.K.," the girl said in a friendly manner. "Mr. Grantley has an account."

"Perhaps you know what sort of roses I should get," Martyn suggested. She felt extraordinarily light and rather loquacious. "You see, I'm Miss Hamilton's dresser but I'm new and I don't know what she likes."

"Red would be quayte in order, I think. There are some lovely Bloody Warriors just in." She caught Martyn's eye and giggled. "Well, they do think of the weirdest names, don't they? Look: aren't they lovelies?"

She held up a group of roses with drops of water clinging to their half-opened petals. "Gorgeous," she said, "aren't they? Such a colour."

Martyn, appalled at the price, took a dozen. The girl looked curiously at her and said: "Miss Hamilton's dresser. Fancy! Aren't you lucky?" and she was vividly reminded of Fred Badger.

"I feel terribly lucky this morning," she said and was going away when the girl, turning pink under her make-up, said: "Pardon me asking, but I don't suppose you could get me Miss Hamilton's autograph. I'd be ever so thrilled."

"I haven't even seen her yet but I'll do my best."

"You *are* a duck. Thanks a million. Of course," the girl added, "I'm a real fan. I never miss any of her pictures and I do think Adam Poole— pardon me, Mr. Poole—is simply mawvellous. I mean to say I think he's just mawvellous. They're so mawvellous together. I suppose he's crazy about her in real life, isn't he? I always say they couldn't act together like that—you know, so gorgeously—unless they had a pretty hot clue on the sayde. Don't you agree?"

Martyn said she hadn't had a chance of forming an opinion as yet and left the florist in pensive contemplation of the remaining Bloody Warriors.

When she got back to the theatre its character had completely changed: it was alive and noisy. The dockdoors were open and sunlight lay in incongruous patches on painted canvas and stacked furniture. Up in the grid there was a sound of hammering. A back-cloth hung diagonally in mid-air and descended in jerks, while a man in shirtsleeves shouted: "Down on yer long. Now yer short. Now bodily. Right-oh! Dead it. Now find yer Number Two."

A chandelier lay in a heap in the middle of the stage, and above it was suspended a batten of spotlights within reach of an elderly mechanist who fitted pink and straw-coloured mediums into their frames. Near the stage-door a group of men stared at a small Empire desk from which a stage-hand had removed a cloth wrapping. A tall young man in spectacles, wearing a red pullover and corduroy trousers, said irritably: "It's too bloody chi-chi. Without a shadow of doubt, he'll hate its guts."

He glanced at Martyn and added: "Put them in her room, dear, will you?"

She hurried to the dressing-room passage and found that here too there was life and movement. A vacuum-cleaner hummed in the Greenroom, a bald man in overalls was tacking cards on the doors, somewhere down the passage an unseen person sang cheerfully and the door next to Miss Hamilton's was open. These signs of preparation awakened in Martyn a sense of urgency. In a sudden fluster she unwrapped her roses and thrust them into the vase. The stalks were too long and she had nothing to cut them with. She ran down the passage to the empty room, and reflected as she rootled in her suitcase that she would be expected to have sewing materials at hand. Here was the housewife an aunt had given her when she left New Zealand but it was depleted and in a muddle. She ran back with it, sawed at the rose stems with her nail-scissors and, when someone in the next room tapped on the wall, inadvertently jammed the points into her hand.

"And how," a disembodied voice inquired, "is La Belle Tansley this morning?"

Sucking her left hand and arranging roses with her right, Martyn wondered how she should respond to this advance. She called out tentatively: "I'm afraid it's not Miss Tansley."

"What's that?" the voice said vaguely, and a moment later she heard the brisk sound of a clothes-brush at work.

The roses were done at last. She stood with the ends of the stalks in her hand and wondered why she had become so nervous.

"Here we go again," a voice said in the doorway. She spun round to face a small man in an alpaca coat with a dinner-jacket in his hands. He stared at her with his jaw dropped. "Pardon me," he said. "I thought you was Miss Tansley."

Martyn explained. "Well!" he said. "That'll be her heart, that will. She ought to have given up before this. I warned her. In hospital, too? T'ch, t'ch, t'ch." He wagged his head and looked, apparently in astonishment, at Martyn. "So that's the story," he continued, "and you've stepped into the breach. Fancy that! Better introduce ourselves, hadn't we? The name's Cringle but Bob'll do as well as anything else. I'm 'is lordship's dresser. How are you?"

Martyn gave him her name and they shook hands. He had a pleasant face covered with a cobweb of fine wrinkles. "Been long at this game?" he asked, and added: "Well, that's a foolish question, isn't it? I should have said: Will this be your first place, or Are you doing it in your school holidays, or something of that sort."

"Do you suppose," Martyn said anxiously, "Miss Hamilton will think I'm too young?"

"Not if you give satisfaction, she won't. She's all right if you give satisfaction. Different from my case. Slave meself dizzy, I can, and if 'is lordship's in one of 'is moods, what do I get for it? Spare me days, I don't know why I put up with it and that's a fact. But *she's* all right if she likes you." He paused and added tentatively: "But you know all about that, I dare say." Martyn was silent and felt his curiosity reach out as if it were something tangible. At last she said desperately: "I'll try. I want to give satisfaction."

He glanced round the room. "Looks nice," he said. "Are you pressed and shook out? Yes, I can see you are. Flowers too. Very nice. Would you be a friend of hers? Doing it to oblige, like?"

"No, no. I've never seen her. Except in the pictures, of course."

"Is that a fact?" His rather bird-like eyes were bright with speculation. "Young ladies," he said, "have to turn their hands to all sorts of work these days, don't they?"

"I suppose so. Yes."

"No offence, I hope, but I was wondering if you come from one of those drama-schools. Hoping to learn a bit, watching from the side, like."

A kind of sheepishness that had hardened into obstinacy prevented her from telling him in a few words why she was there. The impulse of a fortnight ago to rush to somebody—the ship's captain, the High Commissioner for her own country, anyone—and unload her burden of disaster had given place almost at once to a determined silence. This mess was of her own making, she had decided, and she herself would see it out. And throughout the loneliness and panic of her ordeal, to this resolution she had stuck. It had ceased to be a reasoned affair with Martyn: the less she said, the less she wanted to say. She had become crystallized in reticence.

So she met the curiosity of the little dresser with an evasion. "It'd be wonderful," she said, "if I did get the chance."

A deep voice with an unusually vibrant quality called out on the stage. "Bob! Where the devil have you got to? Bob!"

"Cripes!" the little dresser ejaculated. "Here we are *and* in one of our tantrums. *In here, sir! Coming, sir!*"

He darted towards the doorway but before he reached it a man appeared there, a man so tall that for a fraction of a second he looked down over the dresser's head directly into Martyn's eyes.

"This young lady," Bob Cringle explained with an air of discovery, "is the new dresser for Miss Hamilton. I just been showing her the ropes, Mr. Poole, sir."

"You'd much better attend to your work. I want you." He glanced again at Martyn. "Good morning," he said and was gone. "Look at this!" she heard him say angrily in the next room. "Where *are* you!"

Cringle paused in the doorway to turn his thumbs down and his eyes up. "Here we are, sir. What's the little trouble?" he was saying pacifically as he disappeared.

Martyn thought: "The picture in the Greenroom is more like him than the photographs." Preoccupied with this discovery she was only vaguely aware of a fragrance in the air and a new voice in the passage. The next moment her employer came into the dressing-room.

ii

An encounter with a person hitherto only seen and heard on the cinema screen is often disconcerting. It is as if the two-dimensional and enormous image had contracted about a living skeleton and in taking on substance had acquired an embarrassing normality. One is not always glad to change the familiar shadow for the strange reality.

Helena Hamilton was a blonde woman. She had every grace. To set down in detail the perfections of her hair, eyes, mouth and complexion, her shape and the gallantry of her carriage would be to reiterate merely that which everyone had seen in her innumerable pictures. She was, in fact, quite astonishingly beautiful. Even the circumstance of her looking somewhat older than her moving shadow could not modify the shock of finding her its equal in everything but this.

Coupled with her beauty was her charm. This was famous. She could reduce press conferences to a conglomerate of eager, even naïve, males. She could make a curtain-speech that every leading woman in every theatre in the English-speaking world had made before her and persuade the last man in the audience that it was original. She could convince bit-part actresses playing maids in first acts that there, but for the grace of God, went she.

On Martyn, however, taken off her balance and entirely by surprise, it was Miss Hamilton's smell that made the first impression. At ten guineas a moderately sized bottle, she smelt like Master Fenton, all April and May. Martyn was very much shorter than Miss Hamilton but this did not prevent her from feeling cumbersome and out-of-place, as if she had been caught red-handed with her own work in the dressing-room. This awkwardness was in part dispelled by the friendliness of Miss Hamilton's smile and the warmth of her enchanting voice.

"You've come to help me, haven't you?" she said. "Now, that *is* kind. I know all about you from Mr. Grantley and I fully expect we'll get along famously together. The only thing I *don't* know, in fact, is your name."

Martyn wondered if she ought to give only her Christian name or only her surname. She said: "Tarne. Martyn Tarne."

"But what a charming name!" The brilliant eyes looked into Martyn's face and their gaze sharpened. After a fractional pause she repeated: "Really charming," and turned her back.

It took Martyn a moment or two to realize that this was her cue to remove Miss Hamilton's coat. She lifted it from her shoulders—it was made of Persian lamb and smelt delicious—and hung it up. When she turned round she found that her employer was looking at her. She smiled reassuringly at Martyn and said: "You've got everything arranged very nicely. Roses, too. Lovely."

"They're from Mr. Grantley."

"Sweet of him but I bet he sent you to buy them."

"Well—" Martyn began and was saved by the entry of the young man in the red sweater with a dressing-case for which she was given the keys. While she was unpacking it the door opened and a middle-aged, handsome man with a raffish face and an air of boldness came in. She remembered the photographs in the foyer. This was Clark Bennington. He addressed himself to Miss Hamilton.

"Hullo," he said, "I've been talking to John Rutherford."

"What about?" she asked and sounded nervous.

"About that kid. Young Gay. He's been at her again. So's Adam." He glanced at Martyn. "I wanted to talk to you," he added discontentedly.

"Well, so you shall. But I've got to change now, Ben. And look, this is my new dresser, Martyn Tarne."

He eyed Martyn with more attention. "Quite a change from old Tansley," he said. "And a very nice change, too." He turned away. "Is Adam down?" He jerked his head at the wall.

"Yes."

"I'll see you later, then."

"All right, but—yes, all right."

He went out, leaving a faint rumour of alcohol behind him.

She was quite still for a moment after he had gone. Martyn heard her fetch a sigh, a sound half-impatient, half-anxious. "Oh, well," she said, "let's get going, shall we?"

Martyn had been much exercised about the extent of her duties. Did, for instance, a dresser undress her employer? Did she kneel at her feet and roll down her stockings? Did she unhook and unbutton? Or did she stand capably aside while these rites were performed by the principal herself? Miss Hamilton solved the problem by removing her dress, throwing it to Martyn and waiting to be inserted into her dressing-gown. During these operations a rumble of male voices sounded at intervals in the adjoining room. Presently there was a tap at the door. Martyn answered it and found the little dresser with a florist's box in his hands. "Mr. Poole's compliments," he said and winked broadly before retiring.

Miss Hamilton by this time was spreading a yellow film over her face. She asked Martyn to open the box and, on seeing three orchids that lay crisp and fabulous on their mossy bed, sang "Darling!" on two clear notes.

The voice beyond the wall responded. "Hullo?"

"They're quite perfect. Thank you, my sweet."

"Good," the voice said. Martyn laid the box on the dressing-table and saw the card: *Until to-morrow. Adam.*

She got through the next half hour pretty successfully, she hoped. There seemed to be no blunders and Miss Hamilton continued charming and apparently delighted. There were constant visitors. A tap on the door would be followed by a head looking round and always by the invitation to come in. First there was Miss Gay Gainsford, a young and rather intense person with a pretty air of deference, who seemed to be in a state of extreme anxiety.

"Well, darling," Miss Hamilton said, glancing at her in the glass. "Everything under strict control?"

Miss Gainsford said unevenly: "I suppose so. I'm trying to be good and sort of *biddable,* do you know, but underneath I realize that I'm seething like a cauldron. Butterflies the size of *bats* in the stomach."

"Well, of course. But you mustn't be terrified, really, because whatever happens we all know John's written a good play, don't we?"

"I suppose we do."

"We do indeed. And Gay—you're going to make a great personal success in this part. I want you to tell yourself you are. Do you know? *Tell* yourself."

"I wish I could believe it." Miss Gainsford clasped her hands and raised them to her lips. "It's not very easy," she said, "when he—John— Dr. Rutherford—so obviously thinks I'm a misfit. Everybody keeps telling me it's a marvellous part, but for me it's thirteen sides of hopeless hell. Honestly, it is."

"Gay, what *nonsense!* John may seem hard—"

"*Seem!*"

"Well, he may *be* hard, then. He's famous for it, after all. But you'll get your reward, my dear, when the time comes. Remember," said Miss Hamilton with immense gravity, "we all have faith in you."

"Of course," said Miss Gainsford with an increased quaver in her voice, "it's too marvellous your feeling like that about it. You've been so miraculously kind. And Uncle Ben, of course. Both of you. I can't get over it."

"But, my dear, that's utter nonsense. You're going to be one of our rising young actresses."

"You do *really* think so!"

"But yes. We all do." Her voice lost a little colour and then freshened. "We all do," she repeated firmly and turned back to her glass.

Miss Gainsford went to the door and hesitated there. "Adam doesn't," she said loudly.

Miss Hamilton made a quick expressive gesture toward the next dressing-room and put her finger to her lips. "He'll be *really* angry if he hears you say that," she whispered, and added aloud with somewhat forced casualness: "Is John down this morning?"

"He's on-stage. I think he said he'd like to speak to you."

"I want to see him particularly. Will you tell him, darling?"

"Of course, Aunty Helena," Miss Gainsford said rather miserably, and added: "I'm sorry, I forgot. Of course, Helena, darling." With a wan smile she was gone.

"Oh, dear!" Miss Hamilton sighed and catching Martyn's eye in the looking-glass made a rueful face. "If only—" she began and stopped unaccountably, her gaze still fixed on Martyn's image. "Never mind," she said.

There was a noisy footfall in the passage followed by a bang on the door, and, with scarcely a pause for permission, by the entry of a large, florid and angry-looking man wearing a sweater, a leather waistcoat, a muffler and a very old duffel coat.

"Good morning, John darling," said Miss Hamilton gaily and extended her hand. The new-comer planted a smacking kiss on it and fixed Martyn with a china-blue and bulging pair of eyes. Martyn turned away from this embarrassing regard.

"What have we here?" he demanded. His voice was loud and rumbling.

"My new dresser. Dr. Rutherford, Martyn."

"Stay me with flagons!" said Rutherford. He turned on Miss Hamilton. "That fool of a wench Gainsford said you wanted me," he said. "What's up?"

"John, *what* have you been saying to that child?"

"I? Nothing. Nothing to what I could, and, mark you, what I ought to say to her. I merely asked her if, for the sake of my sanity, she'd be good enough to play the central scene without a goddam simper on her fat and wholly unsuitable dial."

"You're frightening her."

"She's terrifying me. She may be your niece, Helena—"

"She's not my niece. She's Ben's niece."

"If she was the Pope's niece she'd still be a goddam pain in the neck. I wrote this part for an intelligent actress who could be made to look reasonably like Adam. What do you give me? A moronic amateur who looks like nothing on God's earth."

"She's extremely pretty."

"Lollypops! Adam's too damn easy on her. The only hope lies in shaking her up. Or kicking her out and I'd do that myself if I had my way. It ought to have been done a month back. Even now—"

"Oh, my *dear* John! We open in two days, you might remember."

"An actress worth her salt'd memorize it in an hour. I told her—"

"I do beg you," she said, "to leave her to Adam. After all he is the producer, John, and he's very wise."

Dr. Rutherford pulled out of some submerged pocket a metal box. From this he extracted a pinch of snuff, which he took with loud and uncouth noises.

"In a moment," he said, "you'll be telling me the author ought to keep out of the theatre."

"That's utter nonsense."

"Let them try to keep *me* out," he said and burst into a neighing laugh.

Miss Hamilton slightly opened her mouth, hardened her upper lip, and with the closest attention painted it a purplish red. "Really," she said briskly, "you'd much better behave prettily, you know. You'll end by having her on your hands with a nervous breakdown."

"The sooner the better if it's a good one."

"Honestly, John, you are the rock *bottom* when you get like this. If you didn't write the plays you do write—if you weren't the greatest dramatist since—"

"Spare me the raptures," he said, "and give me some actors. And while we're on the subject, I may as well tell you that I don't like the way Ben is shaping in the big scene. If Adam doesn't watch him he'll be up to some bloody leading-man hocus-pocus, and by God if he tries that on I'll wring his neck for him."

She turned and faced him. "John, he *won't*. I'm sure he won't."

"No, you're not. You can't be sure. Nor can I. But if there's any sign of it to-night, and Adam doesn't tackle him, I will. I'll tickle his catas-

trophe, by God I will. As for that Mongolian monstrosity, that discard
from the waxworks, Mr. Parry Percival, what devil—will you answer me
—what inverted sadist foisted it on my play?"

"Now, look here, John—" Miss Hamilton began with some warmth,
and was shouted down.

"Have I not stipulated from the beginning of my disastrous association with this ill-fated playhouse that I would have none of these abor-
tions in my works? These Things. These foetid Growths. These
Queers."

"Parry isn't one."

"Yah! He shrieks it. I have an instinct, my girl. I nose them as I go
into the lobby."

She made a gesture of despair. "I give up," she said.

He helped himself to another pinch of snuff. "Hooey!" he snorted.
"You don't do anything of the sort, my sweetie-pie. You're going to
rock 'em, you and Adam. Think of that and preen yourself. And leave
all the rest—to *me*."

"Don't quote from *Macbeth*. If Gay Gainsford heard you doing that
she really would go off at the deep end."

"Which is precisely where I'd like to push her."

"Oh, go away," she cried out impatiently but with an air of good nature. "I've had enough of you. You're wonderful and you're hopeless.
Go away."

"The audience is concluded?" He scraped the parody of a Regency
bow.

"The audience is concluded. The door, Martyn."

Martyn opened the door. Until then, feeling wretchedly in the way,
she had busied herself with the stack of suitcases in the corner of the
room and now, for the first time, came absolutely face to face with the
visitor. He eyed her with an extraordinary air of astonishment.

"Here!" he said. "Hi!"

"No, John," Miss Hamilton said with great determination. "No!"

"*Eureka!*"

"Nothing of the sort. Good morning."

He gave a shrill whistle and swaggered out. Martyn turned back to
find her employer staring into the glass. Her hands trembled and she
clasped them together. "Martyn," she said, "I'm going to call you Martyn because it's such a nice name. You know, a dresser is rather a particular sort of person. She has to be as deaf as a post and as blind as a
bat to almost everything that goes on under her very nose. Dr. Rutherford is, as I expect you know, a most distinguished and brilliant person.

Our Greatest English Playwright. But like many brilliant people," Miss
Hamilton continued, in what Martyn couldn't help thinking a rather too
special voice, "he is *eccentric*. We all understand and we expect you to
do so too. Do you know?"

Martyn said she did.

"Good. Now, put me into that pink thing and let us know the worst
about it, shall we?"

When she was dressed she stood before the cheval-glass and looked
with cold intensity at her image. "My God," she said, "the lighting had
better be good."

Martyn said: "Isn't it right? It looks lovely to me."

"My poor girl!" she muttered. "You run to my husband and ask him
for cigarettes. He's got my case. I need a stimulant."

Martyn hurried into the passage and tapped at the next door. "So
they are married," she thought. "He must be ten years younger than she
is but they're married and he still sends her orchids in the morning."

The deep voice shouted impatiently: "Come!" and she opened the
door and went in.

The little dresser was putting Poole into a dinner jacket. Their backs
were turned to Martyn. "Yes?" Poole said.

"Miss Hamilton would like her cigarette case, if you please."

"I haven't got it," he said and shouted: "Helena!"

"Hullo, darling?"

"I haven't got your case."

There was a considerable pause. The voice beyond the wall called:
"No, no. Ben's got it. Mr. Bennington, Martyn."

"I'm so sorry," Martyn said, and made for the door, conscious of the
little dresser's embarrassment and of Poole's annoyance.

Mr. Clark Bennington's room was on the opposite side of the passage
and next the Greenroom. On her entrance Martyn was abruptly and
most unpleasantly transported into the immediate past—into yesterday
with its exhaustion, muddle and panic, to the moment of extreme humil-
iation when Fred Badger had smelt brandy on her breath. Mr. Bennington's flask was open on his dressing-shelf and he was in the act of entertaining a thick-set gentleman with beautifully groomed white hair,
wearing a monocle in a strikingly handsome face. This person set down
his tumbler and gazed in a startled fashion at Martyn.

"It's not," he said, evidently picking up with some difficulty the conversation she had interrupted, "it's not that I would for the world inter-
fere, Ben, dear boy. Nor do I enjoy raising what is no doubt a delicate
subject in these particular circumstances. But I feel for the child damna-

bly, you know. Damnably. Moreover, it does rather appear that the Doctor never loses an opportunity to upset her."

"I couldn't agree more, old boy, and I'm bloody angry about it. Yes, dear, wait a moment, will you?" Mr. Bennington rejoined, running his speeches together and addressing them to no one in particular. "This is my wife's new dresser, J.G."

"Really?" Mr. J. G. Darcey responded and bowed politely to Martyn. "Good morning, child. See you later, Ben, my boy. Thousand thanks."

He rose, looked kindly at Martyn, dropped his monocle, passed his hand over his hair and went out, breaking into operatic song in the passage.

Mr. Bennington made a half-hearted attempt to put his flask out of sight and addressed himself to Martyn.

"And what," he asked, "can I do for the new dresser?"

Martyn delivered her message. "Cigarette case? Have I got my wife's cigarette case? God, I don't know. Try my overcoat, dear, will you? Behind the door. Inside pocket. No secrets," he added obscurely. "Forgive my asking you. I'm busy."

But he didn't seem particularly busy. He twisted round in his chair and watched Martyn as she made a fruitless search of his overcoat pockets. "This your first job?" he asked. She said it was not and he added: "As a dresser, I mean."

"I've worked in the theatre before."

"And where was that?"

"In New Zealand."

"*Really?*" he said, as if she had answered some vitally important question.

"I'm afraid," Martyn went on quickly, "it's not in the overcoat."

"God, what a bore! Give me my jacket then, would you? The grey flannel."

She handed it to him and he fumbled through the pockets. A pocketbook dropped on the floor, spilling its contents. Martyn gathered them together and he made such a clumsy business of taking them from her that she was obliged to put them on the shelf. Among them was an envelope bearing a foreign stamp and postmark. He snatched it up and it fluttered in his fingers. "Mustn't lose track of that one, must we?" he said and laughed. "All the way from Uncle Tito." He thrust it at Martyn. "Look," he said and steadied his hand against the edge of the shelf. "What d'you think of *that?* Take it."

Troubled at once by the delay and by the oddness of his manner

Martyn took the envelope and saw that it was addressed to Bennington.

"Do you collect autographs," Bennington asked with ridiculous intensity—"or signed letters?"

"No, I'm afraid I don't," she said and put the letter face-down on the shelf.

"There's someone," he said with a jab of his finger at the envelope, "who'd give a hell of a lot for *that* one in there. A hell of a lot."

He burst out laughing, pulled a cigarette case out of the jacket and handed it to her with a flourish. "Purest gold," he said. "Birthday present but not from me. I'm her husband, you know. What the hell! Are you leaving me? Don't go."

Martyn made her escape and ran back to Miss Hamilton's room, where she found her in conference with Adam Poole and a young man of romantic appearance whom she recognized as the original of the last of the photographs in the foyer—Mr. Parry Percival. The instinct that makes us aware of a conversation in which we ourselves have in our absence been involved warned Martyn that they had been talking about her and had broken off on her entrance. After a moment's silence, Mr. Percival, with far too elaborate a nonchalance, said: "Yes. Well, there you have it," and it was obvious that there was a kind of double significance in his remark. Miss Hamilton said: "My poor Martyn, where *have* you been?" with a lightness that was not quite cordial.

"I'm sorry," Martyn said. "Mr. Bennington had trouble in finding the case." She hesitated for a moment and added, "Madam."

"That," Miss Hamilton rejoined, looking at Adam Poole, "rings dismally true. Would you believe it, darling, I became so furious with him for taking it that, most reluctantly, I gave him one for himself. He lost it instantly, of course, and now swears he didn't and mine is his. If you follow me."

"With considerable difficulty," Poole said, "I do."

Parry Percival laughed gracefully. He had a winning, if not altogether authentic, air of ingenuousness, and at the moment seemed to be hovering on the edge of some indiscretion. "I am afraid," he said ruefully to Miss Hamilton, "I'm rather in disgrace myself."

"With me, or with Adam?"

"I hope not with either of you. With Ben." He glanced apologetically at Poole, who did not look at him. "Because of the part, I mean. I suppose I spoke out of turn, but I really did think I could play it—still do for a matter of that, but there it is."

It was obvious that he was speaking at Poole. Martyn saw Miss Hamilton look from one man to the other before she said lightly, "I think you could too, Parry, but as you say, there it is. Ben *has* got a flair, you know."

Percival laughed. "He has indeed," he said. "He has had it for twenty years. Sorry. I shouldn't have said that. Honestly, I *am* sorry."

Poole said: "I dislike post mortems on casting, Parry."

"I know, I *do* apologize." Percival turned ingratiatingly, and the strong light caught his face sideways. Martyn saw with astonishment that under the thin film of greasepaint there was a system of incipient lines, and she realized that he was not, after all, a young man. "I know," he repeated, "I'm being naughty."

Poole said: "We open on Thursday. The whole thing was thrashed out weeks ago. Any discussion now is completely fruitless."

"That," said Miss Hamilton, "is what I have been trying to tell the Doctor."

"John? I heard him bellowing in here," Poole said. "Where's he gone? I want a word with him. And with you, Parry, by the way. It's about that scene at the window in the second act. You're not making your exit line. You must top Ben there. It's most important."

"Look, old boy," Mr. Percival said with agonized intensity, "I *know*. It's just another of those things. Have you *seen* what Ben does? Have you seen that business with my handkerchief? He won't take his hands off me. The whole exit gets messed up."

"I'll see what can be done."

"John," said Miss Hamilton, "is worried about it too, Adam."

Poole said: "Then he should talk to me."

"You know what the Doctor is."

"We all do," said Parry Percival, "and the public, I fear, is beginning to find out. God, there I go again."

Poole looked at him. "You'll get along better, I think, Parry, if you deny yourself these cracks against the rest of the company. Rutherford has written a serious play. It'd be a pity if any of us should lose faith in it."

Percival reddened and made towards the door. "I'm just being a nuisance," he said. "I'll take myself off and be photographed like a good boy." He made an insinuating movement of his shoulders towards Miss Hamilton, and fluttered his hand at her dress. "Marvellous," he said—"a triumph, if the bit-part actor may be allowed to say so."

The door shut crisply behind him, and Miss Hamilton said: "Darling, aren't you rather high and grand with poor Parry?"

"I don't think so. He's behaving like an ass. He couldn't play the part. He was born to be a feed."

"He'd *look* it."

"If all goes well Ben will *be* it."

"If all goes well! Adam, I'm terrified. He's—"

"Are you dressed, Helena? The cameras are ready."

"Shoes, please, Martyn," said Miss Hamilton. "Yes, darling. I'm right."

Martyn fastened her shoes and then opened the door. Miss Hamilton swept out, lifting her skirts with great elegance. Martyn waited for Poole to follow, but he said: "You're meant to be on-stage. Take make-up and a glass and whatever Miss Hamilton may need for her hair."

She thanked him and in a flurry gathered the things together. Poole took the Persian lamb coat and stood by the door. She hesitated, expecting him to precede her, but found that he was looking at the cheval-glass. When she followed his gaze it was to be confronted by their images, side by side in the mirror.

"Extraordinary," he said abruptly, "isn't it?" and motioned her to go out.

iii

When Martyn went out on the stage, she was able for the first time to see the company assembled together, and found it consisted, as far as the players were concerned, of no more than the six persons she had already encountered: first in their fixed professional poses in the show-frame at the front of the house, and later in their dressing-rooms. She had attached mental tags to them and found herself thinking of Helena Hamilton as the Leading Lady, of Gay Gainsford as the Ingenue, of J. G. Darcey as the Character Actor, of Parry Percival as the Juvenile, of Clark Bennington regrettably, perhaps unjustly, as the Drunken Actor, and of Adam Poole—but as yet she had found no label for Poole, unless it was the old-fashioned one of "Governor," which pleased her by its vicarious association with the days of the Victorian actor-managers.

To this actual cast of six she must add a number of satellite figures— the author, Dr. John Rutherford, whose eccentricities seemed to surpass those of his legend, with which she was already acquainted; the man in the red sweater, who was the stage-manager, and was called Clem Smith; his assistant, a morose lurking figure; and the crew of stage-hands, who went about their business or contemplated the actors with equal detachment.

The actors were forming themselves now into a stage "picture" moving in a workman-like manner under the direction of Adam Poole, and watched with restless attentiveness by an elderly, slack-jointed man, carrying a paint pot and brushes. This man, the last of all the figures to appear upon the stage that morning, seemed to have no recognizable jobs but to be concerned in all of them. He was dressed in overalls and a tartan shirt, from which his long neck emerged, bird-like and crepe-y to terminate in a head that wobbled slightly as if its articulation with the top of the spine had loosened with age. He was constantly addressed with exasperated affection as Jacko. Under his direction, bunches of lights were wheeled into position, cameramen peered and muttered, and at his given signal the players, by an easy transition in behaviour and appearance, became larger than life. A gap was left in the middle of the group, and into this when all was ready floated Helena Hamilton, ruffling her plumage, and becoming at once the focal point of the picture.

"Darling," she said, "it's not going to be a flash, is it, with all of you looking like village idiots, and me like the Third Witch on the morning after the cauldron scene?"

"If you can hold it for three seconds," Adam Poole said, "it needn't be a flash."

"I can hold anything, if you come in and help me."

He moved in beside her. "All right," he said, "let's try it. The end of the first act"; and at once she turned upon him a look of tragic and burning intensity. The elderly man wandered across and tweaked at her skirts. Without changing pose or expression, she said: "Isn't it shameful the way Jacko can't keep his hands off me." He grinned and ambled away. Adam Poole said "Right"; the group froze in postures of urgency that led the eye towards the two central figures and the cameras clicked.

Martyn tried, as the morning wore on, to get some idea of the content of the play, but was unable to do so. Occasionally the players would speak snatches of dialogue leading up to the moment when a photograph was to be taken, and from these she gathered that the major conflict of the theme was between the characters played by Adam Poole and Clark Bennington and that this conflict was one of ideas. About a particular shot there was a great deal of difficulty. In this Poole and Gay Gainsford confronted each other, and it was necessary that her posture, the arrested gesture of her hand, and even her expression should be an exact reflection of his.

To Martyn, Poole had seemed to be a short-tempered man, but with Gay Gainsford he showed exemplary patience. "It's the old story, Gay," he said. "You're over-anxious. It's not enough for you to look like me. Let's face it—" he hesitated for a moment and said quickly: "We've had all this, haven't we—but it's worth repeating—you can't look strikingly like me, although Jacko's done wonders. What you've got to do is to *be* me. At this moment, don't you see, you're my heredity, confronting me like a threat. As far as the photograph is concerned, we can cheat—the shot can be taken over your shoulder, but in the performance there can be no cheating, and that is why I'm making such a thing of it. Now let's take it with the line. Your head's on your arms, you raise it slowly to face me. Ready now. Right, up you come."

Miss Gainsford raised her face to his as he leaned across the writing desk and whispered: "Don't you like what you see?" At the same moment there was a cascade of laughter from Miss Hamilton. Poole's voice cracked like a whip-lash: "Helena, please," and she turned from Parry Percival to say: "Darling, I'm so sorry," and in the same breath spoke her line of dialogue: "But it's you, don't you see? You can't escape from it. It's you." Gay Gainsford made a hopeless little gesture and Poole said: "Too late, of course. Try again."

They tried several times, in an atmosphere of increasing tension. The amiable Jacko was called in to make an infinitesimal change in Gay's make-up, and Martyn saw him blot away a tear. At this juncture a disembodied voice roared from the back of the circle:

"Madam, have comfort: all of us have cause
To wail the dimming of our shining star!"

Poole glanced into the auditorium. "Do shut up like a good chap, John," he said.

"Pour all your tears! I am your sorrow's nurse,
And I will pamper it with la-men-ta-ti-ons."

The man called Jacko burst out laughing and was instantly dismissed to the dressing-rooms by Poole.

There followed a quarter of an hour of mounting hysteria on the part of Gay Gainsford and of implacable persistence from Adam Poole. He said suddenly: "All right, we'll cheat. Shift the camera."

The remaining photographs were taken without a great deal of trouble. Miss Gainsford, looking utterly miserable, went off to her dressing-room. The man called Jacko reappeared and ambled across to Miss Hamilton. There was an adjustment in make-up while Martyn held up the mirror.

"Maybe it's lucky," he said, "you don't have to look like somebody else."

"Are you being nice or beastly, Jacko?"

He put a cigarette between her lips and lit it. "The dresses are good," he said. He had a very slight foreign accent.

"You think so, do you?"

"Naturally. I design them for *you*."

"Next time," she said grimly, "you'd better write the play as well."

He was a phenomenally ugly man, but a smile of extraordinary sweetness broke across his face.

"All these agonies!" he murmured. "And on Thursday night everyone will be kissing everyone else and at the Combined Arts Ball we are in triumph and on Friday morning you will be purring over your notices. And you must not be unkind about the play. It is a good play." He grinned again, more broadly. His teeth were enormous and uneven. "Even the little niece of the great husband cannot entirely destroy it."

"Jacko!"

"You may say what you like, it is not intelligent casting."

"Please, Jacko."

"All right, all right. I remind you instead of the Combined Arts Ball, and that no one has decided in what costume we go."

"Nobody has any ideas. Jacko, you must invent something marvellous."

"And in two days I must also create out of air eight marvellous costumes."

"Darling Jacko, how beastly we are to you. But you know you love performing your little wonders."

"I suggest then, that we are characters from Tchekhov as they would be in Hollywood. You absurdly gorgeous, and the little niece still grimly ingenue. Adam perhaps as Vanya if he were played by Boris Karloff. And so on."

"Where shall I get my absurdly gorgeous dress?"

"I paint the design on canvas and cut it out and if I were introduced to your dresser I would persuade her to sew it up." He took the glass from Martyn and said: "No one makes any introductions in this theatre, so we introduce ourselves to each other. I am Jacques Doré, and you are the little chick whom the stork has brought too late, or dropped into the wrong nest. Really," he said, rolling his eyes at Miss Hamilton, "it is the most remarkable coincidence, if it is a coincidence. I am dropping bricks," he added. "I am a very privileged person but one day I drop an outsize brick, and away I go." He made a circle of his thumb and forefinger and looked through it, as though it were a quizzing-glass, at Martyn. "All the same," he said, "it is a pity you are a little dresser and not a little actress."

iv

Between the photograph call and the dress rehearsal, which was timed for seven o'clock, a state of uneven ferment prevailed at the Vulcan. During the rare occasions on which she had time to reflect, Martyn anticipated a sort of personal zero hour, a moment when she would have to take stock, to come to a decision. She had two and fourpence and no place of abode, and she had no idea when she would be paid, or how much she would get. This moment of reckoning, however, she continually postponed. The problem of food was answered for the moment by the announcement that it would be provided for everyone whose work kept them in the theatre throughout the day. As Miss Hamilton had discovered a number of minor alterations to be made in her dresses, Martyn was of this company. Having by this time realized the position of extraordinary ubiquity held by Jacko, she was not surprised to find him cooking a mysterious but savoury mess over the gas ring in Fred Badger's sinkroom.

This concoction was served in enamel mugs, at odd intervals, to anyone who asked for it, and Martyn found herself eating her share in company with Bob Cringle, Mr. Poole's dresser. From him she learnt more about Mr. Jacques Doré. He was responsible for the décor and dressing of all Poole's productions. His official status was that of assistant to Mr. Poole, but in actual fact he seemed to be a kind of superior odd-job man.

"General dogsbody," Cringle gossiped, "that's what Mr. Jacko is. 'Poole's Luck,' people call him, and if the Guv'nor was superstitious about anything, which 'e is *not,* it would be about Mr. Jacko. The lady's the same. Can't do without 'im. As a matter of fact it's on 'er account 'e sticks it out. You might say 'e's 'er property, a kind of pet, if you like to put it that way. Joined up with 'er and 'is nibs when they was in Canada and the Guv'nor still doing the child-wonder at 'is posh college. 'E's a Canadian-Frenchy, Mr. Jacko is. Twenty years ago that must 'ave been, only don't say I said so. It's what they call dog-like devotion, and that's no error. To 'er, *not* to 'is nibs."

"Do you mean Mr. Bennington?" Martyn ventured.

"Clark Bennington, the distinguished character actor, that's right," said Cringle dryly. Evidently he was not inclined to elaborate this theme. He entertained Martyn, instead, with a lively account of the eccentricities of Dr. John Rutherford. "My oaff," he said, "what a daisy! Did you 'ear 'im chi-iking from the front this morning? Typical! We done three of 'is pieces up to date and never a dull moment. Rows and ructions, ructions and rows from the word go. The Guv'nor puts up with it on account he likes the pieces and what a time 'e 'as with 'im, oh dear! It's something shocking the way Doctor cuts up. Dynamite! This time it's the little lady and 'is nibs and Mr. Parry Profile Percival 'e's got it in for. Can't do nothing to please 'im. You should 'ear 'im at rehearsals. 'You're bastardizing my play,' 'e 'owls. 'Get the 'ell aht of it,' 'e shrieks. You never see such an exhibition. Shocking! Then the Guv'nor shuts 'im up and 'e 'as an attack of the willies or what-have-you and keeps aht of the theaytre for a couple of days. Never longer, though, which is very unfortunate for all concerned."

Martyn tried to find out from Cringle what the play was about. He was not very illuminating. "It's 'igh-brow," he said. "Intellectually, it's clarse. 'A Modern Morality' he calls it, the Doctor does. It's all about whether you're brought up right makes any difference to what your old pot 'ands on to you. ''Eredity versus enviroment' they call it. The Guv'nor's enviroment, and all the rest of 'em's 'eredity. And like it always is in clarse plays, the answer's a lemon. Well, I must go on me way rejoicing."

To Martyn, held as she was in a sort of emotional suspension, the lives and events enclosed within the stage walls and curtain of the Vulcan Theatre assumed a greater reality than her own immediate problem. Her existence since five o'clock the previous afternoon, when she had walked into the theatre, had much of the character and substance of a dream with all the shifting values, the passages of confusion and extreme clarity, which make up the texture of a dream. She was in a state of semi-trauma and found it vaguely agreeable. Her jobs would keep her busy all the afternoon and to-night there was the first dress rehearsal.

She could, she thought, tread water indefinitely, half in and half out of her dream, as long as she didn't come face to face with Mr. Adam Poole in any more looking-glasses.

Chapter III

First Dress Rehearsal

Martyn's official jobs were all finished by about three o'clock, but by some curious process of which she herself was scarcely aware she had by that time turned into a sort of odd-job girl, particularly where Jacko was concerned. He was engaged in re-painting a piece of very modern decoration above the main and central entrance of the second act set.

"It was lousy in the design," he said, "and it was therefore twelve times lousier when it was twelve times bigger, so now I make it a little worse. Before the first dress rehearsal it is a good thing to be at one's wits' ends, or else one would lose them altogether. When there is not a job, I invent it, because after all there must be someone sane to watch the dress rehearsal. Now if you pass me up the pot of pink, I make a very civilized little flourish in the mode of the second act, and we take time off for you to tell me how clever I am, and why you are such a simpleton as to turn yourself into a dresser."

"I wish," Martyn said, "I knew what the play was about. Is it really a modern morality and do you think it good?"

"All good plays are moralities," said Jacko sententiously, and he leant so far back on the top of his step-ladder that Martyn hurriedly grasped it. "And this is a good play with a very old theme." He hesitated for a moment and she wondered if she only imagined that he looked worried. "Here is a selected man with new ideas in conflict with people who have very old ones. Adam is the selected man. He has been brought up on an island by a community of idealists; he represents the value of environment. By his own wish he returns to his original habitat, and there he is confronted by his heredity, in the persons of his great-uncle, who is played by J. G. Darcey, his brilliant but unstable cousin, who is played by Clark Bennington, this cousin's wife, who is Helena, and with whom he falls in love, and their daughter, who is freakishly like him, but vicious, and who represents therefore his inescapable heredity. This wretched girl," Jacko continued with great relish, looking at Martyn out of the corner of his eyes, "is engaged to a nonentity but finds herself drawn by a terrible attraction to Adam himself. She is played by Gay Gainsford. Receive again from me the pink pot, and bestow upon me the brown. As I have recited it to you so baldly, without nuance and without detail, you will say perhaps if Ibsen or Kafka or Brecht or even Sartre had written this play it would be a good one."

Inexplicably, he again seemed to be in some sort of distress. "It has, in fact," he said, "a continental flavour. But for those who have ears to hear and eyes to see, it has a wider implication than I have suggested. It is a tale, in point of fact, about the struggle of the human being in the detestable situation in which from the beginning he has found himself. Now I descend." He climbed down his step-ladder, groaning lamentably. "And now," he said, "we have some light, and we see if what I have done is good. Go out into the front of the house and in a moment I join you."

By the time Martyn reached the sixth row of the stalls the stage was fully illuminated, and for the first time she saw the set for Act II as Jacko had intended it.

It was an interior, simple in design and execution, but with an air of being over-civilized and stale. "They are," Jacko explained, slumping into a seat beside her, "bad people who live in it. They are not bad of their own volition, but because they have been set down in this place by their heredity and cannot escape. And now you say, all this is pretentious nonsense, and nobody will notice my set except perhaps a few oddities who come to first nights and in any case will get it all wrong. And now we wash ourselves and go out to a place where I am known, and we eat a little, and you tell me why you look like a puppy who has found his tail but dare not wag it. Come."

The restaurant where Jacko was known turned out to be hard by the theatre, and situated in a basement. He insisted on paying for a surprisingly good meal, and Martyn's two and fourpence remained in her pocket. Whereas the curiosity of Fred Badger and Bob Cringle, and in some degree of the actors, had been covert and indirect, Jacko's was unblushing and persistent.

"Now," he said, over their coffee, "I ask you my questions. If there is a secret you tell me so, and with difficulty I shut myself up. If not, you confide in me, because everybody in the Vulcan makes me their confidant and I am greatly flattered by this. In any case we remain friends, no bones broken, and we repeat our little outings. How old do you think I am?"

With some embarrassment, Martyn looked at his scrawny neck, at the thin lichen-like growth of fuzz on his head, and at his heavily scored and indented face. "Fifty-seven," she ventured.

"Sixty-two," said Jacko complacently. "I am sixty-two years old, and a bit of a character. I have not the talent to make a character of myself for the people who sit in front, so instead I play to actors. A wheel within wheels. For twenty years I have built up my role of confidant, and now if I wanted to I couldn't leave off. For example, I can speak perfect English, but my accent is a feature of the role of Papa Jacko and must be sustained. Everybody knows it is a game and, amiably, everyone pretends with me. It is all rather ham and jejune, but I hope that you are going to play too."

Martyn thought: "It would be pleasant to tell him: I'm sure he's very nice and so why don't I do it? I suppose it's because he looks so very odd." And whether with uncanny intuition or else by a queer coincidence he said: "I'm not nearly as peculiar as I look." Martyn said tentatively: "But I honestly don't know what you want me to tell you."

On the opposite wall of the restaurant there was a tarnished looking-glass, upon the surface of which someone had half-heartedly painted a number of water-lilies and leaves. Among this growth, as if drowned in Edwardiana, Jacko's and Martyn's faces were reflected. He pointed to hers.

"See," he said. "We rehearse a play for which it is necessary a secondary part actress should resemble, strikingly, the leading man. We have auditions, and from the hundreds of anxious ingenues we select the one who is least unlike him, but she is still very unlike him. Incidentally," Jacko continued, looking Martyn very hard in the eye, "she is the niece of Clark Bennington. She is not very like him, either, which is neither here nor there and perhaps fortunate for her. It is her unlikeness to Adam that we must deplore. Moreover, although I am a genius with make-up, there is very little I can do about it. So we depend instead on reflected emotions and echoed mannerisms. But although she is a nice little actress with a nice small talent, she cannot do this very well either. In the meantime our author, who is a person of unbridled passion where his art is in question, becomes incensed with her performance and makes scenes and everybody except her Uncle Bennington retires into corners and tears pieces of their hair out. The little actress also retires into corners and weeps and is comforted by her Uncle Bennington, who nevertheless knows she is not good.

"Upon this scene there enters, in the guise of a dresser—" he jabbed his finger at the fly-blown mirror— "this. Look at it. If I set out to draw the daughter or the young sister of the leading man, that is what I should draw. Everybody has a look at her and retires again into corners to ask what it is about. Because obviously, she is not a dresser. Is she perhaps—and there are many excited speculations. 'A niece for a niece?' we ask ourselves, and there is some mention of Adam's extreme youth—you must excuse me—and the wrong side of the rose-bush, and everybody says it cannot be an accident and waits to see, except Papa Jacko, whose curiosity will not permit him to wait."

Martyn cried out: "I've never seen him before, except in films in New Zealand. He knows nothing about me at all. Nothing. I came here from New Zealand a fortnight ago and I've been looking for a job ever since. I came to the Vulcan looking for a job, that's all there is about it."

"Did you come looking for the job of dresser to Miss Hamilton?"

"For any job," she said desperately. "I heard by accident about the dresser."

"But it was not to be a dresser that you came all the way from New Zealand, and yet it was to work in the theatre, and so perhaps after all you hoped to be an actress."

"Yes," Martyn said, throwing up her hands, "all right, I hoped to be an actress. But please let's forget all about it. You can't imagine how thankful I am to be a dresser, and if you think I'm secretly hoping Miss Gainsford will get laryngitis or break her leg, you couldn't be more mistaken. I don't believe in fairy-tales."

"What humbugs you all are."

"Who?" she demanded indignantly.

"All you Anglo-Saxons. You humbug even yourselves. Conceive for the moment the *mise-en-scène*, the situation, the coincidence, and have you the cheek to tell me again that you came thirteen thousand miles to be an actress and yet do not wish to play this part? Are you a good actress?"

"Don't," Martyn said, "don't. I've got a job and I'm in a sort of a trance. It makes everything very simple and I don't want to come out of it."

Jacko grinned fiendishly. "Just a little touch of laryngitis?" he suggested.

Martyn got up. "Thank you very much for my nice dinner," she said. "I ought to be getting on with my job."

"Little hypocrite. Or perhaps after all you know already you are a very bad actress."

Without answering she walked out ahead of him, and they returned in silence to the Vulcan.

Timed to begin at seven, the dress rehearsal actually started at ten past eight. They were waiting, it appeared, for the author. Miss Hamilton had no changes in the first act, and told Martyn she might watch from the front. She went out and sat at the back of the stalls near the other dressers. There was a sprinkling of onlookers, two of whom were understudies, in the auditorium. About half-way down the centre-aisle Adam Poole, made up and wearing a dressing-gown, sat between Jacko and a young man whom Martyn supposed to be a secretary. Jacko had told her that Poole's first entrance came at the end of the act. The atmosphere that hangs over all dress rehearsals seeped out into the auditorium. The delay seemed interminable. Poole turned from time to time and peered up towards the circle. At last a door slammed upstairs, somebody floundered noisily down the circle steps, a seat banged and a voice—Dr. John James Rutherford's—shouted:

"Hung be the heavens with black, yield day to
    night!
Comets, importing change of times and states,
Brandish your crystal tresses in the sky,
And with them scourge the bad revolting stars—

Repeat," Dr. Rutherford bawled, leaning over the balustrade, "repeat: *bad revolting stars*. I'm here, my hearties. Take it away and burn it."

Martyn saw Poole grin. "You behave yourself, up there," he said. "Have you got your paper and pencil?"

"I am provided in that kind."

"Good."

The lights went up along the fringe of the curtain, Martyn's flesh began to creep. Poole called "All right," and lit a cigarette. Throughout the auditorium other little flames sprang up, illuminating from below, like miniature footlights, the faces of the watchers in front. A remote voice said: "O.K. Take it away"; a band of gold appeared below the fringe of the curtain, widened and grew to a lighted stage. Parry Percival spoke the opening line of Dr. Rutherford's new play.

Martyn liked the first act. It concerned itself with the group of figures Jacko had already described—the old man, his son, his son's wife, their daughter and her fiancé. They were creatures of convention, the wife alone possessed of some inclination to reach out beyond her enclosed and aimless existence. In his production Adam Poole, with Jacko's décor to help him, delicately underlined the playwright's symbolic treatment of his theme. It was, as all first acts should be, anticipatory in character. The group awaited the arrival of the islander, the man from outside. Their behaviour suggested that of caged creatures who were completely resigned to their confinement, and in his arrival already saw a threat to their tranquillity. Again Helena Hamilton, as the wife, alone suggested, and she did so with great artistry, a kind of awareness of their sterility and decadence. Bennington, as her hard-drinking, brilliant and completely defeated husband, was giving an exciting performance, though at times Martyn wondered if he was not playing against his author's intention. Was he not, with facile bits of business and clever, unexpected inflections, superimposing upon the part a false quality? Wouldn't the audience, against the tenor of the play, find themselves liking this man, and become increasingly tolerant of the very traits with which the author sought to disgust them? As his father, J. G. Darcey seemed to Martyn to follow adequately the somewhat conventional die-hard the author had intended. As the completely colourless, almost puppet-like juvenile, Parry Percival with his magazine-cover looks was exactly right in what actors call a most ungrateful part. She could understand his dislike of it.

Gay Gainsford's entry as the daughter was a delayed one, and try as she might not to anticipate it, Martyn felt a sinking in her midriff when at last towards the end of the act Miss Gainsford came on. It was quite a small part but one of immense importance. Of the entire group, the girl represented the third generation, the most completely lost, and in the writing of her part Rutherford displayed the influence of Existentialism. It was clear that with few lines to carry her she must make her mark, and clever production was written over everything she did. Agitated as she was by Jacko's direct attack, Martyn wondered if she only imagined that there was nothing more than production there, and if Miss Gainsford was really as ill at ease as she herself supposed. A specific gesture had been introduced and was evidently important, a sudden thrust of her fingers through her short hair, and she twice used a phrase—"That was not what I meant"—where in the context it was evidently intended to plant a barb of attention in the minds of the audience. When this moment came, Martyn sensed uneasiness among the actors. She glanced at Poole and saw him make the specific gesture he had given Miss Gainsford, a quick thrust of his fingers through his hair.

At this juncture the voice in the circle ejaculated: "Boo!"

"Quiet!" said Poole.

Miss Gainsford hesitated, looked wretchedly into the auditorium, and lost her words. She was twice prompted before she went on again. Bennington crossed the stage, put his arm about her shoulders and glared into the circle. The prompter once more threw out a line, Miss Gainsford repeated it and they were off again. Poole got up and went back-stage through the pass-door. The secretary leant forward and shakily lit one cigarette from the butt of another. For the life of her, Martyn couldn't resist glancing at Jacko. He was slumped back in his stall with his arms folded—deliberately imperturbable, she felt—putting on an act. The light from the stage caught his emu-like head and, as if conscious of her attention, he rolled his eyes round at her. She hastily looked back at the stage.

With Gay Gainsford's exit, Martyn could have sworn a wave of relaxation blessed the actors. The dialogue began to move forward compactly with a firm upward curve towards some well-designed climax. There was an increase in tempo corresponding with the rising suspense. Martyn's blood tingled and her heart thumped. Through which door would the entrance be made? The players began a complex circling movement accompanied by a sharp crescendo in the dialogue. Up and up it soared. "Now," she thought, "now!" The action of the play was held in suspense, poised and adjusted, and into the prepared silence, with judgement and precision, at the head of Jacko's twisted flight of steps, came Adam Poole.

"Is that an entrance," thought Martyn, pressing her hands together, "or is it an entrance?"

The curtain came down almost immediately. The secretary gathered his notes together and went back-stage. Dr. Rutherford shouted: "Hold your horses," thundered out of the circle, reappeared in the stalls, and plunged through the pass-door to back-stage where he could be heard cruelly apostrophizing the Almighty and the actors. Jacko stretched elaborately and slouched down the centre-aisle, saying into the air as he passed Martyn: "You had better get round for the change."

Horrified, Martyn bolted like a rabbit. When she arrived in the dressing-room she found her employer, with a set face, attempting to unhook an elaborate back fastening. Martyn bleated an apology which was cut short.

"I hope," said Miss Hamilton, "you haven't mistaken the nature of your job, Martyn. You are my dresser and as such are expected to be here, in this dressing-room, whenever I return to it. Do you understand?"

Martyn, feeling very sick, said that she did, and with trembling fingers effected the complicated change. Miss Hamilton was completely silent, and to Martyn, humiliated and miserable, the necessary intimacies of her work were particularly mortifying.

A boy's voice in the passage chanted: "Second act, please. Second act," and Miss Hamilton said: "Have you got everything on-stage for the quick change?"

"I think so, madam."

"Very well." She looked at herself coldly and searchingly in the long glass and added: "I will go out."

Martyn opened the door. Her employer glanced critically at her. "You're as white as a sheet," she said. "What's the matter?"

Martyn stammered: "Am I? I'm sorry, madam. It must have been the first act."

"Did you like it?"

"*Like* it?" Martyn repeated. "Oh yes, I liked it."

"As much as that?" As easily as if she had passed from one room into another, Miss Hamilton re-entered her mood of enchantment. "What a ridiculous child you are," she said. "It's only actresses who are allowed to have temperaments."

She went out to the stage, and as Martyn followed her she was surprised to feel in herself a kind of resistance to this woman who could so easily command her own happiness or misery.

An improvised dressing-room had been built on the stage for the quick change, and in or near it Martyn spent the whole of the second act. She was not sure when the quick change came, and didn't like to ask anybody. She therefore spent the first quarter of an hour on tenterhooks, hearing the dialogue, but not seeing anything of the play.

After a short introductory passage the act opened with a long scene between Helena Hamilton and Adam Poole in which their attraction to each other was introduced and established, and her instinctive struggle against her environment made clear and developed. The scene was admirably played by both of them, and carried the play strongly forward. When Miss Hamilton came off she found her dresser bright-eyed and excited. Martyn managed the change without any blunders and in good time. Miss Hamilton's attention seemed to be divided between her clothes and the scene which was now being played between J. G. Darcey, Poole and her husband. This scene built up into a quarrel between Poole and Bennington which at its climax was broken by Poole saying in his normal voice, "I dislike interrupting dress rehearsals, Ben, but we've had this point over and over again. Please take the line as we rehearsed it."

There was complete silence, perhaps for five seconds, and then, unseen, so that Martyn formed no picture of what he was doing or how he looked, Bennington began to giggle. The sound wavered and bubbled into a laugh. Helena Hamilton whispered: "Oh, my *God!*" and went out toward the stage. Martyn heard the stage-hands who had been moving round the set stop dead as if in suspended animation. She saw Parry Percival, waiting off-stage, turn with a look of elaborate concern toward Miss Hamilton and mime bewilderment.

Bennington's laughter broke down into ungainly speech. "I always say," he said, "there is no future in being an actor-manager unless you arrange things your own way. I want to make this chap a human being. You and John say he's to be a monster. All right, all right, dear boy, I won't offend again. He shall be less human than Caliban, and far less sympathetic."

Evidently Poole was standing inside the entrance nearest to the dressing-room, because Martyn heard Bennington cross the stage and when he spoke again he was quite close to her, and had lowered his voice. "You're grabbing everything, aren't you?" the voice wavered. "On and off stage, as you might say—domestically and professionally. The piratical Mr. Poole."

Poole muttered: "If you are not too drunk to think, we'll go on," and pitching his voice threw out a line of dialogue: "If you knew what you wanted, if there was any object, however silly, behind anything you say or do, I could find some excuse for you—"

Martyn heard Helena Hamilton catch her breath in a sob. The next moment she had flung open the door and had made her entrance.

iii

Through the good offices of Jacko, Martyn was able to watch the rest of the act from the side. Evidently he was determined she should see as much as possible of the play. He sent her round a list, scribbled in an elaborate hand, of the warnings and cues for Miss Hamilton's entrances and exits and times when she changed her dress. *Stand in the O.P. corner*, he had written across the paper, *and think of your sins*. She wouldn't have dared to follow his advice if Miss Hamilton, on her first exit, had not said with a sort of irritated good nature: "You needn't wait in the dressing-room perpetually. Just be ready for me, that's all."

So she stood in the shadows of the O.P. corner and saw the one big scene between Adam Poole and Gay Gainsford. The author's intention was clear enough. In this girl, the impure flower of her heredity, the most hopelessly lost of all the group, he sought to show the obverse side of the character Poole presented. She was his twisted shadow, a spiritual incubus. In everything she said and did the audience must see a distortion of Poole himself, until at the end they faced each other across the desk, as in the scene that had been photographed, and Helena Hamilton re-entered to speak the line of climax: *"But it's you, don't you see? You can't escape from it. It's you,"* and the curtain came down.

Gay Gainsford was not good enough. It was not only that she didn't resemble Poole closely: her performance was too anxious, too careful a reproduction of mannerisms without a flame to light them. Martyn burnt in her shadowy corner. The transparent covering in which, like a sea-creature, she had spent her twenty-four hours respite now shrivelled away and she was exposed to the inexorable hunger of an unsatisfied player.

She didn't see Bennington until he put his hand on her arm as the curtain came down, and he startled her so much that she cried out and backed away from him.

"So you think you could do it, dear, do you?" he said.

Martyn stammered: "I'm sorry. Miss Hamilton will want me," and dodged past him towards the improvised dressing-room. He followed, and with a conventionally showy movement barred her entrance.

"Wait a minute, *wait* a minute," he said. "I want to talk to you."

She stood there, afraid of him, conscious of his smell of grease-paint and alcohol, and thinking him a ridiculous as well as an alarming person.

"I'm *so* angry," he said conversationally, "just literally so angry that I'm afraid you're going to find me quite a difficult man. And now we've got that ironed out perhaps you'll tell me who the bloody hell you are."

"You know who I am," Martyn said desperately. "Please let me go in."

"M'wife's dresser?"

He took her chin in his hand and twisted her face to the light. Poole came round the back of the set. Martyn thought: "He'll be sick of the sight of me. Always getting myself into stupid little scenes." Bennington's hand felt wet annd hot round her chin.

"M'wife's dresser," he repeated. "And m'wife's lover's little by-blow. That the story?"

Poole's hand dropped on his arm. "In you go," he said to Martyn, and twisted Bennington away from the door. Martyn slipped through and he shut it behind her. She heard him say: "You're an offensive fellow in your cups, Ben. We'll have this out after rehearsal. Get along and change for the third act."

There was a moment's pause. The door opened and he looked in.

"Are you all right?" he asked.

"Perfectly, thank you," Martyn said, and in an agony of embarrassment added: "I'm sorry to be a nuisance, sir."

"Oh, don't be an ass," he said with great ill humour. The next moment he had gone.

Miss Hamilton, looking desperately worried, came in to change for the third act.

iv

The dress rehearsal ended at midnight in an atmosphere of acute tension. Because she had not yet been paid, Martyn proposed to sleep again in the Greenroom. So easily do our standards adjust themselves to our circumstances that whereas on her first night at the Vulcan the Greenroom had seemed a blessed haven, her hours of precarious security had bred a longing for a bed and ordered cleanliness, and she began to dread the night.

In groups and singly, the actors and stage-staff drifted away. Their voices died out in the alley and passages, and she saw, with dismay, that Fred Badger had emerged from the door of his cubby-hole and now eyed her speculatively. Desolation and fear possessed Martyn. With a show of preoccupation, she hurried away to Miss Hamilton's dressing-room, which she had already set in order. Here she would find a moment's respite. Perhaps in a few minutes she would creep down the passage and lock herself in the empty room and wait there until Fred Badger had gone his rounds. He would think she had found a lodging somewhere and left the theatre. She opened the door of Miss Hamilton's room and went in.

Adam Poole was sitting in front of the gas fire.

Martyn stammered: "I'm sorry," and made for the door.

"Come in," he said and stood up. "I want to see you for a moment."

"Well," Martyn thought sickly, "this is it. I'm to go."

He twisted the chair round and ordered rather than invited her to sit in it. As she did so she thought: "I won't be able to sleep here to-night. When he's sacked me I'll get my suitcase and ask my way to the nearest women's hostel. I'll walk alone through the streets and when I get there the hostel will be shut."

He had turned his back to her and seemed to be examining something on the dressing-shelf.

"I would very much rather have disregarded this business," he said irritably, "but I suppose I can't. For one thing, someone should apologize to you for Bennington's behaviour. He's not likely to do it for himself."

"It really didn't matter."

"Of course it mattered," he said sharply. "It was insufferable. For both of us."

She was too distressed to recognize as one of pleasure the small shock this last phrase gave her.

"You realize, of course, how this nonsense started," he was saying. "You've seen something of the play. You've seen me. It's not a matter for congratulation, I dare say, but you're like enough to be my daughter. You're a New Zealander, I understand. How old are you?"

"Nineteen, sir."

"You needn't bother to pepper your replies with this 'sir' business. It's not in character and it's entirely unconvincing. I'm thirty-eight. I toured New Zealand in my first job twenty years ago, and Bennington was in the company. That, apparently, is good enough for him. Under the circumstances, I hope you won't mind my asking you who your parents are and where you were born."

"I've no objection whatever," said Martyn with spirit. "My father was Martin Tarne. He was the son and grandson of a high-country runholder—a sheepfarmer—in the South Island. He was killed on Crete."

He turned and looked directly at her for the first time since she had come into the room.

"I see. And your mother?"

"She's the daughter of a run-holder in the same district."

"Do you mind telling me her maiden name, if you please?"

Martyn said: "I don't see what good this will do."

"Don't you, indeed? Don't you, after all, resent the sort of conjecture that's brewing among these people?"

"I certainly haven't the smallest desire to be thought your daughter."

"And I couldn't agree more. Good Lord!" he said. "This is a fatheaded way for us to talk. Why don't you want to tell me your mother's maiden name? What was the matter with it?"

"She always thought it sounded silly. It was Paula Poole Passington."

He brought the palm of his hand down crisply on the back of her chair. "And why in the world," he asked, "couldn't you say so at once?" Martyn was silent. "Paula Poole Passington," he repeated. "All right. An old cousin of my father's—Cousin Paula—married someone called Passington and disappeared. I suppose to New Zealand. Why didn't she look me up when I went out there?"

"I believe she didn't care for theatricals," said Martyn. "She was my grandmother. The connection is really quite distant."

"You might at least have mentioned it."

"I preferred not to."

"Too proud?"

"If you like," she said desperately.

"Why did you come to England?"

"To earn my living."

"As a dresser?" She was silent. "Well?" he said.

"As best I could."

"As an actress? Oh, for God's sake," he added, "it's damnably late and I'll be obliged if you'll behave reasonably. I may tell you I've spoken to Jacko. Don't you think you're making an ass of yourself? All this mystery act!"

Martyn got up and faced him. "I'm sorry," she said. "It's a silly business but it's not an act. I didn't want to make a thing of it. I joined an English touring company in New Zealand a year ago and they took me on with them to Australia."

"What company was this? What parts did you play?"

She told him.

"I heard about the tour," he said. "They were a reasonably good company."

"They paid quite well and I did broadcasting too. I saved up enough to keep me in England for six months and got a job as assistant children's minder on a ship coming here. Perhaps I should explain that my father lost pretty well everything in the slump, and we are poor people. I had my money in traveller's cheques and the day we landed they were stolen out of my bag, together with my letters of introduction. The bank will probably be able to stop them and let me have it back, but until they decide, I'm hard up. That's all."

"How long have you been here?"

"A fortnight."

"Where have you tried?"

"Agencies. All the London theatres, I think."

"This one last? Why?"

"One of them had to be last."

"Did you know of this—connection—as you call it?"

"Yes. My mother knew of it."

"And the resemblance?"

"I—we saw your pictures—people sometimes said—"

They looked at each other, warily, with guarded interest.

"And you deliberately fought shy of this theatre because you knew I was playing here?"

"Yes."

"Did you know about this piece? The girl's part?"

Martyn was beginning to be very tired. A weariness of spirit and body seeped up through her being in a sluggish tide. She was near to tears and thrust her hand nervously through her short hair. He made some kind of ejaculation and she said at once: "I didn't mean to do that."

"But you knew about the part when you came here?"

"There's a lot of gossip at the agencies when you're waiting. A girl I stood next to in the queue at Garnet Marks's told me they wanted someone at the Vulcan who could be made up to look like you. She'd got it all muddled up with yesterday's auditions for the touring company in another piece."

"So you thought you'd try?"

"Yes. I was a bit desperate by then. I thought I'd try."

"Without, I suppose, mentioning this famous 'connection'?"

"Yes."

"And finding there was nothing for you in the piece you applied for the job of dresser?"

"Yes."

"Well," he said, "it's fantastic, but at least it's less fantastic than pure coincidence would have been. One rather respects you by the way, if it's not impertinent in a second cousin once removed to say so."

"Thank you," she said vaguely.

"The question is, what are we going to do about it?"

Martyn turned away to the ranks of dresses, and with business-like movements of her trembling hands tweaked at the sheets that covered them. She said briskly: "I realize of course that I'll have to go. Perhaps Miss Hamilton—"

"You think you ought to go?" his voice said behind her. "I suppose you're right. It's an awkward business."

"I'm sorry."

"But I'd like to—it's difficult to suggest—"

"I'll be perfectly all right," she said with savage brightness. "Please don't give it another thought."

"Why, by the way, are you still in the theatre?"

"I was going to sleep here," Martyn said loudly. "I did last night. The night-watchman knows."

"You would be paid on Friday."

"Like the actors?"

"Certainly. How much is there in the exchequer between now and Friday?" Martyn was silent and he said with a complete change of voice: "My manners, you will already have been told, are notoriously offensive, but I don't believe I was going to say anything that would have offended you."

"I've got two and fourpence."

He opened the door and shouted "Jacko!" into the echoing darkness. She heard the Greenroom door creak and in a moment or two Jacko came in. He carried a board with a half-finished drawing pinned to it. This he exhibited to Poole. "Crazy, isn't it?" he said. "Helena's costume for the ball. What must I do but waste my beauty-sleep concocting it. Everybody will have to work very hard if it is to be made. I see you are in need of counsel. What goes on?"

"Against my better judgement," Poole said, "I'm going to follow your advice. You always think you're indispensable at auditions. Give me some light out there and then sit in front."

"It is past midnight. This child has worked and worried herself into a complete *bouleversement*. She is as pale as a Pierrot."

Poole looked at her. "Are you all right?" he asked her. "It won't take ten minutes."

"I don't understand, but I'm all right."

"There you are, Jacko," Poole said and sounded pleased. "It's over to you."

Jacko took her by the shoulders and gently pushed her down on the chair. "*Attention*," he said. "We make a bargain. I live not so far from here in an apartment house kept by a well-disposed French couple. An entirely respectable house, you understand, with no funny business. At the top one finds an attic room as it might be in a tale for children, and so small, it is but twice the size of its nice little bed. The rental is low, within the compass of a silly girl who gets herself into equivocal situations. At my recommendation she will be accommodated in the attic, which is included in my portion of the house, and will pay me the rent at the end of a week. But in exchange for my good offices she does for us a little service. Again, no funny business."

"Oh, dear!" Martyn said. She leant towards the dressing-shelf and propped her face in her hands. "It sounds so wonderful," she said and tried to steady her voice, "a nice little bed."

"All right, Jacko," Poole said. She heard the door open and shut. "I want you to relax for a few minutes," his voice went on. "Relax all over like a cat. Don't think of anything in particular. You're going to sleep sound to-night. All will be well."

The gas fire hummed, the smell of roses and cosmetics filled the warm room. "Do you smoke?" Poole asked.

"Sometimes."

"Here you are."

She drew in the smoke gratefully. He went into the passage and she watched him light his own cigarette. Her thoughts drifted aimlessly about the bony structure of his head and face. Presently a stronger light streamed down the passage. Jacko's voice called something from a great distance.

Poole turned to her. "Come along," he said.

On the stage, dust-thickened rays from pageant-lamps settled in a pool of light about a desk and two chairs. It was like an island in a vague region of blueness. She found herself seated there at the desk, facing him across it. In response to a gesture of Poole's she rested her arms on the desk and her face on her arms.

"Listen," he said, "and don't move. You are in the hall of an old house, beautiful but decaying. You are the girl with the bad heredity. You are the creature who goes round and round in her great empty cage like a stoat filled with a wicked little desire. The object of your desire is the man on the other side of the desk, who is joined to you in blood and of whose face and mind you are the ill reflection. In a moment you will raise your face to his. He will make a gesture and you will make the same gesture. Then you will say: 'Don't you like what you see?' It must be horrible and real. Don't move. Think it. Then raise your head and speak."

There was a kind of voluptuousness in Martyn's fatigue. Only the chair she sat on and the desk that propped her arms and head prevented her, she felt, from slipping to the floor. Into this defencelessness Poole's suggestions entered like those of a mesmerist, and that perfection of duality for which actors pray and which they are so rarely granted now fully invested her. She was herself and she was the girl in the play. She guided the girl and was aware of her and she governed the possession of the girl by the obverse of the man in the play. When at last she raised her face and looked at him and repeated his gesture it seemed to her that she looked into a glass and saw her own reflection and spoke to it.

"Don't you like what you see?" Martyn said.

In the pause that followed, the sound of her own breathing and Poole's returned. She could hear her heart beat.

"Can you do it again?" he said.

"I don't know," she said helplessly. "I don't know at all." She turned away and with a childish gesture hid her face in the crook of her arm. In dismay and shame she let loose the tears she had so long denied herself.

"There, now!" he said, not so much as if to comfort her as to proclaim some private triumph of his own. Out in the dark auditorium Jacko struck his hands together once.

Poole touched her shoulder. "It's nothing," he said. "These are growing pains. They will pass." From the door in the set he said: "You can have the understudy. We'll make terms to-morrow. If you prefer it, the relationship can be forgotten. Good night."

He left her alone and presently Jacko returned to the stage carrying her suitcase.

"Now," he said, "we go home."

Chapter IV

Second Dress Rehearsal

When Martyn opened her eyes on the second morning of her adventure it was with the sensation of having come to rest after a painful journey. At first the events of the previous night seemed to be incorporated in the sleep that had followed them, and her happiness had something of the precarious and transitory quality of a remembered dream. It was difficult to believe that nine hours ago she had faced Adam Poole across a table on the stage of the Vulcan Theatre and had done so, for the moment at least, as an actress. The subsequent drive in a taxi with the unusually silent Jacko, their entrance into a sleeping house, creaking tiptoe up the stairs, the rapture of a hot bath and her subsequent oblivion—all these events flowed together in her memory and she felt she was as yet neither asleep nor fully wakened.

She lay quiet and looked about her. It was a bright morning and the sun came in at the attic window above her bed. The room had an air of great cleanliness and freshness. She remembered now that Jacko had told her he occasionally made use of it and indeed, tiny as it was, it bore his eccentric imprint. A set of designs for *Twelfth Night* was pinned to a wall-board. Ranged along the shelf were a number of figures dressed in paper as the persons in the play and on the wall facing her bed hung a mask of the fool, Feste, looking very like Jacko himself.

"There never was such a little room," Martyn sighed, and began to plan how she would collect and stow away her modest belongings. She was filled with gratitude and with astonished humility.

The bathroom was on the next floor and as she went downstairs she smelt coffee and fresh bread. A door on the landing opened and Jacko's clownish head looked out.

"Breakfast in ten minutes," he said. "Speed is essential."

Of all the amenities, it seemed to Martyn, a hot bath was the most beneficent, and after that a shower under which one could wash one's hair quickly. "Lucky it's short," she thought, and rubbed it dry with her towel.

She was out again in eight minutes to find Jacko on the landing.

"Good," he said. "In your woollen gown you are entirely respectable. A clean school-child. In."

He marshalled her into a largish room set out in an orderly manner as a workshop. Martyn wondered why Jacko, who showed such exquisite neatness in his work, should in his person present such a wild front to the world. He was dressed now in faded cotton trousers, a paint-stained undervest and a tattered dressing-gown. He was unshaven and uncombed and his prominent eyes were slightly bloodshot. His manner, however, was as usual amiable and disarming.

"I propose," he said, "that we breakfast together as a general rule. A light breakfast and supper are included in the arrangement. You will hand me your ration book and I shall shop with discretion. Undoubtedly I am a better cook than you and will therefore make myself responsible for supper. For luncheon you may return if you wish and forage ineffectually for yourself or make what other arrangement seems good to you. Approved?"

Martyn said carefully: "If you please, Jacko, I'm so grateful and so muddled I can't think at all sensibly. You see, I don't know what I shall be earning."

"For your dual and unusual role of understudy and dresser, I imagine about eight pounds a week. Your rental, *demi-pension*, here is two."

"It seems so little," Martyn said timidly. "The rent, I mean."

Jacko tapped the side of the coffee-pot with a spoon.

"*Attention,*" he said. "How often must I repeat. You will have the goodness to understand I am not a dirty old man. It is true that I am virile," he continued with some complacency, "but you are not my type. I prefer the more mature, the more *mondaine*, the—" He stopped short, the spoon with which he had been gesticulating still held aloft. His eyes were fixed on the wall behind Martyn. She turned her head to see a sketch in water-colour of Helena Hamilton. When she faced Jacko again, he was grinning desperately.

"Believe me," he said, "you are in no danger of discomfort from the smallest whisper of scandal. I am notoriously pure. This morning there are eggs and therefore an omelette. Let us observe silence while I make it."

He was gay, in his outlandish fashion, from then onwards. When they had finished their admirable breakfast she helped him wash up and he gave her what he called her orders for the day. She was to go down to the theatre with him, set about her work as a dresser, and at three o'clock she would be given a formal rehearsal as understudy. At night, for the second dress rehearsal, she would again take up her duties as Miss Hamilton's dresser.

"An eccentric arrangement," Jacko said. He groped in the bosom of his undervest and produced a somewhat tattered actor's "part," typewritten and bound in paper. "Only thirteen sides," he said. "A bit-part. You will study the lines while you press and stitch and by this afternoon you are word-perfect, isn't it? You are, of course, delighted?"

"Delighted," Martyn said, "is not exactly the word. I'm flabbergasted and excited and grateful for everything and I just can't believe it's true. But it is a bit worrying to feel I've sort of got in on a fluke and that everybody's wondering what it's all about. They are, you know."

"All that," Jacko said, with an ungainly sweep of his arm, "is of no importance. Gay Gainsford is still to play the part. She will not play it well but she is the niece of the leading lady's husband and she is therefore in a favourable position."

"Yes, but her uncle—"

He said quickly: "Clark Bennington was once a good actor. He is now a stencil. He drinks too much and when he is drunk he is offensive. Forget him." He turned away and with less than his usual deftness began to set out his work-table. Finally, from an adjoining room he said indistinctly: "I advise that which I find difficult to perform. Do not allow yourself to become hag-ridden by this man. It is a great mistake. I myself—" His voice was lost in the spurt of running water. Martyn heard him shout: "Run off and learn your lines. I have a job in hand."

With a feeling of unease she returned to her room. But when she opened her part and began to read the lines, this feeling retreated until it hung like a very small cloud over the hinterland of her mind. The foreground was occupied entirely by the exercise of memorizing and in a few minutes she had almost, but not quite, forgotten her anxiety.

ii

She was given her moves that afternoon by the stage-manager, and at three o'clock rehearsed her scenes with the other two understudies. The remaining parts were read from the script. Jacko pottered about backstage intent on one of his odd jobs: otherwise the theatre seemed to be deserted. Martyn had memorized her lines but inevitably lost them from time to time in her effort to associate them with physical movement. The uncompromising half-light of a working-stage, the mechanical pacing to-and-fro of understudies, the half-muted lines raised to concert-pitch only for cues, and the dead sound of voices in an empty house—all these workaday circumstances, though she was familiar enough with them, after all, laid a weight upon her: she lost her belief in the magic of the previous night. She was oppressed by this anti-climax, and could scarcely summon up the resources of her young experience to meet it.

The positions and moves had been planned with a vivid understanding of the text and seemed to spring out of it. She learnt them readily enough. Rather to her surprise, and, she thought, that of the other understudies, they were finally taken through her scenes at concert-pitch, so that by the end of the rehearsal the visual and aural aspects of her part had fused into a whole. She had got her routine. But it was no more than a routine: she spoke and paused and moved and spoke and there was no reality at all, she felt, in anything she did. Clem Smith, the stage-manager, said nothing about interpretation but, huddled in his overcoat, merely set the moves and then crouched over the script. She was not even a failure, she was just another colourless understudy and nothing had happened.

When it was over, Clem Smith shut the book and said: "Thank you, ladies and gentlemen. Eleven in the morning, if you please." He lit a cigarette and went down into the auditorium and out through the front of the house.

Left alone on the stage, Martyn struggled with an acute attack of deflation. She tried to call herself to order. This in itself was a humiliating, if salutary, exercise. If, she thought savagely, she had been a Victorian young lady, she would at this juncture have locked herself away with a plush-bound journal and, after shedding some mortified tears, forced a confession out of herself. As it was, she set her jaw and worked it out there and then. The truth was, she told herself, she'd been at her old tricks again: she'd indulged in the most blatant kind of daydream. She'd thought up a success-story and dumped herself down in the middle of it with half a dozen pageant-lamps bathing her girlish form. Because she looked like Poole and because last night she'd had a mild success with one line by playing it off her nerves she'd actually had the gall to imagine— Here Martyn felt her scalp creep and her face burn. "Come on," she thought, "out with it."

Very well, then. She'd dreamt up a further rehearsal with Poole. She'd seen herself responding eagerly to his production, she'd heard him say regretfully that if things had been different— She had even— At this point, overtaken with self-loathing, Martyn performed the childish exercise of throwing her part across the stage, stamping violently and thrusting her fingers through her hair.

"Damn and blast and hell," said Martyn, pitching her voice to the back row of the gallery.

"Not quite as bad as all that."

Adam Poole came out of the shadowed pit and down the centre-aisle of the stalls. He rested his hands on the rail of the orchestral well. Martyn gaped at him.

"You've got the mechanics," he said. "Walk through it again by yourself before to-morrow. Then you can begin to think about the girl. Get the lay-out of the house into your head. Know your environment. What has she been doing all day before the play opens? What has she been thinking about? Why does she say the things she says and do the things she does? Listen to the other chaps' lines. Come down here for five minutes and we'll see what you think about acting."

Martyn went down into the house. Of all her experience during these three days at the Vulcan Theatre, she was to remember this most vividly. It was a curious interview. They sat side by side as if waiting for the rise-of-curtain. Their voices were deadened by the plush stalls. Jacko could be heard moving about behind the set and in some distant room back-stage, somebody in desultory fashion hammered and sawed. At first Martyn was ill at ease, unable to dismiss or to reconcile the jumble of distracted notions that beset her. But Poole was talking about theatre and about problems of the actor. He talked well, without particular emphasis but with penetration and authority. Soon she listened with single hearing and with all her attention to what he had to say. Her nervousness and uncertainty were gone, and presently she was able to speak of matters that had exercised her in her own brief experience of the stage. Their conversation was adult and fruitful. It didn't even occur to her that they were getting on rather well together.

Jacko came out on the stage. He shielded his eyes with his hand and peered into the auditorium.

"Adam?" he said.

"Hullo? What is it?"

"It is Helena on the telephone to inquire why have you not rung her at four, the time being now five-thirty. Will you take it in the office?"

"Good Lord!" he ejaculated and got up. Martyn moved into the aisle to let him out.

He said: "All right, Miss Tarne. Work along the lines we've been talking about and you should be able to cope with the job. We take our understudies seriously at the Vulcan and like to feel they're an integral

part of the company. You'll rehearse again tomorrow morning and—"
He stopped unaccountably, and after a moment said hurriedly: "You're
all right, aren't you? I mean you feel quite happy about this arrangement?"

"Yes," she said. "Very happy."

"Good." He hesitated again for a second and then said: "I must go,"
and was off down the aisle to the front of the house. He called out: "I'll
be in the office for some time, Jacko, if anyone wants me."

A door banged. There was a long silence.

Jacko advanced to the footlights. "Where are you?" he asked.

"Here," said Martyn.

"I see you. Or a piece of you. Where is the rest? Reassemble yourself. There is work to be done."

The work turned out to be the sewing together of a fantastic garment
created and tacked up by Jacko himself. It had a flamboyant design,
stencilled in black and yellow, of double-headed eagles, and was made
in part of scenic canvas. There was an electric sewing machine in the
wardrobe-room, which was next to Mr. J. G. Darcey's at the end of the
passage. Here Jacko sat Martyn down, and here for the next hour she
laboured under his exacting direction while he himself crawled about
the floor cutting out further garments for the Combined Arts Ball. At
half past six he went out, saying he would return with food.

Martyn laboured on. Sometimes she repeated the lines of the part,
her voice drowned by the clatter of the machine. Sometimes, when engaged in hand-work, it would seem in the silent room that she had entered into a new existence, as if she had at that moment been born and
was a stranger to her former self. And since this was rather a frightening sensation, though not new to Martyn, she must rouse herself and
make a conscious effort to dispel it. On one of these occasions, when
she had just switched off the machine, she felt something of the impulse
that had guided her first attempt at the scene with Poole. Wishing to re-
tain and strengthen this experience, she set aside her work and rested
her head on her arms as the scene required. She waited in this posture,
summoning her resources, and when she was ready raised her head to
confront her opposite.

Gay Gainsford stood on the other side of the table, watching her.

iii

Martyn's flesh leapt on her bones. She cried out and made a sweeping
gesture with her arms. A pair of scissors clattered to the floor.

"I'm sorry I startled you," said Miss Gainsford. "I came in quietly. I thought you were asleep but I realize now—you were doing that scene. Weren't you?"

"I've been given the understudy," Martyn said.

"You've had an audition and a rehearsal, haven't you?"

"Yes. I was so frightful at rehearsal, I thought I'd have another shot by myself."

"You needn't," Miss Gainsford said, "try to make it easy for me."

Martyn, still shaken and bewildered, looked at her visitor. She saw a pretty face that under its make-up was sodden with tears. Even as she looked, the large photogenic eyes flooded and the small mouth quivered.

"I suppose," Miss Gainsford said, "you know what you're doing to me."

"Good Lord!" Martyn ejaculated. "What *is* all this? What have I done? I've got your understudy. I'm damn thankful to have it and so far I've made a pretty poor showing."

"It's no good taking that line with me. I know what's happening."

"Nothing's happening. Oh, *please,*" Martyn implored, torn between pity and a rising fear, "*please* don't cry. I'm nothing. I'm just an old understudy."

"That's pretty hot, I must say," Miss Gainsford said. Her voice wavered grotesquely between two registers like an adolescent boy's. "To talk about 'an old understudy' when you've got that appearance. What's everyone saying about you when they think I'm not about? 'She's got the appearance!' It doesn't matter to them that I've had to dye my hair because they don't like wigs. I still haven't got the appearance. I'm a shoulder-length natural ash-blonde, and I've had to have an urchin cut and go black and all I get is insults. In any other management," she continued wildly, "the author wouldn't be allowed to speak to the artists as that man speaks to me. In any other management an artist would be protected against that kind of treatment. Adam's worse, if anything. He's so bloody patient and persistent and half the time you don't know what he's talking about."

She drew breath, sobbed and hunted in her bag for her handkerchief.

Martyn said: "I'm so terribly sorry. It's awful when things go badly at rehearsals. But the worst kind of rehearsals *do* have a way of turning into the best kind of performances. And it's a grand play, isn't it?"

"I loathe the play. To me it's a lot of high-brow hokum and I don't care who knows it. Why the hell couldn't Uncle Ben leave me where I was, playing leads and second leads in fortnightly rep? We were a happy family in fortnightly rep; everyone had fun and games and there wasn't this ghastly graveyard atmosphere. I was miserable enough, God knows, before you came but now it's just *more* than I can stand."

"But I'm not going to play the part," Martyn said desperately. "You'll be all right. It's just got you down for the moment. I'd be no good, I expect, anyway."

"It's what they're all saying and thinking. Its a pity, they're saying, that you came too late."

"Nonsense. You only imagine that because of the likeness."

"Do I? Let me tell you I'm not imagining *all* the things they're saying about you. And about Adam. How you *can* stay here and take it! Unless it's true. *Is* it true?"

Martyn closed her hands on the material she had been sewing. "I don't want to know what they're saying. There's nothing unkind that's true for them to say."

"So the likeness is purely an accident? There's no relationship?"

Martyn said: "It seems that we are very distantly related, so distantly that the likeness is a freak. I didn't want to tell anyone about it. It's of no significance at all. I haven't used it to get into the theatre."

"I don't know how and why you got in but I wish to God you'd get out. How you *can* hang on, knowing what they think, if it isn't true! You can't have any pride or decency. It's so cruel. It's so *damnably* cruel."

Martyn looked at the pretty tear-blubbered face and thought in terror that if it had been that of Atropos it could scarcely have offered a more dangerous threat. "Don't!" she cried out. "Please don't say that; I need this job so desperately. Honestly, *honestly* you're making a thing of all this. I'm not hurting you."

"Yes, you are. You're driving me completely frantic. I'm nervously and emotionally exhausted," Miss Gainsford sobbed, with an air of quoting somebody else. "It just needed you to send me over the border-line. Uncle Ben keeps on and on and on about it until I think I'll go mad. This is a beastly unlucky theatre anyway. Everyone knows there's something wrong about it and then you come in like a Jonah and it's the rock *bottom*. If," Miss Gainsford went on, developing a command of histrionic climax of which Martyn would scarcely have suspected her capable, "if you have *any* pity at all, *any* humanity, you'll spare me this awful ordeal."

"But this is all nonsense. You're making a song about nothing. I won't be taken in by it," Martyn said and recognized defeat in her own voice.

Miss Gainsford stared at her with watery indignation and through trembling lips uttered her final cliché. "You can't," she said, "do this thing to me," and broke down completely.

It seemed to Martyn that beyond a facade of stock emotionalism she recognized a real and a profound distress. She thought confusedly that if they had met on some common and reasonable ground she would have been able to put up a better defence. As it was they merely floundered in a welter of unreason. It was intolerably distressing to her. Her precarious happiness died, she wanted to escape, she was lost. With a feeling of nightmarish detachment she heard herself say: "All right. I'll speak to Mr. Poole. I'll say I can't do the understudy."

Miss Gainsford had turned away. She held her handkerchief to her face. Her shoulders and head had been quivering but now they were still. There was a considerable pause. She blew her nose fussily, cleared her throat, and looked up at Martyn.

"But if you're Helena's dresser," she said, "you'll still be *about*."

"You can't mean you want to turn me out of the theatre altogether."

"There's no need," Miss Gainsford mumbled, "to put it like that."

Martyn heard a voice and footsteps in the passage. She didn't want to be confronted with Jacko. She said: "I'll see if Mr. Poole's still in the theatre. I'll speak to him now if he is."

As she made for the door Miss Gainsford snatched at her arm. "Please!" she said. "I *am* grateful. But you will be really generous won't you? Really big? You won't bring me into it, will you? With Adam I mean. Adam wouldn't underst—"

Her face set as if she had been held in suspension, like a motion picture freezing into a still. She didn't even release her hold on Martyn's arm.

Martyn spun round and saw Poole, with Jacko behind him, in the passage. To her own astonishment she burst out laughing.

"No, really!" she stammered. "It's too much! This is the third time. Like the demon-king in pantomime."

"What the devil do you mean?"

"I'm sorry. It's just your flair for popping up in crises. Other people's crises. Mine, in fact."

He grimaced as if he gave her up as a bad job. "What's the present crisis?" he said and looked at Miss Gainsford, who had turned aside and was uneasily painting her mouth. "What is it, Gay?"

"Please!" she choked. "Please let me go. I'm all right, really. Quite all right. I just rather want to be alone."

She achieved a tearful smile at Poole and an imploring glance at

Martyn. Poole stood away from the door and watched her go out with her chin up and with courageous suffering neatly portrayed in every inch of her body.

She disappeared into the passage and a moment later the door of the Greenroom was heard to shut.

"It is a case of mis-casting," said Jacko, coming into the room. "She should be in Hollywood. She has what it takes in Hollywood. What an exit! We have misjudged her."

"Go and see what's the matter."

"She wants," said Jacko, making a dolorous face, "to be alone."

"No, she doesn't. She wants an audience. You're it. Get along and do your stuff."

Jacko put several parcels on the table. "I am the dogsbody," he said, "to end all dogsbodies," and went out.

"Now, then," Poole said.

Martyn gathered up her work and was silent.

"What's the matter? You're as white as a sheet. Sit down. What is all this?"

She sat behind the machine.

"Come on," he said.

"I'm sorry if it's inconvenient for you but I'm afraid I've got to give notice."

"Indeed? As a dresser or as understudy?"

"As both."

"It's extremely inconvenient and I don't accept it."

"But you must. Honestly, you must. I can't go on like this: it isn't fair."

"Do you mean because of that girl?"

"Because of her and because of everything. She'll have a breakdown. There'll be some disaster."

"She doesn't imagine you're going to be given the part over her head, does she?"

"No, no, of course not. It's just that she's finding it hard anyway and the—the sight of me sort of panics her."

"The likeness?"

"Yes."

"She needn't look at you. I'm afraid she's the most complete ass, that girl," he muttered. He picked up a fold of the material Martyn had been sewing, looked absently at it and pushed the whole thing across the table. "Understand," he said, "I won't for a second entertain the idea of your going. For one thing Helena can't do without you, and for another

I will not be dictated to by a minor actress in my own company. Nor," he added with a change of tone, "by anyone else."

"I'm so terribly sorry for her," Martyn said. "She feels there's some sort of underground movement against her. She really feels it."

"And you?"

"I must admit I don't much enjoy the sensation of being in the theatre on sufferance. But I was so thankful—" She caught her breath and stopped.

"Who makes you feel you're on sufferance? Gay? Bennington? Percival?"

"I used a silly phrase. Naturally, they all must think it a bit queer, my turning up. It *looks* queer."

"It'd look a damn sight queerer if you faded out again. I can't think," he said impatiently, "how you could let yourself be bamboozled by that girl."

"But it's *not* all bamboozle. She really is at the end of her tether."

Martyn waited for a moment. She thought inconsequently how strange it was that she should talk like this to Adam Poole, who two days ago had been a celebrated name, a remote legend, seen and heard and felt through a veil of characterization in his films.

"Oh, well," she thought and said aloud: "I'm thinking of the show. It's such a good play. She mustn't be allowed to fail. I'm thinking about that."

He came nearer and looked at her with a sort of incredulity. "Good Lord," he said, "I believe you are! Do you mean to say you haven't considered your own chance if she did crack up? Where's your wishful thinking?"

Martyn slapped her palm down on the table. "But of course I have. Of course I've done my bit of wishful thinking. But don't you see—"

He reached across the table and for a brief moment his hand closed over hers. "I think I do," he said. "I'm beginning, it seems, to get a taste of your quality. How do you suppose the show would get on if you had to play?"

"That's unfair," Martyn cried.

"Well," he said, "don't run out on me. That'd be unfair, if you like. No dresser. No understudy. A damn shabby trick. As for this background music, I know where it arises. It's a more complex business than you may suppose. I shall attend to it." He moved behind her chair, and rested his hands on its back. "Well," he said, "shall we clap hands and a bargain? How say you?"

Martyn said slowly: "I don't see how I can do anything but say yes."

"There's my girl!" His hand brushed across her head and he moved away.

"Though I must say," Martyn added, "you do well to quote Petruchio. And Henry the Fifth, if it comes to that."

"A brace of autocratic male animals? Therefore it must follow you are 'Kate' in two places. And—shrewd Kate, French Kate, kind Kate, but never curst Kate—you will rehearse at eleven to-morrow, hold or cut bow-strings. Agreed?"

"I am content."

"Damned if you look it, however. All right. I'll have a word with that girl. Good day to you, Kate."

"Good day, sir," said Martyn.

iv

That night the second dress rehearsal went through as for performance, without, as far as Martyn knew, any interruption during the action.

She stayed throughout in one or the other of Miss Hamilton's dressing-rooms and, on the occasions when she was in transit, contrived to be out of the way of any of the players. In the second act, her duties kept her in the improvised dressing-room on the stage and she heard a good deal of the dialogue.

There is perhaps nothing that gives one so strong a sense of theatre from the inside as the sound of invisible players in action. The disembodied and remote voices, projected at an unseen mark, the uncanny quiet off-stage, the smells and the feeling that the walls and the dust listen, the sense of a simmering expectancy; all these together make a corporate life so that the theatre itself seems to breathe and pulse and give out a warmth. This warmth communicated itself to Martyn and, in spite of all her misgivings, she glowed and thought to herself, "This is my place. This is where I belong."

Much of the effect of the girl's part in this act depended not so much on what she said, which was little, but on mime and on that integrity of approach which is made manifest in the smallest gesture, the least movement. Listening to Miss Gainsford's slight uncoloured voice, Martyn thought: "But perhaps if one watched her it would be better. Perhaps something is happening that cannot be heard, only seen."

Miss Hamilton, when she came off for her changes, spoke of nothing but the business in hand and said little enough about that. She was in-drawn and formal in her dealings with her dresser. Martyn wondered uneasily how much Poole had told her of their interviews, whether she had any strong views or prejudices about her husband's niece, or shared his resentment that Martyn herself had been cast as an understudy.

The heat radiated by the strong lights of the dressing-rooms in-tensified their characteristic smells. With business-like precision Miss Hamilton would aim an atomizer at her person and spray herself rhyth-mically with scent while Martyn, standing on a chair, waited to slip a dress over her head. After the end of the second act, when she was about this business in the star-room, Poole came in. "That went very nicely, Helena," he said.

Martyn paused with the dress in her hands. Miss Hamilton extended her whitened arms, and with a very beautiful movement turned to him.

"Oh, darling," she said. "Did it? Did it really?"

Martyn thought she had never seen anyone more lovely than her em-ployer was then. Hers was the kind of beauty that declared itself when most simply arrayed. The white cloth that protected her hair added a Holbein-like emphasis to the bones and subtly turning planes of her face. There was a sort of naïveté and warmth in her posture: a touching intimacy. Martyn saw Poole take the hands that were extended to him and she turned her head away, not liking, with the voluminous dress in her arms, to climb down from her station on the chair. She felt suddenly desolate and shrunken within herself.

"Was it *really* right?" Miss Hamilton said.

"You were, at least."

"But—otherwise?"

"Much as one would expect."

"Where's John?"

"In the circle, under oath not to come down until I say so."

"Pray God, he keep his oath!" she quoted sombrely.

"Hullo, Kate," Poole said.

"Kate?" Miss Hamilton asked. "Why Kate?"

"I suspect her," said Poole, "of being a shrew. Get on with your job, Kate. What are you doing up there?"

Miss Hamilton said: "Really, darling!" and moved away to the chair. Martyn slipped the dress over her head, jumped down and began to fas-ten it. She did this to a running accompaniment from Poole. He whis-pered to himself anxiously as if he were Martyn, muttered and grunted as if Miss Hamilton complained that the dress was tight, and thus kept up a preposterous duologue, matching his words to their actions. This was done so quaintly and with so little effort that Martyn had much ado to keep a straight face and Miss Hamilton was moved to exasperated laughter. When she was dressed she took him by the arm. "Since when, my sweet, have you become a dressing-room comedian?"

"Oh God, your only jig-maker."

"Last act, please, last act," said the call-boy in the passage.

"Come on," she said, and they went out together.

When the curtain was up, Martyn returned to the improvised dressing-room on the stage and there, having for the moment no duties, she listened to the invisible play and tried to discipline her most unruly heart.

Bennington's last exit was followed in the play by his suicide, off-stage. Jacko, who had, it seemed, a passion for even the simplest of off-stage stunts, had come round from the front of the house to supervise the gunshot. He stood near the entry into the dressing-room passage with a stage-hand who carried an effects-gun. This was fired at the appropriate moment and, as they were stationed not far from Martyn in her canvas room, she leapt at the report, which was nerve-shatteringly successful. The acrid smell of the discharge drifted into her roofless shelter.

Evidently Bennington was standing nearby. His voice, carefully lowered to a murmur, sounded just beyond the canvas wall. "And that," he said, "takes me *right* off, thank God. Give me a cigarette, Jacko, will you?" There was a pause. The stage-hand moved away. A match scraped and Bennington said: "Come to my room and have a drink."

"Thank you, Ben, not now," Jacko whispered. "The curtain comes down in five minutes."

"Followed by a delicious post mortem conducted by the Great Producer and the Talented Author. Entrancing prospect! How did I go, Jacko?"

"No actor," Jacko returned, "cares to be told how he goes in anything but terms of extravagant praise. You know how clever you always are. You are quite as clever to-night as you have always been. Moreover, you showed some discretion."

Martyn heard Bennington chuckle. "There's still tomorrow," he said. "I reserve my fire, old boy. I bide my time."

There was a pause. Martyn heard one of them fetch a long sigh—Jacko, evidently, because Bennington, as if in answer to it, said: "Oh, nonsense." After a moment he added: "The kid's all right," and when Jacko didn't answer: "Don't you think so?"

"Why, yes," said Jacko.

On the stage the voices of Helena Hamilton and Adam Poole built towards a climax. The call-boy came round behind the set and went down the passage chanting: "All on for the curtain, please. All on."

Martyn shifted the chair in the dressing-room and moved noisily. There was a brief silence.

"I don't give a damn if she can hear," Bennington said more loudly. "Wait a moment. Stay where you are. I was asking you what you thought of Gay's performance. She's all right. Isn't she?"

"Yes, yes. I must go."

"Wait a bit. If the fools left her alone she'd go tremendously. I tell you what, old boy. If our Eccentric Author exercises his talent for wisecracking on that kid to-night I'll damn well take a hand."

"You will precipitate a further scene, and that is to be avoided."

"I'm not going to stand by and hear her bullied. By God, I'm not. I understand you've given harbourage, by the way, to the Mystery Maiden."

"I must get round to the side. By your leave, Ben."

"Plenty of time."

And Martyn knew that Bennington stood in the entry to the passage, barring the way.

"I'm talking," he said, "about this understudy-cum-dresser. Miss X."

"You are prolific in cryptic titles."

"Call her what you like, it's a peculiar business. What is she? You may as well tell me, you know. Some ancient indiscretion of Adam's adolescence come home to roost?"

"Be quiet, Ben."

"For tuppence I'd ask Adam himself. And that's not the only question I'd like to ask him. Do you think I relish my position?"

"They are getting near the tag. It is almost over."

"Why do you suppose I drink a bit? What would you do in my place?"

"Think before I speak," said Jacko, "for one thing."

A buzzer sounded. "There's the curtain," said Jacko. "Look out."

Martyn heard a kind of scuffle followed by an oath from Bennington. There were steps in the passage. The curtain fell with a giant whisper. A gust of air swept through the region back-stage.

"All on," said the stage-manager distantly. Martyn heard the players go on and the curtain rise and fall again.

Poole, on the stage, said: "And that's all of that. All right, everyone. Settle down and I'll take the notes. John will be round in a moment. I'll wait for you, Helena."

Miss Hamilton came into the improvised room. Martyn removed her dress and put her into her gown.

"I'll take my make-up off out there," she said. "Bring the things, Martyn, will you? Grease, towels and my cigarettes?"

Martyn had them ready. She followed Miss Hamilton out and for the first time that night went onto the set.

Poole, wearing a dark dressing-gown, stood with his back to the curtain. The other five members of the cast sat, relaxed but attentive, about the stage. Jacko and Clem Smith waited by the Prompt corner with papers and pencils. Martyn held a looking-glass before Miss Hamilton, who said: "Adam, darling, you don't mind, do you? I mustn't miss a word but I *do* rather want to get on," and began to remove her make-up.

Upon this scene Dr. John James Rutherford erupted. His arrival was prefaced in his usual manner by slammed doors, blundering footsteps and loud ejaculations. He then appeared in the central entrance, flame-headed, unshaven, overcoated, and grasping a sheaf of papers.

"Roast me," he said, "in sulphur! Wash me in steep-down gulfs of liquid fire! 'Ere I again endure the loathy torment of a dress rehearsall What have I done, ye gods, that I should—"

"All right, John," Poole said. "Not yet. Sit down. On some heavy piece of furniture and carefully."

Clem Smith shouted: "Alf! The Doctor's chair."

A large chair with broken springs was brought on and placed with its back to the curtain. Dr. Rutherford hurled himself into it and produced his snuff-box. "I am a child to chiding," he said. "What goes on, chums?"

Poole said: "I'm going to take my stuff. If anything I have to say repeats exactly any of your own notes you might leave it out for the sake of saving time. If you've any objections, be a good chap and save them till I've finished. Agreed?"

"Can't we cut the flummery and get down to business?"

"That's just what I'm suggesting."

"Is it? I wasn't listening. Press on, then, my dear fellow. Press on."

They settled down. Jacko gave Poole a block of notes and he began to work through them. "Nothing much in Act I," he said, "until we get to—" His voice went on evenly. He spoke of details in timing, of orchestration and occasionally of stage-management. Sometimes a player would ask a question and there would be a brief discussion. Sometimes Clem Smith would make a note. For the scenes where Poole had been on, Jacko, it appeared, had taken separate notes. Martyn suddenly remembered that Jacko's official status was that of assistant to Poole, and thought it characteristic of him that he made so little of his authority.

From where she stood, holding the glass for Helena Hamilton, she could see all the players. In the foreground was the alert and beautiful face of her employer, a little older now with its make-up gone, turning at times to the looking-glass and at times, when something in his notes concerned her, towards Poole. Beyond Miss Hamilton sat J. G. Darcey, alone and thoughtfully filling his pipe. He glanced occasionally, with an air of anxious solicitude, at Miss Gainsford. At the far side Parry Percival lay in an armchair looking fretful. Bennington stood near the centre with a towel in his hands. At one moment he came behind his wife. Putting a hand on her shoulder, he reached over it, helped himself to a dollop of grease from a jar in her case and slapped it on his face. She made a slight movement of distaste and immediately afterwards a little secret grimace, as if she had caught herself out in a blunder. For a moment he retained his hold of her shoulder. Then he looked down at her, dragged his clean fingers across her neck and, smearing the grease over his face, returned to his former position and began to clean away his make-up.

Martyn didn't want to look at Gay Gainsford but was unable altogether to avoid doing so. Miss Gainsford sat, at first alone, on a smallish sofa. She seemed to have herself tolerably well in hand, but her eyes were restless and her fingers plaited and replaited the folds of her dress. Bennington watched her from a distance until he had done with his towel. Then he crossed the stage and sat beside her, taking one of the restless hands in his. He looked hard at Martyn, who was visited painfully by a feeling of great compassion for both of them and by a sensation of remorse. She had a notion, which she tried to dismiss as fantastic, that Poole sensed this reaction. His glance rested for a moment on her and she thought: "This is getting too complicated. It's going to be too much for me." She made an involuntary movement and at once Miss Hamilton put out a hand to the glass.

When Poole had dealt with the first act he turned to Dr. Rutherford, who had sat throughout with his legs extended and his chin on his chest, directing from under his brows a glare of extreme malevolence at the entire cast.

"Anything to add to that, John?" Poole asked.

"Apart from a passing observation that I regard the whole thing as a *tour de force* of understatement and with reservations that I keep to myself"—here Dr. Rutherford looked fixedly at Parry Percival—"I am mum. I reserve my fire."

"Act II, then," said Poole, and began again.

Martyn became aware after a few minutes that Dr. Rutherford, like Bennington, was staring at her. She was as horridly fascinated as a bird is said to be by the unwinking gaze of a snake. Do what she could to look elsewhere about the stage, she must after a time steal a glance at him, only to meet again his speculative and blood-shot regard. This alarmed her profoundly. She was persuaded that a feeling of tension had been communicated to the others, and that they too were aware of some kind of impending crisis. This feeling grew in intensity as Poole's voice went steadily on with his notes. He had got about half-way through the second act when Dr. Rutherford ejaculated: "Hi! Wait a bit!" and began a frenzied search through his own notes, which seemed to be in complete disorder. Finally he pounced on a sheet of paper, dragged out a pair of spectacles and, with a hand raised to enjoin silence, read it to himself with strange noises in his breathing. Having scattered the rest of his notes over his person and the floor, he now folded this particular sheet and sat on it.

"Proceed," he said. The cast stirred uneasily. Poole continued. He had come to the scene between himself and Miss Gainsford, and beyond a minor adjustment of position said nothing about it. Miss Hamilton, who had arrived at the final stage of her street make-up, dusted her face with powder, nodded good-humouredly at Martyn and turned to face Poole. Martyn thankfully shut the dressing-case and made for the nearest exit.

At the same moment Poole reached the end of his notes for the second act and Dr. Rutherford shouted: "Hold on! Stop that wench!"

Martyn, with a sensation of falling into chaos, turned in the doorway. She saw nine faces lifted towards her own. They made a pattern against the smoke-thickened air. Her eyes travelled from one to the other and rested finally on Poole's.

"It's all right," he said. "Go home."

"No, you don't," Dr. Rutherford shouted excitedly.

"Indeed she does," said Poole. "Run away home, Kate. Good night to you."

Martyn heard the storm break as she fled down the passage.

Chapter V

Opening Night

From noon until half past six on the opening night of Dr. Rutherford's new play, the persons most concerned in its birth were absent from their theatre. Left to itself, the Vulcan was possessed only by an immense expectancy. It waited. In the auditorium rows of seats, stripped of their dust-cloths, stared at the curtain. The curtain itself presented its reverse side to Jacko's set, closing it in with a stuffy air of secrecy. The stage was dark. Battalions of dead lamps, focussed at crazy angles, overhung it with a promise of light. Cue-sheets, fixed to the switchboard, awaited the electrician, the prompt-script was on its shelf, the properties were ranged on trestle-tables. Everything bided its time in the dark theatre.

To enter into this silent house was to feel as if one surprised a poised and expectant presence. This air of suspense made itself felt to the occasional intruders: to the boy who from time to time came through from the office with telegrams for the dressing-rooms, to the girl from Florian's and the young man from the wig-makers, and to the piano-tuner who for an hour twanged and hammered in the covered well. And to Martyn Tarne who, alone in the ironing-room, set about the final pressing of the dresses under her care.

The offices were already active and behind their sand-blasted glass walls typewriters clattered and telephone bells rang incessantly. The blacked-out box-plan lay across Bob Grantley's desk, and stacked along the wall were rectangular parcels of programmes, fresh from the printer.

And at two o'clock the queues for the early doors began to form in Carpet Street.

ii

It was at two o'clock that Helena Hamilton, after an hour's massage, went to bed. Her husband had telephoned, with a certain air of opulence which she had learnt to dread, that he would lunch at his club and return to their flat during the afternoon to rest.

In her darkened room she followed a practised routine and, relaxing one set of muscles after another, awaited sleep. This time, however, her self-discipline was unsuccessful. If only she could hear him come in, it would be better; if only she could see into what sort of state he'd got himself. She used all her formulae for repose but none of them worked. At three o'clock she was still awake and still miserably anxious.

It was no good trying to cheer herself up by telling over her rosary of romantic memories. Usually this was a successful exercise. She had conducted her affairs of the heart, she knew, with grace and civility. She had almost always managed to keep them on a level of enchantment. She had simply allowed them to occur with the inconsequence and charm of self-sown larkspurs in an otherwise correctly ordered border. They had hung out their gay little banners for a season and then been painlessly tweaked up. Except, perhaps, for Adam. With Adam, she remembered uneasily, it had been different. With Adam, so much her junior, it had been a more deeply rooted affair. It had put an end, finally, to her living with Ben as his wife. It had made an enemy of Ben. And at once her thoughts were infested with worries about the contemporary scene at the theatre. "It's such a muddle," she thought, "and I hate muddles." They'd had nothing but trouble all through rehearsals. Ben fighting with everybody and jealous of Adam. The Doctor bawling everybody out. And that wretchedly unhappy child Gay (who, God knew, would never be an actress as long as she lived) first pitchforked into the part by Ben and now almost bullied out of it by the Doctor. And, last of all, Martyn Tarne.

She had touched the raw centre of her anxiety. Under any other conditions, she told herself, she would have welcomed the appearance out of a clear sky and—one had to face it—under very odd circumstances, of this little antipodean: this throw-back to some forebear that she and Adam were supposed to have in common. She would have been inclined to like Martyn for the resemblance instead of feeling so uncomfortably disturbed by it. Of course she accepted Adam's explanation, but at the same time she thought it rather naïve of him to believe that the girl had actually kept away from the theatre because she didn't want to make capital out of the relationship. That, Helena thought, turning restlessly on her bed, was really too simple of Adam. Moreover, he'd stirred up the already exacerbated nerves of the company by giving this girl the understudy without, until last night, making public the relationship.

There she went, thinking about last night's scene: John Rutherford demanding that even at this stage Martyn should play the part, Gay imploring Adam to release her, Ben saying he'd walk out on the show if

Gay went, and Adam— Adam had done the right thing of course. He'd come down strongly with one of his rare thrusts of anger and reduced them to complete silence. He had then described the circumstances of Martyn's arrival at the theatre, and had added in a voice of ice that there was and could be no question of any change in the cast. He finished his notes and left the theatre, followed by Jacko.

This had been the signal for an extremely messy row in which everybody seemed to bring to light some deep-seated grudge. Ben had quarrelled almost simultaneously with Parry Percival (on the score of technique), with Dr. Rutherford (on the score of casting), with his niece (on the score of humanity) and, unexpectedly, with J. G. Darcey (on the score of Ben bullying Gay). Percival had responded to a witticism of the Doctor's by a stream of shrill invective which astonished everybody, himself included, and Gay had knitted the whole scene into a major climax by having a fit of hysterics from which she was restored with brutal efficiency by Dr. Rutherford himself.

The party had then broken up. J.G. sustained his new role of knightly concern by taking Gay home. Parry Percival left in a recrudescence of fury occasioned by the Doctor flinging after him a composite Shakesperian epithet: "Get you gone, you dwarf; you minimus, of hindering knot-grass made; you bead, you acorn." She herself had retired into the wings. The stage-staff had already disappeared. The Doctor and Ben, finding themselves in undisputed possession of the stage, had squared up to each other with the resolution of all-in wrestlers, and she, being desperately tired, had taken the car home and asked their man to return to the theatre for her husband. When she had awakened late in the morning she was told he had already gone out.

"I wish," a voice cried out in her mind, "I wish to God he'd never come back."

And at that moment she heard him stumble heavily upstairs.

She expected him to go straight to his room and was dismayed when he came to a halt outside her door and, with a clumsy sound that might have been intended for a knock, opened it and came in. The smell of brandy and cigars came in with him and invaded the whole room. It was more than a year since that had happened.

He walked uncertainly to the foot of the bed and leant on it—and she was frightened of him.

"Hullo," he said.

"What is it, Ben? I'm resting."

"I thought you might be interested. There'll be no more nonsense from John about Gay."

"Good," she said.

"He's calmed down. I got him to see reason."

"He's not so bad, really—old John."

"He's had some good news from abroad. About the play."

"Translation rights?"

"Something like that." H was smiling at her, uncertainly. "You look comfy," he said. "All tucked up."

"Why don't you try and get some rest yourself?" He leant over the foot of the bed and said something under his breath. "What?" she said anxiously. "What did you say?"

"I said it's a pity Adam didn't appear a bit sooner, isn't it? I'm so extraneous."

Her heart thumped like a fist inside her ribs. "Ben, *please*," she said.

"And another thing. Do you both imagine I don't see through this dresser-cum-understudy racket? Darling, I don't much enjoy playing the cuckold in your Restoration comedy, but I'm just bloody well furious when you so grossly under-estimate my intelligence. When was it? On the New Zealand tour in 1930?"

"What is this nonsense!" she said breathlessly.

"Sorry. How are you managing to-night? You and Adam?"

"My dear Ben!"

"I'll tell you. You're making shift with me for once in a blue moon. And I'm not talking about to-night."

She recognized this scene. She had dreamt it many times. His face had advanced upon her while she lay inert with terror, as one does in a nightmare. For an infinitesimal moment she was visited by the hope that perhaps after all she had slept and, if she could only scream, would awaken. But she couldn't scream. She was quite helpless.

iii

Adam Poole's telephone rang at half past four. He had gone late to rest and was wakened from a deep sleep. For a second or two he didn't recognize her voice, and she spoke so disjointedly that even when he was broad awake he couldn't make out what she was saying.

"What is it?" he said. "Helena, what's the matter? I can't hear you." Then she spoke more clearly and he understood.

iv

At six o'clock the persons in the play began to move towards the theatre. In their lodgings and flats they bestirred themselves after their several fashions: to drink tea or black coffee, choke down pieces of bread and butter that tasted like sawdust, or swallow aspirin and alcohol. This was their zero hour: the hour of low vitality when the stimulus of the theatre and the last assault of nerves was yet to come. By a quarter past six they were all on their way. Their dressers were already in their rooms and Jacko prowled restlessly about the darkened stage. Dr. John James Rutherford, clad in an evening suit and a boiled shirt garnished with snuff, both of which dated from some distant period when he still attended the annual dinners of the B.M.A., plunged into the office and made such a nuisance of himself that Bob Grantley implored him to go away.

At twenty past six the taxi carrying Gay Gainsford and J. G. Darcey turned into Carpet Street. Darcey sat with his legs crossed elegantly and his hat perched on them. In the half-light his head and profile looked like those of a much younger man.

"It was sweet of you to call for me, J.G.," Gay said unevenly.

He smiled, without looking at her, and patted her hand. "I'm always petrified myself," he said, "on first nights."

"Are you? I suppose a true artist must be."

"Ah, youth, youth!" sighed J.G.—a little stagily perhaps, but, if she hadn't been too preoccupied to notice it, with a certain overtone of genuine nostalgia.

"It's worse than the usual first-night horrors for me," she said. "I'm just boxing on in a private hell of my own."

"My poor child."

She turned a little towards him and leant her head into his shoulder. "Nice!" she murmured and after a moment: "I'm so frightened of him, J.G."

With the practised ease of a good actor, he slipped his arm round her. "I won't have it," he said. "By God, I won't! If he worries you again, author or no author—"

"It's not *him*," she said. "Not the Doctor. Oh, I know he's simply filthy to work with and he does fuss me dreadfully, but it's not the Doctor *really* who's responsible for all my misery."

"No? Who is then?"

"Uncle Ben!" She made a small wailing noise that was muffled by his coat. He bent his head attentively to listen. "J.G., I'm just plain *terrified* of Uncle Ben."

v

Parry Percival always enjoyed his arrival at the theatre when there was a gallery queue to be penetrated. One raised one's hat and said: "Pardon me. Thanks so much," to the gratified ladies. One heard them murmur one's name. It was a heartening little fillip to one's self-esteem.

On this occasion the stimulant didn't work with its normal magic. He was too worried to relish it wholeheartedly. For one thing his row with Dr. Rutherford still lingered like an unpleasant taste in his memory. Apart from the altogether unforgiveable insults the Doctor had levelled at his art, there was one in particular which had been directed at himself as a man and this troubled him deeply. It had almost brought him to the pitch of doing something that he dreaded to do—take stock of himself. Until now he had lived in an indeterminate hinterland, drifting first towards one frontier, then the other, unsure of his impulses and not strongly propelled by them in any one direction. He would, he thought, perhaps have turned out a happier being if he had been born a woman. "Let's face it," he thought uneasily, "I'm interested in their kind of things. I'm intuitive and sensitive in their way." It helped a little to think how intuitive and how sensitive he was. But he was not in any sense a fair target for the sort of veiled insults the Doctor had levelled at him. And as if this weren't enough of a worry, there was the immediate menace of Clark Bennington. Ben, he thought hotly, was insufferable. Every device by which a second-leading man could make a bit-part actor look foolish had been brought into play during rehearsals. Ben had up-staged him, had flurried him by introducing new business, had topped his lines and, even while he was seething with impotent fury, had reduced him to nervous giggles by looking sideways at him. It was the technique with which a schoolmaster could torture a small boy, and it revived in Parry hideous memories of his childhood.

Only partially restored by the evidence of prestige afforded by the gallery queue, he walked down the stage-door alley and into the theatre. He was at once engulfed in its warmth and expectancy.

He passed into the dressing-room passage. Helena Hamilton's door was half-open and the lights were on. He tapped, looked in and was greeted by the smell of greasepaint, powder, wet-white and flowers. The gas fire groaned comfortably. Martyn, who was spreading out towels, turned and found herself confronted by his deceptively boyish face.

"Early at work?" he fluted.

Martyn wished him good evening.

"Helena not down yet?"

"Not yet."

He hung about the dressing-room, fingering photographs and eyeing Martyn.

"I hear you come from Down Under," he said. "I nearly accepted an engagement to go out there last year, but I didn't really like the people so I turned it down. Adam played it in the year dot, I believe. Well, more years ago than he would care to remember, I dare say. Twenty, if we're going to let our back-hair down. Before you were born, I dare say."

"Yes," Martyn agreed. "Just before."

Her answer appeared to give him extraordinary satisfaction. "Just before?" he repeated. "Really?" and Martyn thought: "I mustn't let myself be worried by this."

He seemed to hover on the edge of some further observation and pottered about the dressing-room examining the great mass of flowers. "I'll swear," he said crossly, "those aren't the roses I chose at Florian's. Honestly, that female's an absolute menace."

Martyn, seeing how miserable he looked, felt sorry for him. He muttered: "I do so *abominate* first nights," and she rejoined: "They are pretty ghastly, aren't they?" Because he seemed unable to take himself off, she added with an air of finality: "Anyway, may I wish you luck for this one?"

"Sweet of you," he said. "I'll need it. I'm the stooge of this piece. Well, thanks, anyway."

He drifted into the passage, halted outside the open door of Poole's dressing-room and greeted Bob Cringle. "Governor not down yet?"

"We're on our way, Mr. Percival."

Parry inclined his head and strolled into the room. He stood close to Bob, leaning his back against the dressing-shelf, his legs elegantly crossed.

"Our little stranger," he murmured, "seems to be new-brooming away next door."

"That's right, sir," said Bob. "Settled in very nice."

"Strong resemblance," Parry said invitingly.

"To the Guv'nor, sir?" Bob rejoined cheerfully. "That's right. Quite a coincidence."

"A coincidence!" Parry echoed. "Well, not precisely, Bob. I understand there's a distant relationship. It was mentioned for the first time last night. Which accounts for the set-up, one supposes. Tell me, Bob, have you ever before heard of a dresser doubling as understudy?"

"Worked out very convenient, hasn't it, sir?"

"Oh, very," said Parry discontentedly. "Look, Bob. You were with the Governor on his New Zealand tour in 'thirty, weren't you?"

Bob said woodenly: "That's correct sir. 'E was just a boy in them days. Might I trouble you to move, Mr. Percival? I got my table to lay out."

"Oh, sorry. I'm in the way. As usual. Quite! Quite!" He waved his hand and walked jauntily into the passage.

"Good luck for to-night, sir," said Bob and shut the door after him.

In the room opposite to Poole's and next to the Greenroom, Parry could hear Bennington's dresser moving about whistling softly through his teeth. There is a superstition in the theatre that it's unlucky to whistle in a dressing-room and Parry knew that the man wouldn't do it if Ben had arrived. He didn't much like the sound of it himself, and moved on to J. G. Darcey's room. He tapped, was answered, and went in. J.G. was already embarked on his make-up.

"Bob," said Parry, "refuses to be drawn."

"Good evening, dear boy. About what?"

"Oh, you know. The New Zealand tour and so on."

"Quite right," said J.G. firmly, and added: "He was the merest stripling."

"Well—eighteen," Parry began and then broke off.

"I know, I know. I couldn't care less, actually." He dropped into the only other chair in the room and buried his face in his hands. "Oh, dear," he said, "I'm so bored with it all. By-blow or not, what *does* it matter!"

"It only matters," said J.G., laying down a stick of No. 5, "in so far as it's driving Gay Gainsford pretty close to a nervous breakdown, and to that I do most strongly object."

"Really?" Parry raised his head and stared at him. "How altruistic of you, J.G. Well, I mean, I'm sorry for her, poor child. Naturally. And one trembles for the performance, of course."

"The performance would be all right if people left her alone. Ben, in particular."

"Yes," said Parry with great satisfaction. "The situation appears to be getting under the skin of the great character actor. There is that."

"I'm told," said J.G., "there was a midnight audition. Jacko professes ecstasy."

"My dear J.G., there have been two more-or-less public auditions. The object, no doubt, being to make everything look as clean as a whistle. The second affair was this morning."

"Did you see her?"

"I happened to look in."

"What's she like?"

Parry lit a cigarette. "As you have seen," he said, "she's fantastically like *him*. Which is really the point at issue. But *fantastically* like."

"Can she give a show?"

"Oh, yes," said Parry. He leaned forward and hugged his knees boyishly. "Oh, yes indeed. Indeed she can, my dear J.G. You'd be surprised."

J.G. made a non-committal sound and went on with his make-up.

"This morning," Parry continued, "the Doctor was there. And Ben. Ben, quite obviously devoured with chagrin. I confess I couldn't help rather gloating. As I remarked, it's getting under his skin. Together, no doubt, with vast potations of brandy and soda."

"I hope to God he's all right to-night."

"It appears Gay was in the back of the house, poor thing, while it was going on."

"She didn't tell me that," J.G. said anxiously and, catching Parry's sharpened glance, he added: "I didn't really hear anything about it."

"It was a repetition of last night. Really, one feels quite dizzy. Gay rushed weeping to Adam and again implored him to let her throw in the part. The Doctor, of course, was all for it. Adam was charming, but Uncle Ben produced another temperament. He and the Doctor left simultaneously in a silence more ominous, I assure you, than last night's dog-fight. Ben's not down yet."

"Not yet," J.G. said and repeated: "I hope to God he's all right."

For a moment the two men were united in a common anxiety. J.G. said: "Christ, I wish I didn't get nervous on first nights."

"You, at least, have something to be nervous about. Whereas I half kill myself over the dimmest bit in the West End. When I first saw the part I nearly screamed the place down. I said to Adam if it wasn't that he and Helena had always been very sweet to me—"

J.G. paid this routine plaint the compliment of looking gloomily acquiescent, but he barely listened to it.

"—and anyway," Parry was saying, "what chance has any of us as long as this *fantastic* set-up continues? In Poole-Hamilton pieces the second leads go automatically to the star's husband. I suppose Adam thinks it's the least he can do. Actually, I *know* I'm too young for the part but—"

"I wouldn't say you were," J.G. said, absently. Parry shot an indignant glance at him but he was pressing powder into the sides of his nose.

"If he tries any of his up-stage fun-and-games on me to-night," Parry said, furiously hissing his sibilants, "I'll just simply bitch up his big exit for him. I could, you know. It'd be no trouble at all."

"I wouldn't, dear boy," J.G. said good-naturedly. "It never does one any good, you know. One can't afford these little luxuries, however tempting. Well, that's taken the polish off the knocker on the old front door." He took his nose delicately between his thumb and forefinger. "The play stinks," he said thoughtfully. "In my considered opinion, it stinks."

"Well, I must say you *are* a comfort to us."

"Pay no attention. I always feel like that at about half-hour time."

"Half-hour! God, have they called it?"

"They will in five minutes."

"I must dart to my paints and powders." Parry went out, but re-opened the door to admit his head. "In case I don't see you again, dear J.G., all the very best."

J.G. turned and raised his hand. "And to you the best, of course, dear boy."

Left alone, he sighed rather heavily, looked closely at his carefully made-up face and, with a rueful air, shook his head at himself.

vi

Clark Bennington's dresser, a thin melancholy man, put him into his gown and hovered, expressionless, behind him.

"I shan't need you before the change," said Bennington. "See if you can help Mr. Darcey."

The man went out. Bennington knew he'd guessed the reason for his dismissal. He wondered why he could never bring himself to have a drink in front of his dresser. After all, there was nothing in taking a nip before the show. Adam, of course, chose to make a great thing of never touching it. And at the thought of Adam Poole he felt resentment and fear stir at the back of his mind. He got his flask out of his overcoat pocket and poured a stiff shot of brandy.

"The thing to do," he told himself, "is to wipe this afternoon clean out. Forget it. Forget everything except my work." But he remembered, unexpectedly, the way, fifteen years ago, he used to prepare himself for a first night. He used to make a difficult and intensive approach to his initial entrance so that when he walked out on the stage he was already possessed by a life that had been created in the dressing-room. Took a lot of concentration: Stanislavsky and all that. Hard going, but in those days it had seemed worth the effort. Helena had encouraged him. He had a notion she and Adam still went in for it. But now he'd mastered the easier way—the repeated mannerism, the trick of pause and the unexpected flattening of the voice—the technical box of tricks.

He finished his drink quickly and began to grease his face. He noticed how the flesh had dropped into sad folds under the eyes, had blurred the jaw-line and had sunk into grooves about the nostrils and the corners of the mouth. All right for this part, of course, where he had to make a sight of himself, but he'd been a fine-looking man. Helena had fallen for him in a big way until Adam cut him out. At the thought of Adam he experienced a sort of regurgitation of misery and anger. "I'm a haunted man," he thought suddenly.

He'd let himself get into a state, he knew, because of this afternoon. Helena's face, gaping with terror, like a fish almost, kept rising up in his mind and wouldn't be dismissed. Things always worked like that with him: remorse always turned into nightmare.

It had been a bad week altogether. Rows with everybody; with John Rutherford in particular and with Adam over that blasted little dresser. He felt he was the victim of some elaborate plot. He was fond of Gay; she was a nice friendly little thing—his own flesh and blood. Until he had brought her into this piece she had seemed to like him. Not a bad little artist either, and good enough, by God, for the artsy-craftsy part they'd thrown at her. He thought of her scene with Poole and of her unhappiness in her failure and how, in some damned cockeyed way, they all, including Gay, seemed to blame him for it. He supposed she thought he'd bullied her into hanging on. Perhaps in a way he had, but he felt so much that he was the victim of a combined assault. "Alone," he thought, "I'm so desperately *alone*," and he could almost hear the word as one would say it on the stage, making it echo, forlorn and hopeless and extremely effective.

"I'm giving myself the jim-jams," he thought. He wondered if Helena had told Adam about this afternoon. By God, that'd rock Adam, if she had. And at once a picture rose up to torture him, a picture of Helena weeping in Adam's arms and taking solace there. He saw his forehead grow red in the looking-glass and told himself he'd better steady-up. No good getting into one of his tempers with a first performance ahead of him and everything so tricky with young Gay. There he was, coming back to that girl, that phoney dresser. He poured out another drink and began his make-up.

He recognized with satisfaction a familiar change of mood, and he now indulged himself with a sort of treat. He brought out a little piece of secret knowledge he had stored away. Among this company of enemies there was one over whom he exercised almost complete power. Over one, at least, he had overwhelmingly the whip-hand, and the knowledge of his sovereignty warmed him almost as comfortably as the brandy. He began to think about his part. Ideas, brand new and as clever as paint, crowded each other in his imagination. He anticipated his coming mastery.

His left hand slid towards the flask. "One more," he said, "and I'll be fine."

vii

In her room across the passage, Gay Gainsford faced her own reflection and watched Jacko's hands pass across it. He dabbed with his finger-tips under the cheek-bones and made a droning sound behind his closed lips. He was a very good make-up; it was one of his many talents. At the dress rehearsals the touch of his fingers had soothed rather than exacerbated her nerves, but to-night, evidently she found it almost intolerable.

"Haven't you finished?" she asked.

"Patience, patience. We do not catch a train. Have you never observed the triangular shadows under Adam's cheek-bones? They are yet to be created."

"Poor Jacko," Gay said breathlessly, "this must be such a bore for you! Considering everything."

"Quiet, now. How can I work?"

"No, but I mean it must be so exasperating to think that two doors away there's somebody who wouldn't need your help. Just a straight make-up, wouldn't it be? No trouble."

"I adore making up. It is my most brilliant gift."

"But she's your find in a way, isn't she? You'd like her to have the part, wouldn't you?"

He rested his hands on her shoulders. *"Ne vous dérangez pas,"* he said. "Shut up, in fact. Tranquillize yourself, idiot girl."

"But I want you to tell me."

"Then I tell you. Yes, I would like to see this little freak play your part because she is in fact a little freak. She has dropped into this theatre like an accident in somebody else's dress and the effect is fantastic. But she is well content to remain off-stage and it is you who play, and we have faith in you and wish you well with all our hearts."

"That's very nice of you," Gay said.

"What a sour voice! It is true. And now reflect. Reflect upon the minuteness of Edmund Kean, upon Sarah's one leg and upon Irving's two, upon ugly actresses who convince their audiences they are beautiful and old actors who persuade them they are young. It is all in the mind, the spirit and the preparation. What does Adam say? Think in, and then play out. Do so."

"I can't," Gay said between her teeth. "I can't." She twisted in her chair. He lifted his fingers away from her face quickly, with a wide gesture. "Jacko," she said, "there's a jinx on this night. Jacko, did you know? It was on the night of the Combined Arts Ball that it happened."

"What is this foolishness?"

"You know. Five years ago. The stage-hands were talking about it. I heard them. The gas fire case. The night that man was murdered. Everyone knows."

"Be silent!" Jacko said loudly. "This is idiocy. I forbid you to speak of it. The chatter of morons. The Combined Arts Ball has no fixed date and, if it had, shall an assembly of British bourgeoisie in bad fancy dress control our destiny? I am ashamed of you. You are altogether too stupid. Master yourself."

"It's not only that. It's everything. I can't face it."

His fingers closed down on her shoulders. "Master yourself," he said. "You must. If you cry I shall beat you and wipe your make-up across your face. I defy you to cry."

He cleaned his hands, tipped her head forward and began to massage the nape of her neck. "There are all sorts of things," he said, "that you must remember and as many more to forget. Forget the little freak and the troubles of to-day. Remember to relax all your muscles and also your nerves and your thoughts. Remember the girl in the play and the faith I have in you, and Adam and also your Uncle Bennington."

"Spare me my Uncle Bennington, Jacko. If my Uncle Bennington had left me where I belong, in fortnightly rep, I wouldn't be facing this hell. I know what everyone thinks of Uncle Ben and I agree with them. I never want to see him again. I hate him. He's made me go on with this. I wanted to throw the part in. It's not my part. I loathe it. No, I don't loathe it, that's not true. I loathe myself for letting everybody down. Oh, God, Jacko, what am I going to do?"

Across the bowed head Jacko looked at his own reflection and poked a face at it. "You shall play this part," he said through his teeth.

"Mouse-heart, skunk-girl. You shall play. Think of nothing. Unbridle your infinite capacity for inertia and be dumb."

Watching himself, he arranged his face in an unconvincing glower and fetched up a Shakesperian belly-voice.

"The devil damn thee black, thou cream-faced loon! Where got'st thou that goose look?"

He caught his breath. Beneath his fingers, Gay's neck stiffened. He began to swear elaborately, in French and in a whisper.

"Jacko. *Jacko.* Where does that line come from?"

"I invented it."

"You didn't. You *didn't.* It's *Macbeth,*" she wailed. *"You've quoted from* Macbeth!" and burst into a flurry of terrified weeping.

"Great suffering and all-enduring Saints of God," apostrophized Jacko, "give me some patience with this Quaking Thing."

But Gay's cries mounted in a sharp crescendo. She flung out her arms and beat with her fists on the dressing-table. A bottle of wet-white rocked to and fro, overbalanced, rapped smartly against the looking-glass and fell over. A neatly splintered star frosted the surface of the glass.

Gay pointed to it with an air of crazy triumph, snatched up her towel and scrubbed it across her make-up. She thrust her face, blotched and streaked with black cosmetic, at Jacko.

"Don't you like what you see?" she quoted, and rocketed into genuine hysteria.

Five minutes later Jacko walked down the passage towards Adam Poole's room, leaving J.G., who had rushed to the rescue in his shirt-sleeves, in helpless contemplation of the screaming Gay. Jacko disregarded the open doors and the anxious painted faces that looked out at him.

Bennington shouted from his room: "What the hell goes on? Who *is* that?"

"Listen," Jacko began, thrusting his head in at the door. He looked at Bennington and stopped short. "Stay where you are," he said and crossed the passage to Poole's room.

Poole had swung round in his chair to face the door. Bob Cringle stood beside him, twisting a towel in his hands.

"Well?" Poole said. "What is it? Is it Gay?"

"She's gone up. Sky-high. I can't do anything nor can J.G., and I don't believe anyone can. She refuses to go on."

"Where's John? Is this his doing?"

"God knows. I don't think so. He came in an hour ago and said he'd be back at five to seven."

"Has Ben tried?"

"She does nothing but scream that she never wants to see him again. In my opinion, Ben would be fatal."

"He must be able to hear all this."

"I told him to stay where he is."

Poole looked sharply at Jacko and went out. Gay's laughter had broken down in a storm of irregular sobbing that could be heard quite clearly. Helena Hamilton called out, "Adam, shall I go to her?" and he answered from the passage: "Better not, I think."

He was some time with Gay. They heard her shouting: "No! No! I won't go on! No!" over and over again like an automaton.

When he came out he went to Helena Hamilton's room. She was dressed and made up. Martyn, with an ashen face, stood inside the doorway.

"I'm sorry, darling," Poole said, "but you'll have to do without a dresser."

The call-boy came down the passage chanting: "Half-hour. Half-hour, please."

Poole and Martyn looked at each other.

"You'll be all right," he said.

Chapter VI

Performance

At ten to eight Martyn stood by the entrance.

She was dressed in Gay's clothes and Jacko had made her up very lightly. They had all wished her luck; J.G., Parry Percival, Helena Hamilton, Adam Poole, Clem Smith and even the dressers and stage-hands.

There had been something real and touching in their way of doing this, so that even in her terror she had felt they were good and very kind. Bennington alone had not wished her well but he had kept right away, and this abstention, she thought, showed a certain generosity.

She no longer felt sick but the lining of her mouth and throat was harsh as if, in fact, she had actually vomited. She thought her sense of hearing must have become distorted. The actors' voices on the other side of the canvas wall had the remote quality of voices in a nightmare, whereas the hammer-blows of her heart and the rustle of her dress that accompanied them sounded exceeding loud.

She saw the frames of the set, their lashings and painted legends—ACT I,P.2—and the door which she was to open. She could look into the Prompt corner where the A.S.M. followed the lighted script with his finger, and where, high above him, the electrician leaned over his perch, watching the play. The stage lights were reflected in his face. Everything was monstrous in its preoccupation. Martyn was alone.

She tried to command the upsurge of panic in her heart, to practise an approach to her ordeal, to create, in place of these implacable realities, the reality of the house in the play and that part of it in which now, out of sight of the audience, she must already have her being. This attempt went down before the clamour of her nerves. "I'm going to fail," she thought.

Jacko came round the set. She hoped he wouldn't speak to her and, as if he sensed this wish, he stopped at a distance and waited.

"I must listen," she thought. "I'm not listening. I don't know where they've got to. I've forgotten which way the door opens. I've missed my cue." Her inside deflated and despair griped it like a colic.

She turned and found Poole beside her.

"You're all right," he said. "The door opens on. You can do it. Now, my girl. On you go."

Martyn didn't hear the round of applause with which a London audience greets a player who appears at short notice.

She was on. She had made her entry and was engulfed in the play.

ii

Dr. Rutherford sat in the O.P. box with his massive shoulder turned to the house and his gloved hands folded together on the balustrade. His face was in shadow but the stage lights just touched the bulging curve of his old-fashioned shirt-front. He was monumentally still. One of the critics, an elderly man, said in an aside to a colleague that Rutherford reminded him of Watts's picture of the Minotaur.

For the greater part of the first act he was alone, having, as he had explained in the office, no masochistic itch to invite a guest to a Roman holiday where he himself was the major sacrifice. Towards the end of the act, however, Bob Grantley came into the box and stood behind him. Grantley's attention was divided. Sometimes he looked down through beams of spotlights at the stalls, cobbled with heads, sometimes at the stage and sometimes, sideways and with caution, at the Doctor himself. Really, Grantley thought, he was quite uncomfortably motionless. One couldn't tell what he was thinking and one hesitated, the Lord knew, to ask him.

Down on the stage Clark Bennington, Parry Percival and J. G. Darcey had opened the long crescendo leading to Helena's entrance. Grantley thought suddenly how vividly an actor's nature could be exposed on the stage: there was, for instance, a kind of bed-rock niceness about old J.G., a youthfulness of spirit that declaimed itself through the superimposed make-up, the characterization and J.G.'s indisputable middle age. And Bennington? And Percival? Grantley had begun to consider them in these terms when Percival, speaking one of his colourless lines, turned down-stage. Bennington moved centre, looked at Darcey and neatly sketched a parody of Percival's somewhat finicking movement. The theatre was filled with laughter. Percival turned quickly; Bennington smiled innocently at him, prolonging the laugh.

Grantley looked apprehensively at the Doctor.

"Is that new?" he ventured in a whisper. "That business?"

The Doctor didn't answer, and Grantley wondered if he only imagined that the great hands on the balustrade had closed more tightly over each other.

Helena Hamilton came on to a storm of applause, and with her entrance the action was roused to a new excitement and was intensified with every word she uttered. The theatre grew warm with her presence and with a sense of heightened suspense.

"Now they're all on," Grantley thought, "except Adam and the girl."

He drew a chair forward stealthily and sat behind Rutherford.

"It's going enormously," he murmured to the massive shoulder. "Terrific, old boy." And because he was nervous he added: "This brings the girl on, doesn't it?"

For the first time the Doctor spoke. His lips scarcely moved. A submerged voice uttered within him. "Hence," it said, "heap of wrath, foul indigested lump."

"Sorry, old boy," whispered Grantley, and began to wonder what hope in hell there was of persuading the distinguished author to have a drink in the office during the interval with a hand-picked number of important persons.

He was still preoccupied with this problem when a side door in the set opened and a dark girl with short hair walked out on the stage.

Grantley joined in the kindly applause. The Doctor remained immovable.

The players swept up to their major climax, Adam came on, and five minutes later the curtain fell on the first act. The hands of the audience filled the house with a storm of rain. The storm swelled prodigiously and persisted even after the lights had come up.

"Ah, good girl," Bob Grantley stammered, filled with the sudden and excessive emotion of the theatre. "Good old Adam. Jolly good show!"

Greatly daring, he clapped the Doctor on the shoulder.

The Doctor remained immovable.

Grantley edged away to the back of the box. "I must get back," he said. "Look, John, there are one or two people coming to the office for a drink who would be—"

The Doctor turned massively in his seat and faced him.

"No," he said, "thank you."

"Well, but look, dear boy, it's just one of those things. You know how it is, John, you know how—"

"Shut up," said the Doctor without any particular malice. "I'm going back-stage," he added. He rose and turned away from the audience. "I have no desire to swill tepid spirits with minor celebrities among the backsides of sand-blasted gods. Thank you, however. See you later."

He opened the pass-door at the back of the box.

"You're pleased, aren't you?" Grantley said. "You *must* be pleased."

"Must I? Must I indeed?"

"With the girl, at least? So far?"

"The wench is a good wench. So far. I go to tell her so. By your leave, Robert."

He lumbered through the pass-door and Grantley heard him plunge dangerously down the narrow stairway to the stage.

iii

Dr. Rutherford emerged in a kaleidoscopic world: a world where walls fell softly apart, landscapes ascended into darkness and stairways turned and moved aside. A blue haze rose from the stage, which was itself in motion. Jacko's first set revolved bodily, giving way to a new and more distorted version of itself, which came to rest facing the curtain. Masking pieces were run forward to frame it in. The Doctor started off for the dressing-room passage and was at once involved with moving flats. "If you please, sir." "Stand aside there, *please*." "Clear stage, *by* your leave." His bulky shape was screened and exposed again and again as he plunged forward confusedly. Warning bells rang, the call-boy began to chant: "Second act beginners, please. Second act."

"Lights," Clem Smith said.

The shifting world stood still. Circuit by circuit, the lights came on and bore down on the acting area. The last toggle-line slapped home and was made fast and the sweating stage-hands walked disinterestedly off the set. Clem Smith, with his back to the curtain, made a final check. "Clear stage," he said and looked at his watch. The curtain-hand climbed an iron ladder.

"Six minutes," said the A.S.M. He wrote it on his chart. Clem moved into the Prompt corner. "Right," he said. "Actors, please."

J. G. Darcey and Parry Percival walked onto the set and took up their positions. Helena Hamilton came out of her dressing-room. She stood with her hands clasped lightly at her waist at a little distance from the door by which she must enter. A figure emerged from the shadows near the passage and went up to her.

"Miss Hamilton," Martyn said nervously, "I'm not on for your quick change. I can do it."

Helena turned. She looked at Martyn for a moment with an odd fixedness. Then a smile of extraordinary charm broke across her face and she took Martyn's head lightly between her hands.

"My dear child," she murmured, "my ridiculous child." She hesitated for a moment and then said briskly: "I've got a new dresser."

"A new dresser?"

"Jacko. He's most efficient."

Poole came down the passage. She turned to him and linked her arm through his. "She's going to be splendid in her scene," she said. "Isn't she?"

Poole said: "Keep it up, Kate. All's well." And in the look he gave Helena Hamilton there was something of comradeship, something of compassion and something, perhaps, of gratitude.

Dr. Rutherford emerged from the passage and addressed himself to Martyn. "Here!" he said. "I've been looking for you, my pretty. You might be a lot worse, considering, but you haven't done anything yet. When you play this next scene, my poppet, these few precepts in thy—"

"No, John," Poole and Helena Hamilton said together. "Not now."

He glowered at them. Poole nodded to Martyn, who began to move away but had not got far before she heard Rutherford say. "Have you tackled that fellow? Did you see it? Where is he? By God, when I get at him—"

"Stand by," said Clem Smith.

"Quiet, John," said Poole imperatively. "Back to your box, sir."

The curtain rose on the second act.

For the rest of her life the physical events that were encompassed by the actual performance of the play were to be almost lost for Martyn. That is to say, she was to forget all but a few desultory and quite insignificant details, such as the fact of Jacko kissing her after she came off in the second act (he smelt of toothpaste and nicotine), and of Poole, when the curtain came down, giving her his handkerchief, which surprised her until she found her face was wet with her own tears. He had said something to her, then, with a manner so unlike anything she had found in him before that it had filled her with immense surprise, but she couldn't remember his words and thought: "I shall never know what he said." She knew that when she was not playing and during the intervals, she had stood near the entry to the passage and that people had spoken to her while she was there. But these recollections had no more substance than a dream. Still more unreal was her actual performance: she thought she remembered a sense of security and command that had astonishingly blessed her, but it was as if these things had happened to someone else. Indeed, she could not be perfectly certain that they had happened at all. She might have been under hypnosis or some partial anaesthesia for all the reality they afterwards retained.

This odd condition, which was perhaps the result of some kind of physical compensation for the extreme assault on her nerves and emotions, persisted until she made her final exit in the last act. It happened some time before the curtain. The character she played was the first to relinquish its hold and to fade out of the picture. She came off and returned to her corner near the entry into the passage. The others were all on; the dressers and stage-staff, drawn by the hazards of a first night, watched from the side and Jacko was near the Prompt corner. The passage and dressing-rooms seemed deserted and Martyn was quite alone. She began to emerge from her trance-like suspension. Parry Percival came off and spoke to her.

"Darling," he said incoherently, "you were perfectly splendid. I'm just so angry at the moment I can't speak, but I do congratulate you!"

Martyn saw that he actually trembled with an emotion that was, she must suppose, fury. Out of the dream from which she was not yet fully awakened there came a memory of Gargantuan laughter and she thought she associated it with Bennington and with Percival. He said: "This settles it. I'm taking action. God, this settles it!" and darted down the passage.

Martyn thought, still confusedly, that she should go to the dressing-room and tidy her make-up for the curtain-call. But it was not her dressing-room, it was Gay's and she felt uneasy about it. While she hesitated J. G. Darcey, who had come off, put his hand on her shoulder. "Well done, child," he said. "A very creditable performance."

Martyn thanked him and, on an impulse, added: "Mr. Darcey, is Gay still here? Should I say something to her? I'd like to, but I know how she must feel and I don't want to be clumsy."

He waited for a moment, looking at her. "She's in the Greenroom," he said. "Perhaps later. Not now, I think. Nice of you."

"I won't unless you say so, then."

He made her a little bow. "I am at your service," he said and followed Percival down the passage.

Jacko came round the set with the stage-hand who was to fire the effects-gun. When he saw Martyn his whole face split in a grin. He took her hands in his and kissed them and she was overwhelmed with shyness.

"But your face," he said, wrinkling his own into a monkey's grimace. "It shines like a good deed in a naughty world. Do not touch it yourself.

To your dressing-room. I come in two minutes. Away, before your ears are blasted."

He moved down-stage, applied his eye to a secret hole in the set through which he could watch the action, and held out his arm in warning to the stage-hand, who then lifted the effects-gun. Martyn went down the passage as Bennington came off. He caught her up: "Miss Tarne. Wait a moment, will you?"

Dreading another intolerable encounter, Martyn faced him. His make-up had been designed to exhibit the brutality of the character and did so all too successfully. The lips were painted a florid red, the pouches under the eyes and the sensual drag from the nostrils to the mouth had been carefully emphasized. He was sweating heavily through the greasepaint and his face glistened in the dull light of the passage.

"I just wanted to say—" he began, and at that moment the gun was fired and Martyn gave an involuntary cry. He went on talking. "—when I see it," he was saying. "I suppose you aren't to be blamed for that. You saw your chance and took it. Gay and Adam tell me you offered to get out and were not allowed to go. That may be fair enough, I wouldn't know. But I'm not worrying about that." He spoke disjointedly. It was as if his thoughts were too disordered for any coherent expression. "I just wanted to tell you that you needn't suppose what I'm going to do—you needn't think—I mean—"

He touched his shining face with the palm of his hand. Jacko came down the passage and took Martyn by the elbow. "Quick," he said. "Into your room! You want powdering, Ben. Excuse me."

Bennington went into his own room. Jacko thrust Martyn into hers, and leaving the door open followed Bennington. She heard him say: "Take care with your upper lip. It is dripping with sweat." He darted back to Martyn, stood her near the dressing-shelf and, with an expression of the most ardent concentration, effected a number of what he called running repairs to her make-up and her hair. They heard Percival and Darcey go past on their way to the stage. A humming noise caused by some distant dynamo made itself heard, the tap in the wash-basin dripped, the voices on the stage sounded intermittently. Martyn looked at Gay's make-up box, at her dressing-gown and at the array of mascots on the shelf and wished very heartily that Jacko would have done. Presently the call-boy came down the passage with his summons for the final curtain. "Come," said Jacko.

He took her round to the Prompt side.

Here she found a group already waiting: Darcey and Percival, Clem Smith, the two dressers and, at a distance, one or two stage-hands. They all watched the final scene between Helena Hamilton and Adam Poole. In this scene Rutherford tied up and stated finally the whole thesis of his play. The man was faced with his ultimate decision. Would he stay and attempt, with the woman, to establish a sane and enlightened formula for living in place of the one he himself had destroyed, or would he go back to his island community and attempt a further development within himself and in a less complex environment? As throughout the play, the conflict was set out in terms of human and personal relationships. It could be played like many another love-scene, purely on those terms. Or it could be so handled that the wider implications could be felt by the audience, and in the hands of these two players that was what happened. The play ended with them pledging themselves to each other and to an incredible task. As Poole spoke the last lines, the electrician, with one eye on Clem below, played madly over his switchboard. The entire set changed its aspect, seemed to dissolve, turned threadbare, a skeleton, a wraith, while beyond it a wide stylized landscape was flooded with light and became, as Poole spoke the tag, the background upon which the curtain fell.

"Might as well be back in panto," said the electrician, leaning on his dimmers. "We got the transformation scene. All we want's the bloody fairy queen."

It was at this moment when the applause seemed to surge forward and beat against the curtain, when Clem shouted "All on!" and Dr. Rutherford plunged out of the O.P. pass-door, when the players walked on and linked hands that Poole, looking hurriedly along the line, said: "Where's Ben?"

One of those panic-stricken crises peculiar to the theatre boiled up on the instant. From her position between Darcey and Percival on the stage, Martyn saw the call-boy make some kind of protest to Clem Smith and disappear. Above the applause they heard him hare down the passage yelling: "Mr. Bennington! Mr. Bennington! Please! You're on!"

"We can't wait," Poole shouted. "Take it up, Clem."

The curtain rose and Martyn looked into a sea of faces and hands. She felt herself led forward into the roaring swell, bowed with the others, felt Darcey's and Percival's hands tighten on hers, bowed again and with them retreated a few steps up-stage as the first curtain fell.

"Well?" Poole shouted into the wings. The call-boy could be heard beating on the dressing-room door.

Percival said: "What's the betting he comes on for a star call?"

"He's passed out," said Darcey. "Had one or two more since he came off."

"By God, I wouldn't cry if he never came to."

"Go on, Clem," said Poole.

The curtain rose and fell again, twice. Percival and Darcey took Martyn off and it went up again on Poole and Helena Hamilton, this time to those cries of "Bravo!" that reach the actors as a long open sound like the voice of a singing wind. In the wings Clem Smith, with his eyes on the stage, was saying repeatedly: "He doesn't answer. He's locked in. The b— doesn't answer."

Martyn saw Poole coming towards her and stood aside. He seemed to tower over her as he took her hand. "Come along," he said. Darcey and Percival and the group off-stage began to clap.

Poole led her on. She felt herself resisting and heard him say: "Yes, it's all right."

So bereft was Martyn of her normal stage-wiseness that he had to tell her to bow. She did so, and wondered why there was a warm sound of laughter in the applause. She looked at Poole, found he was bowing to her and bent her head under his smile. He returned her to the wings.

They were all on again. Dr. Rutherford came out from the O.P. corner. The cast joined in the applause. Martyn's heart had begun to sing so loudly that it was like to deafen every emotion but a universal gratitude. She thought Rutherford looked like an old lion standing there in his out-of-date evening clothes, his hair ruffled, his gloved hand touching his bulging shirt, bowing in an unwieldy manner to the audience and to the cast. He moved forward and the theatre was abruptly silent—silent, but for an obscure and intermittent thudding in the dressing-room passage. Clem Smith said something to the A.S.M. and rushed away, jingling keys.

"Hah," said Dr. Rutherford with a preliminary bellow. "Hah— thankee. I'm much obliged to you, ladies and gentlemen, and to the actors. The actors are much obliged, no doubt, to you, but not necessarily to me." Here the audience laughed and the actors smiled. "I am not able to judge," the Doctor continued with a rich roll in his voice, "whether you have extracted from this play the substance of its argument. If you have done so, we may all felicitate each other with the indiscriminate enthusiasm characteristic of these occasions: if you have not, I for my part am not prepared to say where the blame should rest."

A solitary man laughed in the audience. The Doctor rolled an eye at him and, with this clownish trick, brought the house down. "The prettiest epilogue to a play that I am acquainted with," he went on, "is (as I need perhaps hardly mention to so intelligent an audience) that written for a boy actor by William Shakespeare. I am neither a boy nor an actor, but I beg leave to end by quoting it to you. 'If it be true that good wine needs no bush—' "

"Gas!" Parry Percival said under his breath. Martyn, who thought the Doctor was going well, glanced indignantly at Parry and was astonished to see that he looked frightened. " '—therefore,' " the Doctor was saying arrogantly, " 'to beg will not become me—' "

"Gas!" said an imperative voice off-stage and someone else ran noisily round the back of the set.

And then Martyn smelt it. Gas.

iv

To the actors, it seemed afterwards as if they had been fantastically slow to understand that disaster had come upon the theatre. The curtain went down on Dr. Rutherford's last word. There was a further outbreak of applause. Someone off-stage shouted: "The King, for God's sake!" and at once the anthem rolled out disinterestedly in the well. Poole ran off the stage and was met by Clem Smith, who had a bunch of keys in his hand. The rest followed him.

The area back-stage reeked of gas.

It was extraordinary how little was said. The players stood together and looked about them with the question in their faces that they were unable to ask.

Poole said: "Keep all visitors out, Clem. Send them to the foyer." And at once the A.S.M. spoke into the Prompt telephone. Bob Grantley burst through the pass-door, beaming from ear to ear.

"*Stupendous!*" he shouted. "John! Helena! Adam! My God, chaps, you've done it—"

He stood, stock-still, his arms extended, the smile drying on his face.

"Go back, Bob," Poole said. "Cope with the people. Ask our guests to go on and not wait for us. Ben's ill. Clem, get all available doors open. We want air."

Grantley said: "Gas?"

"Quick," Poole said. "Take them with you. Settle them down and explain. He's ill. Then ring me here. But quickly, Bob. Quickly."

Grantley went out without another word.

"Where is he?" Dr. Rutherford demanded.

Helena Hamilton suddenly said: "Adam?"

"Go on to the stage, Helena. It's better you shouldn't be here, believe me. Kate will stay with you. I'll come in a moment."

"Here you are, Doctor," said Clem Smith.

There was a blundering sound in the direction of the passage. Rutherford said "Open the dock-doors," and went behind the set.

Poole thrust Helena through the Prompt entry and shut the door behind her. Draughts of cold air came through the side entrances.

"Kate," Poole said, "go in and keep her there if you can. Will you? And, Kate—"

Rutherford reappeared and with him four stage-hands, bearing with difficulty the inert body of Clark Bennington. The head hung swinging upside down between the two leaders, its mouth wide open.

Poole moved quickly, but he was too late to shield Martyn.

"Never mind," he said. "Go in with Helena."

"Anyone here done respiration for gassed cases?" Dr. Rutherford demanded. "I can start but I'm not good for long."

"I can," said the A.S.M. "I was a warden."

"I can," said Jacko.

"And I," said Poole.

"In the dock, then. Shut these doors and open the outer ones."

Kneeling by Helena Hamilton and holding her hand, Martyn heard the doors roll back and the shambling steps go into the dock. The doors crashed behind them.

Martyn said: "They're giving him respiration. Dr. Rutherford's there."

Helena nodded with an air of sagacity. Her face was quite without expression and she was shivering.

"I'll get your coat," Martyn said. It was in the improvised dressing-room on the O.P. side. She was back in a moment and put Helena into it as if she were a child, guiding her arms and wrapping the fur about her.

A voice off-stage—J. G. Darcey's—said: "Where's Gay? Is Gay still in the Greenroom?"

Martyn was astonished when Helena, behind that mask that had become her face, said loudly: "Yes. She's there. In the Greenroom."

There was a moment's silence and then J.G. said: "She mustn't stay there. Good God—"

They heard him go away.

Parry Percival's voice announced abruptly that he was going to be sick. "But where?" he cried distractedly. "Where?"

"In your dressing-room, for Pete's sake," Clem Smith said.

"It'll be full of gas. Oh, *really!*" There was an agonized and not quite silent interval. "I couldn't be more sorry," Percival said weakly.

"I want," Helena said, "to know what happened. I want to see Adam. Ask him to come, please."

Martyn made for the door, but before she reached it Dr. Rutherford came in, followed by Poole. Rutherford had taken off his coat and was a fantastic sight in boiled shirt, black trousers and red braces.

"Well, Helena," he said, "this is not a nice business. We're doing everything that can be done. I'm getting a new oxygen thing in as quickly as possible. There have been some remarkable saves in these cases. But I think you ought to know it's a thinnish chance. There's no pulse and so on."

"I want," she said, holding out her hand to Poole, "to know what happened."

Poole said gently: "All right, Helena, you shall. It looks as if Ben locked himself in after his exit, and then turned the gas fire off—and on again. When Clem unlocked the door and went in he found Ben on the floor. His head was near the fire and a coat over both. He could only have been like that for quite a short time."

"This theatre," she said. "This awful theatre."

Poole looked as if he would make some kind of protest, but after a moment's hesitation he said: "All right, Helena. Perhaps it did suggest the means, but if he had made up his mind he would, in any case, have found the means."

"Why?" she said. "Why has he done it?"

Dr. Rutherford growled inarticulately and went out. They heard him open and shut the dock-doors. Poole sat down by Helena and took her hands in his. Martyn was going, but he looked up at her and said: "No, don't. Don't go, Kate," and she waited near the door.

"This is no time," Poole said, "to speculate. He may be saved. If he isn't, then we shall of course ask ourselves just why. But he was in a bad way, Helena. He'd gone to pieces and he knew it."

"I wasn't much help," she said, "was I? Though it's true to say I did try for quite a long time."

"Indeed you did. There's one thing you must be told. If it's no go with Ben, we'll have to inform the police."

She put her hand to her forehead as if puzzled. "The police?" she repeated, and stared at him. "No, darling, no!" she cried, and after a moment whispered: "They might think—oh, darling, darling, darling, the Lord knows what they might think!"

The door up-stage opened and Gay Gainsford came in, followed by Darcey.

She was in her street-clothes, and at some time during the evening had made extensive repairs to her face, which wore, at the moment, an expression oddly compounded of triumph and distraction. Before she could speak she was seized with a paroxysm of coughing.

Darcey said: "Is it all right for Gay to wait here?"

"Yes, of course," said Helena.

He went out and Poole followed him, saying he would return.

"Darling," Miss Gainsford gasped, "I knew. I knew as soon as I smelt it. There's a Thing in this theatre. Everything pointed to it. I just sat there and *knew*." She coughed again. "*Oh*, I do feel so sick," she said.

"Gay, for pity's sake, what are you talking about?" Helena said.

"It was Fate, I felt. I wasn't a bit surprised. I just knew something had to happen to-night."

"Do you mean to say," Helena murmured, and the wraith of her gift for irony was on her mouth, "that you just sat in the Greenroom with your finger raised, telling yourself it was Fate?"

"Darling Aunty—I'm sorry. I forgot. Darling Helena, wasn't it amazing?"

Helena made a little gesture of defeat. Miss Gainsford looked at her for a moment and then, with the prettiest air of compassion, knelt at her feet. "Sweet," she said, "I'm so terribly, terribly sorry. We're together in this, aren't we? He was my uncle and your husband."

"True enough," said Helena. She looked at Martyn over the head bent in devoted commiseration, and shook her own helplessly. Gay Gainsford sank into a sitting posture and leant her cheek against Helena's hand. The hand, after a courteous interval, was withdrawn.

There followed a very long silence. Martyn sat at a distance and wondered if there was anything in the world she could do to help. There was an intermittent murmur of voices somewhere off-stage. Gay Gainsford, feeling perhaps that she had sustained her position long enough, moved by gradual degrees away from her aunt by marriage, rose and, sighing heavily, transferred herself to the sofa.

Time dragged on, mostly in silence. Helena lit one cigarette from the butt of another, Gay sighed with infuriating punctuality and Martyn's thoughts drifted sadly about the evaporation of her small triumph.

Presently there were sounds of arrival. One or two persons walked round the set from the outside entry to the dock and were evidently admitted into it.

"Who can that be, I wonder?" Helena Hamilton asked idly, and after a moment: "Is Jacko about?"

"I'll see," said Martyn.

She found Jacko off-stage with Darcey and Parry Percival. Percival was saying: "Well, naturally, nobody wants to go to the party, but I must say that as one is quite evidently useless here, I don't see why one can't go home."

Jacko said: "You would be recalled by the police, I dare say, if you went."

He caught sight of Martyn, who went up to him. His face was beaded with sweat. "What is it, my small?" he asked. "This is a sad epilogue to your success story. Never mind. What is it?"

"I think Miss Hamilton would like to see you."

"Then I come. It is time, in any case."

He took her by the elbow and they went in together. When Helena saw him she seemed to rouse herself. "Jacko?" she said.

He didn't answer and she got up quickly and went to him. "Jacko? What is it? Has it happened?"

Jacko's hands, so refined and delicate that they seemed like those of another woman, touched her hair and her face.

"It has happened," he said. "We have tried very hard but nothing is any good at all, and there is no more to be done. He has taken wing."

Gay Gainsford broke into a fit of sobbing, but Helena stooped her head to Jacko's shoulder and when his arms had closed about her said: "Help me to feel something, Jacko. I'm quite empty of feeling. Help me to be sorry."

Above her head Jacko's face, glistening with sweat, grotesque and primitive, had the fixed inscrutability of a classic mask.

Chapter VII

Disaster

The fact of Bennington's death had the effect of changing the values of other circumstances in the theatre. One after another the members of the company had said what they could to Helena Hamilton, and she had thanked them. She was very tremulous and uncertain of her voice, but she did not break down at any time and seemed, Martyn thought, to be in a kind of trance. At first they were all uncomfortably silent but, as the minutes slipped by, they fell into muted conversation. Most of what they said was singularly aimless. Matters of normal consequence were forgotten, details of behaviour became ridiculously important.

The question, for instance, of where they should assemble exercised the whole company. It was almost eleven o'clock and the stage was beginning to grow cold.

Clem Smith had rung up the police as soon as Dr. Rutherford said that Bennington was beyond recovery, and within five minutes a constable and sergeant had appeared at the stage-door. They went into the dock with Rutherford and then to Bennington's dressing-room, where they remained alone for some time. During this period an aimless discussion developed among the members of the company about where they should go. Clem Smith suggested the Greenroom as the warmest place, and added tactlessly that the fumes had probably dispersed and if so there was no reason why they shouldn't light the fire. Both Parry Percival and Gay Gainsford had made an outcry against this suggestion on the grounds of delicacy and susceptibility. Darcey supported Gay, the A.S.M. suggested the offices and Jacko the auditorium. Dr. Rutherford, who appeared to be less upset than anyone else, merely remarked that "All places that the eye of heaven visits are to a wise man ports and happy havens," which, as Percival said acidly, got them nowhere.

Finally, Poole asked if the central-heating couldn't be stoked up and a stage-hand was dispatched to the underworld to find out. Evidently he met with success as presently the air became less chilled.

They waited in the last-act set, much as they had waited when Poole summed up at the dress rehearsal. In this final scene, which was painted on gauze, Jacko had, by the use of grotesque perspective and exaggerated emphases, achieved a distortion of the second set, which itself was a distortion of the first. The walls and staircase seemed to lean over the actors, crushing them into too small a compass. Martyn became very much aware of this and disliked it.

The resemblance to the dress rehearsal was heightened by Jacko, who had fetched Helena's dressing-case from her room. Again she removed her make-up on the stage, but this time it was Jacko who held the glass for her. He had brought powder and her bag for Martyn and a towel for each of them. With only a spatter of desultory conversation, the players sat about the stage and cleaned their faces. And they listened.

They heard the two men come back along the passage and separate. Then the central door opened and the young constable came in.

He was a tall, good-looking youth with a charming smile.

"The sergeant," he said, "has asked me to explain that he's telephoning Scotland Yard. He couldn't be more sorry, but he's afraid he'll have to ask everybody to wait until he gets his instructions. He's sure you'll understand that it's just a matter of routine."

He might have been apologizing for his mother's late arrival at her own dinner-party.

He was about to withdraw when Dr. Rutherford said: "Hi! Sonny!"

"Yes, sir?" said the young constable obligingly.

"You intrigue me. You talk, as they say, like a book. *None sine dis animosus infans.* You swear with a good grace and wear your boots very smooth, do you not?"

The young constable was, it seemed, only momentarily taken aback. He said: "Well, sir, for my boots, they are after the Dogberry fashion, and for my swearing, sir, it goes by the book."

The Doctor, who until now had seemed to share the general feeling of oppression and shock, appeared to cheer up with indecent haste. He was, in fact, clearly enchanted. "Define, define, well educated infant," he quoted exultantly.

"I mean that in court, sir, we swear by the book. But I'm afraid, sir," added the young constable apologetically, "that I'm not much of a hand at 'Bardinage.' My purse is empty already. If you'll excuse me," he concluded, with a civil glance round the company, "I'll just—"

He was again about to withdraw when his sergeant came in at the O.P. entrance.

"Good evening, ladies and gentlemen," the sergeant said, in what

Martyn, for one, felt was the regulation manner. "Very sorry to keep you, I'm sure. Sad business. In these cases we have to do a routine check-up, as you might say. My superior officers will be here in a moment and then, I hope, we shan't be long. Thank you."

He tramped across the stage, said something inaudible to the constable and was heard to go into the dock. The constable took a chair from the Prompt corner, placed it in the proscenium entrance and, with a modest air, sat on it. His glance fell upon Martyn and he smiled at her. They were the youngest persons there and it was as if they signalled in a friendly manner to each other. In turning away from this pleasant exchange, Martyn found that Poole was watching her with fixed and, it seemed, angry glare. To her fury she found that she was very much disturbed by this circumstance.

They had by this time all cleaned their faces. Helena Hamilton with an unsteady hand put on a light street make-up. The men looked ghastly in the cold working-lights that bleakly illuminated the stage.

Parry Percival said fretfully: "Well, I must say I do *not* see the smallest point in our hanging about like this."

The constable was about to answer when they all heard sounds of arrival at the stage-door. He said: "This will be the party from the Yard, sir," and crossed to the far exit. The sergeant was heard to join him there.

There was a brief conversation off-stage. A voice said: "You two go round with Gibson then, will you? I'll join you in a moment."

The young constable reappeared to usher in a tall man in plain clothes.

"Chief Detective-Inspector Alleyn," he said.

ii

Martyn, in her weary pilgrimage round the West End, had seen men of whom Alleyn at first reminded her. In the neighbourhood of the St. James's Theatre they had emerged from clubs, from restaurants and from enchanting and preposterous shops. There had been something in their bearing and their clothes that gave them a precise definition. But when she looked more closely at Inspector Alleyn's face, this association became modified. It was a spare and scholarly face with a monkish look about it.

Martyn had formed the habit of thinking of people's voices in terms of colour. Helena Hamilton's voice, for instance, was for Martyn golden, Gay Gainsford's pink, Darcey's brown and Adam Poole's violet.

When Alleyn spoke she decided that his voice was a royal blue of the clearest sort.

Reminding herself that this was no time to indulge this freakish habit of classification, she gave him her full attention.

"You will, I'm sure," he was saying, "realize that in these cases our job is simply to determine that they are, on the face of it, what they appear to be. In order to do this effectively we are obliged to make a fairly thorough examination of the scene as we find it. This takes a little time always, but if everything's quite straightforward, as I expect it will be, we won't keep you very long. Is that clear?"

He looked round his small audience. Poole said at once: "Yes, of course. We all understand. At the same time, if it's a matter of taking statements, I'd be grateful if you'd see Miss Hamilton first."

"Miss Hamilton?" Alleyn said, and after a moment's hesitation looked at her.

"I'm his wife," she said. "I'm Helena Bennington."

"I'm so sorry. I didn't know. Yes, I'm sure that can be managed. Probably the best way will be for me to see you all together. If everything seems quite clear there may be no need for further interviews. And now, if you'll excuse me, I'll have a look round and then rejoin you. There is a doctor among you, isn't there? Dr. Rutherford?" Dr. Rutherford cleared his throat portentously. "Are you he, sir? Perhaps you'll join us."

"Indubitably," said the Doctor. "I had so concluded."

"Good," Alleyn said and looked faintly amused. "Will you lead the way?"

They were at the door when Jacko suddenly said: "A moment, if you please, Chief Inspector."

"Yes?"

"I would like permission to make soup. There is a filthy small kitchen-place inhabited only by the night-watchman, where I have waiting a can of prepared soup. Everyone is very cold and fatigued and entirely empty. My name is Jacques Doré, I am dogsbody-in-waiting in this theatre and there is much virtue in my soup."

Alleyn said: "By all means. Is the kitchen-place that small sink-room near the dock with the gas jet in it?"

"But you haven't looked at the place yet!" Parry Percival ejaculated.

"I've been here before," said Alleyn. "I remember the theatre. Shall we get on, Dr. Rutherford?"

They went out. Gay Gainsford, whose particular talent from now onwards was to lie in the voicing of disquieting thoughts which her companions shared but decided to leave unspoken, said in a distracted manner: *"When* was he here before?" And when nobody answered, she said dramatically: "I can see it all! He must be the man they sent that other time." She paused and collected their reluctant attention. She laid her hand on J.G.'s arm and raised her voice. "That's why he's come again," she announced.

"Come now, dear," J.G. murmured inadequately, and Poole said quickly: "My *dear* Gay!"

"But I'm right," she persisted. "I'm sure I'm right. Why else should he know about the sink-room?" She looked about her with an air of terrified complacency.

"And last time," she pointed out, *"it was Murder."*

"Climax," said Jacko. "Picture and Slow Curtain! Put your hands together, ladies and gentlemen, for this clever little artist."

He went out with his eyes turned up.

"Jacko's terribly hard, isn't he?" Gay said to Darcey. "After all, Uncle Ben *was* my uncle." She caught sight of Helena Hamilton. "And your husband," she said hurriedly, "of course, darling."

iii

The stage-hands had set up in the dock one of the trestle-tables used for properties. They had laid Clark Bennington's body on it and had covered it with a sheet from the wardrobe-room. The dock was a tall echoing place, concrete-floored, with stacks of old flats leaning against the walls. A solitary unprotected lamp bulb, dust-encrusted, hung above the table.

A group of four men in dark overcoats and hats stood beside this improvised bier, and it so chanced they had taken up their places at the four corners and looked therefore as if they kept guard over it. Their hats shadowed their faces and they stood in pools of shadow. A fifth man, bareheaded, stood at the foot of the bier and a little removed from it. When the tallest of the men reached out to the margin of the sheet, his arm cast a black bar over its white and eloquent form. His gloved hand dragged down the sheet and exposed a rigid gaping face encrusted with greasepaint. He uncovered his head and the other three, a little awkwardly, followed his example.

"Well, Curtis?" he said.

Dr. Curtis, the police surgeon, bent over the head, blotting it out with his shadow. He took a flash lamp from his pocket and the face, in this changed light, stared out with an altered look as if it had secretly rear-ranged its expression.

"God!" Curtis muttered. "He looks pretty ghastly, doesn't he? What an atrocious make-up!"

From his removed position Dr. Rutherford said loudly: "My dear man, the make-up was required by My Play. It should, in point of fact, be a damn sight more repellent. But—*vanitas vanitatum*. Also: *Mit der Dummheit kämpfen Götter selbst vergebens*. I didn't let them fix him up at all. Thought you'd prefer not." His voice echoed coldly round the dock.

"Quite so," Curtis murmured. "Much better not."

"Smell very noticeable still," a thickset, grizzled man observed. "Always hangs about in these cases," rejoined the sergeant, "doesn't it, Mr. Fox?"

"We worked damn hard on him," Dr. Rutherford said. "It never looked like it from the start. Not a hope."

"Well," said Curtis, drawing back, "it all seems straightforward enough, Alleyn. It doesn't call for a very extensive autopsy, but of course we'll do the usual things."

"Lend me your torch a moment," Alleyn said, and after a moment: "Very heavy make-up, isn't it? He's so thickly powdered."

"He needed it. He sweated," Dr. Rutherford said, "like a pig. Alcohol and a dicky heart."

"Did you look after him, sir?"

"Not I. I don't practise nowadays. The alcohol declared itself and he used to talk about a heart condition. Valvular trouble, I should imagine. I don't know who his medical man was. His wife can tell you."

Dr. Curtis replaced the sheet. "That," he said to Rutherford, "might account for him going quickly."

"Certainly."

"There's a mark on the jaw," Alleyn said. "Did either of you notice it? The make-up is thinner there. Is it a bruise?"

Curtis said: "I saw it, yes. It might be a bruise. We'll see better when we clean him up."

"Right. I'll look at the room," Alleyn said. "Who found him?"

"The stage-manager," said Rutherford.

"Then perhaps you wouldn't mind asking him to come along when you rejoin the others. Thank you so much, Dr. Rutherford. We're glad to have had your report. You'll be called for the inquest, I'm afraid."

"Hell's teeth, I suppose I shall. So be it." He moved to the doors.

The sergeant obligingly rolled them open and he muttered "Thankee," and with an air of dissatisfaction went out.

Dr. Curtis said: "I'd better go and make professional noises at him." "Yes, do," Alleyn said.

On their way to Bennington's room they passed Jacko and a stage-hand bearing a fragrant steaming can and a number of cups to the stage. In his cubby-hole, Fred Badger was entertaining a group of stage-hands and dressers. They had steaming pannikins in their hands and they eyed the police party in silence.

"Smells very tasty, doesn't it?" Detective-Inspector Fox observed rather wistfully.

The young constable, who was stationed by the door through which Martyn had made her entrance, opened it for the soup party and shut it after them.

Fox growled: "Keep your wits about you."

"Yes, sir," said the young constable and exhibited his note-book.

Clem Smith was waiting for them in Bennington's room. The lights were full on and a white glare beat on the dressing-shelf and walls. Bennington's street-clothes and his suit for the first act hung on coat-hangers along the wall. His make-up was laid out on a towel, and the shelf was littered with small objects that in their casual air of usage suggested that he had merely left the room for a moment and would return to take them up again. On the floor, hard by the dead gas fire, lay an overcoat from which the reek of gas, which still hung about the room, seemed to arise. The worn rug was drawn up into wrinkles.

Clem Smith's face was white and anxious under his shock of dark hair. He shook hands jerkily with Alleyn and then looked as if he wondered if he ought to have done so. "This is a pretty ghastly sort of party," he muttered, "isn't it?"

Alleyn said: "It seems that you came in for the worst part of it. Do you mind telling us what happened?"

Fox moved behind Clem and produced his note-book. Sergeant Gibson began to make a list of the objects in the room. Clem watched him with an air of distaste.

"Easy enough to tell you," he said. "He came off about eight minutes before the final curtain and I suppose went straight to this room. When the boy came round for the curtain-call, Ben didn't appear with the others. I didn't notice. There's an important light-cue at the end and I was watching for it. Then, when they all went on, he just wasn't there. We couldn't hold the curtain for long. I sent it up for the first call and the boy went back and hammered on this door. It was locked. He smelt gas and began to yell for Ben and then ran back to tell me what was wrong. I'd got the Doctor on for his speech by that time. I left my A.S.M. in charge, took the bunch of extra keys from the Prompt corner and tore round here."

He wetted his lips and fumbled in his pocket. "Is it safe to smoke?" he asked.

"I'm afraid we'd better wait a little longer," Alleyn said. "Sorry."

"O.K. Well, I unlocked the door. As soon as it opened the stink hit me in the face. I don't know why, but I expected him to be sitting at the shelf. I don't suppose, really, it was long before I saw him, but it seemed fantastically long. He was lying there by the heater. I could only see his legs and the lower half of his body. The rest was hidden by that coat. It was tucked in behind the heater, and over his head and shoulders. It looked like a tent. I heard the hiss going on underneath it." Clem rubbed his mouth. "I don't think," he said, "I was as idiotically slow as all this makes me out to be. I don't think, honestly, it was more than seconds before I went in. Honestly, I don't think so."

"I expect you're right about that. Time goes all relative in a crisis."

"Does it? Good. Well, then: I ran in and hauled the coat away. He was on his left side—his mouth—it was— The lead-in had been disconnected and it was by his mouth, hissing. I turned it off and dragged him by the heels. He sort of stuck on the carpet. Jacko—Jacques Doré bolted in and helped."

"One moment," Alleyn said. "Did you knock over that box of powder on the dressing-table? Either of you?"

Clem Smith stared at it. "That? No, I didn't go near it and I'd got him half-way to the door when Jacko came in. He must have done it himself."

"Right. Sorry. Go on."

"We lifted Ben into the passage and shut his door. At the far end of the passage there's a window, the only one near. We got it open and carried him to it. I think he was dead even then. I'm sure he was. I've seen gassed cases before, in the blitz."

Alleyn said: "You seem to have tackled this one like an old hand, at all events."

"I'm damn glad you think so," said Clem, and sounded it.

Alleyn looked at the Yale lock on the door. "This seems in good enough shape," he said absently.

"It's new," Clem said. "There were pretty extensive renovations and a sort of general clean-up when Mr. Poole took the theatre over. It's useful for the artists to be able to lock up valuables in their rooms and the old locks were clumsy and rusted up. In any case—" He stopped and then said uncomfortably: "The whole place has been repainted and modernized."

"Including the gas installations?"

"Yes," said Clem, not looking at Alleyn. "That's all new, too."

"Two of the old dressing-rooms have been knocked together to form the Greenroom?"

"Yes."

"And there are new dividing walls? And ventilators, now, in the dressing-rooms?"

"Yes," said Clem unhappily and added, "I suppose that's why he used his coat."

"It does look," Alleyn said without stressing it, "as if the general idea was to speed things up, doesn't it? All right, Mr. Smith, thank you. Would you explain to the people on the stage that I'll come as soon as we've finished our job here? It won't be very long. We'll probably ask you to sign a statement of the actual discovery as you've described it to us. You'll be glad to get away frm this room, I expect."

Inspector Fox had secreted his note-book and now ushered Clem Smith out. Clem appeared to go thankfully.

"Plain sailing, wouldn't you say, Mr. Alleyn," said Fox, looking along the passage. "Nobody about," he added. "I'll leave the door open."

Alleyn rubbed his nose. "It looks like plain sailing, Fox, certainly. But in view of the other blasted affair we can't take a damn thing for granted. You weren't on the Jupiter case, were you, Gibson?"

"No, sir," said Gibson, looking up from his note-book. "Homicide dressed up to look like suicide, wasn't it?"

"It was, indeed. The place has been pretty extensively chopped up and rehashed, but the victim was on this side of the passage and in what must have been the room now taken in to make the Greenroom. Next door there was a gas fire backing on to his own. The job was done by blowing down the tube next door. This put out the fire in this room and left the gas on, of course. The one next door was then re-lit. The victim was pretty well dead-drunk and the trick worked. We got the bloke on the traces of crepe hair and greasepaint he left on the tube."

"Very careless," Fox said. "Silly chap, really."

"The theatre," Alleyn said, "was shut up for a long time. Three or four years at least. Then Adam Poole took it, renamed it the Vulcan and got a permit for renovation. I fancy this is only his second production here."

"Perhaps," Fox speculated, "the past history of the place played on deceased's mind and led him to do away with himself after the same fashion."

"Sort of superstitious?" Gibson ventured.

"Not precisely," said Fox majestically. "And yet something after that style of thing. They're a very superstitious mob, actors, Fred. Very. And if he had reason, in any case, to entertain the notion of suicide—"

"He must," Alleyn interjected, "have also entertained the very very nasty notion of throwing suspicion of foul play on his fellow-actors. If there's a gas fire back-to-back with this—"

"And there is," Fox said.

"The devil there is! So what does Bennington do? He re-creates as far as possible the whole set-up, leaves no note, no indication, as far as we can see, of his intention to gas himself, and—who's next door, Fox?"

"A Mr. Parry Percival."

"All right. Bennington pushes off, leaving Mr. Parry Percival ostensibly in the position of the Jupiter murderer. Rotten sort of suicide that'd be, Br'er Fox."

"We don't know anything yet, of course," said Fox.

"We don't, and the crashing hellish bore about the whole business lies in the all-too-obvious fact that we'll have to find out. What's on your inventory, Gibson?"

Sergeant Gibson opened his note-book and adopted his official manner.

"Dressing-table or shelf," he said. "One standing mirror. One cardboard box containing false hair, rouge, substance labelled 'nose-paste,' seven fragments of greasepaint and one unopened box of powder. Shelf. Towel spread out to serve as table-cloth. On towel, one tray containing six sticks of greasepaint. To right of tray, bottle of spirit-adhesive. Bottle containing what appears to be substance known as liquid powder. Open box of powder overturned. Behind box of powder, pile of six pieces of cotton-wool and a roll from which these pieces have been removed." He looked up at Alleyn. "Intended to be used for powdering purposes, Mr. Alleyn."

"That's it," Alleyn said. He was doubled up, peering at the floor under the dressing-shelf. "Nothing there," he grunted. "Go on."

"To left of tray, cigarette case with three cigarettes and open box of fifty. Box of matches. Ash-tray. Towel, stained with greasepaint. Behind mirror, flask—one-sixth full—and used tumbler smelling of spirits."

Alleyn looked behind the standing glass. "Furtive sort of cache," he said. "Go on."

"Considerable quantity of powder spilt on shelf and on adjacent floor area. Considerable quantity of ash. Left wall, clothes. I haven't been through the pockets yet, Mr. Alleyn. There's nothing on the floor but powder and some paper ash, original form undistinguishable. Stain as of something burnt on hearth."

"Go ahead with it then. I wanted," Alleyn said with a discontented air, "to *hear* whether I was wrong."

Fox and Gibson looked placidly at him. "All right," he said, "don't mind me. I'm broody."

He squatted down by the overcoat. "It really is the most obscene smell, gas," he muttered. "How anybody *can* always passes my comprehension." He poked in a gingerly manner at the coat. "Powder over everything," he grumbled. "Where had this coat been? On the empty hanger near the door, presumably. That's damned rum. Check it with his dresser. We'll have to get Bailey along, Fox. And Thompson. Blast!"

"I'll ring the Yard," said Fox and went out.

Alleyn squinted through a lens at the wing-taps of the gas fire. "I can see prints clearly enough," he said, "on both. We can check with Bennington's. There's even a speck or two of powder settled on the taps."

"In the air, sir, I dare say," said Gibson.

"I dare say it was. Like the gas. We can't go any further here until the dabs and flash party has done its stuff. Finished, Gibson?"

"Finished, Mr. Alleyn. Nothing much in the pockets. Bills. Old racing card. Cheque-book and so on. Nothing on the body, by the way, but a handkerchief."

"Come on, then. I've had my belly-full of gas."

But he stood in the doorway eyeing the room and whistling softly.

"I wish I could believe in you," he apostrophized it, "but split me and sink me if I can. No, by all that's phoney, not for one credulous second. Come on, Gibson. Let's talk to these experts."

iv

They all felt a little better for Jacko's soup, which had been laced with something that, as J. G. Darcey said (and looked uncomfortable as soon as he'd said it), went straight to the spot marked X.

Whether it was this potent soup, or whether extreme emotional and physical fatigue had induced in Martyn its familiar complement, an uncanny sharpening of the mind, she began to consider for the first time the general reaction of the company to Bennington's death. She thought: "I don't believe there's one of us who really minds very much. How lonely for him! Perhaps he guessed that was how it would be. Perhaps he felt the awful isolation of a child that knows itself unwanted and thought he'd put himself out of the way of caring."

It was a shock to Martyn when Helena Hamilton suddenly gave voice to her own thoughts. Helena had sat with her chin in her hand, looking at the floor. There was an unerring grace about her and this fireside posture had the beauty of complete relaxation. Without raising her eyes she said: "My dears, my dears, for pity's sake don't let's pretend. Don't let me pretend. I didn't love him. Isn't that sad? We all know and we try to patch up a decorous scene but it won't do. We're shocked and uneasy and dreadfully tired. Don't let's put ourselves to the trouble of pretending. It's so useless."

Gay said, "But I *did* love him!" and J.G. put his arm about her.

"Did you?" Helena murmured. "Perhaps you did, darling. Then you must hug your sorrow to yourself. Because I'm afraid nobody really shares it."

Poole said: "We understand, Helena."

With that familiar gesture, not looking at him, she reached out her hand. When he had taken it in his, she said: "When one is dreadfully tired one talks. I do, at all events. I talk much too easily. Perhaps that's a sign of a shallow woman. You know, my dears, I begin to think I'm only capable of affection. I have a great capacity for affection, but as for my loves, they have no real permanency. None."

Jacko said gently: "Perhaps your talent for affection is equal to other women's knack of loving."

Gay and Parry Percival looked at him in astonishment, but Poole said: "That may well be."

"What I meant to say," Helena went on, "only I do sidetrack myself so awfully, is this. Hadn't we better stop being muted and mournful and talk about what may happen and what we ought to do? Adam, darling, I thought perhaps they might all be respecting my sorrow or something. What should we be talking about? What's the situation?"

Poole moved one of the chairs with its back to the curtain and sat in it. Dr. Rutherford returned and lumped himself down in the corner. "They're talking," he said, "to Clem Smith in the—they're talking to Clem. I've seen the police surgeon, a subfuse exhibit, but one that can tell a hawk from a handsaw if they're held under his nose. He agrees that there was nothing else I could have done, which is no doubt immensely gratifying to me. What are you all talking about? You look like a dress rehearsal."

"We were about to discuss the whole situation," said Poole. "Helena feels it should be discussed and I think we all agree with her."

"What situation pray? Ben's? Or ours? There is no more to be said about Ben's situation. As far as we know, my dear Helena, he has administered to himself a not too uncomfortable and effective anaesthetic which, after he had become entirely unconscious, brought about the end he had in mind. For a man who had decided to shuffle off this mortal coil he behaved very sensibly."

"Oh, *please*," Gay whispered. *"Please!"*

Dr. Rutherford contemplated her in silence for a moment and then said: "What's up, Misery?" Helena, Darcey and Parry Percival made expostulatory noises. Poole said: "See here, John, you'll either pipe down or preserve the decencies."

Gay, fortified perhaps by this common reaction, said loudly: "You might at least have the grace to remember he was my uncle."

"Grace me no grace," Dr. Rutherford quoted inevitably, "and uncle me no uncles." After a moment's reflection, he added: "All right, Thalia, have a good cry. But you must know, if the rudiments of reasoned thinking are within your command, that your Uncle Ben did you a damn shabby turn. A scurvy trick, by God. However, I digress. Get on with the post mortem, Chorus. I am dumb."

"You'll be good enough to remain so," said Poole warmly. "Very well, then. It seems to me, Helena, that Ben took this—this way out—for a number of reasons. I know you want me to speak plainly and I'm going to speak very plainly indeed, my dear."

"Oh, yes," she said. "Please, but—" For a moment they looked at each other. Martyn wondered if she imagined that Poole's head moved in the faintest possible negative. "Yes," Helena said, "very plainly, please."

"Well, then," Poole said, "we know that for the last year Ben, never a very temperate man, has been a desperately intemperate one. We know his habits undermined his health, his character and his integrity as an actor. I think he realized this very thoroughly. He was an unhappy man, who looked back at what he had once been and was appalled. We all know he did things in performance to-night that, from an actor of his standing, were quite beyond the pale."

Parry Percival ejaculated: "Well, I mean to say—oh, well. Never mind."

"Exactly," Poole said. "He had reached a sort of chronic state of instability. We all know he was subject to fits of depression. I believe he did what he did when he was at a low ebb. I believe he would have done it sooner or later by one means or another. And in my view, for what it's worth, that's the whole story. Tragic enough, God knows, but, in its tragedy, simple. I don't know if you agree."

Darcey said: "If there's nothing else. I mean," he said diffidently, glancing at Helena, "if nothing has happened that would seem like a further motive."

Helena's gaze rested for a moment on Poole and then on Darcey. "I think Adam's right," she said. "I'm afraid he was appalled by a sudden realization of himself. I'm afraid he was insufferably lonely."

"Oh, my God!" Gay ejaculated, and having by this means collected their unwilling attention she added: "I shall never forgive myself. Never."

Dr. Rutherford groaned loudly.

"I failed him," Gay announced. "I was a bitter, bitter disappointment to him. I dare say I turned the scale."

"Now in the name of all the gods at once," Dr. Rutherford began, and was brought to a stop by the entry of Clem Smith.

Clem looked uneasily at Helena Hamilton and said: "They're in the dressing-room. He says they won't keep you waiting much longer."

"It's all right, then?" Parry Percival blurted out and added in a flurry: "I mean there won't be a whole lot of formalities. I mean we'll be able to get away. I mean—"

"I've no idea about that," Clem said. "Alleyn just said they'd be here soon." He had brought a cup of soup with him and he withdrew into a corner and began to drink it. The others watched him anxiously but said nothing.

"What did he ask you about?" Jacko demanded suddenly.

"About what we did at the time."

"Anything else?"

"Well, yes. He—well, in point of fact, he seemed to be interested in the alterations to the theatre."

"To the dressing-rooms in particular?" Poole asked quickly.

"Yes," Clem said unhappily. "To them."

There was a long silence, broken by Jacko.

"I find nothing remarkable in this," he said. "Helena has shown us the way with great courage and Adam has spoken his mind. Let us all speak ours. I may resemble an ostrich but I do not propose to imitate its behaviour. Of what do we all think? There is the unpleasing little circumstance of the Jupiter case and we think of that. When Gay mentions it she does so with the air of one who opens a closet and out tumbles a skeleton. But why? It is inevitable that these gentlemen, who also remember the Jupiter case, should wish to inspect the dressing-rooms. They wish, in fact, to make very sure indeed that this is a case of suicide and not of murder. And since we are all quite certain that it is suicide we should not disturb ourselves that they do their duty."

"Exactly," Poole said.

"It's going," Darcey muttered, "to be damn bad publicity."

"Merciful Heavens!" Parry Percival exclaimed. "The Publicity! None of us thought of that!"

"Did we not!" said Poole.

"I must say," Parry complained, "I *would* like to know what's going to happen, Adam. I mean—darling Helena, I know you'll understand—but I mean, about the piece. Do we go on? Or what?"

"Yes," Helena said. "We go on. Please, Adam."

"Helena, I've got to think. There are so many—"

"We go on. Indeed, indeed we do."

Martyn felt rather than saw the sense of relief in Darcey and Percival.

Darcey said: "I'm the understudy, Lord help me," and Percival made a tiny ambiguous sound that might have been one of satisfaction or of chagrin.

"How are you for it, J.G.?" Helena asked.

"I *know* it," he said heavily.

"I'll work whenever you like. We've got the week-end."

"Thank you, Helena."

"Your own understudy's all right," said Clem.

"Good."

It was clear to Martyn that this retreat into professionalism was a great relief to them, and it was clear also that Poole didn't share in their comfort. Watching him, she was reminded of his portrait in the Greenroom: he looked withdrawn and troubled.

A lively and almost cosy discussion about re-casting had developed. Clem Smith, Jacko and Percival were all talking at once when, with her infallible talent for scenes, Gay exclaimed passionately:

"I can't bear it! I think you're all awful!"

They broke off. Having collected their attention, she built rapidly to her climax. "To sit round and talk about the show as if nothing had happened! How you can! When beyond those doors, he's lying there, forgotten. Cold and forgotten! It's the most brutal thing I've ever heard of, and if you think I'm coming near this horrible, fated, *haunted* place again, I'm telling you here and now that wild horses wouldn't drag me inside the theatre once I'm away from it. I suppose someone will find time to tell me when the funeral is going to be. I happen to be just about his only relation."

They all began to expostulate at once, but she topped their lines with the determination of a robust star. "You needn't bother to explain," she shouted. "I understand only too well, thank you." She caught sight of Martyn and pointed wildly at her. "You've angled for this miserable part, and now you've got it. I think it's extremely likely you're responsible for what's happened."

Poole said: "You'll stop at once, Gay. Stop."

"I won't! I won't be gagged! It drove my Uncle Ben to despair and I don't care who knows it."

It was upon this line that Alleyn, as if he had mastered one of the major points of stage technique, made his entrance up-stage and centre.

v

Although he must have heard every word of Gay's final outburst, Alleyn gave no sign of having done so. He and the young constable came in and, as if he had walked into somebody's flat, he took off his hat and put it on a table near the door. The young constable looked round and then went off-stage, returning with two chairs which he placed, one in a central position for Alleyn, and one in the O.P. corner for himself. To Martyn he had fantastically the air of an A.D.C. As he settled himself he gave her another of his friendly smiles.

Clem and Parry had got uncomfortably to their feet and now sat down again in a faintly huffy manner. With the exception of Dr. Rutherford, the company reorientated itself, unobtrusively, on Alleyn.

"Well, now," he said, "I'm afraid the first thing I have to say to you all won't be very pleasant news. We don't look like getting through with our side of this unhappy business as quickly as I hoped. I know you are all desperately tired and very shocked and I'm sorry. But the general circumstances aren't quite as straightforward as, on the face of it, you have probably supposed them to be."

A trickle of ice moved under Martyn's diaphragm. She thought: "No, it's not fair. I can't be made to have two goes of the jim-jams in one night."

Alleyn addressed himself specifically to Helena Hamilton.

"You'll have guessed—of course you will—that one can't overlook the other case of gas poisoning that is associated with this theatre. It must have jumped to everybody's mind almost at once."

"Yes, of course," she said. "We've been talking about it."

The men looked uneasily at her but Alleyn said at once: "I'm sure you have. So have we. And I expect you've wondered, as we have, if the memory of that former case could have influenced your husband."

"I'm certain it did," she said quickly. "We all are."

The others made small affirmative noises. Only Dr. Rutherford was silent. Martyn saw with amazement that his chin had sunk on his rhythmically heaving bosom, his eyes were shut and his lips pursed in the manner of a sleeper who is just not snoring. He was at the back of the group and, she hoped, concealed from Alleyn.

"Have you," Alleyn asked, "any specific argument to support this theory?"

"No *specific* reason. But I know he thought a lot of that other dreadful business. He didn't *like* this theatre. Mr. Alleyn, actors are sensitive to atmosphere. We talk a lot about the theatres we play in and we get very vivid—you would probably think absurdly vivid—impressions of their 'personalities.' My husband felt there was a—an unpleasant atmosphere in this place. He often said so. In a way I think it had a rather horrible fascination for him. We'd a sort of tacit understanding in the Vulcan that its past history wouldn't be discussed among us, but I know he did talk about it. Not to us, but to people who had been concerned in the other affair."

"Yes, I see." Alleyn waited for a moment. The young constable completed a note. His back was now turned to the company. "Did anyone else notice this preoccupation of Mr. Bennington's?"

"Oh, yes!" Gay said with mournful emphasis. "*I* did. He talked to me about it, but when he saw how much it upset me—because I'm so stupidly sensitive to atmosphere—I just can't help it—it's one of those things—but I *am*—because when I first came into the theatre I just knew —you may laugh at me but these things can't be denied—"

"When," Alleyn prompted, "he saw that it upset you?"

"He stopped. I was his niece. It was rather a marvellous relationship."

"He stopped," Alleyn said, "Right." He had a programme in his hand and now glanced at it. "You must be Miss Gainsford, I think. Is that right?"

"Yes, I am. But my name's really Bennington. I'm his only brother's daughter. My father died in the war and Uncle Ben really felt we were awfully near to each other, do you know? That's why it's so devastating for me, because I sensed how wretchedly unhappy he was."

"Do you mind telling us why you thought him so unhappy?"

J. G. Darcey interposed quickly: "I don't think it was more than a general intuitive sort of thing, was it, Gay? Nothing special."

"Well—" Gay said reluctantly, and Helena intervened.

"I don't think any of us have any doubt about my husband's unhappiness, Mr. Alleyn. Before you came in I was saying how most, *most* anxious I am that we should be very frank with each other and of course with you. My husband drank so heavily that he had ruined his health and his work quite completely. I wasn't able to help him and we were not—" The colour died out of her face and she hesitated. "Our life together wasn't true," she said. "It had no reality at all. To-night he behaved very badly on the stage. He coloured his part at the expense of the other actors and I think he was horrified at what he'd done. He was very drunk indeed to-night. I feel he suddenly looked at himself and couldn't face what he saw. I feel that very strongly."

"One *does* sense these things," Gay interjected eagerly, "or I do at any rate."

"I'm sure you do," Alleyn agreed politely. Gay drew breath and was about to go on when he said: "Of course, if any of you can tell us any happenings or remarks or so on that seem to prove that he had this thing in mind, it will be a very great help."

Martyn heard her voice—acting, it seemed, of its own volition. "I think, perhaps—"

Alleyn turned to her and his smile reassured her. "Yes?" he said. "Forgive me, but I don't yet know all your names." He looked again at his programme and then at her. Gay gave a small laugh. Darcey put his hand over hers and said something undistinguishable.

Poole said quickly: "Miss Martyn Tarne. She is, or should be, our heroine to-night. Miss Gainsford was ill and Miss Tarne, who was the understudy, took her part at half-an-hour's notice. We'd all be extremely proud of her if we had the wits to be anything but worried and exhausted."

Martyn's heart seemed to perform some eccentric gyration in the direction of her throat and she thought: "That's done it. Now my voice is going to be ungainly with emotion."

Alleyn said: "That must have been a most terrifying and exciting adventure," and she gulped and nodded. "What had you remembered," he went on after a moment, "that might help us?"

"It was something he said when he came off in the last act."

"For his final exit in the play?"

"Yes."

"I'll be very glad to hear it."

"I'll try to remember exactly what it was," Martyn said carefully. "I was in the dressing-room passage on my way to my—to Miss Gainsford's room and he caught me up. He spoke very disjointedly and strangely, not finishing his sentences. But one thing he said—I think it was the last—I do remember quite distinctly because it puzzled me very much. He said: 'I just wanted to tell you that you needn't suppose what I'm going to do—' and then he stopped as if he was confused and added, I think: 'You needn't suppose—' and broke off again. And then Jacko—Mr. Doré—came and told me to go into the dressing-room to have my make-up attended to and, I think, said something to Mr. Bennington about his."

"I told him he was shining with sweat," said Jacko. "And he went into his room."

"Alone?" Alleyn asked.

"I just looked in to make sure he had heard me. I told him again he needed powder and then went at once to this Infant."

"Miss Tarne, can you remember anything else Mr. Bennington said?"

"Not really. I'm afraid I was rather in a haze myself just then."

"The great adventure?"

"Yes," said Martyn gratefully. "I've an idea he said something about my performance. Perhaps I should explain that I knew he must be very disappointed and upset about my going on instead of Miss Gainsford, but his manner was not unfriendly and I have the impression that he meant to say he didn't bear for me, personally, any kind of resentment. But that's putting it too definitely. I'm not at all sure what he said, except for that one sentence. Of that I'm quite positive."

"Good," Alleyn said. "Thank you. Did you hear his remark, Mr. Doré?"

Jacko said promptly: "But certainly. I was already in the passage and he spoke loudly as I came up."

"Did you form any opinion as to what he meant?"

"I was busy and very pleased with this Infant and I did not concern myself. If I thought at all it was to wonder if he was going to make a scene because the niece had not played. He had a talent for scenes. It appears to be a family trait. I thought perhaps he meant that this Infant would not be included in some scene he planned to make or be scolded for her success."

"Did he seem to you to be upset?"

"Oh, yes. Yes. Upset. Yes."

"Very much distressed, would you say?"

"All his visage wann'd?" inquired a voice in the background. "Tears in his eyes, distraction in's aspect?"

Alleyn moved his position until he could look past Gay and Darcey at the recumbent Doctor. "Or even," he said, "his whole function suiting with forms to his conceit?"

"Hah!" The Doctor ejaculated and sat up. "Upon my soul, the whirligig of time brings in his revenges. Even to the point where dull detection apes at artifice, inspectors echo with informed breath their pasteboard prototypes of fancy wrought. I am amazed and know not what to say." He helped himself to snuff and fell back into a recumbent position.

"Please don't mind him," Helena said, smiling at Alleyn. "He is a very foolish vain old man and has read somewhere that it's clever to quote in a muddled sort of way from the better known bits of the Bard."

"We encourage him too much," Jacko added gloomily.

"We have become too friendly with him," said Poole.

"And figo for thy friendship," said Dr. Rutherford.

Parry Percival sighed ostentatiously and Darcey said: "Couldn't we get on?" Alleyn looked good-humouredly at Jacko and said: "Yes, Mr. Doré?"

"I would agree," Jacko said, "that Ben was very much upset, but that was an almost chronic condition of late with poor Ben. I believe now with Miss Hamilton that he had decided there was little further enjoyment to be found in observing the dissolution of his own character and was about to take the foolproof way of ending it. He wished to assure Martyn that the decision had nothing to do with chagrin over Martyn's success or the failure of his niece. And that, if I am right, was nice of Ben."

"I don't think we need use the word 'failure,' " J.G. objected. "Gay was quite unable to go on."

"I hope you are better now, Miss Gainsford," Alleyn said.

Gay made an eloquent gesture with both hands and let them fall in her lap. "What does it matter?" she said. "Better? Oh, yes, I'm better." And with the closest possible imitation of Helena Hamilton's familiar gesture she extended her hand, without looking at him, to J. G. Darcey. He took it anxiously. "Much better," he said, patting it.

Martyn thought: "Oh, dear, he *is* in love with her. *Poor* J.G.!"

Alleyn looked thoughtfully at them for a moment and then turned to the others.

"There's a general suggestion," he said, "that none of you was very

surprised by this event. May I just—sort of tally-up the general opinion
as far as I've heard it? It helps to keep things tidy, I find. Miss Hamilton, you tell us that your husband had a curious, an almost morbid interest in the Jupiter case. You and Mr. Doré agree that Mr. Bennington
had decided to take his life because he couldn't face the 'dissolution of
his character.' Miss Gainsford, if I understand her, believes he was
deeply disturbed by the *mise-en-scéne* and also by her inability to go on
to-night for this part. Miss Tarne's account of what was probably the
last statement he made suggests that he wanted her to understand that
some action he had in mind had nothing to do with her. Mr. Doré sup-
ports this interpretation and confirms the actual words that were used.
This, as far as it goes, is the only tangible bit of evidence as to intention
that we have."

Poole lifted his head. His face was very white and a lock of black
hair had fallen over his forehead, turning him momentarily into the
likeness, Martyn thought inconsequently, of Michelangelo's Adam. He
said: "There's the fact itself, Alleyn. There's what he did."

Alleyn said carefully: "There's an interval of perhaps eight minutes
between what he said and when he was found."

"Look here—" Parry Percival began, and then relapsed. "Let it
pass," he said. "I wouldn't know."

"Pipe up, Narcissus," Dr. Rutherford adjured him, "the Inspector
won't bite you."

"Oh, shut up!" Parry shouted, and was awarded a complete and astonished silence. He rose and addressed himself to the players. "You're
all being so bloody frank and sensible about this suicide," he said.
"You're *so* anxious to show everybody how honest you are. The Doctor's *so* unconcerned he can even spare a moment to indulge in his
favourite pastime of me-baiting. I know what the Doctor thinks about
me and it doesn't say much for his talents as a diagnostician. But if it's
queer to feel desperately sorry for a man who was miserable enough to
choke himself to death at a gas jet, if it's queer to be physically and
mentally sick at the thought of it, then, by God, I'd rather be queer than
normal. Now!"

There followed a silence broken only by the faint whisper of the
young constable's pencil.

Dr. Rutherford struggled to his feet and lumbered down to Parry.

"Your argument, my young coxcomb," he said thoughtfully, "is as
sea-worthy as a sieve. As for my diagnosis, if you're the normal man
you'd have me believe, why the hell don't you show like one? You exhibit the stigmata of that water-fly whom it is a vice to know, and fly

into a fit when the inevitable conclusion is drawn." He took Parry by the elbow and addressed himself to the company in the manner of a lecturer. "A phenomenon," he said, "that is not without its dim interest. I invite your attention. Here is an alleged actor who, an hour or two since, was made a public and egregious figure of fun by the deceased. Who was roasted by the deceased before an audience of a thousand whinnying nincompoops. Who allowed his performance to be prostituted by the deceased before this audience. Who before his final and most welcome exit suffered himself to be tripped up contemptuously by the deceased, and who fell on his painted face before this audience. Here is this phenomenon, ladies and gents, who now proposes himself as Exhibit A in the Compassion Stakes. I invite your—"

Poole said *"Quiet!"* and when Dr. Rutherford grinned at him added: "I meant it, John. You will be quiet if you please."

Parry wrenched himself free from the Doctor and turned on Alleyn. "You're supposed to be in charge here—" he began, and Poole said quickly: "Yes, Alleyn, I really do think that this discussion is getting quite fantastically out of hand. If we're all satisfied that this is a case of suicide—"

"Which," Alleyn said, "we are not."

They were all talking at once: Helena, the Doctor, Parry, Gay and Darcey. They were like a disorderly chorus in a verse-play. Martyn, who had been watching Alleyn, was terrified. She saw him glance at the constable. Then he stood up.

"One moment," he said. The chorus broke off as inconsequently as it had begun.

"We've reached a point," Alleyn said, "where it's my duty to tell you I'm by no means satisfied that this is, in fact, a case of suicide."

Martyn was actually conscious, in some kind, of a sense of relief. She could find no look either of surprise or of anger in any of her fellowplayers. Their faces were so many white discs and they were motionless and silent. At last Clem Smith said with an indecent lack of conviction: "He was horribly careless about things like that—taps, I mean—" His voice sank to a murmur. They heard the word "accident."

"Is it not strange," Jacko said loudly, "how loath one is to pronounce the word that is in all our minds. And truth to tell, it has a soft and ugly character." His lips closed over his fantastic teeth. He used the exaggerated articulation of an old actor. "Murder," he said. "So beastly, isn't it?"

It was at this point that one of the stage-hands, following, no doubt, his routine for the night, pulled up the curtain and exhibited the scene of climax to the deserted auditorium.

Chapter VIII

Afterpiece

From this time onward, through the watches of that night, it seemed to Martyn that a second play was acted out in the Vulcan: a play that wrote itself as it went along, with many excursions into irrelevance, with countless *longueurs* and with occasional unanticipated scenes of climax. She was unable to dismiss the sense of an audience that watched in the shrouded seats, or the notion that the theatre itself was attentive to the action on its stage.

This illusion was in some sort created by the players, for it seemed to Martyn that each of them was acting a part. She was not on this account repelled by any of them, but rather felt drawn towards them all as one is to people with whom one shares a common danger. They were of one guild. Even Gay Gainsford's excesses were at first a cause only of resigned irritation, and Parry Percivul's outburst, Martyn felt, was understandable. On the whole she thought the better of him for it.

When she considered them all as they sat about their own working-stage, bruised by anxiety and fatigue, Jacko's ugly word sounded not so much frightening as preposterous. It was unthinkable that it could kindle even a bat-light of fear in any of their hearts. "And yet," thought Martyn, "it has done so. There are little points of terror burning in all of us like match-flames."

After Jacko had spoken there was a long silence, broken at last by Adam Poole, who asked temperately: "Are we to understand, Alleyn, that you have quite ruled out the possibility of suicide?"

"By no means," Alleyn rejoined. "I still hope you may be able, among you, to show that there is at least a clear enough probability of suicide for us to leave the case as it stands until the inquest. But where there are strong indications that it may *not* be suicide we can't risk waiting as long as that without a pretty exhaustive look round."

"And there are such indications?"

"There are indeed."

"Strong?"

Alleyn waited a moment. "Sufficiently strong," he said.

"What are they?" Dr. Rutherford demanded.

"It must suffice," Alleyn quibbled politely, "that they are sufficient."

"An elegant sufficiency, by God!"

"But, Mr. Alleyn," Helena cried out, "what can we tell you. Except that we all most sincerely believe that Ben did this himself. Because we know him to have been bitterly unhappy. What else is there for us to say?"

"It will help, you know, when we get a clear picture of what you were all doing and where you were between the time he left the stage and the time he was found. Inspector Fox is checking now with the stage-staff. I propose to do so with the players."

"I see," she said. She leant forward and her air of reasonableness and attention was beautifully executed. "You want to find out which of us had the opportunity to murder Ben."

Gay Gainsford and Parry began an outcry, but Helena raised her hand and they were quiet. "That's it, isn't it?" she said.

"Yes," Alleyn said, "that really is it. I fancy you would rather be spared the stock evasions about routine enquiries and all the rest of it."

"Much rather."

"I was sure of it," Alleyn said. "Then shall we start with you, if you please?"

"I was on the stage for the whole of that time, Mr. Alleyn. There's a scene, before Ben's exit, between J.G.—that's Mr. Darcey over there—Parry, Adam, Ben and myself. First Parry and then J.G. goes off and Ben follows a moment later. Adam and I finish the play."

"So you, too," Alleyn said to Poole, "were here, on the stage, for the whole of this period?"

"I go off for a moment after his exit. It's a strange, rather horridly strange, coincidence that in the play he—the character he played, I mean —does commit suicide off-stage. He shoots himself. When I hear the shot I go off. The two other men have already made their exits. They remain off but I come on again almost immediately. I wait outside the door on the left from a position where I can watch Miss Hamilton, and I re-enter on a 'business' cue from her."

"How long would this take?"

"Shall we show you?" Helena suggested. She got up and moved to the centre of the stage. She raised her clasped hands to her mouth and stood motionless. She was another woman.

As if Clem had called "Clear stage"—and indeed he looked about him with an air of authority—Martyn, Jacko and Gay moved into the wings. Parry and J.G. went to the foot of the stairs and Poole crossed to above Helena. They placed themselves thus in the business-like manner of a rehearsal. The Doctor, however, remained prone on his sofa, breathing deeply and completely disregarded by everybody. Helena glanced at Clem Smith, who went to the book.

"From Ben's exit, Clem," Poole said, and after a moment Helena turned and addressed herself to the empty stage on her left.

"I've only one thing to say, but it's between the three of us." She turned to Parry and Darcey. "Do you mind?" she asked them.

Parry said: "I don't understand and I'm past minding."

Darcey said: "My head is buzzing with a sense of my own inadequacy. I shall be glad to be alone."

They went out, each on his own line, leaving Helena, Adam, and the ghost of Bennington on the stage.

Helena spoke again to vacancy. "It must be clear to you, now. It's the end, isn't it?"

"Yes," Clem's voice said. "I understand you perfectly. Good-bye, my dear."

They watched the door on the left. Alleyn took out his watch. Helena made a quick movement as if to prevent the departure of an unseen person and Poole laid his hand on her arm. They brought dead Ben back to the stage by their mime and dismissed him as vividly. It seemed that the door must open and shut for him as he went out.

Poole said: "And now I must speak to you alone." There followed a short passage of dialogue which he and Helena played *a tempo* but with muted voices. Jacko, in the wings, clapped his hands and the report was as startling as a gun-shot. Poole ran out through the left-hand door.

Helena traced a series of movements about the stage. Her gestures were made in the manner of an exercise but the shadow of their significance was reflected in her face. Finally she moved into the window and seemed to compel herself to look out. Poole re-entered.

"Thank you," Alleyn said, shutting his watch. "Fifty seconds. Will you all come on again, if you please?"

When they had assembled in their old positions, he said: "Did anyone notice Mr. Poole as he waited by the door for his re-entry?"

"The door's recessed," Poole said. "I was more or less screened."

"Someone off-stage may have noticed, however." He looked from Darcey to Percival.

"We went straight to our rooms," said Parry.

"Together?"

"I was first. Miss Tarne was in the entrance to the passage and I spoke to her for a moment. J.G. followed me, I think."

"Do you remember this, Miss Tarne?"

It had been at the time when Martyn had begun to come back to earth. It was like a recollection from a dream. "Yes," she said. "I remember. They both spoke to me."

"And went on down the passage?"

"Yes."

"To be followed in a short time by yourself and Mr. Bennington?"

"Yes."

"And then Mr. Doré joined you and you went to your rooms?"

"Yes."

"So that after Mr. Bennington had gone to his room, you, Mr. Percival, were in your dressing-room, which is next door to his, Mr. Darcey was in his room which is on the far side of Mr. Percival's, and Miss Tarne was in her room—or more correctly, perhaps, Miss Gainsford's—with Mr. Doré, who joined her there after looking in on Mr. Bennington. Right?"

They murmured an uneasy assent.

"How long were you all in these rooms?"

Jacko said: "I believe I have said I adjusted this Infant's make-up and returned with her to the stage."

"I think," said Martyn, "that the other two went out to the stage before we did. I remember hearing them go up the passage together. That was before the call for the final curtain. We went out after the call, didn't we, Jacko?"

"Certainly, my Infant. And by that time you were a little more awake, isn't it? The pink clouds had receded a certain distance?"

Martyn nodded, feeling foolish. Poole came behind her and rested his hands on her shoulders. "So there would appear at least to be an alibi for the Infant Phenomenon," he said. It was the most natural and inevitable thing in the world for her to lean back. His hands moved to her arms and he held her to him for an uncharted second while a spring of well-being broke over her astounded heart.

Alleyn looked from her face to Poole's and she guessed that he wondered about their likeness to each other. Poole, answering her thoughts and Alleyn's unspoken question, said: "We are remotely related, but I am not allowed to mention it. She's ashamed of the connection."

"That's unlucky," Alleyn said with a smile, "since it declares itself so unequivocally."

Gay Gainsford said loudly to Darcey: "Do you suppose, darling, they'd let me get my cigarettes?"

Helena said: "Here you are, Gay." Darcey had already opened his case and held it out to her in his right hand. His left hand was in his trousers pocket. His posture was elegant and modish, out of keeping with his look of anxiety and watchfulness.

"Where are your cigarettes?" Alleyn asked and Gay said quickly: "It doesn't matter, thank you. I've got one. I won't bother. I'm sorry I interrupted."

"But where are they?"

"I don't really know what I've done with them."

"Where were you during the performance?"

She said impatiently: "It *really* doesn't matter. I'll look for them later or something."

"Gay," said Jacko, "was in the Greenroom throughout the show."

"Lamprey will see if he can find them."

The young constable said: "Yes, of course, sir," and went out.

"In the Greenroom?" Alleyn said. "Were you there all the time, Miss Gainsford?"

Standing in front of her with his back to Alleyn, Darcey held a light to her cigarette. She inhaled and coughed violently. He said: "Gay didn't feel fit enough to move. She curled up in a chair in the Greenroom. I was to take her home after the show."

"When did you leave the Greenroom, Miss Gainsford?"

But it seemed that Gay had half-asphyxiated herself with her cigarette. She handed it wildly to Darcey, buried her face in her handkerchief and was madly convulsed. P. C. Lamprey returned with a packet of cigarettes, was waved away with vehemence, gave them to Darcey and on his own initiative fetched a cup of water.

"If the face is congested," Dr. Rutherford advised from the sofa, "hold her up by the heels." His eyes remained closed.

Whether it was the possibility of being subjected to this treatment or the sip of water that Darcey persuaded her to take or the generous thumps on her back, administered by Jacko, that effected a cure, the paroxysm abated. Alleyn, who had watched this scene thoughtfully, said: "If you are quite yourself again, Miss Gainsford, will you try to remember when you left the Greenroom?"

She shook her head weakly and said in an invalid's voice: "Please, I honestly don't remember. Is it very important?"

"Oh, for pity's sake, Gay!" cried Helena, with every sign of the liveliest irritation. "Do stop being such an unmitigated ass. You're not choking: if you were your eyes would water and you'd probably dribble. Of course it's important. You were in the Greenroom and next door to Ben. Think!"

"But you can't imagine—" Gay said wildly. "Oh, Aunty—I'm sorry, I mean Helena—I do think that's a frightful thing to suggest."

"My dear Gay," Poole said, "I don't suppose Helena or Mr. Alleyn or any of us imagines you went into Ben's room, knocked him senseless with a straight left to the jaw and then turned the gas on. We merely want to know what you did do."

J.G., who had given a sharp ejaculation and half risen from his chair, now sank back.

Alleyn said: "It would also be interesting, Mr. Poole, to hear how you knew about the straight left to the jaw."

ii

Poole was behind Martyn and a little removed from her. She felt his stillness in her own bones. When he spoke it was a shock rather than a relief to hear how easy and relaxed his voice sounded.

"Do you realize, Alleyn," he said, "you've given me an opportunity to use, in reverse, a really smashing detective's cliché: 'I didn't know. You have just told me!' "

"And that," Alleyn said with some relish, "as I believe you would say in the profession, takes me off with a hollow laugh and a faint hiss. So you merely guessed at the straight left?"

"If Ben was killed, and I don't believe he was, it seemed to me to be the only way this murder could be brought about."

"Surely not," Alleyn said without emphasis. "There is the method that was used before in this theatre with complete success."

"I don't know that I would describe as completely successful a method that ended with the arrest of its employer."

"Oh," Alleyn said lightly, "that's another story. He underestimated our methods."

"A good enough warning to anyone else not to follow his plan of action."

"Or perhaps merely a hint that it could be improved upon," Alleyn said. "What do you think, Mr. Darcey?"

"I?" J.G. sounded bewildered. "I don't know. I'm afraid I haven't followed the argument."

"You were still thinking about the straight-left theory, perhaps?"

"I believe with the others that it was suicide," said J.G. He had sat down again beside Gay. His legs were stretched out before him and crossed at the ankles, his hands were in his trousers pockets and his chin on his chest. It was the attitude of a distinguished M.P. during a damaging speech from the opposite side of the House.

Alleyn said: "And we still don't know when Miss Gainsford left the Greenroom."

"Oh, *lawks!*" Parry ejaculated. "This is *too* tiresome. J.G., you looked in at the Greenroom door when we came back for the curtain-call, don't you remember? Was she there then? Were you there then, Gay darling?"

Gay opened her mouth to speak but J.G. said quickly: "Yes, of course I did. Stupid of me to forget. Gay was sound asleep in the armchair, Mr. Alleyn. I didn't disturb her." He passed his right hand over his beautifully groomed head. "It's a most extraordinary thing," he said vexedly, "that I should have forgotten this. Of course she was asleep. Because later, when—well, when, in point of fact, the discovery had been made—I asked where Gay was and someone said she was still in the Greenroom, and I was naturally worried and went to fetch her. She was still asleep and the Greenroom, by that time, reeking with gas. I brought her back here."

"Have you any idea, Miss Gainsford," Alleyn asked, "about when you dropped off?"

"I was exhausted, Mr Alleyn. Physically and emotionally exhausted. I still am."

"Was it, for instance, before the beginning of the last act?"

"N—n—no. No. Because J.G. came in to see how I was in the second interval. Didn't you, darling? And I was exhausted, wasn't I?"

"Yes, dear."

"And he gave me some aspirins and I took two. And I suppose, in that state of utter exhaustion, they worked. So I fell into a sleep—an exhausted sleep, it was."

"Naturally," Helena murmured with a glance at Alleyn, "it would be exhausted."

"Undoubtedly," said Jacko, "it was exhausted."

"Well, it was," said Gay crossly. "Because I was. Utterly."

"Did anyone else beside Mr. Darcey go into the Greenroom during the second interval?"

Gay looked quickly at J.G. "Honestly," she said, "I'm so muddled about times it really isn't safe to ask me. I'm sure to be wrong."

"Mr. Darcey?"

"No," J.G. said.

"Well, my dearest J.G.," Parry said, "I couldn't be more reluctant to keep popping in like one of the Eumenides in that utterly incomprehensible play, but I do assure you that you're at fault here. Ben went into the Greenroom in the second interval."

"Dear Heaven!" Helena said, on a note of desperation. "What has happened to us all!"

"I'm terribly sorry, Helena darling," Parry said, and sounded it.

"But why should you be sorry? Why shouldn't Ben go and see his niece in the interval? He played the whole of the third act afterwards. Of course you should say so, Parry, if you know what you're talking about. Shouldn't he, Adam? Shouldn't he, Mr. Alleyn?"

Poole was looking with a sort of incredulous astonishment at Darcey. "I think he should," he said slowly.

"And you, Mr. Darcey?" asked Alleyn.

"All right, Parry," said J.G., "go on."

"There's not much more to be said, and anyway I don't suppose it matters. It was before they'd called the third act. Helena and Adam and Martyn had gone out. They begin the act. I come on a bit later and Ben after me and J.G. later still. I wanted to see how the show was going and I was on my way in the passage when Ben came out of his room and went into the Greenroom next door. The act was called soon after that."

"Did you speak to him?" Alleyn asked.

"I did not," said Parry with some emphasis. "I merely went out to the stage and joined Jacko and the two dressers and the call-boy, who were watching from the Prompt side, and Clem."

"That's right," Clem Smith said. "I remember telling you all to keep away from the bunches. The boy called J.G. and Ben about five minutes later."

"Were you still in the Greenroom when you were called, Mr. Darcey?"

"Yes."

"With Mr. Bennington?"

"He'd gone to his room."

"Not for the life of me," Helena said wearily, "can I see why you had to be so mysterious, J.G."

"Perhaps," Alleyn said, "the reason is in your left trousers pocket, Mr. Darcey."

J.G. didn't take his hand out of his pocket. He stood up and addressed himself directly to Alleyn.

"May I speak to you privately?" he asked.

"Of course," Alleyn said. "Shall we go to the Greenroom?"

iii

In the Greenroom and in the presence of Alleyn and of Fox, who had joined them there, J. G. Darcey took his left hand out of his trousers pocket and extended it palm downwards for their inspection. It was a well-shaped and well-kept hand but the knuckles were grazed. A trace of blood had seeped out round the greasepaint and powder which had been daubed over the raw skin.

"I suppose I've behaved very stupidly," he said. "But I hoped there would be no need for this to come out. It has no bearing whatever on his death."

"In that case," Alleyn said, "it will not be brought out. But you'll do well to be frank."

"I dare say," said J.G. wryly.

"There's a bruise on the deceased's jaw on the right side that could well have been caused by that straight left Mr. Poole talked about. Now, we can of course determine whether make-up from your left fist is mixed with Bennington's own make-up over this bruise. If you tell me you didn't let drive at him we'll make this experiment."

"I assure you that you don't need to do any such thing. I'll willingly admit that I hit him," J.G. said with a shudder.

"And also why you hit him?"

"Oh, yes, if I can. If I can," he repeated and pressed his hand to his eyes. "D'you mind if we sit down, Alleyn? I'm a bit tired."

"Do."

J.G. sat in the leather armchair where Martyn, and, in her turn, Gay Gainsford had slept. In the dim light of the Greenroom his face looked wan and shadowed. "Not the chicken I was," he said, and it was an admission actors do not love to make.

Alleyn faced him. Fox sat down behind him, flattened his note-book on the table and placed his spectacles across his nose. There was something cosy about Fox when he took notes. Alleyn remembered absently that his wife had once observed that Mr. Fox was a cross between a bear and a baby and exhibited the most pleasing traits of both creatures.

The masked light above Jacko's sketch of Adam Poole shone down upon it, and it thus was given considerable emphasis in an otherwise shadowed room.

"If you want a short statement," J.G. said, "I can give it to you in a sentence. I hit Ben on the jaw in this room during the second act wait. I didn't knock him out but he was so astonished he took himself off. I was a handy amateur welter-weight in my young days but it must be twenty years or more since I put up my hands. I must say I rather enjoyed it."

"What sort of condition was he in?"

"Damned unpleasant. Oh, you mean drunk or sober? I should say ugly-drunk. Ben was a soak. I've never seen him incapacitated, but really I've hardly ever seen him stone-cold either. He was in his second degree of drunkenness: offensive, outrageous and incalculable. He'd behaved atrociously throughout the first and second acts."

"In what way?"

"As only a clever actor with too much drink in him can behave. Scoring off other people. Playing for cheap laughs. Doing unrehearsed bits of business that made nonsense of the production. Upon my word," said J.G. thoughtfully, "I wonder Adam or the Doctor or poor little Parry, if he'd had the guts, didn't get in first and give him what he deserved. A perfectly bloody fellow."

"Was it because of his performance that you hit him?"

J.G. looked at his finger-nails and seemed to ponder. "No," he said at last. "Or not directly. If I thought you'd believe me I'd say yes, but no doubt you'll talk to her and she's so upset anyway—"

"You mean Miss Gainsford?"

"Yes," said J.G. with the oddest air of pride and embarrassment. "I mean Gay."

"Was it on her account you dotted him one?"

"It was. He was damned offensive."

"I'm sorry," Alleyn said, "but you'll realize that we do want to be told a little more than that about it."

"I suppose so." He clasped his hands and examined his bruised knuckles. "Although I find it extremely difficult and unpleasant to go into the wretched business. It's only because I hope you'll let Gay off, as far as possible, if you know the whole story. That's why I asked to see you alone." He slewed round and looked discontentedly at Fox.

"Inspector Fox," Alleyn said, "is almost pathologically discreet."

"Glad to hear it. Well, as you've heard, I'd managed to get hold of a bottle of aspirins and I brought them to her, here, in the second interval. Gay was sitting in this chair. She was still terribly upset. Crying. I don't know if you've realized why she didn't go on for the part?"

"No. I'd be glad to have the whole story."

J.G. embarked on it, with obvious reluctance, but as he talked his hesitancy lessened and he even seemed to find some kind of ease in speaking. He described Gay's part and her struggle at rehearsals. It was clear that, however unwillingly, he shared the general opinion of her limited talent. "She'd have given a reasonable show," he said, "if she'd been given a reasonable chance but from the beginning the part got her down. She's a natural ingenue and this thing's really 'character.' It was bad casting. Adam kept the Doctor at bay as much as possible but she knew what he thought. She didn't *want* the part. She was happy where she was in repertory but Ben dragged her in. He saw himself as a sort of fairy-godfather-uncle and when she found the part difficult he turned obstinate and wouldn't let her throw it in. Out of vanity really. He was very vain. She's a frail little thing, you know, all heart and sensitivity, and between them they've brought her to the edge of a breakdown. It didn't help matters when Miss Martyn Tarne appeared out of a clear sky, first as Helena Hamilton's dresser and then as Gay's understudy and then—mysteriously, as some of the cast, Ben in particular, thought— as Adam's distant cousin. You noticed the uncanny resemblance but you may not know the part in the play requires it. That was the last straw for Gay. She'd been ill with nerves and fright and to-night she cracked up completely and wouldn't—couldn't go on. When I saw her in the first interval she was a bit quieter but in the second act little Miss Tarne did very well indeed. Quite startling, it was. Incidentally, I suppose her success infuriated Ben. And Gay heard everybody raving about her as they came off. Naturally that upset her again. So she was in tears when I came in."

He leant forward and rested his head in his hands. His voice was less distinct. "I'm fond of her," he said. "She's got used to me being about. When I came in she ran to me and—I needn't go into the way I felt. There's no explaining those things. She was sobbing in my arms, poor bird, and God knows my heart had turned over. Ben came in. He went for her like a pickpocket. He was crazy. I tried to shut him up. He didn't make a noise—I don't mean that—matter of fact what he said streamed out of him in a whisper. He was quite off his head and began talking about Helena—about his wife. He used straight-out obscenities. There'd been an episode in the afternoon and—well, he used the sort of generalization that Lear and Othello and Leontes use, if you remember your Shakespeare."

"Yes."

"Gay was still clinging to me and he began to talk the same sort of stuff about her. I'm not going into details. I put her away from me and quite deliberately gave him what was coming to him. I don't remember what I said. I don't think any of us said anything. So he went out nursing his jaw and they called me for the last act and I went out too. During this last act, when we were on together, I could see the bruise coming out under his make-up."

"What was his general behaviour like during the final act?"

"As far as I was concerned he behaved in the way people do when they play opposite someone they've had a row with off-stage. He didn't look me in the eye. He looked at my forehead or ears. It doesn't show from the front. He played fairly soundly until poor Parry got out of position. Parry is his butt in the piece, but of course what Ben did was outrageous. He stuck out his foot as Parry moved and brought him down. That was not long before his own exit. I never saw him again after that until he was carried out. That's all. I don't know if you've believed me but I hope you'll let Gay off any more of this stuff."

Alleyn didn't answer. He looked at the young-old actor for a moment. J.G. was lighting a cigarette with that trained economy and grace of movement that were part of his stock-in-trade. His head was stooped, and Alleyn saw how carefully the silver hair had been distributed over the scalp. The hands were slightly tremulous. How old was J.G.? Fifty? Fifty-five? Sixty? Was he the victim of that Indian Summer that can so unmercifully visit an ageing man?

"It's the very devil, in these cases," Alleyn said, "how one has to plug away at everyone in turn. Not that it helps to say so. There's one more question that I'm afraid you won't enjoy at all. Can you tell me more specifically what Bennington said about—I think you called it an episode—of the afternoon, in which his wife was concerned?"

"No, by God, I can't," said J.G. hotly.

"He spoke about it in front of Miss Gainsford, didn't he?"

"You can't possibly ask Gay about it. It's out of the question."

"Not, I'm afraid, for an investigating officer," said Alleyn, who thought that J.G.'s delicacy, if delicacy were in question, was possibly a good deal more sensitive than Miss Gainsford's. "Do you suppose Bennington talked about this episode to other people?"

"In the condition he was in I should think it possible."

"Well," Alleyn said, "we shall have to find out."

"See here, Alleyn. What happened, if he spoke the truth, was something entirely between himself and his wife and it's on her account that I can't repeat what he said. You know she and Poole were on-stage at the crucial time and that there's no sense in thinking of motive, if that's what you're after, where they are concerned."

Alleyn said: "This episode might constitute a motive for suicide, however."

J.G. looked up quickly. "Suicide? But—why?"

"Shame?" Alleyn suggested. "Self-loathing if he sobered up after you hit him and took stock of himself? I imagine they've been virtually separated for some time."

"I see you have a talent," said J.G., "for reading between the lines."

"Let us rather call it an ugly little knack. Thank you, Mr. Darcey, I don't think I need bother you any more for the moment."

J.G. went slowly to the door. He hesitated for a moment and then said: "If you're looking for motive, Alleyn, you'll find it in a sort of way all over the place. He wasn't a likeable chap and he'd antagonized everyone. Even poor little Parry came off breathing revenge after the way he'd been handled, but, my God, actors do that kind of thing only too often. Feeling runs high, you know, on first nights."

"So it would seem."

"Can I take that child home?"

"I'm sorry," Alleyn said, "not yet. Not just yet."

vi

"Well," Alleyn said when J.G. had gone, "what have you got at your end of the table, Br'er Fox?"

Fox turned back the pages of his note-book.

"What you might call negative evidence, on the whole, Mr. Alleyn. Clearance for the understudies, who watched the show from the back of the circle and then went home. Clearance for the two dressers (male), the stage-manager and his assistant, the stage-hands and the night-watchman. They were all watching the play or on their jobs. On statements taken independently, they clear each other."

"That's something."

"No female dresser," Mr. Fox observed. "Which seems odd."

"Miss Tarne was the sole female dresser and she's been promoted overnight to what I believe I should call starletdom. Which in itself seems to me to be a rum go. I've always imagined female dressers to be cups-of-tea in alpaca aprons and not embryo actresses. I don't think Miss Tarne could have done the job, but she comes into the picture as the supplanter of Uncle Ben's dear little niece, whom I find an extremely irritating ass with a certain amount of low cunning. Miss Tarne, on the other hand, seems pleasant and intelligent and looks nice. You must allow me my prejudices, Br'er Fox."

"She's Mr. Poole's third cousin or something."

"The case reeks with obscure relationships—blood, marital and illicit, as far as one can see. Did you get anything from Bennington's dresser?"

"Nothing much," said Fox, sighing. "It seems the deceased didn't like him to hang about on account of being a secret drinker. He was in the dressing-room up to about seven and was then told to go and see if he could be of any use to the other gentlemen, and not to come back till the first interval when the deceased changed his clothes. I must say that chap earns his wages pretty easily. As far as I could make out the rest of his duties for the night consisted in tearing off chunks of cotton-wool for the deceased to do up his face with. I checked his visits to the dressing-room by that. The last time he looked in was after the deceased went on the stage in the third act. He cleared away the used cotton-wool and powdered a clean bit. In the normal course of events I suppose he'd have put Mr. Bennington into the fancy dress he was going to wear to the ball and then gone home quite worn out."

"Was he at all talkative?"

"Not got enough energy, Mr. Alleyn. Nothing to say for himself barring the opinion that deceased was almost on the D.T. mark. The other dresser, Cringle, seems a bright little chap. He just works for Mr. Poole."

"Have you let them go?"

"Yes, sir, I have. And the stage-hands. We can look them out again if we want them, but for the moment I think we've just about cleaned them up. I've let the assistant stage-manager—A.S.M. they call him—get away, too. Wife's expecting any time and he never left the prompting book."

"That reduces the mixed bag a bit. You've been through all the rooms, of course, but before we do anything else, Br'er Fox, let's have a prowl."

They went into the passage. Fox jerked his thumb at Bennington's room. "Gibson's doing a fly-crawl in there," he said. "If there's anything, he'll find it. That dresser-chap didn't clear anything up except his used powder-puffs."

They passed Bennington's room and went into Parry Percival's, next door. Here they found Detective-Sergeants Thompson and Bailey, the one a photographic and the other a finger-print expert. They were packing up their gear.

"Well, Bailey?" Alleyn asked.

Bailey looked morosely at his superior. "It's there all right, sir," he said grudgingly. "Complete prints, very near, and a check-up all over the shop."

"What about next door?"

"Deceased's room, sir? His prints on the wing-tap and the tube.

Trace of red greasepaint on the rubber connection at the end of the tube. Matches paint on deceased's lips."

"Very painstaking," said Alleyn. "Have you tried the experiment?"

"Seeing the fires are back-to-back, sir," Fox said, "we have. Sergeant Gibson blew down this tube and deceased's fire went out. As in former case."

"Well," Alleyn said, "there you are. Personally I don't believe a word of it, either way." He looked, without interest, at the telegrams stuck round the frame of Parry's looking-glass and at his costume for the ball. "*Very* fancy," he muttered. "Who's in the next room?"

"Mr. J. G. Darcey," said Thompson.

They went into J.G.'s room, which was neat and impersonal in character and contained nothing, it seemed, of interest, unless a photograph of Miss Gainsford looking *insouciante* could be so regarded.

In the last room on this side of the passage they saw the electric sewing-machine, some rough sketches, scraps of material and other evidences of Martyn's sewing-party for Jacko. Alleyn glanced round it, crossed the passage and looked into the empty room opposite. "Dismal little cells when they're unoccupied, aren't they?" he said, and moved on to Gay Gainsford's room.

He stood there, his hands in his pockets, with Fox at his elbow. "This one suffers from the fashionable complaint, Fox," he said. "Schizophrenia. It's got a split personality. On my left a rather too-smart overcoat, a frisky hat, chi-chi gloves, a pansy purse-bag, a large bottle of one of the less reputable scents, a gaggle of mascots, a bouquet from the management and orchids from—who do you suppose?" He turned over the card. "Yes. Alas, yes, with love and a thousand good wishes from her devoted J.G. On my right a well-worn and modest little topcoat, a pair of carefully tended shoes and gloves that remind one of the White Rabbit, a grey skirt and beret and a yellow jumper. A handbag that contains, I'm sure, one of those rather heartrending little purses and—what else?" He explored the bag. "A New Zealand passport issued this year in which one finds Miss Tarne is nineteen years old and an actress. So the dresser's job was—what? The result of an appeal to the celebrated third cousin? But why not give her the understudy at once? She's fantastically like him and I'll be sworn he's mightily catched with her. What's more, even old Darcey says she's a damn good actress." He turned the leaves of the passport. "She only arrived in England seventeen days ago. Can that account for the oddness of the set-up? Anyway, I don't suppose it matters. Let's go next door, shall we?"

Cringle had left Poole's room in exquisite order. Telegrams were pinned in rows on the walls. A towel was spread over the make-up. A cigarette had been half-extracted from a packet and a match left ready on the top of its box. A framed photograph of Helena Hamilton stood near the glass. Beside it a tiny clock with a gay face ticked feverishly. It stood on a card. Alleyn moved it delicately and read the inscription. *From Helena. To-night and to-morrow and always—bless you.*

"The standard for first-night keepsakes seems to be set at a high level," Alleyn muttered. "This is a French clock, Fox, with a Sèvres face encircled with garnets. What do you suppose the gentleman gave the lady?"

"Would a tiara be common?" asked Fox.

"Let's go next door and see."

Helena's room smelt and looked like a conservatory. A table had been brought in to carry the flowers. Jacko had set out the inevitable telegrams and had hung up the dresses under their dust sheets.

"Here we are," Alleyn said. "A sort of jeroboam of the most expensive scent on the market. Price, I should say, round about thirty pounds. 'From Adam.' Why don't you give me presents when we solve a petty larceny, Foxkin? Now, I may be fanciful, but this looks to me like the gift of a man who's at his wit's end and plumps for the expensive, the easy and the obvious. Here's something entirely different. Look at this, Fox."

It was a necklace of six wooden medallions strung between jade rings. Each plaque was most delicately carved in the likeness of a head in profile and each head was a portrait of one of the company of players. The card bore the date and the inscription: *From J.*

"Must have taken a long time to do," observed Fox. "That'll be the foreign gentleman's work, no doubt. Mr. Doré."

"No doubt. I wonder if love's labour has been altogether lost," said Alleyn. "I hope she appreciates it."

He took up the leather case with its two photographs of Poole. "He's a remarkable looking chap," he said. "If there's anything to be made of faces in terms of character, and I still like to pretend there is, what's to be made of this one? It's what they call a heart-shaped face, broad across the eyes with a firmly moulded chin and a generous but delicate mouth. Reminds one of a Holbein drawing. Doré's sketch in the Greenroom is damn good. Doré crops up all over the place, doesn't he? Designs their fancy dresses. Paints their faces, in a double sense. Does their décor and, with complete self-effacement, loves their leading lady."

"Do you reckon?"

"I do indeed, Br'er Fox," Alleyn said and rubbed his nose vexedly. "However. Gibson's done all the usual things in these rooms, I suppose?"

"Yes, Mr. Alleyn. Pockets, suitcases and boxes. Nothing to show for it."

"We can let them come home to roost fairly soon, then. We'll start now to see them separately. Blast! I suppose I'll have to begin with checking Darcey's statement with the Gainsford. She gives me the horrors, that young woman."

"Shall I see her, Mr. Alleyn?"

"You can stay and take your notes. I'll see her in the Greenroom. No, wait a bit. You stay with the others, Fox, and send young Lamprey along with her. And you might try again if you can dig up anything that sounds at all off-key with Bennington over the last few days. Anything that distressed or excited him."

"He seems to have been rather easily excited."

"He does, doesn't he, but you never know. I don't believe it was suicide, Fox, and I'm not yet satisfied that we've unearthed anything that's good enough for a motive for murder. Trip away, Foxkin. Ply your craft."

Fox went out sedately. Alleyn crossed the passage and opened the door of Bennington's room. Sergeant Gibson was discovered, squatting on his haunches before the dead gas fire.

"Anything?" Alleyn asked.

"There's this bit of a stain that looks like a scorch on the hearth, sir."

"Yes, I saw that. Any deposit?"

"We-ll—"

"We may have to try."

"The powder pads deceased's dresser cleared away were in the rubbish bin on the stage where he said he put them. Nothing else in the bin. There's this burnt paper on the floor, but it's in small flakes—powder almost."

"All right. Seal the room when you've finished. And Gibson, don't let the mortuary van go without telling me."

"Very good, sir."

Alleyn returned to the Greenroom. He heard Miss Gainsford approaching under the wing of P. C. Lamprey. She spoke in a high grand voice that seemed to come out a drawing-room comedy of the twenties.

"I think you're *too* intrepid," she was saying, "to start from rock bottom like this. It must be so devastatingly boring for you, though I will say it's rather a comfort to think one is in the hands of, to coin a phrase, a gent. Two gents, in fact."

"Chief Inspector Alleyn," said P. C. Lamprey, "is in the Greenroom I think, Miss."

"My dear, you do it quite marvellously. You ought, again to coin a phrase, to go on the stage."

Evidently Miss Gainsford lingered in the passage.

Alleyn heard his subordinate murmur: "Shall I go first?" His regulation boots clumped firmly to the door, which he now opened.

"Will you see Miss Gainsford, sir?" asked P. C. Lamprey, who was pink in the face.

"All right, Mike," Alleyn said. "Show her in and take notes."

"Will you come this way, Miss?"

Miss Gainsford made her entrance with a Mayfairish gallantry that was singularly dated. Alleyn wondered if she had decided that her first reading of her new role was mistaken. "She's abandoned the brave little woman for the suffering *mondaine* who goes down with an epigram," he thought, and sure enough, Miss Gainsford addressed herself to him with staccato utterance and brittle high-handedness.

"Ought one to be terribly flattered because one is the first to be grilled?" she asked. "Or is it a sinister little hint that one is top of the suspect list?"

"We have to start somewhere," Alleyn said. "I thought it might be convenient to see you first. Will you sit down, Miss Gainsford?"

She did so elaborately, gave herself a cigarette, and turned to P. C. Lamprey. "May one ask The Force for a light," she asked, "or would that be against the rules?"

Alleyn lit her cigarette while his unhappy subordinate retired to the table. She turned in her chair to watch him. "Is he going to take me down and use it all in evidence against me?" she asked. Her nostrils dilated, she raised her chin and added jerkily, "That's what's called the Usual Warning, isn't it?"

"A warning is given in police practice," Alleyn said as woodenly as possible, "if there is any chance that the person under interrogation will make a statement that is damaging to himself. Lamprey will note down this interview and, if it seems advisable, you will be asked later on to give a signed statement."

"If that was meant to be reassuring," said Miss Gainsford, "I can't have heard it properly. Could we get cracking?"

"Certainly. Miss Gainsford, you were in the Greenroom throughout the performance. During the last interval you were visited by Mr. J. G.

Darcey and by your uncle. Do you agree that as the result of something
the deceased said, Mr. Darcey hit him on the jaw?"

She said: "Wasn't it too embarrassing! I mean the Gorgeous Primitive Beast is one thing, but one old gentleman banging another about is
so utterly another. I'm afraid I didn't put that very clearly."

"You agree that Mr. Darcey hit Mr. Bennington?"

"But madly. Like a sledge-hammer. I found it so difficult to know
what to say. There just seemed to be no clue to further conversation."

"It is the conversation before than after the blow that I should like to
hear about, if you please."

Alleyn had turned away from her and was looking at Jacko's portrait
of Poole. He waited for some moments before she said sharply: "I suppose you think because I talk like this about it I've got no feeling. You
couldn't be more at fault." It was as if she called his attention to her
performance.

He said, without turning: "I assure you I hadn't given it a thought.
What did your uncle say that angered Mr. Darcey?"

"He was upset," she said sulkily, "because I was ill and couldn't
play."

"Hardly an occasion for hitting him."

"J.G. is very sensitive about me. He treats me like a piece of china."

"Which is more than he did for your uncle, it seems."

"Uncle Ben talked rather wildly." Miss Gainsford seemed to grope
for her poise and made a half-hearted return to her brittle manner.
"Let's face it," she said, "he was stinking, poor pet."

"You mean he was drunk?"

"Yes, I do."

"And abusive?"

"I didn't care. I understood him."

"Did he talk about Miss Hamilton?"

"Obviously J.G.'s already told you he did, so why ask me?"

"We like to get confirmation of statements."

"Well, you tell me what he said and I'll see about confirming it."

For the first time Alleyn looked at her. She wore an expression of
rather frightened impertinence. "I'm afraid," he said, "that won't quite
do. I'm sure you're very anxious to get away from the theatre, Miss
Gainsford, and we've still a lot of work before us. If you will give me
your account of this conversation I shall be glad to hear it; if you prefer
not to do so I'll take note of your refusal and keep you no longer."

She gaped slightly, attempted a laugh and seemed to gather up the
rags of her impersonation.

"Oh, but I'll tell you," she said. "Why not? It's only that there's so pathetically little to tell. I can't help feeling darling Aunty—she likes me to call her Helena—was *too* Pinero and Galsworthy about it. It appears that poorest Uncle Ben came in from his club and found her in a suitable setting and—well, there you are, and—well, really, even after all these years of segregation, you couldn't call it a seduction. Or could you? Anyway, she chose to treat it as such and raised the most piercing hue-and-cry and he went all primitive and when he came in here he was evidently in the throes of a sort of hangover, and seeing J.G. was being rather sweet to me he put a sinister interpretation on it and described the whole incident and was rather rude about women generally and me and Aunty in particular. And J.G. took a gloomy view of his attitude and hit him. And, I mean, taking it by and large one can't help feeling: *what* a song and dance about nothing in particular. Is that all you wanted to know?"

"Do you think any other members of the company know of all this?"

She looked genuinely surprised. "Oh yes," she said. "Adam and Jacko, anyway. I mean Uncle Ben appeared to have a sort of nation-wide hook-up idea about it but even if *he* didn't mention it, *she'd* naturally tell Adam, wouldn't you think? And Jacko, because everybody tells Jacko everything. And he was doing dresser for her. Yes, I'd certainly think she'd tell Jacko."

"I see. Thank you, Miss Gainsford. That's all."

"Really?" She was on her feet. "I can go home?"

Alleyn answered her as he had answered J.G. "I'm sorry, not yet. Not just yet."

P. C. Lamprey opened the door. Inevitably, she paused on the threshold. "Never tell *me* there's nothing in atmosphere," she said. "I *knew* when I came into this theatre. As if the very walls screamed it at me. I *knew*."

She went out.

"Tell me, Mike," Alleyn said, "are many young women of your generation like that?"

"Well, no, sir. She's what one might call a composite picture, don't you think?"

"I do, indeed. And I fancy she's got her genres a bit confused."

"She tells me she's been playing in *Private Lives, The Second Mrs. Tanqueray* and *Sleeping Partners* in the provinces."

"That may account for it," said Alleyn.

An agitated voice—Parry Percival's—was raised in the passage, to be answered in a more subdued manner by Sergeant Gibson's.

"Go and see what it is, Mike," Alleyn said.

But before Lamprey could reach the door it was flung open and Parry burst in, slamming it in Gibson's affronted face. He addressed himself instantly and breathlessly to Alleyn.

"I'm sorry," he said, "but I've just remembered something. I've been so *hideously* upset, I just simply never gave it a thought. It was when I smelt gas. When I went back to my room, I smelt gas and I turned off my fire. I ought to have told you. I've just realized."

"I think perhaps what you have just realized," Alleyn said, "is the probability of our testing your gas fire for finger-prints and finding your own."

Chapter IX

The Shadow of Otto Brod

Parry stood inside the door and pinched his lips as if he realized they were white and hoped to restore their colour.

"I don't know anything about finger-prints," he said. "I never read about crime. I don't know anything about it. When I came off after my final exit I went to my room. I was just going back for the call when I smelt gas. We're all nervous about gas in this theatre and anyway the room was frightfully hot. I turned the thing off. That's all."

"This was after Bennington tripped you up?"

"I've told you. It was after my last exit and before the call. It wasn't—"

He walked forward very slowly and sat down in front of Alleyn. "You can't think that sort of thing about me," he said, and sounded as if he was moved more by astonishment than by any other emotion. "My God, *look* at me. I'm so hopelessly harmless. I'm not vicious. I'm not even odd. I'm just harmless."

"Why didn't you tell me at once that you noticed the smell of gas?"

"Because, as I've tried to suggest, I'm no good at this sort of thing. The Doctor got me all upset and in any case the whole show was so unspeakable." He stared at Alleyn and, as if that explained everything, said: "I saw him. I saw him when they carried him out. I've never been much good about dead people. In the blitz I sort of managed but I never got used to it."

"Was the smell of gas very strong in your room?"

"No. Not strong at all. But in this theatre—we were all thinking about that other time, and I just thought it was too bad of the management to have anything faulty in the system considering the history of the place. I don't know that I thought anything more than that: I smelt it and remembered, and got a spasm of the horrors. Then I felt angry at being given a shock and then I turned my fire off and went out. It was rather like not looking at the new moon through glass. You don't really believe it can do anything but you avoid it. I forgot all about the gas as soon as

I got on-stage. I didn't give it another thought until I smelt it again during the Doctor's speech."

"Yes, I see."

"You do, really, don't you? After all, suppose I—suppose I had thought I'd copy that other awful thing—well, I'd scarcely be fool enough to leave my finger-prints on the tap, would I?"

"But you tell me," Alleyn said, not making too much of it, "that you don't know anything about finger-prints."

"God!" Parry whispered, staring at him. "You do frighten me. It's not fair. You frighten me."

"Believe me, there's no need for an innocent man to be frightened."

"How can you be so sure of yourselves? Do you never make mistakes?"

"We do indeed. But not," Alleyn said, "in the end. Not nowadays on these sorts of cases."

"What do you mean these sorts of cases!"

"Why, I mean on what may turn out to be a capital charge."

"I can't believe it!" Parry cried out. "I shall never believe it. We're not like that. We're kind, rather simple people. We wear our hearts on our sleeves. We're not complicated enough to kill each other."

Alleyn said with a smile: "You're quite complicated enough for us at the moment. Is there anything else you've remembered that you think perhaps you ought to tell me about?"

Parry shook his head and dragged himself to his feet. Alleyn saw, as Martyn had seen before him, that he was not an exceedingly young man. "No," he said. "There's nothing I can think of."

"You may go to your dressing-room now, if you'd like to change into —what should I say?—into plain clothes?"

"Thank you. I simply loathe the thought of my room after all this but I shall be glad to change."

"Do you mind if Lamprey does a routine search before you go? We'll ask this of all of you."

Parry showed the whites of his eyes but said at once: "Why should I mind?"

Alleyn nodded to young Lamprey, who advanced upon Parry with an apologetic smile.

"It's a painless extraction, sir," he said.

Parry raised his arms in a curve with his white hands held like a dancer's above his head. There was a silence and a swift, efficient exploration. "Thank you so much, sir," said Mike Lamprey. "Cigarette case, lighter and handkerchief, Mr. Alleyn."

"Right. Take Mr. Percival along to his room, will you?"

Parry said: "There couldn't be a more fruitless question but it would be nice to know, one way or the other, if you have believed me."

"There couldn't be a more unorthodox answer," Alleyn rejoined, "but at the moment I see no reason to disbelieve you, Mr. Percival."

When Lamprey came back he found his senior officer looking wistfully at his pipe and whistling under his breath.

"Mike," Alleyn said, "the nastiest cases in our game are very often the simplest. There's something sticking out under my nose in this theatre and I can't see it. I know it's there because of another thing that, Lord pity us all, Fox and I can see."

"Really, sir? Am I allowed to ask what it is?"

"You're getting on in the service, now. What have you spotted on your own account?"

"Is it something to do with Bennington's behaviour, sir?"

"It is indeed. If a man's going to commit suicide, Mike, and his face is made up to look loathsome, what does he do about it? If he's a vain man (and Bennington appears to have had his share of professional vanity), if he minds about the appearance of his own corpse, he cleans off the greasepaint. If he doesn't give a damn, he leaves it as it is. But with time running short, he does *not* carefully and heavily powder his unbecoming make-up for all the world as if he meant to go on and take his curtain-call with the rest of them. Now, does he?"

"Well, no sir," said Mike. "If you put it like that, I don't believe he does."

ii

By half past twelve most of the company on the stage seemed to be asleep or dozing. Dr. Rutherford on his couch occasionally lapsed into bouts of snoring from which he would rouse a little, groan, take snuff and then settle down again. Helena lay in a deep chair with her feet on a stool. Her eyes were closed but Martyn thought that if she slept it was but lightly. Clem had made himself a bed of some old curtains and was curled up on it beyond the twisting stairway. Jacko, having tucked Helena up in her fur coat, settled himself on the stage beside her, dozing, Martyn thought, like some eccentric watch-dog at his post. After J.G. silently returned from the Greenroom, Gay Gainsford was summoned and in her turn came back—not silently, but with some attempt at conversation. In the presence of the watchful Mr. Fox this soon petered out. Presently she, too, fell to nodding. Immediately after her return

Parry Percival suddenly made an inarticulate ejaculation and, before Fox could move, darted off the stage. Sergeant Gibson was heard to accost him in the passage. Fox remained where he was and there was another long silence.

Adam Poole and Martyn looked into each other's faces. He crossed the stage to where she sat, on the left side, which was the farthest removed from Fox. He pulled up a small chair and sat facing her.

"Kate," he muttered, "I'm so sorry about all this. There are hare's-foot shadows under your eyes, your mouth droops, your hands are anxious and your hair is limp, though not at all unbecoming. You should be sound asleep in Jacko's garret under the stars and there should be the sound of applause in your dreams. Really, it's too bad."

Martyn said: "It's nice of you to think so but you have other things to consider."

"I'm glad to have my thoughts interrupted."

"Then I still have my uses."

"You can see that chunk of a man over there. Is he watching us?"

"Yes. With an air of absent-mindedness which I'm not at all inclined to misunderstand."

"I don't think he can hear us, though it's a pity my diction is so good. If I take your hand perhaps he'll suppose I'm making love to you and feel some slight constabular delicacy."

"I hardly think so," Martyn whispered, and tried to make nothing of his lips against her palm.

"Will you believe, Kate, that I am not in the habit of making passes at young ladies in my company?"

Martyn found herself looking at the back of Helena's chair.

"Oh yes," Poole said. "There's that, too. I make no bones about that. It's another and a long and a fading story. On both parts. Fading on both parts, Kate. I have been very much honoured."

"I can't help feeling this scene is being played at the wrong time, in the wrong place and before the wrong audience. And I doubt," Martyn said, not looking at him, "if it should be played at all."

"But I can't be mistaken. It has happened for us, Martyn. Hasn't it? Suddenly, preposterously, almost at first sight we blinked and looked again and there we were. Tell me it's happened. The bird under your wrist is so wildly agitated. Is that only because you are frightened?"

"I am frightened. I wanted to ask your advice and now you make it impossible."

"I'll give you my advice. There. Now you are alone again. But for the sake of the law's peace of mind as well as my own you must take a firm line about your blushing."

"It was something he said to me that morning," she murmured in the lowest voice she could command.

"Do you mean the morning when I first saw you?"

"I mean," Martyn said desperately, "the morning the photographs were taken. I had to go to his dressing-room."

"I remember very well. You came to mine too."

"He said something, then. He was very odd in his manner. They've asked us to try and remember anything at all unusual."

"Are you going to tell me what it was?"

In a few words and under her breath she did so.

Poole said: "Perhaps you should tell them. Yes, I think you should. In a moment I'll do something about it, but there's one thing more I must say to you. Do you know I'm glad this scene has been played so awkwardly—inaudible, huddled up, inauspicious and uneffective. Technically altogether bad. It gives it a kind of authority, I hope. Martyn, are you very much surprised? Please look at me."

She did as he asked and discovered an expression of such doubt and anxiety in his face that to her own astonishment she put her hand against his cheek and he held it there for a second. "God," he said, "what a thing to happen!" He got up abruptly and crossed the stage.

"Inspector," he said, "Miss Tarne has remembered an incident three days old which we both think might possibly be of some help. What should we do about it?"

The others stirred a little. J.G. opened his eyes.

Fox got up. "Thank you very much, sir," he said. "When Mr. Alleyn is disengaged I'm sure he'll— Yes? What is it?"

P. C. Lamprey had come in. He delivered a message that the dressing-rooms were now open for the use of their occupants. At the sound of his brisk and loudish voice they all stirred. Helena and Darcey got to their feet. Jacko sat up. Clem, Gay and Dr. Rutherford opened their eyes, listened to the announcement and went to sleep again.

Fox said: "You can take this young lady along to the Chief in three minutes, Lamprey. Now, ladies and gentlemen, if you'd care to go to your rooms."

He shepherded Helena and Darcey through the door and looked back at Poole. "What about you, sir?"

Poole, with his eyes on Martyn, said: "Yes, I'm coming." Fox waited stolidly at the door for him and, after a moment's hesitation, Poole followed the others. Fox went with them.

Mike Lamprey said: "We'll let them get settled, Miss Tarne, and then I'll take you along to Mr. Alleyn. You must be getting very bored with all this hanging about."

Martyn, whose emotional processes were in a state of chaos, replied with a vague smile. She wondered disjointedly if constables of P. C. Lamprey's class were a commonplace in the English Force. He glanced good-humouredly at Gay and the three dozing men and evidently felt obliged to make further conversation.

"I heard someone say," he began, "that you are a New Zealander. I was out there as a small boy."

"Were you, really?" Martyn said, and wondered confusedly if he could have been the son of a former governor-general.

"We had a place out there on a mountain. Mount Silver, it was. Would that be anywhere near your part of the world?"

Something clicked in Martyn's memory. "Oh yes!" she said. "I've heard about the Lampreys of Mount Silver, I'm sure, and—" Her recollection clarified a little. "Yes, indeed," she added lamely.

"No doubt," said Mike with a cheerful laugh, "a legend of lunacy has survived us. We came Home when I was about eight, and soon afterwards my uncle happened to get murdered in our flat and Mr. Alleyn handled the case. I thought at the time I'd like to go into the Force and the idea sort of persisted. And there you are, you know. Potted autobiography. Shall we go along and see if he's free?"

He escorted her down the passage to the Greenroom door, past Sergeant Gibson, who seemed to be on guard there. Mike chatted freely as they went, rather as if he were taking her into supper after a successful dance. The star-bemused Martyn found herself brightly chatting back at him.

This social atmosphere was not entirely dispelled, she felt, by Alleyn himself, who received her rather as a distinguished surgeon might greet a patient.

"Come in, Miss Tarne," he said cordially. "I hear you've thought of something to tell us about this wretched business. Do sit down."

She sat in her old chair, facing the gas fire and with her back to the table. Only when she looked up involuntarily at the sketch of Adam Poole did she realize that young Lamprey had settled himself at the table and taken out a note-book. She could see his image reflected in the glass.

Inspector Fox came in and went quietly to the far end of the room, where he sat in a shadowed corner and appeared to consult his own note-book.

"Well," Alleyn said, "what's it all about?"

"You'll probably think it's about nothing," Martyn began, "and if you do I shall be sorry I've bothered you with it. But I thought—just in case—"

"You were perfectly right. Believe me, we are 'conditioned,' if that's the beastly word, to blind alleys. Let's have it."

"On my first morning in this theatre," Martyn said, "which was the day before yesterday . . . no, if it's past midnight, the day before that."

"Tuesday?"

"Yes. On that morning I went to Mr. Bennington's room to fetch Miss Hamilton's cigarette case. He was rather strange in his manner, but at first I thought that was because—I thought he'd noticed my likeness to Mr. Poole. He couldn't find the case and in hunting through the pockets of a jacket, he dropped a letter to the floor. I picked it up and he drew my attention to it in the oddest sort of way. I'd describe his manner almost as triumphant. He said something about autographs. I think he asked me if I collected autographs or autographed letters. He pointed to the envelope, which I still had in my hand, and said there was somebody who'd give a hell of a lot for that one. Those, I'm almost sure, were his exact words."

"Did you look at the letter?"

"Yes, I did, because of what he said. It was addressed to him and it had a foreign stamp on it. The writing was very bold and it seemed to me foreign-looking. I put it on the shelf face downwards and he drew my attention to it again by stabbing at it with his finger. The name of the sender was written on the back."

"Do you remember it?"

"Yes, I do, because of his insistence."

"Good girl," said Alleyn quietly.

"It was Otto Brod and the address was a theatre in Prague. I'm afraid I don't remember the name of the theatre or the street. I *ought* to remember the theatre. It was a French name, Théâtre de—something. *Why* can't I remember!"

"You haven't done badly. Was there something in the envelope?"

"Yes. It wasn't anything fat. One sheet of paper, I should think."

"And his manner was triumphant?"

"I thought so. He was just rather odd about it. He'd been drinking—brandy, I thought—the tumbler was on the dressing-shelf and he made as if to put the flask behind his looking-glass."

"Did you think he was at all the worse for wear?"

"I wondered if it accounted for his queer behaviour."

"Can you tell me anything else he said? The whole conversation if you remember it."

Martyn thought back, and it seemed she had journeyed half a lifetime in three days. There was the room. There was J.G. going out and leaving her with Bennington, and there was Bennington staring at her and talking about the cigarette case. There was also something else, buried away behind her thoughts, of which the memory now returned. She was made miserable by it.

"He said, I think, something about the cigarette case. That he himself hadn't given it to Miss Hamilton."

"Did he say who gave it to her?"

"No," Martyn said, "I don't think he said that. Just that *he* didn't."

"And was his manner of saying this strange?"

"I thought his manner throughout was—uncomfortable and odd. He seemed to me to be a very unhappy man."

"Yet you used the word 'triumphant'?"

"There can be unhappy victories."

"True for you. There can, indeed. Tell me one thing more. Do you connect the two conversations? I mean, do you think what he said about the cigarette case had anything to do with what he said about the letter?"

"I should say nothing. Nothing at all."

"Oh Lord!" Alleyn said resignedly and called out: "Have you got all that, Mike?"

"Coming up the straight, sir."

"Put it into longhand, now, will you, and we'll ask Miss Tarne to have a look at it and see if she's been misrepresented. Do you mind waiting a minute or two, Miss Tarne? It'll save you coming back."

"No, of course not," said Martyn, whose ideas of police investigation were undergoing a private revolution. Alleyn offered her a cigarette and lit it for her. The consultation, she felt, was over, and the famous surgeon was putting his patient at her ease.

"I gather from Lamprey's far-reaching conversation that you are a New Zealander," he said. "If I may say so, you seem to have dropped out of a clear sky into your own success-story. Have you been long at the Vulcan, Miss Tarne?"

"A little over three days."

"Good Lord! And in that time you've migrated from dresser to what sounds like minor stardom. Success-story, indeed!"

"Yes, but—" Martyn hesitated. For the first time since she walked into the Vulcan she felt able to talk about herself. It didn't occur to her that it was odd for her confidant to be a police officer.

"It's all been very eccentric," she said. "I only reached England a little over a fortnight ago and my money was stolen in the ship, so I had to get some sort of job rather quickly."

"Did you report the theft to the police?"

"No. The purser said he didn't think it would do any good."

"So much," said Alleyn with a wry look, "for the police!"

"I'm sorry—" Martyn began and he said: "Never mind. It's not an uncommon attitude, I'm afraid. So you had a rather unhappy arrival. Lucky there was your cousin to come to your rescue."

"But—no—I mean—" Martyn felt herself blushing and plunged on. "That's just what I didn't want to do. I mean I didn't want to go to him at all. He didn't know of my existence. You see—"

It was part of Alleyn's professional equipment that something in his make-up invited confidence. Mr. Fox once said of his superior that he would be able to get himself worked up over the life-story of a mollusc, provided the narrative was obtained first-hand. He heard Martyn's story with the liveliest interest up to the point where she entered the theatre. He didn't seem to think it queer that she should have been anxious to conceal her relationship to Poole, or that she was stupid to avoid the Vulcan in her search for a job. She was describing her interview with Bob Grantley on Monday night when Sergeant Gibson's voice sounded in the passage. He tapped on the door and came in.

"Excuse me, sir," he said, "but could you see the night-watchman? He seems to think it's important."

He'd got as far as this when he was elbowed aside by Fred Badger, who came angrily into the room.

" 'Ere!" he said. "Are you the guv-nor of this 'owd'yerdo?"

"Yes," said Alleyn.

"Well, look. You can lay orf this young lady, see? No call to get nosey on account of what she done, see? I don't know nothink abaht the law, see, but I'm in charge 'ere of a night and what she done she done wiv my permission. Nah!"

"Just a moment—" Alleyn began and was roared down.

"Suppose it was an offence! What abaht it! She never done no 'arm. No offence taken where none was intended, that's correct, ain't it! Nah ven!"

"What," Alleyn said turning to Martyn, "is this about?"

"I'm afraid it's about me sleeping in the theatre that first night. I'd nowhere to go and it was very late. Mr. Badger very kindly—didn't turn me out."

"I see. Where did you sleep?"

"Here. In this chair."

"Like a charld," Fred Badger interposed. "Slep' like a charld all night. I looked in on me rahnds and seen 'er laying safe in the arms of Morpus. Innercent. And if anyone tells you different you can refer 'im to me. Badger's the name."

"All right, Badger."

"If you put me pot on with the management fer what I done, leaving 'er to lay—all right. Aht! Finish! There's better jobs rahnd the corner."

"Yes. All right. I don't think we'll take it up."

"Awright. Fair enough." He addressed himself to Martyn. "And what was mentioned between you and me in a friendly manner needn't be mentioned no more. Let bygones be bygones." He returned to Alleyn. "She's as innercent as a babe. Arst 'is nibs."

Alleyn waited for a moment and then said: "Thank you." Gibson succeeded in removing Fred Badger, but not before he had directed at Martyn that peculiar clicking sound of approval which is accompanied by a significant jerk of the head.

When he had gone Alleyn said: "I think I'd better ask you to interpret. What was his exquisite meaning?"

Martyn felt a dryness in her mouth. "I think," she said, "he's afraid he'll get into trouble for letting me sleep in here that night and I think he's afraid I'll get into trouble if I tell you that he showed me how the murder in the Jupiter case was accomplished."

"That seems a little far-fetched."

Martyn said rapidly: "I suppose it's idiotic of me to say this, but I'd rather say it. Mr. Bennington very naturally resented my luck in this theatre. He tackled me about it and he was pretty truculent. I expect the stage-hands have gossiped to Badger and he thinks you might—might—"

"Smell a motive?"

"Yes," said Martyn.

"Did Bennington threaten you?"

"I don't remember exactly what he said. His manner was threatening. He frightened me."

"Where did this happen?"

"Off-stage, during the first dress rehearsal."

"Was anyone present when he tackled you?"

The image of Poole rose in Martyn's memory. She saw him take Bennington by the arm and twist him away from her.

"There were people about," she said. "They were changing the set. I should think it very likely—I mean it was a very public sort of encounter."

He looked thoughtfully at her and she wondered if she had changed colour. "This," he said, "was before it was decided you were to play the part?"

"Oh, yes. That was only decided half an hour before the show went on."

"So it was. Did he do anything about this decision? Go for you again?"

"He didn't come near me until I'd finished. And knowing how much he must mind, I was grateful for that."

Alleyn said: "You've been very sensible to tell me this, Miss Tarne."

Martyn swallowed hard. "I don't know," she said, "that I would have told you if it hadn't been for Fred Badger."

"Ah, well," Alleyn said, "one mustn't expect too much. How about that statement, Mike?"

"Here we are, sir. I hope you can read my writing, Miss Tarne."

When she took the paper, Martyn found her hands were not steady. Alleyn moved away to the table with his subordinate. She sat down again and read the large schoolboyish writing. It was a short and accurate résumé of the incident of the letter from Prague.

"It's quite right," she said. "Am I to sign it?"

"If you please. There will be statements for most of the others to sign later on, but yours is so short I thought we might as well get it over now."

He gave her his pen and she went to the table and signed. P. C. Lamprey smiled reassuringly at her and escorted her to the door.

Alleyn said: "Thank you so much, Miss Tarne. Do you live far from here?"

"Not very far. A quarter of an hour's walk."

"I wish I could let you go home now but I don't quite like to do that. Something might crop up that we'd want to refer to you."

"Might it?"

"You never know," he said. "Anyway, you can change now." Lamprey opened the door and she went to the dressing-room.

When she had gone, Alleyn said: "What did you make of her, Mike?"

"I thought she was rather a sweetie-pie, sir," said P. C. Lamprey. Fox, in his disregarded corner, snorted loudly.

"That was all too obvious," said Alleyn. "Sweetness apart, did you find her truthful?"

"I'd have said so, sir, yes."

"What about you, Br'er Fox? Come out of cover and declare yourself."

Fox rose, removed his spectacles and advanced upon them. "There was something," he observed, "about that business of when deceased went for her."

"There was indeed. Not exactly lying, wouldn't you think, so much as leaving something out?"

"Particularly in respect of whether there was a witness."

"She had her back to you but she looked at this portrait of Adam Poole. I'd make a long bet Poole found Bennington slanging that child and ordered him off."

"Very possibly, Mr. Alleyn. He's sweet on the young lady. That's plain to see. *And* she on him."

"Good Lord!" Mike Lamprey ejaculated. "He must be forty! I'm sorry, sir."

Mr. Fox began a stately reproof but Alleyn said: "Go away, Mike. Go back to the stage. Wake Dr. Rutherford and ask him to come here. I want a change from actors."

iii

Dr. Rutherford, on his entry into the Greenroom, was a figure of high fantasy. For his greater ease in sleeping he had pulled his boiled shirt from its confinement and it dangled fore and aft like a crumpled tabard. Restrained only by his slackened braces, it formed a mask, Alleyn conjectured, for a free adjustment of the Doctor's trousers buttoning. He had removed his jacket and assumed an overcoat. His collar was released and his tie dangled on his bosom. His head was tousled and his face blotched.

He paused in the doorway while Lamprey announced him and then, with a dismissive gesture, addressed himself to Alleyn and Fox.

"Calling my officers about me in my branched velvet gown," he shouted, "having come from a day-bed where I left Miss Gainsford sleeping, I present myself as a brand for the constabular burning. What's cooking, my hearties?"

He stood there, puffing and blowing, and eyed them with an expression of extreme impertinence. If he had been an actor, Alleyn thought, he would have been cast, and cast ideally, for Falstaff. He fished under his shirt-tail, produced his snuff-box, and helped himself, with a parody of Regency deportment, to a generous pinch. "Speak!" he said. "Pronounce! Propound! I am all ears."

"I have nothing, I'm afraid, to propound," Alleyn said cheerfully, "and am therefore unable to pronounce. As for speaking, I hope you'll do most of that yourself, Dr. Rutherford. Will you sit down?"

Dr. Rutherford, with his usual precipitancy, hurled himself into the nearest armchair. As an afterthought he spread his shirt-tail with ridiculous finicking movements across his lap. "I am a thought down-gyved," he observed. "My points are untrussed. Forgive me."

"Tell me," Alleyn said. "Do you think Bennington was murdered?"

The Doctor opened his eyes very wide, folded his hands on his stomach, revolved his thumbs and said "No."

"No?"

"No."

"We do."

"Why?"

"I'll come to that when I'm quite sure you may be put into the impossible class."

"Am I a suspect, by all that's pettifogging?"

"Not if you can prove yourself otherwise."

"By God," said Dr. Rutherford deeply, "if I'd thought I could get away with it, be damned if I wouldn't have had a shot. He was an unconscionable rogue, was Ben."

"In what way?"

"In every way, by Janus. A drunkard. A wife-terrorist. An exhibitionist. And what's more," he went on with rising intensity, "a damned wrecker of plays. A yea-forsooth knavish pander, by Heaven! I tell you this, and I tell you plainly, if I, sitting in my O.P. box, could have persuaded the Lord to stoop out of the firmament and drop a tidy thunderbolt on Ben, I would have done it with bells on. Joyously!"

"A thunderbolt," Alleyn said, "is one of the few means of dispatch that we have not seriously considered. Would you mind telling me where you were between the time when he made his last exit and the time when you appeared before the audience?"

"Brief let me be. In my box. On the stairs. Off-stage. On the stage."

"Can you tell me exactly when you left your box?"

"While they were making their initial mops and mows at the audience."

"Did you meet anyone or notice anything at all remarkable during this period?"

"Nothing, and nobody whatever."

"From which side did you enter for your own call?"

"The O.P., which is actors' right."

"So you merely emerged from the stairs that lead from the box to the stage and found yourself hard by the entrance?"

"Precisely."

"Have you any witness to all this, sir?"

"To my knowledge," said the Doctor, "none whatever. There may have been a rude mechanical or so."

"As far as your presence in the box is concerned, there was the audience. Nine hundred of them."

"In spite of its mangling at the hands of two of the actors, I believe the attention of the audience to have been upon My Play. In any case," the Doctor added, helping himself to a particularly large pinch of snuff and holding it poised before his face, "I had shrunk in modest confusion behind the curtain."

"Perhaps someone visited you?"

"Not after the first act. I locked myself in," he added, taking his snuff with uncouth noises, "as a precautionary measure. I loathe company."

"Did you come back stage at any other time during the performance?"

"I did. I came back in both intervals. Primarily to see the little wench."

"Miss Tarne?" Alleyn ventured.

"She. A tidy little wench it is and will make a good player. If she doesn't allow herself to be debauched by the sissies that rule the roost in our lamentable theatre."

"Did you, during either of these intervals, visit the dressing-rooms?"

"I went to the Usual Office at the end of the passage, if you call that a dressing-room."

"And returned to your box—when?"

"As soon as the curtain went up."

"I see." Alleyn thought for a moment and then said: "Dr. Rutherford, do you know anything about a man called Otto Brod?"

The Doctor gave a formidable gasp. His eyes bulged, his nostrils wrinkled and his jaw dropped. This grimace turned out to be the preliminary spasm to a Gargantuan sneeze. A handkerchief not being at his disposal, he snatched up the tail of his shirt, clapped it to his face and revealed a state of astonishing disorder below the waist.

"Otto Brod?" he repeated, looking at Alleyn over his shirt-tail as if it were an improvised yashmak. "Never heard of him."

"His correspondence seems to be of some value," Alleyn said vaguely but the Doctor merely gaped at him. "I don't," he said flatly, "know what you're talking about."

Alleyn gave up Otto Brod. "You'll have guessed," he said, "that I've already heard a good deal about the events of the last few days: I mean as they concerned the final rehearsals and the change in casting."

"Indeed? Then you will have heard that Ben and I had one flaming row after another. If you're looking for motive," said Dr. Rutherford with an expansive gesture, "I'm lousy with it. We hated each other's guts, Ben and I. Of the two I should say, however, that he was the more murderously inclined."

"Was this feeling chiefly on account of the part his niece was to have played?"

"Fundamentally it was the fine flower of a natural antipathy. The contributive elements were his behaviour as an actor in My Play and the obvious and immediate necessity to return his niece to her squalid little *métier* and replace her by the wench. We had at each other on that issue," said Dr. Rutherford with relish, "after both auditions and on every other occasion that presented itself."

"And in the end, it seems, you won?"

"Pah!" said the Doctor with a dismissive wave of his hand. "Cat's meat!"

Alleyn looked a little dubiously at the chaotic disarray of his garments. "Have you any objection," he asked, "to being searched?"

"Not I," cried the Doctor and hauled himself up from his chair. Fox approached him.

"By the way," Alleyn said, "as a medical man, would you say that a punch on the jaw such as Bennington was given could have been the cause of his fainting some time afterwards? Remembering his general condition?"

"Who says he had a punch on the jaw? It's probably a hypostatic discolouration. What do you want?" Dr. Rutherford demanded of Fox.

"If you wouldn't mind taking your hands out of your pockets, sir," Fox suggested.

The Doctor said: "Let not us that are squires of the night's body be called thieves of the day's beauty," and obligingly withdrew his hands from his trousers pockets. Unfortunately he pulled the linings out of them.

A number of objects fell about his feet—pencils, his snuff-box, scraps of paper, a pill-box, a programme, a note-book and a half-eaten cake of chocolate. A small cloud of snuff floated above this collection. Fox bent down and made a clucking sound of disapproval. He began to collect the scattered objects, inhaled snuff and was seized with a paroxysm of sneezing. The Doctor broke into a fit of uncouth laughter and floundered damagingly among the exhibits.

"Dr. Rutherford," Alleyn said with an air of the liveliest exasperation, "I would be immensely obliged to you if you'd have the goodness to stop behaving like a Pantaloon. Get off those things, if you please."

The Doctor backed away into his chair and examined an unlovely mess of chocolate and cardboard on the sole of his boot. "But, blast your lights, my good ass," he said, "there goes my spare ration. An ounce of the best rappee, by Heaven!" Fox began to pick the fragments of the pill-box from his boot. Having collected and laid aside the dropped possessions, he scraped up a heap of snuff. "It's no good now, Dogberry," said the Doctor with an air of intense disapproval. Fox tipped the scrapings into an envelope.

Alleyn stood over the Doctor. "I think," he said, "you had better give this up, you know."

The Doctor favoured him with an antic grimace but said nothing. "You're putting on an act, Dr. Rutherford, and I do assure you it's not at all convincing. As a red herring it stinks to high Heaven. Let me tell you this. We now know that Bennington was hit over the jaw. We know when it happened. We know that the bruise was afterwards camouflaged with make-up. I want you to come with me while I remove this make-up. Where's your jacket?"

"Give me my robe; put on my crown; I have immortal longings in me . . ."

Fox went out and returned with a tail-coat that was in great disorder. "Nothing in the pockets, Mr. Alleyn," he said briefly. Alleyn nodded and he handed it to Dr. Rutherford, who slung it over his shoulder.

Alleyn led the way down the passage, where Gibson was still on guard, and round the back of the stage to the dock. P. C. Lamprey came off the set and rolled the doors back.

Bennington had stiffened a little since they last looked at him. His face bore the expression of knowledgeable acquiescence that is so often seen in the dead. Using the back of a knife-blade, Alleyn scraped away the greasepaint from the right jaw. Fox held a piece of card for him and he laid smears of greasepaint on it in the manner of a painter setting his palette. The discoloured mark on the jaw showed clearly.

"There it is," Alleyn said, and stood aside for Dr. Rutherford.

"A tidy buffet, if buffet it was. Who gave it him?"

Alleyn didn't answer. He moved round to the other side and went on cleaning the face.

"The notion that it could have contributed to his death," the Doctor said, "is preposterous. If, as you say, there was an interval between the blow and the supposed collapse. Preposterous!"

Fox had brought cream and a towel, with which Alleyn now completed his task. The Doctor watched him with an air of impatience and unease. "Damned if I know why you keep me hanging about," he grumbled at last.

"I wanted your opinion on the bruise. That's all, Fox. Is the mortuary van here?"

"On its way, sir," said Fox, who was wrapping his piece of card in paper.

Alleyn looked at the Doctor. "Do you think," he said, "that his wife will want to see him?"

"She won't want to. She may think she ought to. Humbug, in my opinion. Distress herself for nothing. What good does it do anybody?"

"I think, however, I should at least ask her."

"Why the blazes you can't let her go home passes my comprehension. And where do I go, now? I'm getting damn bored with Ben's company."

"You may wait either on the stage or, if you'd rather, in the unoccupied dressing-room. Or the office, I think, is open."

"Can I have my snuff back?" Dr. Rutherford asked with something of the shamefaced air of a small boy wanting a favour.

"I think we might let you do that," Alleyn said. "Fox, will you give Dr. Rutherford his snuff-box?"

Dr. Rutherford lumbered uncertainly to the door. He stood there with his chin on his chest and his hands in his pockets.

"See here, Alleyn," he said, looking from under his eyebrows at him. "Suppose I told you it was I who gave Ben that wallop on his mug. What then?"

"Why," Alleyn said, "I shouldn't believe you, you know."

Chapter X

Summing Up

Alleyn saw Helena Hamilton in her dressing-room. It was an oddly exotic setting. The scent of banked flowers, of tobacco smoke and of cosmetics was exceedingly heavy, the air hot and exhausted. She had changed into her street-clothes and sat in an armchair that had been turned with its back to the door, so that when he entered he saw nothing of her but her right hand trailing near the floor with a cigarette between her fingers. She called: "Come in, Mr. Alleyn," in a warm voice as if he were an especially welcome visitor. He would not have guessed from this greeting that when he faced her he would find her looking so desperately tired.

As if she read his thoughts she put her hands to her eyes and said: "My goodness, this is a long night, isn't it?"

"I hope that for you, at least, it is nearing its end," he said. "I've come to tell you that we are ready to take him away."

"Does that mean I ought to—to look at him?"

"Only if you feel you want to. I can see no absolute need at all, if I may say so."

"I don't want to," she whispered and added in a stronger voice: "It would be a pretence. I have no real sorrow and I have never seen the dead. I should only be frightened and confused."

Alleyn went to the door and looked into the passage, where Fox waited with Gibson. He shook his head and Fox went away. When Alleyn came back to her she looked up at him and said: "What else?"

"A question or two. Have you ever known or heard of a man called Otto Brod?"

Her eyes widened. "But what a strange question!" she said. "Otto Brod? Yes. He's a Czech or an Austrian, I don't remember which. An intellectual. We met him three years ago when we did a tour of the continent. He had written a play and asked my husband to read it. It was in German and Ben's German wasn't up to it. The idea was that he should get someone over here to look at it, but he was dreadfully bad at keeping those sorts of promises and I don't think he ever did anything about it."

"Have they kept in touch, do you know?"

"Oddly enough, Ben said a few days ago that he'd heard from Otto. I think he'd written from time to time for news of his play but I don't suppose Ben answered." She pressed her thumb and fingers on her eyes. "If you want to see the letter," she said, "it's in his coat."

Alleyn said carefully: "You mean the jacket he wore to the theatre? Or his overcoat?"

"The jacket. He was always taking my cigarette case in mistake for his own. He took it out of his breast-pocket when he was leaving for the theatre and the letter was with it." She waited for a moment and then said: "He was rather odd about it."

"In what way?" Alleyn asked. She had used Martyn's very phrase, and now when she spoke again it was with the uncanny precision of a delayed echo: "He was rather strange in his manner. He held the letter out with the cigarette case and drew my attention to it. He said, I think: 'That's my trump card.' He seemed to be pleased in a not very attractive way. I took my case. He put the letter back in his pocket and went straight out."

"Did you get the impression he meant it was a trump card he could use against somebody?"

"Yes. I think I did."

"And did you form any idea who that person could be?"

She leant forward and cupped her face in her hands. "Oh yes," she said. "It seemed to me that it was I myself he meant. Or Adam. Or both of us. It sounded like a threat." She looked up at Alleyn. "We've both got alibis, haven't we? If it was murder."

"You have, undoubtedly," Alleyn said, and she looked frightened.

He asked her why she thought her husband had meant that the letter was a threat to herself or to Poole but she evaded this question, saying vaguely that she had felt it to be so.

"You didn't come down to the theatre with your husband?" Alleyn said.

"No. He was ready before I was. And in any case—" She made a slight expressive gesture and didn't complete her sentence. Alleyn said: "I think I must tell you that I know something of what happened during the afternoon."

The colour that flooded her face ebbed painfully and left it very white. She said: "How do you know that? You can't know." She stopped and seemed to listen. They could just hear Poole in the next room. He sounded as if he was moving about irresolutely. She caught her breath and after a moment she said loudly: "Was it Jacko? No, no, it was never Jacko."

"Your husband himself—" Alleyn began and she caught him up quickly. "Ben? Ah, I can believe that. I can believe he would boast of it. To one of the men. To J.G.? Was it J.G.? Or perhaps even to Gay?"

Alleyn said gently: "You must know I can't answer questions like these."

"It was never Jacko," she repeated positively and he said: "I haven't interviewed Mr. Doré yet."

"Haven't you? Good."

"Did you like Otto Brod?"

She smiled slightly and lifted herself in her chair. Her face became secret and brilliant. "For a little while," she said, "he was a fortunate man."

"Fortunate?"

"For a little while I loved him."

"Fortunate indeed," said Alleyn.

"You put that very civilly, Mr. Alleyn."

"Do you think there was some connection here? I mean between your relationship with Brod and the apparent threat when your husband showed you the letter?"

She shook her head. "I don't know. I don't think Ben realized. It was as brief as summer lightning, our affair."

"On both parts?"

"Oh no," she said, as if he had asked a foolish question. "Otto was very young, rather violent and dreadfully faithful, poor sweet. You are looking at me in an equivocal manner, Mr. Alleyn. Do you disapprove?"

Alleyn said formally: "Let us say that I am quite out of my depth with—"

"Why do you hesitate? With what?"

"I was going to say with a *femme fatale*," said Alleyn.

"Have I been complimented again?"

He didn't answer and after a moment she turned away as if she suddenly lost heart in some unguessed-at object she had had in mind.

"I suppose," she said, "I may not ask you why you believe Ben was murdered?"

"I think you may. For one reason: his last act in the dressing-room was not consistent with suicide. He refurbished his make-up."

"That's penetrating of you," she said. "It was an unsympathetic make-up. But I still believe he killed himself. He had much to regret and nothing in the wide world to look forward to. Except discomfiture."

"The performance to-night, among other things, to regret?"

"Among all the other things. The change in casting, for one. It must have upset him very much. Because yesterday he thought he'd stopped what he called John's nonsense about Gay. And there was his own behaviour, his hopeless, *hopeless* degradation. He had given up, Mr. Alleyn. Believe me, he had quite given up. You will find I'm right, I promise you."

"I wish I may," Alleyn said. "And I think that's all at the moment. If you'll excuse me, I'll get on with my job."

"Get on with it, then," she said and looked amused. She watched him go and he wondered after he'd shut the door if her expression had changed.

ii

Adam Poole greeted Alleyn with a sort of controlled impatience. He had changed and was on his feet. Apparently Alleyn had interrupted an aimless promenade about the room.

"Well?" he said. "Are you any further on? Or am I not supposed to ask?"

"A good deal further, I think," Alleyn said. "I want a word with you, if I may have it, and then with Mr. Doré. I shall then have something to say to all of you. After that I think we shall know where we are."

"And you're convinced, are you, that Bennington was murdered?"

"Yes, I'm quite convinced of that."

"I wish to God I knew why."

"I'll tell you," Alleyn said, "before the night is out."

Poole faced him. "I can't believe it," he said, "of any of us. It's quite incredible." He looked at the wall between his own room and Helena's. "I could hear your voices in there," he said. "Is she all right?"

"She's perfectly composed."

"I don't know why you wanted to talk to her at all."

"I had three things to say to Miss Hamilton. I asked her if she wanted to see her husband before he was taken away. She didn't want to do so. Then I told her that I knew about an event of yesterday afternoon."

"What event?" Poole demanded sharply.

"I mean an encounter between her husband and herself."

"How the hell did you hear about that?"

"You know of it yourself, evidently."

Poole said: "Yes, all right. I knew," and then, as if the notion had just come to him and filled him with astonishment, he exclaimed: "Good God, I believe you think it's a motive for *me!*" He thrust his hand through his hair. "That's about as ironical an idea as one could possibly imagine." He stared at Alleyn. An onlooker coming into the room at that moment would have thought that the two men had something in common and a liking for each other. "You can't imagine," Poole said, "how inappropriate *that* idea is."

"I haven't yet said I entertain it, you know."

"It's not surprising if you do. After all, I suppose I could, fantastically, have galloped from the stage to Ben's room, laid him out, turned the gas on and doubled back in time to re-enter! Do you know what my line of re-entry is in the play?"

"No."

"I come in, shut the door, go up to Helena, and say: 'You've guessed, haven't you? He's taken the only way out. I suppose we must be said to be free.' It all seems to fit so very neatly, doesn't it? Except that for us it's a year or more out of date." He looked at Alleyn. "I really don't know," he added, "why I'm talking like this. It's probably most injudicious. But I've had a good deal to think about the last two days and Ben's death has more or less put the crown on it. What am I to do about this theatre? What are we to do about the show? What's going to happen about—" He broke off and looked at the wall that separated his room from Martyn's. "Look here, Alleyn," he said. "You've no doubt heard all there is to hear, and more, about my private life. And Helena's. It's the curse of this job that one is perpetually in the spotlight."

He seemed to expect some comment on this. Alleyn said lightly: "The curse of greatness?"

"Nothing like it, I'm afraid. See here, Alleyn. There are some women who just can't be fitted into any kind of ethical or sociological pigeonhole. Ellen Terry was one of them. It's not that they are above reproach in the sense most people mean by the phrase, but that they are outside it. They behave naturally in an artificial set-up. When an attachment comes to an end, it does so without any regrets or recrimination. Often, with an abiding affection on both sides. Do you agree?"

"That there are such women? Yes."

"Helena is one. I'm not doing this very well but I do want you to believe that she's right outside this beastly thing. It won't get you any further and it may hurt her profoundly if you try to establish some link between her relationship with her husband or anyone else and the circumstances of his death. I don't know what you said to each other, but I do know it would never occur to her to be on guard for her own sake."

"I asked her to tell me about Otto Brod."

Poole's reaction to this was surprising. He looked exasperated. "There you are!" he said. "That's exactly what I mean. Otto Brod! A fantastic irresponsible affair that floated out of some midsummer notion of Vienna and Strauss waltzes. How the devil you heard of it I don't know, though I've no doubt that at the time she fluttered him like a plume in her bonnet for all to see. I never met him but I understand he was some young intellectual with a pale face, no money and an over-developed faculty for symbolic tragedy. Why bring him in?"

Alleyn told him that Bennington, when he came down to the theatre, had had a letter from Brod in his pocket and Poole said angrily: "Why the hell shouldn't he? What of it?"

"The letter is not to be found."

"My dear chap, I suppose he chucked it out or burnt it or something."

"I hardly think so," said Alleyn. "He told Miss Hamilton it was his trump card."

Poole was completely still for some moments. Then he turned away to the dressing-shelf and looked for his cigarettes.

"Now what in the wide world," he said with his back to Alleyn, "could he have meant by a trump card?"

"That," said Alleyn, "is what, above everything else, I should very much like to know."

"I don't suppose it means a damn thing, after all. It certainly doesn't to me."

He turned to offer his cigarettes but found that Alleyn had his own case open in his hands. "I'd ask you to have a drink," Poole said, "but I don't keep it in the dressing-room during the show. If you'd come to the office—"

"Nothing I'd like more but we don't have it in the working hours either."

"Of course not. Stupid of me." Poole glanced at his dress for the ball and then at his watch. "I hope," he said, "that my business manager is enjoying himself with my guests at my party."

"He rang up some time ago to enquire. There was no message for you."

"Thank you." Poole leant against the dressing-shelf and lit his cigarette.

"It seems to me," Alleyn said, "that there is something you want to say to me. I've not brought a witness in here. If what you say is likely to be wanted as evidence I'll ask you to repeat it formally. If not, it will have no official significance."

"You're very perceptive. I'm damned if I know why I should want to tell you this, but I do. Just out of earshot behind these two walls are two women. Of my relation with the one, you seem to have heard. I imagine it's pretty generally known. I've tried to suggest that it has come to its end as simply, if that's not too fancy a way of putting it, as a flower relinquishes its petals. For a time I've pretended their colour had not faded and I've watched them fall with regret. But from the beginning we both knew it was that sort of affair. She didn't pretend at all. She's quite above any of the usual subterfuges and it's some weeks ago that she let me know it was almost over for her. I think we both kept it up out of politeness more than anything else. When she told me of Ben's unspeakable behaviour yesterday, I felt as one must feel about an outrage to a woman whom one knows very well and likes very much. I was appalled to discover in myself no stronger emotion than this. It was precisely this discovery that told me that the last petal had indeed fallen and now—" He lifted his hands. "Now Ben gets himself murdered, you say, and I've run out of the appropriate emotions."

Alleyn said: "We are creatures of convention and like our tragedies to take a recognizable form."

"I'm afraid this is not even a tragedy. Unless—" He turned his head and looked at the other wall. "I haven't seen Martyn," he said, "since you spoke to her. She's all right, isn't she?" Before Alleyn could answer he went on: "I suppose she's told you about herself—her arrival out of a clear sky and all the rest of it?"

"Everything, I think."

"I hope to God— I want to see her, Alleyn. She's alone in there. She may be frightened. I don't suppose you understand."

"She's told me of the relationship between you."

"The *relationship!*" he said quickly. "You mean—"

"She's told me you are related. It's natural that you should be concerned about her."

Poole stared at him. "My good ass," he said, "I'm nineteen years her senior and I love her like a boy of her own age."

"In that case," Alleyn remarked, "you can *not* be said to have run out of the appropriate emotions."

He grinned at Poole in a friendly manner and, accompanied by Fox, went to his final interview—with Jacques Doré.

iii

It took place on the stage. Dr. Rutherford had elected to retire into the office to effect, he had told Fox, a few paltry adjustments of his costume. The players, too, were all in their several rooms and Clem Smith had been wakened, re-examined by Fox, and allowed to go home.

So Jacko was alone in the tortured scene he had himself designed.

He looked a frightful scarecrow in his working clothes, with grey stubble on his chin, grey bags under his eyes and grey fuzz standing up on his head. His long crepe-y neck stuck out of the open collar of his tartan shirt. His eyes were bloodshot and his delicate hands were filthy.

"I have slept," he announced, rising from the heap of old curtains which Clem had transformed into a bed, "like the Holy Innocents, though it is possible that I do not resemble any of them. However deceptive the outward man may be, gentlemen, the inner is entirely at your service." He smiled ingratiatingly at them. His lips curled back and exposed teeth like a row of yellow pegs in a dice box. "What do we talk about?" he asked, and began to roll himself a cigarette.

"First of all," Alleyn said, "I must tell you that I am asking for a general search through the clothes that have been worn in the theatre. We have no warrant at this stage but so far no one has objected."

"Then who am I to do so?"

Fox went through his pockets and found a number of curious objects —chalk, pencils, a rubber, a surgeon's scalpel which Jacko said he used for wood carving, and which was protected by a sheath, a pocket-book with money, a photograph of Helena Hamilton, various scraps of paper with drawings on them, pieces of cotton-wool and an empty bottle smelling strongly of ether. This, he told Alleyn, had contained a fluid used for cleaning purposes. "Always they are messing themselves and always I am removing the mess. My overcoat is in the junk room. It contains merely a filthy handkerchief, I believe."

Alleyn thanked him and returned the scalpel, the pocket-book and drawing materials. Fox laid the other things aside, sat down and opened his note-book.

"Next," Alleyn said, "I think I'd better ask you what your official job is in this theatre. I see by the programme—"

"The programme," Jacko said, "is euphemistic. 'Assistant to Adam Poole,' is it not? Let us rather say: Dogsbody in Ordinary to the Vulcan

Theatre. Henchman Extraordinary to Mr. Adam Poole. At the moment, dresser to Miss Helena Hamilton. Confidant to all and sundry. Johannes Factotum and not without bells on. *Le* Vulcan, *c'est moi,* in a shabby manner of speaking. Also: *j'y suis, j'y reste.* I hope."

"Judging by this scenery," Alleyn rejoined, "and by an enchanting necklace which I think is your work, there shouldn't be much doubt about that. But your association with the management goes farther back than the Vulcan, doesn't it?"

"Twenty years," Jacko said, licking his cigarette paper. "For twenty years I improvise my role of Pantaloon for them. Foolishness, but such is my deplorable type. The eternal doormat. What can I do for you?"

Alleyn said: "You can tell me if you still think Bennington committed suicide."

Jacko lit his cigarette. "Certainly," he said. "You are wasting your time."

"Was he a vain man?"

"Immensely. And he knew he was artistically sunk."

"Vain in his looks?"

"But yes, *yes!*" Jacko said with great emphasis, and then looked very sharply at Alleyn. "Why, of his looks?"

"Did he object to his make-up in this play? It seemed to me a particularly repulsive one."

"He disliked it, yes. He exhibited the vanity of the failing actor in this. Always, always he must be sympathetic. Fortunately Adam insisted on the make-up."

"I think you told me that you noticed his face was shining with sweat before he went for the last time to his room?"

"I did."

"And you advised him to remedy this? You even looked into his room to make sure?"

"Yes," Jacko agreed after a pause, "I did."

"So when you had gone he sat at his dressing-table and carefully furbished up his repellent make-up as if for the curtain-call. And then gassed himself?"

"The impulse perhaps came very suddenly." Jacko half-closed his eyes and looked through their sandy lashes at his cigarette smoke. "Ah, yes," he said softly. "Listen. He repairs his face. He has a last look at himself. He is about to get up when his attention sharpens. He continues to stare. He sees the ruin of his face. He was once a coarsely handsome fellow, was Ben, with a bold rakehelly air. The coarseness has increased, but where, he asks himself, are the looks? Pouches, grooves, veins, yellow eyeballs—and all emphasized most hideously by the make-up. This is what he has become, he thinks, he has become the man he has been playing. And his heart descends into his belly. He knows despair and he makes up his mind. There is hardly time to do it. In a minute or two he will be called. So quickly, quickly he lies on the floor, with trembling hands he pulls his coat over his head and puts the end of the gas tube in his mouth."

"You knew how he was found, then?"

"Clem told me. I envisage everything. He enters a world of whirling dreams. And in a little while he is dead. I see it very clearly."

"Almost as if you'd been there," Alleyn said lightly. "Is this, do you argue, his sole motive? What about the quarrels that had been going on? The change of cast at the last moment? The handing over of Miss Gainsford's part to Miss Tarne? He was very much upset by that, wasn't he?"

Jacko doubled himself up like an ungainly animal and squatted on a stool. "Too much has been made of the change of casting," he said. "He accepted it in the end. He made a friendly gesture. On thinking it over I have decided we were all wrong to lay so much emphasis on this controversy." He peered sideways at Alleyn. "It was the disintegration of his artistic integrity that did it," he said. "I now consider the change of casting to be of no significance."

Alleyn looked him very hard in the eye. "And that," he said, "is where we disagree. I consider it to be of the most complete significance: the key, in fact, to the whole puzzle of his death."

"I cannot agree," said Jacko. "I am sorry."

Alleyn waited for a moment and then—and for the last time—asked the now familiar question.

"Do you know anything about a man called Otto Brod?"

There was a long silence. Jacko's back was bent and his head almost between his knees.

"I have heard of him," he said at last.

"Did you know him?"

"I have never met him. Never."

"Perhaps you have seen some of his work?"

Jacko was silent.

"*Können Sie Deutsch lesen?*"

Fox looked up from his notes with an expression of blank surprise. They heard a car turn in from Carpet Street and come up the side lane with a chime of bells. It stopped and a door slammed.

"*Jawohl,*" Jacko whispered.

The outside doors of the dock were rolled back. The sound resembled stage-thunder. Then the inner and nearer doors opened heavily and someone walked round the back of the set. Young Lamprey came through the Prompt entrance. "The mortuary van, sir," he said.

"All right. They can go ahead."

He went out again. There was a sound of voices and of boots on concrete. A cold draught of night air blew in from the dock and set the borders creaking. A rope tapped against canvas and a sighing breath wandered about the grid. The doors were rolled together. The engine started up and, to another chime of bells, Bennington made his final exit from the Vulcan. The theatre settled back into its night-watch.

Jacko's cigarette had burnt his lip. He spat it out and got slowly to his feet.

"You have been very clever," he said. He spoke as if his lips were stiff with cold.

"Did Bennington tell you how he would, if necessary, play his trump card?"

"Not until after he had decided to play it."

"But you had recognized the possibility?"

"Yes."

Alleyn nodded to Fox, who shut his note-book, removed his spectacles and went out.

"What now?" Jacko asked.

"All on," Alleyn said. "A company call. This is the curtain speech, Mr. Doré."

iv

Lamprey had called them and then retired. They found an empty stage awaiting them. It was from force of habit, Martyn supposed, that they took up, for the last time, their after-rehearsal positions on the stage. Helena lay back in her deep chair with Jacko on the floor at her feet. When he settled himself there, she touched his cheek and he turned his lips to her hand. Martyn wondered if he was ill. He saw that she looked at him and made his clown's grimace. She supposed that, like everybody else, he was merely exhausted. Darcey and Gay Gainsford sat together on the small settee and Parry Percival on his upright chair behind them. At the back, Dr. Rutherford lay on the sofa with a newspaper spread over his face. Martyn had returned to her old seat near the Prompt corner and Poole to his central chair facing the group. "We have come out of our rooms," Martyn thought, "like rabbits from their burrows." Through the Prompt entrance she could see Fred Badger, lurking anxiously in the shadows.

Alleyn and his subordinates stood in a group near the dock doors. On the wall close by them was the baize rack with criss-crossed tapes in which two receipts and a number of commercial cards were exhibited. Fox had read them all. He now replaced the last and looked through the Prompt corner to the stage.

"Are they all on?" Alleyn asked.

"All present and correct, sir."

"Do you think I'm taking a very risky line, Br'er Fox?"

"Well, sir," said Fox uneasily, "it's a very unusual sort of procedure, isn't it?"

"It's a very unusual case," Alleyn rejoined, and after a moment's reflection he took Fox by the arm. "Come on, old trooper," he said. "Let's get it over."

He walked onto the stage almost as if, like Poole, he were going to sum up a rehearsal. Fox went to his old chair near the back entrance. Martyn heard the other men move round behind the set. They took up positions, she thought, outside the entrances and it was unpleasant to think of them waiting there, unseen.

Alleyn stood with his back to the curtain and Poole at once slewed his chair round to face him. With the exception of Jacko, who was rolling a cigarette, they all watched Alleyn. Even the Doctor removed his newspaper, sat up, stared, groaned and returned ostentatiously to his former position.

For a moment Alleyn looked round the group, and to Martyn he seemed to have an air of compassion. When he began to speak his manner was informal but extremely deliberate.

"In asking you to come here together," he said, "I've taken an unorthodox line. I don't myself know whether I am justified in taking it, and I shan't know until those of you who are free to do so have gone home. That will be in a few minutes, I think.

"I have to tell you that your fellow-player has been murdered. All of you must know that we've formed this opinion, and I think most of you know that I was first inclined to it by the circumstance of his behaviour on returning to his dressing-room. His last conscious act was to repair his stage make-up. While that seemed to me to be inconsistent with suicide, it was, on the other hand, much too slender a thread to tie up a case for homicide. But there is more conclusive evidence and I'm going to put it before you. He powdered his face. His dresser had already removed the pieces of cotton-wool that had been used earlier in the evening and put out a fresh pad. Yet after his death there was no used pad of cotton-wool anywhere in the room. There is, on the other hand, a fresh stain near the gas fire which may, on analysis, turn out to have been caused by such a pad having been burnt on the hearth. The box of powder has been overturned on the shelf and there is a deposit of powder all over that corner of the room. As you know, his head and shoulders were covered, tentwise, with his overcoat. There was powder on this coat and over his finger-prints on the top of the gas fire. The coat had hung near the door and would, while it was there, have been out of range of any powder flying about. The powder, it is clear, had been scattered after and not before he was gassed. If he was, in fact, gassed."

Poole and Darcey made simultaneous ejaculations. Helena and Gay looked bewildered, and Percival incredulous. Jacko stared at the floor and the Doctor groaned under his newspaper.

"The post mortem," Alleyn said, "will of course settle this one way or the other. It will be exhaustive. No, it's quite certain that the dresser didn't go into the room after Mr. Bennington entered it this last time, and it is equally certain that the dresser left it in good order—the powder-pad prepared, the clothes hung up, the fire burning and the door unlocked. It is also certain that the powder was not overturned by the men who carried Mr. Bennington out. It was spilt by someone who was in the room after he was on the floor with the coat over his head. This person, the police will maintain, was his murderer. Now the question arises, doesn't it, how it came about that he was in such a condition —comatose or unconscious—that it was possible to get him down on the floor, put out the gas fire, and then disengage the connecting tube, put the rubber end in his mouth and turn the gas on again, get his finger prints on the wing-tap and cover him with his own overcoat. There is still about one-sixth of brandy left in his flask. He was not too drunk to make up his own face and he was more or less his own man, though not completely so, when he spoke to Miss Tarne just before he went into his room. During the second interval Mr. Darcey hit him on the jaw and raised a bruise. I suppose it is possible that his murderer hit him again on the same spot—there is no other bruise—and knocked him out. A closer examination of the bruise may show if this was so. In that case the murderer would need to pay only one visit to the room: he would simply walk in a few minutes before the final curtain, knock his victim out and set the stage for apparent suicide.

"On the other hand, it's possible that he was drugged."

He waited for a moment. Helena Hamilton said: "I don't believe in all this. I don't mean, Mr. Alleyn, that I think you're wrong: I mean it just sounds unreal and rather commonplace like a case reported in a newspaper. One knows that probably it's all happened but one doesn't actively believe it. I'm sorry. I interrupted."

"I hope," Alleyn said, "you will all feel perfectly free to interrupt at any point. About this possibility of drugging. If the brandy was drugged, then of course we shall find out. Moreover, it must have been tinkered with after he went on for his final scene. Indeed, any use of a drug, and one cannot disregard the possibility of even the most fantastic methods, must surely have been prepared while he was on the stage during the last act. We shall, of course, have a chemical analysis made of everything he used—the brandy, his tumbler, his cigarettes, his make-ups and even the greasepaint on his face. I tell you, quite frankly, that I've no idea at all whether this will get us any further."

Fox cleared his throat. This modest sound drew the attention of the company upon him but he merely looked gravely preoccupied and they turned back to Alleyn.

"Following out this line of thought, it seems clear," he said, "that two visits would have to be made to the dressing-room. The first, during his scene in the last act, and the second, after he had come off and be-fore the smell of gas was first noticed—by Mr. Parry Percival."

Percival said in a high voice: "I knew this was coming." Gay Gains-ford turned and looked at him with an expression of the liveliest horror. He caught her eye and said: "Oh, don't be fantastic, Gay darling. *Honestly!*"

"Mr. Percival," Alleyn said, "whose room is next to Mr. Benning-ton's and whose fire backs on his, noticed a smell of gas when he was about to go out for the curtain-call. He tells us he is particularly sensi-tive to the smell because of its associations in this theatre and that he turned his own fire off and went out. Thus his finger-prints were found on the tap."

"Well, naturally they were," Parry said angrily. "Really, Gay!"

"This, of course," Alleyn went on, "was reminiscent of the Jupiter case, but in that case the tube was not disconnected because the mur-derer never entered the room. He blew down the next-door tube and the fire went out. In that instance the victim was comatose from alcohol. Now, it seems quite clear to us that while this thing was planned with one eye on the Jupiter case, there was no intention to throw the blame upon anyone else and that Mr. Percival's reaction to the smell was not foreseen by the planner. What the planner hoped to emphasize was Mr. Bennington's absorption in the former case. We were to suppose that when he decided to take his own life he used the method by which he was obsessed. Suppose this to have been so. Wouldn't we, remembering the former case, suspect that it was not suicide at all and look for what my colleague likes to call funny business? On the other hand . . ." Alleyn paused. Percival, who was obviously lost in his sense of release, and Gay Gainsford, who equally obviously was in a high state of confusion, both seemed to pull themselves together.

"On the other hand," Alleyn repeated, "suppose this hypothetical planner was none other than Bennington himself?"

v

Their response to this statement had a delayed action. They behaved as actors do when they make what is technically known as a "double take." There were a few seconds of blank witlessness followed by a sudden and violent reaction. Darcey and Percival shouted together that it would be exactly like Ben, Helena cried out inarticulately and Poole gave a violent ejaculation. The Doctor crackled his newspaper and Martyn's thoughts tumbled about in her head like dice. Jacko alone stared incredulously at Alleyn.

"Do you mean," Jacko asked, "that we are to understand that Ben killed himself in such a way as to throw suspicion of murder upon one of us? Is that your meaning?"

"No. For a time we wondered if this might be so, but the state of the dressing-room, as I'd hoped I'd made clear, flatly contradicts any such theory. No. I believe the planner based the method on Bennington's preoccupation with the other case and hoped we would be led to some such conclusion. If powder had not been spilt on the overcoat we might well have done so."

"So we are still—in the dark," Helena said, and gave the commonplace phrase a most sombre colour.

"Not altogether. I needn't go over the collection of near-motives that have cropped up in the course of our interviews. Some of them sound far-fetched, others at least possible. It's not generally recognized that, given a certain temperament, the motive for homicide can be astonishingly unconvincing. Men have been killed from petty covetousness, out of fright, vanity, jealousy, boredom or sheer hatred. One or other of these motives lies at the back of this case. You all, I think, had cause to dislike this man. In one of you the cause was wedded to that particular kink which distinguishes murderers from the rest of mankind. With such beings there is usually some, shall I say, explosive agency—a sort of fuse—which, if it is touched off, sets them going as murder-machines. In this case I believe the fuse to have been a letter written by Otto Brod to Clark Bennington. This letter has disappeared and was probably burnt in his dressing-room. As the powder-pad may have been burnt. By his murderer."

Poole said: "I can't begin to see the sense of all this," and Helena said drearily: "Dark. In the dark."

Alleyn seemed to be lost in thought. Martyn, alone of all the company, looked at him. She thought she had never seen a face as withdrawn and—incongruously the word flashed up again—compassionate. She wondered if he had come to some crucial point and she watched anxiously for the sign of a decision. But at this moment she felt Poole's eyes upon her, and when she looked at him they exchanged the delighted smiles of lovers. "How *can* we," she thought, and tried to feel guilty. But she hadn't heard Alleyn speak and he was half-way through his first sentence before she gave him her attention.

"—so far about opportunity," he was saying. "If there were two visits to the dressing-room during the last act I think probably all of you except Miss Hamilton could have made the earlier one. But for the second visit there is a more restricted field. Shall I take you in the order in which you are sitting? Miss Tarne, in that case, comes first."

Martyn thought: "I ought to feel frightened again."

"Miss Tarne has told us that after she left the stage, and she was the first to leave it, she stood at the entry to the dressing-room passage. She was in a rather bemused state of mind and doesn't remember much about it until Mr. Percival, Mr. Darcey and Mr. Bennington himself came past. All three spoke to her in turn and went on down the passage. It is now that the crucial period begins. Mr. Doré was near by, and after directing the gun-shot took her to her dressing-room. On the way he looked in for a few seconds on Mr. Bennington, who had just gone to his own room. After Miss Tarne and Mr. Doré had both heard Mr. Darcey and Mr. Percival return to the stage, they followed them out. They gave each other near-alibis up to this point and the stage-hands extend Miss Tarne's alibi to beyond the crucial time. She is, I think, out of the picture."

Gay Gainsford stared at Martyn. "That," she said, "must be quite a change for you."

"Miss Gainsford comes next," Alleyn said as if he had not heard her. "She was in the Greenroom throughout the crucial period and tells us she was asleep. There is no witness to this."

"George!" said Gay Gainsford wildly and turned to Darcey, thus revealing for the first time his Christian name. "It's all right, dear," he said. "Don't be frightened. It's all right."

"Mr. Darcey and Mr. Percival are also in the list of persons without alibis. They left the stage and returned to it, together, or nearly so. But they went of course to separate rooms. Mr. Percival is the only one who noticed the smell of gas. Dr. Rutherford," Alleyn went on, moving slightly in order to see the Doctor, "could certainly have visited the room during this period, as at any other stage of the performance. He could have come down from his box, passed unobserved round the back of the scenery, taken cover and gone in after these four persons were in their own rooms."

He waited politely, but the Doctor's newspaper rose and fell rhythmically. Alleyn raised his voice slightly. "He could have returned to his O.P. stairs when the rest of you were collected on the Prompt side and he could have made an official entry in the character of Author." He waited for a moment. The others looked in a scandalized manner at the recumbent Doctor but said nothing.

"Mr. Poole has himself pointed out that he could have darted to the room during his brief period off-stage. He could not, in my opinion, have effected all that had to be done, and if he had missed his re-entry he would have drawn immediate attention to himself.

"Mr. Doré is in a somewhat different category from the rest," Alleyn continued. "We know he came away from her dressing-room with Miss Tarne, but although he was seen with the others on the Prompt side, he was at the back of the group and in the shadows. Everyone's attention at this period was riveted on the stage. The call-boy checked over the players for the curtain-call and noticed Mr Bennington had not yet appeared. Neither he nor anyone else had reason to check Mr. Doré's movements."

Jacko said: "I remind you that Parry said he smelt gas while I was still with Miss Tarne in her room."

"I have remembered," Alleyn answered, "what Mr. Percival said." He looked at Helena Hamilton. "And while all this was happening," he concluded, "Miss Hamilton was on the stage holding the attention of a great cloud of witnesses in what I think must have been a most remarkable play."

There was a long silence.

"That's all I have to say." Alleyn's voice changed its colour a little. "I'm going to ask you to return to your rooms. You'll want to do so in any case to collect your coats and so on. If you would like to talk things over among yourselves you are quite free to do so. We shall be in the

Greenroom. If each of you will come in and leave us an address and telephone number I'll be grateful." He looked round them for a moment. Perhaps deliberately he repeated the stage-manager's customary dismissal: "Thank you, ladies and gentlemen. That will be all."

Chapter XI

Last Act

Alleyn stood in front of Adam Poole's portrait and looked at his little group of fellow-policemen.

"Well," he said, "I've done it."

"Very unusual," said Fox.

Bailey and Thompson stared at the floor.

Gibson blew out a long breath and wiped his forehead.

P. C. Lamprey looked as if he would like to speak but knew his place too well. Alleyn caught his eye. "That, Mike," he said, "was an almost flawless example of how an investigating officer is not meant to behave. You will be good enough to forget it."

"Certainly, sir."

"What do you reckon, Mr. Alleyn?" Fox asked. "A confession? Brazen it out? Attempt to escape? Or what?"

"There'll be no escape, Mr. Fox," Gibson said. "We've got the place plastered outside. No cars without supervision within a quarter of a mile and a full description."

"I said 'attempt,' Fred," Mr. Fox pointed out majestically.

"If I've bungled," Alleyn muttered, "I've at least bungled in a big way. A monumental mess."

They looked uneasily at him. Bailey astonished everybody by saying to his boots, with all his customary moroseness: "That'll be the day."

"Don't talk Australian," Mr. Fox chided immediately, but he looked upon Bailey with approval.

A door in the passage opened and shut.

"Here we go," said Alleyn.

A moment later there was a tap at the Greenroom door and Parry Percival came in. He wore a dark overcoat, a brilliant scarf, yellow gloves and a green hat.

"If I'm still under suspicion," he said, "I'd like to know but I suppose no one will tell me."

Fox said heartily: "I shouldn't worry about that if I were you, sir. If you'd just give me your address and 'phone number. Purely as a reference."

Parry gave them and Lamprey wrote them down.

"Thank you, Mr. Percival," Alleyn said. "Good night." Parry walked to the door. "They all seem to be going home in twos except me," he said. "Which is rather dreary. I hope no one gets coshed for his pains. Considering one of them seems to be a murderer it's not too fantastic a notion, though I suppose you know your own business. Oh well. Good night."

Evidently he collided with Gay Gainsford in the passage. They heard her ejaculation and his fretful apology. She came in followed by Darcey.

"I couldn't face this alone," she said and looked genuinely frightened. "So George brought me."

"Perfectly in order, Miss Gainsford," Fox assured her.

Darcey, whose face was drawn and white, stood near the door. She looked appealingly at him and he came forward and gave their addresses and telephone numbers. His voice sounded old. "I should like to see this lady home," he said and was at once given leave to do so. Alleyn opened the door for them and they went out, arm in arm.

Poole came next. He gave a quick look round the room and addressed himself to Alleyn. "I don't understand all this," he said, "but if any member of my company is to be arrested, I'd rather stay here. I'd like to see Martyn Tarne home—she lives only a few minutes away—but if it's all right with you, I'll come back." He hesitated and then said quickly: "I've spoken to Jacques Doré."

Alleyn waited for a moment. "Yes," he said at last, "I'd be glad if you'd come back."

"Will you see Helena now? She's had about all she can take."

"Yes, of course."

"I'll get her," Poole said and crossed the passage. They heard him call: "Helena?" and in a moment he re-opened the door for her.

She had put a velvet beret on her head and had pulled the fullness forward so that her eyes were shadowed. Her mouth drooped with fatigue but it had been carefully painted. Fox took her address and number.

"Is the car here?" she asked, and Fox said: "Yes, madam, in the yard. The constable will show you out."

"I'll take you, Helena," Poole said. "Or would you rather be alone?"

She turned to Alleyn. "I thought," she said, "that if I'm allowed, I'd

rather like to take Jacko. If he's still about. Would you mind telling
him? I'll wait in the car."

"There's no one," Alleyn asked, "that you'd like us to send for? Or
ring up?"

"No, thank you," she said. "I'd just rather like to have old Jacko."

She gave him her hand. "I believe," she said, "that when I can think
at all sensibly about all this, I'll know you've been kind and consid-
erate."

Poole went out with her and Lamprey followed them.

A moment later, Martyn came in.

As she stood at the table and watched Fox write out her address she
felt how little she believed in herself here, in this quietly fantastic setting. Fox and his two silent and soberly dressed associates were so incredibly what she had always pictured plain-clothes detectives to be,
and Alleyn, on the contrary, so completely unlike. She was much occupied with this notion and almost forgot to give him her message.

"Jacko," she said, "asked me to say his address is the same as mine.
I have a room in the house where he lodges." She felt there might be
some ambiguity in this statement and was about to amend it when
Alleyn asked: "Has Mr. Doré gone?"

"I think he's waiting for Miss Hamilton in her car."

"I see," Alleyn said. "And I believe Mr. Poole is waiting for you.
Good-bye, Miss Tarne, and good luck."

Her face broke into a smile. "Thank you *very* much," said Martyn.

Poole's voice called in the passage: "Where are you, Kate?"

She said good night and went out.

Their steps died away down the passage and across the stage. A door
slammed and the theatre was silent.

"Come on," said Alleyn.

He led the way round the back of Jacko's set to the Prompt corner.
Only the off-stage working-lights were alive. The stage itself was almost as shadowy as it was when Martyn first set foot on it. A dust-
begrimed lamp above the letter-rack cast a yellow light over its surface.

In the centre, conspicuous in its fresh whiteness, was an envelope
that had not been there before.

It was addressed in a spidery hand to Chief Detective-Inspector
Alleyn.

He took it from the rack. "So he did it this way," he said, and without another word led them onto the stage.

Jacko's twisted stairway rose out of the shadows like a crazy ejaculation. At its base, untenanted chairs faced each other in silent communion. The sofa was in the darkest place of all.

Young Lamprey began to climb the iron steps to the switch-board. The rest used their flash-lamps. Five pencils of light interlaced, hovered and met at their tips on a crumpled newspaper. They advanced upon the sofa as if it housed an enemy, but when Alleyn lifted the newspaper and the five lights enlarged themselves on Dr. Rutherford's face, it was clearly to be seen that he was dead.

ii

The little group of men stood together in the now fully lit stage while Alleyn read the letter. It was written on official theatre paper and headed: "The Office. 1:45 A.M."

DEAR ALLEYN,

I cry you patience if this letter is but disjointedly patched together. Time presses and I seem to hear the clink of constabular bracelets.

Otto Brod wrote a play which he asked Clark Bennington to read and help him improve. Ben showed it to the two persons of his acquaintance who could read German and had some judgement. I refer to Doré and myself. The play we presented last night was my own free adaptation of Brod's piece made without his consent or knowledge. Base is the slave that pays. In every way mine is an improvement. Was it George Moore who said that the difference between his quotations and those of the next man was that he left out the inverted commas? I am in full agreement with this attitude and so, by the way, was Will Shakespeare. Doré, however, is a bourgeois where the arts are in question. He recognized the source, disapproved, but had the grace to remain mum. The British critics, like Doré, would take the uncivilized view and Ben knew it. He suspected the original authorship, wrote to Brod and three days ago got an answer confirming his suspicions. This letter he proposed to use as an instrument of blackmail. I told Ben, which was no more than the truth, that I intended to make things right with Brod, who, if he's not a popinjay, would be well content with the honour done him and the arrangement proposed. Ben would have none of this. He threatened to publish Brod's letter if a certain change was made in the casting. The day before yesterday, under duress, I submitted and no longer pressed for this change.

However, owing to Miss G.'s highstrikes, it was, after all, effected. Five minutes before the curtain went up on the first act, Ben informed me, with, ho! such bugs and goblins in my life, that at the final curtain he intended to advance to the footlights and tell the audience I'd pinched the play. Knowing Ben meant business, I acted: in a manner which, it appears, you have rumbled and which will be fully revealed by your analysis of the greasepaint on his unlovely mug.

He powdered his face with pethidine-hydrochloride, an effective analgesic drug now in fashion, of which the maximum therapeutic dose is 100 milligrams. Ben got about 2 grams on his sweaty upper lip. I loaded his prepared powder-pad with pethidine (forgive the nauseating alliteration) while he was on in the last act and burnt the pad when I returned, immediately before the curtain-call. He was then comatose and I doubt if the gassing was necessary. However, I wished to suggest suicide. I overturned his powder-box in opening out his overcoat. My own vestment being habitually besprinkled with snuff was none the worse, but the powder must have settled on his coat after I had covered his head. Unfortunate. I fancy that with unexpected penetration you have in all respects hit on the *modus operandi*. Pity we couldn't share the curtain-call.

It may interest you to know that I have formed the habit of pepping up my snuff with this admirable drug and had provided myself with a princely quantity in the powder form used for dispensing purposes. One never knew which way the cat would jump with Ben. I have been equipped for action since he threatened to use his precious letter. By the way, it would amuse me to know if you first dropped to it when I trampled on my pethidine box in the Greenroom. Dogberry, I perceived, collected the pieces.

My other spare part is secreted in the groove of the sofa. I shall now return to the sofa, listen to your oration and if, as I suspect, it comes close to the facts, will take the necessary and final step. I shall instruct the moronic and repellent Badger to place this letter in the rack if I am still asleep when the party breaks up. Pray do not attempt artificial respiration. I assure you I shall be as dead as a doornail. While I could triumphantly justify my use of Brod's play, I decline the mortification of the inevitable publicity, more particularly as it would reflect upon persons other than myself. If you wish to hang a motive on my closed file you may make it vanity.

Let me conclude with a final quotation from my fellow-plagiarist.

> *And sometimes we are devils to ourselves,*
> *When we will tempt the frailty of our powers,*
> *Presuming on their changeful potency.*

I hear the summons to return. *Moriturus*—to coin, as Miss G. would say, a phrase—*te saluto, Caesar.*

Yours, etc., on the edge of the viewless winds.

JOHN JAMES RUTHERFORD

iii

Alleyn folded the letter and gave it to Fox. He walked back to the sofa and stood looking down at its burden for some time.

"Well, Fox," he said at last, "he diddled us in the end, didn't he?"

"Did he, Mr. Alleyn?" asked Fox woodenly.

Bailey and Thompson moved tactfully off-stage. Young Lamprey came on with a sheet from one of the dressing-rooms. Fox took it and dismissed him with a jerk of his head. When the sheet was decently bestowed, Alleyn and Fox looked at each other.

"Oh, let us yet be merciful!" Alleyn said, and it is uncertain whether this quotation from the Doctor's favourite source was intended as an epitaph or an observation upon police procedure.

iv

Poole switched off his engine outside Jacko's house. Martyn stirred and he said: "Do you want to go in at once? We haven't said a word to each other. Are you deadly tired?"

"No more than everybody else but—yes. Aren't you? You must," she said drowsily, "be so dreadfully puzzled and worried."

"I suppose so. No. Not really. Not now. But you must sleep, Martyn. Martyn. There, now I've used your Christian name again. Do you know that I called you Kate because I felt it wasn't time yet, for the other? That astonished me. In the theatre we be-darling and be-Christian-name each other at the drop of a hat. But it wouldn't do with you."

He looked down at her. She thought: "I really must rouse myself," but bodily inertia, linked with a sort of purification of the spirit, flooded through her and she was still.

"It isn't fair," Poole said, "when your eyelids are so heavy, to ask you if I've made a mistake. Perhaps to-morrow you will think you dreamed this, but Martyn, before many more days are out, I shall ask you to marry me. I do love you so very much."

To Martyn his voice seemed to come from an immensely long way away but it brought her a feeling of great content and refreshment. It was as if her spirit burgeoned and flowered into complete happiness. She tried to express something of this but her voice stumbled over a few disjointed words and she gave it up. She heard him laugh and felt him move away. In a moment he was standing with the door open. He took her keys from her hand.

"Shall I carry you in? I must go back to the theatre."

The cold night air joined with this reminder of their ordeal to awaken her completely. She got out and waited anxiously beside him while he opened the house door.

"Is it awful to feel so happy?" she asked. "With such a terror waiting? Why must you go to the theatre?" And after a moment "Do you know?"

"It's not awful. The terrors are over. Alleyn said I might return. And I think I do know. There. Good night. Quickly, quickly, my darling heart, good night and good morning."

He waited until the door shut behind her and then drove back to the theatre.

The pass-door into the foyer was open and the young policeman stood beside it.

"Mr. Alleyn is in here, sir," he said.

Poole went in and found Alleyn with his hands in his pockets in front of the great frame of photographs on their easel.

"I'm afraid I've got news," he said, "that may be a shock to you."

"I don't think so," Poole said. "Jacko spoke to me before I left. He knew about the play: I didn't. And we both thought John's sleep was much too sound."

They stood side by side and looked at the legend over the photographs.

Opening at this theatre
on
THURSDAY, MAY 11TH
THUS TO REVISIT
—*A New Play*—
by
JOHN JAMES RUTHERFORD

KILLER
DOLPHIN

Contents

Cast of Characters

A clerk
Peregrine Jay   Playwright and Theatre Director
Henry Jobbins   Caretaker
Mr. Vassily Conducis
His Chauffeur
Mawson   His manservant
Jeremy Jones   Designer
Mr. Greenslade   Solicitor to Mr. Conducis
An Expert on Historic Costume
Winter Meyer   Manager, Dolphin Theatre
Marcus Knight   ⎤ "Shakespeare" in Peregrine's play
Destiny Meade | "The Dark Lady"   "   "
W. Hartly Grove | "The Rival"   "   "
Gertrude Bracey   ⎬ "Ann Hathaway"   "   "
Emily Dunne | "Joan Hart"   "   "
Charles Random | "Dr. Hall"   "   "
Trevor Vere   ⎦ "Hamnet"   "   "
Mrs. Blewett   Trevor's mother
Superintendent Roderick Alleyn C. I. D.
Hawkins   A Security Officer
A Police Sergeant
P. C. Grantley
Divisional-Superintendent Gibson
A Divisional-Surgeon
Inspector Fox C. I. D.
Detective-Sergeant Bailey C. I. D.
Detective-Sergeant Thompson C. I. D.
Mrs. Guzmann   An American millionairess

Chapter I

Mr. Conducis

"Dolphin?" the clerk repeated. "Dolphin. Well, yerse. We hold the keys. Were you wanting to view?"

"If I might, I was," Peregrine Jay mumbled, wondering why such conversations should always be conducted in the past tense. "I mean," he added boldly, "I did and I still do. I want to view, if you please."

The clerk made a little face that might have been a sneer or an occupational tic. He glanced at Peregrine, who supposed his appearance was not glossy enough to make him a likely prospect.

"It *is* for sale, I believe?" Peregrine said.

"Oh, it's for *sale,* all right," the clerk agreed contemptuously. He re-examined some document that he had on his desk.

"May I view?"

"*Now?*"

"If it's possible."

"Well—I don't know, reely, if we've anybody free at the moment," said the clerk and frowned at the rain streaming dirtily down the windows of his office.

Peregrine said, "Look. The Dolphin is an old theatre. I am a man of the theatre. Here is my card. If you care to telephone my agents or the management of my current production at The Unicorn they will tell you that I am honest, sober and industrious, a bloody good director and playwright and possessed of whatever further attributes may move you to lend me the keys of The Dolphin for an hour. I would like to view it."

The clerk's face became inscrutable. "Oh, quite," he muttered and edged Peregrine's card across his desk, looking sideways at it as if it might scuttle. He retired within himself and seemed to arrive at a guarded conclusion.

"Yerse. Well, O.K., Mr.—er. It's not usually done but we try to oblige." He turned to a dirty-white board where keys hung like black tufts on a piece of disreputable ermine.

"Dolphin," said the clerk. "Aeo, yerse. Here we are." He unhooked a bunch of keys and pushed them across the desk. "You may find them a bit hard to turn," he said. "We don't keep *on* oiling the locks. There aren't all that many inquiries." He made what seemed to be a kind of a joke. "It's quite a time since the blitz," he said.

"Quarter of a century," said Peregrine, taking the keys.

"That's right. What a spectacle! I was a kid. Know your way I suppose, Mr.—er—Jay?"

"Thank you, yes."

"Thank *you*, sir," said the clerk, suddenly plumping for deference, but establishing at the same time his utter disbelief in Peregrine as a client. "Terrible weather. You *will* return the keys?"

"Indubitably," said Peregrine, aping, he knew not why, Mr. Robertson Hare.

He got as far as the door when the clerk said: "Oh, by-the-way, Mr. —er—Jay. You *will* watch how you go. Underfoot. On stage particularly. There was considerable damage."

"Thank you. I'll be careful."

"The hole *was* covered over but that was some time ago. Like a well," the clerk added, worrying his first finger. "Something of the sort. Just watch it."

"I will."

"I—er—I don't answer for what you'll find," the clerk said. "Tramps get in, you know. They *will* do it. One died a year or so back."

"Oh."

"Not that it's likely to happen twice."

"I hope not."

"Well, *we* couldn't help it," the clerk said crossly. "I don't know how they effect an entrance, reely. Broken window or something. You can't be expected to attend to everything."

"No," Peregrine agreed and let himself out.

Rain drove up Wharfingers Lane in a slanting wall. It shot off the pavement, pattering against doors and windows, and hit Peregrine's umbrella so hard that he thought it would split. He lowered it in front of him and below its scalloped and bearded margin saw, as if at rise of curtain in a cinema, the Thames, rain-pocked and choppy on its ebb-tide.

There were not a great many people about. Vans passed him grinding uphill in low gear. The buildings were ambiguous: warehouses? wharfingers' offices? Further down he saw the blue lamp of a River Police Station. He passed a doorway with a neat legend: PORT OF

LONDON AUTHORITY and another with old-fashioned lettering: CAMPERDOWN AND CARBOYS RIVERCRAFT COMPANY. DEMURRAGE. WHARFAGE. INQUIRIES.

The lane turned sharply to the left, it now ran parallel with the river. He lifted his umbrella. Up it went, like a curtain, on The Dolphin. At that moment, abruptly, there was no more rain.

There was even sunshine. It washed thinly across the stagehouse of The Dolphin and picked it out for Peregrine's avid attention. There it stood: high, square and unbecoming, the object of his greed and deep desire. Intervening buildings hid the rest of the theatre except for the wrought-iron ornament at the top of a tower. He hurried on until, on his left, he came to a pub called The Wharfinger's Friend and then the bombsite and then, fully displayed, the wounded Dolphin itself.

On a fine day, Peregrine thought, a hundred years ago, watermen and bargees, ship's chandlers, business gents, deepwater sailors from foreign parts and riverside riff-raff looked up and saw The Dolphin. They saw its flag snapping and admired its caryatids touched up on the ringlets and nipples with tasteful gilt. Mr. Adolphus Ruby, your very own Mr. Ruby, stood here in Wharfingers Lane with his thumbs in his armholes, his cigar at one angle and his hat at the other and feasted his pop eyes on his very own palace of refined and original entertainment. "Oh, oh!" thought Peregrine. "And here I stand but not, alas, in Mr. Ruby's lacquered highlows. And the caryatids have the emptiest look in their blank eyes for me."

They were still there, though, two on each side of the portico. They finished at their waists, petering out with grimy discretion in pastrycook's scrolls. They supported with their sooty heads and arms a lovely wrought-iron balcony and although there were occasional gaps in their plaster foliations they were still in pretty good trim. Peregrine's envious thoughts restored, too, the elegant sign supported above the portico by two prancing cetaceous mammals, and regilded its lettering: THE DOLPHIN THEATRE.

For a minute or two he looked at it from the far side of the lane. The sun shone brightly now. River, shipping and wet roofs reflected it and the cobblestones in front of the theatre began to send up a thin vapour. A sweep of seagulls broke into atmospheric background noises and a barge honked.

Peregrine crossed the wet little street and entered the portico.

It was stuck over with old bills including the agents' notice which had evidently been there for a very long time and was torn and discoloured. "This Valuable Commercial Site," it said.

"In that case," Peregrine wondered, "why hasn't it been sold? Why has no forward-looking commercial enterprise snapped up the Valuable Site and sent The Dolphin Theatre crashing about its own ears?"

There were other moribund bills. "Sensational!" one of them proclaimed but the remainder was gone and it was anybody's guess what sensation it had once recommended. "Go home——" was chalked across one of the doors but somebody had rubbed out the rest of the legend and substituted graffiti of a more or less predictable kind. It was all very dismal.

But as Peregrine approached the doors he found, on the frontage itself, high up and well protected, the tatter of a playbill. It was the kind of thing that patrons of the Players Theatre cherish and Kensington art shops turn into lampshades.

> THE BEGGAR GIRL'S WEDDING
> IN RESPONSE TO
> OVERWHELMING SOLICITATION!!—
> MR. ADOLPHUS RUBY
> PRESENTS
> A RETURN PERFORMA—

The rest was gone.

When, Peregrine speculated, could this overwhelming solicitation have moved Mr. Ruby? In the eighties? He knew that Mr. Ruby had lived to within ten years of the turn of the century and in his heyday had bought, altered, restored and embellished The Dolphin, adding his plaster and jute caryatids, his swags, his supporting marine mammals and cornucopia, his touches of gilt and lollypink to the older and more modest elegance of wrought iron and unmolested surfaces. When did he make all these changes? Did he, upon his decline, sell The Dolphin and, if so, to whom? It was reputed to have been in use at the outbreak of the Second World War as a rag-dealer's storehouse.

Who was the ground landlord now?

He confronted the main entrance and its great mortice lock for which he had no trouble in selecting the appropriate key. It was big enough to have hung at the girdle of one of Mr. Ruby's very own stage-gaolers. The key went home and engaged but refused to turn. Why had Peregrine not asked the clerk to lend him an oil-can?

He struggled for some time and a voice at his back said, "Got it all on yer own, mate, aincher?"

Peregrine turned to discover a man wearing a peaked cap like a waterman's and a shiny blue suit. He was a middle-aged man with a high colour, blue eyes and a look of cheeky equability.

"You want a touch of the old free-in-one," he said. He had a gritty hoarseness in his voice. Peregrine gaped at him. "Oil, mate. Loobrication," the man explained.

"Oh. Yes, indeed, I know I do."

"What's the story, anyway? Casing the joint?"

"I want to look at it," Peregrine grunted. "Oh, damn, I'd better try the stage-door."

"Let's take a butcher's."

Peregrine stood back and the man stooped. He tried the key, delicately at first and then with force. "Not a hope," he wheezed. "'Alf a mo'."

He walked away, crossed the street and disappeared between two low buildings and down a narrow passageway that seemed to lead to the river.

"Damnation!" Peregrine thought. "He's taken the key!"

Two gigantic lorries with canvas-covered loads roared down Wharfingers Lane and past the theatre. The great locked doors shook and rattled and a flake of plaster fell on Peregrine's hand. "It's dying slowly," he thought in a panic. "The Dolphin is being shaken to death."

When the second lorry had gone by, there was the man again with a tin and a feather in one hand and the key in the other. He re-crossed the street and came through the portico.

"I'm very much obliged to you," Peregrine said.

"No trouble, yer Royal 'Ighness," said the man. He oiled the lock and after a little manipulation turned the key. "Kiss yer 'and," he said. Then he pulled back the knob. The tongue inside the lock shifted with a loud clunk. He pushed the door and it moved a little. "Sweet as a nut," said the man, and stepped away. "Well, dooty calls as the bloke said on 'is way to the gallers."

"Wait a bit—" Peregrine said, "you must have a drink on me. Here." He pushed three half-crowns into the man's hand.

"Never say no to that one, Mister. Fanks. Jolly good luck."

Peregrine longed to open the door but thought the man, who was evidently a curious fellow, might attach himself. He wanted to be alone in The Dolphin.

"Your job's somewhere round about here?" he asked.

"Dahn Carboy Stairs. Phipps Bros. Drugs and that. Jobbins is the name. Caretaker. Uster be a lighterman but it done no good to me

chubes. Well, so long, sir. Hope you give yerself a treat among them
spooks. Best of British luck."

"Goodbye, and thank you."

The door opened with a protracted groan and Peregrine entered The
Dolphin.

ii

The windows were unshuttered and though masked by dirt let enough
light into the foyer for him to see it quite distinctly. It was surprisingly
big. Two flights of stairs with the prettiest wrought-iron balustrades
curved up into darkness. At the back and deep in shadow, passages led
off on either side giving entrance no doubt to boxes and orchestral
stalls. The Pit entrance must be from somewhere outside.

On Peregrine's right stood a very rococo box-office introduced, he
felt sure, by Mr. Ruby. A brace of consequential plaster putty hovered
upside down with fat-faced insouciance above the grill and must have
looked in their prime as if they were counting the door sales. A fibre-
plaster bust of Shakespeare on a tortuous pedestal lurked in the shadows. The filthy walls were elegantly panelled and he thought must have
originally been painted pink and gilded.

There was nothing between Peregrine and the topmost ceiling. The
circle landing, again with a wrought-iron balustrade, reached less than
halfway across the well. He stared up into darkness and fancied he
could distinguish a chandelier. The stench was frightful: rats, rot, general dirt and, he thought, an unspeakable aftermath of the hobos that
the clerk had talked about. But how lovely it must have been in its early
Victorian elegance and even with Mr. Ruby's preposterous additions.
And how surprisingly undamaged it seemed to be.

He turned to the righthand flight of stairs and found two notices:
DRESS CIRCLE and TO THE PARIS BAR. The signwriter had added
pointing hands with frills round their wrists. Upstairs first, or into the
stalls? Up.

He passed by grimed and flaking panels, noticing the graceful airiness
of plaster ornament that separated them. He trailed a finger on the iron
balustrade but withdrew it quickly at the thick touch of occulted dust.
Here was the circle foyer. The double flight of stairs actually came out
on either side of a balcony landing that projected beyond the main landing and formed the roof of a portico over the lower foyer. Flights of
three shallow steps led up from three sides of this "half-landing" to the

top level. The entire structure was supported by very elegant iron pillars.

It was much darker up there and he could only just make out the Paris Bar. The shelves were visible but the counter had gone. A nice piece of mahogany it may have been—something to sell or steal. Carpet lay underfoot in moth-eaten tatters and the remains of curtains hung before the windows. These must be unbroken because the sound of the world outside was so very faint. Boarded up, perhaps. It was extraordinary how quiet it was, how stale, how stifling, how dead.

"Not a mouse stirring," he thought and at that moment heard a rapid patter. Something scuttled across his foot. Peregrine was astonished to find himself jolted by a violent shudder. He stamped with both feet and was at once half-stifled by the frightful cloud of dust he raised.

He walked towards the Paris Bar.

A man with a shaded face moved towards him.

"Euh!" Peregrine said in his throat. He stopped and so did the man. He could not have told how many heart thuds passed before he saw it was himself.

The bar was backed by a sheet of looking-glass.

Peregrine had recently given up smoking. If he had now had access to a cigarette he would have devoured it. Instead, he whistled, and the sound in that muffled place was so lacking in resonance, so dull, that he fell silent and crossed the foyer to the nearest door into the auditorium There were two, one on each side of the sunken half-landing. He passed into the circle.

The first impression was dramatic. He had forgotten about the bomb damage. A long shaft of sunlight from a gap in the roof of the stage-house took him by surprise. It produced the effect of a wartime blitz drawing in charcoal and, like a spotlight, found its mark on the empty stage. There, in a pool of mild sunlight, stood a broken chair still waiting, Peregrine thought, for one of Mr. Ruby's very own actors. Behind the chair lay a black patch that looked as if a paint pot had been upset on the stage. It took Peregrine a moment or two to realize that this must be the hole the clerk had talked about. It was difficult to see it distinctly through the shaft of light.

Against this one note of brilliance the rest of the house looked black. It was in the classic horseshoe form and must have seated, Peregrine thought, about five hundred. He saw that the chairs had little iron trimmings above their plushy backs and that there were four boxes. A loop of fringe dangled from the top of the proscenium and this was all that could be seen of the curtain.

Peregrine moved round the circle and entered the O.P. box, which stank. He backed out of it, opened a door in the circle wall and found an iron stair leading to the stage.

He climbed down. Even these iron steps were muffled with dust and they gave out a half-choked clang as if he were soft-pedaling them.

Now he was onstage, as a man of the theatre should be, and at once he felt much easier—exhilarated even, as if some kind of authority had passed to him by right of entry. He peered through the shaft of sunshine which he saw was dense with motes that floated, danced and veered in response to his own movement. He walked into it, stood by the broken chair and faced the auditorium. Quite dazzled and bemused by the strange tricks of light, he saw the front of the house as something insubstantial and could easily people it with Mr. Ruby's patrons. Beavers, bonnets, ulsters, shawls. A flutter of programmes. Rows of pale discs that were faces. "Oh, wonderful!" Peregrine thought, and in order to embrace it all, took a pace backward.

iii

To fall without warning, even by the height of a single step, is disturbing. To fall, as he did, now, by his height and the length of his arms into cold, stinking water is monstrous, nightmarish, like a small death. For a moment he only knew that he had been physically insulted. He stared into the shaft of light with its madly jerking molecules, felt wood slip under his gloved fingers and tightened his grip. At the same time he was disgustingly invaded, saturated up to the collarbone in icy stagnant water. He hung at arm's length.

"Oh God!" Peregrine thought. "Why aren't I a bloody Bond? Why can't I make my bloody arms hitch me up? Oh God, don't let me drown in this unspeakable muck. Oh God, let me keep my head."

Well, of course, he thought, his hands and arms didn't have to support his entire weight. Eleven stone. He was buoyed up by whatever he had fallen into. What? a dressing-room turned into a well for surface water? Better not speculate. Better explore. He moved his legs and dreadful ambiguous waves lapped up to his chin. He could find nothing firm with his feet. He thought: "How long can I hang on like this?" And a line of words floated in: *"How long will a man lie i' the earth ere he rot?"*

What *should* he do? Perhaps a frog-like upward thing? Try it and at least gain a better finger hold? He tried it: he kicked at the water, pulled and clawed at the stage. For a moment he thought he had gained, but his palms slid back, scraping on the edge and sucking back his soaked gloves. He was again suspended. The clerk? If he could hang on, would the clerk send someone to find out why he hadn't returned the keys? When? *When?* Why in God's name had he shaken off the man with the oil can from Phipps Bros.? Jobbins. Suppose he were to yell? Was there indeed a broken window where tramps crept in? He took a deep breath and, being thus inflated, rose a little in the water. He yelled.

"Hullo! Hullo! Jobbins!"

His voice was silly and uncannily stifled. Deflated, he sank to his former disgusting level.

He had disturbed more than water when he tried his leap. An anonymous soft object bobbed against his chin. The stench was outrageous. I can't, he thought, I can't stay like this. Already his fingers had grown cold and his arms were racked. Presently—soon—he would no longer feel the edge, he would only feel pain and his fingers would slip away. And what then? Float on his back in this unspeakable water and gradually freeze? He concentrated on his hands, tipping his head back to look up the length of his stretched arms at them. The details of his predicament now declared themselves: the pull on his pectoral muscles, on his biceps and forearms, and the terrible strain on his gloved fingers. The creeping obscenity of the water. He hung on for some incalculable age and realized that he was coming to a crisis when his body would no longer be controllable. Something must be done. Now. Another attempt? If there were anything solid to push against. Suppose, after all, his feet were only a few inches from the bottom? But what bottom? The floor of a dressing-room? An understage passage? A boxed-in trap? He stretched his feet and touched nothing. The water rose to his mouth. He flexed his legs, kicked, hauled on the edge and bobbed upwards. The auditorium appeared. If he could get his elbows on the edge. No.

But at the moment when the confusion of circle and stalls shot up before his eyes, he had heard a sound that he recognized, a protracted groan, and at the penultimate second, he had seen—what? a splinter of light? And heard? Somebody cough?

"Hi!" Peregrine shouted. "Here! Quick! Help!"

He sank and hung again by his fingers. But someone was coming through the house. Muffled steps on the rags of carpet.

"Here!! Come here, will you? Onstage."

The steps halted.

"Look here! I say! Look, for God's sake come up. I've fallen through the stage, I'll drown. Why don't you answer, whoever you are?"

The footsteps started again. A door opened nearby. Pass-door in the

Prompt-side box, he thought. Steps up. Now: crossing the stage. Now.

"Who are you?" Peregrine said. "Look out. Look out for the hole. *Look out for my hands. I've got gloves on. Don't tread on my hands.* Help me out of this. But look out. And say something."

He flung his head back and stared into the shaft of light. Hands covered his hands and then closed about his wrists. At the same time heavy shoulders and a head wearing a hat came as a black silhouette between him and the light. He stared into a face he could not distinguish.

"It doesn't need much," he chattered. "If you could just give me a heave I can do it."

The head was withdrawn. The hands changed their grip. At last the man spoke.

"Very well," said a voice. "Now."

He gave his last frog leap, was heaved up, was sprawled across the edge and had crawled back on the stage to the feet of the man. He saw beautiful shoes, sharp trouser ends and the edge of a fine overcoat. He was shivering from head to foot.

"Thank you," he said. "I couldn't be more grateful. My God, how I stink."

He got to his feet.

The man was, he thought, about sixty years old. Peregrine could see his face now. It was extremely pale. He wore a bowler hat and was impeccably dressed.

"You are Mr. Peregrine Jay, I think," said the man. His voice was toneless, educated and negative.

"Yes—I—I?"

"The people at the estate agents told me. You should have a bath and change. My car is outside."

"I can't get into anyone's car in this state. I'm very sorry, sir," Peregrine said. His teeth were going like castanets. "You're awfully kind but—"

"Wait a moment. Or no. Come to the front of the theatre."

In answer to a gesture, Peregrine walked through the pass-door down into the house and was followed. Stagnant water poured off him. It ran out of his gloved finger-tips and squelched and spurted in his shoes. He went through a box and along a passage and came into the foyer. "Please stay here. I shall only be a moment," said his rescuer.

He went into the portico, leaving the door open. Out in Wharfingers Lane Peregrine saw a Daimler with a chauffeur. He began to jump and thrash his arms. Water splashed out of him and clouds of dust settled upon his drenched clothes. The man returned with the chauffeur, who carried a fur rug and a heavy mackintosh.

"I suggest you strip and put this on and wrap the rug round you," the man said. He stretched out his arms as if he were actually thinking of laying hands on Peregrine. He seemed to be suspended between attraction and repulsion. He looked, it struck Peregrine, as if he were making some kind of appeal. "Let me—" he said.

"But, sir, you can't. I'm disgusting."

"Please."

"No, no—really."

The man walked away. His hands were clasped behind him. Peregrine saw, with a kind of fuddled astonishment, that they were trembling. "My God!" Peregrine thought. "This is a morning and a half. I'd better get out of this one pretty smartly but how the hell—"

"Let me give you a hand, sir," said the chauffeur to Peregrine. "You're that cold, aren't you?"

"I can manage. If only I could wash."

"Never mind, sir. That's the idea. Leave them there, sir. I'll attend to them. Better keep your shoes on, hadn't you? The coat'll be a bit of help and the rug's warm. Ready sir?"

"If I could just have a taxi, I wouldn't be such an infernal nuisance."

His rescuer turned and looked, not fully at him but at his shoulder. "I beg you to come," he said.

Greatly worried by the extravagance of the phrase Peregrine said no more.

The chauffeur went ahead quickly and opened the doors of the car. Peregrine saw that newspaper had been spread over the floor and back seat.

"Please go," his rescuer said, "I'll follow."

Peregrine shambled across the portico and jumped in at the back. The lining of the mackintosh stuck to his body. He hitched the rug around him and tried to clench his chattering jaw.

A boy's voice in the street called, "Hey, look! Look at that bloke." The caretaker from Phipps Bros. had appeared at the top of the alley and stared into the car. One or two people stopped and pointed Peregrine out to each other.

As his master crossed the portico the chauffeur locked the theatre doors. Holding Peregrine's unspeakable clothes at arm's length he put them in the boot of the car and got into the driver's seat. In another moment they were moving up Wharfingers Lane.

His rescuer did not turn his head or speak. Peregrine waited for a moment or two and then, controlling his voice with some success, said, "I'm giving you far too much trouble."

"No."

"If—if you would be so very kind as to drop me at The Unicorn Theatre I think I could—"

Still without turning his head the man said with extreme formality, "I really do beg that you will allow me to—" he stopped for an unaccountably long time and then said loudly "—to rescue you. I mean to take you to my house and set you right. I shall be most upset otherwise. Dreadfully upset."

Now he turned and Peregrine had never seen an odder look in anyone's face. It was an expression almost, he thought, of despair.

"I am responsible," said his extraordinary host. "Unless you allow me to make amends I shall—I shall feel—very guilty."

"*Responsible?* But—"

"It will not take very long, I hope. Drury Place."

"Oh Lord!" Peregrine thought. "What poshery." He wondered, suddenly, if perhaps the all too obvious explanation was the wrong one and if his rescuer was a slightly demented gentleman and the chauffeur his keeper.

"I really don't see, sir—" he began, but an inaudible conversation was taking place in the front seat.

"Certainly, sir," said the chauffeur and drew up outside the estate agents. He pulled the keys out of his pocket as he entered. In a moment or two the clerk's face appeared looking anxiously and crossly over the painted lower pane of his window. He disappeared and in a moment came running out and round to the passenger's side.

"Well, sir," he obsequiously gabbled, "I'm sure I'm very sorry this has occurred. Very regrettable, I'm sure. But as I was saying to your driver, sir, I did warn the viewer." He had not yet looked at Peregrine but he did so now, resentfully. "I warned you," he said.

"Yes, yes," Peregrine said. "You did."

"Yes, well, thank you. But I'm sure—"

"That will do. There has been gross negligence. Good morning." The voice was so changed, so brutally icy that Peregrine stared and the clerk drew back as if he'd been stung. They moved off.

The car's heating system built up. By the time they had crossed the river Peregrine was a little less cold and beginning to feel drowsy. His host offered no further remarks. Once when Peregrine happened to look at the rear-vision glass on the passenger's side he found he was being observed, apparently with extreme distaste. Or no. Almost with fear. He looked away quickly but out of the tail of his eye saw a gloved hand change the angle of the glass.

"Oh, well," he thought bemusedly. "I'm bigger and younger than he is. I suppose I can look after myself, but how tricky it all is. Take away a man's clothes, after all, and you make a monkey of him. What sort of public image will I present, fleeing down Park Lane in a gent's mac and a fur rug, both the property of my pursuer?"

They were in Park Lane now and soon turned off into a side street and thence into the cul-de-sac called Drury Place. The car pulled up. The chauffeur got out and rang the bell of No. 7. As he returned to the car, the house door was opened by a manservant.

Peregrine's host said in a comparatively cheerful voice, "Not far to go. Up the steps and straight in."

The chauffeur opened the door. "Now, sir," he said, "shan't be long, shall we?"

There really was nothing else for it. Three impeccable men, an errand boy and a tightly encased lady carrying a little dog walked down the footpath. Peregrine got out and instead of bolting into the house made an entrance of it. He ascended the steps with deliberation, leaving a trail of filthy footprints behind him and dragging his fur rug like a ceremonial train. The manservant stood aside.

"Thank you," Peregrine said grandly. "I have fallen, as you see, into dirty water."

"Quite so, sir."

"Up to my neck."

"Very unfortunate, sir."

"For all concerned," said Peregrine.

His host had arrived.

"First of all, of course, a bath," he was saying, "and something to defeat that shivering. Mawson?"

"Certainly, sir."

"And then come and see me."

"Very good, sir."

The man went upstairs. Peregrine's host was now behaving in so normal a manner that he began to wonder if he himself had perhaps been bemused by his hideous experience. There was some talk of the efficacy of Epsom Salts in a hot bath and of coffee laced with rum. Peregrine listened in a trance.

"Do forgive me for bossing you about like this. You must be feeling ghastly and really, I *do* blame myself."

"But *why?*"

"Yes, Mawson?"

"If the gentleman will walk up, sir."

"Quite so. Quite so. Good."

Peregrine walked up and was shown into a steaming and aromatic bathroom.

"I thought pine, sir, would be appropriate," said Mawson. "I hope the temperature is as you like it. May I suggest a long, hot soak, sir?"

"You may indeed," said Peregrine warmly.

"Perhaps I may take your rug and coat. And shoes," said Mawson with an involuntary change of voice. "You will find a bath wrap on the rail and a hot rum and lemon within easy reach. If you would be good enough to ring, sir, when you are ready."

"Ready for what?"

"To dress, sir."

It seemed a waste of time to say, "In what?" so Peregrine merely said "Thank you" and Mawson said "Thank you" and withdrew.

It was rapture beyond compare in the bath. Essence of pine. A lovely long-handled brush. Pine-smelling soap. And the hot rum and lemon. He left off shivering, soaped himself all over, including his head, scrubbed himself scarlet, submerged completely, rose, drank and tried to take a responsible view of the situation. In this he failed. Too much had occurred. He realized after a time that he was becoming light-headed and without at all fancying the idea took a hard-hitting cold shower. This restored him. Rough-dried and wrapped in a towelling bathrobe he rang the bell. He felt wonderful.

Mawson came and Peregrine said he would like to telephone for some clothes, though when he thought about it he didn't quite know where he would ring. Jeremy Jones with whom he shared a flat would certainly be out and it wasn't the morning for their charlady. The Unicorn Theatre? *Somebody* would be there, of course, but who?

Mawson showed him to a bedroom where there was a telephone.

There were also clothes laid out on the bed. "I think they are approximately your size, sir. It is hoped that you will have no objection to making use of them in the meantime," said Mawson.

"Yes, but look here—"

"It will be much appreciated if you make use of them. Will there be anything else, sir?"

"I—honestly—I—"

"Mr. Conducis sends his compliments, sir, and hopes you will join him in the library."

Peregrine's jaw dropped.

"Thank you, sir," said Mawson neatly and withdrew.

Conducis? *Conducis!* It was as if Mawson had said "Mr. Onassis." Could this possibly be Mr. Vassily Conducis? The more Peregrine thought about it the more he decided that it could. But what in the wide world would Mr. Vassily Conducis be up to in a derelict theatre on the South Bank at half past ten in the morning when he ought to have been abominably lolling on his yacht in the Aegean? And what was *he,* Peregrine, up to in Mr. Conducis's house which (it now dawned upon him) was on a scale of insolently quiet grandeur such as he had never expected to encounter outside the sort of book which, in any case, he never read.

Peregrine looked round the room and felt he ought to curl his lip at it. After all he *did* read his *New Statesman.* He then looked at the clothes on the bed and found them to be on an equal footing with what, being a man of the theatre, he thought of as the decor. Absently, he picked up a gayish tie that was laid out beside a heavy silk shirt. "Charvet," said the label. Where had he read of Charvet?

"I don't want any part of this," he thought. He sat on the bed and dialed several numbers without success. The Theatre didn't answer. He put on the clothes and saw that though they were conservative in style he looked startlingly presentable in them. Even the shoes fitted.

He rehearsed a short speech and went downstairs, where he found Mawson waiting for him.

He said, "Did you say—Mr. Conducis?"

"Yes, sir, Mr. Vassily Conducis. Will you step this way, sir?"

Mr. Conducis stood in front of his library fire and Peregrine wondered how on earth he had failed to recognize a face that had been so widely publicized with, it was reported, such determined opposition from its owner. Mr. Conducis had an olive, indeed a swarthy, complexion and unexpectedly pale eyes. These were merely facial adjuncts and might, Peregrine afterwards thought, have been mass produced for all the speculation they inspired. The mouth, however, was disturbing, being, or so Peregrine thought, both ruthless and vulnerable. The chin was heavy. Mr. Conducis had curly black hair going predictably gray at the temples. He looked, by and large, enormously expensive.

"Come in," he said. "Yes. Come in." His voice was a light tenor. Was there a faintly foreign inflection? A slight lisp, perhaps.

As Peregrine approached, Mr. Conducis looked fixedly at his guest's hands.

"You are well?" he asked. "Recovered?"

"Yes, indeed. I can't thank you enough, sir. As for—well, as for lending me these things—I really do feel—!"

"Do they fit?"

"Yes. Very well."

"That is all that is necessary."

"Except that after all they *are* yours," Peregrine said and tried a light laugh in order not to sound pompous.

"I have told you. I am responsible. You might—" Mr. Conducis's voice faded but his lips soundlessly completed the sentence "—have been drowned."

"But honestly, sir!" Peregrine launched himself on his little speech. "You've saved my life, you know. I would have just hung on by my fingers until they gave out and then—and then—well, finally and disgustingly drowned as you say."

Almost soundlessly Mr. Conducis said, "I should have blamed myself."

"But why on earth! For a hole in The Dolphin stage?"

"It is my property."

"Oh!" Peregrine ejaculated before he could stop himself. "How splendid!"

"Why do you say that?"

"I mean: how splendid to own it. It's such an adorable little playhouse."

Mr. Conducis looked at him without expression. "Indeed?" he said. "Splendid? Adorable? You make a study of theatres, perhaps?"

"Not really. I mean I'm not an expert. Good Lord, no! But I earn my living in theatres and I am enormously attracted by old ones."

"Yes. Will you join me in a drink?" Mr. Conducis said in his wooden manner. "I am sure you will." He moved to a tray on a sidetable.

"Your man has already given me a very strong and wonderfully restoring hot rum and lemon."

"I am sure that you will have another. The ingredients are here."

"A very small one, please," Peregrine said. There was a singing sensation in his veins and a slight thrumming in his ears but he still felt wonderful. Mr. Conducis busied himself at the tray. He returned with a reeking tumbler for Peregrine and something that he had poured out of a jug for himself. Could it be barley water?

"Shall we sit down," he suggested. When they had done so he gave Peregrine a hurried, blank glance and said, "You wonder why I was at the theatre perhaps. There is some question of demolishing it and building on the site. An idea that I have been turning over for some time. I wanted to refresh my memory. The agents told my man you were there." He put two fingers in a waistcoat pocket and Peregrine saw his own card had been withdrawn. It looked incredibly grubby.

"You—you're going to pull it down?" he said and heard a horribly false jauntiness in his own unsteady voice. He took a pull at his rum. It was extremely strong.

"You dislike the proposal," Mr. Conducis observed, making it a statement rather than a question. "Have you any reason other than a general interest in such buildings?"

If Peregrine had been absolutely sober and dressed in his own clothes it is probable that he would have mumbled something ineffectual and somehow or another made an exit from Mr. Conducis's house and from all further congress with its owner. He was a little removed, however, from his surroundings and the garments in which he found himself.

He began to talk excitedly. He talked about The Dolphin and about how it must have looked after Mr. Adolphus Ruby had gloriously tarted it up. He described how, before he fell into the well, he had imagined the house: clean, sparkling with lights from chandeliers, full, warm, buzzing and expectant. He said that it was the last of its kind and so well designed with such a surprisingly large stage that it would be very possible to mount big productions there.

He forgot about Mr. Conducis and also about not drinking any more rum. He talked widely and distractedly.

"Think what a thing it would be," Peregrine cried, "to do a season of Shakespeare's comedies! Imagine *Love's Labour's* there. Perhaps one could have a barge—yes. *The Grey Dolphin*—and people could take water to go to the play. When the play was about to begin he would run up a flag with a terribly intelligent dolphin on it. And we'd do them quickly and lightly and with elegance and—oh!" cried Peregrine, "and with that little catch in the breath that never, *never* comes in the same way with any other playwright."

He was now walking about Mr. Conducis's library. He saw, without seeing, the tooled spines of collected editions and a picture that he would remember afterwards with astonishment. He waved his arms. He shouted.

"There was never such a plan," shouted Peregrine. "Never in all London since Burbage moved the first theatre from Shoreditch to Southwark." He found himself near his drink and tossed it off. "And not too fancy," he said, "mind you. Not twee. God, no! Not a pastiche either. Just a good theatre doing the job it was meant to do. And doing the stuff that doesn't belong to any bloody Method or Movement or Trend or Period of what-have-you. Mind that."

"You refer to Shakespeare again?" said Mr. Conducis's voice. "If I follow you."

"Of course I do!" Peregrine suddenly became fully aware of Mr. Conducis. "Oh dear!" he said.

"Is something the matter?"

"I'm afraid I'm a bit tight, sir. Not *really* tight but a bit uninhibited. I'm awfully sorry. I think perhaps I'd better take myself off and I'll return all these things you've so kindly lent me. I'll return them as soon as possible, of course. So, if you'll forgive me—"

"What do you do in the theatre?"

"I direct plays and I've written two."

"I know nothing of the theatre," Mr. Conducis said heavily. "You are reasonably successful?"

"Well, sir, yes. I think so. It's a jungle of course. I'm not at all affluent but I make out. I've had as much work as I could cope with over the last three months and I think my mana's going up. I hope so. Goodbye, sir."

He held out his hand. Mr. Conducis, with an expression that really might have been described as one of horror, backed away from it.

"Before you go," he said, "I have something that may be of interest to you. You can spare a moment?"

"Of course."

"It is in this room," Mr. Conducis muttered and went to a bureau that must, Peregrine thought, be of fabulous distinction. He followed his host and watched him pull out a silky, exquisitely inlaid drawer.

"How lovely that is," he said.

"Lovely?" Mr. Conducis echoed as he had echoed before. "You mean the bureau? Yes. It was found for me. I understand nothing of such matters. That is not what I wished to show you. Will you look at this? Shall we move to a table?"

He had taken from the drawer a very small wooden Victorian hand-desk, extremely shabby, much stained, and Peregrine thought, of no particular distinction. A child's possession perhaps. He laid it on a table under a window and motioned to a chair beside it. Peregrine now felt as if he was playing a part in somebody else's dream. "But I'm all right," he thought. "I'm not really drunk. I'm in that pitiable but enviable condition when all things seem to work together for good."

He sat before the table and Mr. Conducis, standing well away from him, opened the little desk, pressed inside with his white, flat thumb and revealed a false bottom. It was a commonplace device and Peregrine wondered if he was meant to exclaim at it. He saw that in the exposed cavity there was a packet no bigger than a half-herring and much the same shape. It was wrapped in discoloured yellow-brown silk and tied with a morsel of tarnished ribbon. Mr. Conducis had a paper knife in his hand. "Everything he possesses," Peregrine thought, "is on museum-piece level. It's stifling." His host used the paper knife as a sort of server, lifting the little silk packet out on its blade and, as it were, helping Peregrine to it like a waiter.

It slid from the blade and with it, falling to one side, a discoloured card upon which it had lain. Peregrine, whose vision had turned swimmy, saw that this card was a menu and bore a date some six years past. The heading, THE STEAM YACHT KALLIOPE. GALA DIN NER, floated tipsily into view with a flamboyant and illegible signature that was sprawled across it above a dozen others when a short white hand swiftly covered and then removed the card.

"That is nothing," Mr. Conducis said. "It is of no consequence." He went to the fire. A bluish flame sprang up and turned red. Mr. Conducis returned.

"It is the packet that may be of interest. Will you open it?" he said.

Peregrine pulled gingerly at the ribbon ends and turned back the silk wrapping.

He had exposed a glove.

A child's glove. Stained as if by water, it was the colour of old parchment and finely wrinkled like an old, old face. It had been elegantly embroidered, with tiny roses in gold and scarlet. A gold tassel, now blackened and partly unravelled, was attached to the tapered gauntlet. It was the most heartrending object Peregrine had ever seen.

Underneath it lay two pieces of folded paper, very much discoloured.

"Will you read the papers?" Mr. Conducis invited. He had returned to the fireplace.

Peregrine felt an extraordinary delicacy in touching the glove. "Cheveril," he thought. "It's a cheveril glove. Has it gone brittle with age?" No. To his fingertip it was flaccid: uncannily so, as if it had only just died. He slipped the papers out from beneath it. They had split along the folds and were foxed and faded. He opened the larger with great care and it lay broken before him. He pulled himself together and managed to read it.

This little glove and accompanying note were given to my Great-Great Grandmother by her Beft Friend: A Mifs or Mrs. J.

Hart. My dear Grandmother always infifted that it had belonged to the Poet N.B. mark infide gauntlet.

M.E. 23 April 1830

The accompanying note was no more than a slip of paper. The writing on it was much faded and so extraordinarily crabbed and tortuous that he thought at first it must be hieroglyphic and that he therefore would never make it out. Then it seemed to him that there was something almost familiar about it. And then, gradually, words began to emerge. Everything was quiet. He heard the fire settle. Someone crossed the room above the library. He heard his own heart thud.

He read.

Mayd by my father for my sonne on his XI birthedy and never worne butte ync

Peregrine sat in a kind of trance and looked at the little glove and the documents. Mr. Conducis had left the paper knife on the table. Peregrine slid the ivory tip into the gauntlet and very slowly lifted and turned it. There was the mark, in the same crabbed hand: *H.S.*

"But where—" Peregrine heard his own voice saying, "where did it come from? Whose is it?"

"It is mine," Mr. Conducis said and his voice seemed to come from a great distance. "Naturally."

"But—where did you find it?"

A long silence.

"At sea."

"At sea?"

"During a voyage six years ago. I bought it."

Peregrine looked at his host. How pale Mr. Conducis was and how odd was his manner!

He said: "The box—it is some kind of portable writing-desk—was a family possession. The former owner did not discover the false bottom until—" He stopped.

"Until—?" Peregrine said.

"Until shortly before he died."

Peregrine said, "Has it been shown to an authority?"

"No. I should, no doubt, get an opinion from some museum or perhaps from Sotheby's."

His manner was so completely negative, so toneless that Peregrine wondered if by any extraordinary chance he did not understand the full implication. He was wondering how, without offense, he could find out, when Mr. Conducis continued.

"I have not looked it all up but I understand the age of the boy at the time of his death is consistent with the evidence and that the grandfather was in fact a glover."

"Yes."

"And the initials inside the gauntlet do in fact correspond with the child's initials."

"Yes. Hamnet Shakespeare."

"Quite so," said Mr. Conducis.

Chapter II

Mr. Greenslade

"I know that," Peregrine said. "You don't need to keep on at it, Jer. I know there's always been a Bardic racket and that since the quatro-centenary it's probably been stepped up. I *know* about the tarting-up of old portraits with dome foreheads and the fake signatures and 'stol'n and surreptitious copies' and phoney 'discovered' documents and all that carry-on. I *know* the overwhelming odds are against this glove being anything but a fake. I merely ask you to accept that with the things lying there in front of me, I was knocked all of a heap."

"Not only by them, I understand. You were half-drowned, half-drunk, dressed up in a millionaire's clobber and not knowing whether the owner was making a queer pass at you or not."

"I'm almost certain, not."

"His behaviour, on your own account, seems to have been, to say the least of it, strange."

"Bloody strange but not, I have decided, queer."

"Well, you're the judge," said Jeremy Jones. He bent over his work-table and made a delicate slit down a piece of thin cardboard. He was building a set to scale for a theatre-club production of *Venice Observed*. After a moment he laid aside his razor-blade and looked up at Peregrine. "Could you make a drawing of it?" he said.

"I can try."

Peregrine tried. He remembered the glove very clearly indeed and produced a reasonable sketch.

"It *looks* O.K.," Jeremy said. "Late sixteenth century. Elaborate in the right way. Tabbed. Embroidered. Tapering to the wrist. And the leather?"

"Oh, fine as fine. Yellow and soft and wrinkled and old, old, old."

"It may be an Elizabethan or Jacobean glove but the letter could be a forgery."

"But why? Nobody's tried to cash in on it."

"You don't know. You don't know anything. Who was this chum Conducis bought it from?"

"He didn't say."

"And who was M.E. whose dear grandma insisted it had belonged to the Poet?"

"Why ask me? You might remember that the great-*great*-grandmother was left it by a Mrs. J. Hart. And that Joan Hart—"

"Nee Shakespeare, was left wearing-apparel by her brother. Yes. The sort of corroborative details any good faker would cook up. But, of course, the whole thing should be tackled by experts."

"I told you: I said so. I said wouldn't he take it to the V. and A., and he gave me one of his weird looks; furtive, scared, blank—I don't know how you'd describe them—and shut up like a clam."

"Suspicious in itself." Jeremy grinned at his friend and then said, " '*I would I had been there.*' "

"Well, at that, '*I would have much amazed you.*' "

" '*Very like. Very like.*' What do we know about Conducis?"

"I can't remember with any accuracy," Peregrine said. "He's an all-time-high for money, isn't he? There was a piece in one of the Sunday supplements some time back. About how he loathes publicity and does a Garbo and leaves Mr. Gulbenkian wondering what it was that passed him. And how he doesn't join in any of the joy and is thought to be a fabulous anonymous philanthropist. A Russian mum, I think it said, and an Anglo-Rumanian papa."

"Where does he get his pelf?"

"I don't remember. Isn't it always oil? 'Mystery Midas' it was headed and there was a photograph of him looking livid and trying to dodge the camera on the steps of his Bank and a story about how the photographer made his kill. I read it at the dentist's."

"Unmarried?"

"I think so."

"How did you part company?"

"He just walked out of the room. Then his man came in and said the car was waiting to bring me home. He gave me back my revolting, stinking pocketbook and said my clothes had gone to the cleaner and were thought to be beyond salvation. I said something about Mr. Conducis and the man said Mr. Conducis was taking a call from New York and would 'quite understand.' Upon which hint, off I slunk. I'd better write a sort of bread-and-butter, hadn't I?"

"I expect so. And he owns The Dolphin and is going to pull it down and put up, one supposes, another waffle-iron on the South Bank?"

"He's 'turning over the idea' in his mind."

"May it choke him," said Jeremy Jones.

"Jer," Peregrine said. "You *must* go and look at it. It'll slay you. Wrought iron. Cherubs. Caryatids. A wonderful sort of potpourri of early and mid-Vic and designed by an angel. Oh God, God, when I think of what could be done with it."

"And this ghastly old Croesus—"

"I know. I know."

And they stared at each other with the companionable indignation and despair of two young men whose unfulfilled enthusiasms coincide.

They had been at the same drama school together and had both decided that they were inclined by temperament, interest and ability to production rather than performance in the theatre. Jeremy finally settled for design and Peregrine for direction. They had worked together and apart in weekly and fortnightly repertory and had progressed to more distinguished provincial theatres and thence, precariously, to London. Each was now tolerably well known as a coming man and both were occasionally subjected to nerve-racking longeurs of unemployment. At the present juncture Peregrine had just brought to an auspicious opening the current production at The Unicorn and had seen his own first play through a trial run out of London. Jeremy was contemplating a decor for a masque which he would submit to an international competition for theatrical design.

He had recently bought a partnership in a small shop in Walton Street where they sold what he described as "very superior tatt. Jacobean purses, stomachers and the odd codpiece." He was a fanatic on authenticity and had begun to acquire a reputation as an expert.

Jeremy and Peregrine had spent most of what they had saved on leasing and furnishing their studio flat and had got closer than was comfortable to a financial crisis. Jeremy had recently become separated from a blonde lady of uncertain temper: a disentanglement that was rather a relief to Peregrine, who had been obliged to adjust to her unpredictable descents upon their flat.

Peregrine himself had brought to uneventful dissolution an affair with an actress who had luckily discovered in herself the same degree of boredom that he, for his part, had hesitated to disclose. They had broken up with the minimum of ill-feeling on either part and he was, at the moment, heart-free and glad of it.

Peregrine was dark, tall and rather mischievous in appearance. Jeremy was of medium stature, reddish in complexion and fairly truculent. Behind a prim demeanour he concealed an amorous inclination.

They were of the same age: twenty-seven. Their flat occupied the top story of a converted warehouse on Thames-side east of Blackfriars. It was from their studio window, about a week ago, that Peregrine, idly exploring the South Bank through a pair of field-glasses, had spotted the stage-house of The Dolphin, recognized it for what it was and hunted it down. He now walked over to the window.

"I can just see it," he said. "There it is. I spent the most hideous half hour of my life, so far, inside that theatre. I ought to hate the sight of it but, by God, I yearn after it as I've never yearned after anything ever before. You know, if Conducis does pull it down I honestly don't believe I'll be able to stay here and see it happen."

"Shall we wait upon him and crash down on our knees before him crying, 'Oh, sir, please sir, spare The Dolphin, pray do, sir'?"

"I can tell you exactly what the reaction would be. He'd back away as if we smelt and say in that deadpan voice of his that he knew nothing of such matters."

"I wonder what it would cost."

"To restore it? Hundreds of thousands no doubt," Peregrine said gloomily. "I wonder if National Theatre has so much as thought of it. Or *somebody*. Isn't there a society that preserves Ancient Monuments?"

"Yes. But 'I know nothing of such matters,'" mocked Jeremy. He turned back to his model. With a degree of regret to which wild horses wouldn't have persuaded him to confess, Peregrine began packing Mr. Conducis's suit. It was a dark charcoal tweed and had been made by a princely tailor. He had washed and ironed the socks, undergarments and shirt that he had worn for about forty minutes and had taken a box that Jeremy was hoarding to make up the parcel.

"I'll get a messenger to deliver it," he said.

"Why on earth?"

"I don't know. Too bloody shy to go myself."

"You'd only have to hand it over to the gilded lackey."

"I'd feel an ass."

"You're mad," said Jeremy briefly.

"I don't want to go back there. It was all so rum. Rather wonderful, of course, but in a way rather sinister. Like some wish-fulfillment novel."

"The wide-eyed young dramatist and the kindly recluse."

"I don't think Conducis is kindly but I will allow and must admit I was wide-eyed over the glove. You know what?"

"What?"

"It's given me an idea."

"Has it, now? Idea for what?"

"A play. I don't want to discuss it."

"One must never discuss too soon, of course," Jeremy agreed. "That way abortion lies."

"You have your points."

In the silence that followed they both heard the metallic clap of the letter box downstairs.

"Post," said Jeremy.

"Won't be anything for us."

"Bills."

"I don't count them. I daren't," said Peregrine.

"There might be a letter from Mr. Conducis offering to adopt you."

"Heh, heh, heh."

"Do go and see," Jeremy said. "I find you rather oppressive when you're clucky. The run downstairs will do you good."

Peregrine wandered twice round the room and absently out at the door. He went slowly down their decrepit staircase and fished in their letter box. There were three bills (two, he saw, for himself), a circular and a typed letter.

"Peregrine Jay, Esq. By Hand."

For some reason that he could not have defined, he didn't open the letter. He went out-of-doors and walked along their uneventful street until he came to a gap through which one could look across the river to Southwark. He remembered afterwards that his bitch-muse as he liked to call her was winding her claws in his hair. He stared unseeing at a warehouse that from here partly obscured The Dolphin: Phipps Bros., perhaps, where the man with the oil can—Jobbins—worked. A wind off the river whipped his hair back. Somewhere downstream a hooting set up. Why, he wondered idly, do river-craft set up gaggles of hooting all at once? His right hand was in his jacket pocket and his fingers played with the letter.

With an odd sensation of taking some prodigious step he suddenly pulled it out of his pocket and opened it.

Five minutes later Jeremy heard their front door slam and Peregrine come plunging up the stairs. He arrived, white-faced and apparently without the power of speech.

"What now, for pity's sake," Jeremy asked. "Has Conducis tried to kidnap you?"

Peregrine thrust a sheet of letter paper into his hand.

"Go on," he said. "Bloody read it, will you. Go on." Jeremy read.

Dear Sir,

I am directed by Mr. V. M. G. Conducis to inform you that he has given some consideration to the matter of The Dolphin Theatre, Wharfingers Lane, which he had occasion to discuss with you this morning. Mr. Conducis would be interested to have the matter examined in greater detail. He suggests, therefore, that to this end you call at the offices of Consolidated Oils, Pty. Ltd., and speak to Mr. S. Greenslade who has been fully informed of the subject in question. I enclose for your convenience a card with the address and a note of introduction.

I have ventured to make an appointment for you with Mr. Greenslade for 11:30 tomorrow (Wednesday). If this is not a convenient time, perhaps you will be good enough to telephone Mr. Greenslade's secretary before 5:30 this evening.

Mr. Conducis asks me to beg that you will not trouble yourself to return the things he was glad to be able to offer after your most disagreeable accident for which, as he no doubt explained, he feels a deep sense of responsibility. He understands that your own clothes have been irretrievably spoilt and hopes that you will allow him to make what he feels is a most inadequate gesture by way of compensation. The clothes, by the way, have not been worn. If, however, you would prefer it, he hopes that you will allow him to replace your loss in a more conventional manner.

Mr. Conducis will not himself take a direct part in any developments that may arise in respect of The Dolphin and does not wish at any juncture to be approached in the matter. Mr. Greenslade has full authority to negotiate for him at all levels,

With compliments, I am.

Yours truly,

M. SMYTHIMAN
Private Secretary to Mr. Conducis

"Not true," Jeremy said, looking over the tops of his spectacles.

"True. Apparently. As far as it goes."

Jeremy read it again. "Well," he said, "at least he doesn't want you to approach him. We've done him wrong, there."

"He doesn't want to set eyes on me, thank God."

"Were you passionately eloquent, my poor Peregrine?"

"It looks as if I must have been, doesn't it? I was plastered, of course."

"I have a notion," Jeremy said with inconsequence, "that he was once wrecked at sea."

"Who?"

"Conducis, you dolt. Who but? In his yacht."

"Was his yacht called *Kalliope?*"

"I rather think so. I'm sure it went down."

"Perhaps my predicament reminded him of the experience."

"You know," Jeremy said, "I can't really imagine why we're making such a thing of this. After all, what's happened? You look at a derelict theatre. You fall into a fetid well from which you are extricated by the owner who is a multimillionaire. You urge in your simple way the graces and excellence of the theatre. He wonders if before he pulls it down, it might just be worth getting another opinion. He turns you over to one of his myrmidons. Where's the need for all the agitation?"

"I wonder if I should like M. Smythiman if I met him and if I shall take against S. Greenslade at first sight. Or he against me, of course."

"What the hell does that matter? You place far too much importance upon personal relationships. Look at the fatuous way you go on about your women. And then suspecting poor Mr. Conducis of improper intentions when he never wants to look upon your like again!"

"Do you suggest that I accept his gorgeous apparel?" Peregrine asked on an incredulous note.

"Certainly, I do. It would be rude and ungenerous and rather vulgar to return it with a po-faced note. The old boy wants to give you his brand new clobber because you mucked up your own in his dirty great well. You should take it and not slap him back as if he'd tried to tip you."

"If you had seen him you would not call him an old boy. He is the uncosiest human being I have ever encountered."

"Be that as it may, you'd better posh yourself up and wait upon S. Greenslade on the stroke of eleven-thirty."

Peregrine said, after a pause, "I shall do so, of course. He says nothing about the letter and glove, you observe."

"Nothing."

"I shall urge S. Greenslade to get it vetted at the V. and A."

"You jolly well do."

"Yes, I will. Well, Jer, as you say, why make a thing? If by some wild, rapturous falling-out of chance, I could do anything to save the life of The Dolphin, I would count myself amply rewarded. But it will, of course, only be a rum little interlude and in the meantime, here's the latest batch of bills."

"At least," Jeremy said, "there won't be a new one from your tailors for some time to come."

ii

Mr. S. Greenslade was bald, pale, well-dressed and unremarkable. His office was quietly sumptuous and he was reached through a hinterland of equally conservative but impressive approaches. He now sat, with a file under his hand, a distinguished painting behind him, and before him, Peregrine, summoning all the techniques of the theatre in order to achieve relaxation.

"Mr. Jay," Mr. Greenslade said, "you appreciate, of course, the fact that your meeting yesterday with Mr. Conducis has led to this appointment."

"I suppose so. Yes."

"Quite. I have here a digest, as it were, of a—shall I say a suggestion you made to Mr. Conducis as he recollects it. Here it is."

Mr. Greenslade put on his spectacles and read from the paper before him.

"Mr. Jay proposed that The Dolphin Theatre should be restored to its former condition and that a company should be established there performing Shakespeare and other plays of a high cultural quality. Mr. Jay suggested that The Dolphin is a building of some cultural worth and that, historically speaking, it is of considerable interest."

Mr. Greenslade looked up at Peregrine. "That was, in fact, your suggestion?"

"Yes. Yes. It was. Except that I hate the word culture."

"Mr. Jay, I don't know if you are at all informed about Mr. Conducis's interests."

"I—no—I only know he's—he's—"

"Extremely wealthy and something of a recluse?" Mr. Greenslade suggested with a slight, practiced smile.

"Yes."

"Yes." Mr. Greenslade removed his spectacles and placed them delicately in the centre of his writing pad. Peregrine thought he must be going to make some profound revelation about his principal. Instead he merely said "Quite" again and after a dignified silence asked Peregrine if he would be good enough to tell him something about himself. His schooling, for example, and later career. He was extremely calm in making this request.

Peregrine said he had been born and educated in New Zealand, had come to England on a drama bursary and had remained there.

"I am aware, of course, of your success in the theatrical field," said Mr. Greenslade and Peregrine supposed that he had been making some kind of confidential inquiries.

"Mr. Jay," said Mr. Greenslade, "I am instructed to make you an offer. It is, you may think, a little precipitant: Mr. Conducis is a man of quick decisions. It is this. Mr. Conducis is prepared to consider the rehabilitation of the theatre, subject, of course, to favourable opinions from an architect and from building authorities and to the granting of necessary permits. He will finance this undertaking. On one condition." Mr. Greenslade paused.

"On one condition?" Peregrine repeated in a voice that cracked like an adolescent's.

"Exactly. It is this. That you yourself will undertake the working management of The Dolphin. Mr. Conducis offers you, upon terms to be arrived at, the post of organizing the running of the theatre, planning its artistic policy, engaging the company and directing the productions. You would be given a free hand to do this within certain limits of expenditure which would be set down in this contract. I shall be glad to hear what your reactions are to this, at its present stage, necessarily tentative proposal."

Peregrine suppressed a frightening inclination towards giving himself over to manic laughter. He looked for a moment into Mr. Greenslade's shrewd and well-insulated face and he said: "It would be ridiculous of me to pretend that I am anything but astonished and delighted."

"Are you?" Mr. Greenslade rejoined. "Good. In that case I shall proceed with the preliminary investigations. I, by the way, am the solicitor for a number of Mr. Conducis's interests. If and when it comes to drawing up contracts I presume I should negotiate with your agents?"

"Yes. They are—"

"Thank you," said Mr. Greenslade. "Messrs. Slade and Oppinger, I believe?"

"Yes," said Peregrine, wondering if at any stage of his tipsy rhapsody he had mentioned them to Mr. Conducis and rather concluding that he hadn't.

"There is one other matter." Mr. Greenslade opened a drawer in his desk with an uncanny reenacting of his principal's gestures on the previous morning, withdrew from it the small Victorian writing-desk. "You are already familiar with the contents, I understand, and expressed some anxiety about their authenticity."

"I said I wished they could be shown to an expert."

"Quite. Mr. Conducis has taken your point, Mr. Jay, and wonders if you yourself would be so obliging as to act for him in this respect."

Peregrine, in a kind of trance, said: "Are the glove and documents insured?"

"They are covered by a general policy, but they have not been specifically insured since their value is unknown."

"I feel the responsibility would be—"

"I appreciate your hesitation and I may say I put the point to Mr. Conducis. He still wishes me to ask you to undertake this mission."

There was a short silence.

"Sir," said Peregrine, "why is Mr. Conducis doing all this? Why is he giving me at least the chance of undertaking such fantastically responsible jobs? What possible motive can he have? I hope," Peregrine continued with a forthrightness that became him very well, "that I'm not such an ass as to suppose I can have made an impression in the least degree commensurable with the proposals you've put before me and I—I—" He felt himself reddening and ran out of words.

Mr. Greenslade had watched him, he thought with renewed attention. He now lifted his spectacles with both hands, held them poised daintily over his blotter and said, apparently to them: "A reasonable query."

"Well—I hope so."

"And one which I am unable to answer."

"Oh?"

"Yes. I will," said Mr. Greenslade, evenly, "be frank with you, Mr. Jay. I am at a loss to know why Mr. Conducis is taking this action. If, however, I have interpreted your misgivings correctly I can assure you they are misplaced." Suddenly, almost dramatically, Mr. Greenslade became human, good-tempered and coarse. "He's not that way inclined," he said and laid down his spectacles.

"I'm extremely glad to hear it."

"You will undertake the commission?"

"Yes, I will."

"Splendid."

iii

The expert folded his hands and leaned back in his chair.

"Well," he said, "I think we may say with certainty this is a glove of late sixteenth- or early seventeenth-century workmanship. It has, at some time, been exposed to salt-water but not extensively. One might surmise that it was protected. The little desk is very much stained. Upon the letters H.S. inside the gauntlet I am unable to give an authoritative opinion but could, of course, obtain one. As for these two really rather startling documents: they can be examined and submitted to a number of tests—infra-red, spectography and so on—not in my province, you know. If they've been concocted it will certainly be discovered."

"Would you tell me how I can get the full treatment for them?"

"Oh, I think we could arrange that, you know. But we would want written permission from the owner, full insurance and so on. You've told me nothing, so far, of the history, have you?"

"No," Peregrine said. "But I will. With this proviso, if you don't mind: the owner, or rather his solicitor on his behalf, has given me permission to disclose his name to you on your undertaking to keep it to yourself until you have come to a conclusion about these things. He has a—an almost morbid dread of publicity which you'll understand, I think, when you learn who he is."

The expert looked very steadily at Peregrine. After a considerable silence he said: "Very well. I am prepared to treat the matter confidentially as far as your principal's name is concerned."

"He is Mr. Vassily Conducis."

"Good God."

"Quite," said Peregrine, doing a Greenslade. "I shall now tell you as much as is known of the history. Here goes."

And he did in considerable detail.

The expert listened in a startled manner.

"Really, very odd," he said when Peregrine had finished.

"I assure you I'm not making it up."

"No, no. I'm sure. I've heard of Conducis, of course. Who hasn't? You do realize what a—what a really flabbergasting thing this would be if it turned out to be genuine?"

"I can think of nothing else. I mean: there they lie—a child's glove and a letter asking one to suppose that on a summer's morning in the year 1596 a master-craftsman of Stratford made a pair of gloves and gave them to his grandson, who wore them for a day and then—"

"Grief filled the room up of an absent child?"

"Yes. And a long time afterwards—twenty years—the father made his will—I wonder he didn't chuck in a ghastly pun—Will's Will—don't you? And he left his apparel to his sister Joan Hart. And for her information wrote that note there. I mean—*his* hand moved across that bit of paper. If it's genuine. And then two centuries go by and somebody called M.E. puts the glove and paper in a Victorian desk with the information that

her great-great-grandmother had them from J. Hart and her grandmother insisted they were the Poet's. It *could* have *been* Joan Hart. She
died in 1664."

"I shouldn't build on it," the expert said dryly.

"Of course not!"

"Has Mr. Conducis said anything about their value? I mean—even if
there's only a remote chance they will be worth—well, I can't begin to
say what their monetary value might be, but I know what *we'd* feel
about it, here."

Peregrine and the expert eyed each other for a moment or two. "I
suppose," Peregrine said, "he's thought of that, but I must say he's
behaved pretty casually over it."

"Well, *we* shan't," said the expert. "I'll give you your receipt and ask
you to stay and see things safely stowed."

He stopped for a moment over the little dead, wrinkled glove. "If it
were true!" he murmured.

"I know, I know," Peregrine cried. "It's frightening to think what
would happen. The avid attention, the passionate greed for possession."

"There's been murder done for less," said the expert lightly.

iv

Five weeks later Peregrine, looking rather white about the gills and
brownish under the eyes, wrote the last word of his play and underneath
it: *Curtain.* That night he read it to Jeremy, who thought well of it.

There had been no word from Mr. Greenslade. The stage-house of
The Dolphin could still be seen on Bankside. Jeremy had asked at the
estate agents for permission to view and had been told that the theatre
was no longer in their hands and they believed had been withdrawn
from the market. Their manner was stuffy.

From time to time the two young men talked about The Dolphin, but
a veil of unreality seemed to have fallen between Peregrine and his
strange interlude: so much so that he sometimes almost felt as if he had
invented it.

In an interim report on the glove and documents, the museum had
said that preliminary tests had given no evidence of spurious inks or
paper and so far nothing inconsistent with their supposed antiquity had
been discovered. An expert on the handwriting of ancient documents, at
present in America, would be consulted on his return. If his report was
favourable, Peregrine gathered, a conference of authorities would be
called.

"Well," Jeremy said, "they haven't laughed it out of court, evidently."

"Evidently."

"You'll send the report to the man Greenslade?"

"Yes, of course."

Jeremy put his freckled hand on Peregrine's manuscript.

"What about opening at The Dolphin this time next year with *The Glove,* a new play by Peregrine Jay?"

"Gatcha!"

"Well—why not? For the hell of it," Jeremy said, "let's do a shadow casting. Come on."

"I have."

"Give us a look."

Peregrine produced a battered sheet of paper covered in his irregular handwriting.

"Listen," he said. "I know what would be said. That it's been done before. Clemence Dane for one. And more than that: it'd be a standing target for wonderful cracks of synthetic Bardery. The very sight of the cast. Ann Hathaway and all that lot. You know? It'd be held to stink. Sunk before it started."

"I for one don't find any derry-down tatt in the dialogue."

"Yes: but to cast 'Shakespeare.' What gall!"

"*He* did that sort of thing. You might as well say: 'Oo-er! To cast Henry VIII!' Come on: who *would* you cast for Shakespeare?"

"It sticks out a mile, doesn't it?"

"Elizabethan Angry, really isn't he? Lonely. Chancy. Tricky. Bright as the sun. A Pegasus in the Hathaway stable? Enormously over-sexed and looking like the Grafton portrait. In which I entirely believe."

"And I. All right. Who looks and plays like that?"

"Oh God!" Jeremy said, reading the casting list.

"Yes," Peregrine rejoined. "What I said. It sticks out a mile."

"Marcus Knight. My God."

"Of course. He *is* the Grafton portrait, and as for fire! Think of his Hotspur. And Harry Five. And Mercutio. And, by heaven, his Hamlet. Remember the Peer Gynt?"

"What's his age?"

"Whatever it is he doesn't show it. He can look like a stripling."

"He'd cost the earth."

"This is only mock-up, anyway."

"Has he ever been known to get through a production without creating a procession of dirty big rows?"

"Never."

"Custom-built to wreck the morale of any given company?"

"That's Marco."

"Remember the occasion when he broke off and told latecomers after the interval to sit down or get the hell out of it?"

"Vividly."

"And when the rest of the cast threw in their parts as one man?"

"I directed the fiasco."

"He's said to be more than usually explosive just now on account of no knighthood last batch."

"He is, I understand, apoplectic, under that heading."

"Well," said Jeremy, "it's your play. I see you've settled for rolling the lovely boy and the seduced fair friend and 'Mr. W.H.' all up in one character."

"So I have."

"How you dared!" Jeremy muttered.

"There have been madder notions over the centuries."

"True enough. It adds up to a damn good part. How do you see him?"

"Very blond. Very male. Very impertinent."

"W. Hartly Grove?"

"Might be. Type casting."

"Isn't he held to be a bad citizen?"

"Bit of a nuisance."

"What about your Dark Lady? The Rosaline? Destiny Meade, I see you've got here."

"I rather thought Destiny. She's cement from the eyes up but she gives a great impression of smoldering depths and really inexhaustible sex. She can produce what's called for in any department as long as it's put to her in basic English and very, very slowly. And she lives, by the way, with Marco."

"That might or might not be handy. And Ann H?"

"Oh, any sound, unsympathetic actress with good attack," Peregrine said.

"Like Gertie Bracey?"

"Yes."

"Joan Hart's a nice bit. I tell you who'd be good as Joan. Emily Dunne. You know? She's been helping in our shop. You liked her in that T.V. show. She did some very nice Celias and Nerissas and Hermias at Stratford. Prick her down on your list."

"I shall. See, with a blot I damn her."

"The others seem to present no difficulty, but the spirit sinks at an infant phenomenon."

"He dies before the end of Act I."

"Not a moment too soon. I am greatly perturbed by the vision of some stunted teen-ager acting its pants off!"

"It'll be called Gary, of course."

"Or Trevor."

"Never mind."

"Would you give me the designing of the show?"

"Don't be a bloody ass."

"It'd be fun," Jeremy said, grinning at him. "Face it: it *would* be fun."

"Don't worry, it won't happen. I have an instinct and I know it won't. None of it: the glove, the theatre, the play. It's all a sort of miasma. It won't happen."

The post box slapped.

"There you are. Fate knocking at the door," said Jeremy.

"I don't even wonder if it might be, now," Peregrine said. "However, out of sheer kindness I'll get the letters."

He went downstairs, collected the mail and found nothing for himself. He climbed up again slowly. As he opened the door, he said: "As I foretold you. No joy. All over. Like an insubstantial pageant faded. The mail is as dull as ditchwater and all for you. Oh, sorry!"

Jeremy was talking on the telephone.

He said, "Here he is, now. Would you wait a second?"

He held out the receiver with one hand over the mouthpiece.

"Mr. Greenslade," he said, "wishes to speak to you. Ducky—this is it."

Chapter III

Party

"A year ago," Peregrine thought, "I stood in this very spot on a February morning. The sun came out and gilded the stage tower of the injured Dolphin and I lusted after it. I thought of Adolphus Ruby and wished I was like him possessed. And here I am again, as the Lord's my judge, a little jumped-up Cinderella-man in Mr. Ruby's varnished boots."

He looked at the restored caryatids, the bouncing cetaceans and their golden legend, and the immaculate white frontage and elegance of ironwork and he adored them all.

He thought: "Whatever happens, this is, so far, the best time of my life. Whatever happens I'll look back at today, for instance, and say: 'Oh *that* was the morning when I knew what's meant by bliss.'"

While he stood there the man from Phipps Bros. came out of Phipps Passage.

"Morning, guvnor," he said.

"Good morning, Jobbins."

"Looks a treat, dunnit?"

"Lovely."

"Ah. Different. From what it was when you took the plunge."

"Yes: indeed."

"Yus. You wouldn't be looking for a watchman, I suppose? Now she's near finished-like? Night or day. Any time?"

"I expect we *shall* want someone. Why? Do you know of a good man?"

"Self-praise, no recommendation's what they say, ainnit?"

"Do you mean you'd take it on?"

"Not to deceive yer, guvnor, that *was* the idea. Dahn the Passage in our place, it's too damp for me chubes, see? Somethink chronic. I got good references, guvnor. Plenty'd speak up for me. 'Ow's it strike yer? Wiv a sickening thud or favourable?"

"Why," said Peregrine. "Favourably, I believe."

"Will you bear me in mind, then?"

"I'll do that thing," said Peregrine.

"Gor' bless yer, guv," said Jobbins and retired down Phipps Passage.

Peregrine crossed the lane and entered the portico of his theater. He looked at the framed notice:

DOLPHIN THEATRE
REOPENING SHORTLY
UNDER NEW MANAGEMENT

It hung immediately under the tattered Victorian playbill that he had seen on his first remarkable visit.

THE BEGGAR GIRL'S WEDDING
IN RESPONSE TO
OVERWHELMING SOLICITATION!!—
MR. ADOLPHUS RUBY . . .

When the painters cleaned and resurfaced the facade Peregrine had made them work all round that precarious fragment without touching it. "It shall stay here," he had said to Jeremy Jones, "as long as I do."

He opened the front doors. They had new locks and the doors themselves had been stripped and scraped and restored to their original dignity.

The foyer was alive. It was being painted, gilded, polished and furbished. There were men on scaffolds, on long ladders, on pendant platforms. A great chandelier lay in a sparkling heap on the floor. The two fat cherubim, washed and garnished, beamed upside-down into the resuscitated box-office.

Peregrine said good morning to the workmen and mounted the gently curving stairs.

There was still a flower-engraved looking-glass behind the bar, but now he advanced towards himself across shining mahogany, framed by brass. The bar was all golden syrup and molasses in colour. "Plain, serviceable, no tatt," Peregrine muttered.

The renovations had been completed up here and soon a carpet would be laid. He and Jeremy and the young decorator had settled in the end for the classic crimson, white and gilt, and the panelling blossomed, Peregrine thought, with the glorious vulgarity of a damask rose. He crossed the foyer to a door inscribed MANAGEMENT and went in.

The Dolphin was under the control of "Dolphin Theatres Incorporated." This was a subsidiary of Consolidated Oils. It had been created, broadly speaking, by Mr. Greenslade, to encompass the development of The Dolphin project. Behind his new desk in the office sat Mr. Winter Meyer, an extremely able theatrical business manager. He had been wooed into the service by Mr. Greenslade upon Peregrine's suggestion, after a number of interviews and, Peregrine felt sure, exhaustive inquiries. Throughout these preliminaries, Mr. Conducis had remained, as it were, the mere effluvium: far from anxious and so potent that a kind of plushy assurance seemed to permeate the last detail of renaissance in The Dolphin.

Mr. Meyer had now under his hand an entire scheme for promotion, presentation and maintenance embracing contracts with actors, designers, costumiers, front-of-house staff, stage-crew and press agents and the delicate manipulation of such elements as might be propitious to the general mana of the enterprise.

He was a short, pale and restless man with rich curly hair, who, in what little private life belonged to him, collected bric-a-brac.

"Good morning, Winty."

"Perry," said Mr. Meyer as a definitive statement rather than a greeting.

"And joy?"

Mr. Meyer lolled his head from side to side.

"Before I forget. Do we want a caretaker, watchman, day or night, stage-door keeper or any other lowly bod about the house?"

"We shall in a couple of days."

Peregrine told him about Mr. Jobbins.

"All right," said Mr. Meyer. "If the references are good. Now, it's my turn. Are you fully cast?"

"Not quite. I'm hovering."

"What do you think of Harry Grove?"

"As an actor?"

"Yes."

"As an actor I think a lot of him."

"Just as well. You've got him."

"Winty, what the hell do you mean?"

"A directive, dear boy: or what amounts to it. From Head Office."

"About *W. Hartly Grove?*"

"You'll probably find something in your mail."

Peregrine went to his desk. He was now very familiar with the look of Mr. Greenslade's communications and hurriedly extracted the latest from the pile.

Dear Peregrine Jay,

Your preliminaries seem to be going forward smoothly and according to plan. We are all very happy with the general shaping
and development of the original project and are satisfied that the
decision to open with your own play is a sound one, especially in
view of your current success at The Unicorn. This is merely an informal note to bring to your notice Mr. W. Hartly Grove, an actor,
as you will of course know, of repute and experience. Mr. Conducis personally will be very pleased if you give favourable attention to Mr. Grove when forming your company.

With kind regards,

Yours sincerely,

                                        STANLEY GREENSLADE

When Peregrine read this note he was visited by a sense of misgiving
so acute as to be quite disproportionate to its cause. In no profession
are personal introductions and dearboymanship more busily exploited
than in the theatre. For an actor to get the ear of the casting authority
through an introduction to regisseur or management is a commonplace
manoeuvre. For a second or two, Peregrine wondered with dismay if he
could possibly be moved by jealousy and if the power so strangely, so
inexplicably put into his hands had perhaps already sown a detestable
seed of corruption. But no, he thought, on consideration, there were
grounds more relative than that for his reaction, and he turned to Meyer
to find the latter watching him with a half-smile.

"I don't like this," Peregrine said.

"So I see, dear boy. May one know why?"

"Of course. I don't like W. Hartly Grove's reputation. I try to be
madly impervious to gossip in the theatre and I don't know that I believe what they say about Harry Grove."

"What do they say?"

"Vaguely shady behaviour. I've directed him once and knew him before that. He taught voice production at my drama school and disappeared over a weekend. Undefined scandal. Most women find him attractive, I believe. I can't say," Peregrine added, rumpling up his hair,
"that he did anything specifically objectionable in the later production
and I must allow that personally I found him an amusing fellow. But
apart from the two women in the company nobody liked him. *They* said
they didn't but you could see them eyeing him and knowing he eyed
them."

"This," said Meyer, raising a letter that lay on his desk, "is practi-
cally an order. I suppose yours is, too."

"Yes, blast it."

"You've been given a fabulously free hand up to now, Perry. No business of mine, of course, dear boy, but frankly I've never seen anything like it. General management, director, author—the lot. Staggering."

"I hope," Peregrine said with a very direct look at his manager, "staggering though it may be, I got it on my reputation as a director and playwright. I believe I did. There is no other conceivable explanation, Winty."

"No, no, old boy, of course not," said Winter Meyer in a hurry.

"As for W. Hartly Grove, I suppose I can't jib. As a matter of fact he would be well cast as Mr. W.H. It's his sort of thing. But I don't like it. My God," Peregrine said, "haven't I stuck my neck out far enough with Marcus Knight in the lead and liable to throw an average of three dirty great temperaments per rehearsal? What have I done to deserve Harry Grove as a bonus?"

"The Great Star's shaping up for trouble already. He's calling me twice a day to make difficulties over his contract."

"Who's winning?"

"I am," said Winter Meyer. "So far."

"Good for you."

"I'm getting sick of it," Meyer said. "Matter of fact it's on my desk now." He lifted a sheet of blotting paper and riffled the pages of the typewritten document he exposed. "Still," he said, "he's signed and he can't get past that one. We almost had to provide an extra page for it. Take a gander."

The enormous and completely illegible signature did indeed occupy a surprising area. Peregrine glanced at it and then looked more closely.

"I've seen that before," he said. "It looks like a cyclone."

"Once seen never forgotten."

"I've seen it," Peregrine said, "recently. *Where,* I wonder."

Winter Meyer looked bored.

"Did he sign your autograph book?" he asked bitterly.

"It was somewhere unexpected. Ah, well. Never mind. The fun will start with the first rehearsal. He'll want me to rewrite his part, of course, adding great hunks of ham and corn and any amount of fat. It's tricky enough as it is. Strictly speaking, a playwright shouldn't direct his own stuff. He's too tender with it. But it's been done before and by the Lord I mean to do it again. Marco or no Marco. He looks like the Grafton portrait of Shakespeare. He's got the voice of an angel and colossal prestige. He's a brilliant actor and this is a part he can play. It'll be a ding-dong go which of us wins but by heaven I'm game if he is."

"Fair enough," said Meyer. "Live for ever, dear boy. Live for ever."

They settled at their respective desks. Presently Peregrine's buzzer rang and a young woman provided by the management and secreted in an auxiliary cubby-hole said: "Victoria and Albert for you, Mr. Jay."

Peregrine refrained from saying: "Always available to Her Majesty and the Prince Consort." He was too apprehensive. He said: "Oh yes. Right. Thank you," and was put into communication with the expert.

"Mr. Jay," the expert said, "is this a convenient time for you to speak?"

"Certainly."

"I thought it best to have a word with you. We will, of course, write formally with full reports for you to hand to your principal but I felt— really," said the expert and his voice, Peregrine noticed with mounting excitement, was trembling, "really it is the most remarkable thing. I—well, to be brief with you, the writing in question has been exhaustively examined. It has been compared by three experts with the known signatures and they find enough coincidence to give the strongest presumption of identical authorship. They are perfectly satisfied as to the age of the cheveril and the writing materials and that apart from saltwater stains there has been no subsequent interference. In fact, my dear Mr. Jay, incredible as one might think it, the glove and the document actually seem to be what they purport to be."

Peregrine said, "I've always felt this would happen and now I can't believe it."

"The question is: what is to be done with them?"

"You will keep them for the time being?"

"We are prepared to do so. We would very much like," said the expert, and Peregrine caught the wraith of a chuckle in the receiver, "to keep them altogether. However! I think my principals will, after consultation, make an approach to—er—the owner. Through you, of course, and—I imagine this would be the correct proceeding—Mr. Greenslade."

"Yes. And—no publicity?"

"Good God, no!" the expert exclaimed quite shrilly. "I should hope not. Imagine!" There was a long pause. "Have you any idea," the expert said, "whenever he will contemplate selling?"

"No more than you have."

"No. I see. Well: you will have the reports and a full statement from us within the next week. I—must confess—I—I have rung you up simply because I—in short—I am, as you obviously are, a devotee."

"I've written a play about the glove," Peregrine said impulsively. "We're opening here with it."

"Really? A play," said the expert and his voice flattened.

"It isn't cheek!" Peregrine shouted into the telephone. "In its way it's a tribute. A play! Yes, a play."

"Oh, please! Of course. Of course."

"Well, thank you for telling me."

"No, no."

"Goodbye."

"What? Oh, yes. Of course. Goodbye."

Peregrine put down the receiver and found Winter Meyer staring at him.

"You'll have to know about this, Winty," he said. "But as you heard —no publicity. It concerns the Great Person, so that's for sure. Further it must not go."

"All right. If you say so: not an inch."

"Top secret?"

"Top secret, as you say. Word of honour."

So Peregrine told him. When he had finished Meyer ran his white fingers through his black curls and lamented. "But listen, but listen, listen, listen. What material! What a talking line! The play's *about* it. Listen: it's *called The Glove*. We've *got* it. Greatest Shakespeare relic of all time. The *Dolphin* Glove. American offers. Letters to the papers: 'Keep the Dolphin Glove in Shakespeare's England.' 'New fabulous offer for Dolphin Glove!' Public subscriptions. The lot! Ah, Perry, cherub, dear, *dear* Perry. All this lovely publicity and we should keep it secret!"

"It's no good going on like that."

"How do you expect me to go on? The Great Person must be handled over this one. He must be seen. He must be made to work. What makes him work? You've seen him. Look: he's a financial wizard: he *knows*. He knows what's good business. Listen: if this was handled right and we broke the whole story at the psychological moment: you know, *with* the publicity, the right kind of class publicity . . . Look—"

"Do pipe down," Peregrine said.

"Ah! Ah! Ah!"

"I'll tell you what my guess is, Winty. He'll take it all back to his iron bosom and lock it away in his Louis-the-Somethingth bureau and that's the last any of us will ever see of young Hamnet Shakespeare's cheveril glove."

In this assumption, however, Peregrine was entirely mistaken.

ii

"But that's all one," Marcus Knight read in his beautiful voice. *"Put it away somewhere. I shall not look at it again. Put it away."*

He laid his copy of Peregrine's play down, and the six remaining members of the company followed his example. A little slap of typescripts ran round the table.

"Thank you," Peregrine said. "That was a great help to me. It was well read."

He looked round the table. Destiny Meade's enormous black eyes were fixed upon him with the determined adulation of some mixed-up and sexy mediaeval saint. This meant, as he knew, nothing. Catching his eye, she raised her fingers to her lips and then in slow motion extended them to him.

"Darling Perry," she murmured in her celebrated hoarse voice, "what can we say? It's all too much. Too much." She made an appealing helpless little gesture to the company at large. They responded with suitable if ambiguous noises.

"My dear Peregrine," Marcus Knight said (and Peregrine thought: "His voice is like no other actor's"), "I like it. I see great possibilities. I saw them as soon as I read the play. Naturally, that was why I accepted the role. My opinion, I promise you, is unchanged. I look forward with interest to creating this part." Royalty could not have been more gracious.

"I'm so glad, Marco," Peregrine said.

Trevor Vere, whose age, professionally, was eleven, winked abominably across the table at Miss Emily Dunne, who disregarded him. She did not try to catch Peregrine's eye and seemed to be disregardful of her companions. He thought that perhaps she really had been moved.

W. Hartly Grove leaned back in his chair with some elegance. His fingers tapped the typescript. His knuckles, Peregrine absently noted, were like those of a Regency prizefighter. His eyebrows were raised and a faint smile hung about his mouth. He was a blond man, very comely, with light blue eyes, set far apart, and an indefinable expression of impertinence. "I think it's fabulous," he said. "And I like my Mr. W.H."

Gertrude Bracey, patting her hair and settling her shoulders, said: "I *am* right, aren't I, Perry? Ann Hathaway *shouldn't* be played unsympathetically. I mean: definitely *not* a bitch?"

Peregrine thought: "Trouble with this one: I foresee trouble."

He said cautiously: "She's had a raw deal, of course."

Charles Random said: "I wonder what Joan Hart did with the gloves?" and gave Peregrine a shock.

"But there weren't any gloves, *really,*" Destiny Meade said, "were there, darling? Or were there? Is it historical?"

"No, no, love," Charles Random said. "I was talking inside the play. Or out of wishful thinking. I'm sorry."

Marcus Knight gave him a look that said it was not usual for secondary parts to offer gratuitous observations round the conference table. Random, who was a very pale young man, reddened. He was to play Dr. Hall in the first act.

"I see," Destiny said. "So, I mean there weren't *really* any gloves? In Stratford or anywhere real?"

Peregrine looked at her and marvelled. She was lovely beyond compare and as simple as a sheep. The planes of her face might have been carved by an angel. Her eyes were wells of beauty. Her mouth, when it broke into a smile, would turn a man's heart over and, although she was possessed of more than her fair share of commonsense, professional cunning and instinctive technique, her brain took one idea at a time and reduced each to the comprehension level of a baby. If she were to walk out on any given stage and stand in the least advantageous place on it in a contemptible lack of light and with nothing to say, she would draw all eyes. At this very moment, fully aware of her basic foolishness, Marcus Knight, W. Hartly Grove and, Peregrine observed with dismay, Jeremy Jones, all stared at her with the solemn awareness that was her habitual tribute, while Gertrude Bracey looked at her with something very like impotent fury.

The moment had come when Peregrine must launch himself into one of those pre-production pep-talks upon which a company sets a certain amount of store. More, however, was expected of him, now, than the usual helping of "We're all going to love this, so let's get cracking" sort of thing. For once he felt a full validity in his own words when he clasped his hands over his play and said: "This is a great occasion for me." He waited for a second and then, abandoning everything he had so carefully planned, went on. "It's a great occasion for me because it marks the rebirth of an entrancing playhouse: something I'd longed for and dreamed of and never, never thought to see. And then: to be given the job I have been given of shaping the policy and directing the productions and—as a final and incredible *bon-bouche*—the invitation to open with my own play. I do hope you'll believe me when I say all this makes me feel not only immensely proud but extremely surprised and—although it's not a common or even appropriate emotion in a director-playwright—very humble.

"It might have been more politic to behave as if I took it all as a matter of course and no more than my due, but I'd rather, at the outset, and probably for the last time, say that I can't get over my good fortune. I'm not the first dramatist to have a bash at the man from Warwickshire and I'm sure I won't be the last. In this piece I've—well, you've seen, I hope, what I've tried to do. Show the sort of combustion that built up in that unique personality: the terrifying sensuality that lies beyond the utterly unsentimental lyricism—gilded flies under daisies pied and violets blue. His only release, his only *relief,* you might say, has been his love for the boy Hamnet. It's his son's death that brings about the frightful explosion in his own personality, and the moment when Rosaline (I have always believed the Dark Lady was a Rosaline) pulls Hamnet's glove on her hand is the climax of the entire action. The physical intrusion and his consent to it brings him to the condition that spewed up Timon of Athens and was seared out of him by his own disgust. I've tried to suggest that for such a man the only possible release is through his work. He would like to be an Antony to Rosalind's Cleopatra, but between himself and that sort of surrender stands his genius. And—incidentally—the hard-headed bourgeois of Stratford which also, he is."

Peregrine hesitated. Had he said anything? Was it any good trying to take it further? No.

"I won't elaborate," he said. "I can only hope that we'll find out what it's all about as we work together." He felt the abrupt upsurge of warmth that is peculiarly of the theatre.

"I hope, too, very much," he said, "that we're going to agree together. It's a great thing to be starting a playhouse on its way. They say dolphins are intelligent and gregarious creatures. Let us be good Dolphins and perform well together. Bless you all."

They responded at once and all blessed him in return and for the occasion, at least, felt uplifted and stimulated and, in themselves, vaguely noble.

"And now," he said, "let's look at Jeremy Jones's sets and then it'll be almost time to drink a health to our enterprise. This is a great day."

iii

Following the reading there was a small party, thrown by the Management and thrown with a good deal of quiet splendour. It was held in the circle foyer with the bar in full array. The barman wore a snowy white shirt, flamboyant waistcoat and gold albert. There was a pot-boy with his sleeves rolled up to his shoulders like the one in *Our Mutual Friend.* The waiters were conventionally dressed but with a slight Victorian emphasis. Champagne in brass-bound ice buckets stood along the mahogany bar and the flowers, exclusively, were crimson roses set in fern leaves.

Mr. Greenslade was the host. Apart from the company, Jeremy, Winter Meyer, the publicity agents and the stage-director and his assistant, there were six personages of startling importance from the worlds of theatre, finance, the press and what Mr. Meyer, wide-eyed, described as "the sort you can't, socially speaking, look any higher than." From a remark let fall by Mr. Greenslade, Peregrine was led to suppose that behind their presence could be discerned the figure of Mr. Conducis who, of course, did not attend. Indeed it was clear from the conversation of the most exalted of these guests that Mr. Conducis was perfectly well known to be the presiding genius of The Dolphin.

"A new departure for V.M.C.," this personage said. "We were all astonished." (Who were "we"?) "Still, like the rest of us, one supposes, he must have his toys."

Peregrine wondered if it would have been possible for him to have heard a more innocently offensive comment.

"It's a matter of life and death to us," he said. The personage looked at him with amusement.

"Is it really?" he said. "Well, yes. I can see that it is. I hope all goes well. But I am still surprised by the turn of V.M.C.'s fancy. I didn't think he had any fancies."

"I don't really know him," said Peregrine.

"Which of us does?" the personage rejoined. "He's a legend in his own lifetime and the remarkable thing about *that* is: the legend is perfectly accurate." Well content with this aphorism he chuckled and passed superbly on, leaving an aftermath of cigar, champagne and the very best unguents for the Man.

"If I were to become as fabulously rich as that," Peregrine wondered, "would I turn into just such another? Can it be avoided?"

He found himself alongside Emily Dunne, who helped in Jeremy's shop and was to play Joan Hart in *The Glove*. She had got the part by audition and on her performance, which Peregrine had seen, of Hermia in *A Midsummer Night's Dream*.

She had a pale face with dark eyes and a welcoming mouth. He thought she looked very intelligent and liked her voice, which was deepish.

"Have you got some champagne?" asked Peregrine. "And would you like something to eat?"

"Yes and no, thank you," said Emily. "It's a wonderful play. I can't get over my luck, being in it. And I can't get over The Dolphin, either."

"I thought you looked as if you were quite enjoying it. You read Joan exactly right. One wants to feel it's a pity she's Will's sister because she's the only kind of woman who would ever suit him as a wife."

"I think before they were both married she probably let him in by a side-window when he came home to Henley Street in the early hours after a night on the tiles."

"Yes, of course she did. How right you are. Do you like cocktail parties?"

"Not really, but I always hope I will."

"I've given that up, even."

"Do you know, when I was playing at The Mermaid over a year ago, I used to look across the river to The Dolphin, and then one day I walked over Blackfriars Bridge and stood in Wharfingers Lane and stared at it. And then an old, old stagehand I knew told me his father had been on the curtain there in the days of Adolphus Ruby. I got a sort of thing about it. I found a book in a sixpenny rack called *The Buskin and the Boards*. It was published in 1860 and it's all about contemporary theatres and actors. *Terribly* badly written, you know, but there are some good pictures and The Dolphin's one of the best."

"Do let me see it."

"Of course."

"I had a thing about The Dolphin, too. What a pity we didn't meet in Wharfingers Lane," said Peregrine. "Do you like Jeremy's models? Let's go and look at them."

They were placed about the foyer and were tactfully lit. Jeremy had been very intelligent: the sets made single uncomplicated gestures and were light and strong-looking and beautifully balanced. Peregrine and Emily had examined them at some length when it came to him that he should be moving among the guests. Emily seemed to be visited by the same notion. She said: "I think Marcus Knight is wanting to catch your eye. He looks a bit portentous to me."

"Gosh! So he does. Thank you."

As he edged through the party towards Marcus Knight, Peregrine thought: "That's a pleasing girl."

Knight received him with an air that seemed to be compounded of graciousness and overtones of huff. He was the centre of a group: Winter Meyer, Mrs. Greenslade, who acted as hostess and was beautifully dressed and excessively poised, Destiny Meade and one of the personages, who wore an expansive air of having acquired her.

"Ah, Perry, dear boy," Marcus Knight said, raising his glass to salute. "I wondered if I should manage to have a word with you. Do forgive me," he said jollily to the group. "If I don't fasten my hooks in him now he'll escape me altogether." Somewhat, Peregrine thought, to her astonishment, Knight kissed Mrs. Greenslade's hand. "Lovely, lovely party," he said and moved away. Peregrine saw Mrs. Greenslade open her eyes very widely for a fraction of a second at the personage. "We're amusing her," he thought sourly.

"Perry," Knight said, taking him by the elbow. "May we have a long, long talk about your wonderful play? And I mean that, dear boy. Your *wonderful* play."

"Thank you, Marco."

"Not here, of course," Knight said, waving his disengaged hand, "not now. But soon. And, in the meantime, a thought."

"Oops!" Peregrine thought. "Here we go."

"Just a thought. I throw it out for what it's worth. Don't you feel— and I'm speaking absolutely disinterestedly—don't you feel that in your Act Two, *dear* Perry, you keep Will Shakespeare offstage for *rather* a long time? I mean, having built up this tremendous tension—"

Peregrine listened to the celebrated voice and as he listened he looked at the really beautiful face with its noble brow and delicate bone structure. He watched the mouth and thought how markedly an exaggerated dip in the bow of the upper lip resembled that of the Droushout engraving and the so-called Grafton portrait. "I must put up with him," Peregrine thought. "He's got the prestige, he's got the looks and his voice is like no other voice. God give me strength."

"I'll think very carefully about it, Marco," he said and he knew that Knight knew he was going to do nothing of the sort. Knight, in a grand seignorial manner, clapped him on the shoulder. "We shall agree," he cried, "like birds in their little nest."

"I'm sure of it," said Peregrine.

"One other thing, dear boy, and this is your private ear." He steered Peregrine by the elbow into a corridor leading off to the boxes. "I find with some surprise," he said, muting the exquisite voice, "that we are to have W. Hartly Grove in our company."

"I thought he read Mr. W.H. quite well, didn't you?"

"I could scarcely bring myself to listen," said Knight.

"Oh," Peregrine said coolly. "Why?"

"My dear man, do you know anything at all about Mr. Harry Grove?"

"Only that he is a reasonably good actor. Marco," Peregrine said, "don't let's start any anti-Grove thing. For your information, and I'd be terribly grateful if you'd treat this as strictly—very strictly, Marco—be-tween ourselves, I've had no hand in this piece of casting. It was done at the desire of the Management. They have been generous to a degree in every other respect and even if I'd wanted to I couldn't have opposed them."

"You had this person *thrust* upon you?"

"If you like to put it that way."

"You should have refused."

"I had no valid reason for doing so. It is a good piece of casting. I beg you, Marco, not to raise a rumpus at the outset. Time enough when anything happens to justify it."

For a moment he wondered if Knight was going to produce a temperament then and there and throw in his part. But Peregrine felt sure Knight had a great desire to play Will Shakespeare and although, in the shadowy passage, he could see the danger signal of mounting purple in the oval face, the usual outburst did not follow this phenomenon.

Instead, Knight said: "Listen. You think I am unreasonable. Allow me to tell you, Perry—"

"I don't want to listen to gossip, Marco."

"*Gossip!* My God! Anyone who accuses me of gossip does me an injury I won't stomach. *Gossip!* Let me tell you I know for a fact that Harry Grove—" The carpet was heavy and they had heard no sound of an approach. The worst would have happened if Peregrine had not seen a shadow move across the gilt panelling. He closed his hand round Knight's arm and stopped him.

"What are you two up to, may I ask?" said Harry Grove. "Scandal-mongering?"

He had a light, bantering way with him and a boldish stare that was somehow very far from being offensive. "Perry," he said, "this is an enchanting theatre. I want to explore, I want to see everything. Why don't we have a bacchanal and go in Doric procession through and about the house, tossing down great bumpers of champagne and chanting some madly improper hymn? Led, of course, by our great, *great* star. Or should it be by Mr. and Mrs. Greensleeves?"

He made his preposterous suggestion so quaintly that in spite of himself and out of sheer nerves Peregrine burst out laughing. Knight said, "Excuse me," with a good deal of ostentation and walked off.

"'*It is offended,*'" Grove said. "'*See, it stalks away.*' It dislikes me, you know. Intensely."

"In that case don't exasperate it, Harry."

"Me? You think better not? Rather tempting though, I must say. Still, you're quite right, of course. Apart from everything else, I can't afford to. Mr. Greengage might give me the sack," Grove said with one of his bold looks at Peregrine.

"If he didn't, I might. Do behave prettily, Harry. And I must get back into the scrum."

"I shall do everything that is expected of me, Perry dear. I nearly always do."

Peregrine wondered if there was a menacing note behind this apparently frank undertaking.

When he returned to the foyer it was to find that the party had attained its apogee. Its component bodies had almost all reached points farthest removed from their normal behaviour. Everybody was now obliged to scream if he or she wished to be heard and almost everybody would have been glad to sit down. The personages were clustered together in a flushed galaxy and the theatre people excitedly shouted shop. Mrs. Greenslade could be seen saying something to her husband and Peregrine was sure it was to the effect that she felt it was time their guests began to go away. It would be best, Peregrine thought, if Destiny Meade and Marcus Knight were to give a lead. They were together on the outskirts and Peregrine knew, as certainly as if he had been beside them, that Knight was angrily telling Destiny how he felt about W. Hartly Grove. She gazed at him with her look of hypersensitive and at the same time sexy understanding but every now and then her eyes swivelled a little and always in the same direction. There was a slightly furtive air about this manoeuvre.

Peregrine turned to discover what could be thus attracting her attention and there, in the entrance to the passage, stood Harry Grove with wide-open eyes and a cheerful smile, staring at her. *"Damn,"* thought Peregrine. "Now what?"

Emily Dunne, Charles Random and Gertie Bracey were all talking to Jeremy Jones. Jeremy's crest of red hair bobbed up and down and he waved his glass recklessly. He threw back his head and his roar of laughter could be heard above the general din. As he always laughed a great deal when he was about to fall in love, Peregrine wondered if he was attracted by Emily and hoped he was not. It could hardly be Gertie. Perhaps he was merely plastered.

But no. Jeremy's green and rather prominent gaze was directed over the heads of his group and was undoubtedly fixed upon Destiny Meade.

"He *couldn't* be such an ass," Peregrine thought uneasily. "Or could he?"

His awareness of undefined hazards were not at all abated when he turned his attention to Gertie Bracey. He began, in fact, to feel as if he stood in a field of fiercely concentrated shafts of criss-cross searchlights. Like searchlights, the glances of his company wandered, interlaced, selected and darted. There, for example, was Gertie with her rather hatchet-jawed intensity stabbing her beam at Harry Grove. Peregrine recollected, with a jolt, that somebody had told him they had been lovers and were now breaking up. He had paid no attention to this rumour. Supposing it was true, would this be one more personality problem on his plate?

"Or am I," he wondered, "getting some kind of director's neurosis? Do I merely imagine that Jeremy eyes Destiny and Destiny and Harry ogle each other and Gertie glares hell's fury at Harry and Marcus has his paw on Destiny and that's why he resents Harry? Or is it all an unexpected back-kick from the Conducis champagne?"

He edged round to Destiny and suggested that perhaps they ought to make a break and that people were waiting for a lead from her and Marcus. This pleased both of them. They collected themselves as they did offstage before a big entrance and, with the expertise of rugby halfbacks, took advantage of a gap and swept through it to Mrs. Greenslade.

Peregrine ran straight into their child actor, Master Trevor Vere, and his mama, who was a dreadful lady called Mrs. Blewitt. She had to be asked and it was God's mercy that she seemed to be comparatively sober. She was dressed in a black satin shift with emerald fringe and she wore a very strange green toque on her pale corn hair. Trevor, in the classic tradition of infant phenomena, was youthfully got up in some sort of contemporary equivalent of a Fauntleroy suit. There were overtones of the Mod. His hair was waved back from his rather pretty face and he wore a flowing cravat. Peregrine knew that Trevor was not as old as his manner and his face suggested because he came under the legal restrictions imposed upon child performers. It was therefore lucky in more ways than one that he died early in the first act.

Mrs. Blewitt smiled and smiled at Peregrine with the deadly knowingness of the professional mum and Trevor linked his arm in hers and smiled, too. There are many extremely nice children in the professional theatre. They have been well brought up by excellent parents. But none of these had been available to play Hamnet Shakespeare and Trevor, it had to be faced, was talented to an unusual degree. He had made a great hit on cinema in a biblical epic as the Infant Samuel.

"Mrs. Blewitt," said Peregrine.

"I was just hoping for a chance to say how much we appreciate the compliment," said Mrs. Blewitt with an air of conspiracy. "It's not a big role, of course, not like Trev's accustomed to. Trev's accustomed to leading child-juves, Mr. Jay. We was offered—"

It went on predictably for some time. Trevor, it appeared, had developed a heart condition. Nothing, Mrs. Blewitt hurriedly assured Peregrine, to worry about really because Trev would never let a show down, never, but the doctor under whom Trev was and under whom she herself was—a monstrous picture presented itself—had advised against another big, emotionally exhausting role—

"Why bring that up, Mummy?" Trevor piped with one of his atrocious winks at Peregrine. Peregrine excused himself, saying that they must all be getting along, mustn't they, and he wanted to catch Miss Dunne before she left.

This was true. He had thought it would be pleasant to take Emily back to their studio for supper with him and Jeremy. Before he could get to her he was trapped by Gertrude Bracey.

She said: "Have you seen Harry anywhere?"

"I saw him a minute or two ago. I think perhaps he's gone."

"I think perhaps you're right," she said with such venom that Peregrine blinked. He saw that Gertrude's mouth was unsteady. Her eyes were not quite in focus and were blurred with tears.

"Shall I see if I can find him?" he offered.

"God, no," she said. "I know better than that, I hope, thank you very much." She seemed to make a painful effort to present a more conventional front. "It doesn't matter two hoots, darling," she said. "It was nothing. Fabulous party. Can't wait to begin work. I see great things in poor Ann, you know."

She walked over to the balustrade and looked down into the lower foyer which was populous with departing guests. She was not entirely steady on her pins, he thought. The last pair of personages was going downstairs and of the company only Charles Random and Gertrude remained. She leaned over the balustrade, holding to it with both hands. If she was looking for Harry Grove, Peregrine thought, she hadn't found him. With an uncoordinated swing she turned, flapped a long black glove at Peregrine and plunged downstairs. Almost certainly she had not said goodbye to her host and hostess but, on the whole, perhaps that was just as well. He wondered if he ought to put her in a taxi but heard Charles Random shout: "Hi, Gertie love. Give you a lift?"

Jeremy was waiting for him but Emily Dunne had gone. Almost everybody had gone. His spirits plummeted abysmally. Unpredictably, his heart was in his boots.

He went up to Mrs. Greenslade with extended hand.

"Wonderful," he said. "How can we thank you."

Chapter IV

Rehearsal

"Who is this comes hopping up the lane?"

"Hopping? Where? Oh, I see. A lady dressed for riding. She's lame, Master Will. She's hurt. She can't put her foot to the ground."

"She makes a grace of her ungainliness. There's a stain across her face. And in her bosom. A raven's feather in a valley of snow."

"Earth. Mire. On her habit, too. She must have fallen."

"Often enough, I dare swear."

"She's coming in at the gate."

"Will! Where ARE *you.* WILL!*"*

"We'll have to stop again, I'm afraid," Peregrine said. "Gertie! Ask her to come on, will you, Charles?"

Charles Random opened the door on the Prompt side. "Gertie! Oh, dear."

Gertrude Bracey entered with her jaw set and the light of battle in her eyes. Peregrine walked down the centre aisle and put his hands on the rail of the orchestral well.

"Gertie, love," he said, "it went back again, didn't it? It was all honey and sweet reasonableness and it wouldn't have risen one solitary hackle. She *must* grate. She *must* be bossy. He's looking down the lane at that dark, pale creature who comes hopping into his life with such deadly seduction. And while he's quivering, slap bang into this disturbance of—of his whole personality—comes your voice: scolding, demanding, possessive, always too loud. It *must* be like that, Gertie. Don't you *see?* You must hurt. You must jangle."

He waited. She said nothing.

"I can't have it any other way," Peregrine said.

Nothing.

"Well, let's build it again, shall we? Back to *'Who is this,'* please, Marco. You're off, please, Gertie."

She walked off.

Marcus Knight cast up his eyes in elaborate resignation, raised his arms and let them flop.

"Very well, dear boy," he said, "as often as you like, of course. One grows a little jaded but never mind."

Marco was not the only one, Peregrine thought, to feel jaded: Gertie was enough to reduce an author-director to despair. She had after a short tour of the States become wedded to Method acting. This involved endless huddles with whoever would listen to her and a remorseless scavenging through her emotional past for fragments that could start her off on some astonishing association with her performance.

"It's like a bargain basement," Harry Grove said to Peregrine. "The things Gertie digs up and tries on are really *too* rococo. We get a new look every day."

It was a slow process and the unplotted pauses she took in which to bring the truth to light were utterly destructive to concerted playing. "If she goes on like this," Peregrine thought, "she'll tear herself to tatters and leave the audience merely wishing she wouldn't."

As for Marcus Knight, the danger signals for a major temperament had already been flown. There was a certain thunderous quietude which Peregrine thought it best to disregard.

Really, for him, Peregrine thought, Marco was behaving rather well, and he tried to ignore the little hammer that pounded away under Marco's oval cheek.

"*Who is this—*"

Again they built up to her line. When it came it was merely shouted offstage without meaning and apparently without intention.

"Great Christ in Heaven!" Marcus Knight suddenly bellowed. "How long must this endure! What, in the name of all the suffering clans of martyrdom, am I expected to *do*? Am I coupled with a harridan or a bloody dove? My author, my producer, my *art* tell me that here is a great moment. I should be fed, by Heaven, fed: I should be led up to. I have my line to make. I must show what I am. My whole being should be lacerated. And so, God knows it is, but by what!" He strode to the door and flung it wide. Gertrude Bracey was exposed looking both terrified and determined. "By a drivelling, piping pea-hen!" he roared, straight into her face. "What sort of an actress are you, dear? Are you a woman, dear? Has anybody ever slighted you, trifled with you, deserted you? Have you no conception of the gnawing serpent that ravages a woman scorned?"

Somewhere in the front of the house Harry Grove laughed. Unmistakably, it was he. He had a light, mocking, derisive laugh, highly infec-

tious to anybody who had not inspired it. Unhappily both Knight and
Gertrude Bracey, for utterly opposed reasons, took it as a direct personal affront. Knight spun round on his heel, advanced to the edge of
the stage and roared into the darkness of the auditorium. "Who is that!
Who is it! I demand an answer."

The laughter ran up to a falsetto climax and somewhere in the shadows Harry Grove said delightedly: "Oh dear me, dear me, how very entertaining. The King Dolphin in a rage."

"Harry," Peregrine said, turning his back on the stage and vainly trying to discern the offender. "You are a professional actor. You know
perfectly well that you are behaving inexcusably. I must ask you to
apologize to the company."

"To the *whole* company, Perry dear? Or just to Gertie for laughing
about her not being a woman scorned?"

Before Peregrine could reply Gertrude re-entered, looking wildly
about the house. Having at last distinguished Grove in the back stalls,
she pointed to him and screamed out with a virtuosity that she had
hitherto denied herself: "This is a deliberate insult." She then burst into
tears.

There followed a phenomenon that would have been incomprehensible to anybody who was not intimately concerned with the professional theatre. Knight and Miss Bracey were suddenly allied. Insults
of the immediate past were as if they had never been. They both began
acting beautifully for each other: Gertrude making big eloquent piteous
gestures and Marcus responding with massive understanding. She wept.
He kissed her hand. They turned with the precision of variety artists to
the auditorium and simultaneously shaded their eyes like comic sailors.
Grove came gaily down the aisle saying: "I apologize. Marcus and
Gerts. Everybody. I really *do* apologize. In seventeen plastic and entirely different positions. I shall go and be devoured backstage by the
worm of contrition. What more can I do? I cannot say with even mar-
ginal accuracy that it's all a mistake and that you're not at all funny. But
anything else. Anything else."

"Be quiet," Peregrine said, forcing a note of domineering authority
which was entirely foreign to him. "You will certainly go backstage,
since you are needed. I will see you after we break. In the meantime I
wish neither to see nor hear from you until you make your entrance. Is
that understood?"

"I'm sorry," Grove said quietly. "I really am." And he went backstage by the pass-door that Mr. Conducis had used when he pulled
Peregrine out of the well.

"Marco and Gertie," Peregrine said, and they turned blackly upon him. "I hope you'll be very generous and do something nobody has a right to ask of you. I hope you'll dismiss this lamentable incident as if it had never happened."

"It is either that person or me. Never in the entire course of my professional experience—"

The Knight temperament raged on. Gertrude listened with gloomy approval and repaired her face. The rest of the company were still as mice. At last Peregrine managed to bring about a truce and eventually they began again at: *"Who is this comes hopping up the lane?"*

The row had had one startling and most desirable effect. Gertrude, perhaps by some process of emotive transference, now gave out her offstage line with all the venom of a fishwife.

"But *darling*," reasoned Destiny Meade, a few minutes later, devouring Peregrine with her great black lamps. *"Hopping.* Me? On my first entrance? I mean—actually? I mean what an *entrance! Hopping!"*

"Destiny, love, it's like I said. He had a thing about it."

"Who did?"

"Shakespeare, darling. About a breathless, panting, jigging, hopping woman with a white face and pitchball eyes and blue veins."

"How peculiar of him."

"The thing is, for him it was all an expression of sexual attraction."

"I don't see how I can do a sexy thing if I come on playing hopscotch and puffing and blowing like a whale. Truly."

"Destiny: listen to what he wrote. Listen.

> *'I saw her once*
> *Hop forty paces through the public street;*
> *And having lost her breath, she spoke, and panted,*
> *That she did make defect perfection,*
> *And, breathless, power breathe forth.'*

"That's why I've made her fall off her horse and come hopping up the lane."

"Was he sort of kinky?"

"Certainly not," Marcus interrupted.

"Well, I only wondered. Gloves and everything."

"Listen, darling. Here you are. Laughing and out of breath—"

"And hopping. *Honestly!"*

"All *right*," said Marcus. "We know what you mean, but listen. You're marvellous. Your colour's coming and going and your bosom's heaving. He has an entirely normal reaction, Destiny darling: you *send* him. You do see, don't you? *You* send *me*."

"With my hopping?"

"*Yes*," he said irritably. "That and all the rest of it. Come on, darling, do. Make your entrance to me."

"Yes, Destiny," Peregrine said. "Destiny, listen. You're in a velvet habit with your bosom exposed, a little plumed hat and soft little boots and you're lovely, lovely, lovely. And young Dr. Hall has gone out to help you and is supporting you. Charles—come and support her. Yes: like that. Leave her as free as possible. Now: the door opens and we see you. Fabulous. You're in a shaft of sunlight. And *he* sees you. Shakespeare does. And you speak. Right? Right, Destiny? You say—go on, dear."

"*Here I come upon your privacy, Master Shakespeare, hopping over your doorstep like a starling.*"

"Yes, and at once, at that very moment, you know you've limed him."

"Limed?"

"Caught."

"Am I keen?"

"Yes. You're pleased. You know he's famous. And you want to show him off to W.H. You come forward, Marco, under compulsion, and offer your help. Staring at her. And you go to him, Destiny, and skip and half-fall and fetch up laughing and clinging to him. He's terribly, terribly still. Oh, *yes,* Marco, yes. Dead right. Wonderful. And Destiny, darling, that's *right*. You know? It's right. It's what we want."

"Can I sit down or do I keep going indefinitely panting away on his chest?"

"Look into his face. Give him the whole job. Laugh. No, not that sort of a laugh, dear. Not loud. Deep down in your throat!"

"More sexy?"

"Yes," Peregrine said and ran his hands through his hair. "*That's* right. More sexy."

"And then I sit down?"

"Yes. He helps you down. Centre. Hall pushes the chair forward. Charles?"

"Could it," Marcus intervened, "be left of centre, dear boy? I mean I only suggest it because it'll be easier for Dessy and I *think* it'll make a better picture. I can put her down. Like this." He did so with infinite grace and himself occupied centre stage.

"I think I like it better the other way, Marco, darling. Could we try it the other way, Perry? This feels false, a bit, to me."

They jockeyed about for star positions. Peregrine made the final decision in Knight's favour. It really was better that way. Gertrude came on and then Emily, very nice as Joan Hart, and finally Harry Grove, behaving himself and giving a bright, glancing indication of Mr. W.H. Peregrine began to feel that perhaps he had not written a bad play and that, given a bit of luck, he might, after all, hold the company together.

He was aware, in the back of his consciousness, that someone had come into the stalls. The actors were all onstage and he supposed it must be Winter Meyer or perhaps Jeremy, who often looked in, particularly when Destiny was rehearsing.

They ran the whole scene without interruption and followed it with an earlier one between Emily, Marcus and the ineffable Trevor in which the boy Hamnet, on his eleventh birthday, received and wore his grandfather's present of a pair of embroidered cheveril gloves. Marcus and Peregrine had succeeded in cowing the more offensive exhibitionisms of Trevor and the scene went quite well. They broke for luncheon. Peregrine kept Harry Grove back and gave him a wigging which he took so cheerfully that it lost half its sting. He then left and Peregrine saw with concern that Destiny had waited for him. Where then was Marcus Knight and what had become of his proprietary interest in his leading lady? As if in explanation, Peregrine heard Destiny say: "Darling, the King Dolphin's got a pompous feast with someone at the Garrick. Where shall we go?"

The new curtain was half-lowered, the working lights went out, the stage-manager left and the stage-door banged distantly.

Peregrine turned to go out by front-of-house.

He came face to face with Mr. Conducis.

ii

It was exactly as if the clock had been set back a year and three weeks and he again dripped fetid water along the aisle of a bombed theatre. Mr. Conducis seemed to wear the same impeccable clothes and to be seized with the same indefinable oddness of behaviour. He even took the same involuntary step backwards, almost as if Peregrine was going to accuse him of something.

"I have watched your practice," he said as if Peregrine were learning the piano. "If you have a moment to spare there is a matter I want to discuss with you. Perhaps in your office?"

"Of course, sir," Peregrine said. "I'm sorry I didn't see you had come in."

Mr. Conducis paid no attention to this. He was looking, without evidence of any kind of reaction, at the now resplendent auditorium: at the crimson curtain, the chandeliers, the freshly gilt scrollwork, and the shrouded and expectant stalls.

"The restoration is satisfactory?" he asked.

"Entirely so. We shall be ready on time, sir."

"Will you lead the way?"

Peregrine remembered that on their former encounter Mr. Conducis had seemed to dislike being followed. He led the way upstairs to the office, opened the door and found Winter Meyer in residence, dictating letters. Peregrine made a complicated but apparently eloquent face and Meyer got to his feet in a hurry.

Mr. Conducis walked in looking at nothing and nobody.

"This is our Manager, sir. Mr. Winter Meyer, Mr. Conducis."

"Oh, yes. Good morning," said Mr. Conducis. Without giving an impression of discourtesy he turned away. "Really, old boy," as Mr. Meyer afterwards remarked. "He might have been giving me the chance to follow my own big nose instead of backing out of The Presence."

In a matter of seconds Mr. Meyer and the secretary had gone to lunch.

"Will you sit down, sir?"

"No, thank you. I shall not be long. In reference to the glove and documents: I am told that their authenticity is established."

"Yes."

"You have based your piece upon these objects?"

"Yes."

"I have gone into the matter of promotion with Greenslade and with two persons of my acquaintance who are conversant with this type of enterprise." He mentioned two colossi of the theatre. "And have given some thought to preliminary treatment. It occurs to me that, properly manipulated, the glove and its discovery and so on might be introduced as a major theme in promotion."

"Indeed it might," Peregrine said fervently.

"You agree with me? I have thought that perhaps some consideration should be given to the possibility of timing the release of the glove story with the opening of the theatre and of displaying the glove and documents, suitably protected and housed, in the foyer. Peregrine said with what he hoped was a show of dispassionate judgment that surely, as a piece of pre-production advertising, this gesture would be unique. Mr.

Conducis looked quickly at him and away again. Peregrine asked him if he felt happy about the security of the treasure. Mr. Conducis replied with a short exegesis upon wall safes of a certain type in which, or so Peregrine confusedly gathered, he held a controlling interest.

"Your public relations and press executive," Mr. Conducis stated in his dead fish voice, "is a Mr. Conway Boome."

"Yes. It's his own name," Peregrine ventured, wondering for a moment if he had caught a glint of something that might be sardonic humour, but Mr. Conducis merely said: "I daresay. I understand," he added, "that he is experienced in theatrical promotion, but I have suggested to Greenslade that having regard for the somewhat unusual character of the type of material we propose to use, it might be as well if Mr. Boome were to be associated with Maitland Advertising, which is one of my subsidiaries. He is agreeable."

"I'll be bound he is," Peregrine thought.

"I am also taking advice on the security aspect from an acquaintance at Scotland Yard, a Superintendent Alleyn."

"Oh, yes."

"Yes. The matter of insurance is somewhat involved, the commercial worth of the objects being impossible to define. I am informed that as soon as their existence is made known there is likely to be an unprecedented response. Particularly from the United States of America."

There followed a short silence.

"Mr. Conducis," Peregrine said, "I can't help asking you this. I know it's no business of mine but I really can't help it. Are you—have you—I mean, would you feel at all concerned about whether the letters and glove stay in the country of their owner or not?"

"In my country?" Mr. Conducis asked as if he wasn't sure that he had one.

"I'm sorry, no. I meant the original owner."

Peregrine hesitated for a moment and then found himself embarked upon an excitable plea for the retention of the documents and glove. He felt he was making no impression whatever and wished he could stop. There was some indefinable and faintly disgusting taint in the situation.

With a closed face Mr. Conducis waited for Peregrine to stop and then said: "That is a sentimental approach to what is at this juncture a matter for financial consideration. I cannot speak under any other heading: historical, romantic, nationalistic or sentimental. I know," Mr. Conducis predictably added, "nothing of such matters."

He then startled Peregrine quite shockingly by saying with an indefinable change in his voice: "I dislike pale gloves. Intensely."

For one moment Peregrine thought he saw something like anguish in this extraordinary man's face and at the next that he had been mad to suppose anything of the sort. Mr. Conducis made a slight movement indicating the interview was at an end. Peregrine opened the door, changed his mind and shut it again.

"Sir," he said. "One other question. May I tell the company about the letters and glove? The gloves that we use on the stage will be made by the designer, Jeremy Jones—who is an expert in such matters. If we are to show the original in the front-of-house he should copy it as accurately as possible. He should go to the museum and examine it. And he will be so very much excited by the whole thing that I can't guarantee his keeping quiet about it. In any case, sir, I myself spoke to him about the glove on the day you showed it to me. You will remember you did not impose secrecy at that time. Since the report came through I have not spoken of it to anyone except Meyer and Jones."

Mr. Conducis said, "A certain amount of leakage at this stage is probably inevitable and if correctly handled may do no harm. You may inform your company of all the circumstances. With a strong warning that the information is, for the time being, confidential and with this proviso: I wish to remain completely untroubled by the entire business. I realize that my ownership may well become known—is known in fact, already, to a certain number of people. This is unavoidable. But under no circumstances will I give statements, submit to interviews or be quoted. My staff will see to this at my end. I hope you will observe the same care, here. Mr. Boome will be instructed. Good morning. Will you—?"

He made that slight gesture for Peregrine to precede him. Peregrine did so.

He went out on the circle landing and ran straight into Harry Grove.

"Hall-lo, dear boy," said Harry, beaming at him. "I just darted back to use the telephone. Destiny and I—" He stopped short, bobbed playfully round Peregrine at Mr. Conducis and said: *"Now,* see what I've done! A genius for getting myself in wrong. My only talent."

Mr. Conducis said: "Good morning to you, Grove." He stood in the doorway looking straight in front of him.

"And to you, wonderful fairy godfather, patron, guiding light and all those things," Harry said. "Have you come to see your latest offspring, your very own performing Dolphins?"

"Yes," said Mr. Conducis.

"Look at dear Perry!" Harry said. "He's stricken dumb at my misplaced familiarity. Aren't you, Perry?"

"Not for the first time," Peregrine said and felt himself to be the victim of a situation he should have controlled.

"Well!" Harry said, glancing with evident amusement from one to the other of his hearers. "I mustn't double-blot my copybook, must I? Nor must I keep lovely ladies waiting." He turned to Mr. Conducis with an air of rueful deference. "I do hope you'll be pleased with us, sir," he said. "It must be wonderful to be the sort of man who uses his power to rescue a drowning theatre instead of slapping it under. All the more wonderful since you have no personal interest in our disreputable trade, have you?"

"I have little or no knowledge of it."

"No. Like vinegar, it doesn't readily mix with Oil," Harry said. "Or is it Shipping? I always forget. Doing any yachting lately? But I mustn't go on being a nuisance. Goodbye, sir. Do remember me to Mrs. G. See you later, Perry, dear boy."

He ran downstairs and out by the main door.

Mr. Conducis said: "I am late. Shall we—?" They went downstairs and crossed the foyer to the portico. There was the Daimler and, at its door, Peregrine's friend the chauffeur. It gave him quite a shock to see them again and he wondered for a dotty moment if he would be haled away once more to Drury Place.

"Good morning," Mr. Conducis said again. He was driven away and Peregrine joined Jeremy Jones at their habitual chop-house on the Surrey Side.

iii

He told the company and Jeremy Jones about the glove before afternoon rehearsal. They all made interested noises. Destiny Meade became very excited and confused on learning that the glove was "historic" and persisted in thinking they would use it as a prop in the production. Marcus Knight was clearly too angry to pay more than token attention. He had seen Destiny return, five minutes late and in hilarious company with W. Hartly Grove. Gertrude Bracey was equally disgruntled by the same phenomenon.

When Harry Grove heard about the glove he professed the greatest interest and explained, in his skittish manner, "Someone ought to tell Mrs. Constantia Guzmann about this."

"Who in earth," Peregrine had asked, "is Mrs. Constantia Guzmann?"

"Inquire of the King Dolphin," Harry rejoined. He insisted on referring to Marcus Knight in these terms, to the latter's evident annoyance. Peregrine saw Knight turn crimson to the roots of his hair and thought it better to ignore Harry.

The two members of the company who were whole-heartedly moved by Peregrine's announcement were Emily Dunne and Charles Random and their reaction was entirely satisfactory. Random kept saying: "Not true! Well, of *course.* Now, we know what inspired you. No—it's incredible. It's too much."

He was agreeably incoherent.

Emily's cheeks were pink and her eyes bright, and that, too, was eminently satisfactory.

Winter Meyer, who was invited to the meeting, was in ecstasy.

"So what have we got?" he asked at large. "We have got a story to make the front pages wish they were double elephants."

Master Trevor Vere was not present at this rehearsal.

Peregrine promised Jeremy that he would arrange for him to see the glove as often as he wanted to, at the museum. Meyer was to get in touch with Mr. Greenslade about safe-housing it in the theatre and the actors were warned about secrecy for the time being, although the undercover thought had clearly been that a little leakage might be far from undesirable as long as Mr. Conducis was not troubled by it.

Stimulated perhaps by the news of the glove, the company worked well that afternoon. Peregrine began to block the tricky second act and became excited about the way Marcus Knight approached his part.

Marcus was an actor of whom it was impossible to say where hard thinking and technique left off and the pulsing glow that actors call star-quality began. At earlier rehearsals he would do extraordinary things: shout, lay violent emphasis on oddly selected words, make strange, almost occult gestures and embarrass his fellow players by speaking with his eyes shut and his hands clasped in front of his mouth as if he prayed. Out of all this inwardness there would occasionally dart a flash of the really staggering element that had placed him, still a young man, so high in his chancy profession. When the period of incubation had gone by the whole performance would step forward into full light. "And," Peregrine thought, "there's going to be much joy about this one."

Act Two encompassed the giving of the dead child Hamnet's gloves on her demand to the Dark Lady: a black echo, this, of Bertram's and Bassanio's rings and of Berowne's speculation as to the whiteness of his wanton's hand. It continued with the entertainment of the poet by the infamously gloved lady and his emergence from "the expense of passion in a waste of shame." It ended with his savage reading of the sonnet to her and to W.H. Marcus Knight did this superbly.

W. Hartly Grove lounged in a window seat as Mr. W.H. and, already mingling glances with Rosaline, played secretly with the gloved hand. The curtain came down on a sudden cascade of his laughter. Peregrine spared a moment to reflect that here, as not infrequently in the theatre, a situation in a play reflected in a cock-eyed fashion the emotional relationships between the actors themselves. He had a theory that, contrary to popular fancy, this kind of overlap between the reality of their personalities in and out of their roles was an artistic handicap. An actor, he considered, was embarrassed rather than released by unsublimated chunks of raw association. If Marcus Knight was enraged by the successful blandishments of Harry Grove upon Destiny Meade, this reaction would be liable to upset his balance and bedevil his performance as Shakespeare, deceived by Rosaline with W.H.

And yet, apparently, it had not done so. They were all going great guns and Destiny, with only the most rudimentary understanding of the scene, distilled an erotic compulsion that would have peeled the gloves off the hands of the dead child as easily as she filched them from his supersensitive father. "She really *is*," Jeremy Jones had said, "the original overproof *femme fatale*. It's just there. Whether she's a goose or a genius doesn't matter. There's something solemn about that sort of attraction."

Peregrine had said, "I wish you'd just try and think of her in twenty years' time with china-boys in her jaws and her chaps hitched up above her lugs and her wee token brain shrank to the size of a pea."

"Rail on," Jeremy had said. "I am unmoved."

"You don't suppose you'll have any luck?"

"That's right. I don't. She is busily engaged in shuffling off the great star and teaming up with the bounding Grove. Not a nook or cranny left for me."

"Oh, dear, oh dear, oh dear," Peregrine had remarked and they let it go at that.

On this particular evening Peregrine himself had at last succeeded after several rather baffling refusals in persuading Emily Dunne to come back to supper at the studio. Jeremy, who supervised and took part in the construction and painting of his sets at a warehouse not far away, was to look in at The Dolphin and walk home with them over Blackfriars Bridge. It had appeared to Peregrine that this circumstance, when she heard of it, had been the cause of Emily's acceptance. Indeed, he heard her remark in answer to some question from Charles Random: "I'm going to Jeremy's." This annoyed Peregrine extremely.

Jeremy duly appeared five minutes before the rehearsal ended and sat in the front stalls. When they broke, Destiny beckoned to him and he went up to the stage through the pass-door. Peregrine saw her lay her hands on Jeremy's coat and talk into his eyes. He saw Jeremy flush up to the roots of his red hair and glance quickly at him. Then he saw Destiny link her arm in Jeremy's and lead him upstage, talking hard. After a moment or two they parted and Jeremy returned to Peregrine.

"Look," he said in stage Cockney. "Do me a favour. Be a pal."

"What's all this?"

"Destiny's got a sudden party and she's asked me. Look, Perry, you don't mind if I go? The food's all right at the studio. You and Emily can do very nicely without me: damn sight better than with."

"She'll think you're bloody rude," Peregrine said angrily, "and she won't be far wrong, at that."

"Not at all. She'll be enchanted. It's you she's coming to see."

"I'm not so sure."

"Properly speaking, you ought to be jolly grateful."

"Emily'll think it's a put-up job."

"So what? She'll be pleased as Punch. Look, Perry, I—I can't wait. Destiny's driving us all and she's ready to go. Look, I'll have a word with Emily."

"You'd damn well better, though what in decency's name you can find to say!"

"It'll be as right as a bank. I promise."

"So *you* say," Peregrine contemplated his friend, whose freckled face was pink, excited and dreadfully vulnerable. "All right," he said. "Make your excuse to Emily. Go to your party. I think you're heading for trouble but that's your business."

"I only hope I'm heading for *something*," Jeremy said. "Fanks, mate. You're a chum."

"I very much doubt it," said Peregrine.

He stayed front-of-house and saw Jeremy talk to Emily onstage. Emily's back was towards him and he was unable to gauge her reaction but Jeremy was all smiles. Peregrine had been wondering what on earth he could say to her when it dawned upon him that, come hell or high water, he could not equivocate with Emily.

Destiny was up there acting her boots off with Marcus, Harry Grove, and now Jeremy, for an audience. Marcus maintained a proprietary air, to which she responded like a docile concubine, Peregrine thought. But he noticed that she managed quite often to glance at Harry with a slight widening of her eyes and an air of decorum that was rather more provocative than if she'd hung round his neck and said: "Now." She also beamed upon poor Jeremy. They all talked excitedly, making plans for their party. Soon they had gone away by the stage-door.

Emily was still onstage.

"Well," Peregrine thought, "here goes."

He walked down the aisle and crossed to the pass-door in the box on the Prompt side. He never went backstage by this route without a kind of aftertaste of his first visit to The Dolphin. Always, behind the sound of his own footsteps on the uncarpeted stairway, Peregrine caught an echo of Mr. Conducis coming invisibly to his rescue.

It was a slight shock now, therefore, to hear, as he shut the pass-door behind him, actual footsteps beyond the turn in this narrow, dark and widening stair.

"Hullo?" he said. "Who's that?"

The steps halted.

"Coming up," Peregrine said, not wanting to collide.

He went on up the little stairway and turned the corner.

The door leading onto the stage opened slightly, admitting a blade of light. He saw that somebody moved uncertainly as if in doubt whether to descend or not and he got the impression that whoever it was had actually been standing in the dark behind the door.

Gertrude Bracey said, "I was just coming down."

She pushed open the door and went onstage to make way for him. As he came up with her, she put her hand on his arm.

"Aren't you going to Destiny's sinister little party?" she asked.

"Not I," he said.

"Unasked? Like me?"

"That's right," he said lightly and wished she wouldn't stare at him like that. She leaned towards him.

"Do you know what I think of Mr. W. Hartly Grove?" she asked quietly. Peregrine shook his head and she then told him. Peregrine was used to uninhibited language in the theatre but Gertrude Bracey's eight words on Harry Grove made him blink.

"Gertie, *dear!*"

"Oh, yes," she said. "Gertie, dear. And Gertie dear knows what she's talking about, don't you worry."

She turned her back on him and walked away.

iv

"Emily,". Peregrine said as they climbed up Wharfingers Lane, "I hope you don't mind it just being me. And I hope you don't think there's any skulduggery at work. Such as me getting rid of Jer in order to make a heavy pass at you. Not, mark you, that I wouldn't like to but that I really wouldn't have the nerve to try such an obvious ploy."

"I should hope not," said Emily with composure.

"Well, I wouldn't. I suppose you've seen how it is with Jeremy?"

"One could hardly miss it."

"One couldn't, could one?" he agreed politely.

Suddenly for no particular reason they both burst out laughing and he took her arm.

"Imagine!" he said. "Here we are on Bankside, not much more than a stone's throw from The Swan and The Rose and The Globe. Shakespeare must have come this way a thousand times after rehearsals had finished for the day. We're doing just what he did and I do wish, Emily, that we could take water for Blackfriars."

"It's pleasant," Emily said, "to be in company that isn't self-conscious about him and doesn't mistake devotion for idolatry."

"Well, he *is* unique, so what's the matter with being devoted? Have you observed, Emily, that talent only fluctuates about its own middle line whereas genius nearly always makes great walloping bloomers?"

"Like Agnes Pointing Upwards and bits of *Cymbeline?*"

"Yes. I think, perhaps, genius is nearly always slightly lacking in taste."

"Anyway, without intellectual snobbery?"

"Oh that, certainly."

"Are you pleased with rehearsals, so far?"

"On the whole."

"I suppose it's always a bit of a shock bringing something you've written to the melting pot or forge or whatever the theatre is. Particularly when, as producer, you yourself *are* the melting pot."

"Yes, it is. You see your darling child being processed, being filtered through the personalities of the actors and turning into something different on the way. And you've got to accept all that because a great many of the changes are for the good. I get the oddest sort of feeling sometimes, that, as producer, I've stepped outside myself as playwright. I begin to wonder if I ever knew what the play is about."

"I can imagine."

They walked on in companionship: two thinking ants moving eastward against the evening out-swarm from the City. When they reached Blackfriars it had already grown quiet there and the little street where Jeremy and Peregrine lived was quite deserted. They climbed up to the studio and sat in the window drinking dry martinis and trying to see The Dolphin on the far side of the river.

"We haven't talked about the letter and the glove," Emily said. "Why, I wonder, when it's such a tremendous thing. You must have felt like a high-pressure cooker with it all bottled up inside you."

"Well, there was Jeremy to explode to. And of course the expert."

"How strange it is," Emily said. She knelt on the window-seat with her arms folded on the ledge and her chin on her arms. Her heartshaped face looked very young. Peregrine knew that he must find out about her: about how she thought and what she liked and disliked and where she came from and whether she was or had been in love and if so what she did about it. "How strange," she repeated, "to think of John Shakespeare over in Henley Street making them for his grandson. Would he make them himself or did he have a foreman-glover?"

"He made them himself. The note says 'Mayde by my father.'"

"Is the writing all crabbed and squiggly like his signatures?"

"Yes. But not exactly like any of them. People's writing isn't always like their signatures. The handwriting experts have all found what they call 'definitive' points of agreement."

"*What* will happen to them, Perry? Will he sell to the highest bidder or will he have any ideas about keeping them here? Oh," Emily cried, "they *should* be kept here."

"I tried to say as much but he shut up like a springtrap."

"Jeremy," Emily said, "will probably go stark ravers if they're sold out of the country."

"Jeremy?"

"Yes. He's got a manic thing about the draining away of national treasures, hasn't he? I wouldn't have been in the least surprised, would you, if it had turned out to be Jeremy who stole the Goya Wellington. Simply to keep it in England, you know." Emily chuckled indulgently and Peregrine thought he detected the proprietary air of romance and was greatly put out. Emily went on and on about Jeremy Jones and his treasures and how moved and disturbed he was by the new resolution. "Don't you feel he is perfectly capable," she said, "of bearding Mr. Conducis in his den and telling him he mustn't let them go?"

"I do hope you're exaggerating."

"I really don't believe I am. He's a fanatic."

"You know him very well, don't you?"

"Quite well. I help in their shop sometimes. They *are* experts, aren't they, on old costume? Of course Jeremy has to leave most of it to his partner because of work in the theatre but in between engagements he does quite a lot. I'm learning how to do all kinds of jobs from him like putting old tinsel on pictures and repairing bindings. He's got some wonderful prints and books."

"I know," Peregrine said rather shortly. "I've been there."

She turned her head and looked thoughtfully at him. "He's madly excited about making the gloves for the show. He was saying just now he's got a pair of Jacobean gloves, quite small, and he thinks they might be suitable if he took the existing beadwork off and copied the embroidery off Hamnet's glove onto them."

"I know, he told me."

"He's letting me help with that, too."

"Fun for you."

"Yes. I like him very much. I do hope if he's madly in love with Destiny that it works out but I'm afraid I rather doubt it."

"Why?"

"He's a darling but he hasn't got anything like enough of what it takes. Well, I wouldn't have thought so."

"Really?" Peregrine quite shouted in an excess of relief. He began to talk very fast about the glove and the play and what they should have for dinner. He had been wildly extravagant and had bought all the things he himself liked best: smoked salmon with caviar folded inside, cold partridge and the ingredients for two kinds of salad. It was lucky that his choice seemed to coincide with Emily's. They had Bernkasteler Doktor with the smoked salmon and it was so good they went on drinking it with the partridge. Because of Jeremy's defection there was rather a lot of everything and they ate and drank it all up.

When they had cleared away they returned to the window-seat and watched the Thames darken and the lights come up on Bankside. Peregrine began to think how much he wanted to make love to Emily. He watched her and talked less and less. Presently he closed his hand over hers. Emily turned her hand, gave his fingers a brief matter-of-fact squeeze and then withdrew.

"I'm having a lovely time," she said, "but I'm not going to stay very late. It takes ages to get back to Hampstead."

"But I'll drive you. Jeremy hasn't taken the car. It lives in a little yard round the corner."

"Well, that'll be grand. But I still won't stay very late."

"I'd like you to stay forever and a day."

"That sounds like a theme song from a rather twee musical."

"Emily: have you got a young man?"

"No."

"Do you have a waiting list, at all?"

"No, Peregrine."

"No preferential booking?"

"I'm afraid not."

"Are you ever so non-wanton?"

"Ever so."

"Well," he sighed, "it's original, of course."

"It's not meant to madden and inflame."

"That was what I feared. Well, O.K. I'll turn up the lights and show you my photographs."

"You jolly well do," said Emily.

So they looked at Peregrine's and Jeremy's scrapbooks and talked interminable theatre shop and presently Emily stood up and said now she must go.

Peregrine helped her into her coat with rather a perfunctory air and banged round the flat getting his own coat and shutting drawers.

When he came back and found Emily with her hands in her pockets looking out of the window he said loudly: "All the same, it's scarcely fair to have cloudy hair and a husky voice and your sort of face and body and intelligence and not even *think* about being provocative."

"I do apologize."

"I suppose I can't just give you 'a single famished kiss'?"

"All right," said Emily. "But not too famished."

"*Emily!*" Peregrine muttered and became, to his astonishment, breathless.

When they arrived at her flat in Hampstead she thanked him again for her party and he kissed her again, but lightly this time. "For my own peace of mind," he said. "Dear Emily, goodnight."

"Goodnight, dear Peregrine."

"Do you know something?"

"What?"

"We open a fortnight tonight."

v

BLISS FOR BARDOLITERS
STAGGERING DISCOVERY
Absolutely Priceless Say Experts

MYSTERY GLOVE
WHO FOUND IT?
Dolphin Discovery

FIND OF FOUR CENTURIES
NO FAKING SAY EGG-HEADS
Shakespeare's Dying Son

"IN HIS OWN WRITE"
BARD'S HAND AND NO KIDDING
Inspires Playwright Jay

IMPORTANT DISCOVERY
Exhaustive tests have satisfied the most distinguished scholars and experts of the authenticity . . .

GLOVE–LETTER–SENSATION
"It's the most exciting thing that has ever happened to me," says tall, gangling playwright Peregrine Jay.

WHO OWNS THE DOLPHIN GLOVE?
WE GIVE YOU ONE GUESS
"No Comment"—Conducis

FABULOUS OFFER FROM U.S.A.

AMAZING DEVELOPMENTS
DOLPHIN GLOVE MYSTERY
Spokesman for Conducis Says No Decision on Sale. May Go to States.

COMING EVENTS
The restored Dolphin Theatre on Bankside will open on Thursday with a new play, *The Glove,* written and directed by Peregrine Jay and inspired, it is generally understood, by the momentous discovery of . . .

OPENING TOMORROW
At The Dolphin. Bankside. Under Royal Patronage. *The Glove* by Peregrine Jay. The Dolphin Glove with Documents will be on view

in the foyer. Completely sold out for the next four weeks. Waiting list now open.

vi

"You've been so very obliging," Jeremy Jones said to the learned young assistant at the museum, "letting us have access to the glove and take up so much of your time, that Miss Dunne suggested you might like to see the finished copies."

"That's very nice of you. I shall be most interested."

"They're only stage-props, you know," Jeremy said, opening a cardboard box. "But I've taken a little more trouble than usual because the front row of the stalls will be comparing them to the real thing "

"*And* because it was a labour of love," Emily said. "Mostly that, Jeremy, now, wasn't it?"

"Well, perhaps. There you are."

He turned back a piece of old silk and exposed the gloves lying neatly, side by side. The assistant bent over them. "I should think the front row of the stalls will be perfectly satisfied," he said. "They are really *very* good copies. Accurate in the broad essentials and beautifully worked. Where did you get your materials?"

"From stock. A thread of silk here, a seed-pearl there. Most of it's false, of course. The sequins are Victorian, as you see."

"They fill the bill quite well, however, at a distance. I hope you never feel tempted," the assistant said with pedantic archness, "to go in for antiquarian forgery, Mr. Jones. You'd be much too successful."

"To me," Jeremy said, "it seems a singularly revolting form of chicanery."

"Good. I understand that a car will be sent here to collect the glove tomorrow. I am to deliver it at the theatre and to see it safely housed. I believe you have designed the setting. Perhaps you would call in here and we can go together. I would prefer to have someone with me. Unnecessarily particular, I dare say, but there's been so much publicity."

"I will be delighted to come," said Jeremy.

There is to be another observer at the theatre, I understand, to witness the procedure and inspect the safety precautions. Somebody from the police, I think it is."

"So I hear," said Jeremy. "I'm glad to know they are being careful."

vii

The Malaise of First Night Nerves had gripped Peregrine, not tragically and aesthetically by the throat but, as is its habit, shamefully in the guts.

At half past six on Thursday morning he caught sight of himself in the bathroom shaving-glass. He saw, with revulsion, a long, livid face, pinched up into untimely wrinkles and strange dun-coloured pouches. The stubbled jaw sagged and the lips were pallid. There was a general suggestion of repulsive pigheadedness and a terrible dearth of charm.

The final dress-rehearsal had ended five hours ago. In fourteen hours the curtain would rise and in twenty-four hours he would be quivering under the lash of the morning critics.

"Oh God, God, why, why have I done this fearful thing."

Every prospect of the coming day and night was of an excursion with Torquemada: the hours when there was nothing to do were as baleful as those when he would be occupied. He would order flowers, send telegrams, receive telegrams, answer telephone calls. He would prowl to and fro and up and down all alone in his lovely theatre, unable to rest, unable to think coherently, and when he met anybody—Winty Meyer or the stage-director or the S.M. or some hellish gossip hound—he would be cool and detached. At intervals he would take great nauseating swigs from a bottle of viscous white medicine.

He tried going back to bed but hated it. After a time he got up, shaved his awful face, bathed, dressed, suddenly was invaded by a profound inertia and sleepiness, lay down and was instantly possessed of a compulsion to walk.

He rose, listened at Jeremy's door, heard him snore and stole downstairs. He let himself out into London.

Into the early morning sounds and sights of the river and of the lanes and steps and streets. The day was fresh and sunny and would presently be warm. He walked to the gap where he could look across the Thames to Southwark. The newly painted stage-house and dome of The Dolphin showed up clearly now and the gilded flagpole glittered so brightly it might have been illuminated.

As he stared at it a bundle ran up and opened out into their new flag: a black dolphin on a gold ground. Jobbins was on his mark in good time. Big Ben and all the clocks in the City struck eight and Peregrine's heart's blood rose and pounded in his ears. The glory of London was upon him. A kind of rarefied joy possessed him, a trembling anticipation of good fortune that he was scared to acknowledge.

He was piercingly happy. He loved all mankind with indiscriminate embracement and more particularly Emily Dunne. He ran back to the flat and sang *Rigoletto* on his way upstairs.

"You look," Jeremy said, "like the dog's dinner and you sound like nothing on earth. Can you be joyful?"

"I can and I am."

"Long may it last."

"Amen."

He could eat no breakfast. Even black coffee disgusted him. He went over to the theatre at nine o'clock. Jeremy was to come in at ten with Emily and the assistant from the museum to see the installation of the glove and documents. He, too, crackled like a cat's fur with First Night Nerves.

When Peregrine arrived at The Dolphin it was alive with cleaners and florists' assistants. As he went upstairs he heard the telephone ring, stop and ring again. The bar was in a state of crates, cartons and men in shirtsleeves, and on the top landing itself two packing cases had been opened and their contents displayed: a pair of wrought-iron pedestals upon which were mounted two bronze dolphins stylized and sleek. They were a gift from Mr. Conducis, who had no doubt commissioned Mr. Greenslade to go to "the best man." This he might be said to have done with the result that while the dolphins were entirely out of style with their company and setting they were good enough to hold their own without causing themselves or their surroundings to become ridiculous.

Peregrine suggested that they should be placed in the circle foyer. One on each side of the steps from the sunken landing.

He crossed the foyer and went into the office.

Winter Meyer was behind his desk. He was not alone. A very tall man with an air of elegance and authority stood up as Peregrine entered.

"Oh Lord," Peregrine thought. "Another of the Conducis swells, or is it somebody to check up on how we behave with the Royals? Or what?"

" 'Morning, Perry old boy," said Meyer. "Glad you've come in. Mr. Peregrine Jay, Superintendent Alleyn."

Chapter V

Climax

Alleyn was not altogether unused to the theatrical scene or to theatrical people. He had been concerned in four police investigations in which actors had played—and "played" had been the operative word—leading roles. As a result of these cases he was sardonically regarded at the Yard as something of an expert on the species.

It was not entirely on this score, however, that he had been sent to The Dolphin. Some five years ago Mr. Vassily Conducis had been burgled in Drury Place. Alleyn had been sent in and had made a smartish catch and recovered the entire haul within twenty-four hours. Mr. Conducis was away at the time but on his return had asked Alleyn to call, probably with the idea of making a tangible acknowledgement. Possibly Alleyn's manner had made him change his mind and substitute a number of singularly unsparkling congratulations delivered in a stifled tone from somewhere in the region of his epiglottis. Alleyn had left, uncharmed by Mr. Conducis.

Their next encounter was the result of a letter to Alleyn's Great White Chief signed by Mr. Conducis and requesting advice and protection for the Shakespeare documents and glove.

"He's asked for you, Rory," the Great White Chief said. "No regard for your rank and status, of course. Very cool. In other respects, I suppose you *are* the man for the job: what with your theatrical past and your dotage on the Bard. These damned objects seem to be worth the spoils of the Great Train Robbery. Tell him to buy protection from a reputable firm and leave us alone, by Heaven."

"I'd be delighted."

"No, you wouldn't. You're hell bent on getting a look at the things."

"I'm not hell bent on getting another look at Conducis."

"No? What's wrong with him, apart from stinking of money?"

"Nothing, I daresay."

"Well, you'd better find out when these things are going to be trans-

ferred and check up on the security. We don't want another bloody
Goya and worse on our hands."

So Alleyn went to The Dolphin at nine o'clock on the morning of the
opening performance.

The housing for the glove and letters was in a cavity made in the auditorium wall above the sunken landing which was, itself, three steps
below the level of the circle foyer. In this wall was ledged a large steel
safe, with convex plate glass replacing the outward side. The door of
the safe, opposite this window, was reached from the back of the circle
and concealed by a panel in the wall. Between the window and the exte-
rior face of the wall were sliding steel doors, opened electrically by a
switch at the back of the cavity. Concealed lighting came up when the
doors were opened. Thus the glove and letters would be exposed to patrons on the stairs, the landing and, more distantly, in the foyer.

The safe was a make well enough known to Alleyn. It carried a five
figure lock. This combination could be chosen by the purchaser. It was
sometimes based on a key word and a very simple code. For instance,
the numbers from one to zero might be placed under the letters of the
alphabet from A to J and again from K to T and again from U to Z.
Each number had therefore two and in the case of 1–6, three corresponding letters. Thus, if the key word was "night" the number of the
combination would be 49780.

Jeremy had caused the steel safe to be lined with padded yellow silk.
On its floor was a book-hinged unit covered with black velvet. It had a
variable tilt and was large enough to display the glove and two documents. He had made a beautifully lettered legend which had been
framed and would be hung below the wall cavity. During performances
the sliding doors would be retracted and the plate glass window exposed.

Alleyn made a very thorough inspection and found the precautions
rather more efficient than might have been expected. There were not, at
large, many criminal virtuosi of the combination lock who would be
equal to this one. It would have to be a cracksman's job. An efficient
burglar alarm had been installed and would go into action at the first attempt at entry into the theatre. Once the glove and documents were
housed the safe would not be re-opened, the interior lighting and sliding
doors in front of the glass panel being operated from a switch inside the
wall cavity. He pointed out that one man on another man's shoulders
could effect a smash, snatch and grab and asked about watchmen. He
was told that for as long as the objects were in the theatre, there would
be a man on the landing. Jobbins, late Phipps Bros., was revealed in a

brand new uniform. He was to be on duty from four up to midnight, when he would be relieved by a trained man from a security organization. Jobbins would sleep on the premises in an unused dressing-room and could be roused in case of need. A second man already on duty would take over at 8 A.M. and remain in the foyer until Jobbins returned at four. The burglar alarm would be switched on by Jobbins after the show when he locked up for the night.

Alleyn had been fully informed of these arrangements when Peregrine walked into the office. As they shook hands he saw the pallor and the shadows under the eyes and thought: "First night terrors, poor chap."

"Mr. Alleyn's had a look at our security measures," Meyer said, "and thinks they'll pass muster. He's going to wait and see the treasure safely stored." His telephone rang. "Excuse me."

Alleyn said to Peregrine: "You're all in the throes of every kind of preoccupation. Don't pay any attention to me. If I may, while I'm waiting I'll look at this enchanting theatre. What a superb job you've done."

This was unlike Peregrine's idea of a plainclothes policeman. Alleyn had reached the door before he said: "I'll show you round, sir."

"I wouldn't dream of it. If I may just wander. You're up to your neck, I'm sure."

"On the contrary. Meyer is, but my problem," Peregrine said, "is not having anything real to do. I'd like to show you The Dolphin."

"Well, in that case—"

It was a comprehensive tour. Alleyn was so clearly interested and so surprisingly well-informed that Peregrine actually enjoyed himself. He found himself talking about the play and what he had tried to do with it and how it had been born of his first sight of Hamnet Shakespeare's glove.

Alleyn knew about the terms of the will and about Joan Hart getting the wearing apparel. Indeed, Peregrine would have betted, Alleyn knew as much as he did about Shakespearean scholarship and was as familiar with the plays as he was himself.

For his part, Alleyn liked this strained, intelligent and modest young man. He hoped Peregrine had written and produced a good play. Alleyn asked one or two questions, and since he was a trained investigator and was personally attracted by the matter in hand, Peregrine found himself talking about his work with an ease that he would never have thought possible on a ten minutes' acquaintance. He began to speak quickly and excitedly, his words tumbling over each other. His love of The Dolphin welled up into his voice.

"Shall we go backstage?" he said. "Or—wait a moment. I'll take the Iron up and you can see Jeremy Jones's set for the first act."

He left Alleyn in the stalls, went through the pass-door, and sent up the elegantly painted fireproof curtain. He then moved onstage and faced the house. He had run up the pass-door passage very quickly and his blood pounded in his ears. Nervous exhaustion, wasn't it called? He even felt a bit dizzy.

The cleaners upstairs had unshuttered a window and a shaft of sunlight struck down upon the stage. It was peopled by dancing motes.

"Is anything the matter?" an unusually deep voice asked quite close at hand. Alleyn had come down the centre aisle. Peregrine, dazzled, thought he was leaning on the rail of the orchestra well.

"No—I mean—no, nothing. It's just that I was reminded of my first visit to The Dolphin."

Was it because the reminder had been so abrupt or because over the last week Peregrine had eaten very little and slept hardly at all that he felt so monstrously unsure of himself. Alleyn wouldn't have thought it was possible for a young man to turn any whiter in the face than Peregrine already was but somehow he now contrived to do so. He sat down on Jeremy's Elizabethan dower chest and wiped his hand across his mouth. When he looked up Alleyn stood in front of him. "Just where the hole was," Peregrine thought.

He said: "Do you know, underneath your feet there's a little stone well with a door. It was there that the trap used to work. Up and down, you know, for Harlequin and Hamlet's Ghost and I daresay for a Lupino or a Lane of that vintage. Or perhaps both. Oh dear."

"Stay where you are for the moment. You've been overdoing things."

"Do you think so? I don't know. But I tell you what. Through all the years after the bomb that well gradually filled with stinking water and then one morning I nearly drowned in it."

Alleyn listened to Peregrine's voice going on and on and Peregrine listened to it, too, as if it belonged to someone else. He realized with complete detachment that for a year and three months some rather terrible notion about Mr. Conducis had been stuffed away at the back of the mind that was Peregrine. It had been, and still was, undefined and unacknowledged but because he was so tired and ravaged by anxiety it had almost come out to declare itself. He was very relieved to hear himself telling this unusual policeman exactly what had happened that morning. When he had related everything down to the last detail he said: "And it was all to be kept quiet, except for Jeremy Jones, so now

I've broken faith, I suppose, and I couldn't care, by and large, less. I feel better," said Peregrine loudly.

"I must say you look several shades less green about the gills. You've half killed yourself over this production, haven't you?"

"Well, one does, you know."

"I'm sorry I dragged you up and down all those stairs. Where does that iron curtain work from? The Prompt side. Oh, yes, I see. Don't move. I'll do it. Dead against the union rules, I expect, but never mind."

The fire curtain inched its way down. Alleyn glanced at his watch. Any time now the party from the museum should arrive.

He said: "That was an extraordinary encounter, I must say. But out of it—presumably—has grown all this: the theatre—your play. And now: tonight."

"And now tonight. Oh God!"

"Would it be a good idea for you to go home and put your boots up for an hour or two?"

"No, thank you. I'm perfectly all right. Sorry to have behaved so oddly," Peregrine said, rubbing his head. "I simply have no notion why I bored you with my saga. You won't, I trust, tell Mr. Conducis."

"I shall," Alleyn said lightly, "preserve an absolute silence."

"I can't begin to explain what an odd man he is."

"I have met Mr. Conducis."

"Did you think him at all dotty? Or sinister? Or merely plutocratic?"

"I was quite unable to classify him."

"When I asked him where he found the treasure he said: at sea. Just that: at sea. It sounded rum."

"Not in the yacht *Kalliope* by any chance?"

"The yacht—*Kalliope*. Wait a moment—what is there about the yacht *Kalliope?*" Peregrine asked. He felt detached from his surroundings, garrulous and in an odd way rather comfortable but not quite sure that if he stood up he might not turn dizzy. "The yacht *Kalliope,*" he repeated.

"It was his private yacht and it was run down and split in two in a fog off Cape St. Vincent."

"*Now* I remember. Good Lord—"

A commotion of voices broke out in the entrance.

"I think," Alleyn said, "that the treasure has arrived. Will you stay here for a breather? Or come and receive it?"

"I'll come."

When they reached the foyer, Emily and Jeremy Jones and the assistant from the museum had arrived. The assistant carried a metal case.

Winter Meyer had run downstairs to meet them. They all went up to the office and the whole affair became rather formal and portentous. The assistant was introduced to everybody. He laid his metal case on Peregrine's desk, unlocked and opened it and stood back.

"Perhaps," he said, looking round the little group and settling on Peregrine, "we should have formal possession taken. If you will just examine the contents and accept them as being in good order."

"Jeremy's the expert," Peregrine said. "He must know every stitch and stain on the glove by this time, I should think."

"Indeed, yes," said the assistant warmly. "Mr. Jones, then—will you?"

Jeremy said: "I'd love to."

He removed the little desk from the case and laid it on the desk.

Peregrine caught Alleyn's eye. "Stained, as you see," he murmured, "with water. They say: sea-water."

Jeremy opened the desk. His delicate, nicotine-stained fingers folded back the covering tissues and exposed the little wrinkled glove and two scraps of documents.

"There you are," he said. "Shall I?"

"Please do."

With great delicacy he lifted them from their housing and laid them on the desk.

"And this," said the assistant pleasantly, "is when I bow myself out. Here is an official receipt, Mr. Meyer, if you will be good enough to sign it."

While Meyer was doing this Peregrine said to Alleyn: "Come and look."

Alleyn moved forward. He noticed as he did so that Peregrine stationed himself beside Miss Emily Dunne, that there was a glint of fanaticism in the devouring stare that Jeremy Jones bent upon the glove, that Winter Meyer expanded as if he had some proprietary rights over it and that Emily Dunne appeared to unfold a little at the approach of Peregrine. Alleyn then stooped over the notes and the glove and wished that he could have been alone. There could, at such a moment, be too much anticipation, too much pumping up of appropriate reactions. The emotion the relics were expected to arouse was delicate, chancy and tenuous. It was not much good thinking: "But the Hand of Glory moved warmly across that paper and four centuries ago a small boy's sick fist filled out that glove and somewhere between then and now a lady called M.E. wrote a tidy little memorandum for posterity." Alleyn found himself wishing very heartily that Peregrine's play would perform the miracle of awareness which would take the sense of death away from Shakespeare's note and young Hamnet's glove.

He looked up at Peregrine. "Thank you for letting me come so close," he said.

"You must see them safely stowed."

"If I may."

Winter Meyer became expansive and a little fussy. Jeremy, after a hesitant glance, laid the treasure on Peregrine's blotter. There was a discussion with the museum man about temperature and fire risks and then a procession of sorts formed up and they all went into the back of the circle, Jeremy carrying the blotter.

"On your right," Meyer said unnecessarily.

The panel in the circle wall was opened and so was the door of the safe. Jeremy drew out the black velvet easel-shaped unit, tenderly disposed the glove upon its sloping surface and flanked the glove with the two documents.

"I hope the nap of the velvet will hold them," he said. "I've tilted the surface like this to give a good view. Here goes."

He gently pushed the unit into the safe.

"How do the front doors work?" he asked.

"On your left," Meyer fussed. "On the inside surface of the wall. Shall I?"

"Please, Winty."

Meyer slipped his fingers between the safe and the circle wall. Concealed lighting appeared and with a very slight whisper the steel panels on the far side slid back.

"Now!" he said. "Isn't that quite something?"

"We can't *see* from here, though, Winty," Peregrine said. "Let's go out and see."

"I know," Jeremy agreed. "Look, would you all go out and tell me if it works or if the background ought to be more tilted? Sort of spread yourselves."

" 'Some to kill cankers in the moss-rose buds'?" Alleyn asked mildly. Jeremy looked at him in a startled manner and then grinned.

"The Superintendent," he said, "is making a nonsense of us. Emily, would you stay in the doorway, love, and be a liaison between me in the circle and the others outside?"

"Yes. All right."

The men filed out. Meyer crossed the circle foyer. Peregrine stood on the landing and the man from the museum a little below him. Alleyn strolled to the door, passed it and remained in the circle. He was conscious that none of these people except, of course, the museum man, was behaving in his or her customary manner but that each was screwed up to a degree of inward tension over which a stringent self-discipline was imposed. "And for them," he thought, "this sort of thing occurs quite often, it's a regular occupational hazard. They are seasoned troops and about to go into action."

"It should be more tilted, Jer," Peregrine's voice was saying. "And the things'll have to be higher up on the easel."

The museum assistant, down on the first flight, said something nasal and indistinguishable.

"What's he talking about?" Jeremy demanded.

"He says it doesn't show much from down below but he supposes that is unavoidable," said Emily.

"Wait a bit," Jeremy reached inside the safe. "More tilt," he said. "Oh, *blast,* it's collapsed."

"Can I help?" Emily asked.

"Not really. Tell them to stay where they are."

Alleyn walked over to the safe. Jeremy Jones was on his knees gingerly smoothing out the glove and the documents on the velvet surface. "I'll have to use *beastly* polythene and I hoped not," he said crossly. He laid a sheet of it over the treasures and fastened it with black velvet-covered drawing pins. Then he replaced the easel in the safe at an almost vertical angle. There was a general shout of approval from the observers.

"They say: much joy," Emily told him.

"Shall I shut the doors and all?"

"Yes."

"Twiddle the thing and all?"

"Winty says yes."

Jeremy shut the steel door and spun the lock.

"Now let's look."

He and Emily went out.

Alleyn came from the shadows, opened the wall panel and looked at the safe. It was well and truly locked. He shut the panel and turned to find that at a distance of about thirty feet down the passageway leading to the boxes, a boy stood with his hands in his pockets, watching him: a small boy, he thought at first, of about twelve, dressed in over-smart clothes.

"Hullo," Alleyn said. "Where did you spring from?"

"That's my problem," said the boy. *"Would* you mind."

Alleyn walked across to him. He was a pretty boy with big eyes and an impertinent, rather vicious mouth. *"Would* you mind!" he said again. "Who are you staring at? *If* it's not a rude question?"

The consonants and vowels were given full attention.

"At you," Alleyn said.

Peregrine's voice outside on the landing asked: "Where's Superintendent Alleyn?"

"Here!" Alleyn called. He turned to go.

"Aeoh, I *beg* pardon I'm sure," said Trevor Vere. "You must be the bogey from the Yard. What could I have been thinking of! Manners."

Alleyn went out to the front. He found that Marcus Knight and Destiny Meade had arrived and joined the company of viewers.

Above the sunken landing where the two flights of stairs came out was an illuminated peepshow. Yellow and black for the heraldic colours of a gentleman from Warwickshire, two scraps of faded writing and a small boy's glove.

Jeremy fetched his framed legend from the office and fixed it in position underneath.

"Exactly right," said the man from the museum. "I congratulate you, Mr. Jones. It couldn't be better displayed."

He put his receipt in his breast pocket and took his leave of them.

"It's perfect, Jer," said Peregrine.

Trevor Vere strolled across the landing and leaned gracefully on the balustrade.

"I reckon," he observed at large, "any old duff could crack that peter with his eyes shut. Kid stakes."

Peregrine said, "What are you doing here, Trevor? You're not called."

"I just looked in for my mail, Mr. Jay."

"Why aren't you at school?"

"I took one of my turns last night, Mr. Jay. They quite understand at school."

"You're not needed here. Much better go home and rest."

"Yes, Mr. Jay." A terribly winning smile illuminated Trevor's photogenic face. "I wanted to wish you and the play and everybody the most fabulous luck. Mummy joins me."

"Thank you. The time for that is later. Off you go."

Trevor, still smiling, drifted downstairs.

"Dear little mannikin," Jeremy said with venom.

Emily said: "Men and cameras, Winty, in the lane."

"The press, darling," Meyer said. "Shots of people looking at the glove. Destiny and Marcus are going to make a picture."

"It won't be all that easy to get a shot," Knight pointed out, "with the things skied up there."

"Should we have them down again?"

"I trust," Jeremy said suddenly, "that somebody knows how to work the safe. I've locked it, you might remember."

"Don't worry," said little Meyer, whose reaction to opening nights took the form of getting slightly above himself. "I know. It was all cooked up at the offices and Greenslade, of course, told me. Actually The Great Man himself suggested the type of code. It's all done on a *word*. You see? You think of a *word* of five letters—"

Down below the front doors had opened to admit a number of people and two cameras.

"—and each letter stands for a figure. Mr. Conducis said he thought easily the most appropriate word would be—"

"*Mr. Meyer.*"

Winter Meyer stopped short and swung around. Alleyn moved out on the landing.

"Tell me," he said. "How long has this safe been in position?"

"Some days. Three or four. Why?"

"Have you discussed the lock mechanism with your colleagues?"

"Well—I—well I only vaguely, you know, only vaguely."

"Don't you think that it might be quite a good idea if you kept your five-letter word to yourself?"

"Well I—well, we're all well "

"It really is the normal practice, you know."

"Yes—but we're different. I mean—we're all—"

"Just to persuade you," Alleyn said, and wrote on the back of an envelope. "Is the combination one of these?"

Meyer looked at the envelope.

"*Christ,*" he said.

Alleyn said, "If I were you I'd get a less obvious code word and a new combination and keep them strictly under your Elizabethan bonnet. I seriously advise you to do this." He took the envelope back, blacked out what he had written and put it in his breast pocket.

"You have visitors," he said, amiably.

He waited while the pictures were taken and was not at all surprised when Trevor Vere reappeared, chatted shyly to the pressman whom he had instinctively recognized as the authority and ended up gravely contemplating the glove with Destiny Meade's arm about him and his cheek against hers while lamps flashed and cameras clicked.

The picture, which was much the best taken that morning, appeared with the caption: *Child player, Trevor Vere, with Destiny Meade, and the Shakespeare glove. "It makes me feel kinda funny like I want to cry," says young Trevor.*

ii

Peregrine answered half-a-dozen extremely intelligent questions and for the rest of his life would never know in what words. He bowed and stood back. He saw himself doing it in the glass behind the bar: a tall, lank, terrified young man in tails. The doors were swung open and he heard the house rise with a strange composite whispering sound.

Mr. Conducis, who wore a number of orders, turned to him.

"I must wish you success," he said.

"Sir—I can't thank you—"

"Not at all. I must follow."

Mr. Conducis was to sit in the Royal box.

Peregrine made for the left-hand doors into the circle.

"Every possible good luck," a deep voice said.

He looked up and saw a grandee who turned out to be Superintendent Alleyn in a white tie with a lovely lady on his arm.

They had gone.

Peregrine heard the anthem through closed doors. He was the loneliest being on earth.

As the house settled he slipped into the circle and down to the box on the O.P. side. Jeremy was there.

"Here we go," he said.

"Here we go."

iii

Mr. Peregrine Jay successfully negotiates the tight-rope between Tudor-type schmaltz and unconvincing modernization. His dialogue has an honest sound and constantly surprises by its penetration. Sentimentality is nimbly avoided. The rancour of the insulted sensualist has never been more searchingly displayed since Sonnet CXXIX was written.

After all the gratuitous build-up and deeply suspect antics of the promotion boys I dreaded this exhibit at the newly tarted-up Dolphin. In the event it gave no offense. It pleased. It even stimulated. Who would have thought—

Marcus Knight performs the impossible. He makes a credible being of the Bard.

For once phenomenal advance-promotion has not foisted upon us an inferior product. This play may stand on its own merits.

Wot, no four letter words? No drag? No kinks? Right. But hold on, mate—

Peregrine Jay's sensitive, unfettered and almost clinical examination of Shakespeare is shattering in its dramatic intensity. Disturbing and delightful.

Without explicitly declaring itself, the play adds up to a searching attack upon British middle-class mores.

—Met in the foyer by Mr. Vassily Conducis and escorted to a box stunningly tricked out with lilies of the valley, she wore—

It will run.

iv

Six months later Peregrine put a letter down on the breakfast table and looked across at Jeremy.

"This is it," he said.

"What?"

"The decision. Conducis is going to sell out. To an American collector."

"My God!"

"Greenslade, as usual, breaks the news. The negotiations have reached a point where he thinks it appropriate to advise me there is every possibility that they will go through."

The unbecoming mauvish-pink that belongs to red hair and freckles suffused Jeremy's cheeks and mounted to his brow. "I tell you what," he said. "This can't happen. This can't be allowed to happen. This man's a monster."

"It appears that the B.M. and the V. and A. have shot their bolts. So has the British syndicate that was set up."

Jeremy raised the cry of the passionately committed artist against the rest of the world. "But *why!* He's lousy with money. He's got so much it must have stopped meaning anything. What'll he *do* with this lot? Look, suppose he gives it away? So what! Let him give William Shakespeare's handwriting and Hamnet Shakespeare's glove away. Let him give them to Stratford or the V. and A. Let him give them to the nation. Fine. He'll be made a bloody peer and good luck to him."

"Let him do this and let him do that. He'll do what he's worked out for himself."

"*You'll* have to see him, Perry. After all he's got a good thing out of you and The Dolphin. Capacity business for six months and booked out for weeks ahead. Small cast. Massive prestige. The lot."

"And a company of Kilkenny cats as far as good relations are concerned?"

"What do you mean?"

"You know jolly well. Destiny waltzing over to Harry Grove. Gertrude and Marco reacting like furies." Peregrine hesitated. "And so on," he said.

"You mean me lusting after Destiny and getting nowhere? Don't let it give you a moment's pause. I make no trouble among the giants, I assure you."

"I'm sorry, Jer."

"No, no. Forget it. Just you wade in to Conducis."

"I can't."

"For God's sake! Why?"

"Jer, I've told you. He gives me the jim-jams. I owe him nothing and I don't want to owe him anything. Still less do I want to go hat in hand asking for anything. *Anything.*"

"Why the hell not?"

"Because I might get it."

"Well, if he's not an old queer and you say you don't believe he is, what the hell? You feel like I do about the glove and the letter. You *say* you do. That they ought to be here among Shakespeare's people in his own city or country town—*here*. Well?"

"I can't go pleading again. I did try, remember, when he came to The Dolphin. I made a big song and dance and got slapped right down for my trouble. I won't do it again."

Jeremy now lost his temper.

"Then, by God, I will," he shouted.

"You won't get an interview."

"I'll stage a sit-down on his steps."

"Shall you carry a banner?"

"If necessary I'll carry a sledgehammer."

This was so startlingly in accord with Emily's half-joking prediction that Peregrine said loudly: "For the Lord's sake pipe down. That's a damn silly sort of thing to say and you know it."

They had both lost their tempers and shouted foolishly at each other. An all-day and very superior help was now in their employment and they had to quiet down when she came in. They walked about their refurnished and admirably decorated studio, smoking their pipes and not looking at each other. Peregrine began to feel remorseful. He himself was so far in love with Emily Dunne and had been given such moderate encouragement that he sympathized with Jeremy in his bondage and yet thought what a disaster it was for him to succumb to Destiny. They were, in common with most men of their age, rather owlish in their affairs of the heart and a good deal less sophisticated than their conversation seemed to suggest.

Presently Jeremy halted in his walk and said:

"Hi."

"Hi."

"Look, I have been a morsel precipitate."

Peregrine said: "Not at all, Jer."

"Yes. I don't really envisage a sit-down strike."

"No?"

"No." Jeremy looked fixedly at his friend. "On the whole," he said, and there was a curious undertone in his voice, "I believe it would be a superfluous exercise."

"You *do!* But—well really, I do *not* understand you."

"Think no more of it."

"Very well," said the astonished Peregrine. "I might as well mention that the things are to be removed from the safe on this day week and will be replaced by a blown-up photograph. Greenslade is sending two men from the office to take delivery."

"Where are they to go?"

"He says for the time being to safe storage at his offices. They'll probably be sold by private treaty but if they are put up at Sotheby's the result will be the same. The client's hell bent on getting them."

Jeremy burst out laughing.

"I think you must be mad," said Peregrine.

v

The night before the Shakespeare relics were to be removed from The Dolphin Theatre was warm and very still with a feeling of thunder in the air which, late in the evening, came to fulfillment. During the third act, at an uncannily appropriate moment a great clap and clatter broke out in the heavens and directly over the theatre.

"Going too far with the thunder-sheet up there," Meyer said to Peregrine, who was having a drink with him in the office.

There were several formidable outbreaks followed by the characteristic downpour. Peregrine went out to the circle foyer. Jobbins was at his post on the half-landing under the treasure.

Peregrine listened at the double doors into the circle and could just hear his own dialogue spoken by strange disembodied voices. He glanced at his watch. Half past ten. On time.

"Goodnight, Jobbins," he said and went downstairs. Cars, already waiting in Wharfingers Lane, glistened in the downpour. He could hear the sound of water hitting water on the ebony night tide. The stalls attendant stood by to open the doors. Peregrine slipped in to the back of the house. There was a man of Stratford, his head bent over his sonnet: sitting in the bow window of a house in Warwickshire. The scratch of his quill on parchment could be clearly heard as the curtain came down.

Seven curtains and they could easily have taken more. One or two women in the back row were crying. They blew their noses, got rid of their handkerchiefs and clapped.

Peregrine went out quickly. The rain stopped as he ran down the side alleyway to the stage-door. A light cue had been missed and he wanted a word with the stage-director.

When he had had it he stood where he was and listened absently to the familiar sounds of voices and movement in the dressing-rooms and front-of-house. Because of the treasure a systematic search of the theatre was conducted after each performance, and he had seen to it that this was thoroughly performed. He could hear the staff talking as they moved about the stalls and circle and spread their dust sheets. The assistant stage-manager organized the backstage procedure. When this was completed he and the stagecrew left. A trickle of backstage visitors came through and groped their alien way out. How incongruous they always seemed.

Destiny was entertaining in her dressing-room. He could hear Harry Grove's light impertinent laughter and the ejaculations of the guests.

Gertrude Bracey and, a little later, Marcus Knight appeared, each of them looking furious. Peregrine advised them to go through the front of the house and thus avoid the puddles and overflowing gutters in the stage-door alleyway.

They edged through the pass-door and down the stairs into the stalls. There seemed to be a kind of wary alliance between them. Peregrine thought they probably went into little indignation huddles over Destiny and Harry Grove.

Charles Random, quiet and detached as usual, left by the stage-door and then Emily came out.

"Hullo," she said, "are you benighted?"

"I'm waiting for you. Would you come and have supper at that new bistro near the top of Wharfingers Lane? 'The Younger Dolphin' it's artily called. It's got an extension license till twelve for its little tiny opening thing and it's asked me to look in. Do come, Emily."

"Thank you," she said. "I'd be proud."

"How lovely!" Peregrine exclaimed. "And it's stopped raining, I think. Wait a jiffy and I'll see."

He ran to the stage-door. Water still dripped from the gutters in the alleyway but the stars shone overhead. Destiny and her smart friends came out, making a great to-do. When she saw Peregrine she stopped them all and introduced him. They said things like: "Absolutely riveting" and "Loved your play" and "Heaven." They made off, warning each other about the puddles. Harry Grove said: "I'll go on, then, and fetch it, if you really want me to. See you later, angel."

"Don't be too long, now," Destiny called after him. Peregrine heard Harry's sports car start up.

Peregrine told the stage-door keeper he could shut up shop and go. He returned to Emily. As he walked towards the darkened set he was aware of a slight movement and thought it must have been the pass-door into front-of-house. As if somebody had just gone through and softly closed it. A backstage draught no doubt.

Emily was on the set. It was shut in by the fire curtain and lit only by a dim infiltration from a working lamp backstage: a dark, warm, still place.

"I always think it feels so strange," she said, "after we've left it to itself. As if it's got a life of its own. Always waiting for us."

"Another kind of reality?"

"Yes. A more impressive kind. You can almost imagine it breathes."

A soughing movement of air up in the grill gave momentary confirmation of Emily's fancy.

"Come on," Peregrine said. "It's a fine starry night and no distance at all to the top of Wharfingers Lane." He had taken her arm and was guiding her to the pass-door when they both heard a thud.

They stood still and asked each other: "What was that?"

"Front-of-house?" Emily said.

"Yes. Winty or someone, I suppose."

"Wouldn't they all have gone?"

"I'd have thought so."

"What *was* it? The noise?"

Peregrine said, "It sounded like a seat flapping up."

"Yes. It did sound like that."

"Wait a bit."

"Where are you going?" she said anxiously.

"Not far. Just to have a look."

"All right."

He opened the pass-door. The little twisting stair was in darkness but he had a torch in his pocket. Steps led down to the stalls box and up from where he stood to the box in the circle. He went down and then out into the stall's. They were in darkness. He flapped a seat down and let it spring back. That was the sound.

Peregrine called: "Hullo. Anyone there?" but his voice fell dead in an upholstered silence.

He flashed his torch across walls and shrouded seats. He walked up the new central aisle and into the foyer. It was deserted and dimly lit and the street doors were shut. Peregrine called up the stairs.

"Jobbins."

"Eh?" Jobbins's voice said. "That you, guv? Anything up?"

"I heard a seat flap. In front."

"*Did*jer, guv?"

Jobbins appeared on the stairs. He wore an extremely loud brown, black and white checked overcoat, a woollen cap and carpet slippers.

"Good Lord!" Peregrine ejaculated. "Are you going to the Dogs or Ally Pally or what? Where's your brown bowler?"

"You again, guv?" Jobbins wheezed. "I'd of 'eld back me quick change if I'd known. Pardon the dish-bill. Present from a toff this 'ere coat is and very welcome. Gets chilly," he said, descending, "between nah and the witching ar, when my relief comes in. What's this abaht a seat?"

Peregrine explained. To his astonishment Jobbins pushed the doors open, strode into the auditorium and uttered in a sort of hoarse bellow—

"Nah then. Out of it. Come on. You 'eard."

Silence.

Then Emily's voice sounding worried and lonely: "What goes on?" She had groped her way down into the house.

"It's all right," Peregrine shouted. "Won't be long." And to Jobbins: "What *does* go on. You sound as if you're used to this."

"*Which* I am," Jobbins sourly endorsed. "It's that perishing child-wonder, that's what it is. 'E done it before and 'e'll do it again *and* once too often."

"Done what?"

"'Angs abaht. 'Is mum plays the steel guitar in a caff see, acrost the river. She knocks off at eleven and 'er'earts-delight sallies forth to greet 'er at the top of the lane. And 'e fills in the gap, buggering rhand the theyater trying to make out 'e's a robber or a spectrum. 'E knows full well I can't leave me post so 'e 'ides isself in various dark regions. ''Ands up,' 'e yells. 'Stick 'em up,' 'e 'owls, and crawls under the seats making noises like 'e's bein' strangulated *which* 'e will be if ever I lay me 'ands on 'im. Innit marvellous?"

From somewhere backstage a single plangent sound rang out and faded. It was followed by an eldritch screech of laughter, a catcall and a loud slam.

"There 'e goes," said Jobbins and flung an ejaculation of startling obscenity into the auditorium.

"I'll get that little bastard," Peregrine said. He foolishly made a dash for the treble-locked doors into the portico.

"You'll never catch 'im, guv," Jobbins said. His voice had almost vanished with excessive vocal exercise. "'E'll be 'alf-way up the lane and going strong. His mum meets 'im at the top when she's sober."

"I'll have the hide off him tomorrow," Peregrine said. "All right, Jobbins. I'll see you're not pestered again. And anyway as far as the treasure is concerned this is your last watch."

"That's right, sir. Positively the last appearance in this epoch-making role."

"Goodnight again."

"Goodnight, guv. Best of British luck."

Peregrine went into the stalls. "Emily!" he called. "Where are you, my poor girl?"

"Here," Emily said, coming up the aisle.

"Did you see the little swine?"

"No I was in front. He came down from the circle. I could hear him on the steps."

Peregrine looked at his watch. Five past eleven. He took her arm.

"Let's forget him," he said, "and sling our hooks. We've wasted ages. They shut at midnight. Come on."

They slammed the stage-door behind them. The night was still fine and quite warm. They climbed Wharfingers Lane and went in under the illuminated sign of the new bistro: THE YOUNGER DOLPHIN.

It was crowded, noisy and extremely dark. The two waiters were dressed as fishermen in tight jeans, striped jumpers and jelly bag caps. A bas-relief of a dolphin wearing a mortar-board was lit from below.

As their eyes adjusted to the gloom they saw that Destiny and her three audience friends were established at a table under the dolphin and had the air of slumming. Destiny waggled her fingers at them and made faces to indicate that she couldn't imagine why she was there.

They ate grilled sole, drank lager, danced together on a pocket-handkerchief and greatly enjoyed themselves. Presently Destiny and her friends left. As they passed Emily and Peregrine, she said: "Darlings! we thought we would but oh, no, no." They went away talking loudly about what they would have to eat when they got to Destiny's flat in Chelsea. At ten to twelve Peregrine said: "Emily: why are you so stand-offish in the elder Dolphin and so come-toish in the younger one?"

"Partly because of your prestige and anyway I'm not all that oncoming, even here."

"Yes, you are. You are when we're dancing. Not at first but suddenly, about ten minutes ago."

"I'm having fun and I'm obliged to you for providing it."

"Do you at all fancy me?"

"Very much indeed."

"Don't say it brightly like that: it's insufferable."

"Sorry."

"And what do you mean, my prestige. Are you afraid people like Gertie, for example, will say you're having an advantageous carry-on with the author-producer?"

"Yes, I am."

"How bloody silly. *'They say. What say they? Let them say.'*"

"That aphorism was coined by a murdering cad."

"What of it? Emily: I find you more attractive than any of my former girls. Now, don't flush up and bridle. I know you're not my girl, in actual fact. Emily," Peregrine shouted against a screaming crescendo from the saxophonist, "Emily, listen to me. I believe I love you."

The little band had crashed to its climax and was silent. Peregrine's declaration rang out as a solo performance.

"After that," Emily said, "I almost think we had better ask for the bill, don't you?"

Peregrine was so put out that he did so. They left The Younger Dolphin assuring the anxious proprietor that they would certainly return.

Their plan had been to stroll over to Blackfriars, pick up Peregrine's and Jeremy's car and drive to Hampstead.

They walked out of The Younger Dolphin into a deluge.

Neither of them had a mackintosh or an umbrella. They huddled in the entrance and discussed the likelihood of raising a cab. Peregrine went back and telephoned a radio-taxi number to be told nothing would be available for at least twenty minutes. When he rejoined Emily the rain had eased off a little.

"I tell you what," he said. "I've got a gamp and a mac in the office. Let's run down the hill, beat Jobbins up and collect them. Look, it's almost stopped."

"Come on, then."

"Mind you don't slip."

Hand in hand they ran wildly and noisily down Wharfingers Lane. They reached the turning at the bottom, rounded the corner and pulled up outside The Dolphin. They laughed and were exhilarated.

"Listen!" Emily exclaimed. "Peregrine, listen. Somebody else is running in the rain."

"It's someone in the stage-door alley."

"So it is."

The other runner's footsteps rang out louder and louder on the wet cobblestones. He came out of the alley into the lane and his face was open-mouthed like a gargoyle.

He saw them and he flung himself upon Peregrine, pawed at his coat and jabbered into his face. It was the night watchman who relieved Jobbins.

"For Gawsake!" he said. "Oh, my Gawd, Mr. Jay, for Gawsake."

"What the devil's the matter? *What is it? What's happened!*"

"Murder," the man said, and his lips flabbered over the word. "That's what happened, Mr. Jay. Murder."

Chapter VI

Disaster

While he let them in at the stage-door the man—he was called Hawkins —said over and over again in a shrill whine that it wasn't his fault if he was late getting down to the theatre. Nobody, he said, could blame him. He turned queer, as was well known, at the sight of blood. It was as much as Peregrine could do to get the victim's name out of him. He had gone completely to pieces.

They went through the stage-door into the dark house, and up the aisle and so to the foyer. It was as if they had never left the theatre.

Peregrine said to Emily: "Wait here. By the box-office. Don't come any further."

"I'll come if you want me."

"Oh Gawd no. Oh Gawd no, Miss."

"Stay here, Emily. Or wait in front. Yes. Just wait in front." He opened the doors into the stalls and fastened them back. She went in. "Now, Hawkins," Peregrine said.

"You go, Mr. Jay. Up there. I don't 'ave to go. I can't do nothing. I'd vomit. Honest I would."

Peregrine ran up the graceful stairway towards the sunken landing: under the treasure where both flights emerged. It was dark up there but he had a *torch* and used it. The beam shot out and found an object.

There, on its back in a loud overcoat and slippers lay the shell of Jobbins. The woollen cap had not fallen from the skull but had been stove into it. Out of what had been a face, broken like a crust now, and glistening red, one eye stared at nothing.

Beside this outrage lay a bronze dolphin, grinning away for all it was worth through a wet, unspeakable mask.

Everything round Peregrine seemed to shift a little as if his vision had swiveled like a movie camera. He saw without comprehension a square of reflected light on the far wall and its source above the landing. He saw, down below him, the top of Hawkins's head. He moved to the balustrade, held on to it and with difficulty controlled an upsurge of nausea. He fetched a voice out of himself.

"Have you rung the police?"

"I better had, didn't I? I better report, didn't I?" Hawkins gabbled without moving.

"Stay where you are. I'll do it."

There was a general purposes telephone in the downstairs foyer outside the box-office. He ran down to it and, controlling his hand, dialed the so celebrated number. How instant and how cool the response.

"No possibility of survival, sir?"

"God, no. I told you—"

"Please leave everything as it is. You will be relieved in a few minutes. Which entrance is available? Thank you."

Peregrine hung up. "Hawkins," he said. "Go back to the stage-door and let the police in. Go on."

"Yes. O.K. Yes, Mr. Jay."

"Well, go *on,* damn you."

Was there an independent switch anywhere in the foyer for front-of-house lighting or was it all controlled from backstage? Surely not. He couldn't remember. Ridiculous. Emily was out there in the darkened stalls. He went in and found her standing just inside the doors.

"Emily?"

"Yes. All right. Here I am."

He felt her hands in his. "This is a bad thing," he said hurriedly. "It's a very bad thing, Emily."

"I heard what you said on the telephone."

"They'll be here almost at once."

"I see. Murder," Emily said, trying the word.

"We can't be sure."

They spoke aimlessly. Peregrine heard a high-pitched whine inside his own head and felt sickeningly cold. He wondered if he was going to faint and groped for Emily. They put their arms about each other. "We must behave," Peregrine said, "in whatever way one is expected to behave. You know? Calm? Collected? All the things people like us are meant not to be."

"That's right. Well, so we will."

He stooped his head to hers. "Can this be you?" he said.

A sound crept into their silence: a breathy intermittent sound with infinitesimal interruptions that seemed to have some sort of vocal quality. They told each other to listen.

With a thick premonition of what was to come, Peregrine put Emily away from him.

He switched on his *torch* and followed its beam down the centre aisle. He was under the overhang of the dress-circle but moved on until its rim was above his head. It was here, in the centre aisle of the stalls and below the circle balustrade, that his *torch*light came to rest on a small, breathing, faintly audible heap which, as he knelt beside it, revealed itself as an unconscious boy.

"Trevor," Peregrine said. *"Trevor."*

Emily behind him said, "Has he been killed? Is he dying?"

"I don't know. What should we do? Ring for the ambulance? Ring the Yard again? Which?"

"Don't move him. I'll ring Ambulance."

"Yes."

"Listen. Sirens."

"Police."

Emily said: "I'll ring, all the same," and was gone.

There seemed to be no interval of time between this moment and the occupation of The Dolphin by uniformed policemen with heavy necks and shoulders and quiet voices. Peregrine met the Sergeant.

"Are you in charge? There's something else since I telephoned. A boy. Hurt but alive. Will you look?"

The Sergeant looked. He said: "This might be serious. You haven't touched him, sir?"

"No. Emily—Miss Dunne who is with us—is ringing Ambulance."

"Can we have some light?"

Peregrine, remembering at last where they were, put the houselights on. More police were coming in at the stage-door. He rejoined the Sergeant. A constable was told to stay by the boy and report any change.

"I'll take a look at this body, if you please," the Sergeant said.

Emily was at the telephone in the foyer saying, "It's very urgent. It's really urgent. Please."

"If you don't mind, Miss," said the Sergeant and took the receiver. "Police here," he said and was authoritative. "They'll be round in five minutes," he said to Emily.

"Thank God."

"Now then, Mr. Jay." He'd got Peregrine's name as he came in.

"May I go back to the boy?" Emily asked. "In case he regains consciousness and is frightened? I know him."

"Good idea," said the Sergeant with a kind of routine heartiness. "You just stay there with the boy, Miss—?"

"Dunne."

"Miss Dunne. Members of the company here, would it be?"

"Yes," Peregrine said. "We were at the new restaurant in Wharfingers Lane and came back to shelter from the rain."

"Is that so? I see. Well, Miss Dunne, you just stay with the boy and tell the Ambulance all you know. Now, Mr. Jay."

A return to the sunken landing was a monstrous thing to contemplate. Peregrine said, "Yes, I'll show you. If you don't mind, I won't—" and reminded himself of Hawkins. "It's terrible," he said. "I'm sorry to baulk. This way."

"Up the stairs?" the Sergeant asked conversationally, as if he inquired his way to the Usual Offices. "Don't trouble to come up again, Mr. Jay. The less traffic, you know, the better we like it."

"Yes, of course. I forgot."

"If you'll just wait down here."

"Yes. Thank you."

The Sergeant was not long on the landing. Peregrine could not help looking up at him and saw that, like himself, the Sergeant did not go beyond the top step. He returned and went to the telephone. As he passed Peregrine he said: "Very nasty, sir, isn't it," in a preoccupied voice.

Peregrine couldn't hear much of what the Sergeant said into the telephone. "Some kind of caretaker—Jobbins—and a young lad—looks like it. Very good, sir. Yes. Yes. Very good." And then after a pause and in a mumble of words, one that came through very clearly:

"—robbery—"

Never in the wide world would Peregrine have believed it of himself that a shock, however acute, or a slight, however appalling, could have so bludgeoned his wits. There, there on the wall opposite the one in which the treasure was housed, shone the telltale square of reflected light and there above his head as he stood on the stairs had been the exposed casket—exposed and brightly lit when it should have been shut off and—

He gave a kind of stifled cry and started up the stairs.

"Just a moment, sir. If you please."

"The glove," Peregrine said. "The letters and the glove. I must see. I must look."

The Sergeant was beside him. A great hand closed without undue force round his upper arm.

"All right, sir. All right. But you can't go up there yet, you know. You join your young lady and the sick kiddy. And if you're referring to the contents of that glassed-in cabinet up there, I can tell you right away. It's been opened from the back and they seem to have gone."

Peregrine let out an incoherent cry and blundered into the stalls to tell Emily.

For him and for Emily the next half-hour was one of frustration, confusion and despair. They had to collect themselves and give statements to the Sergeant who entered them at an even pace in his notebook. Peregrine talked about hours and duties and who ought to be informed and Mr. Greenslade and Mr. Conducis, and he stared at the Sergeant's enormous forefinger, flattened across the image of a crown on a blue cover. Peregrine didn't know who Jobbins's next-of-kin might be. He said, as if that would help: "He was a nice chap. He was a bit of a character. A nice chap."

The theatre continually acquired more police: plainclothes, unhurried men, the most authoritative of whom was referred to by the Sergeant as the Div-Super and addressed as Mr. Gibson. Peregrine and Emily heard him taking a statement from Hawkins, who cried very much and said it wasn't a fair go.

The ambulance came. Peregrine and Emily stood by while Trevor, the whites of his eyes showing under his heavy lashes and his breathing very heavy, was gently examined. A doctor appeared: the divisional-surgeon, Peregrine heard someone say. Mr. Gibson asked him if there was any chance of a return to consciousness and he said something about Trevor being deeply concussed.

"He's got broken ribs and a broken right leg," he said, "and an unbroken bruise on his jaw. It's a wonder he's alive. We won't know about the extent of internal injuries until we've had a look-see," said the divisional-surgeon. "Get him into St. Terence's at once." He turned to Peregrine. "Would you know the next-of-kin?"

Peregrine was about to say: "Only too well," but checked himself. "Yes," he said, "his mother."

"Would you have the address?" asked Mr. Gibson. "And the telephone number."

"In the office. Upstairs. No, wait a moment. I've a cast list in my pocketbook. Here it is: Mrs. Blewitt."

"Perhaps you'd be so kind as to ring her, Mr. Jay. She ought to be told at once. What's the matter, Mr. Jay?"

"She meets him, usually. At the top of the lane. I—Oh God, poor Jobbins told me that. I wonder what she did when Trevor didn't turn up. You'd have thought she'd have come to the theatre."

"Can we get this boy away?" asked the divisional-surgeon crisply.

"O.K., Doc. You better go with them," Mr. Gibson said to the constable who had stayed by Trevor. "Keep your ears open. Anything. Whisper. Anything. Don't let some starched battleaxe push you about. We want to know what hit him. Don't leave him, now."

Mr. Gibson had a piece of chalk in his hand. He ran it round Trevor's little heap of a body, grinding it into the carpet. "O.K.," he said and Trevor was taken away.

The divisional-surgeon said he'd take a look-see at the body and went off with the Sergeant. Superintendent Gibson was about to accompany them when Peregrine and Emily, who had been in consultation, said: "Er—" and he turned back.

"Yes, Mr. Jay? Miss Dunne? Was there something?"

"It's just," Emily said, "—we wondered if you knew that Mr. Roderick Alleyn—I mean Superintendent Alleyn—supervised the installation of the things that were in the wall-safe. The things that have been stolen."

"Rory *Alleyn!*" the Superintendent ejaculated. "Is that so? Now, why was that, I wonder?"

Peregrine explained. "I think," he said finally, "that Mr. Vassily Conducis, who owns the things—"

"So I understand."

"—asked Mr. Alleyn to do it as a special favour. Mr. Alleyn was very much interested in the things."

"He would be. Well, thank you," said Mr. Gibson rather heavily. "And now, if you'd phone this Mrs. Blewitt. Lives in my Division, I see. Close to our headquarters. If she can't get transport to the hospital tell her, if you please, that we'll lay something on. No, wait on. Second thoughts. I'll send a policewoman round from the station if one's available. Less of a shock."

"Shouldn't we ring her up—just to warn her someone's coming?" Emily asked. "Should I offer to go?"

Mr. Gibson stared at her and said that he thought on the whole it would be better if Peregrine and Emily remained in the theatre a little longer, but, yes, they could telephone to Mrs. Blewitt after he himself had made one or two little calls. He padded off—not fast, not slow—towards the foyer. Peregrine and Emily talked disjointedly. After some minutes they heard sounds of new arrivals by the main entrance and of Superintendent Gibson greeting them.

"None of this is real," Emily said presently.

"Are you exhausted?"

"I don't think so."

"I ought to tell Greenslade," Peregrine ejaculated. "He ought to be told, good God!"

"And Mr. Conducis? After all, it's his affair."

"Greenslade can tackle that one. Emily, are you in a muddle like me? I can't get on top of this. Jobbins. That appalling kid. Shakespeare's note and the glove. All broken or destroyed or stolen. Isn't it beastly, all of it? What *are* human beings? What's the thing that makes monsters of us all?"

"It's out of our country. We'll have to play it by ear."

"No, but we *act* it. It's our raw material. Murder. Violence. Theft. Sexual greed. They're commonplace to us. We do our Stanislavsky over them. We search out motives and associate experiences. We try to think our way into Macbeth or Othello or a witch-hunt or an Inquisitor or a killer-doctor at Auschwitz and sometimes we think we've succeeded. But confront us with the thing itself! It's as if a tractor had rolled over us. *We're* nothing. Superintendent Gibson is there instead to put it all on a sensible, factual basis."

"Good luck to him," said Emily rather desperately.

"Good luck? You think? All right, if you say so."

"Perhaps I can now ring up Mrs. Blewitt."

"I'll come with you."

The foyer was brilliantly lit and there were voices and movement upstairs where Jobbins lay. Cameramen's lamps flashed and grotesquely reminded Peregrine of the opening night of his play. Superintendent Gibson's voice and that of the divisional-surgeon were clearly distinguishable. There was also a new rather comfortable voice. Downstairs, a constable stood in front of the main doors. Peregrine told him that Mr. Gibson had said they might use the telephone, and the constable replied pleasantly that it would be quite all right he was sure.

Peregrine watched Emily dial the number and wait with the receiver to her ear. How pale she was. Her hair was the kind that goes into a mist after it has been out in the rain and her wide mouth drooped at the corners like a child's. He could hear the buzzer ringing, on and on. Emily had just shaken her head at him when the telephone quacked angrily. She spoke for some time, evidently to no avail and at last hung up.

"A man," she said. "A landlord, I should think. He was livid. He says Mrs. Blewitt went to a party after her show and didn't meet Trevor tonight. He says she's 'flat out to it' and nothing would rouse her. So he hung up."

"The policewoman will have to cope. I'd better rouse Greenslade, I suppose. He lives at some godawful place in the stockbrokers' belt. Here goes."

Evidently Mr. and Mrs. Greenslade had a bedside telephone. She could be heard, querulous and half asleep, in the background. Mr. Greenslade said: "Shut up, darling. Very well, Jay, I'll come down. Does Alleyn know?"

"I—don't suppose so. I told the Superintendent that Alleyn would be concerned."

"He should have been told. Find out, will you? I'll come at once."

"*Find out,*" Peregrine angrily repeated to Emily. "I can't go telling the police who they ought to call in, blast it. How can I *find out* if Alleyn's been told?"

"Easily," Emily rejoined with a flicker of a smile. "Because, look."

The constable had opened the pass-door in the main entrance and now admitted Superintendent Alleyn in the nearest he ever got to a filthy temper.

ii

Alleyn had worked late and unfruitfully at the Yard in company with Inspector Fox. As he let himself into his own house he heard the telephone ring, swore loudly and got to it just as his wife, Troy, took the receiver off in their bedroom.

It was the Chief Commander who was his immediate senior at the Yard. Alleyn listened with disgust to his story. "—and so Fred Gibson thought that as you know Conducis and had a hand in the installation, he'd better call us. He just missed you at the Yard. All things considered I think you'd better take over, Rory. It's a big one. Murder. Double, if the boy dies. And robbery of these bloody, fabulous museum pieces."

"Very good," Alleyn said. "All right. Yes."

"Got your car out or garaged?"

"Thank you. Out."

It was nothing new to turn round in his tracks after one gruelling day and work through till the next. He took five minutes to have a word with Troy and a rapid shave and was back in the car and heading for the Borough within half an hour of leaving the Yard. The rain had lifted but the empty streets glistened under their lamps.

He could have kicked himself from Whitehall to Bankside. Why, why, why hadn't he put his foot down about the safe and its silly window and bloody futile combination lock? Why hadn't he said that he would on no account recommend it? He reminded himself that he had given sundry warnings but snapped back at himself that he should have gone further. He should have telephoned Conducis and advised him not to go on with the public display of the Shakespeare treasures. He should have insisted on that ass of a business manager scrapping his imbecile code word, penetrable in five minutes by a certified moron, and should have demanded a new combination. The fact that he had been given no authority to do so and had nevertheless urged precisely this action upon Mr. Winter Meyer made no difference. He should have thrown his weight about.

And now some poor damned commissionaire had been murdered. Also, quite probably, that unspeakably ghastly little boy who had cheeked him in The Dolphin. And Hamnet Shakespeare's glove and Hamnet's father's message had inspired these atrocities and were gone. Really, Alleyn thought, as he drew up by the portico of The Dolphin Theatre, he hadn't been so disgruntled since he took a trip to Cape Town with a homicidal pervert.

Then he entered the theatre and came face-to-face with Peregrine and Emily and saw how white and desperate they looked and recognized the odd vagueness that so often overcomes people who have been suddenly confronted with a crime of violence. He swallowed his chagrin and summoned up the professionalism that he had once sourily defined as an infinite capacity to notice less and less with more and more accuracy.

He said: "This is no good at all, is it? What are you two doing here?"

"We got here," Peregrine said, "just after."

"You look as if you'd better go and sit down somewhere. 'Morning, Fred," Alleyn said, meeting Superintendent Gibson at the foot of the stair. "What's first?" He looked towards the half-landing and without waiting for an answer walked upstairs followed by Gibson.

Among the group of men and cameras was an elderly thick-set man with a grizzled moustache and bright eyes.

"Hullo," Alleyn said. "You again."

"That's right, Mr. Alleyn," said Inspector Fox. "Just beat you to it. I was still at the Yard when they rang up so the C.C. said I might as well join in. Don't quite know why and I daresay Fred doesn't either."

"More the merrier," Mr. Gibson rejoined gloomily. "This looks like being an extra curly one."

"Well," Alleyn said, "I'd better see."

"We covered him," Gibson said. "With a dust sheet. It's about as bad as they come. Worst *I've* ever seen. Now!"

"Very nasty," Fox said. He nodded to one of the men. "O.K., Bailey."

Detective-Sergeant Bailey, a finger-print expert, uncovered the body of Jobbins.

It was lying on its back with the glittering mask and single eye appallingly exposed. The loudly checked coat was open and dragged back into what must be a knotted lump under the small of the back. Between the coat and the dirty white sweater there was a rather stylish yellow scarf. The letter H had been embroidered on it. It was blotted and smeared. The sweater itself was soaked in patches of red and had ridden up over the chest. There was something almost homely and normal in the look of a tartan shirt running in sharp folds under the belted trousers that were strained across the crotch by spread-eagled legs.

Alleyn looked, waited an appreciable time and then said: "Has he been photographed? Printed?"

"The lot," somebody said.

"I want to take some measurements. Then he can be moved. I see you've got a mortuary van outside. Get the men up." The Sergeant moved to the stairhead. "Just make sure those two young people are out of the way," Alleyn said.

He held out his hand and Fox gave him a steel springtape. They measured the distance from that frightful head to the three shallow steps that led up to the circle foyer and marked the position of the body. When Jobbins was gone and the divisional-surgeon after him, Alleyn looked at the bronze dolphin, glistening on the carpet.

"There's your weapon," Gibson said unnecessarily.

The pedestal had been knocked over and lay across the shallow steps at the left-hand corner. The dolphin, detached, lay below it on the landing, close to a dark blot on the crimson carpet where Jobbins's head had been. Its companion piece still made an elegant arc on the top of its own pedestal near the wall. They had stood to left and right at the head of the stairs in the circle foyer. Four steps below the landing lay a thick cup in a wet patch and below it another one and a small tin tray.

"His post," Alleyn said, "was on this sunken landing under—"

He looked up. There, still brilliantly lit, was the exposed casket, empty.

"That's correct," Gibson said. "He was supposed to stay there until he was relieved by this chap Hawkins at midnight."

"Where is this Hawkins?"

"Ah," Gibson said disgustedly, "sobbing his little heart out in the gent's cloaks. He's gone to pieces."

Fox said austerely, "He seems to have acted very foolishly from the start. Comes in late. Walks up here. Sees deceased and goes yelling out of the building."

"That's right," Gibson agreed. "And if he hadn't run into this Mr. Jay and his lady friend he might be running still and us none the wiser."

"So it was Jay who rang police?" Alleyn interjected.

"That's correct."

"What about their burglar alarm?"

"Off. The switch is back of the box-office."

"I know. They showed me. What then, Fred?"

"The Sergeant's sent in and gets support. I get the office and I come in and we set up a search. Thought our man might be hiding on the premises but not. Either got out of it before Hawkins arrived or slipped away while he was making an exhibition of himself. The pass-door in the main entrance was shut but not locked. It had *been* locked, they say, so it looked as if that was his way out."

"And the boy?"

"Yes. Well, now. The boy. Mr. Jay says the boy's a bit of a young limb. Got into the habit of hanging round after the show and acting the goat. Jobbins complained of him making spook noises and that. He was at it before Mr. Jay and Miss Dunne left the theatre to go out to supper. Mr. Jay tried to find him but it was dark and he let out a catcall or two and then they heard the stage-door slam and reckoned he'd gone. Not, as it turns out."

"Evidently. I'll see Hawkins now, Fred."

Hawkins was produced in the downstage foyer. He was a plain man made plainer by bloodshot eyes, a reddened nose and a loose mouth. He gazed lugubriously at Alleyn, spoke of shattered nerves and soon began to cry.

"Who's going to pitch into me next?" he asked. "I ought to be getting hospital attention, the shock I've had, and not subjected to treatment that'd bring about an inquiry if I made complaints. I ought to be home in bed getting looked after."

"So you shall be," Alleyn said. "We'll send you home in style when you've just told me quietly what happened."

"I have! I have told. I've told them others."

"All right. I know you're feeling rotten and it's a damn shame to keep you but you see you're the chap we're looking to for help."

"Don't you use that yarn to me. I know what the police mean when they talk about help. Next thing it'll be the Usual Bloody Warning."

"No, it won't. Look here—I'll say what I think happened and you jump on me if I'm wrong. All right?"

"How do I know if it's all right!"

"Nobody suspects you, you silly chap," Fox said. "How many more times!"

"Never mind," Alleyn soothed. "Now, listen, Hawkins. You come down to the theatre. When? About ten past twelve?"

Hawkins began a great outcry against buses and thunderstorms but was finally induced to say he heard the hour strike as he walked down the lane.

"And you came in by the stage-door. Who let you in?"

Nobody, it appeared. He had a key. He banged it shut and gave a whistle and shouted. Pretty loudly, Alleyn gathered, because Jobbins was always at his post on the half-landing and he wanted to let him know he'd arrived. He came in, locked the door and shot the bolt. He supposed Jobbins was fed up with him for being late. This account was produced piecemeal and with many lamentable excursions. Hawkins now became extremely agitated and said what followed had probably made a wreck of him for the rest of his life. Alleyn displayed sympathy and interest, however, and was flattering in his encouragement. Hawkins gazed upon him with watering eyes and said that what followed was something chronic. He had seen no light in the Property Room so had switched his *torch* on and gone out to front-of-house. As soon as he got there he noticed a dim light in the circle. And there—it had given him a turn—in the front row, looking down at him was Henry Jobbins in his flash new overcoat.

"You never told us this!" Gibson exclaimed.

"You never arst me."

Fox and Gibson swore quietly together.

"Go on," Alleyn said.

"I said: 'That you, Hen?' and he says 'Who d'yer think it is' and I said I was sorry I was late and should I make the tea and he said yes. So I went into the Props Room and made it."

"How long would that take?"

"It's an old electric jug. Bit slow."

"Yes? And then?"

"Oh Gawd. Oh Gawd."

"I know. But go on."

He had carried the two cups of tea through the house to the front foyer and up the stairs.

Here Hawkins broke down again in a big way but finally divulged that he had seen the body, dropped the tray, tried to claw his way out at the front, run by the side aisle through the stalls and pass-door, out of the stage-door and down the alley, where he ran into Peregrine and Emily. Alleyn got his address and sent him home.

"What a little beauty," Fred Gibson said.

"You tell me," Alleyn observed, "that you've searched the theatre. What kind of search, Fred?"

"How d'you mean?"

"Well—obviously, as you say, for the killer. But have they looked for the stuff?"

"Stuff?"

"For a glove, for instance and two scraps of writing?"

There was a very short silence and then Gibson said: "There hasn't really been time. We would, of course."

Fox said, "If he was surprised, you mean, and dropped them? Something of that nature?"

"It's a forlorn hope, no doubt," Alleyn said. He looked at Sergeant Bailey and the cameraman who was Sergeant Thompson—both of the Yard. "Have you tackled this dolphin?"

"Just going to when you arrived, sir," Thompson said.

"Take it as it lies before you touch it. It's in a ghastly state but there may be something. And the pedestal, of course. What's the thing weigh?"

He went to the top of the stairs, took the other dolphin from its base, balanced and hefted it. "A tidy lump," he said.

"Do you reckon it could have been used as a kind of club?" Fox asked.

"Only by a remarkably well-muscled-up specimen, Br'er Fox." Alleyn replaced the dolphin and looked at it. "Nice," he said. "He does that sort of thing beautifully." He turned to Gibson. "What about routine, Fred?"

"We're putting it round the divisions. Anybody seen in the precincts of The Dolphin or the Borough or further out. Might be bloody, might be nervous. That's the story. I'd be just as glad to get back, Rory. We've got a busy night in my Div as it happens. Bottle fight at the Cat and Crow with a punch-up and knives. Probable fatality and three break-and-enters. *And* a suspected arson. You're fully equipped, aren't you?"

"Yes. All right, Fred, cut away. I'll keep in touch."

"Goodnight, then. Thanks."

When Gibson had gone Alleyn said: "We'll see where the boy was and then have a word with Peregrine Jay and Miss Dunne. How many chaps have you got here?" he asked the Sergeant.

"Four at present, sir. One in the foyer, one at the stage-door, one with Hawkins and another just keeping an eye, like, on Mr. Jay and Miss Dunne."

"Right. Leave the stage-door man and get the others going on a thorough search. Start in the circle. Where was this boy?"

"In the stalls, sir. Centre aisle and just under the edge of the circle."

"Tell them not to touch the balustrade. Come on, Fox."

When Alleyn and Fox went into the now fully lit stalls the first thing they noticed was a rather touching group made by Peregrine and Emily. They sat in the back row by the aisle. Peregrine's head had inclined to Emily's shoulder and her arm was about his neck. He was fast asleep. Emily stared at Alleyn, who nodded. He and Fox walked down the aisle to the chalk outline of Trevor's body.

"And the doctor says a cut on the head, broken thigh and ribs, a bruise on the jaw and possible internal injuries?"

"That's correct," Fox agreed.

Alleyn looked at the back of the aisle seat above the trace of the boy's head. "See here, Fox."

"Yes. Stain all right. Still damp, isn't it?"

"I think so. Yes."

They both moved a step or two down the aisle and looked up at the circle. Three policemen and the Sergeant with Thompson and Bailey were engaged in a methodical search.

"Bailey," Alleyn said, raising his voice very slightly.

"Sir?"

"Have a look at the balustrade above us here. Look at the pile in the velvet. Use your *torch* if necessary."

There was a longish silence broken by Emily's saying quietly: "It's all right. Go to sleep again."

Bailey moved to one side and looked down into the stalls. "We got something here, Mr. Alleyn," he said. "Two sets of tracks with the pile dragged slantways in a long diagonal line outwards towards the edge. Some of it removed. Looks like fingernails. Trace of something that might be shoe-polish."

"All right. Deal with it, you and Thompson."

Fox said, "Well, well: a fall, eh?"

"Looks that way, doesn't it? A fall from the circle about twenty feet. I suppose nobody looked at the boy's fingernails. Who found him?"

Fox, with a jerk of his head, indicated Peregrine and Emily. "They'd been sent in here," he said, "to get them out of the way."

"We'll talk to them now, Fox."

Peregrine was awake. He and Emily sat hand-in-hand and looked more like displaced persons than anything else, an effect that was heightened by the blueness of Peregrine's jaws and the shadows under their eyes.

Alleyn said: "I'm sorry you've been kept so long. It's been a beastly business for both of you. Now, I'm going to ask Mr. Fox to read over what you have already said to Mr. Gibson and his Sergeant and you shall tell us if, on consideration, this is a fair statement."

Fox did this and they nodded and said yes: that was it.

"Good," Alleyn said. "Then there's only one other question. Did either of you happen to notice Trevor Vere's fingernails?"

They stared at him and both repeated in pallid voices: "His fingernails?"

"Yes. You found him and I think you, Miss Dunne, stayed with him until he was taken away."

Emily rubbed her knuckles in her eyes. "Oh dear," she said, "I *must* pull myself together. Yes. Yes, of course I did. I stayed with him."

"Perhaps you held his hand as one does with a sick child?"

"It's hard to think of Trevor as a child," Peregrine said. "He was born elderly. Sorry."

"But I did," Emily exclaimed. "You're right. I felt his pulse and then, you know, I just went on holding his hand."

"Looking at it?"

"Not specially. Not *glaring* at it. Although—"

"Yes?"

"Well, I remember I did sort of look at it. I moved it between my own hands and I remember noticing how grubby it was, which made it childish and—then—there was something—" She hesitated.

"Yes?"

"I thought he'd got rouge or carmine make-up under his nails and then I saw it wasn't grease. It was fluff."

"I tell you what," Alleyn said. "We'll put you up for the Police Medal, you excellent girl. Fox: get on to St. Terence's Hospital and tell them it's as much as their life is worth to dig out that boy's nails. Tell our chap there he can clean them himself and put the harvest in an envelope and get a witness to it. Throw your bulk about. Get the top battleaxe and give her fits. Fly."

Fox went off at a stately double.

"Now," Alleyn said. "You may go, both of you. Where do you live?"
They told him. Blackfriars and Hampstead, respectively.

"We could shake you down, Emily," Peregrine said. "Jeremy and I."

"I'd like to go home, please, Perry. Could you call a taxi?"

"I think we can send you," Alleyn said. "I shan't need a car yet awhile and there's a gaggle of them out there."

Peregrine said: "I ought to wait for Greenslade, Emily."

"Yes, of course you ought."

"Well," Alleyn said. "We'll bundle you off to Hampstead, Miss Dunne. Where's the Sergeant?"

"Here, sir," said the Sergeant unexpectedly. He had come in from the foyer.

"What's the matter?" Alleyn asked. "What've you got there?"

The Sergeant's enormous hands were clapped together in front of him and arched a little as if they enclosed something that fluttered and might escape.

"Seventh row of the stalls, sir," he said, "centre aisle. On the floor about six foot from where the boy lay. There was a black velvet kind of easel affair and a sheet of polythene laying near them."

He opened his palms like a book and disclosed a little wrinkled glove and two scraps of paper.

"Would they be what was wanted?" asked the Sergeant.

iii

"To me," said Mr. Greenslade with palpable self-restraint, "there can be only one explanation, my dear Alleyn. The boy, who is, as Jay informs us, an unpleasant and mischievous boy, banged the door to suggest he'd gone but actually stayed behind and, having by some means learned the number of the combination, robbed the safe of its contents. He was caught in the act by Jobbins, who must have seen him from his post on the half-landing. As Jobbins made for him the boy, possibly by accident, overturned the pedestal. Jobbins was felled by the dolphin and the boy, terrified, ran into the circle and down the centre aisle. In his panic he ran too fast, stumbled across the balustrade, clutched at the velvet top and fell into the stalls. As he fell he let go the easel with the glove and papers and they dropped, as he did, into the aisle."

Mr. Greenslade, looking, in his unshaven state, strangely unlike himself, spread his hands and threw himself back in Winter Meyer's office chair. Peregrine sat behind his own desk and Alleyn and Fox in two of the modish seats reserved for visitors. The time was twelve minutes past three and the air stale with the aftermath of managerial cigarettes and drinks.

"You say nothing," Mr. Greenslade observed. "You disagree?"

Alleyn said: "As an open-and-shut theory it has its attractions. It's tidy. It's simple. It means that we all sit back and hope for the boy to recover consciousness and health so that we can send him up to the Juvenile Court for manslaughter."

"What I can't quite see—" Peregrine began and then said, "Sorry."

"No. Go on," Alleyn said.

"I can't see why the boy, having got the documents and glove, should come out to the circle foyer where he'd be sure to be seen by Jobbins on the half-landing. Why didn't he go down through the circle by the box, stairs, and pass-door to the stage and let himself out by the stage-door?"

"He might have wanted to show off. He might have—I am persuaded," Mr. Greenslade said crossly, "that your objections can be met."

"There's another thing," Peregrine said, "and I should have thought of it before. At midnight, Jobbins had to make a routine report to police and fire-station. He'd do it from the open telephone in the downstairs foyer."

"Very well," said Mr. Greenslade. "That would give the boy his opportunity. What do you say, Alleyn?"

"As an investigating officer I'm supposed to say nothing," Alleyn said lightly. "But since the people at the bistro up the lane and the wretched Hawkins all put Jay out of the picture as a suspect and you yourself appear to have been some thirty miles away—"

"Well, I must say!"

"—there's no reason why I shouldn't ask you to consider under what circumstances the boy, still clutching his booty, could have fallen from the circle with his face towards the balustrade and as he fell have clawed at the velvet top, palms down in such a posture that he's left nail-tracks almost parallel with the balustrade but slanting towards the outside. There are also traces of boot polish that suggest one of his feet brushed back the pile at the same time. I cannot, myself, reconcile these traces with a nose-dive over the balustrade. I can relate them to a blow to the jaw, a fall across the balustrade, a lift, a sidelong drag and a drop. I also think Jay's objections are very well urged. There may be answers to them but at the moment I can't think of any. What's more, if the boy's the thief and killer, who unshot the bolts and unslipped the iron bar on the little pass-door in the main front entrance? Who left the key in the lock and banged the door shut from outside?"

"*Did* someone do this?"

"That's how things were when the police arrived."

"I—I didn't notice. I didn't notice that," Peregrine said, putting his hand to his eyes. "It was the shock, I suppose."

"I expect it was."

"Jobbins would have bolted the little door and dropped the bar when everyone had gone and I think he always hung the key in the corner beyond the box-office. No," Peregrine said slowly, "I can't see the boy doing that thing with the door. It doesn't add up."

"Not really, does it?" Alleyn said mildly.

"What action," Mr. Greenslade asked, "do you propose to take?"

"The usual routine, and a very tedious affair it's likely to prove. There may be useful prints on the pedestal or the dolphin itself but I'm inclined to think that the best we can hope for there is negative evidence. There may be prints on the safe but so far Sergeant Bailey has found none. The injuries to the boy's face are interesting."

"If he recovers consciousness," Peregrine said, "he'll tell the whole story."

"Not if he's responsible," Mr. Greenslade said obstinately.

"Concussion," Alleyn said, "can be extremely tricky. In the meantime, of course, we'll have to find out about all the members of the company and the front-of-house staff and so on."

"Find out?"

"Their movements for one thing. You may be able to help us here," Alleyn said to Peregrine. "It seems that apart from the boy, you and Miss Dunne were the last to leave the theatre. Unless, of course, somebody lay doggo until you'd gone. Which may well be the case. Can you tell us anything about how and when and by what door the other members of the cast went out?"

"I think I can," Peregrine said. He was now invested with the kind of haggard vivacity that follows emotional exhaustion: a febrile alertness such as he had often felt after some hideously protracted dress-rehearsal. He described the precautions taken at the close of every performance to insure that nobody was left on the premises. A thorough search of the house was made by backstage and front-of-house staff. He was certain it would have been quite impossible for anybody in the audience to hide anywhere in the theatre.

He related rapidly and accurately how the stage-crew left the theater in a bunch and how Gertrude Bracey and Marcus Knight went out together through the auditorium to escape the wet. They had been followed by Charles Random, who was alone and used the stage-door, and then by Emily, who stayed offstage with Peregrine.

"And then," Peregrine said, "Destiny Meade and Harry Grove came out with a clutch of friends. They were evidently going on to a party. They went down the stage-door alley and I heard Harry call out that he'd fetch something or another and Destiny tell him not to be too long. And it was then—I'd come back from having a look at the weather—it was then that I fancied—" He stopped.

"Yes?"

"I thought that the pass-door from stage to front-of-house moved. It was out of the tail of my eye, sort of. If I'm right, and I think I am, it must have been that wretched kid, I suppose."

"But you never saw him?"

"Never. No. Only heard him." And Peregrine described how he had gone out to the front and his subsequent interview with Jobbins. Alleyn took him over this again because, so he said, he wanted to make sure he'd got it right. "You shaped up to chasing the boy, did you? After you heard him catcall and slam the stage-door?"

"Yes. But Jobbins pointed out he'd be well on his way. So we said goodnight and—"

"Yes?"

"I've just remembered. Do you know what we said to each other? I said: 'This is your last watch,' and he said: 'That's right. Positively the last appearance.' Because the treasure was to be taken away today, you see. And after that Jobbins wouldn't have had to be glued to the half-landing."

Greenslade and Fox made slight appropriate noises. Alleyn waited for a moment and then said: "And so you said goodnight and you and Miss Dunne left? By the stage-door?"

"Yes."

"Was it locked? Before you left?"

"No. Wait a moment, though. I think the Yale lock was on but certainly not the bolts. Hawkins came in by the stage-door. He had a key. He's a responsible man from a good firm, though you wouldn't think it from his behaviour tonight. He let himself in and then shot the bolts."

"Yes," Alleyn said. "We got that much out of him. Nothing else you can tell us?"

Peregrine said: "Not as far as I can think. But all the same I've got a sort of notion that there's some damn thing I've forgotten. Some detail."

"To do with what? Any idea?"

"To do with—I don't know. The boy, I think."

"The boy?"

"I fancy I was thinking about a production of *The Cherry Orchard,* but—no, it's gone and I daresay it's of no consequence."

Mr. Greenslade said: "I know this is not your concern, Alleyn, but I hope you don't mind my raising the point with Jay. I should like to know what happens to the play. Does the season continue? I am unfamiliar with theatrical practice."

Peregrine said with some acidity: "Theatrical practice doesn't habitually cover the death by violence of one of its employees."

"Quite."

"But all the same," Peregrine said, "there *is* a certain attitude—"

"Quite. Yes. The—er—'the show,'" quoted Mr. Greenslade self-consciously, "'must go on.'"

"I *think* we *should go* on. The boy's understudy's all right. Tomorrow—no, today's Sunday, which gives us a chance to collect ourselves." Peregrine fetched up short and turned to Alleyn. "Unless," he said, "the police have any objection."

"It's a bit difficult to say at this juncture, you know, but we should be well out of The Dolphin by Monday night. Tomorrow night, in fact. You want an answer long before that, of course. I think I may suggest that you carry on as if for performance. If anything crops up to change the situation we shall let you know at once."

With an air of shocked discovery Peregrine said: "There's a great deal to be done. There's that—that—that—dreadful state of affairs on the half-landing."

"I'm afraid we shall have to take up a section of the carpet. My chaps will do that. Can you get it replaced in time?"

"I suppose so," Peregrine said, rubbing his hand across his face. "Yes. Yes, we can do something about it."

"We've removed the bronze dolphin."

Peregrine told himself that he mustn't think about that. He must keep in the right gear and, oh God, he mustn't be sick.

He muttered: "Have you? I suppose so. Yes."

Mr. Greenslade said, "If there's nothing more one can do—" and stood up. "One has to inform Mr. Conducis," he sighed and was evidently struck by a deadly thought. "The press!" he cried. "My God, the press!"

"The press," Alleyn rejoined, "is in full lurk outside the theatre. We have issued a statement to the effect that a night watchman at The Dolphin has met with a fatal accident but that there is no further indication at the moment of how this came about."

"*That* won't last long," Mr. Greenslade grunted as he struggled into his overcoat. He gave Alleyn his telephone numbers, gloomily told Peregrine he supposed they would be in touch and took his leave.

"I shan't keep you any longer," Alleyn said to Peregrine. "But I shall want to talk to all the members of the cast and staff during the day. I see there's a list of addresses and telephone numbers here. If none of them objects I shall ask them to come here to The Dolphin, rather than call on them severally. It will save time."

"Shall I tell them?"

"That's jolly helpful of you but I think it had better be official."

"Oh. Oh, yes. Of course."

"I expect you'll want to tell them what's happened and warn them they'll be needed, but we'll organize the actual interviews. Eleven o'clock this morning, perhaps."

"I must be with them," Peregrine said. "If you please."

"Yes, of course." Alleyn said. "Goodnight."

Peregrine thought absently that he had never seen a face so transformed by a far from excessive smile. Quite heartened by this phenomenon he held out his hand.

"Goodnight," he said. "There's one saving grace at least in all this horror."

"Yes?"

"Oh, *yes*," Peregrine said warmly and looked at a small glove and two scraps of writing that lay before Alleyn on Winter Meyer's desk. "You know," he said, "if they had been lost I really think I might have gone completely bonkers. You—you will take care of them?"

"Great care," Alleyn said.

When Peregrine had gone Alleyn sat motionless and silent for so long that Fox was moved to clear his throat.

Alleyn bent over the treasure. He took a jeweller's eyeglass out of his pocket. He inserted a long index finger in the glove and turned back the gauntlet. He examined the letters H.S. and then the seams of the glove and then the work on the back.

"What's up, Mr. Alleyn?" Fox asked. "Anything wrong?"

"Oh, my dear Br'er Fox, I'm afraid so. I'm afraid there's no saving grace in this catastrophe, after all, for Peregrine Jay."

Chapter VII

Sunday Morning

"I didn't knock you up when I came in," Peregrine said. "There seemed no point. It was getting light. I just thought I'd leave the note to wake me at seven. And oddly enough I did sleep. Heavily."

Jeremy stood with his back to Peregrine, looking out of the bedroom window. "Is that all?" he asked.

"All?"

"That happened?"

"I should have thought it was enough, my God!"

"I know," Jeremy said without turning. "I only meant: did you look at the glove?"

"I saw it, I told you: the Sergeant brought it to Alleyn with the two documents and afterwards Alleyn laid them out on Winty's desk."

"I wondered if it was damaged."

"I don't think so. I didn't *examine* it. I wouldn't have been let. Fingerprints and all that. It seems they really do fuss away about fingerprints."

"What'll they do with the things?"

"I don't know. Lock them up at the Yard, I imagine, until they've finished with them and then return them to Conducis."

"To Conducis. Yes."

"I must get up, Jer. I've got to ring Winty and the cast and the understudy and find out about the boy's condition. Look, you know the man who did the carpets. Could you ring him up at wherever he lives and tell him he simply must send men in, first thing tomorrow or if necessary tonight, to replace about two or three square yards of carpet on the half-landing. We'll pay overtime and time again and whatever."

"The half-landing?"

Peregrine said very rapidly in a high-pitched voice: "Yes. The carpet. On the half-landing. It's got Jobbins's blood and brains all over it. The carpet."

Jeremy turned gray and said: "I'm sorry. I'll do that thing," and walked out of the room.

When Peregrine had bathed and shaved he swallowed with loathing two raw eggs in Worcestershire sauce and addressed himself to the telephone. The time was now twenty past seven.

On the South Bank in the borough of Southwark, Superintendent Alleyn, having left Inspector Fox to arrange the day's business, drove over Blackfriars Bridge to St. Terence's Hospital and was conducted to a ward where Trevor Vere, screened from general view and deeply sighing, lay absorbed in the enigma of unconsciousness. At his bedside sat a uniformed constable with his helmet under his chair and a notebook in his hand. Alleyn was escorted by the ward sister and a house-surgeon.

"As you see, he's deeply concussed," said the house-surgeon. "He fell on his feet and drove his spine into the base of his head and probably crashed the back of a seat. As far as we can tell there's no profound injury internally. Right femur and two ribs broken. Extensive bruising. You may say he was bloody lucky. A twenty foot fall, I understand."

"The bruise on his jaw?"

"That's a bit of a puzzle. It doesn't look like the back or arm of a seat. It's got all the characteristics of a nice hook to the jaw. I wouldn't care to say definitely, of course. Sir James has seen him." (Sir James Curtis was the Home Office pathologist.) "*He* thinks it looks like a punch."

"Ah. Yes, so he said. It's no use my asking, of course, when the boy may recover consciousness? Or how much he will remember?"

"The usual thing is complete loss of memory for events occurring just before the accident."

"Alas."

"What? Oh, quite. You must find that sort of thing very frustrating."

"Very. I wonder if it would be possible to take the boy's height and length of his arms, would it?"

"He can't be disturbed."

"I know. But if he might be uncovered for a moment. It really is important."

The young house-surgeon thought for a moment and then nodded to the sister, who folded back the bed-clothes.

"I'm very much obliged to you," Alleyn said three minutes later and replaced the clothes.

"Well, if that's all—?"

"Yes. Thank you very much. I mustn't keep you. Thank you, Sister. I'll just have a word with the constable, here, before I go."

The constable had withdrawn to the far side of the bed.

"You're the chap who came here with the ambulance, aren't you?" Alleyn asked.

"Yes, sir."

"You should have been relieved. You heard about instructions from Mr. Fox concerning the boy's fingernails?"

"Yes, I did, sir, but only after he'd been cleaned up."

Alleyn swore in a whisper.

"But I'd happened to notice—" The constable—wooden-faced—produced from a pocket in his tunic a folded paper. "It was in the ambulance, sir. While they were putting a blanket over him. They were going to tuck his hands under and I noticed they were a bit dirty like a boy's often are but the fingernails had been manicured. Colourless varnish and all. And then I saw two were broken back and the others kind of choked up with red fluff and I cleaned them out with my penknife." He modestly proffered his little folded paper.

"What's your name?" Alleyn asked.

"Grantley, sir."

"Want to move out of the uniformed arm?"

"I'd like to."

"Yes. Well, come and see me if you apply for a transfer."

"Thank you, sir."

Trevor Vere sighed lengthily in his breathing. Alleyn looked at the not-quite-closed eyes, the long lashes and the full mouth that had smirked so unpleasingly at him that morning in The Dolphin. It was merely childish now. He touched the forehead which was cool and dampish.

"Where's his mother?" Alleyn asked.

"They say, on her way."

"She's difficult, I'm told. Don't leave the boy before you're relieved. If he speaks: get it."

"They say he's not likely to speak, sir."

"I know. I know."

A nurse approached with a covered object. "All right," Alleyn said, "I'm off."

He went to the Yard, treating himself to coffee and bacon and eggs on the way.

Fox, he was told, had come in. He arrived in Alleyn's office looking, as always, neat, reasonable, solid and extremely clean. He made a succinct report. Jobbins appeared to have no near relations, but the landlady at The Wharfinger's Friend had heard him mention a cousin who was lockkeeper near Marlow. The stage-crew and front-of-house people had been checked and were out of the picture. The routine search before locking up seemed to have been extremely thorough.

Bailey and Thompson had finished at the theatre, where nothing of much significance had emerged. The dressing-rooms had yielded little beyond a note from Harry Grove that Destiny Meade had carelessly tucked into her make-up box.

"Very frank affair," Mr. Fox said primly.

"Frank about what?"

"Sex."

"Oh. No joy for us?"

"Not in the way you mean, Mr. Alleyn."

"What about the boy's room?"

"He shares with Mr. Charles Random. A lot of horror comics including some of the American type that come within the meaning of the act respecting the importation of juvenile reading. One strip was about a well-developed female character called Slash who's really a vampire. She carves up Olympic athletes and leaves her mark on them—'Slash,' in blood. It seems the lad was quite struck with this. He's scrawled 'Slash' across the dressing-room looking-glass with red greasepaint and we found the same thing on the front-of-house lavatory mirrors and on the wall of one of the upstairs boxes. The one on the audience's left."

"Poor little swine."

"The landlady at The Wharfinger's Friend reckons he'll come to no good and blames the mother, who plays the steel guitar at that strip-tease joint behind Magpie Alley. Half the time she doesn't pick the kid up after his show and he gets round the place till all hours, Mrs. Jancy says."

"Mrs.—?"

"Jancy. The landlady. Nice woman. The Blewitts don't live far off as it happens. Somewhere behind Tabard Street at the back of the Borough."

"Anything more?"

"Well—dabs. Nothing very startling. Bailey's been able to pick up some nice, clean, control specimens from the dressing-rooms. The top of the pedestal's a mess of the public's prints, half dusted off by the cleaners."

"Nothing to the purpose?"

"Not really. And you would expect," Fox said with his customary air of placid good sense, "if the boy acted vindictively, to find his dabs—two palms together where he pushed the thing over. Nothing of the kind, however, nice shiny surface and all. The carpet's hopeless, of course. Our chaps have taken up the soiled area. Is anything the matter, Mr. Alleyn?"

"Nothing, Br'er Fox, except the word 'soiled.' "

"It's not too *strong*," Fox said, contemplating it with surprise.

"No. It's dreadfully moderate."

"Well," Fox said, after a moment's consideration, "you have a feeling for words, of course."

"Which gives me no excuse to talk like a pompous ass. Can you do some telephoning? And, by the way, have you had any breakfast? Don't tell me. The landlady of The Wharfinger's Friend stuffed you full of new-laid eggs."

"Mrs. Jancy was obliging enough to make the offer."

"In that case here is the cast and management list with telephone numbers. You take the first half and I'll do the rest. Ask them with all your celebrated tact to come to the theatre at eleven. I think we'll find that Peregrine Jay has already warned them."

But Peregrine had not warned Jeremy because it had not occurred to him that Alleyn would want to see him. When the telephone rang it was Jeremy who answered it; Peregrine saw his face bleach. He thought, "How extraordinary: I believe his pupils have contracted." And he felt within himself a cold sliding sensation which he refused to acknowledge.

Jeremy said: "Yes, of course. Yes," and put the receiver down. "It seems they want me to go to the theatre, too," he said.

"I don't know why. You weren't there last night."

"No. I was here. Working."

"Perhaps they want you to check that the glove's all right."

Jeremy made a slight movement, almost as if a nerve had been flicked. He pursed his lips and raised his sandy brows. "Perhaps," he said and returned to his work-table at the far end of the room.

Peregrine, with some difficulty, got Mrs. Blewitt on the telephone and was subjected to a tirade in which speculation and avid cupidity were but thinly disguised under a mask of sorrow. She suffered, unmistakably from a formidable hangover. He arranged for a meeting, told her what the hospital had told him and assured her that everything possible would be done for the boy.

"Will they catch whoever done it?"

"It may have been an accident, Mrs. Blewitt."

"If it was, the Management's responsible," she said, "and don't forget it."

They rang off.

Peregrine turned to Jeremy, who was bent over his table but did not seem to be working.

"Are you all right, Jer?"

"All right?"

"I thought you looked a bit poorly."

"There's nothing the matter with me. You look pretty sickly, yourself."

"I daresay I do."

Peregrine waited for a moment and then said: "When will you go to The Dolphin?"

"I'm commanded for eleven."

"I thought I'd go over early. Alleyn will use our office and the company can sit about the circle foyer or go to their dressing-rooms."

"They may be locked up," Jeremy said.

"Who—the actors?"

"The dressing-rooms, half-wit."

"I can't imagine why, but you may be right. Routine's what they talk about, isn't it?"

Jeremy did not answer. Peregrine saw him wipe his hand across his mouth and briefly close his eyes. Then he stooped over his work: he was shaping a piece of balsa wood with a mounted razor blade. His hand jerked and the blade slipped. Peregrine let out an involuntary ejaculation. Jeremy swung round on his stool and faced him. "Do me a profound kindness and get the hell out of it, will you, Perry?"

"All right. See you later."

Peregrine, perturbed and greatly puzzled, went out into the weekend emptiness of Blackfriars. An uncoordinated insistence of church bells jangled across the Sunday quietude.

He had nothing to do between now and eleven o'clock. "One might go into the church," he thought but the idea dropped blankly on a field of inertia. "I can't imagine why I feel like this," he thought. "I'm used to taking decisions, to keeping on top of a situation." But there were no decisions to take and the situation was out of his control. He couldn't think of Superintendent Alleyn in terms of a recalcitrant actor.

He thought: "I know what I'll do. I've got two hours. I'll walk, like a character in Fielding or in Dickens. I'll walk northwards, towards Hampstead and Emily. If I get blisters I'll take the bus or a tube and if there's not enough time left for that I'll take a taxi. And Emily and I will go down to The Dolphin together."

Having come to this decision his spirits lifted. He crossed Blackfriars

Bridge and made his way through Bloomsbury towards Marylebone and Maida Vale.

His thoughts were divided between Emily, The Dolphin and Jeremy Jones.

ii

Gertrude Bracey had a mannerism. She would glance pretty sharply at a companion but only for a second and would then, with a brusque turn of the head, look away. The effect was disconcerting and suggested not shiftiness so much as a profound distaste for her company. She smiled readily but with a derisive air and she had a sharp edge to her tongue. Alleyn, who never relied upon first impressions, supposed her to be vindictive.

He found support for this opinion in the demeanour of her associates. They sat round the office in The Dolphin on that Sunday afternoon, with all the conditioned ease of their training but with restless eyes and overtones of discretion in their beautifully controlled voices. This air of guardedness was most noticeable, because it was least disguised, in Destiny Meade. Sleek with fur, not so much dressed as gloved, she sat back in her chair and looked from time to time at Harry Grove who, on the few occasions when he caught her eye, smiled brilliantly in return. When Alleyn began to question Miss Bracey, Destiny Meade and Harry Grove exchanged one of these glances: on her part with brows raised significantly and on his with an appearance of amusement and anticipation.

Marcus Knight looked as if someone had affronted him and also as if he was afraid Miss Bracey was about to go too far in some unspecified direction.

Charles Random watched her with an expression of nervous distaste, and Emily Dunne with evident distress. Winter Meyer seemed to be ravaged by anxiety and inward speculation. He looked restlessly at Miss Bracey as if she had interrupted him in some desperate calculation. Peregrine, sitting by Emily, stared at his own clasped hands and occasionally at her. He listened carefully to Alleyn's questions and Miss Bracey's replies. Jeremy Jones, a little removed from the others, sat bolt upright in his chair and stared at Alleyn.

The characteristic that all these people had in common was that of extreme pallor, guessed at in the women and self-evident in the men.

Alleyn opened with a brief survey of the events in their succession, checked the order in which the members of the company had left the theatre, and was now engaged upon extracting confirmation of their movements from Gertrude Bracey, with the reactions among his hearers that have been indicated.

"Miss Bracey, I think you and Mr. Knight left the theatre together. Is that right?" They both agreed.

"And you left by the auditorium, not by the stage-door?"

"At Perry's suggestion," Marcus Knight said.

"To avoid the puddles," Miss Bracey explained.

"And you went out together through the front doors?"

"No," they said in unison, and she added: "Mr. Knight was calling on the Management."

She didn't actually sniff over this statement but contrived to suggest that there was something to be sneered at in the circumstance.

"I looked in at the office," Knight loftily said, "on a matter of business."

"This office? And to see Mr. Meyer?"

"Yes," Winter Meyer said. Knight inclined his head in stately acquiescence.

"So you passed Jobbins on your way upstairs?"

"I—ah—yes. He was on the half-landing under the treasure."

"I saw him up there," Miss Bracey said.

"How was he dressed?"

"As usual," they said, with evident surprise. "In uniform."

"Miss Bracey, how did you leave?"

"By the pass-door in the main entrance. I let myself out and slammed it shut after me."

"Locking it?"

"No."

"Are you sure?"

"Yes. As a matter of fact I—I re-opened it."

"Why?"

"I wanted to see the time," she said awkwardly, "by the clock in the foyer."

"Jobbins," Winter Meyer said, "barred and bolted this door after everyone had left."

"When would that be?"

"Not more than ten minutes later. Marco—Mr. Knight—and I had a drink and left together. Jobbins came after us and I heard him drop the bar across and shoot the bolts. My God!" Meyer suddenly exclaimed.

"Yes?"

"The alarm! The burglar alarm. He'd switch it on when he'd locked up. Why didn't it work?"

"Because somebody had switched it off."

"My God!"

"May we return to Jobbins? How was he dressed when you left?"

Meyer said with an air of patience under trying circumstances, "I didn't see him as we came down. He may have been in the men's lavatory. I called out goodnight and he answered from up above. We stood for a moment in the portico and that's when I heard him bolt the door."

"When you saw him, perhaps ten minutes later, Mr. Jay, he was wearing an overcoat and slippers?"

"Yes," said Peregrine.

"Yes. Thank you. How do you get home, Miss Bracey?"

She had a mini-car, she said, which she parked in the converted bombsite between the pub and the theatre.

"Were there other cars parked in this area belonging to the theatre people?"

"Naturally," she said. "Since I was the first to leave."

"You noticed and recognized them?"

"Oh, *really*, I *suppose* I noticed them. There were a number of strange cars still there but—yes, I saw—" she looked at Knight: her manner suggested a grudging alliance "—*your* car, Marcus."

"What make of car is Mr. Knight's?"

"I've no idea. What is it, dear?"

"A Jag, dear," said Knight.

"Any others?" Alleyn persisted.

"I *really* don't know. I think I noticed—yours, Charles," she said, glancing at Random. "Yes, I did, because it *is* rather conspicuous."

"What is it?"

"I've no idea."

"A very, very old, old, old souped-up Morris sports," said Random. "Painted scarlet."

"And Miss Meade's car?"

Destiny Meade opened her eyes very wide and raised her elegantly gloved and braceleted hands to her furs. She gently shook her head. The gesture suggested utter bewilderment. Before she could speak Gertrude Bracey gave her small, contemptuous laugh.

"Oh, *that*," she said. "Yes, indeed. Drawn up in glossy state under the portico. As for Royalty."

She did not look at Destiny.

Harry Grove said: "Destiny uses a hire-service, don't you, love?" His manner, gay and proprietary, had an immediate effect upon Marcus Knight and Gertrude Bracey, who both stared lividly at nothing.

"Any other cars, Miss Bracey? Mr. Meyer's?"

"I don't remember. I didn't go peering about for cars. I don't notice them."

"It was there," Winter Meyer said. "Parked at the back and rather in the dark."

"When you left, Mr. Meyer, were there any other cars apart from your own and Mr. Knight's?"

"I really don't know. There might have been. Do you remember, Marco?"

"No," he said, widely and vaguely. "No, I don't remember. As you say: it was dark."

"I had an idea I saw your mini, Gertie," Meyer said, "but I suppose I couldn't have. You'd gone by then, of course."

Gertrude Bracey darted a glance at Alleyn.

"I can't swear to all this sort of thing," she said angrily. "I—I didn't notice the cars and I had—" She stopped and made a sharp movement with her hands. "I had other things to think of," she said.

"I understand," Alleyn said, "that Miss Dunne and Mr. Jay didn't have cars at the theatre?"

"That's right," Emily said. "I haven't got one anyway."

"I left mine at home," said Peregrine.

"Where it remained?" Alleyn remarked. "Unless Mr. Jones took it out?"

"Which I didn't," Jeremy said. "I was at home, working, all the evening."

"Alone?"

"Entirely."

"As far as cars are concerned that leaves only Mr. Grove. Did you by any chance notice Mr. Grove's car in the bombsite, Miss Bracey?"

"Oh, yes!" she said loudly and threw him one of her brief, disfavoring looks. "I saw *that* one."

"What is it?"

"A Panther '55," she said instantly. "An open sports car."

"You know it quite well," Alleyn lightly observed.

"Know it? Oh, yes," Gertrude Bracey repeated with a sharp cackle. "I *know* it. Or you may say I used to."

"You don't think well, perhaps, of Mr. Grove's Panther?"

"There's nothing the matter with the *car*."

Harry Grove said: "Darling, what an infallible ear you have for inflection. Did you go to R.A.D.A.?"

Destiny Meade let out half a cascade of her celebrated laughter and then appeared to swallow the remainder. Meyer gave a repressed snort.

Marcus Knight said, "This is the wrong occasion, in my opinion, for mistimed comedy."

"Of course," Grove said warmly. "I do so agree. But when is the right occasion?"

"If I am to be publicly insulted—" Miss Bracey began on a high note. Peregrine cut in.

"Look," he said. "Shouldn't we all remember this is a police inquiry into something that may turn out to be murder?"

They gazed at him as if he'd committed a social enormity.

"Mr. Alleyn," Peregrine went on, "tells us he's decided to cover the first stages as a sort of company call: everybody who was in the theatre last night and left immediately, or not long before the event. That's right isn't it?" he asked Alleyn.

"Certainly," Alleyn agreed and reflected sourly that Peregrine, possibly with the best will in the world, had effectually choked what might have been a useful and revealing dust-up. He must make the best of it.

"This procedure," he said, "if satisfactorily conducted, should save a great deal of checking and counter-checking and reduce the amount of your time taken up by the police. The alternative is to ask you all to wait in the foyer while I see each of you separately."

There was a brief pause broken by Winter Meyer.

"Fair enough," Meyer said and there was a slight murmur of agreement from the company. "Don't let's start throwing temperaments right and left, chaps," Mr. Meyer added. "It's not the time for it."

Alleyn could have kicked him. "How right you are," he said. "Shall we press on? I'm sure you all see the point of this car business. It's essential that we make out when and in what order you left the theatre and whether any of you could have returned within the crucial time. Yes, Miss Meade?"

"I don't want to interrupt," Destiny Meade said. She caught her underlip between her teeth and gazed helplessly at Alleyn. "Only: I don't *quite* understand."

"Please go on."

"May I? Well, you see, it's just that everybody says Trevor, who is generally admitted to be rather a beastly little boy, stole the treasure and then killed poor Jobbins. I *do* admit he's got some rather awful ways with him and of course one never knows so one wonders why, that being the case, it matters where we all went or what sort of cars we went in."

Alleyn said carefully that so far no hard and fast conclusion could be drawn and that he hoped they would all welcome the opportunity of proving that they were away from the theatre during the crucial period, which was between eleven o'clock, when Peregrine and Emily left the theatre, and about five past twelve, when Hawkins came running down the stage-door alleyway and told them of his discovery.

"So far," Alleyn said, "we've only got as far as learning that when Miss Bracey left the theatre the rest of you were still inside it."

"Not I," Jeremy said. "I've told you, I think, that I was at home."

"So you have," Alleyn agreed. "It would help if you could substantiate the statement. Did anyone ring you up, for instance?"

"If they did, I don't remember."

"I see," said Alleyn.

He plodded back through the order of departure until it was established beyond question that Gertrude and Marcus had been followed by Charles Random, who had driven to a pub on the South Bank where he was living for the duration of the play. He had been given his usual late supper. He was followed by Destiny Meade and her friends, all of whom left by the stage-door and spent about an hour at The Younger Dolphin and then drove to her flat in Cheyne Walk where they were joined, she said, by dozens of vague chums, and by Harry Grove, who left the theatre at the same time as they did, fetched his guitar from his own flat in Canonbury, and then joined them in Chelsea. It appeared that Harry Grove was celebrated for a song sequence in which, Destiny said, obviously quoting someone else, he sent the sacred cows up so high that they remained in orbit forevermore.

"Quite a loss to the nightclubs," Marcus Knight said to nobody in particular. "One wonders why the legitimate theatre should still attract."

"I assure you, Marco dear," Grove rejoined, "only the Lord Chamberlain stands between me and untold affluence."

"Or you might call it dirty-pay," said Knight. It was Miss Bracey's turn to laugh very musically.

"Did any of you," Alleyn went on, "at any time after the fall of curtain see or speak to Trevor Vere?"

"I did, of course," Charles Random said. He had an impatient, rather injured manner which it would have been going too far to call feminine. "He dresses with me. And without wanting to appear utterly brutal I must say it would take nothing less than a twenty foot drop into the stalls to stop him talking."

"Does he write on the looking-glass?"

Random looked surprised. "No," he said. "Write what? Graffiti?"

"Not precisely. The word 'Slash.' In red greasepaint."

"He's always shrieking 'Slash.' Making a great mouthful of it. Something to do with his horror comics, one imagines."

"Does he ever talk about the treasure?"

"Well, yes," Random said uneasily. "He flaunts away about how—well, about how any fool could pinch it and—and: no, it's of no importance."

"Suppose we just hear about it?"

"He was simply putting on his act but he did say anyone with any sense could guess the combination of the lock."

"Intimating that he had, in fact, guessed it?"

"Well—actually—yes."

"And did he divulge what it was?"

Random was of a sanguine complexion. He now lost something of his colour. "He did not," Random said, "and if he had, I should have paid no attention. I don't believe for a moment he knew the combination."

"And *you* ought to know, dear, oughtn't you?" Destiny said with the gracious condescension of stardom to bit-part competence. "Always doing those ghastly puzzles in your intellectual papers. *Right* up your alleyway."

This observation brought about its own reaction of discomfort and silence.

Alleyn said to Winter Meyer, "I remember I suggested that you would be well advised to make the five-letter key group rather less predictable. Was it in fact changed?"

Winter Meyer raised his eyebrows, wagged his head and his hands and said: "I was always going to. And then when we knew they were to go—one of those things." He covered his face for a moment. "One of those things," he repeated and everybody looked deeply uncomfortable.

Alleyn said, "On that morning, besides yourself and the boy, there were present, I think, everybody who is here now except Miss Bracey, Mr. Random and Mr. Grove. Is that right? Miss Bracey?"

"Oh, yes," she said with predictable acidity. "It was a photograph call, I believe. I was *not* required."

"It was just for two pictures, dear," little Meyer said. "Destiny and Marco with the glove. You know?"

"Oh, quite. Quite."

"And the kid turned up so they used him."

"I seem to remember," Harry Grove observed, "that Trevor was quoted in the daily journals as saying that the glove made him feel kinda funny like he wanted to cry."

"Am I wrong," Marcus Knight suddenly demanded of no one in particular, "in believing that this boy is in Critical Condition and May Die? Mr.—ah—Superintendent—ah—Alleyn?"

"He is still on the danger list," Alleyn said.

"Thank you. Has anybody else got something funny to say about the boy?" Knight demanded. "Or has the fount of comedy dried at its source?"

"If," Grove rejoined, without rancour, "you mean me, it's dry as a bone. No more jokes."

Marcus Knight folded his arms.

Alleyn said, "Miss Meade, Miss Dunne, Mr. Knight, Mr. Jay and Mr. Jones—and the boy of course—were all present when the matter of the lock was discussed. Not for the first time, I understand. The safe had been installed for some days and the locking system had been widely canvassed among you. You had heard from Mr. Meyer that it carried a five-number combination and that this was based on a five-letter key word and a very commonplace code. Mr. Meyer also said, before I stopped him, that an obvious key word had been suggested by Mr. Conducis. Had any of you already speculated upon what this word might be? Or discussed the matter?"

There was a long silence.

Destiny Meade said plaintively: "Naturally we *discussed* it. The men seemed to know what it was all about. The alphabet and numbers and not enough numbers for all the letters or something. And anyway it wasn't as if any of us were going to *do* anything, was it? But everyone *thought—*"

"What everyone thought—" Marcus Knight began, but she looked coldly upon him and said: "Please don't butt in, Marco. You've got such a way of butting in. Do you mind?"

"My *God!*" he said with all the repose of an unexploded land mine.

"Everyone thought," Destiny continued, gazing at Alleyn, "that this obvious five-letter *word* would be 'glove.' But as far as *I* could see that didn't get one any nearer to a five-figure *number*."

Harry Grove burst out laughing. "Darling!" he said. "I adore you better than life itself." He picked up her gloved hand and kissed it, peeled back the gauntlet, kissed the inside of her wrist and then remarked to the company in general that he wouldn't exchange her for a wilderness of monkeys. Gertrude Bracey violently re-crossed her legs. Marcus Knight rose, turned his face to the wall and with frightful disengagement made as if to examine a framed drawing of The Dolphin in the days of Adolphus Ruby. A pulse beat rapidly under his empurpled cheek.

"Very well," Alleyn said. "You all thought that 'glove' was a likely word and so indeed it was. Did anyone arrive at the code and produce the combination?"

"Dilly, dilly, dilly, come and be killed," cried Harry.

"Not at all," Alleyn rejoined. "Unless (the security aspect of this affair being evidently laughable) you formed yourselves into a syndicate for robbery. If anyone did arrive at the combination it seems highly unlikely that he or she kept it to himself. Yes, Mr. Random?"

Charles Random had made an indeterminate sound. He looked up quickly at Alleyn, hesitated and then said rapidly, "As a matter of fact, I did. I've always been mildly interested in codes and I heard everybody muttering away about the lock on the safe and how the word might be 'glove.' I have to do a lot of waiting about in my dressing-room and thought I'd try to work it out. I thought it might be one of the sorts where you write down numerals from 1 to 0 in three rows one under another and put in succession under each row the letters of the alphabet, adding an extra A B C D to make up the last line. Then you can read the numbers off from the letters."

"Quite so. And you got—? From the word 'glove'?"

"Seven-two-five-two-five, or, if the alphabet was written from right to left, four-nine-six-nine-six."

"And if the alphabet ran from right to left and then, at K, from left to right and finally, at U, from right to left again?"

"Four-two-five-nine-six, which seemed to me more likely as there are no repeated figures."

"Fancy you *remembering* them like that!" Destiny ejaculated, and appealed to the company. "I mean isn't it? I can't so much as remember anyone's telephone number—scarcely even my own."

Winter Meyer moved his hands, palms up, and looked at Alleyn. "But, of course," Random said, "there are any number of variants in this type of code. I might have been *all* wrong."

"Tell me," Alleyn said, "are you and the boy on in the same scenes? I seem to remember that you are."

"Yes," Peregrine and Random said together, and Random added: "I didn't leave any notes about that Trevor could have read. He tried to pump me. I thought it would be extremely unwise to tell him."

"Did you, in fact, tell anybody of your solutions?"

"No," Random said, looking straight in front of him. "I discussed the code with nobody." He looked at his fellow players. "You can all bear me out in this," he said.

"Well, I must say!" Gertrude Bracey remarked, and laughed.

"A wise decision," Alleyn murmured, and Random glanced at him. "I wonder," he said, fretfully.

"I think there's something else you have to tell me, isn't there?"

In the interval that followed Destiny said with an air of discovery: "No, but you must all admit it's terribly *clever* of Charles."

Random said, "Perhaps it's unnecessary to point out that if I had tried to steal the treasure I would certainly not have told you what I *have* told you; still less what I'm going to tell you."

Another pause was broken by Inspector Fox, who sat by the door and had contrived to be forgotten. "Fair enough," he said.

"Thank you," said Random, startled.

"What *are* you going to tell us, Mr. Random?"

"That, whatever the combination may be, Trevor didn't know it. He's not really as sharp as he sounds. It was all bluff. When he kept on about how easy it was I got irritated—I find him extremely tiresome, that boy—and I said I'd give him a pound if he could tell me and he did a sort of 'Yah-yah-yah, I'm not going to be caught like that' act." Random made a slight, rather finicky movement of his shoulders and his voice became petulant. "He'd been helping himself to my make-up and I was livid with him. It blew up into quite a thing and—well, it doesn't matter but in the end I shook him and he blurted out a number—five-five-five-three-one. Then we were called for the opening."

"When was this?"

"Before last night's show." Random turned to Miss Bracey. "Gertie dresses next door to me," he said. "I daresay she heard the ongoings."

"I certainly *did*. *Not* very helpful when one is making one's preparation which I, at any rate, like to do."

"Method in her madness. Or is it," Harry Grove asked, "madness in her Method?"

"That will do, Harry."

"Dear Perry. Of course."

"You told us a moment ago, Mr. Random," Alleyn said, "that the boy didn't reveal the number."

"Nor did he. Not the correct number," Random said quickly.

Destiny Meade said: "Yes, but why were you so sure it was the wrong number?"

"It's the Dolphin telephone number, darling," Grove said. "Five-five-five-three-one. Remember?"

"Is it? Oh, yes. Of course it is."

"First thing to enter his head in his fright, I suppose," Random said.

"You really frightened him?" asked Alleyn.

"Yes, I did. Little horror. He'd have told me if he'd known." Random added loudly: "He didn't know the combination and he couldn't have opened the lock."

"He was forever badgering me to drop a hint," Winter Meyer said. "Needless to say, I didn't."

"Precisely," said Random.

Peregrine said: "I don't see how you can be so sure, Charlie. He might simply have been holding out on you."

"If he knew the combination and meant to commit the theft," Knight said, flinging himself down into his chair again, "he certainly wouldn't tell you what it was."

There was a general murmur of fervent agreement. "And after all," Harry Grove pointed out, "you couldn't have been absolutely sure, could you, Charles, that you hit on the right number yourself or even the right type of code? Or could you?" He grinned at Random. "Did you *try?*" he asked. "Did you *prove* it, Charles? Did you have a little twiddle? *Before* the treasure went in?"

For a moment Random looked as if he would like to hit him but he tucked in his lips, gave himself time and then spoke exclusively to Alleyn.

He said: "I do *not* believe that Trevor opened the safe and consequently I'm absolutely certain he didn't kill Henry Jobbins." He settled his shoulders and looked defiant.

Winter Meyer said: "I suppose you realize the implication of what you're saying, Charles?"

"I think so."

"Then I must say you've an odd notion of loyalty to your colleagues."

"It doesn't arise."

"*Doesn't* it!" Meyer cried and looked restively at Alleyn.

Alleyn made no answer to this. He sat with his long hands linked together on Peregrine's desk.

The superb voice of Marcus Knight broke the silence.

"I may be very dense," he said, collecting his audience, "but I cannot see where this pronouncement of Charles's leads us. If, as the investigation seems to establish, the boy never left the theatre and if the theatre was locked up and only Hawkins had the key to the stage-door: then how the hell did a third person get in?"

"Might he have been someone in the audience who stayed behind?" Destiny asked, brightly. "You know? Lurked?"

Peregrine said, "The ushers, the commissionaire, Jobbins and the A.S.M. did a thorough search front and back after every performance."

"Well, then, perhaps *Hawkins* is the murderer," she said, exactly as if a mystery-story were under discussion. "Has anyone thought of *that?*" She appealed to Alleyn, who thought it better to disregard her.

"Well, *I* don't know," Destiny rambled on. "Who *could* it be if it's not Trevor? That's what we've got to ask ourselves. Perhaps, though I'm sure I can't think why, and say what you like motive *is* important—" She broke off and made an enchanting little grimace at Harry Grove. "Now don't *you* laugh," she said. "But for all that just *suppose*. Just suppose—it was Mr. Conducis."

"My dear girl—"

"Destiny, honestly."

"Oh for God's sake, darling—"

"I know it sounds silly," Destiny said, "but nobody seems to have any other suggestion and after all he was *there*."

iii

The silence that followed Destiny's remark was so profound that Alleyn heard Fox's pencil skate over a page in his notebook.

He said, "You mean, Miss Meade, that Mr. Conducis was in the audience? Not backstage?"

"That's right. In front. In the upstairs O.P. box. I noticed him when I made my first entrance. I mentioned it to you, Charles, didn't I, when you were holding me up. 'There's God,' I said, 'in the O.P. box.'"

"Mr. Meyer, did you know Mr. Conducis was in front?"

"No, I didn't. But he's got the O.P. box forever," Meyer said. "It's his whenever he likes to use it. He lends it to friends and for all I know occasionally slips in himself. He doesn't let us know if he's coming. He doesn't like a fuss."

"Nobody saw him come or go?"

"Not that I know."

Gertrude Bracey said loudly: "I thought our mysterious Mr. W.H. was supposed to be particularly favoured by Our Patron. Quite a Shakespearean situation or so one hears. Perhaps he can shed light."

"My dear Gertie," Harry Grove said cheerfully, "you really should try to keep a splenetic fancy within reasonable bounds. Miss Bracey," he said, turning to Alleyn, "refers, I *think,* to the undoubted fact that Mr. Conducis very kindly recommended me to the Management. I did him a slight service once upon a time and he is obliging enough to *be* obliged. I had no idea he was in front, Gertie dear, until I heard you hissing away about it as you lay on the King Dolphin's bosom at the end of Act I."

"Mr. Knight," Alleyn asked, "did you know Mr. Conducis was there?"

Knight looked straight in front of him and said with exaggerated clarity as if voicing an affront, "It became evident."

Destiny Meade, also looking neither to left nor right and speaking clearly, remarked: "The loss said about *that* the better."

"Undoubtedly," Knight savagely agreed.

She laughed.

Winter Meyer said: "Yes, but—" and stopped short. "It's nothing," he said. "As you were."

"But in any case it can be of no conceivable significance," Jeremy Jones said impatiently. He had been silent for so long that his intervention caused a minor stir.

Alleyn rose to his considerable height and moved out into the room. "I think," he said, "that we've gone as far as we can, satisfactorily, in a joint discussion. I'm going to ask Inspector Fox to read over his notes. If there is anything any of you wishes to amend will you say so?"

Fox read his notes in a cosy voice and nobody objected to a word of them. When he had finished Alleyn said to Peregrine: "I daresay you'll want to make your own arrangements with the company."

"May I?" said Peregrine. "Thank you."

Alleyn and Fox withdrew to the distant end of the office and conferred together. The company, far from concerning themselves with the proximity of the police, orientated as one man upon Peregrine, who explained that Trevor Vere's understudy would carry on and that his scenes would be rehearsed in the morning. "Everybody concerned, please, at ten o'clock," Peregrine said. "And look: about the press. We've got to be very careful with this one, haven't we, Winty?"

Winter Meyer joined him, assuming at once his occupational manner of knowing how to be tactful with actors. They didn't, any of them, did they, he asked, want the wrong kind of stories to get into the press. There was no doubt they would be badgered. He himself had been rung up repeatedly. The line was regret and no comment. "You'd all gone,"

Meyer said. "You weren't there. You've heard about it, of course, but you've no ideas." Here everybody looked at Destiny.

He continued in this vein and it became evident that this able, essentially kind little man was at considerable pains to stop short of the suggestion that, properly controlled, the disaster, from a box-office angle, might turn out to be no such thing. "But we don't *need* it," he said unguardedly and embarrassed himself and most of his hearers. Harry Grove, however, gave one of his little chuckles.

"Well, that's all perfectly splendid," he said. "Everybody happy. We've no need of bloody murder to boost our door sales and wee Trevor can recover his wits as slowly as he likes. Grand." He placed his arm about Destiny Meade, who gave him a mock-reproachful look, tapped his hand and freed herself.

"Darling, *do* be good," she said. She moved away from him, caught Gertrude Bracey's baleful eye and said with extreme graciousness: "Isn't he *too* frightful?" Miss Bracey was speechless.

"I can see I've fallen under the imperial displeasure," Grove murmured in a too-audible aside. "The Great King Dolphin looks as if it's going to combust."

Knight walked across the office and confronted Grove, who was some three inches shorter than himself. Alleyn was uncannily reminded of a scene between them in Peregrine's play when the man of Stratford confronted the man of fashion while the Dark Lady, so very much more subtle than the actress who beautifully portrayed her, watched catlike in the shadow.

"You really are," Marcus Knight announced, magnificently inflecting, "the most objectionable person—I will not honour you by calling you an actor—with whom it has been my deep, deep misfortune to appear in any production."

"Well," Grove remarked with perfect good humour, "it's nice to head the dishonours list, isn't it? Not having prospects in the other direction. Unlike yourself, Mr. Knight. *Mr. Knight,*" he continued, beaming at Destiny. "A contradiction in terms when one comes to think of it. Never mind: it simply *must* turn into Sir M. Knight (Knight) before many *more* New Years have passed."

Peregrine said: "I am sick of telling you to apologize, Harry, for grossly unprofessional behaviour and begin to think you must be an amateur, after all. Please wait outside in the foyer until Mr. Alleyn wants you. No. Not another word. Out."

Harry looked at Destiny, made a rueful grimace and walked off.

Peregrine went to Alleyn: "I'm sorry," he muttered, "about that little dust-up. We've finished. What would you like us to do?"

"I'd like the women and Random to take themselves off and the rest of the men to wait outside on the landing."

"Me included?"

"If you don't mind."

"Of course not."

"As a sort of control."

"In the chemical sense?"

"Well—"

"O.K.," Peregrine said. "What's the form?"

"Just that." Alleyn returned to the group of players. "If you wouldn't mind moving out to the circle foyer," he said. "Mr. Jay will explain the procedure."

Peregrine marshalled them out.

They stood in a knot in front of the shuttered bar and they tried not to look down in the direction of the half-landing. The lowest of the three steps from the foyer to the half-landing, and the area where Jobbins had lain, were stripped of carpet. The police had put down canvas sheeting. The steel doors of the wall safe above the landing were shut. Between the back of the landing and the wall, three steps led up to a narrow strip of floor connecting the two halves of the foyer, each with its own door into the circle.

Destiny Meade said, "I'm not going down those stairs."

"We can walk across the back to the other flight," Emily suggested.

"I'd still have to set foot on the landing. I can't do it. Harry!" She turned with her air of expecting everyone to be where she required them and found that Harry Grove had not heard her. He stood with his hands in his pockets contemplating the shut door of the office.

Marcus Knight, flushed and angry, said: "Perhaps you'd like me to take you down," and laughed very unpleasantly.

She looked coolly at him. "Sweet of you," she said. "I wouldn't dream of it," and turned away to find herself face-to-face with Jeremy Jones. His freckled face was pink and anxious and his manner diffident. "There's the circle," he said, "and the pass-door. Could I—?"

"Jeremy, *darling*. Yes—please, please. I know I'm a fool but, well, it's just how one's made, isn't it? *Thank* you, my angel." She slipped her arm into his.

They went into the circle and could be heard moving round the back towards the prompt-side box.

Charles Random said, "Well, I'll be off," hesitated for a moment, and then ran down the canvas-covered steps, turned on the landing and descended to the ground floor. Gertrude Bracey stood at the top near the remaining bronze dolphin. She looked at it and then at the mark in the carpet where its companion had stood. She compressed her lips, lifted her head and walked down with perfect deliberation.

All this was observed by Peregrine Jay.

He stopped Emily, who had made as if to follow. "Are you all right, Emily?"

"Yes, quite all right. You?"

"All the better for seeing you. Shall we take lunch together? But I don't know how long I'll be. Were you thinking of lunch later on?"

"I can't say I'm wolfishly ravenous."

"One must eat."

Emily said, "You can't possibly tell when you'll get off. The pub's no good, nor is The Younger Dolphin. They'll both be seething with curiosity and reporters. I'll buy some ham rolls and go down to the wharf below Phipps Passage. There's a bit of a wall one can sit on."

"I'll join you if I can. Don't bolt your rolls and hurry away. It's a golden day on the river."

"Look," Emily said. "What's Harry up to *now!*"

Harry was tapping on the office door. Apparently in answer to a summons he opened it and went in.

Emily left the theatre by the circle and pass-door. Peregrine joined a smouldering Marcus Knight and an anxious Winter Meyer. Presently Jeremy returned, obviously flown with gratification.

On the far side of the office door Harry Grove confronted Alleyn.

His manner quite changed. He was quiet and direct and spoke without affectation.

"I daresay," he said, "I haven't commended myself to you as a maker of statements, but a minute or two ago—after I had been sent out in disgrace, you know—I remembered something. It may have no bearing on the case whatever but I think perhaps I ought to leave it to you to decide."

"That," Alleyn said, "by and large, is the general idea we like to establish."

Harry smiled. "Well then," he said, "here goes. It's rumoured that when the night watchman, whatever he's called—"

"Hawkins."

"That when Hawkins found Jobbins and, I suppose, when you saw him, he was wearing a light overcoat."

"Yes."

"Was it a rather large brown and white check with an overcheck of black?"

"It was."

"Loudish, one might say?"

"One might, indeed."

"Yes. Well, I gave him that coat on Friday evening."

"Your name is still on the inside pocket tag."

Harry's jaw dropped. "The wind," he said, "to coin a phrase, has departed from my sails. I'd better chug off under my own steam. I'm sorry, Mr. Alleyn. Exit actor, looking crestfallen."

"No, wait a bit, as you are here. I'd like to know what bearing you think this might have on the case. Sit down. Confide in us."

"May I?" Harry said, surprised. "Thank you, I'd like to."

He sat down and looked fully at Alleyn. "I don't always mean to behave as badly as in fact I do," he said and went on quickly: "About the coat. I don't think I attached any great importance to it. But just now you did rather seem to make a point of what he was wearing. I couldn't quite see what the point *was* but it seemed to me I'd better tell you that until Friday evening the coat had been mine."

"Why on earth didn't you say so there and then?"

Harry flushed scarlet. His chin lifted and he spoke rapidly as if by compulsion. "Everybody," he said, "was fabulously amusing about my coat. In the hearty, public-school manner, you know. Frightfully nice chaps. Jolly good show. I need not, of course, tell you that I am not even a product of one of our Dear Old Minor Public Schools. Or, if it comes to that, of a county school like the Great King Dolphin."

"Knight?"

"That's right but it's slipped his memory."

"You *do* dislike him, don't you?"

"Not half as heartily as he dislikes me," Harry said and gave a short laugh. "I know I sound disagreeable. You see before you, Superintendent, yet another slum kid with a chip like a Yule log on his shoulder. I take it out in clowning."

"But," Alleyn said mildly, "is your profession absolutely riddled with old Etonians?"

Harry grinned. "Well, no," he said. "But I assure you there are enough more striking and less illustrious O. B. ties to strangle all the extras in a battle scene for Armageddon. As a rank outsider I find the network nauseating. Sorry. No doubt you're a product yourself. Of Eton, I mean."

"So you're a post-Angry at heart? Is that it?"

"Only sometimes. I compensate. They're afraid of my tongue, or I like to think they are."

He waited for a moment and then said: "None of this, by the way and for what it's worth, applies to Peregrine Jay. I've no complaints about him: he has not roused my lower-middle-class rancour and I do not try to score off him. He's a gifted playwright, a good producer and a very decent citizen. Perry's all right."

"Good. Let's get back to the others. They were arrogant about your coat, you considered?"

"The comedy line was relentlessly pursued. Charles affected to have the dazzles. Gertrude, dear girl, shuddered like a castanet. There were lots of asides. And even the lady of my heart professed distaste and begged me to shuffle off my checkered career-coat. So I did. Henry Jobbins was wheezing away at the stage-door saying his chubes were chronic and believe it or not I did a sort of your-need-is-greater-than-mine thing, which I could, of course, perfectly well afford. I took it off there and then and gave it to him. There was," Harry said loudly, "and is, absolutely no merit in this gesture. I simply off-loaded an irksome vulgar mistaken choice on somebody who happened to find it acceptable. He was a good bloke, was old Henry. A good bloke."

"Did anyone know of this spontaneous gift?"

"No. Oh, I suppose the man that relieved him did. Hawkins. Henry Jobbins told me this chap had been struck all of a heap by the overcoat when he came in on Friday night."

"But nobody else, you think, knew of the exchange?"

"I asked Jobbins not to say anything. I really could *not* have stomached the recrudescence of comedy that the incident would have evoked." Harry looked side-long at Alleyn. "You're a dangerous man, Superintendent. You've missed your vocation. You'd have been a wow on the receiving side of the confessional grille."

"No comment," said Alleyn and they both laughed.

Alleyn said, "Look here. Would anyone expect to find *you* in the realm of the front foyer after the show?"

"I suppose so," he said. "Immediately after. Winty Meyer for one. I've been working in a T.V. show and there's been a lot of carry-on about calls. In the event of any last-minute changes I arranged for them to ring this theatre and I've been looking in at the office after the show in case there was a message."

"Yes, I see."

"Last night, though, I didn't go round because the telly thing's finished. And anyway I was bound for Dessy Meade's party. She commanded me, as you've heard, to fetch my guitar and I lit off for Canonbury to get it."

"Did you arrive at Miss Meade's flat in Cheyne Walk before or after she and her other guests did?"

"Almost a dead heat. I was parking when they arrived. They'd been to the little joint in Wharfingers Lane, I understand."

"Anyone hear or see you at your own flat in Canonbury?"

"The man in the flat overhead may have heard me. He complains that I wake him up every night. The telephone rang while I was in the loo. That would be round about eleven. Wrong number. I daresay it woke him but I don't know. I was only there long enough to give myself a drink, have a wash, pick up the guitar and out."

"What's this other flatter's name?"

Harry gave it. "Well," he said cheerfully. "I hope I *did* wake him, poor bugger."

"We'll find out, shall we? Fox?"

Mr. Fox telephoned Harry's neighbour, explaining that he was a telephone operative checking a faulty line. He extracted the information that Harry's telephone had indeed rung just as the neighbour had turned his light off at eleven o'clock.

"Well, God bless him, anyway," said Harry.

"To go back to your overcoat. Was there a yellow silk scarf in the pocket?"

"There was indeed. With an elegant H embroidered by a devoted if slightly witchlike and acquisitive hand. The initial was appropriate at least. Henry J. was as pleased as punch, poor old donkey."

"You liked him very much, didn't you?"

"As I said, he was a good bloke. We used to have a pint at the pub and he'd talk about his days on the river. Oddly enough I think he rather liked me."

"Why should that be so odd?"

"Oh," Harry said. "I'm hideously unpopular, you know. I really *am* disliked. I have a talent for arousing extremes of antipathy, I promise you. Even Mr. Conducis," Harry said, opening his eyes very wide, "although he feels obliged to be helpful, quite hates my guts, I assure you."

"Have you seen him lately?"

"Friday afternoon," Harry said promptly.

"Really?"

"Yes. I call on him from time to time as a matter of duty. After all, he got me this job. Did I mention that we are distantly related? Repeat: *distantly.*"

"No."

"No. I don't mention it very much. Even I," Harry said, "draw the line somewhere, you know."

Chapter VIII

Sunday Afternoon

"What did you think of that little party, Br'er Fox?"

"Odd chap, isn't he? Very different in his manner to when he was annoying his colleagues. One of these inferiority complexes, I suppose. You brought him out, of course."

"Do you think he's dropped to the obvious speculation?"

"About the coat? I don't fancy he'd thought of that one, Mr. Alleyn, and if I've got you right I must say it strikes me as being very far-fetched. You might as well say—well," Fox said in his scandalized manner, "you might as well suspect I don't know who. Mr. Knight. The sharp-faced lady Miss Bracey, or even Mr. Conducis."

"Well, Fox, they all come into the field of vision, don't they? Overcoat or no overcoat."

"That's so," Fox heavily agreed. "So they do. So they do." He sighed and after a moment said majestically, "D'you reckon he was trying to pull our legs?"

"I wouldn't put it past him. All the same there *is* a point, you know, Fox. The landing was very dim even when the safe was open and lit."

"How *does* that interior lighting work? I haven't had a look, yet."

"There's a switch inside the hole in the wall on the circle side. What the thief couldn't have realized is the fact that this switch works the sliding steel front door and that in its turn puts on the light."

"Like a fridge."

"Yes. What might have happened is something like this. The doors from the circle into the upper foyer were shut and the auditorium was in darkness. The thief lay doggo in the circle. He heard Jay and Miss Dunne go out and bang the stage-door. He waited until midnight and then crept up to the door nearest the hole in the wall and listened for Jobbins to put through his midnight report to Fire and Police. You've checked that he made this call. We're on firm ground there, at least."

"And the chap at the Fire Station, which was the second of his two calls, reckons he broke off a bit abruptly."

"Exactly. Now, if I'm right so far—and I know damn well I'm going to speculate—our man would choose this moment to open the wall panel —it doesn't lock—and manipulate the combination. He's already cut the burglar alarm off at the main. He must have had a *torch,* but I wouldn't mind betting that by intention or accident he touched the inner switch button and, without knowing he'd done so, rolled back the front door, which in its turn put on the interior lighting. If it was accidental he wouldn't realize what he'd done until he'd opened the back of the safe and removed the black velvet display stand with its contents and found himself looking through a peep-hole across the upper foyer and sunken landing."

"With the square of light reflected on the opposite wall."

"As bright as ninepence. Quite bright enough to attract Jobbins's attention."

"Now it gets a bit dicey."

"Don't I know it."

"What happens? This chap reckons he'd better make a bolt for it. But why does he come out here to the foyer?" Fox placidly regarded his chief. "This," he continued, "would be asking for it. This would be balmy. He knows Jobbins is somewhere out here."

"I can only cook up one answer to that, Fox. He's got the loot. He intends to shut the safe, fore and aft, and spin the lock. He means to remove the loot from the display stand but at this point he's interrupted. He hears a voice, a catcall, a movement. Something. He turns round to find young Trevor Vere watching him. He thinks Jobbins is down below at the telephone. He bolts through the door from the circle to this end of the foyer meaning to duck into the loo before Jobbins gets up. Jobbins would then go into the circle and find young Trevor and assume he was the culprit. But he's too late. Jobbins, having seen the open safe, comes thundering up from below. He makes for this chap, who gives a violent shove to the pedestal, and the dolphin lays Jobbins flat. Trevor comes out to the foyer and sees this. Our chap goes for him. The boy runs back through the door and down the central aisle with his pursuer hard on his heels. He's caught at the foot of the steps. There's a struggle during which the boy grabs at the display stand. The polythene cover is dislodged, the treasure falls overboard with it. The boy is hit on the face. He falls across the balustrade, face down, clinging to it. He's picked up by the seat of his trousers, swung sideways and heaved over, his nails dragging semi-diagonally across the velvet pile as he goes. At this point Hawkins comes down the stage-door alley."

"You *are* having yourself a ball," said Mr. Fox, who liked occasionally to employ the contemporary idiom. "How long does all this take?"

"From the time he works the combination it *needn't* take more than five minutes. If that. Might be less."

"So the time's now—say—five past midnight."

"Say between twelve and twelve-ten."

"Yerse," said Fox and a look of mild gratification settled upon his respectable face. "And at twelve-five, or -ten or thereabouts Hawkins comes in by the stage-door, goes into the stalls and has a little chat with the deceased, who is looking over the circle balustrade."

"I see you are in merry pin," Alleyn remarked. "Hawkins, Mr. Smartypants, has a little chat with somebody wearing Jobbins's new coat which Hawkins is just able to recognize in the scarcely lit circle. This is not, of necessity, Jobbins. So, you see, Harry Grove had a point about the coat."

"Now then, now then."

"Going too far, you consider?"

"So do you, Mr. Alleyn."

"Well, of course I do. All this is purest fantasy. If you can think of a better one, have a go yourself."

"If only," Fox grumbled, "that kid could recover his wits, we'd all know where we were."

"We might."

"About this howd'yedo with the overcoat. Is your story something to this effect? The killer loses his loot, heaves the kid overboard and hears Hawkins at the stage-door. All right! He bolts back to the circle foyer. Why doesn't he do a bunk by the pass-door in the front entrance?"

"No time. He knows that in a matter of seconds Hawkins will come through the auditorium into the front foyer. Consider the door. A mortice lock with the key kept on a hook behind the office. Two dirty great bolts and an iron bar. No time."

"So you're making out he grabs the coat off the body, puts it on, all mucky as it is with blood and Gawd knows what—"

"Only on the outside. And I fancy he took the scarf from the overcoat pocket and used it to protect his own clothes."

"Ah. So you say he dolls himself up and goes back to the circle and tells Hawkins to make the tea?"

"In a croaking bronchial voice, we must suppose."

"Then what? Humour me, Mr. Alleyn. Don't stop."

"Hawkins goes off to the Property Room and makes the tea. This will take at least five minutes. Our customer returns to the body and redresses it in the coat and puts the scarf round the neck. You noticed how the coat was: bunched up and stuffed under the small of the back. It couldn't have got like that by him falling in it."

"Damn, I missed that one. It's an easy one, too."

"Having done this he goes downstairs, gets the key, unlocks the pass-door in the front entrance, pulls the bolts, unslips the iron bar, lets himself out and slams the door. There's a good chance that Hawkins, busily boiling up on the far side of the iron curtain, won't hear it or if he does won't worry. He's a coolish customer, is our customer, but the arrival of Trevor and then Hawkins and still more the knowledge of what he has done—he didn't plan to murder—having rattled him. He can't do one thing."

"Pick up the swag?"

"Just that. It's gone overboard with Trevor."

"Maddening for him," said Mr. Fox primly. He contemplated Alleyn for some seconds.

"Mind you," he said, "I'll give you this. If it *was* Jobbins and not a murderer rigged out in Jobbins's coat we're left with a crime that took place after Jobbins talked to Hawkins and before Hawkins came round with the tea and found the body."

"And with a murderer who was close by during the conversation and managed to work the combination, open the safe, extract the loot, kill Jobbins, half kill Trevor, do his stuff with the door and sling his hook—all within the five minutes it took Hawkins to boil up."

"Well," Fox said after consideration, "it's impossible, I'll say that for it. It's impossible. And what's *that* look mean, I wonder," he added.

"Get young Jeremy Jones in and find out," said Alleyn.

ii

When Harry Grove came out of the office he was all smiles. "I bet you lot wonder if I've been putting your pots on," he said brightly. "I haven't really. I mean not beyond mentioning that you all hate my guts, which they could hardly avoid detecting, one would think."

"They can't detect something that's nonexistent," Peregrine said crisply. "I don't hate your silly guts, Harry. I think you're a bloody bore when you do your *enfant terrible* stuff. I think you can be quite idiotically mischievous and more than a little spiteful. But I don't hate your guts: I rather like you."

"Perry: how splendidly detached! And Jeremy?"

Jeremy, looking as if he found the conversation unpalatable, said impatiently: "Good God, what's it matter! What a lot of balls."

"And Winty?" Harry said.

Meyer looked very coolly at him. "I should waste my time hating your guts?" He spread his hands. "What nonsense," he said. "I am much too busy."

"So, in the absence of Charlie and the girls, we find ourselves left with the King Dolphin."

As soon as Harry had reappeared Marcus Knight had moved to the far end of the circle foyer. He now turned and said with dignity: "I absolutely refuse to have any part of this," and ruined everything by shouting: "And I will not suffer this senseless, this insolent, this insufferable name-coining."

"Ping!" said Harry. "Great strength rings the bell. I wonder if the Elegant Rozzer in there heard you. I must be off. Best of British luck—" he caught himself up on this familiar quotation from Jobbins and looked miserable. "That," he said, "was *not* intentional," and took himself off.

Marcus Knight at once went into what Peregrine had come to think of as his First Degree of temperament. It took the outward form of sweet reason. He spoke in a deathly quiet voice, used only restrained gesture and, although that nerve jumped up and down under his empurpled cheek, maintained a dreadful show of equanimity.

"This may not be, indeed emphatically is *not*, an appropriate moment to speculate upon the continued employment of this person. One has been given to understand that the policy is adopted at the instigation of the Management. I will be obliged, Winter, if at the first opportunity, you convey to the Management my intention, unless Hartly Grove is relieved of his part, of bringing my contract to its earliest possible conclusion. My agents will deal with the formalities."

At this point, under normal circumstances he would undoubtedly have effected a smashing exit. He looked restlessly at the doors and stairways and, as an alternative, flung himself into one of the Victorian settees that Jeremy had caused to be placed about the circle foyer. Here he adopted a civilized and faintly Corinthian posture but looked, nevertheless, as if he would sizzle when touched.

"My dear, *dear* Perry and my dear Winty," he said. "Please do take this as definite. I am sorry, sorry, sorry that it should be so. But there it is."

Perry and Meyer exchanged wary glances. Jeremy, who had looked utterly miserable from the time he came in, sighed deeply.

Peregrine said, "Marco, may we, of your charity, discuss this a little later? The horrible thing that happened last night is such a *black* problem for all of us. I concede everything you may say about Harry. He behaves atrociously and under normal circumstances would have been given his marching orders long ago. If there's any more of this sort of thing I'll speak about it to Greenslade and if he feels he can't take a hand I shall—I'll go to Conducis himself and tell him I can no longer stomach his protégé. But in the meantime—*please* be patient, Marco."

Marcus waved his hand. The gesture was beautiful and ambiguous. It might have indicated dismissal, magniloquence or implacable fury. He gazed at the ceiling, folded his arms and crossed his legs.

Winter Meyer stared at Peregrine and then cast up his eyes and very, very slightly rolled his head.

Inspector Fox came out of the office and said that if Mr. Jeremy Jones was free Superintendent Alleyn would be grateful if he could spare him a moment.

Peregrine, watching Jeremy go, suffered pangs of an undefined anxiety.

When Jeremy came into the office he found Alleyn seated at Winter Meyer's desk with his investigation kit open before him and, alongside that, a copy of *The Times*. Jeremy stood very still just inside the door. Alleyn asked him to sit down and offered him a cigarette.

"I've changed to a pipe. Thank you, though."

"So have I. Go ahead, if you want to."

Jeremy pulled out his pipe and tobacco pouch. His hands were steady but looked self-conscious.

"I've asked you to come in," Alleyn said, "on a notion that may quite possibly turn out to be totally irrelevant. If so you'll have to excuse me. You did the decor for this production didn't you?"

"Yes."

"If I may say so it seemed to me to be extraordinarily right. It always fascinates me to see the tone and character of a play reflected by its background without the background itself becoming too insistent."

"It often does."

"Not in this instance, I thought. You and Jay share a flat, don't you? I suppose you collaborated over the whole job?"

"Oh, yes," Jeremy said and, as if aware of being unforthcoming, he added: "It worked all right."

"They tell me you've got a piece of that nice shop in Walton Street and are an authority on historic costume."

"That's putting it much too high."

"Well, anyway, you designed the clothes and props for this show?"

"Yes."

"The gloves for instance," Alleyn said and lifted his copy of *The Times* from the desk. The gloves used in the play lay neatly together on Winter Meyer's blotting pad.

Jeremy said nothing.

"Wonderfully accurate copies. And, of course," Alleyn went on, "I saw you arranging the real glove and the documents on the velvet easel and putting them in the safe. That morning in the theatre some six months ago. I was there, you may remember."

Jeremy half rose and then checked himself. "That's right," he said.

Alleyn lifted a tissue paper packet out of his open case, put it near Jeremy on the desk and carefully folded back the wrapping. He exposed a small, wrinkled, stained, embroidered and tasselled glove.

"This would be it?" he asked.

"I—yes," said Jeremy, as white as a sheet.

"The glove you arranged on its velvet background with the two documents and covered with a sheet of polythene fastened with velvet-covered drawing pins?"

"Yes."

"And then from the panel opening in the circle wall, you put this whole arrangement into the cache that you yourself had lined so prettily with padded gold silk. You used the switch that operates the sliding steel door in the foyer wall. It opened and the interior lights went on behind the convex plate-glass front of the cache. Then you shut the back door and spun the combination lock. And Peregrine Jay, Winter Meyer, Marcus Knight, young Trevor Vere, Miss Destiny Meade and Miss Emily Dunne all stood about, at your suggestion, in the circle foyer or the sunken landing and they all greatly admired the arrangement. That right?"

"You were there, after all."

"As I reminded you. I stayed in the circle, you know, and joined you when you were re-arranging the exhibits on their background." He gave Jeremy a moment or two and, as he said nothing, continued.

"Last night the exhibits and their velvet background with the transparent cover were found in the centre aisle of the stalls, not far from where the boy lay. They had become detached from the black velvet display easel. I brought the glove in here and examined it very closely."

"I know," Jeremy said, "what you are going to say."

"I expect you do. To begin with I was a bit worried about the smell. I've got a keen nose for my job and I seemed to get something foreign to the odour of antiquity, if one may call it that. There was a faint whiff of fish glue and paint which suggested another sort of occupational smell, clinging perhaps to somebody's hands."

Jeremy's fingers curled. The nails were coloured rather as Trevor's had been but not with velvet pile.

"So this morning I got my lens out and I went over the glove. I turned it inside out. Sacrilege, you may think. Undoubtedly, I thought, it really is a very old glove indeed and seems to have been worked over and redecorated at some time. And then, on the inside of the back where all the embroidery is—look, I'll show you."

He manipulated the glove, delicately turning it back on itself.

"Can you see? It's been caught down by a stitch and firmly anchored and it's very fine indeed. A single hair, human and—quite distinctly—red."

He let the glove fall on its tissue paper. "This is a much better copy than the property ones and they're pretty good. It's a wonderful job and would convince anyone, I'd have thought, from the distance at which it was seen." He looked up at Jeremy. "Why did you do it?" asked Alleyn.

iii

Jeremy sat with his forearms resting on his thighs and stared at his clasped hands. His carroty head was very conspicuous. Alleyn noticed that one or two hairs had fallen on the shoulders of his suede jerkin.

He said: "I swear it's got nothing to do with Jobbins or the boy."

"That, of course, is our chief concern at the moment."

"May Perry come in, please?"

Alleyn thought that one over and then nodded to Fox, who went out.

"I'd rather be heard now than any other way," Jeremy said.

Peregrine came in, looked at Jeremy and went to him.

"What's up?" he said.

"I imagine I'm going to make a statement. I want you to hear it."

"For God's sake, Jer, don't make a fool of yourself. A statement? What about? Why?"

He saw the crumpled glove lying on the desk and the two prop gloves where Alleyn had displayed them. "What's all this?" he demanded. "Who's been manhandling Hamnet's glove?"

"Nobody," Jeremy said. "It's not Hamnet's glove. It's a bloody good fake. I did it and I ought to know." A long silence followed.

"You fool, Jer," Peregrine said slowly. "You unspeakable fool."

"Do you want to tell us about it, Mr. Jones?"

"Yes. The whole thing. It's better."

"Inspector Fox will take notes and you will be asked to sign them. If in the course of your statement I think you are going to incriminate yourself to the point of an arrest I shall warn you of this."

"Yes. All right." Jeremy looked up at Peregrine. "It's O.K.," he said. "I won't. And don't, for God's sake, gawk at me like that. Go and sit down somewhere. And listen."

Peregrine sat on the edge of his own desk.

"It began," Jeremy said, "when I was going to the Vic and Alb to make drawings of the glove for the two props. Emily Dunne sometimes helps in the shop and she turned out a whole mass of old tatt we've accumulated to see what there was in the way of material. We found that pair over there and a lot of old embroidery silks and gold wire and some fake jewellery that was near enough for the props. But in the course of the hunt I came across"—he pointed—"that one. It's genuine as far as age goes and within fifty years of the original. A small woman's hand. It had the gauntlet and tassel but the embroidery was entirely different. I—I suppose I got sort of besotted on the real glove. I made a very, very elaborate drawing of it. Almost a *trompe l'oeil* job, isn't it, Perry? And all the time I was working on the props there was this talk of Conducis selling the glove to a private collection in the U.S.A."

Jeremy now spoke rapidly and directly to Alleyn.

"I've got a maggot about historic treasures going out of their native setting. I'd give back the Elgin Marbles to Athens tomorrow if I could. I started on the copy; first of all just for the hell of it. I even thought I might pull Peregrine's leg with it when it was done or try it out on the expert at the Vic and Alb. I was lucky in the hunt for silks and for gold and silver wire and all. The real stuff. I did it almost under your silly great beak, Perry. You nearly caught me at it lots of times. I'd no intention, then, absolutely none, of trying substitution."

"What *did* you mean to do with it ultimately? Apart from leg-pulling," said Alleyn.

Jeremy blushed to the roots of his betraying hair. "I rather thought," he said, "of giving it to Destiny Meade."

Peregrine made a slight moaning sound.

"And what made you change your mind?"

"As you've guessed, I imagine, it was on the morning the original was brought here and they asked me to see it housed. I'd brought my copy with me. I thought I might just try my joke experiment. So I grabbed my chance and did a little sleight-of-hand. It was terribly easy: nobody, not even you, noticed. I was going to display the whole thing and if nobody spotted the fake, take the original out of my pocket, do my funny man ha-ha ever-been-had stuff, reswitch the gloves and give Destiny the copy. I thought it'd be rather diverting to have you and the expert and everybody doting and ongoing and the cameramen milling round and Marcus striking wonderful attitudes: all at my fake. You know?"

Peregrine said, "Very quaint and inventive. You ought to go into business with Harry Grove."

"Well, then I heard all the chat about whether the cache was really safe and what you, Mr. Alleyn, said to Winty about the lock and how you guessed the combination. I thought: But this is terrifying. It's asking for trouble. There'll be another Goya's Duke but this time it'll go for keeps. I felt sure Winty wouldn't get around to changing the combination. And then—absolutely on the spur of the moment—it was some kind of compulsive behaviour, I suppose—I decided not to tell about my fake. I decided to leave it on show in the theatre and to take charge of the original myself. It's in a safe-deposit and very carefully packed. I promise you. I was going to replace it as soon as the exhibits were to be removed. I knew I'd be put in charge again and I could easily reverse the former procedure and switch back the genuine article. And then—then—there was the abominable bombshell."

"And I suppose," Peregrine observed, "I now understand your extraordinary behaviour on Friday."

"You may suppose so. On Friday," Jeremy turned to Alleyn, "Peregrine informed me that Conducis *had* sold or as good as sold, to a private collector in the U.S.A."

Jeremy got up and walked distractedly about the office. Alleyn rested his chin in his hand, Fox looked over the top of his spectacles and Peregrine ran his hands through his hair.

"You must have been out of your wits," he said.

"Put it like that if you want to. You don't need to tell me what I've done. Virtually, I've stolen the glove."

"Virtually?" Alleyn repeated. "There's no 'virtually' about it. That is precisely what you've done. If I understand you, you now decided to keep the real glove and let the collector spend a fortune on a fake."

Jeremy threw up his hands: "I don't know," he said. "I hadn't decided anything."

"You don't know what you proposed to do with young Hamnet Shakespeare's glove?"

"Exactly. If this thing hadn't happened to Jobbins and the boy and I'd been responsible for handing over the treasure: I *don't know,* now, what I'd have done. I'd have brought Hamnet's glove with me, I think. But whether I'd have replaced it—I expect I would but—I just *do not know."*

"Did you seriously consider any other line of action? Suppose you hadn't replaced the real glove—what then? You'd have stuck to it? Hoarded it for the rest of your life?"

"NO!" Jeremy shouted. *"NO!* Not that, I wouldn't have done that. I'd have waited to see what happened, I think, and then—and then."

"You realize that if the purchaser had your copy, good as it is, examined by an expert it would be spotted in no time?"

Jeremy actually grinned. "And I wonder what the Great God Conducis would have done about that one," he said. "Return the money or brazen it out that he sold in good faith on the highest authority?"

"What *you* would have done is more to the point."

"I tell you I don't know. Would I let it ride? See what happened? Do a kidnap sort of thing perhaps? Phoney voice on the telephone saying if he swore to give it to the Nation it would be returned? Then Conducis could do what he liked about it."

"Swear, collect and sell," Peregrine said. "You must be demented."

"Where is this safe-deposit?" Alleyn asked. Jeremy told him. Not far from their flat in Blackfriars.

"Tell me," Alleyn went on, "how am I to know you've been speaking the truth? After all you've only handed us this rigmarole after I'd discovered the fake. How am I to know you didn't mean to flog the glove on the freak black market? Do you know there is such a market in historic treasures?"

Jeremy said loudly, "Yes, I do. Perfectly well."

"For God's sake, Jer, shut up. *Shut up."*

"No, I won't. Why should I? I'm not the only one in the company to hear of Mrs. Constantia Guzmann."

"Mrs. Constantia Guzmann?" Alleyn repeated.

"She's a slightly mad millionairess with a flair for antiquities."

"Yes?"

"Yes. Harry Grove knows all about her. So," added Jeremy defiantly, "do Marco and Charlie Random."

"What is the Guzmann story?"

"According to Harry," Jeremy began in a high voice and with what sounded like insecure irony, "she entertained Marco very lavishly when he had that phenomenal season in New York three years ago. Harry was in the company. It appears that Mrs. Guzmann, who is fifty-five, as ugly as sin and terrifying, fell madly in love with Marco. Literally—*madly* in love. She's got a famous collection of pictures and objects d'art. Well, she threw a fabulous party—fabulous even for her—and when it was all over she kept Marco back. As a sort of woo she took him into a private room and showed him a collection of treasures that she said nobody else had ever seen." Jeremy stopped short. The corner of Alleyn's mouth twitched and his right eyebrow rose. Fox cleared his throat. Peregrine said wearily, "Ah, my God."

"I mean," Jeremy said with dignity, "precisely and literally what I say. Behind locked doors Mrs. Guzmann showed Marcus Knight jewels, snuff-boxes, rare books, Fauberge trinkets: all as hot as hell. Every one a historic collector's item. And the whole shooting-match, she confided, bought on a sort of underground international black market. Lots of them had at some time been stolen. She had agents all over Europe and the Far East. She kept all these things simply to gloat over in secret and she told Marco she had shown them to him because she wanted to feel she was in his power. And with that she set upon him in no mean style. She carried the weight and he made his escape, or so he says, by the narrowest of margins and in a cold sweat. He got on quite well with Harry in those days. One evening when he'd had one or two drinks, he told Harry all about this adventure."

"And how did you hear of it?"

Peregrine ejaculated: "I remember! When I told the company about the glove!"

"That's right. Harry said Mrs. Constantia Guzmann ought to know of it. He said it with one of his glances—perhaps they should be called 'mocking'—at Marcus, who turned purple. Harry and Charlie Random and I had drinks in the pub that evening and he told us the Guzmann yarn. I must say he was frightfully funny doing an imitation of Mrs. Guzmann saying: 'But I *vish* to be at your bercy. I log to be in your power. Ach, if you vould only betray be. Ach, but you have so beautiful a botty.'"

Peregrine made an exasperated noise.

"Yes," said Jeremy. "Well knowing your views on theatre gossip, I didn't relay the story to you."

"Have other people in the company heard it?" Alleyn asked.

Jeremy said, "Oh, yes. I imagine so."

Peregrine said, "No doubt Harry has told Destiny," and Jeremy looked miserable. "Yes," he said. "He did. At a party."

Alleyn said, "You will be required to go to your safe-deposit with two C.I.D. officers, uplift the glove and hand it over to them. You will also be asked to sign a full statement as to your activities. Whether a charge will be laid I can't at the moment tell you. Your ongoings, in my opinion, fall little short of lunacy. Technically, on your own showing, you're a thief."

Jeremy, now so white that his freckles looked like brown confetti, turned on Peregrine and stammered: "I've been so bloody miserable. It was a kind of diversion. I've been so filthily unhappy."

He made for the door. Fox, a big man who moved quickly, was there before him. "Just a minute, sir, if you don't mind," he said mildly.

Alleyn said: "All right, Fox. Mr. Jones: will you go now to the safe-deposit? Two of our men will meet you there, take possession of the glove and ask you to return with them to the Yard. For the moment, that's all that'll happen. Good-day to you."

Jeremy went out quickly. They heard him cross the foyer and run downstairs.

"Wait a moment, will you, Jay?" Alleyn said. "Fox, lay that on, please."

Fox went to the telephone and established a subfusc conversation with the Yard.

"That young booby's a close friend of yours, I gather," Alleyn said.

"Yes, he is. Mr. Alleyn, I realize I've no hope of getting anywhere with this but if I may just say one thing—"

"Of course, why not?"

"Well," Peregrine said, rather surprised, "thank you. Well, it's two things, actually. First: from what Jeremy's told you, there isn't any motive whatever for him to burgle the safe last night. Is there?"

"If everything he has said is true—no. If he has only admitted what we were bound to find out and distorted the rest, it's not difficult to imagine a motive. Motives, however, are a secondary consideration in police work. At the moment, we want a workable assemblage of cogent facts. What's your second observation?"

"Not very compelling, I'm afraid, in the light of what you've just said. He is, as you've noticed, my closest friend and I must therefore be supposed to be prejudiced. But I do, all the same, want to put it on record that he's one of the most non-violent men you could wish to meet. Impulsive. Hot-tempered in a sort of sudden red-headed way. Vulnerable. But essentially gentle. Essentially incapable of the kind of thing that was perpetrated in this theatre last night. I *know* this of Jeremy, as well as I know it of myself. I'm sorry," Peregrine said rather grandly. "I realize that kind of reasoning won't make a dent in a police investigation. But if you would like to question anyone else who's acquainted with the fool, I'm sure you'll get the same reaction."

"Speaking as a brutal and hide-bound policeman," Alleyn said cheerfully, "I'm much obliged to you. It isn't always the disinterested witness who offers the soundest observations and I'm glad to have your account of Jeremy Jones."

Peregrine stared at him. "I beg your pardon," he said.

"What for? Before we press on, though, I wonder if you'd feel inclined to comment on the Knight-Meade-Bracey-Grove situation. What's it all about? A character actress scorned and a leading gent slighted? A leading lady beguiled and a second juvenile in the ascendant? Or what?"

"I wonder you bother to ask me since you've got it off so pat," said Peregrine tartly.

"And a brilliant young designer in thrall with no prospect of delight?"

"Yes. Very well."

"All right," Alleyn said. "Let him be for the moment. Have you any idea who the U.S. customer for the treasure might be?"

"No. It wasn't for publication. Or so I understood from Greenslade."

"Not Mrs. Constantia Guzmann by any chance?"

"Good God, *I* don't know," Peregrine said. "I've no notion. Mr. Conducis may not so much as know her. Not that that would signify."

"I think he does, however. She was one of his guests in the *Kalliope* at the time of the disaster. One of the few to escape, if I remember rightly."

"Wait a bit. There's something. Wait a bit."

"With pleasure."

"No, but it's just that I've remembered—it might not be of the smallest significance—but I *have* remembered one incident, during rehearsals when Conducis came in to tell me we could use the treasure for publicity. Harry walked in here while we were talking. He was as bright as a button, as usual, and not at all disconcerted. He greeted Mr. Conducis like a long lost uncle, asked him if he'd been yachting lately and said something like: remember him to Mrs. G. Of course there are a thousand and one Mrs. G's but when you mentioned the yacht—"

"Yes, indeed. How did Conducis take this?"

"Like he takes everything. Dead pan."

"Any idea what the obligation was that Grove seems to have laid upon him?"

"Not a notion."

"Blackmail by any chance, would you think?"

"Ah, *no!* And Conducis is *not* a queer in my opinion if that's what you're working up to. Nor, good Lord, is Harry! And not, I'm quite sure, is Harry a blackmailer. He's a rum customer and he's a bloody nuisance in a company. Like a wasp. But I don't believe he's a bad lot. Not really."

"Why?"

Peregrine thought for a moment. "I suppose," he said at last, with an air of surprise, "that it must be because, to me, he really *is* funny. When he plays up in the theatre I become furious and go for him like a pickpocket and then he says something outrageous that catches me on the hop and makes me want to laugh." He looked from Alleyn to Fox. "Has either of you," Peregrine asked, "ever brought a clown like Harry to book for murder?"

Alleyn and Fox appeared severally to take glimpses into their professional pasts.

"I can't recall," Fox said cautiously, "ever finding much fun in a convicted homicide, can you, Mr. Alleyn?"

"Not really," Alleyn agreed, "but I hardly think the presence or absence of the Comic Muse can be regarded as an acid test."

Peregrine, for the first time, looked amused.

"Did you," Alleyn said, "know that Mr. Grove is distantly related to Mr. Conducis?"

"I did *not*," Peregrine shouted. "Who told you this?"

"He did."

"You amaze me. It must be a tarradiddle. Though, of course," Peregrine said, after a long pause, "it would account for everything. Or would it?"

"Everything?"

"The mailed fist of Management. The recommendation for him to be cast."

"Ah, yes. What's Grove's background, by the way?"

"He refers to himself as an Old Borstalian but I don't for a moment suppose it's true. He's a bit of an inverted snob, is Harry."

"Very much so, I'm sure."

"I rather think he started in the R.A.F. and then drifted on and off the boards until he got a big break a couple of years ago in *Cellar Stairs*. He was out of a shop, he once told me, for so long that he got jobs as a lorry-driver, a steward and a waiter in a strip-tease joint. He said he took more in tips than he ever made speaking lines."

"When was that?"

"Just before his break, he said. About six years ago. He signed off one job and before signing on for another took a trip round the agents and landed star-billing in *Cellar Stairs*. Such is theatre."

"Yes, indeed."

"Is that all?" Peregrine asked after a silence.

"I'm going to ask you to do something else for me. I know you've got the change of casting and internal affairs on your hands, but as soon as you can manage it I wonder if you'd take an hour to think back over your encounters with Mr. Conducis and your adventures of last night, and note down everything you can remember. Everything. And any other item, by the way, that you may have overlooked in the excitement."

"Do you really think Conducis has got anything to do with last night?"

"I've no idea. He occurs. He'll have to be found irrelevant before we may ignore him. Will you do this?"

"I must say it's distasteful."

"So," said Alleyn, "is Jobbins's corpse."

"Whatever happened," Peregrine said, looking sick, "and whoever overturned the bronze dolphin, I don't believe it was deliberate, cold-blooded murder. I think he saw Jobbins coming at him and overturned the pedestal in a sort of blind attempt to stop him. That's what I think and, my God," Peregrine said, "I must say I do *not* welcome an invitation to have any part in hunting him down: whoever it was, the boy or anyone else."

"All right. And if it wasn't the boy, what *about* the boy? How do you fit him in as a useful buffer between your distaste and the protection of the common man? How do you think the boy came to be dropped over the circle? And believe me he was *dropped*. He escaped, by a hundred-to-one chance, being spilt like an egg over the stalls. Yes," Alleyn said, watching Peregrine, "that's a remark in bad taste, isn't it? Murder's a crime in bad taste. You've seen it, now. You ought to know." He waited for a moment and then said, "That was cheating and I apologize."

Peregrine said, "You needn't be so bloody upright. It's nauseating."

"All right. Go away and vomit. But if you have second thoughts, sit down and write out every damn thing you remember of Conducis and all the rest of it. And now, if you want to go—go. Get the hell out of it."

"Out of my own office, I'd have you remember. To kick my heels on the landing."

Alleyn broke into laughter. "You have me there," he said. "Never mind. It's better, believe me, than kicking them in a waiting-room at the

Yard. But all right, we'll have another go. What can you tell me, if your stomach is equal to it, of the background of the other members of your company." Alleyn raised a hand. "I know you have a loyalty to them and I'm not asking you to abuse it. I do remind you, Jay, that suspicion about this crime will fall inside your guild, your mystery, if I may put it like that, and that there's going to be a great deal of talk and speculation. With the exception of yourself and Miss Dunne and Miss Meade, whose alibis seem to us to be satisfactory, and possibly Harry Grove, there isn't one of the company, and I'm including Winter Meyer and Jeremy Jones, who absolutely could *not* have killed Jobbins and attacked the boy."

"I can't see how you make it out. They were all, except Trevor, seen to leave. *I* saw them go. The doors were locked and bolted and barred."

"The stage-door was locked but not bolted and barred. Hawkins unlocked it with his own key. The small pass-door in the front was unlocked when Miss Bracey left and was not bolted and barred until after Meyer and Knight left. They heard Jobbins drop the bar."

"That cuts them out, then, surely."

"Look," Alleyn said. "Put this situation to yourself and see how you like it. Jobbins is still alive. Somebody knocks on the pass-door in the front entrance. He goes down. A recognized voice asks him to open up —an actor has left his money in his dressing-room or some such story. Jobbins lets him in. The visitor goes backstage saying he'll let himself out at the stage-door. Jobbins takes up his post. At midnight he does his routine telephoning and the sequel follows."

"How do you know all this?"

"God bless my soul, my dear chap, for a brilliant playwright you've a quaint approach to logic. I *don't* know it. I merely advance it as a way in which your lock-up theory could be made to vanish. There is at least one other, even simpler solution, which is probably the true one. The only point I'm trying to make is this. If you clamp down on telling me anything at all about any member of your company, you may be very fastidious and loyal and you may be protecting the actual butcher, but you're not exactly helping to clear the other six—even if you count Conducis."

Peregrine thought it over. "I think," he said at last, "that's probably a lot of sophistical hooey but I get your point. But I ought to warn you, you've picked a dud for the job. I've got a notoriously bad memory. There are things," Peregrine said slowly, "at the back of my mind that have been worrying me ever since this catastrophe fell upon us. Do you think I can fetch them up? Not I."

"What do you connect them with?"

"With noises made by Trevor, I think. And then, with Conducis. With that morning when he showed me the treasure. But of course *then* I was drunk so I'm unreliable in any case. However, tell me what you want to know and I'll see about answering."

"Too kind," said Alleyn dryly. "Start with—anyone you like. Marcus Knight. What's his background apart from the press hand-outs? I know all about his old man's stationer's shop in West Ham and how he went to a county school and rose to fame. Is it true he's temperamental?"

Peregrine looked relieved. "If it's only *that* sort of thing! He's hell and well-known for it but he's such a superb actor we all do our best to lump the temperament. He's a jolly nice man really, I daresay, and collects stamps, but he can't take the lightest criticism without going up like a rocket. An unfavourable notice is death to him and he's as vain as a peacock. But people say he's a sweetie at bottom even if it's a fair way to bottom."

Alleyn had strolled over to a display of photographs on the far wall: all the members of the cast in character with their signatures appended. Marcus Knight had been treated to a montage with his own image startlingly echoed by the Grafton portrait and the Droushout engraving. Peregrine joined him.

"Extraordinary," Alleyn said. "The likeness. What a piece of luck!" He turned to Peregrine and found him staring, not at the picture but at the signature.

"Bold!" Alleyn said dryly.

"Yes. But it's not that. There's something about it. Damn! I thought so before. Something I've forgotten."

"You may yet remember. Leave it. Tell me: is the sort of ribbing Knight got from Grove just now their usual form? All the King Dolphin nonsense?"

"Pretty much. It goes on."

"If he's as touchy as you say, why on earth hasn't Knight shaken the Dolphin dust off his boots? Why does he stand it for one second?"

"I think," Peregrine said with great simplicity, "he likes his part. I think that might be it."

"My dear Jay, I really do apologize: of course he does. It's no doubt the best role, outside Shakespeare, that he'll ever play."

"You think so? Really?"

"Indeed I do."

Peregrine suddenly looked deeply happy. "Now, of course," he said, "I'm completely wooed."

"What can it matter what I think! You must know how good your play is."

"Yes, but I like to be told. From which," Peregrine said, "you may gather that I have a temperamental link with Marco Knight."

"Were he and Destiny Meade lovers?"

"Oh yes. Going steady, it seemed, until Harry chucked poor Gertie and came rollicking in. We thought the casting was going to work out very cosily with Dessy and Marco as happy as Larry on the one hand and Gertie and Harry nicely fixed on the other. Maddening, this dodging round in a company. It always makes trouble. And with Marco's capacity to cut up plug-ugly at the drop of a hat—anything might happen. We can only keep our fingers crossed."

"Miss Meade is—she's—I imagine, not an intellectual type."

"She's *so* stupid," Peregrine said thoughtfully. "But so, *so* stupid it's a kind of miracle. Darling Dessy. And yet," he added, "there's an element of cunning, too. Certainly, there's an element of cunning."

"What a problem for her director, in such a subtle role!"

"Not really. You just say: 'Darling, you're sad. You're heartbroken. You can't bear it,' and up come the welling tears. Or: 'Darling, you've been clever, don't you see, you've been one too many for them,' and she turns as shrewd as a marmoset. Or, simplest of all. 'Darling, you're sending him in a big way,' and as she never does anything else it works like a charm. *She does* the things: the audience *thinks* them."

"Temperamental?"

"Only for form's sake when she fancies it's about time she showed up. She's quite good-natured."

"Did she slap Knight back smartly or gradually?"

"Gradually. You could see it coming at rehearsals. In their love scenes. She began looking at her fingernails over his shoulder and pulling bits of mascara off her eyelashes. And then she took to saying could they just walk it because she was rethinking her approach. She talks like that but of course she never has an approach. Only an instinct backed up by superb techniques and great dollops of star-quality."

"She divorced her second husband, I believe, and lives alone?"

"Well—yes. Officially."

"Anything else about her?"

"She's a terrific gambler, is Dessy. On the share-market, with the bookies and anything on the side that offers. That's really what broke up the second marriage. He couldn't do with all the roulette-party and poker-dice carry-on."

"Is she a successful gambler?"

"I daresay she herself scarcely knows, so vague are her ways."

"And Miss Bracey?"

"That's a very different story. I don't know anything about Gertie's background but she really does bear out the Woman Scorned crack. She's—she's not all that charitably disposed at any time, perhaps, and this thing's stirred her up like a wasp's nest. She and Marco exhibit the heads-and-tails of despised love. Marco is a sort of walking example of outraged vanity and incredulous mortification. He can't believe it and yet there it is. Rather touchingly, *I* think, he doesn't until today seem to have taken against Dessy. But I've trembled lest he should suddenly rear back and have a wallop at Harry."

"Hit him?"

"Yes. Bang-bang. Whereas Gertie doesn't vent all she's got on her rival but hisses and stings away at the faithless one."

"And so Miss Meade is let off lightly at both ends and Grove is the object of a dual resentment?"

"And that's throwing roses at it," said Peregrine.

"Knight and Miss Bracey have a real, solid hatred for him? Is that putting it too high?"

"No, it's not but—" Peregrine said quickly: "What is all this? What's it matter how Marco and Gertie feel about Harry?"

"Nothing at all, I daresay. What about Random? Any comment on character?"

"Charlie? No trouble to anyone. Not, as you may have discerned, a hundred per cent he-man, but what of that? He doesn't bring it into the theatre. It was quite all right to let him dress with the boy, for instance."

"Hobbies?"

"Well, as you've heard: Ximenes-class crosswords. Cyphers. And old manuscripts. He's quite an antiquarian, I'm told, is Charles. Jer says he's one of those characters who possess an infallible nose for a rare item. He spends half his time among the sixpenny and shilling bins in Long Acre and the Charing Cross Road. Good, conscientious actor. Minor public school and drama academy."

"Did all the members of the company know each other before this production?"

"Oh, yes. Except Emily. She's at the beginning," Peregrine said tenderly, "and doesn't know many people in the West End yet."

"Tell me, are you familiar with Harry Grove's overcoats?"

"I caught sight of him going away the other night wearing a contraption that screamed its way up the lane like a fire-engine and heard a lot of carry-on about it among the company."

"What was it?"

"I wasn't close enough to—" Peregrine's voice faded. He gaped at Alleyn. "Oh *no!*" he cried. "It can't be. It's not possible."

"What?"

"On—on Henry Jobbins?"

"Grove gave his overcoat to Jobbins on Friday evening. He said nobody seemed to like it. Didn't you know?"

Peregrine shook his head.

"I can't imagine," he said slowly, "I simply cannot imagine why I didn't recognize it on poor Jobbins. I actually cracked a joke about it and he said it was a present."

"Perhaps the scarf made a difference."

"Scarf? I don't think he had a scarf on."

"Did he not? A bright yellow scarf?"

"Wait. Yes," said Peregrine, looking sick, "of course. I—I remember. Afterwards."

"But not before? When you spoke to him?"

"I don't remember it then. It wasn't showing."

"Please say nothing about the overcoat, Jay. It's of the first importance that you don't. Not even," Alleyn said with a friendly air, "to your Emily."

"Very well. May I know why it matters so much?"

Alleyn told him.

"Yes, I see. But it won't really get you much further, will it?"

"If nobody knows of the transfer—"

"Yes, of course. Stupid of me."

"And that really is all. I'm sorry to have kept you such an unconscionable time."

Peregrine went to the door, hesitated and turned back.

"I'll do my best," he said, "to write down my Conduciae or should it be Conducii?"

"Or Conduciosis? Never mind. I'm glad you've decided to help. Thank you. Could you let me have it as soon as it's ready?"

"Yes. All right. Where will you be?"

"Here for another hour I should think. And then wherever developments send me. We'll leave a P.C. on duty in the theatre. If I've gone he'll take a message. Do you really mind doing this?"

"No. Not if it's remotely useful."

"There now!" said Alleyn. "Goodbye for the moment, then. On your way out, would you ask Mr. Knight to come in?"

"Certainly. It's half past twelve," Peregrine said. "He'll have got a bit restive, I daresay."

"Will he indeed?" said Alleyn. "Send him in."

Chapter IX

Knight Rampant

Marcus Knight was not so much restive as portentous. He had the air of a man who is making enormous concessions. When Alleyn apologized for keeping him waiting so long, he waved his hand as if to say: "Think no more of it. Nevertheless "

"One can't tell," Alleyn said, "in our job, how long any given interview will last."

"It didn't escape my notice," Knight said, "that you were honoured with an earlier visit."

"From Hartly Grove? Yes. He had," Alleyn said, "thought of something."

"He thinks of a number of things, most of them highly offensive."

"Really? This was quite harmless. I wonder if you've noticed his overcoat."

Mr. Knight had noticed Mr. Grove's overcoat and said so briefly and with immeasurable distaste. "One is not surprised, however," he said. "One recognizes the form. It is entirely consistent. My God, what a garment! How he dares!"

It became evident that he did not know that the coat had been given to Jobbins.

Alleyn briefly re-checked Knight's movements. He had driven his Jaguar from the theatre to his house in Montpelier Square where he was given supper as usual by the Italian couple who looked after him. He thought it was probably about ten past eleven when he got in. He did not go out again but could not absolutely prove it.

Extreme, wholly male beauty is not a commonplace phenomenon. Marcus Knight possessed it to a generous degree. His oval face, with its subtly turned planes, his delicate nose, slightly tilted eyes and glossy hair might have been dreamed up by an artist of the Renaissance or indeed by the unknown painter of that unknown man whom many observers call the Grafton Shakespeare. He had the bodily harmony that declares itself through its covering and he moved like a panther. How old was he? Middle thirties? Younger? Forty, perhaps? It didn't matter.

Alleyn led him cautiously by way of his own exquisite performance to the work of his fellow players. He uncovered a completely egotistic but shrewd appreciation of the play and a raw patch of professional jealousy when the work of his associates, particularly of Harry Grove, came into question. Grove's Mr. W.H., it seemed, was not a true reading. It was showy. It was vulgar. It was even rather camp, said Marcus Knight.

Alleyn spoke of the theft of the glove and documents. Knight rejoiced that they had been recovered. He gazed with passionate concern at Alleyn. Was it certain they were uninjured? Was it quite, quite certain? Alleyn said it was and began to talk of their unequalled worth. Knight nodded several times very slowly in that larger-than-life manner that Alleyn associated with persons of his profession. It was more like a series of bows.

"Unique," he said, on two mellifluous notes. "U-nique!"

Alleyn wondered what he would say if he knew of Jeremy's substitution.

"Well," he said lightly. "At least Mr. Conducis and the American purchaser can breathe again. I can't help wondering who she may be."

"She?"

"Now, why did I say 'she'?" Alleyn ejaculated. "I suppose I must have been thinking of Mrs. Constantia Guzmann?"

It was formidable to see how rapidly, with what virtuosity, Knight changed colour from deepest plum to parchment and back again. He drew his brows together. He retracted his upper lip. It crossed Alleyn's mind that it was a pity the role of William Shakespeare didn't offer an opportunity for a display of these physical demonstrations of fury.

"What," he asked, rising and looming over Alleyn, "has that person —Grove—said to you? I demand an answer. What has he said?"

"About Mrs. Constantia Guzmann, do you mean? Nothing. Why?"

"You lie!"

"I don't, you know," Alleyn said composedly. "Grove didn't mention her to me. Really. She's an extremely well-known collector. What's the matter?"

Knight glowered at him in silence for some time. Fox cleared his throat.

"Do you swear," Knight began in the lowest register of his voice, building up a crescendo as he went on. "Do you swear the name of Guzmann has not—ah—has not been—ah—mentioned to you in connection with My Own. Here in this room. Today. Do you swear to this? Hah?"

"No, I don't do that, either. It has."

"*All!*" he bellowed suddenly. "*The lot. The whole pack of them!* He's lunched and bloody dined on it. Don't attempt to contradict me. He's betrayed a deeply, *deeply* regretted confidence. A moment of weakness. On my part. Before I knew him for what he is: a false, *false* man." He pointed at Alleyn. "Has he—has he told—her? Miss Meade? Destiny? You need not answer. I see it in your face. He has."

"I've not spoken with Miss Meade," Alleyn said.

"They've laughed together," he roared. "At Me!"

"Perfectly maddening for you if they have," Alleyn said, "but, if you'll forgive me, it isn't, as far as I know, entirely relevant to the business under discussion."

"Yes, it is," Knight passionately contradicted. "By God it is and I'll tell you why. I've put a restraint upon myself. I have not allowed myself to speak about this man. I have been scrupulous lest I should be thought biased. But now *now! I* tell you this and I speak from absolute conviction: if, as you hold, that appalling boy is not guilty and recovers his wits, and if he was attacked by the man who killed Jobbins, and if he *remembers who attacked him,* it will be at W. Hartly Grove he points his finger. *Now!*"

Alleyn, who had seen this pronouncement blowing up for the past five minutes, allowed himself as many seconds in which to be dumb-founded and then asked Marcus if he had any reasons, other, he hastily added, than those already adduced, for making this statement about Harry Grove. Nothing very specific emerged. There were dark and vague allusions to reputation and an ambiguous past. As his temper abated, and it did seem to abate gradually, Knight appeared to lose the fine edge of his argument. He talked of Trevor Vere and said he couldn't understand why Alleyn dismissed the possibility that the boy had been caught out by Jobbins, overturned the dolphin and then run so fast down the circle aisle that he couldn't prevent himself diving over the balustrade. Alleyn once again advanced the logical arguments against this theory.

"And there's no possibility of some member of the public's having hidden during performance?"

"Jay assures me not. A thorough routine search is made and the staff on both sides of the curtain confirm this. This is virtually a 'new' theatre. There are no stacks of scenery or properties or neglected hiding places."

"You are saying," said Knight, beginning portentously to nod again, "that this thing must have been done by One of Us."

"That's how it looks."

"I am faced," Knight said, "with a frightful dilemma." He immediately became a man faced with a frightful dilemma and looked quite haggard. "Alleyn: what can one do? Idle for me to pretend I don't feel as I do about this man. I *know* him to be a worthless, despicable person. I know him—"

"One moment. This is still Harry Grove?"

"Yes." (Several nods.) "Yes. I am aware that the personal injuries he has inflicted upon me must be thought to prejudice my opinion."

"I assure you—"

"And *I* am assuring *you*—oh with such deadly certainty—that there is only one among us who is capable of the crime."

He gazed fixedly into Alleyn's face. "I studied physiognomy," he surprisingly said. "When I was in New York"—for a moment he looked hideously put out but instantly recovered—"I met a most distinguished authority—Earl P. Van Smidt—and I became seriously interested in the science. I have studied and observed and I have proved my conclusions. Over and again. I have completely satisfied myself—but com-pletely—that when you see a pair of unusually round eyes, rather wide apart, very light blue and without depth—look out. *Look out!*" he repeated and flung himself into the chair he had vacated.

"What for?" Alleyn inquired.

"Treachery. Shiftiness. Utter unscrupulousness. Complete lack of ethical values. I quote from Van Smidt."

"Dear me."

"As for Conducis! But no matter. No matter."

"Do you discover the same traits in Mr. Conducis?"

"I—I—am not familiar with Mr. Conducis."

"You have met him, surely?"

"Formal meeting. On the opening night."

"But never before that?"

"I may have done so. Years ago. I prefer—" Knight said surprisingly —"to forget the occurrence." He swept it away.

"May I ask why?"

There was an appreciable pause before he said: "I was once his guest, if you can call it that, and I was subjected to an insolent disregard which I would have interpreted more readily if I had at that time been acquainted with Smidt. In my opinion," Knight said, "Smidt

should be compulsory reading for all police forces. You don't mind my
saying this?" he added in a casual, lordly manner.

"Indeed no."

"Good. Want me any more, dear boy?" he asked, suddenly gracious.

"I think not. Unless—and believe me I wouldn't ask if the question
was irrelevant to the case—unless you care to tell me if Mrs. Constantia
Guzmann really confided to you that she is a buyer of hot objects d'art
on the intercontinental black market."

It was no good. Back in a flash came the empurpled visage and
the flashing eye. Back, too, came an unmistakable background of
sheepishness and discomfort.

"No comment," said Marcus Knight.

"No? Not even a tiny hint?"

"You are mad to expect it," he said, and with that they had to let
him go.

ii

"Well, Br'er Fox, we've caught a snarled up little job this time,
haven't we?"

"We have that," Fox agreed warmly. "It'd be nice," he added wistfully, "if we could put it down to simple theft, discovery and violence."

"It'd be lovely but we can't, you know. We can't. For one thing the
theft of a famous object is always bedevilled by the circumstance of its
being indisposable through the usual channels. No normal high-class
fence, unless he's got very special contacts, is going to touch Shakespeare's note or his son's glove."

"So, for a start you've got either a crank who steals and gloats or a
crank of the type of young Jones who steals to keep the swag in England or a thorough wised-up, high grade professional in touch with the
top international racket. And at the receiving end somebody of the nature of this Mrs. Guzmann, who's a millionaire crank in her own right
and doesn't care how she gets her stuff."

"That's right. Or a kidnapper who holds the stuff for ransom. And
you *might* have a non-professional thief who knows all about Mrs. G.
and believes she'll play and he'll make a pocket."

"That seems to take in the entire boiling of this lot, seeing Mr.
Grove's broadcast the Guzmann-Knight anecdote for all it's worth. I tell
you what, Mr. Alleyn: it wouldn't be the most astonishing event in my
working life if Mr. Knight took to Mr. Grove. Mr. Grove's teasing ways
seem to put him out to a remarkable degree, don't you think?"

"I think," Alleyn said, "we'd better, both of us, remind ourselves about actors."

"You do? What about them?"

"One must always remember that they're trained to convey emotion. On or off the stage, they make the most of everything they feel. Now this doesn't mean they express their feelings up to saturation point. When you and I and all the rest of the non-actors do our damnedest to understate and be ironical about our emotional reflexes, the actor, even when he underplays them, does so with such expertise that he convinces us laymen that he's *in extremis*. He isn't. He's only being professionally articulate about something that happens offstage instead of in front of an official audience."

"How does all this apply to Mr. Knight, then?"

"When he turns purple and roars anathemas against Grove it means A: that he's hot-tempered, pathologically vain and going through a momentary hell and B: that he's letting you know up to the nth degree just *how* angry and dangerous he's feeling. It doesn't necessarily mean that once his present emotion has subsided he will do anything further about it, and nor does it mean that he's superficial or a hypocrite. It's his job to take the micky out of an audience, and even in the throes of a completely genuine emotional crisis, he does just that thing if it's only an audience of one."

"Is this what they call being an extrovert?"

"Yes, Br'er Fox, I expect it is. But the interesting thing about Knight, I thought, was that when it came to Conducis he turned uncommunicative and cagey."

"Fancied himself slighted over something, it seemed. Do you reckon Knight believes all that about Grove? Being a homicidal type? All that stuff about pale eyes etcetera. Because," Fox said with great emphasis, "it's all poppycock: there aren't any facial characteristics for murder. What's that you're always quoting about there being no art to find the mind's construction in the face? I reckon it's fair enough where homicide's concerned. Although," Fox added, opening his own eyes very wide, "I always fancy there's a kind of look about sex offenders of a certain type. That I will allow."

"Be that as it may it doesn't get us much further along our present road. No news from the hospital?"

"No. They'd ring through at once if there was."

"I know. I know."

"What do we do about Mr. Jeremy Jones?"

"Oh, blast! What indeed! I think we take delivery of the glove and documents, give him hell and go no further. I'll talk to the A.C. about him and I rather *think* I'll have to tell Conducis as soon as possible. Who've we got left here? Only little Meyer. Ask him into his own office, Br'er Fox. We needn't keep him long, I think."

Winter Meyer came in quoting Queen Mary. "This," he said wearily, "is a pretty kettle of fish. This is a carry-on. I'm not complaining, mind, and I'm not blaming anybody but what, oh what, has set Marco off again? Sorry. Not your headache, old boy."

Alleyn uttered consolatory phrases, sat him at his own desk, checked his alibi, which was no better and no worse than anyone else's in that after he left the theatre with Knight he drove to his house at Golders Green where his wife and family were all in bed. When he wound up his watch he noticed it said ten to twelve. He had heard the Knight-Guzmann story. "I thought it bloody sad," he said. "Poor woman. Terrible, you know, the problem of the plain, highly sexed woman. Marco ought to have held his tongue. He ought never to have told Harry. Of course Harry made it sound a bit of a yell, but I didn't like Marco telling about it. I don't think that sort of thing's funny."

"It does appear that on her own admission to Knight, she's a buyer on a colossal scale under the museum piece counter."

Winter Meyer spread his hands. "We all have our weaknesses," he said. "So she likes nice things and she can pay for them. Marcus Knight should complain!"

"Well!" Alleyn ejaculated. "That's one way of looking the Big Black Market in the eyes, I must say! Have you ever met Mrs. Guzmann, by the way?"

Winter Meyer had rather white eyelids. They now dropped a little. "No," he said, "not in person. Her husband was a most brilliant man. The equal and more of Conducis."

"Self made?"

"Shall we say self-created? It was a superb achievement."

Alleyn looked his enjoyment of this phrase and Meyer answered his look with a little sigh. "Ah yes!" he said. "These colossi! How marvellous!"

"In your opinion," Alleyn said, "without prejudice and within these four walls and all that: how many people in this theatre know the combination of that lock?"

Meyer blushed. "Yes," he said. "Well. This is where I don't exactly shine with a clear white radiance, isn't it? Well, as he's told you, Charlie Random for one. Got it right, as you no doubt observed. He says he didn't pass it on and personally I believe that. He's a very quiet type,

Charlie. Never opens up about his own or anybody else's business. I'm sure he's dead right about the boy not knowing the combination."

"You are? Why?"

"Because as I said, the bloody kid was always pestering me about it."

"And so you would have been pretty sure, would you, that only you yourself, Random, and Mr. Conducis knew the combination?"

"I don't say that," Meyer said unhappily. "You see, after that morning they did all know about the five-letter word being an obvious one and—and—well, Dessy did say one day, 'Is it "glove," Winty? We all think it might be? Do you swear it's not "glove."' Well, you know Dessy. She'd woo the Grand Master to let the goat out of the Lodge. I suppose I boggled a bit and she laughed and kissed me. I know. I know. I ought to have had it changed. I meant to. But—in the theatre we don't go about wondering if someone in the company's a big-time bandit."

"No, of course you don't, Mr. Meyer: thank you very much. I think we can now return your office to you. It was more than kind to suggest that we use it."

"There hasn't been that much for me to do. The press is our big worry but we're booked out solid for another four months. Unless people get it into their heads to cancel we *should* make out. You never know, though, which way a thing like this will take the public."

They left him in a state of controlled preoccupation.

The circle foyer was deserted, now. Alleyn paused for a moment. He looked at the shuttered bar, at the three shallow steps leading on three sides from the top down to the half-landing and the two flights that curved down from there to the main entrance; at the closed safe in the wall above the landing, the solitary bronze dolphin and the two doors into the circle. Everything was quiet, a bit muffled and stuffily chilly.

He and Fox walked down the three canvas-covered steps to the landing. A very slight sound caught Alleyn's ear. Instead of going on down he crossed to the front of the landing, rested his hands on its elegant iron balustrade and looked into the main entrance below.

His gaze lighted on the crown of a smart black hat and the violently foreshortened figure of a thin woman.

For a second or two the figure made no move. Then the hat tipped back and gave way to a face like a white disc, turned up to his own.

"Do you want to see me, Miss Bracey?"

The face tipped backwards and forwards in assent. The lips moved, but if she spoke her voice was inaudible.

Alleyn motioned to Fox to stay where he was and himself went down the curving right-hand stairway.

There she stood, motionless. The fat upsidedown cupids over the box-office and blandly helpful caryatids supporting the landing made an incongruous background for that spare figure and yet, it crossed Alleyn's mind, her general appearance was evocative, in a cock-eyed way, of the period: of some repressed female character from a Victorian play or novel. Rosa Dartle, he thought, that was the sort of thing: Rosa Dartle.

"What is it?" Alleyn asked. "Are you unwell?"

She looked really ill. He wondered if he had imagined that she had swayed very slightly, and then pulled herself together.

"You must sit down," he said. "Let me help you."

When he went up to her he smelt brandy and saw that her eyes were off-focus. She said nothing but let him propel her to Jeremy Jones's plushy settee alongside the wall. She sat bolt upright. One corner of her mouth drooped a little as if pulled down by an invisible hook. She groped in her handbag, fetched up a packet of cigarettes and fumbled one out. Alleyn lit it for her. She made a great business of this. She's had a lot more than's good for her, he thought, and wondered where, on a Sunday afternoon, she'd get hold of it. Perhaps Fox's Mrs. Jancy at The Wharfinger's Friend had obliged.

"Now," he said, "what's the trouble?"

"Trouble? What trouble? I know trouble when I see it," she said. "I'm saturated in it."

"Do you want to tell me about it?"

"Not a question of me telling you. It's what *he* told you. That's what matters."

"Mr. Grove?"

"Mr. W. Hartly Grove. You know what? He's a monster. You know? Not a man but a monster. Cruel. My God," she said and the corner of her mouth jerked again, "how cruel that man can be!"

Looking at her, Alleyn thought there was not much evidence of loving-kindness in her own demeanour.

"What," she asked with laborious articulation, "did he say about me? What did he say?"

"Miss Bracey, we didn't speak of you at all."

"What *did* you speak about? Why did he stay behind to speak to you. He did, didn't he? Why?"

"He told me about his overcoat."

She glowered at him and sucked at her cigarette as if it were a respirator. "Did he tell you about his scarf?" she asked.

"The yellow one with H. on it?"

She gave a sort of laugh. "Embroidered," she said. "By his devoted Gerts. God, what a fool! And he goes on wearing it. Slung round his neck like a halter and I wish it'd throttle him."

She leaned back, rested her head against the crimson plush and shut her eyes. Her left hand slid from her lap and the cigarette fell from her fingers. Alleyn picked it up and threw it into a nearby sandbox. "Thanks," she said without opening her eyes.

"Why did you stay behind? What do you want to tell me?"

"Stay behind? When?"

"Now."

"*Then,* you mean."

The clock above the box-office ticked. The theatre made a settling noise up in its ceiling. Miss Bracey sighed.

"Did you go back into the theatre?"

"Loo. Downstairs cloaks."

"Why didn't you tell me this before?"

She said very distinctly: "Because it didn't matter."

"Or because it mattered too much?"

"*No.*"

"Did you see or hear anyone while you were in the downstairs foyer?"

"No. Yes, I did. I heard Winty and Marco in the office upstairs. They came out. And I left, then. I went away. Before they saw me."

"Was there someone else you saw? Jobbins?"

"No," she said at once.

"There was someone, wasn't there?"

"No. No. *No.*"

"Why does all this distress you so much?"

She opened her mouth and then covered it with her hand. She rose and swayed very slightly. As he put out a hand to steady her she broke from him and ran hazardously to the pass-door. It was unlocked. She pulled it open and left it so. "Why does all this distress you so much?"

She opened her mouth and then covered it with her hand. She rose and swayed very slightly. As he put out a hand to steady her she broke from him and ran hazardously to the pass-door. It was unlocked. She pulled it open and left it so. Alleyn stood in the doorway and she backed away from him across the portico. When she realized he wasn't going to follow she flapped her hand in a lunatic fashion and ran towards the car park. He was in time to see her scramble into her minicar. Someone was sitting in the passenger seat who caught sight of Alleyn and turned away. It was Charles Random.

"Do you want her held?" Fox said at his elbow.

"No. What for? Let her go."

iii

"I *think* that's the lot," Peregrine said. He laid down his pen, eased his fingers and looked up at Emily.

The bottom of Phipps Passage having turned out to be windy and rich in dubious smells, they had crossed the bridge and retired upon the flat. Emily got their lunch ready while Peregrine laboured to set down everything he could remember of his encounters with Mr. Conducis. Of Jeremy there was nothing to be seen.

Emily said: "'What I did in the Hols. Keep it bright, brief and descriptive.'"

"I seem to have done an unconscionable lot," Peregrine rejoined. "It's far from brief. Look."

"No doubt Mr. Alleyn will mark it for you. 'Quite G. but should take more pains with his writing.' Are you sure you haven't forgotten the one apparently trifling clue round which the whole mystery revolves?"

"You're very jokey, aren't you? I'm far from sure. The near-drowning incident's all complete, I think, but I'm not so sure about the visit to Drury Place. Of course, I was drunk by the time that was over. How *extraordinary* it was," Peregrine said. "Really, he *was* rum. Do you know, Emmy, darling, it seems to me now as if he acted throughout on some kind of compulsion. As if it had been he, not I, who was half-drowned and behaving (to mix my metaphor, you pedantic girl) like a duck that's had its head chopped off. *He* was obsessed while *I* was merely plastered. Or so it seems, now."

"But what did he *do* that was so odd?"

"Do? He—well, there was an old menu card from the yacht *Kalliope*. It was in the desk and he snatched it up and burnt it."

"I suppose if your yacht's wrecked under your feet you don't much enjoy being reminded of it."

"No, but I got the impression it was something *on* the card—" Peregrine went into a stare and after a long pause said in a rather glazed manner: "I think I've remembered."

"What?"

"On the menu. Signatures: you know? And, Emmy, listen."

Emily listened. "Well," she said. "For what it's worth, put it in."

Peregrine put it in. "There's one other thing," he said. "It's about last night. I think it was when I was in front and you had come through from backstage. There was the disturbance by the boy—catcalls and the door-slamming. Somewhere about then, it was, that I remember thinking of *The Cherry Orchard*. Not *consciously* but with one of those sort of momentary, back-of-the-mind things."

"*The Cherry Orchard?*"

"Yes, and Miss Joan Littlewood."

"Funny mixture. She's never produced it, has she?"

"I don't think so. Oh, *damn,* I wish I could get it. Yes," Peregrine said excitedly. "And with it there was a floating remembrance, I'm sure —of what? A quotation: *'Vanished with a*—something *perfume and a most melodious*—' what? I think it was used somewhere by Walter de la Mare. It was hanging about like the half-recollection of a dream when we walked up the puddled alleyway and into Wharfingers Lane. Why? What started it up?"

"It mightn't have anything to do with Trevor or Jobbins."

"I know. But I've got this silly feeling it has."

"Don't *try* to remember and then you may."

"All right. Anyway the End of Hols essay's ready for what it's worth. I wonder if Alleyn's still at the theatre."

"Ring up."

"O.K. What's that parcel you've been carting about all day?"

"I'll show you when you've rung up."

A policeman answered from The Dolphin and said that Alleyn was at the Yard. Peregrine got through with startling promptitude.

"I've done this thing," he said. "Would you like me to bring it over to you?"

"I would indeed. Thank you, Jay. Remembered anything new?"

"Not much, I'm afraid." The telephone made a complicated jangling sound.

"What?" Alleyn asked. "Sorry about that twang. What did you say? Nothing new?"

"Yes!" Peregrine suddenly bawled into the receiver. "Yes. You've done it yourself. I'll put it in. Yes. Yes. Yes."

"You sound like a pop singer. I'll be here for the next hour or so. Ask at the Yard entrance and they'll send you up. 'Bye."

"You've remembered?" Emily cried. "What is it? You've remembered."

And when Peregrine told her, she remembered, too.

He re-opened his report and wrote feverishly. Emily unwrapped her parcel. When Peregrine had finished his additions and swung round in his chair he found, staring portentously at him, a water-colour drawing of a florid gentleman. His hair was curled into a cocks-comb. His whiskers sprang from his jowls like steel wool and his prominent eyes proudly glared from beneath immensely luxuriant brows. He wore a frock coat with satin reveres, a brilliant waistcoat, three alberts, a diamond tie-pin and any quantity of rings. His pantaloons were strapped under varnished boots, and beneath his elegantly arched arm his lilac-gloved hand supported a topper with a curly brim. He stood with one leg straight and the other bent. He was superb.

And behind, lightly but unmistakably sketched in, was a familiar, an adorable facade.

"Emily? It isn't—? It must be—?"

"Look."

Peregrine came closer. Yes, scribbled in faded pencil at the bottom of the work: *Mr. Adolphus Ruby of The Dolphin Theatre, "Histrionic Portraits" series, 23 April 1855.*

"It's a present," Emily said. "It was meant, under less ghastly circs, to celebrate The Dolphin's first six months. I thought I'd get it suitably framed but then I decided to give it to you now to cheer you up a little."

Peregrine began kissing her very industriously.

"Hi!" she said. "Steady."

"Where, you darling love, did you get it?"

"Charlie Random told me about it. He'd seen it in one of his prowls in a print shop off Long Acre. Isn't he odd? He didn't seem to want it himself. He goes in for nothing later than 1815, he said. So, I got it."

"It's not a print, by Heaven, it's an original. It's a Phiz original, Emmy. Oh we shall frame it so beautifully and hang it—" He stopped for a second. "Hang it," he said, "in the best possible place. Gosh, won't it send old Jer sky high!"

"Where is he?"

Peregrine said, "He had a thing to do. He ought to be back by now. Emily, I couldn't have ever imagined myself telling anybody what I'm going to tell you so it's a sort of compliment. Do you know what Jer did?"

And he told Emily about Jeremy and the glove.

"He must have been demented," she said flatly.

"I know. And what Alleyn's decided to do about him, who can tell? You don't sound as flabbergasted as I expected."

"Don't I? No, well—I'm not altogether. When we were making the props Jeremy used to talk incessantly about the glove. He's got a real fixation on the ownership business, hasn't he? It really is almost a kink, don't you feel? Harry was saying something the other day about after all the value of those kinds of jobs was purely artificial and fundamentally rather silly. If he was trying to get a rise out of Jeremy, he certainly succeeded. Jeremy was livid. I thought there'd be a punch-up before we were through. Perry, what's the matter? Have I been beastly?"

"No, no. Of course not."

"I *have*," she said contritely. "He's your great friend and I've been talking about him as if he's a specimen. I *am* sorry."

"You needn't be. I know what he's like. Only I do *wish* he hadn't done this."

Peregrine walked over to the window and stared across the river towards The Dolphin. Last night, he thought, only sixteen hours ago, in that darkened house, a grotesque overcoat had moved in and out of shadow. Last night—He looked down into the street below. There from the direction of the bridge came a ginger head, thrust forward above heavy shoulders and adorned, like a classic ewer, with a pair of outstanding ears.

"Here he comes," Peregrine said. "They haven't run him in as yet, it seems."

"I'll take myself off."

"No, you don't. I've got to drop this stuff at the Yard. Come with me. We'll take the car and I'll run you home."

"Haven't you got things you ought to do? Telephonings and fussings? What about Trevor?"

"I've done that. No change. Big trouble with Mum. Compensation. It's Greenslade's and Winty's headache, thank God. We want to do what's right and a tidy bit more but she's out for the earth."

"Oh dear."

"Here's Jer."

He came in looking chilled and rather sickly. "I'm sorry," he said. "I didn't know you had—oh hullo, Em."

"Hullo, Jer."

"I've told her," Peregrine said.

"Thank you very much."

"There's no need to take it grandly, is there?"

"Jeremy, you needn't mind my knowing. Truly."

"I don't in the least mind," he said in a high voice. "No doubt you'll both be surprised to learn I've been released with a blackguarding that would scour the hide off an alligator."

"Surprised and delighted," Peregrine said. "Where's the loot?"

"At the Yard."

Jeremy stood with his hands in his pockets as if waiting for something irritating to occur.

"Do you want the car, Jer? I'm going to the Yard now," Peregrine said and explained why. Jeremy remarked that Peregrine was welcome to the car and added that he was evidently quite the white-haired Trusty of the Establishment. He stood in the middle of the room and watched them go.

"He *is* in a rage?" Emily said as they went to the car.

"I don't know what he's in but he's bloody lucky it's not the lock-up. Come on."

iv

Alleyn put down Peregrine's report and gave it a definitive slap. "It's useful, Fox," he said. "You'd better read it."

He dropped it on the desk before his colleague, filled his pipe and strolled over to the window. Like Peregrine Jay, an hour earlier, he looked down at the Thames and he thought how closely this case clung to the river as if it had been washed up by the incoming tide and left high-and-dry for their inspection. Henry Jobbins of Phipps Passage was a waterside character if ever there was one. Peregrine Jay and Jeremy Jones were not far east along the Embankment. Opposite them The Dolphin pushed up its stage-house and flagstaff with a traditional flourish on Bankside. Behind Tabard Lane in the Borough lurked Mrs. Blewitt while her terrible Trevor, still on the South Bank, languished in St. Terence's. And as if to top it off, he thought idly, here *we* are at the Yard, hard by the river.

"But with Conducis," Alleyn muttered, "we move west and, I suspect, a good deal further away than Mayfair."

He looked at Fox who, with eyebrows raised high above his spectacles in his stuffy reading-expression, concerned himself with Peregrine's report.

The telephone rang and Fox reached for it. "Super's room," he said. "Yes? I'll just see."

He laid his great palm across the mouthpiece. "It's Miss Destiny Meade," he said, "for you."

"Is it, by gum! What's she up to, I wonder. All right. I'd better."

"Look," cried Destiny, when he had answered. "I know you're a kind, *kind* man."

"Do you?" Alleyn said. "How?"

"I have a sixth sense about people. Now, you won't laugh at me, will you? Promise."

"I've no inclination to do so, believe me."

"And you won't slap me back? You'll come and have a delicious little dinky at six, or even earlier or whenever it suits, and tell me I'm being as stupid as an owl. Now, do, do, do, do, do. Please, please, please."

"Miss Meade," Alleyn said, "it's extremely kind of you but I'm on duty and I'm afraid I can't."

"On duty! But you've been on duty all *day*. That's worse than being an actor and you can't possibly mean it."

"Have you thought of something that may concern this case?"

"It concerns *me*," she cried and he could imagine how widely her eyes opened at the telephone.

"Perhaps if you would just say what it is," Alleyn suggested. He looked across at Fox who, with his spectacles halfway down his nose, blankly contemplated his superior and listened at the other telephone. Alleyn crossed his eyes and protruded his tongue.

"—I can't really, not on the telephone. It's too complicated. Look— I'm *sure* you're up to your ears and not for the wide, wide world—" The lovely voice moved unexpectedly into its higher and less mellifluous register. "I'm nervous," it said rapidly. "I'm afraid. I'm terrified. I'm being threatened." Alleyn heard a distant bang and a male voice. Destiny Meade whispered in his ear, *"Please come. Please come."* Her receiver clicked and the dialling tone set in.

"Now who in Melpomene's dear name," Alleyn said, "does that lovely lady think she's leading down the garden path? Or is she? By gum, if she *is*," he said, "she's going to get such a tap on the temperament as hasn't come her way since she hit the headlines. When are we due with Conducis? Five o'clock. It's not half past two. Find us a car, Br'er Fox, we're off to Cheyne Walk."

Fifteen minutes later they were shown into Miss Destiny Meade's drawing-room.

It was sumptuous to a degree and in maddeningly good taste: an affair of mushroom-coloured curtains, dashes of Schiaparelli pink, dull satin, Severes plaques and an unusual number of orchids. In the middle of it all was Destiny, wearing a heavy sleeveless sheath with a mink collar: and not at all pleased to see Inspector Fox.

"Kind, kind," she said, holding out her hand at her white arm's length for Alleyn to do what he thought best with. "Good afternoon," she said to Mr. Fox.

"Now, Miss Meade," Alleyn said briskly, "what's the matter?" He reminded himself of a mature Hamlet.

"Please sit down. No, please. I've been so terribly distressed and I need your advice so desperately."

Alleyn sat, as she had indicated it, in a pink velvet buttoned chair. Mr. Fox took the least luxurious of the other chairs and Miss Meade herself sank upon a couch, tucked up her feet, which were beautiful, and leaned superbly over the arm to gaze at Alleyn. Her hair, coloured raven black for the Dark Lady, hung like a curtain over her right jaw and half her cheek. She raised a hand to it and then drew the hand away as if it had hurt her. Her left ear was exposed and embellished with a massive diamond pendant.

"This is so difficult," she said.

"Perhaps we could fire point-blank."

"Fire? Oh, I see. Yes. Yes, I must try, mustn't I?"

"If you please."

Her eyes never left Alleyn's face. "It's about—" she began and her voice resentfully indicated the presence of Mr. Fox. "It's about *me?*"

"Yes?"

"Yes. I'm afraid I must be terribly frank. Or no. Why do I say that? To you of all people who, of course, understand—" she executed a circular movement of her arm—"everything. I know you do. I wouldn't have asked you if I hadn't known. And you see I have Nowhere to Turn."

"Oh, surely!"

"No. I mean that," she said with great intensity. "I mean it. No-where. No one. It's all so utterly unexpected. Everything seemed to be going along quite naturally and taking the inevitable course. Because—I know you'll agree with this—one shouldn't—indeed one can't resist the inevitable. One is fated and when this new thing came into our lives we both faced up to it, he and I, oh, over and over again. It's like," she rather surprisingly added, "Antony and Cleopatra. I forget the exact line. I think, actually, that in the production it was cut but it puts the whole thing in a nutshell, and I told him so. Ah, Cleopatra," she mused, and such was her beauty and professional expertise that, there and then, lying (advantageously of course) on her sofa she became for a fleeting moment the Serpent of the old Nile. "But now," she added crossly as she indicated a box of cigarettes that was not quite within her reach, "now, with him turning peculiar and violent like this I feel I simply don't *know* him. I can't cope. As I told you on the telephone, I'm terrified."

When Alleyn leaned forward to light her cigarette he fancied that he caught a glint of appraisal and of wariness, but she blinked, moved her face nearer to his and gave him a look that was a masterpiece.

"Can you," Alleyn said, "perhaps come to the point and tell us precisely why and of whom you are frightened, Miss Meade?"

"Wouldn't one be? It was so utterly beyond the bounds of anything one could possibly anticipate. To come in almost without warning and I must tell you that of course he has his own key and by a hideous chance my married couple are out this afternoon. And then, after all that has passed between us to—to—"

She turned her head aside, swept back the heavy wing of her hair and superbly presented herself to Alleyn's gaze.

"Look," she said.

Unmistakably someone had slapped Miss Meade very smartly indeed across the right-hand rearward aspect of her face. She had removed the diamond earring on this side but its pendant had cut her skin behind the point of the jaw, and the red beginnings of a bruise showed across the cheek.

"What do you think of that?" she said.

"Did Grove do this?" Alleyn ejaculated.

She stared at him. An indescribable look of—what: pity? contempt? mere astonishment?—broke across her face. Her mouth twisted and she began to laugh.

"Oh you poor darling," said Destiny Meade. "Harry? He wouldn't hurt a fly. No, no, no, my dear, this is Mr. Marcus Knight. His Mark."

Alleyn digested this information and Miss Meade watched him apparently with some relish.

"Do you mind telling me," he said at length, "why all this blew up? I mean, *specifically* why. If, as I understand, you have finally broke with Knight."

"*I* had," she said, "but you see *he* hadn't. Which made things so very tricky. And then he wouldn't give me back the key. He has, now. He threw it at me." She looked vaguely round the drawing-room. "It's somewhere about," she said. "It might have gone anywhere or broken anything. He's so *egotistic.*"

"What had precipitated this final explosion, do you think?"

"Well—" She dropped the raven wing over her cheek again. "This and that. Harry, of course, has driven him quite frantic. It's very bad of Harry and I never cease telling him so. And then it really was *too* unfortunate last night about the orchids."

"The orchids?" Alleyn's gaze travelled to a magnificent stand of them in a Venetian goblet.

"Yes, those," she said. "Vass had them sent round during the show. I tucked his card in my décolletage like a sort of Victorian courtesan, you know, and in the big love scene Marco spotted it and whipped it out before I could do a thing. It wouldn't have been so bad if they hadn't had that flare-up in the yacht a thousand years ago. He hadn't realized before that I knew Vass so well. Personally, I mean. Vassy has got this thing about no publicity and of course I *respect* it. I understand. We just see each other quietly from time to time. He has a wonderful brain."

" 'Vassy'? 'Vass'?"

"Vassily, really. I call him Vass. Mr. Conducis."

Chapter X

Monday

As Fox and Alleyn left the flat in Cheyne Walk they encountered in the downstairs entrance a little old man in a fusty overcoat and decrepit bowler. He seemed to be consulting a large envelope.

"Excuse me, gentlemen," he said, touching the brim of the bowler, "but can you tell me if a lady be-the-namer Meade resides in these apartments? It seems to be the number but I can't discover a name board or indication of any sort."

Fox told him and he was much obliged.

When they were in the street Alleyn said: "Did you recognize him?"

"I had a sort of notion," Fox said, "that I ought to. Who is he? He looks like a bum."

"Which is what he is. He's a Mr. Grimball who, twenty years ago and more, was the man in possession at the Lampreys."

"God bless my soul!" Fox said. "Your memory!"

"Peregrine Jay did tell us that the Meade's a compulsive gambler, didn't he?"

"Well, I'll be blowed! Fancy that! On top of all the other lot—in Queer Street. Wonder if Mr. Conducis—"

Fox continued in a series of scandalized ejaculations.

"We're not due with Conducis for another hour and a half," Alleyn said. "Stop clucking and get into the car. We'll drive to the nearest box and ring the Yard in case there's anything."

"About the boy?"

"Yes. Yes. About the boy. Come on."

Fox returned from the telephone box in measured haste.

"Hospital's just rung through," he said. "They think he's coming round."

"Quick as we can," Alleyn said to the driver, and in fifteen minutes, with the sister and house-surgeon in attendance, they walked round the screens that hid Trevor's bed in the children's casualty ward at St. Terence's.

P.C. Grantley had returned to duty. When he saw Alleyn he hurriedly vacated his chair and Alleyn slipped into it.

"Anything?"

Grantley showed his notebook.

"*It's a pretty glove,*" Alleyn read, "*but it doesn't warm my hand. Take it off.*"

"He said that?"

"Yes, sir. Nothing else, sir. Just that."

"It's a quotation from his part."

Trevor's eyes were closed and he breathed evenly. The sister brushed back his curls.

"He's asleep," the doctor said. "We must let him waken in his own time. He'll probably be normal when he does."

"Except for the blackout period?"

"Quite."

Ten minutes slipped by in near silence.

"Mum," Trevor said. "Hey, Mum."

He opened his eyes and stared at Alleyn. "What's up?" he asked and then saw Grantley's tunic. "That's a rozzer," he said. "I haven't done a thing."

"You're all right," said the doctor. "You had a nasty fall and we're looking after you."

"Oh," Trevor said profoundly and shut his eyes.

"Gawd, he's off again," Grantley whispered, distractedly. "Innit marvellous."

"Now then," Fox said austerely.

"Pardon, Mr. Fox."

Alleyn said, "May he be spoken to?"

"He shouldn't be worried. If it's important—"

"It could hardly be more so."

"*Nosey Super,*" Trevor said, and Alleyn turned back to find himself being stared at.

"That's right," he said. "We've met before."

"Yeah. Where though?"

"In The Dolphin. Upstairs in the circle."

"Yeah," Trevor said, wanly tough. A look of doubt came into his eyes. He frowned. "In the circle," he repeated uneasily.

"Things happen up there in the circle, don't they?"

Complacency and still that look of uncertainty. "You can say that again," said Trevor. "All over the house."

"*Slash?*"

"Yeah. *Slash,*" he agreed and grinned.

"You had old Jobbins guessing?"

"And that's no error."

"What did you do?"

Trevor stretched his mouth and produced a wailing sound: *"Wheeeee."*

"Make like spooks," he said. "See?"

"Anything else?"

There was a longish pause. Grantley lifted his head. Somewhere beyond the screens a trolley jingled down the ward.

"Ping."

"That must have rocked them," Alleyn said.

" 'Can say that again. What a turn-up! Oh, dear!"

"How did you do it? Just like that? With your mouth?"

The house-surgeon stirred restively. The sister gave a starched little cough.

"Do you *mind,*" Trevor said. "My mum plays the old steely," he added, and then, with a puzzled look: "Hey! Was that when I got knocked out or something! Was it?"

"That was a bit later. You had a fall. Can you remember where you went after you banged the stage-door?"

"No," he said impatiently. He sighed and shut his eyes. "Do me a favour and pack it up, will you?" he said and went to sleep again.

"I'm afraid that's it," said the house-surgeon.

Alleyn said: "May I have a word with you?"

"Oh, certainly. Yes, of course. Carry on, Sister, will you? He's quite all right."

Alleyn said, "Stick it out, Grantley."

The house-surgeon led him into an office at the entrance to the ward. He was a young man and, although he observed a markedly professional attitude, he was clearly intrigued by the situation.

"Look here," Alleyn said, "I want you to give me your cold-blooded, considered opinion. You tell me the boy is unlikely to remember what happened just before he went overboard. I gather he may recall events up to within a few minutes of the fall?"

"He may, yes. The length of the 'lost' period can vary."

"Did you think he was on the edge of remembering a little further just now?"

"One can't say. One got the impression that he hadn't the energy to try and remember."

"Do you think that if he were faced with the person whom he saw attacking the caretaker, he would recognize him and remember what he saw?"

"I don't know. I'm not a specialist in amnesia or the after-effects of cranial injury. You should ask someone who is." The doctor hesitated and then said slowly: "You mean would the shock of seeing the assailant stimulate the boy's memory?"

"Not of the assault upon himself but of the earlier assault upon Jobbins which may be on the fringe of his recollection—which may lie just this side of the blackout."

"I can't give you an answer to that one."

"Will you move the boy into a separate room—say tomorrow—and allow him to see three—perhaps four—visitors: one after another? For five minutes each."

"No. I'm sorry. Not yet."

"Look," Alleyn said, "can it really do any harm? *Really?*"

"I have not the authority."

"Who has?"

The house-surgeon breathed an Olympian name.

"Is he in the hospital? Now?"

The house-surgeon looked at his watch.

"There's been a board meeting. He may be in his room."

"I'll beard him there. Where is it?"

"Yes, but look here—"

"God bless my soul," Alleyn ejaculated. "I'll rant as well as he. Lead me to him."

ii

"Ten past four," Alleyn said, checking with Big Ben. "Let's do a bit of stocktaking." They had returned to the car.

"You got it fixed up for this show with the boy, Mr. Alleyn?"

"Oh, yes. The great panjandrum turned out to be very mild and a former acquaintance. An instance, I'm afraid, of Harry Grove's detested old-boymanship. I must say I see Harry's point. We went to the ward and he inspected young Trevor who was awake, as bright as a button, extremely full of himself and demanding a nice dinner. The expert decided in our favour. We may arrange the visits for tomorrow at noon. *Out* of visiting hours. We'll get Peregrine Jay to call the actors and arrange the timetable. I don't want us to come into it at this juncture. We'll just occur at the event. Jay is to tell them the truth: that the boy can't remember what happened and that it's hoped the encounters with the rest of the cast may set up some chain of association that could lead to a recovery of memory."

"One of them won't fancy *that* idea."

"No. But it wouldn't do to refuse."

"The nerve might crack. There might be a bolt. With that sort of temperament," Fox said, "you can't tell what may happen. Still, we're well provided."

"If anybody's nerve cracks it won't be Miss Destiny Meade's. What did you make of that scene in her flat, Fox?"

"Well: to begin with, the lady was very much put out by my being there. In *my* view, Mr. Alleyn, she didn't fancy police protection within the meaning of the code to anything like the extent that she fancied it coming in a personal way from yourself. Talk about the go-ahead signal! It was hung out like the week's wash," said Mr. Fox.

"Control yourself, Fox."

"Now, on what she said we only missed Mr. Knight by seconds. She makes out he rang up and abused her to such an extent that she decided to call you and that he walked in while she was still talking to you."

"Yes. And they went bang off into a roaring row which culminated in him handing her a tuppenny one to the jaw after which he flung out and we, within a couple of minutes minced in."

"No thought in her mind, it appears," Fox suggested, "of ringing Mr. Grove up to come and protect her. Only you."

"I daresay she's doing that very thing at this moment. I must say, I hope he knows how to cope with her."

"Only one thing to do with that type of lady," Fox said, "and I don't mean a tuppenny one to the jaw. He'll cope."

"We'll be talking to Conducis in half an hour, Fox, and it's going to be tricky."

"I should damn well think so," Fox warmly agreed. "What with orchids and her just seeing him quietly from time to time. Hi!" he ejaculated. "Would Mr. Grove know about Mr. Conducis and would Mr. Conducis know about Mr. Grove?"

"Who is, remember, his distant relation. Search me, Fox. The thing at the moment seems to be that Knight knows about them both and acts accordingly. Big stuff."

"How a gang like this hangs together beats me. You'd think the resignations'd be falling in like autumn leaves. What they always tell you, I suppose," Fox said. "The Show Must Go On."

"And it happens to be a highly successful show with fat parts and much prestige. But I should think that even they won't be able to sustain the racket indefinitely at this pitch."

"Why are we going to see Mr. Conducis, I ask myself. How do we shape up to him? Does he matter, as far as the case is concerned?"

"In so far as he was in the theatre and knows the combination, yes."

"I suppose so."

"I thought him an exceedingly rum personage, Fox. A cold fish and yet a far from insensitive fish. No indication of any background other than wealth, or of any particular race. He carries a British passport. He inherited one fortune and made Lord knows how many more, each about a hundred per cent fatter than the last. He's spent most of his time abroad and a lot of it in the *Kalliope,* until she was cut in half in a heavy fog under his feet. That was six years ago. What did you make of Jay's account of the menu card?"

"Rather surprising if he's right. Rather a coincidence, two of our names cropping up in that direction."

"We can check the passenger list with the records. But it's not really a coincidence. People in Conducis's world tend to move about expensively in a tight group. There was, of course, an inquiry after the disaster and Conducis was reported to be unable to appear. He was in a nursing home on the Côte d'Azur suffering from exhaustion, exposure and severe shock."

"Bluff?"

"Perhaps. He certainly is a rum 'un and no mistake. Jay's account of his behaviour that morning—by *George,*" Alleyn said suddenly. "Hell's boots and gaiters!"

"What's all this, now?" Fox asked placidly.

"So much hokum I daresay, but listen, all the same."

Fox listened.

"Well," he said. "You always say don't conjecture but personally, Mr. Alleyn, when you get one of your hunches in this sort of way I reckon it's safe to go nap on it. Not that this one really gets us any nearer an arrest."

"I wonder if you're right about that. I wonder."

They talked for another five minutes, going over Peregrine's notes, and then Alleyn looked at his watch and said they must be off. When they were halfway to Park Lane he said: "You went over all the properties in the theatre, didn't you? No musical instruments?"

"None."

"He might have had Will singing 'Take, oh take those lips away' to the Dark Lady. Accompanying himself on a lute. But he didn't."

"Perhaps Mr. Knight can't sing."

"You may be right at that."

They drove into Park Lane and turned into Drury Place.

"I'm going," Alleyn said, "to cling to Peregrine Jay's notes as Mr. Conducis was reported to have clung to his raft."

"I still don't know *exactly* what line we take," Fox objected.

"We let him dictate it," Alleyn rejoined. "At first. Come on."

Mawson admitted them to that so arrogantly unobtrusive interior, and a pale young man advanced to meet them. Alleyn remembered him from his former visit. The secretary.

"Mr. Alleyn. And—er?"

"Inspector Fox."

"Yes. How do you do? Mr. Conducis is in the library. He's been very much distressed by this business. Awfully upset. Particularly about the boy. We've sent flowers and all that nonsense, of course, and we're in touch with the theatre people. Mr. Conducis is most anxious that everything possible should be done. Well—shall we? You'll find him, perhaps, rather nervous, Mr. Alleyn. He has been so very distressed."

They walked soundlessly to the library door. A clock mellifluously struck five.

"Here is Superintendent Alleyn, sir, and Inspector Fox."

"Yes. Thank you."

Mr. Conducis was standing at the far end of the library. He had been looking out of the window, it seemed. In the evening light the long room resembled an interior by some defunct academician: Orchardson, perhaps, or the Hon. John Collier. The details were of an undated excellence but the general effect was strangely Edwardian and so was Mr. Conducis. He might have been a deliberately underslated monument to Affluence.

As he moved towards them Alleyn wondered if Mr. Conducis was ill or if his pallor was brought about by some refraction of light from the apple-green walls. He wore a gardenia in his coat and an edge of crimson silk showed above his breast pocket.

"Good evening," he said. "I am pleased that you were able to come. Glad to see you again."

He offered his hand. Large and white, it withdrew itself—it almost snatched itself away—from contact.

Mawson came in with a drinks tray, put it down, hovered, was glanced at and withdrew.

"You will have a drink," Mr. Conducis stated.

"Thank you, but no," Alleyn said. "Not on duty, I'm afraid. This won't stop you from having one, of course."

"I am an abstainer," said Mr. Conducis. "Shall we sit down?"

They did so. The crimson leather chairs received them like sultans.

Alleyn said, "You sent word you wanted to see us, sir, but we would in any case have asked for an interview. Perhaps the best way of tackling this unhappy business will be for us to hear any questions that it may have occurred to you to ask. We will then, if you please, continue the conversation of what I can only call routine investigation lines."

Mr. Conducis raised his clasped hands to his mouth and glanced briefly over them at Alleyn. He then lowered his gaze to his fingers. Alleyn thought: "I suppose that's how he looks when he's manipulating his gargantuan undertakings."

Mr. Conducis said, "I am concerned with this affair. The theatre is my property and the enterprise is under my control. I have financed it. The glove and documents are mine. I trust, therefore, that I am entitled to a detailed statement upon the case as it appears to your Department. Or rather, since you are in charge of the investigation, as it appears to you."

This was said with an air of absolute authority. Alleyn was conscious, abruptly, of the extraordinary force that resided in Mr. Conducis.

He said very amiably: "We are not authorized, I'm afraid, to make detailed statements on demand—not even to entrepreneurs of businesses and owners of property, especially where a fatality has occurred on that property and a crime of violence may be suspected. On the other hand, I will, as I have suggested, be glad to consider any questions you like to put to me."

And he thought: "He's like a lizard or a chameleon or whatever the animal is that blinks slowly. It's what people mean when they talk about hooded eyes."

Mr. Conducis did not argue or protest. For all the reaction he gave, he might not have heard what Alleyn said.

"In your opinion," he said, "were the fatality and the injury to the boy caused by an act of violence?"

"Yes."

"Both by the same hand?"

"Yes."

"Have you formed an opinion on why it was done?"

"We have arrived at a working hypothesis."

"What is it?"

"I can go so far as to say that I think both were defensive actions."

"By a person caught in the act of robbery?"

"I believe so, yes."

"Do you think you know who this person is?"

"I am almost sure that I do. I am not positive."

"Who?"

"That," Alleyn said, "I am not at liberty to tell you. Yet."

Mr. Conducis looked fully at him, if the fact that those extraordinarily blank eyes were focussed on his face could justify this assertion.

"You said you wished to see me. Why?"

"For several reasons. The first concerns your property: the glove and the documents. As you know they have been recovered, but I think you should also know by what means."

He told the story of Jeremy Jones and the substitution and he could have sworn that as he did so the sweet comfort of a reprieve flooded through Conducis. The thick white hands relaxed. He gave an almost inaudible but long sigh.

"Have you arrested him?"

"No. We have, of course, uplifted the glove. It is in a safe at the Yard with the documents."

"I cannot believe, Superintendent Alleyn, that you give any credence to his story."

"I am inclined to believe it."

"Then in my opinion you are either incredibly stupid or needlessly evasive. In either case, incompetent."

This attack surprised Alleyn. He had not expected his slow-blinking opponent to dart his tongue so soon. As if sensing his reaction Mr. Conducis recrossed his legs and said: "I am too severe. I beg your pardon. Let me explain myself. Can you not see that Jones's story was an impromptu invention? He did not substitute the faked glove for the real glove six months ago. He substituted it last night and was discovered in the act. He killed Jobbins, was seen by the boy and tried to kill him. He left the copy behind—no doubt if he had not been interrupted he would have put it in the safe—and he took the real glove to the safe-deposit."

"First packing it with most elaborate care in an insulated box with four wrappings, all sealed."

"Done in the night. Before Jay got home."

"We can check, you know, with the safe-deposit people. He says he had a witness when he deposited the glove six months ago."

"A witness to a dummy package, no doubt."

"If you consider," Alleyn said, "I'm sure you will come to the conclusion that this theory won't answer. It really won't, you know."

"Why not?"

"Do you want me to spell it out, sir? If, as he states, he transposed the gloves six months ago and intended to maintain the deception, he had no need to do anything further. If the theft was a last-minute notion, he could perfectly well have effected the transposition today or tomorrow, when he performed his authorized job of removing the treasure from the safe. There was no need for him to sneak back into the theatre at dead of night and risk discovery. Why on earth, six months ago, should he go through an elaborate hocus-pocus of renting a safe-deposit and lodging a fake parcel in it?"

"He's a fanatic. He has written to me expostulating about the sale of the items to an American purchaser. He even tried, I am told, to secure an interview. My secretary can show you his letter. It is most extravagant."

"I shall be interested to see it."

A brief silence followed this exchange. Alleyn thought: "He's formidable but he's not as tough as I expected. He's shaken."

"Have you any other questions?" Alleyn asked.

He wondered if the long, unheralded silence was one of Mr. Conducis's strategic weapons: whether it was or not, he now employed it and Alleyn, with every appearance of tranquillity, sat it out. The light had changed in the long green room and the sky outside the far windows had darkened. Beneath them, at the exquisite table, Peregrine Jay had first examined the documents and the glove. And against the left-hand wall under a picture—surely a Kandinsky—stood the bureau, an Oeben or Riesener perhaps, from which Mr. Conducis had withdrawn his treasures. Fox, who in a distant chair had performed his little miracle of self-effacement, gave a slight cough.

Mr. Conducis said without moving, "I would ask for information as to the continued running of the play and the situation of the players."

"I understand the season will go on: we've taken no action that might prevent it."

"You will do so if you arrest a member of the company."

"He or she would be replaced by an understudy."

"She," Mr. Conducis said in a voice utterly devoid of inflection. "That, of course, need not be considered."

He waited, but Alleyn thought it was his turn to initiate a silence and made no comment.

"Miss Destiny Meade has spoken to me," Mr. Conducis said. "She is very much distressed by the whole affair. She tells me you called upon her this afternoon and she finds herself, as a result, quite prostrated. Surely there is no need for her to be pestered like this."

For a split second Alleyn wondered what on earth Mr. Conducis would think if he and Fox went into fits of laughter. He said: "Miss Meade was extremely helpful and perfectly frank. I am sorry she found the exercise fatiguing."

"I have no more to say," Mr. Conducis said and stood up. So did Alleyn.

"I'm afraid that I have," he said. "I'm on duty, sir, and this *is* an investigation."

"I have nothing to bring to it."

"When we are convinced of that we will stop bothering you. I'm sure you'd prefer us to deal with the whole matter here rather than at the Yard. Wouldn't you?"

Mr. Conducis went to the drinks tray and poured himself a glass of water. He took a minute gold case from a waistcoat pocket, shook a tablet on his palm, swallowed it and chased it down.

"Excuse me," he said, "it was time."

Ulcers? wondered Alleyn.

Mr. Conducis returned and faced him. "By all means," he said. "I am perfectly ready to help you and only regret that I am unlikely to be able to do so to any effect. I have, from the time I decided to promote The Dolphin undertaking, acted solely through my executives. Apart from an initial meeting and one brief discussion with Mr. Jay I have virtually no personal contacts with members of the management and company."

"With the exception, perhaps, of Miss Meade?"

"Quite so."

"And Mr. Grove."

"He was already known to me. I except him."

"I understand you are related?"

"A distant connection."

"So he said," Alleyn lightly agreed. "I understand," he added, "that you were formerly acquainted with Mr. Marcus Knight."

"What makes you think so?"

"Peregrine Jay recognized his signature on the menu you destroyed in his presence."

"Mr. Jay was not himself that morning."

"Do you mean, sir, that he made a mistake and Knight was not a guest in the *Kalliope?*"

After a long pause Mr. Conducis said: "He was a guest. He behaved badly. He took offense at an imagined slight. He left the yacht, at my suggestion, at Villefranche."

"And so escaped the disaster?"

"Yes."

Mr. Conducis had seated himself again: this time in an upright chair. He sat rigidly erect, but as if conscious of this, crossed his legs and put his hands in his trouser pockets. Alleyn stood a short distance from him.

"I am going to ask you," he said, "to talk about something that may be painful to you. I want you to tell me about the night of the fancy-dress dinner party on board the *Kalliope*."

Alleyn had seen people sit with the particular kind of stillness that now invested Mr. Conducis. They sat like that in the cells underneath the dock while they waited for the jury to come back. In the days of capital punishment, he had been told by a warder that they sat like that while they waited to hear if they were reprieved. He could see a very slight rhythmic movement of the crimson silk handkerchief and he could hear, ever so faintly, the breathing of Mr. Conducis.

"It was six years ago, wasn't it?" Alleyn said. "And the dinner party took place on the night of the disaster?"

Mr. Conducis's eyes closed in a momentary assent but he did not speak.

"Was Mrs. Constantia Guzmann one of your guests in the yacht?"

"Yes," he said indifferently.

"You told Mr. Jay, I believe, that you bought the Shakespeare relics six years ago?"

"That is so."

"Had you this treasure on board the yacht?"

"Why should you think so?"

"Because Jay found under the glove the menu for a dinner in the *Kalliope*—he thinks it was headed 'Villefranche.' Which you burnt in the fireplace over there."

"The menu must have been dropped in the desk. It was an unpleasant reminder of a painful event."

"So the desk and its contents *were* in the yacht?"

"Yes."

"May I ask why, sir?"

Mr. Conducis's lips moved, were compressed and moved again. "I bought them," he said, "from—" he gave a grotesque little cough— "from a person in the yacht."

"Who was this person, if you please?"

"I have forgotten."

"Forgotten?"

"The name."

"Was it Knight?"

"*No.*"

"There are maritime records. We shall be able to trace it. Will you go on, please?"

"He was a member of the ship's complement. He asked to see me and showed me the desk which he said he wanted to sell. I understand that it had been given him by the proprietress of a lodging-house. I thought the contents were almost certainly worthless but I gave him what he asked for them."

"Which was—?"

"Thirty pounds."

"What became of this man?"

"Drowned," said a voice from somewhere inside Mr. Conducis.

"How did it come about that the desk and its contents were saved?"

"I cannot conjecture by what fantastic process of thought you imagine any of this relates to your inquiry."

"I hope to show that it does. I believe it does."

"I had the desk on deck. I had shown the contents, as a matter of curiosity, to some of my guests."

"Did Mrs. Guzmann see it, perhaps?"

"Perhaps."

"Was she interested?"

A look which Alleyn afterwards described as being profoundly professional drifted into Mr. Conducis's face.

He said, "She is a collector."

"Did she make an offer?"

"She did. I was not inclined to sell."

Alleyn was visited by a strange notion.

"Tell me," he said, "were you both in fancy dress?"

Mr. Conducis looked at him with an air of wondering contempt. "Mrs. Guzmann," he said, "was in costume: Andalusian, I understand. I wore a domino over evening dress."

"Gloved, either of you?"

"No!" he said loudly and added: "We had been playing bridge."

"Were any of the others gloved?"

"A ridiculous question. Some may have been."

"Were the ship's company in fancy dress?"

"Certainly not!"

"The stewards?"

"As eighteenth-century flunkeys."

"Gloved?"

"I do not remember."

"Why do you dislike pale gloves, Mr. Conducis?"

"I have no idea," he said breathlessly, "what you mean."

"You told Peregrine Jay that you dislike them."

"A personal prejudice. I cannot account for it."

"Were there gloved hands that disturbed you on the night of the disaster? Mr. Conducis, are you ill?"

"I—no. No, I am well. You insist on questioning me about an episode which distressed me, which was painful, tragic, an outrage to one's sensibilities."

"I would avoid it if I could. I'm afraid I must go further. Will you tell me exactly what happened at the moment of disaster: to you, I mean, and to whoever was near you then or later?"

For a moment Alleyn thought he was going to refuse. He wondered if there would be a sudden outbreak or whether Mr. Conducis would merely walk out of the room and leave them to take what action they chose. He did none of these things. He embarked upon a toneless, rapid recital of facts. Of the fact of fog, the sudden looming of the tanker, the splitting apart of the *Kalliope*. Of the fact of fire breaking out. Of oil on the water and of how he found himself looking down on the wooden raft from the swimming pool and of how the deck turned into a precipice and he slid from it and landed on the raft.

"Still with the little desk?"

Yes. Clutched under his left arm, it seemed, but with no consciousness of this. He had lain across the raft with the desk underneath him. It had bruised him very badly. He gripped a rope loop at the side with his right hand. Mrs. Guzmann had appeared beside the raft and was clinging to one of the loops. Alleyn had a mental picture of an enormous nose, an open mouth, a mantilla plastered over a big head and a floundering mass of wet black lace and white flesh.

The recital stopped as abruptly as it had begun.

"That is all. We were picked up by the tanker."

"Were there other people on the raft?"

"I believe so. My memory is not clear. I lost consciousness."

"Men? Mrs. Guzmann?"

"I believe so. I was told so."

"Pretty hazardous, I should have thought. It wouldn't accommodate more than—how many?"

"I don't know. I don't know. I don't know."

"Mr. Conducis, when you saw Peregrine Jay's gloved hands clinging to the edge of that hole in the stage at The Dolphin and heard him call out that he would drown if you didn't save him—were you reminded—"

Mr. Conducis had risen and now began to move backwards, like an image in slow motion, towards the bureau. Fox rose, too, and shifted in front of it. Mr. Conducis drew his crimson silk handkerchief from his breast pocket and pressed it against his mouth, and above it his upper lip glistened. His brows were defined by beaded margins and the dark skin of his face was stretched too tight and had blanched over the bones.

"Be quiet," he said. "No. Be quiet."

Somebody had come into the house. A distant voice spoke loudly but indistinguishably.

The door opened and the visitor came in.

Mr. Conducis screamed: "You've told them. You've betrayed me. I wish to Christ I'd killed you."

Fox took him from behind. Almost at once he stopped struggling.

iii

Trevor could be, as Alleyn put it, bent at the waist. He had been so bent and was propped up in a sitting position in his private room. A bed-tray on legs was arranged across his stomach, ready for any offerings that might be forthcoming. His condition had markedly improved since Alleyn's visit of the day before, and he was inclined, though still feebly, to throw his weight about.

The private room was small but there was a hospital screen in one corner of it and behind the screen, secreted there before Trevor was wheeled in, sat Inspector Fox, his large, decent feet concealed by Trevor's suitcase. Alleyn occupied the bedside chair.

On receiving assurances from Alleyn that the police were not on his tracks Trevor reported, with more fluency, his previous account of his antics in the deserted auditorium, but he would not or could not carry the recital beyond the point when he was in the circle and heard a distant telephone ring. "I don't remember another thing," he said importantly. "I've blacked out. I was concussed. The doc says I was very badly concussed. Here! *Where* did I fall, Super? What's the story?"

"You fell into the stalls."

"Would you mind!"

"True."

"Into the *stalls!* Cripes! *Why?"*

"That's what I want to find out."

Trevor looked sideways. "Did old Henry Jobbins lay into me?" he asked.

"No."

"Or Chas Random?"

A knowledgeable look: a disfiguring look of veiled gratification, perhaps, appeared like a blemish on Trevor's pageboy face. He giggled.

"He was wild with me, Chas was. Listen: Chas had it in for me, Super, really he did. I got that camp's goat, actually, good and proper."

Alleyn listened and absently noted how underlying Cockney seeped up through superimposed drama academy. Behind carefully turned vowel and consonant jibed a Southward urchin. "Goo' 'un prop-*per,"* Trevor was really saying, however classy the delivery.

"Some of the company are coming in to see you," Alleyn said. "They may only stay for a minute or two but they'd like to say hullo."

"I'd be pleased," Trevor graciously admitted. He was extremely complacent.

Alleyn watched him and talked to him for a little while longer and then, conscious of making a decision that might turn out most lamentably, he said: "Look here, young Trevor, I'm going to ask you to help me in a very tricky and important business. If you don't like the suggestion you needn't have anything to do with it. On the other hand—"

He paused. Trevor gave him a sharp look.

"Nothing comes to the dumb," he said. "What seems to be the trouble? Come in and give."

Ten minutes later his visitors began to arrive, ushered in by Peregrine Jay. "Just tell them," Alleyn had said, "that he'd like to see them for a few minutes and arrange the timetable. You can pen them up in the waiting-room at the end of the corridor."

They brought presents. Winter Meyer came first with a box of crystallized fruit. He put it on the tray and then stood at the foot of the bed wearing his shepherd's plaid suit and his dark red tie. His hair, beautifully cut, waved above and behind the ears. He leaned his head to one side and looked at Trevor.

"Well, well, well," he said. "So the great star is receiving. How does it feel to be famous?"

Trevor was languid and gracious, but before the prescribed five minutes had elapsed he mentioned that his agent would be waiting upon

Mr. Meyer with reference to the Management, as he put it, seeing him right.

"We don't," Winter Meyer said, eyeing him warily, "need to worry just yet about that one. Do we?"

"I hope not, Mr. Meyer," Trevor said. He leaned his head back against the pillows and closed his eyes. "Funny how faint I appear to get," he murmured. "I hope it won't be kind of permanent. My doctors seem to take a grave view. Funny thing."

Mr. Meyer said, "You played that line just like the end of Act I, but I mustn't tire you."

He tiptoed elaborately away from the bed and, as he passed Alleyn, let droop a heavy white eyelid.

Jeremy Jones had made a group of tiny effigies representing the characters in the play and had mounted them on a minuscule stage. "Everso quaint," Trevor said. "Ta, Mr. Jones. You *have* been busy. Put it on my tray, would you?"

Jeremy put his offering on the tray. Trevor gazed into his face as he did so. "You *are* clever with your fingers," he said. "Aren't you, Mr. Jones?"

Jeremy looked suspiciously at him, turned scarlet and said to Alleyn: "I mustn't stay too long."

"Don't go," said Trevor. "Yet."

Jeremy lingered, with one eye on Alleyn and awkwardly at a loss for anything to say. Peregrine tapped on the door, looked in, said: "Oh, sorry," when he saw his friend and retired.

"I want to see Mr. Jay," Trevor said. "Here! Call him back."

Jeremy fetched Peregrine and seized the opportunity, after a nod from Alleyn, to make his own escape. Peregrine, having already done his duty in that respect, brought no offering.

"Here!" Trevor said. "What price that kid? My understudy. Is he going on tonight?"

"Yes. He's all right," Peregrine said. "Word perfect and going to give quite a nice show. You needn't worry."

Trevor glowered at him. "What about the billing, Mr. Jay? What about the programmes?"

"They've been slipped. 'During your indisposition the part will be played—' You know?"

"Anything in the press? They haven't brought me any papers," the feeble voice grumbled. "What's my agent doing? My mum says they don't want me to see the papers. Look, Mr. Jay—"

Alleyn said: "You'll see the papers."

Peregrine waited until Charles Random arrived. "If you want me," he then said to Alleyn, "I'll be in the corridor."

Random brought a number of dubious-looking comics. "Knowing your taste in literature," he said to Trevor. "Not that I approve."

Trevor indicated his tray. As Random approached him, he put on a sly look. "Really," he said, "you shouldn't have troubled, Mr. Random."

They stared at each other, their faces quite close together—Random's guarded, shuttered, wary and Trevor's faintly impertinent.

"You've got a bruise on your cheekbone," Random said.

"That's nothing. You should see the rest."

"Keep you quiet for a bit."

"That's right."

Random turned his head slowly and looked at Alleyn. "Police are taking a great interest, I see," he said.

"Routine," Alleyn rejoined. "Merely routine."

"At a high level." Random drew back quickly from Trevor, who giggled and opened his bundle of comics. "Oh, fabulous," he said. "It's 'Slash.' Z-z-z-z-yock!" He became absorbed.

"That being that," Random said, "I shall bow myself off. Unless," he added, "the Superintendent is going to arrest me."

Trevor, absorbed in his comic, said: "You never know, do you? Cheerie-bye and ta."

Random moved towards the door. "Get better quick," he murmured. Trevor looked up and winked. "What do you think?" he said.

Random opened the door and disclosed Miss Bracey on the threshold.

They said, "Oh, hullo, dear," simultaneously and Random added: "This gets more like a French farce every second. Everyone popping in and out. Wonderful timing."

They both laughed with accomplishment and he went away.

Gertrude behaved as if she and Alleyn had never met. She said good morning in a poised voice and clearly expected him to leave. He responded politely, indicated the bedside chair, called Trevor's attention to his visitor and himself withdrew to the window.

Miss Bracey said, "You *have* been in the wars, dear, haven't you?" She advanced to the bedside and placed a small parcel on the table. Trevor lifted his face to hers, inviting an embrace. Their faces came together and parted and Miss Bracey sank into the chair.

"I mustn't stay too long: you're not to be tired," she said. She was quite composed. Only that occasional drag at the corner of her mouth suggested to Alleyn that she had fortified herself. She made the conventional inquiries as to Trevor's progress and he responded with an enthusiastic account of his condition. The worst case of concussion, he said importantly, that they'd ever seen in the ward.

"Like what you read about," he said, "I was—"

He stopped short and for a moment looked puzzled. "I was having a bit of fun," he began again. "You know, Miss Bracey. Just for giggles. I was having old Jobbins on."

"Yes?" said Miss Bracey. "That was naughty of you, dear, wasn't it?"

"But," Trevor said, frowning. "You know. You were there, weren't you?" he added doubtfully.

She looked anywhere but at Alleyn. "You're still confused," she said. "You mustn't worry about it."

"But weren't you, Miss Bracey? Down there? In front? Weren't you?"

"I don't know when you mean, dear."

"Neither do I. Not quite. But you were there."

"I was in the downstairs foyer on Saturday night for a minute or two," she said loudly. "As I told the Superintendent."

"Yeah, I know you were," Trevor said. "But where was I?"

"You didn't see me. You weren't there. Don't worry about it."

"I was. I was."

"I'd better go," she said and rose.

"*No*," Trevor almost shouted. He brought his small fist down on the bed-tray and Jeremy's microcosms fell on their faces. "*No!* You've got to stay till I remember."

"I think you should stay, Miss Bracey," Alleyn said. "Really."

She backed away from the bed. Trevor gave a little cry. "There!" he said. "That's it. That's what you did. And you were looking up—at him. Looking up and backing away and kind of blubbing."

"Trevor, be quiet. *Be quiet*. You don't know. You've forgotten."

"Like what you're always doing, Miss Bracey. Chasing him. That's right, isn't it, Miss Bracey? Tagging old Harry. You'd come out of the downstairs lav and you looked up and saw him. And then the office door opened and it was Mr. Meyer and Mr. Knight and you done—you did a quick scarper, Miss Bracey. And so did I! Back into the circle, smartly. I got it, now," Trevor said with infinite satisfaction. "I got it."

"How," Alleyn said, "did you know who he was? It must have been dark up there."

"Him? Harry? By his flash coat. Cripey, what a dazzler!"

"It's not true," she gabbled and stumbled across the room. She

pawed at Alleyn's coat. "It's not true. He doesn't know what he's saying. It wasn't Harry. Don't listen. I swear it wasn't Harry."

"You're quite right," Alleyn said. "You thought it was Harry Grove
but it was Jobbins you saw on the landing. Grove had given Jobbins his
overcoat."

Her hands continued for a second or two to scrabble at his coat and
then fell away. She looked into his face and her own crumpled into a
weeping mask.

Alleyn said: "You've been having a bad time. An awful time. But it
will ease up. It won't always be as bad as this."

"Let me go. Please let me go."

"Yes," he said. "You may go now."

And when she had gone, blowing her nose, squaring her shoulders
and making, instinctively he supposed, quite an exit, he turned to Trevor
and found him, with every sign of gratification, deep in his comics.

"Do I have to see the others?" he asked. "It's getting a bit of a drag."

"Are you tired?"

"No. I'm reading." His eye lit on Gertrude Bracey's parcel. "Might
as well look it over," he said and unwrapped a tie. "Where'd she dig
that up?" he wondered and returned to his comic.

"You are a young toad, aren't you?" Alleyn remarked. "How old are
you, in Heaven's name?"

"Eleven and three months," Trevor said. He was helping himself to a
crystallized plum.

A slight rumpus broke out in the passage. Peregrine put his head
round the door. "Marco and Harry are both here," he said and cast up
his eyes.

When Alleyn joined him at the door he muttered: "Marco won't
wait. He didn't want to come. And Harry says he got here first. He's up
to his usual game," Peregrine said. "Knight-baiting."

"Tell *him* to shut up and wait or I'll run him in."

"I wish to Heaven you would, at that."

"Ask Knight to come along."

"Yes. All right."

"No sign of Conducis as yet?"

"No."

When Marcus Knight came in he did not exhibit his usual signs of
emotional disturbance: the flashing eye, the empurpled cheek, the
throbbing pulse and the ringing tone. On the contrary he was pale and
as near to being subdued, Alleyn felt, as he could be. He laid his offering upon the now filled-to-capacity bed-tray. Fruit: in season and a

gilded basket. He brusquely ran his fingers through Trevor's curls and Trevor immediately responded with a look that successfully combined young Hamnet and Paul Dombey.

"Oh Mr. Knight," he said, "you honestly shouldn't. You *are* kind. Grapes! How fab!"

A rather stilted bedside conversation followed, during which Knight gave at least half his uneasy attention to Alleyn. Presently Trevor complained that he had slipped down in his bed and asked his illustrious guest to help him up. When Knight with an ill-grace bent over him, Trevor gazed admiringly into his face and wreathed his arms round his neck. "Just like the end of Act I come true," he said, "isn't it, Mr. Knight? I ought to be wearing the glove."

Knight hurriedly extricated himself. A look of doubt crossed Trevor's face. "*The glove,*" he repeated. "There's something about the real one— isn't there? Something?"

Knight looked a question at Alleyn, who said: "Trevor doesn't recall the latter part of his adventures in the theatre on Saturday night. I think Jay has explained that we hope one of you may help to restore his memory."

"I *am* remembering more," Trevor said importantly. "I remember hearing Mr. Knight in the office with Mr. Meyer."

Marcus Knight stiffened. "I believe you are aware, Alleyn, that I left with Meyer at about eleven."

"He has told us so," Alleyn said.

"Very well," Knight stood over Trevor and imposed upon himself, evidently with difficulty, an air of sweet reasonableness. "If," he said, "dear boy, you were spying about in front while I was with Mr. Meyer in his office, and if you heard our voices, you doubtless also saw us leave the theatre."

Trevor nodded.

"Precisely," Knight said and spread his hands at Alleyn.

"*People come back,*" said the treble voice. Alleyn turned to find Trevor, the picture of puzzled innocence, frowning, his fingers at his lips.

"What the hell do you mean by that!" Knight ejaculated.

"It's part of what I can't remember. Somebody came back."

"I really cannot imagine, Alleyn—" Knight began.

"*I-don't-think-I-want-to-remember.*"

"There you are, you see. This is infamous. The boy will be harmed. I absolutely refuse to take part in a dangerous and unwarranted experiment. Don't worry yourself, boy. You are perfectly right. Don't try to remember."

"Why?"

"Because I tell you," Knight roared and strode to the door. Here he paused. "I am an artist," he said, suddenly adopting a muted voice that was rather more awful than a piercing scream. "In eight hours' time I appear before the public in a most exhausting role. Moreover I shall be saddled throughout a poignant, delicate and exacting scene with the incompetence of some revolting child-actor of whose excesses I am as yet ignorant. My nerves have been exacerbated. For the past forty-eight hours I have suffered the torments of hell. Slighted. Betrayed. Derided. Threatened. And now—this ludicrous, useless and important summons by the police. Very well, Superintendent Alleyn. There shall be no more of it. I shall lodge a formal complaint. In the meantime—*Goodbye.*"

The door was opened with violence and shut—not slammed—with well-judged temperance.

"Lovely eggzit," said Trevor, yawning and reading his comic.

From outside in the corridor came the sound of applause, an oath, and rapidly retreating footsteps.

Alleyn reopened the door to disclose Harry Grove, gently clapping his hands, and Marcus Knight striding down the corridor.

Harry said, "Isn't he *superb?* Honestly, you have to hand it to him." He drew a parcel from his pocket. "Baby roulette," he said. "Trevor can work out systems. It is true that this is a sort of identification parade?"

"You could put it like that, I suppose," Alleyn agreed.

"Do you mean," Harry said, changing colour, "that this unfortunate but nauseating little boy may suddenly point his finger at one of us and enunciate in ringing tones: 'It all comes back to me. He dunnit.'"

"That, roughly, is the idea."

"Then I freely confess it terrifies me."

"Come inside and get it over."

"Very well. But I'd have you know that he's quite capable of putting on a false show of recovery smartly followed up by a still falser accusation. Particularly," Harry said grimly, "in my case when he knows the act would draw loud cheers and much laughter from all hands and the cook."

"We'll have to risk it. In you go."

Alleyn opened the door and followed Harry into the room.

Trevor had slithered down again in his bed and had dropped off into a convalescent cat-nap. Harry stopped short and stared at him.

"He looks," he whispered, "as if he was quite a nice little boy, doesn't he? You'd say butter wouldn't melt. Is he really asleep or is it an act?"

"He dozes. If you just lean over him he'll wake."

"It seems a damn shame, I must say."

"All the same I'll ask you to do it, if you will. There's a bruise on the cheekbone that mystifies us all. I wonder if you've any ideas. Have a look at it."

A trolley jingled past the door and down the corridor. Outside on the river a barge hooted. Against the multiple, shapeless voice of London, Big Ben struck one o'clock.

Harry put his parcel on the tray.

"Look at the bruise on his face. His hair's fallen across it. Move his hair back and look."

Harry stooped over the boy and put out his left hand.

From behind the screen in the corner there rang out a single, plangent note. *"Twang."*

Trevor opened his eyes, looked into Harry's face and screamed.

Chapter XI

The Show Will Go On

Harry Grove had given no trouble. When Trevor screamed he stepped back from him. He was sheet-white but he achieved a kind of smile.

"No doubt," he had said to Alleyn, "you will now issue the usual warning and invite me to accompany you to the nearest police station. May I suggest that Perry should be informed. He'll want to get hold of my understudy."

And as this was the normal procedure it had been carried out.

So now, at Alleyn's suggestion, they had returned, not to the Yard but to The Dolphin. Here for the first time Mr. Conducis kept company with the actors that he employed. They sat round the circle foyer while, down below, the public began to cue up for the early doors.

Peregrine had called Harry Grove's understudy and he and the new child-actor were being rehearsed behind the fire curtain by the stage-director.

"I think," Alleyn said, "it is only fair to give you all some explanation since each of you has to some extent been involved. These, as I believe, are the facts about Saturday night. I may say that Hartly Grove has admitted to them in substance.

"Grove left the theatre with Miss Meade and her party, saying he would go to Canonbury and pick up his guitar. He had in fact brought his guitar to the theatre and had hidden it in a broom cupboard in the Property Room where it was found, in the course of his illicit explorations, by Trevor. Grove got into his open sports car, drove around the block and parked the car in Phipps Passage. He re-entered the theatre by the pass-door while Mr. Meyer and Mr. Knight were in the office. He may have been seen by Jobbins, who would think nothing of it as Grove was in the habit of coming round for messages. He was not seen by Miss Bracey who mistook Jobbins for him because of the coat.

"Grove remained hidden throughout the rumpus about Trevor until, as he thought, the theatre was deserted except for Jobbins. At eleven o'clock he dialled his own number and let it ring just long enough for his wakeful neighbour to hear it and suppose it had been answered.

"It must have given him a shock when he heard Trevor, in the course of his fooling, pluck the guitar string. It was that scrap of evidence, by the way, when you remembered it, Jay, that set me wondering if Grove had left his instrument in the theatre and not gone to Canonbury. A moment later he heard the stage-door slam and thought, as Mr. Jay and Miss Dunne and Jobbins did, that Trevor had gone. But Trevor had sneaked back and was himself hiding and dodging about the auditorium. He saw Miss Bracey during his activities. Later, he tells us, he caught sight of Harry Grove and began to stalk him like one of his comic-strip heroes. We have the odd picture of Grove stealing to the broom-cupboard to collect his guitar, flitting like a shadow down a side passage, leaving the instrument ready to hand near the front foyer. Inadvertently, perhaps, causing it to emit that twanging sound."

Peregrine gave a short ejaculation but when Alleyn looked at him said: "No. Go on. Go on."

"Having dumped the guitar Grove returned to the stairway from the stage to the circle, climbed it and waited for midnight in the upper box. And, throughout this performance, Trevor peeped, followed, listened, spied.

"At midnight Jobbins left his post under the treasure and went downstairs to ring Police and Fire. Grove darted to the wall panel, opened it, used his torch and manipulated the combination. There had been a lot of talk about the lock after the safe was installed and before the treasure was put into it. At that time it was not guarded and I think he may have done a bit of experimenting, after hours, on the possible 'glove' combination."

Winter Meyer knocked on his forehead and groaned. Marcus Knight said: "Oh God!"

"He opened the safe, removed the display-stand with its contents and I think only then realized he had engaged the switch that operates the front doors and the interior lighting. At that moment Trevor, who had stolen quite close (just as he did to me when I looked at the safe), said —it is his favourite noise at the moment—'Z-z-z-z-yock. Slash.'

"It must have given Grove a nightmarish jolt. He turned, saw the boy standing there in the darkened circle and bolted into the foyer clutching his loot. Only to find Jobbins rushing upstairs at him. He pushed the dolphin pedestal over and down. As Jobbins fell, Trevor came out of the circle and saw it all. Trevor is still not quite clear here but he thinks he screamed. He knows Grove made for him and he remembers plunging down the central steps in the circle. Grove caught him at the bottom. Trevor says—and this may be true—that he snatched the display-stand and threw it overboard before Grove could recover it. The last thing he remembers now is Grove's face close to his own. It was the sight of it this morning, near to him, in association with the single twang effected by my colleague, Inspector Fox, who was modestly concealed behind a screen, that bridged the gap in Trevor's memory."

"*A faint perfume,*" Peregrine said loudly, "*and a most melodious twang.*"

"That's Aubrey, isn't it?" Alleyn asked. "But shouldn't it be a *curious* perfume? Or not?"

Peregrine stared at him. "It is," he said, "and it should. You're dead right and why the hell it's eluded me I cannot imagine. I heard it, you know, when Jobbins was hunting the boy."

Emily said: "And, of course, it's a single plangent note that brings down the curtain on *The Cherry Orchard.*"

"You see, Emily?" said Peregrine.

"I see," she said.

"What the hell *is* all this?" Knight asked plaintively.

"I'll get on with it," Alleyn said. "After a brief struggle Grove, now desperate, rids himself of Trevor by precipitating him into the stalls. He hears Hawkins at the stage-door and once again bolts into the circle foyer. He knows Hawkins will come straight through to the front and he hasn't time to retrieve his guitar, get the key, unlock, unbolt and unbar the pass-door. There lies the body, dressed in his own outlandish coat. He strips off the coat, takes the scarf from the pocket to protect his own clothes and re-enters the darkened circle, to all intents and purposes Jobbins. Hawkins, now in the stalls, sees him, addresses him as Jobbins, and is told to make the tea. He goes backstage. Grove has time, now, to bundle the body back into the coat, fetch his guitar and let himself out. He drives to Chelsea and gets there fully equipped to be the life and soul of Miss Meade's party."

"And he *was,* you know," Destiny said. "He *was.*"

She clasped her hands, raised them to her face and began to weep. Knight gave an inarticulate cry and went to her.

"Never mind, my darling," he said. "Never mind. We must rise above. We must forget."

Mr. Conducis cleared his throat. Destiny threw him a glance that was madly eloquent of some ineffable generalization. He avoided it.

"The motive," Alleyn said, "was, of course, theft. Harry Grove knew a great deal about Mrs. Constantia Guzmann. He knew that if the treasure was stolen she would give a fortune under the counter for it."

Knight, who was kissing Destiny's hands, groaned slightly and shuddered.

"But I think he knew more about her than that," Alleyn went on. "She was a guest of Mr. Conducis's six years ago in the *Kalliope,* when the yacht was wrecked off Cape St. Vincent. At that time, six years ago, Grove was going through a bad patch and taking any jobs he could get. Lorry-driving. Waiter in a strip-joint. And steward."

He turned to Mr. Conducis. "I was about to ask you yesterday when Grove himself interrupted us: was he a steward on board the *Kalliope?*"

Nobody looked at Mr. Conducis.

"Yes," he said.

"How did that come about?"

"He brought himself to my notice. His father was a distant and unsatisfactory connection of mine. I considered this to be no reason for employing him but he satisfied me of his usefulness."

"And he sold you the glove and documents?"

"Yes."

"For thirty pounds?"

"I have already said so."

Marcus Knight, whose manner towards Mr. Conducis had been an extraordinary blend of hauteur and embarrassment, now said loudly: "I don't believe it."

"You don't believe what, Mr. Knight?" Alleyn asked.

"That he was aboard that—vessel."

"You were scarcely there long enough to notice," Mr. Conducis said coldly.

"I was there long enough—" Marcus began on a high note, and dried. "But no matter," he said. "No matter."

Alleyn stood up and so did everybody else except Mr. Conducis.

"I won't keep you any longer," Alleyn said. "I would like to say how sorry I am that this has happened and how much I hope your play and your theatre will ride out the storm. I'm sure they will. I'm taking an unorthodox line when I tell you that Grove has said he will not contest the accusations of assault. He will, he states, admit to taking the treasure, overturning the bronze dolphin and struggling with the boy. He will plead that these were instinctive, self-protective actions committed without intention to kill. This defense, if adhered to, will mean a short trial with little evidence being called and, I think, not a great deal of publicity."

Little Meyer said: "Why's he taking that line? Why isn't he going all out for an acquittal?"

"I asked him that. He said he was suddenly sick of the whole thing. And he added," Alleyn said with a curious twist in his voice, "that he thought it would work out better that way for William Shakespeare, Mr. Peregrine Jay and The Dolphin."

He saw then the eyes of all the company had filled with tears.

When they had gone he turned back to Mr. Conducis. "You said, sir, that you had something you wished to tell me."

"I have something I wish to ask you. Has he said anything about me?"

"A little. He said you owed each other nothing."

"I will pay for his defense. Let him know that."

"Very well."

"Anything else?"

"He said that as far as he is concerned—this was his phrase—he would keep the glove over his knuckles and I could tell you so. He asked me to give you this."

Alleyn gave Mr. Conducis an envelope. He was about to put it in his pocket but changed his mind, opened it and read the short message it contained. He held out the paper to Alleyn.

"*It seems,*" Alleyn read, "*that we are both the victims of irresistible impulse. Which leads me to the ludicrous notion that you will, as they say, 'understand.' You needn't worry. I'm bored with it all and intend to drop it.*"

Down below someone whistled, crossed the foyer and slammed the front doors. The Dolphin was very quiet.

"He clung to the raft," said Mr. Conducis, "and tried to climb aboard it. He would have overturned it. I smashed his knuckles with the writing-desk and thought I'd drowned him. His hands were gloved. They curled and opened and slid away in their own blood. Nobody saw. He has blackmailed me ever since."

ii

"They are not cancelling," said Winter Meyer, giving the box-office plans a smart slap. "And there's very little publicity. I can't understand it."

"Could it be the hand of Conducis?"

"Could be, dear boy. Could be. Power," said little Meyer, "corrupts, didn't somebody say? It may do: but it comes in handy, dear boy, it comes in handy."

He ran upstairs to his office and could be heard singing.

"All the same," Peregrine said to Emily, "I hope it's *not* the hand of Conducis. I hope it's The Dolphin. And us. You know," he went on, "I'm sure he stayed behind to unburden himself to Alleyn."

"What of?"

"Who can tell! I've got a feeling it was something to do with his yacht. He's behaved so very oddly whenever it came up."

"Perhaps," Emily speculated idly, "you reminded him of it. That morning."

"I? How?"

"Oh," she said vaguely, "people drowning, you know, or nearly drowning, or hanging on to bits of wreckage. Perhaps he was glad he rescued you. Or something."

"You never know," Peregrine said.

He put his arm round her and she leaned against him. They had become engaged and were happy.

They looked round them at the upsidedown cupids, the caryatids, the portrait of Mr. Adolphus Ruby, now prominently displayed, and the graceful double flight of stairs. The bronze dolphins were gone and where the safe had been was a montage of the Grafton portrait overlaid by Kean, Garrick, Siddons, Irving and the present great Shakespeareans, all very excitingly treated by Jeremy Jones.

"If you belong to the theatre," Peregrine said, "you belong utterly."

They went out to the portico.

Here they found an enormous Daimler and a chauffeur. It was like a recurrent symbol in a time play and for a moment Peregrine felt as if Mr. Conducis had called again to take him to Drury Place.

"Is that Dessy's car?" Emily said.

But it wasn't Destiny Meade in the back seat. It was an enormous and definitively hideous lady flashing with diamonds, lapped in mink and topped with feathers.

She tapped on the glass and beckoned.

When Peregrine approached, she let down the window and, in a deep voice, addressed him.

"You can perhaps assizt me. I have this morning arrived from America. I vish to inquire about the Shakespearean Religs. I am Mrs. Constantia Guzmann."